FOX PO

GEMMA HOPPER

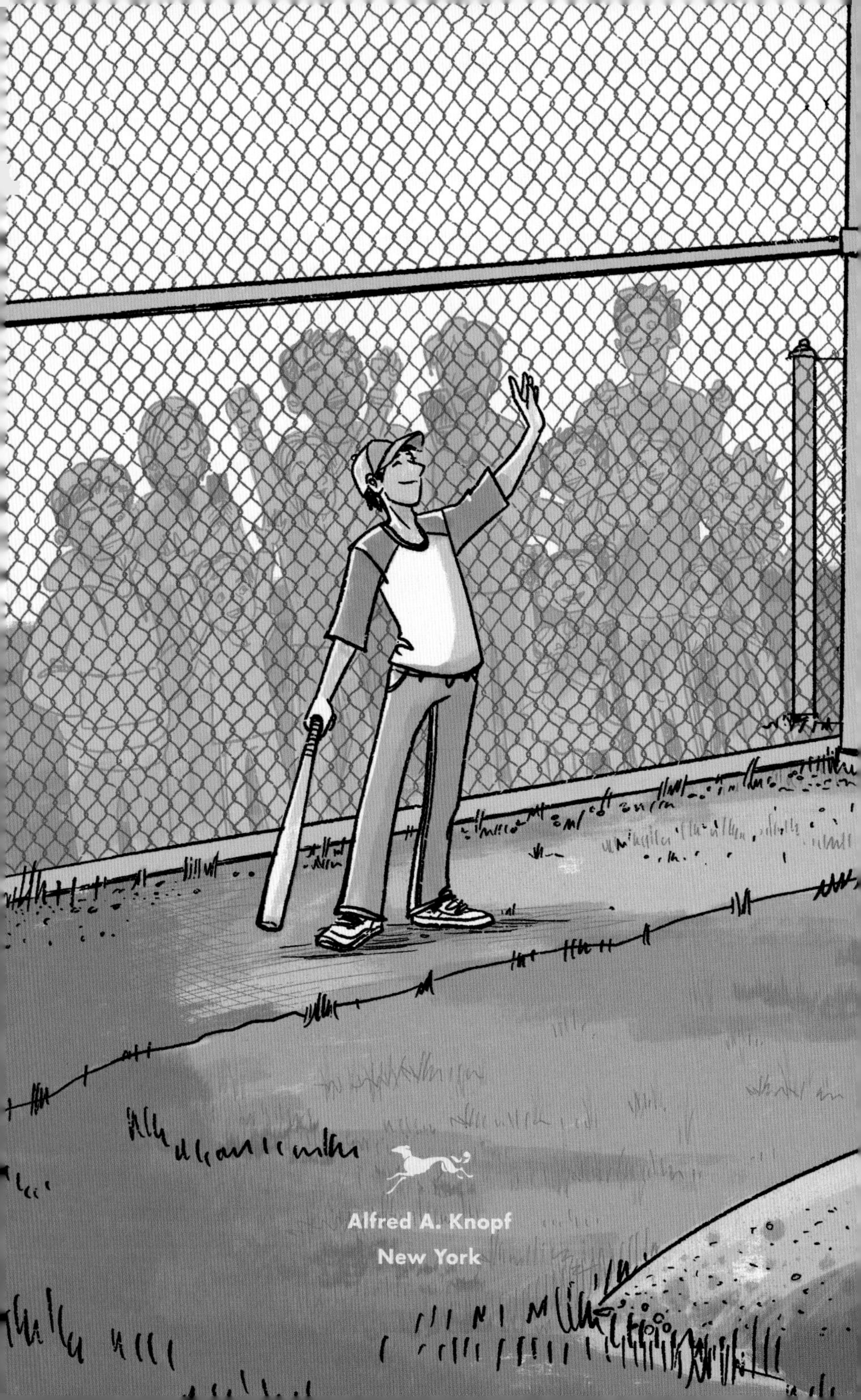

Alfred A. Knopf
New York

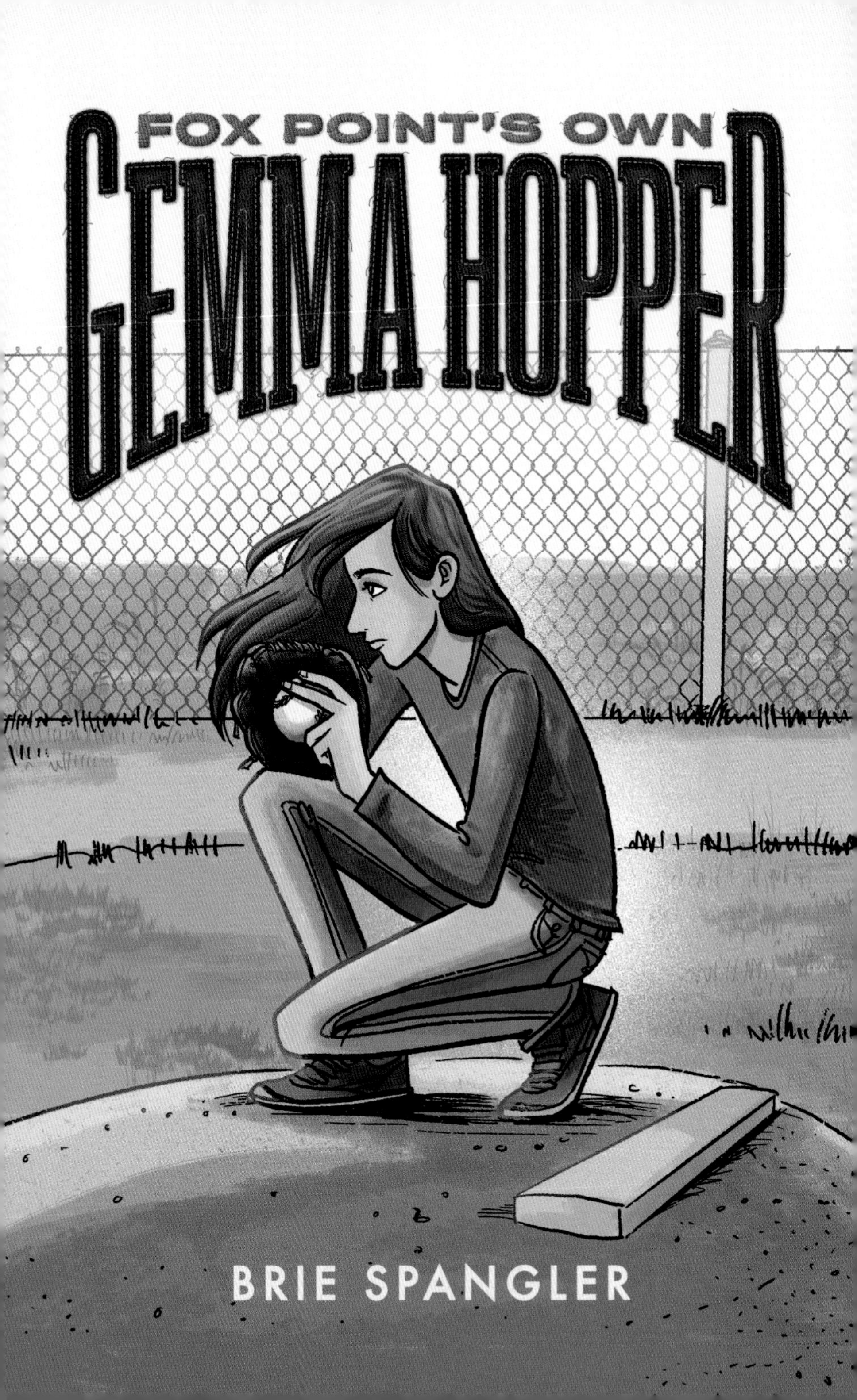
FOX POINT'S OWN
GEMMA HOPPER
BRIE SPANGLER

THIS IS A BORZOI BOOK PUBLISHED BY ALFRED A. KNOPF

Visit us on the Web! rhcbooks.com
Educators and librarians, for a variety of teaching tools, visit us at RHTeachersLibrarians.com

Library of Congress Cataloging-in-Publication Data
Names: Spangler, Brie, author, illustrator.
Title: Fox Point's own Gemma Hopper / Brie Spangler.
Description: First edition. | New York : Alfred A. Knopf, [2023] |
Audience: Ages 8–12. | Summary: "Gemma Hopper is obsessed with baseball but is too busy helping out at home and navigating the perils of friendship to try out for a team."—Provided by publisher.
Identifiers: LCCN 2022023293 (print) | LCCN 2022023294 (ebook) |
ISBN 978-0-593-42849-8 (hardcover) | ISBN 978-0-593-42848-1 (trade paperback) |
ISBN 978-0-593-42850-4 (ebook)
Subjects: CYAC: Graphic novels. | Baseball—Fiction. |
Middle schools—Fiction. | Schools—Fiction. | Friendship—Fiction. |
Family life—Fiction. | LCGFT: Sports fiction. | Graphic novels.
Classification: LCC PZ7.7.S6466 Fo 2023 (print) | LCC PZ7.7.S6466 (ebook) |
DDC 741.5/973—dc23/eng/20220728

The text of this book is set in 9.5-point Sunbird.
Book design by Jen Valero

MANUFACTURED IN CHINA
10 9 8 7 6 5 4 3 2 1
First Edition

To my mom and dad,
thank you for everything.

FOX POINT'S OWN
GEMMA HOPPER

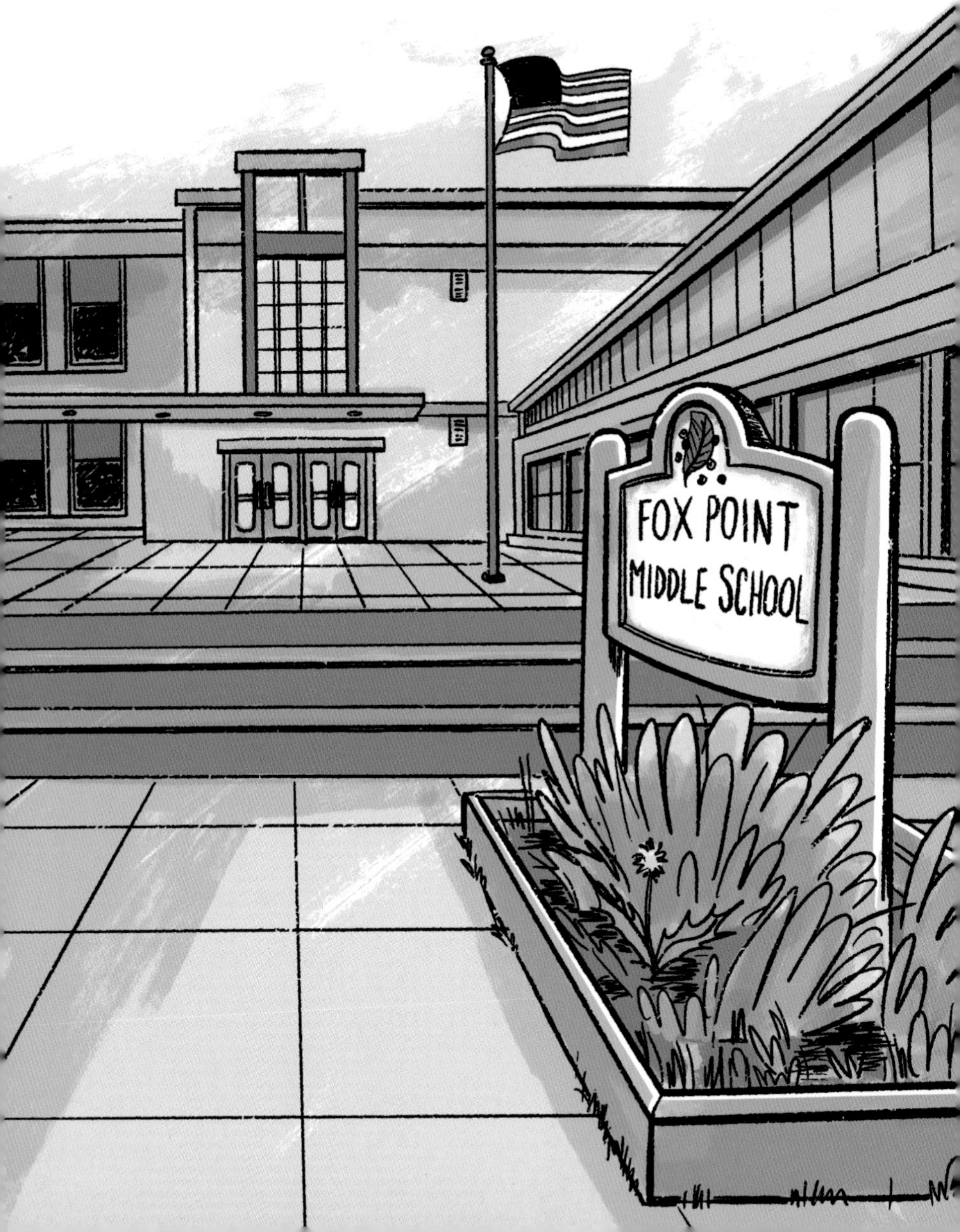
FOX POINT
MIDDLE SCHOOL

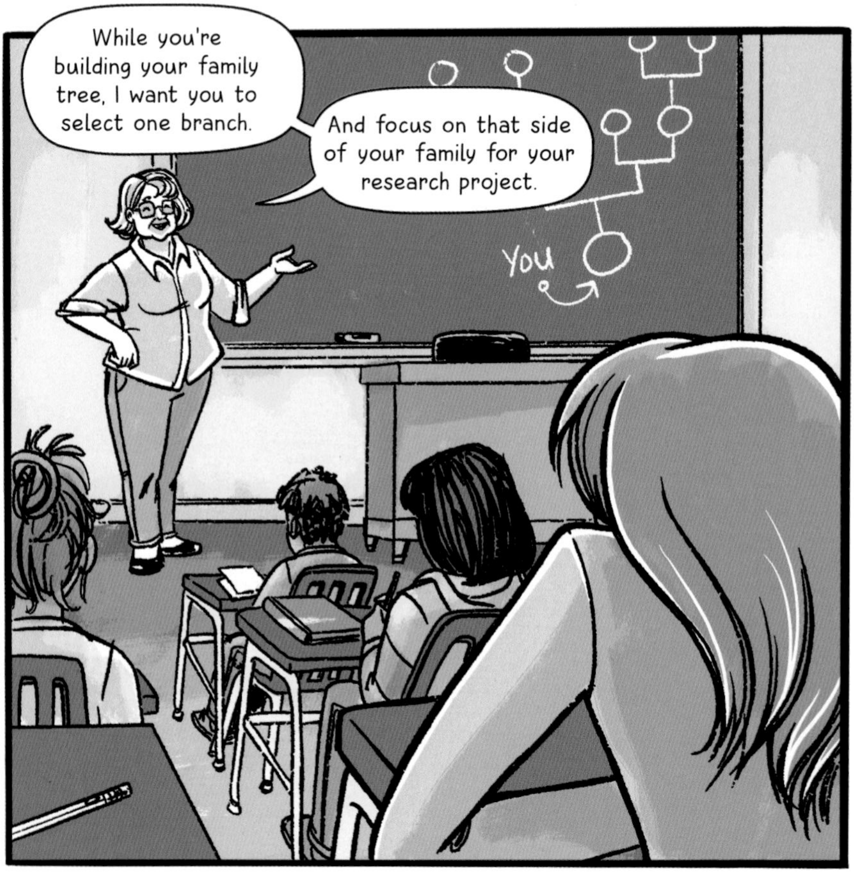
While you're building your family tree, I want you to select one branch.
And focus on that side of your family for your research project.
YOU

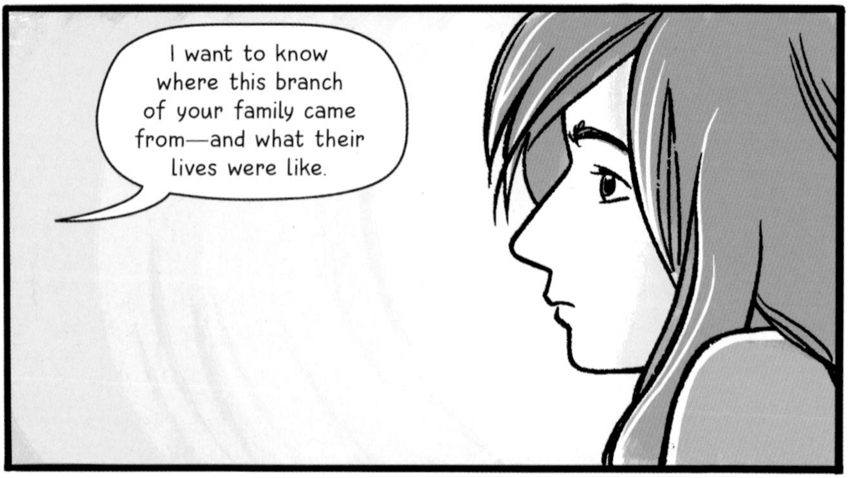
I want to know where this branch of your family came from—and what their lives were like.

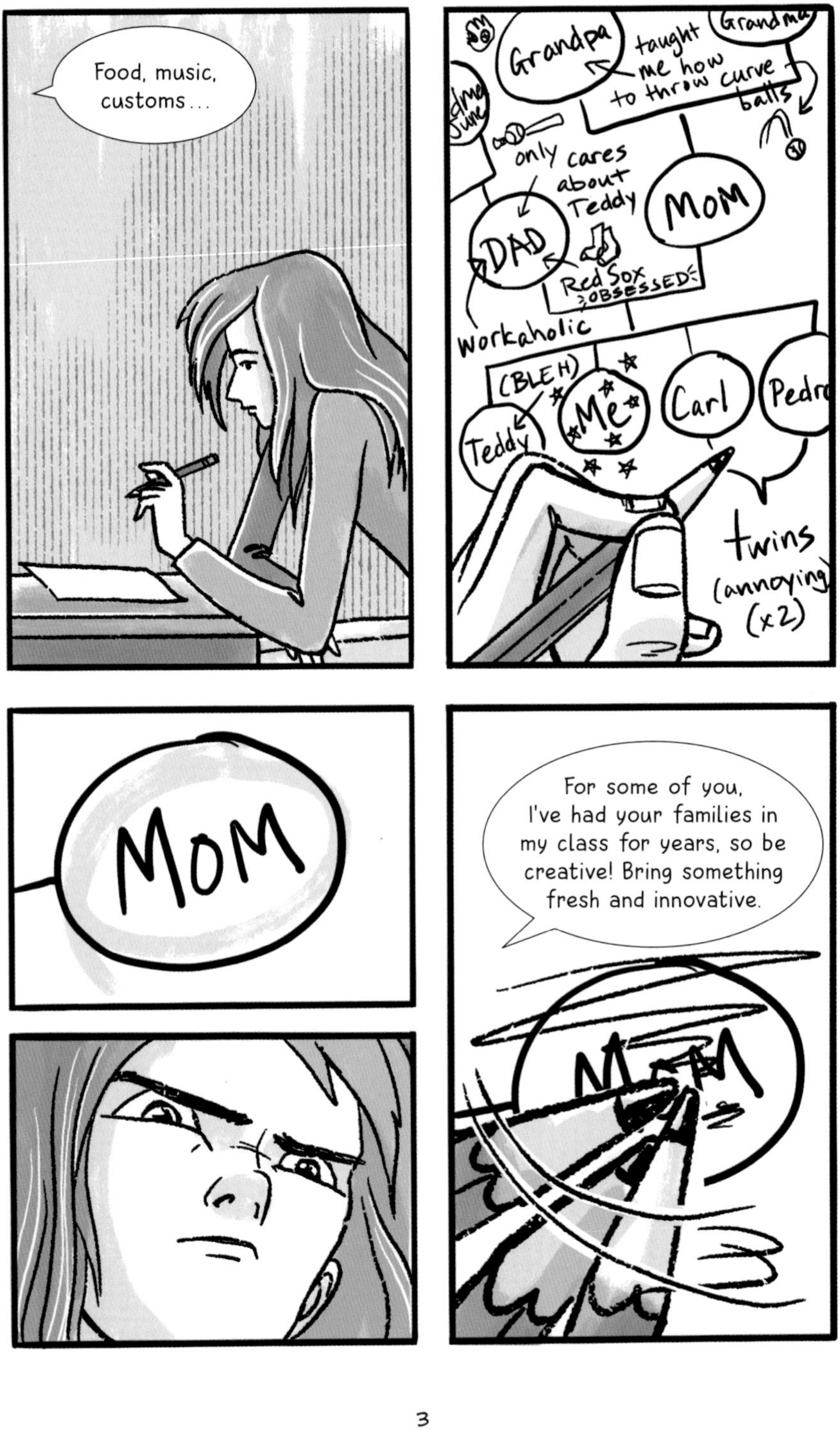
Food, music, customs...
Grandpa
Grandma
taught me how to throw curve balls
only cares about Teddy
DAD
MOM
Red Sox OBSESSED
workaholic
(BLEH)
Teddy
Me
Carl
twins (annoying) (x2)
MOM
For some of you, I've had your families in my class for years, so be creative! Bring something fresh and innovative.

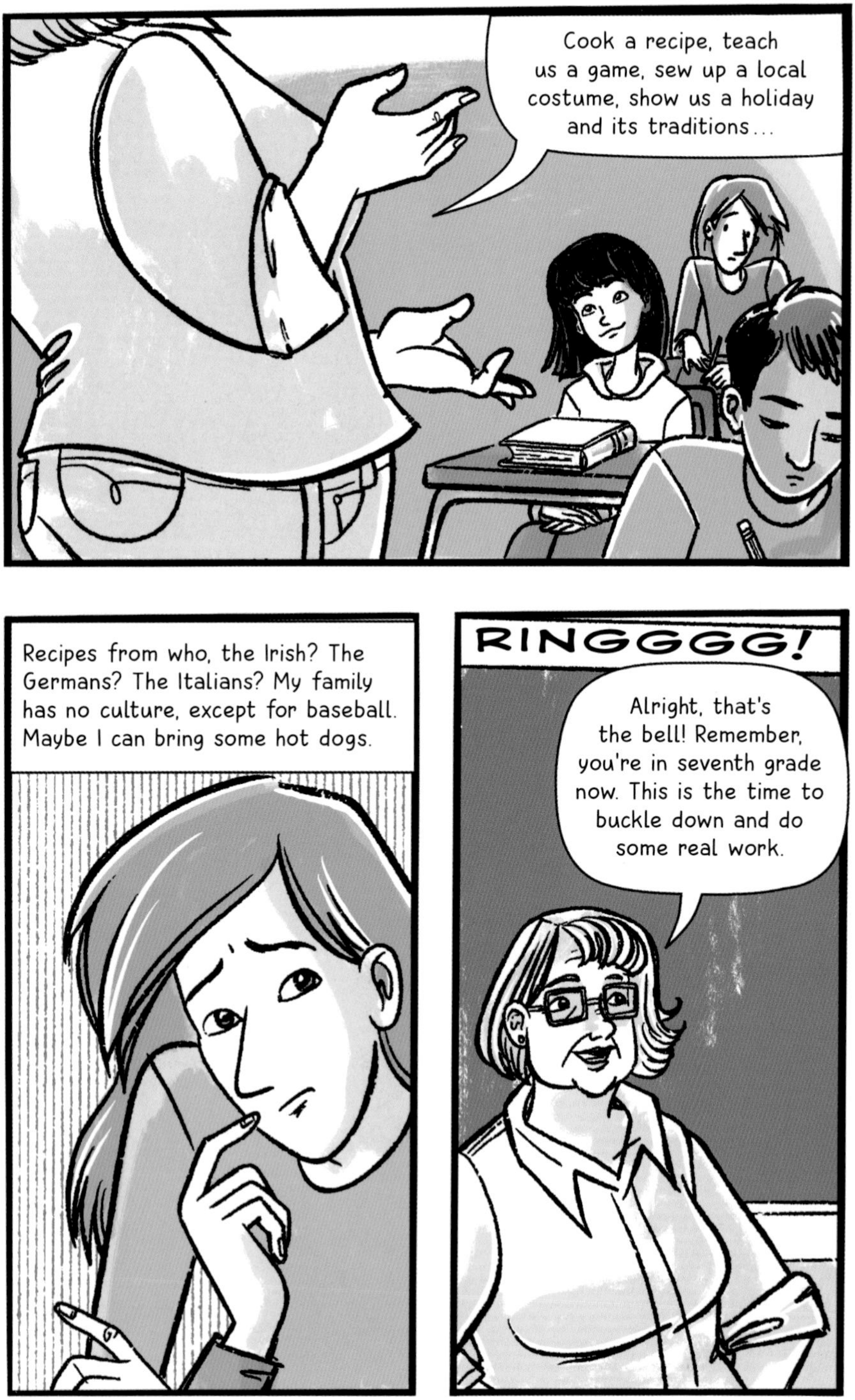

Cook a recipe, teach us a game, sew up a local costume, show us a holiday and its traditions...
Recipes from who, the Irish? The Germans? The Italians? My family has no culture, except for baseball. Maybe I can bring some hot dogs.
RINGGGG!
Alright, that's the bell! Remember, you're in seventh grade now. This is the time to buckle down and do some real work.

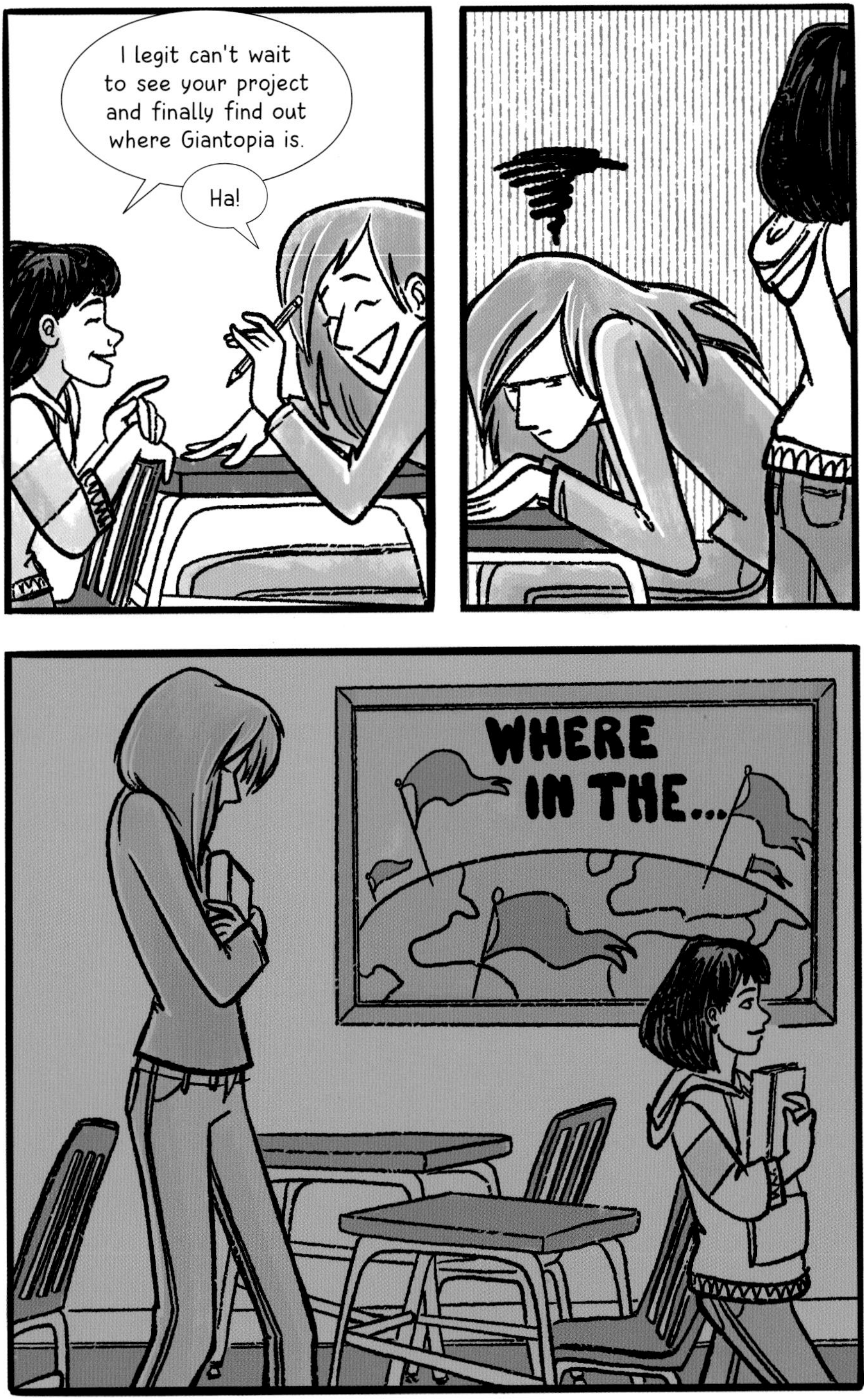
I legit can't wait to see your project and finally find out where Giantopia is.
Ha!
WHERE IN THE...

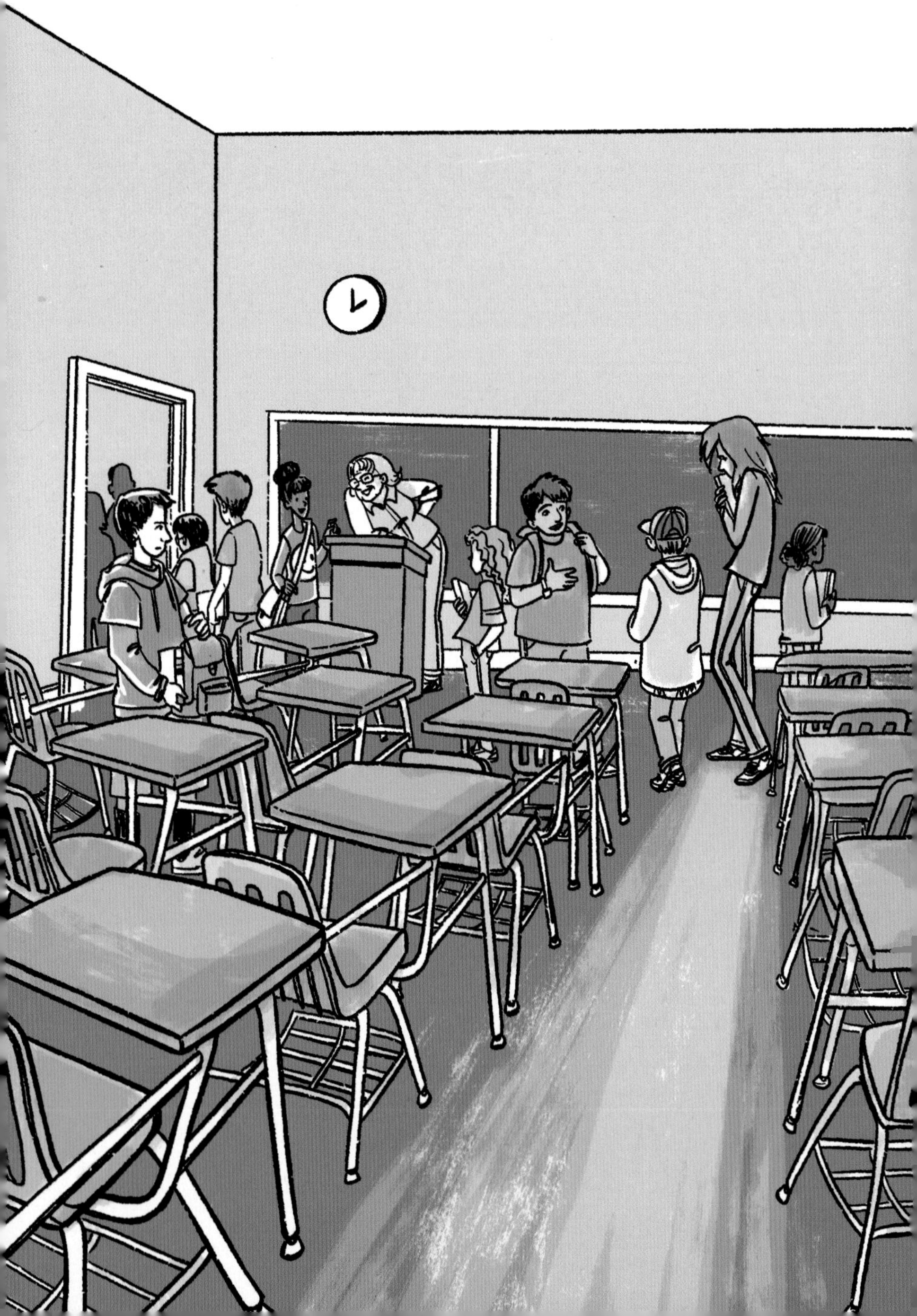

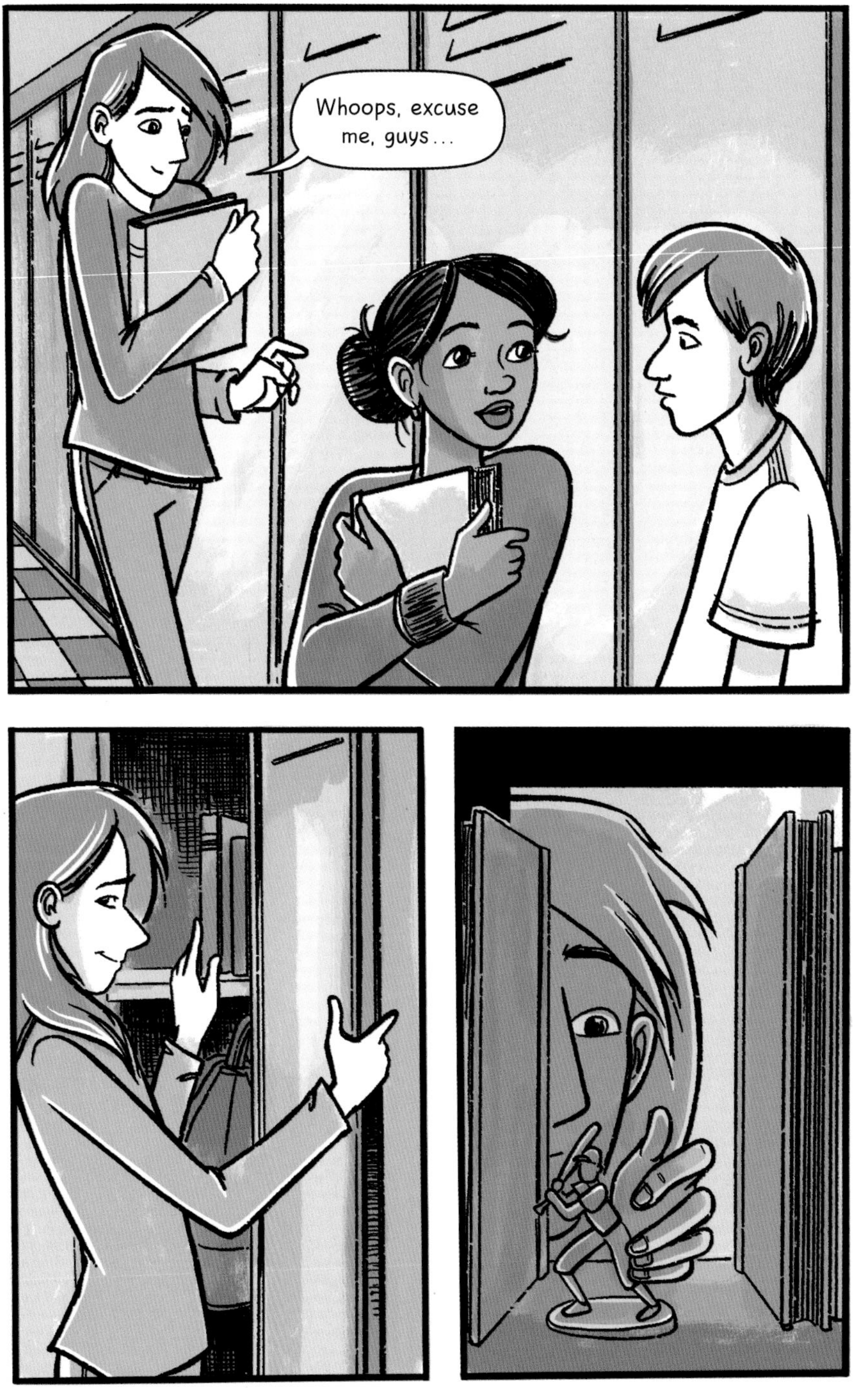
Whoops, excuse me, guys...

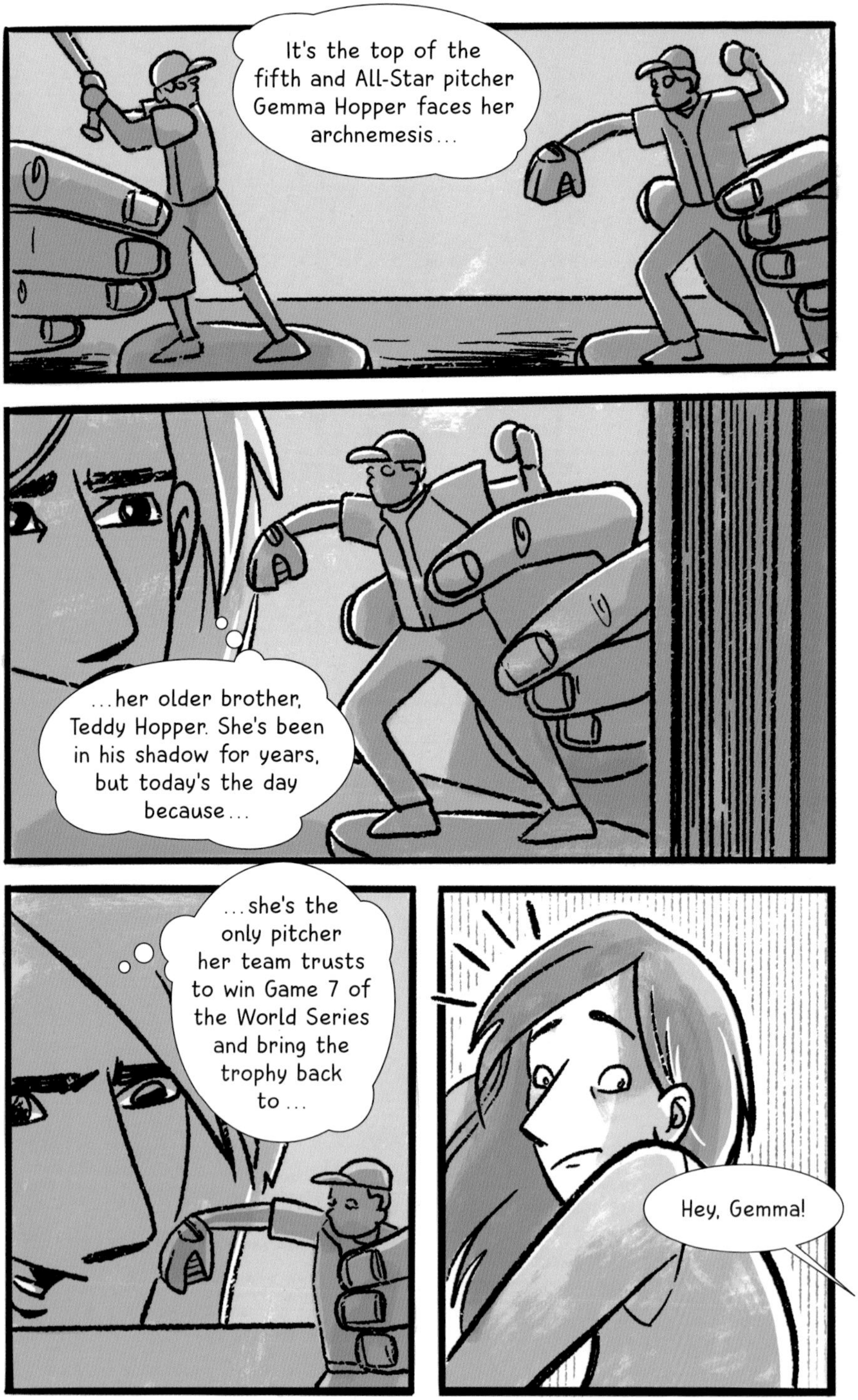
It's the top of the fifth and All-Star pitcher Gemma Hopper faces her archnemesis...
...her older brother, Teddy Hopper. She's been in his shadow for years, but today's the day because...
...she's the only pitcher her team trusts to win Game 7 of the World Series and bring the trophy back to...
Hey, Gemma!

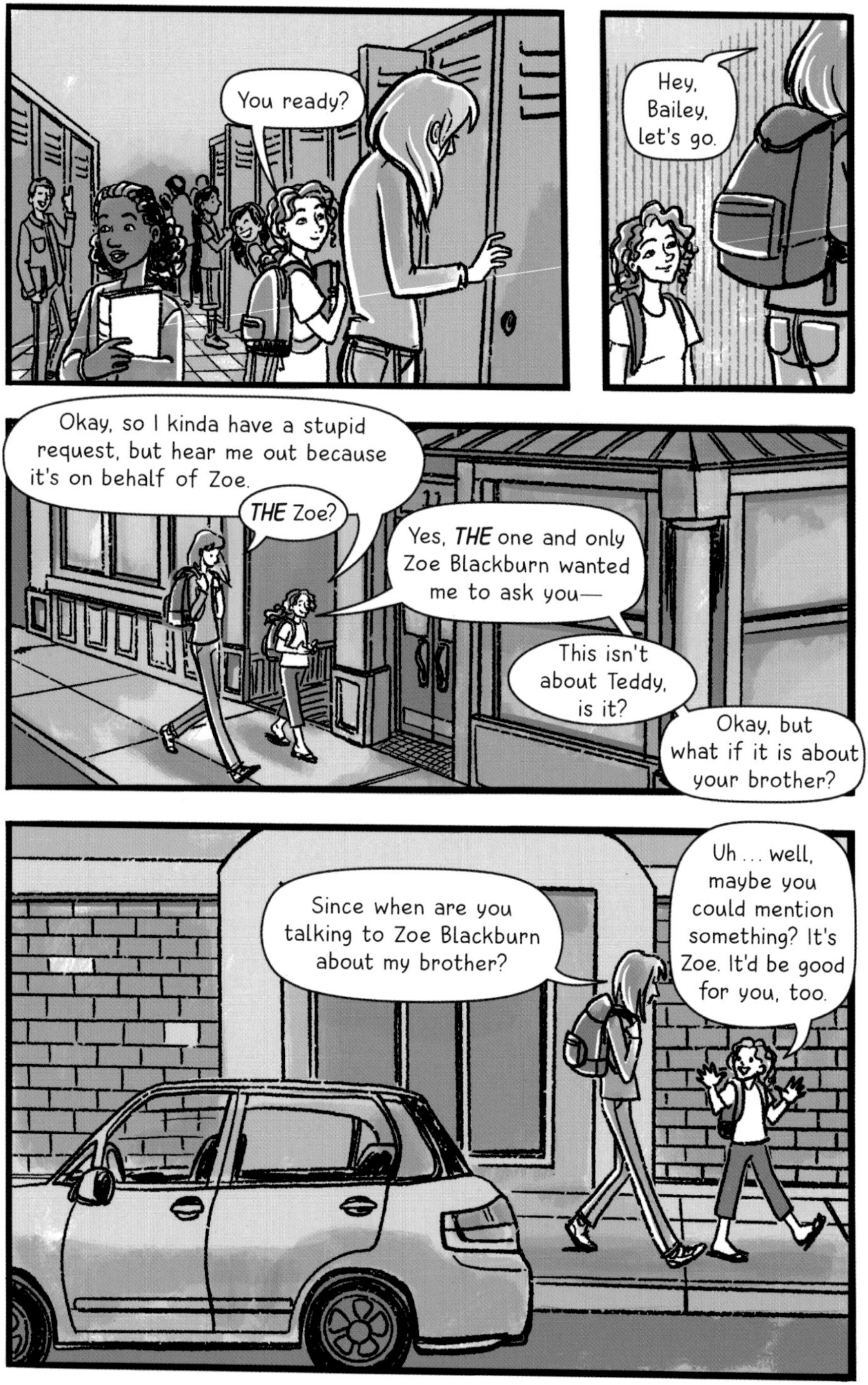
You ready?
Hey, Bailey, let's go.
Okay, so I kinda have a stupid request, but hear me out because it's on behalf of Zoe.
THE Zoe?
Yes, THE one and only Zoe Blackburn wanted me to ask you—
This isn't about Teddy, is it?
Okay, but what if it is about your brother?
Since when are you talking to Zoe Blackburn about my brother?
Uh . . . well, maybe you could mention something? It's Zoe. It'd be good for you, too.

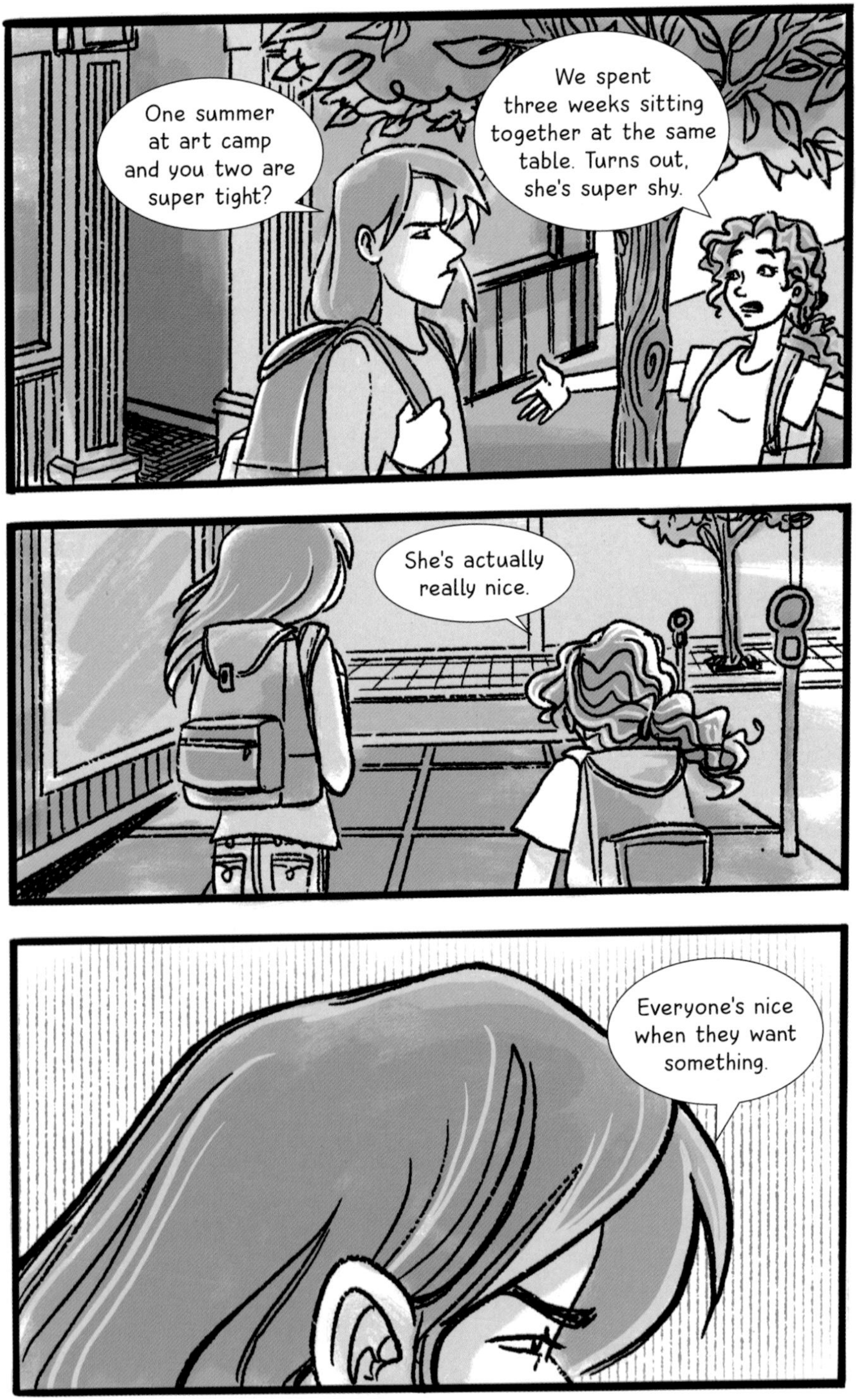
One summer at art camp and you two are super tight?
We spent three weeks sitting together at the same table. Turns out, she's super shy.
She's actually really nice.
Everyone's nice when they want something.

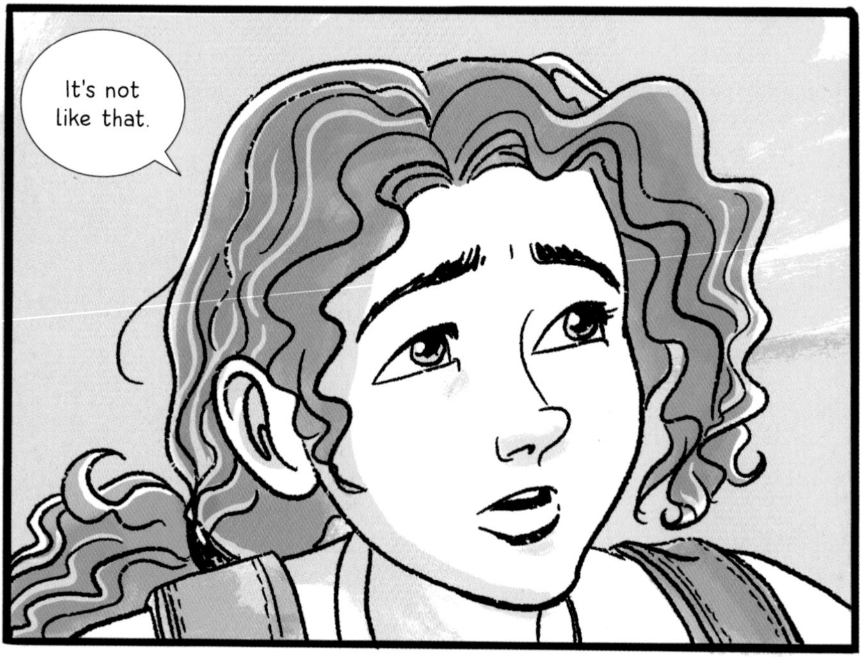
It's not like that.

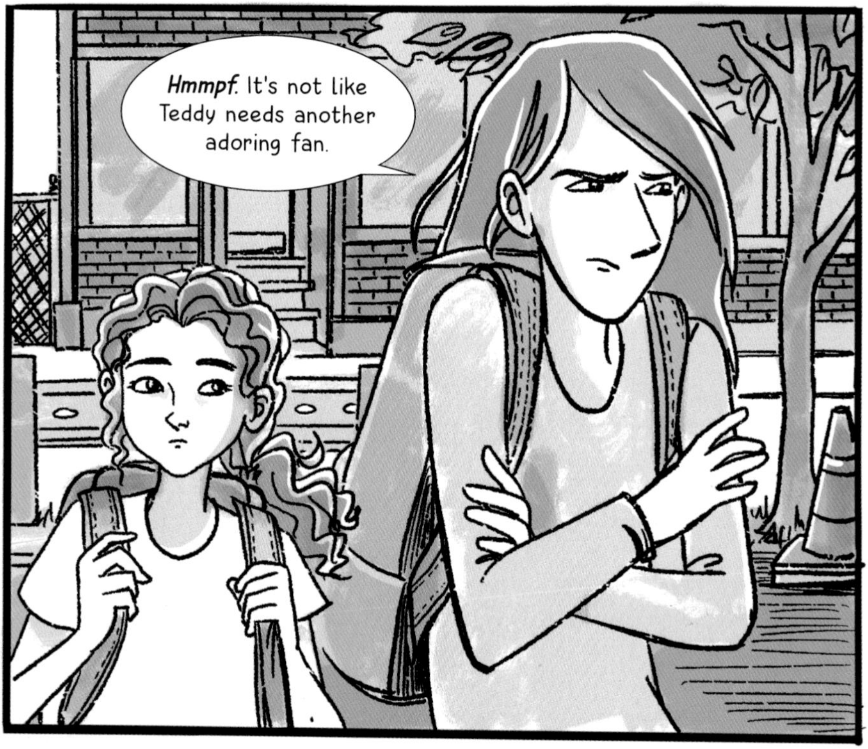
Hmmpf. It's not like Teddy needs another adoring fan.

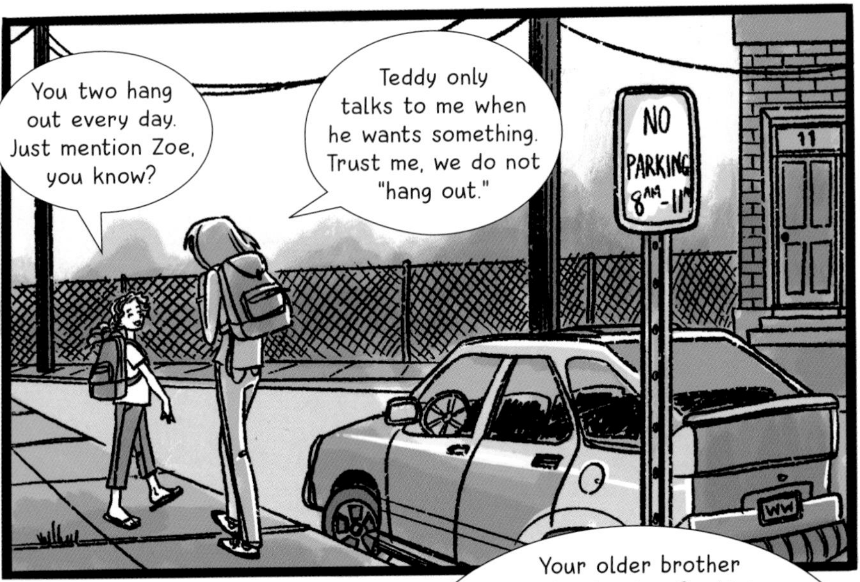
You two hang out every day. Just mention Zoe, you know?
Teddy only talks to me when he wants something. Trust me, we do not "hang out."
NO PARKING 8AM-11

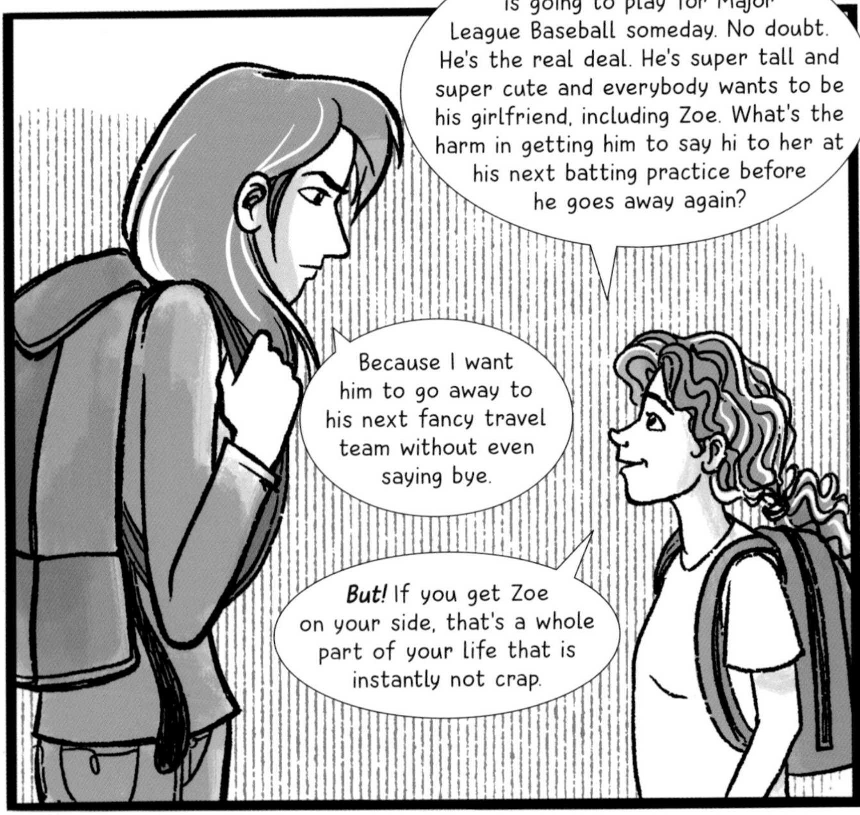
Your older brother is going to play for Major League Baseball someday. No doubt. He's the real deal. He's super tall and super cute and everybody wants to be his girlfriend, including Zoe. What's the harm in getting him to say hi to her at his next batting practice before he goes away again?
Because I want him to go away to his next fancy travel team without even saying bye.
But! If you get Zoe on your side, that's a whole part of your life that is instantly not crap.

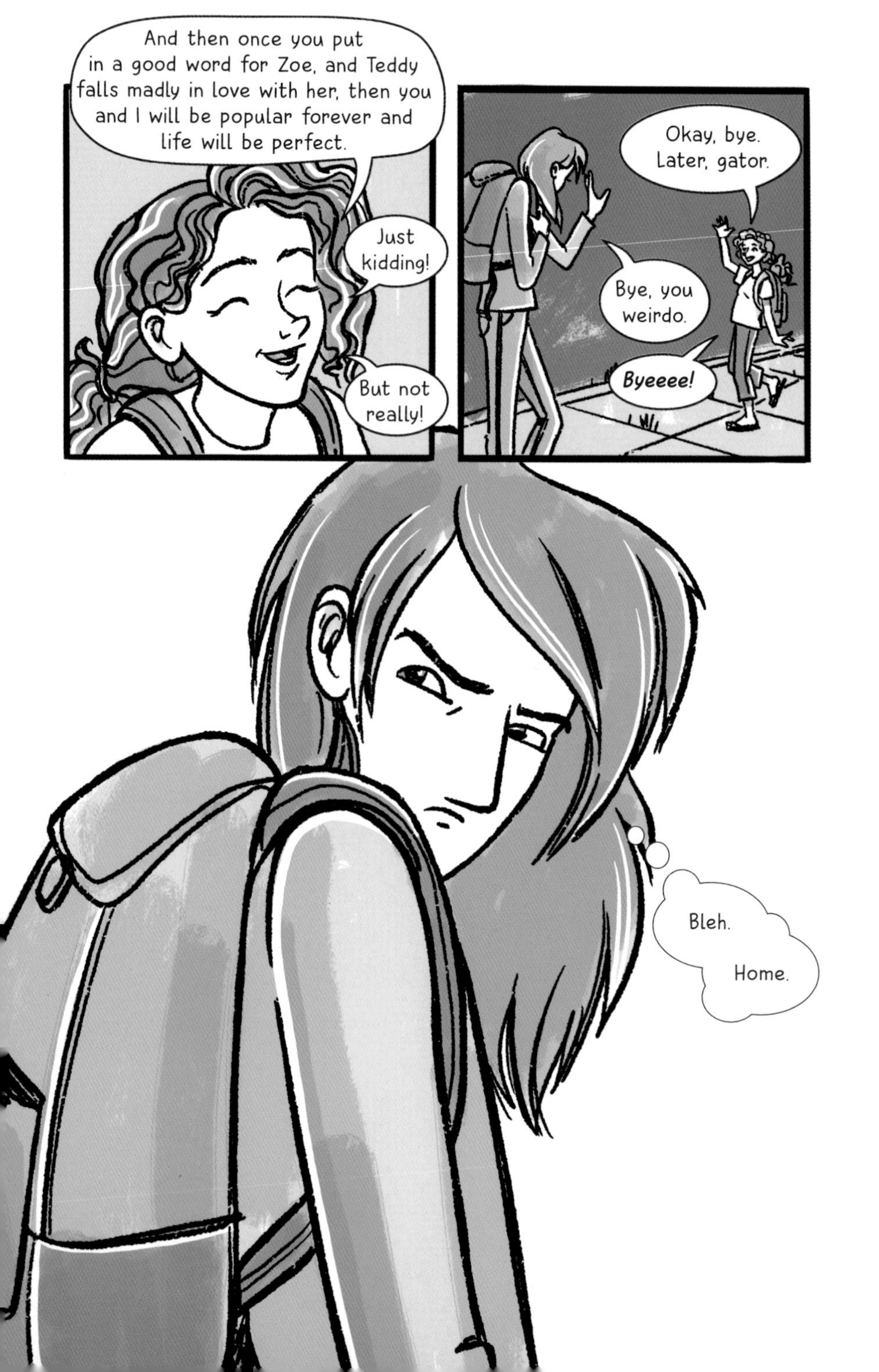
And then once you put in a good word for Zoe, and Teddy falls madly in love with her, then you and I will be popular forever and life will be perfect.
Just kidding!
But not really!
Okay, bye. Later, gator.
Bye, you weirdo.
Byeeee!
Bleh.
Home.

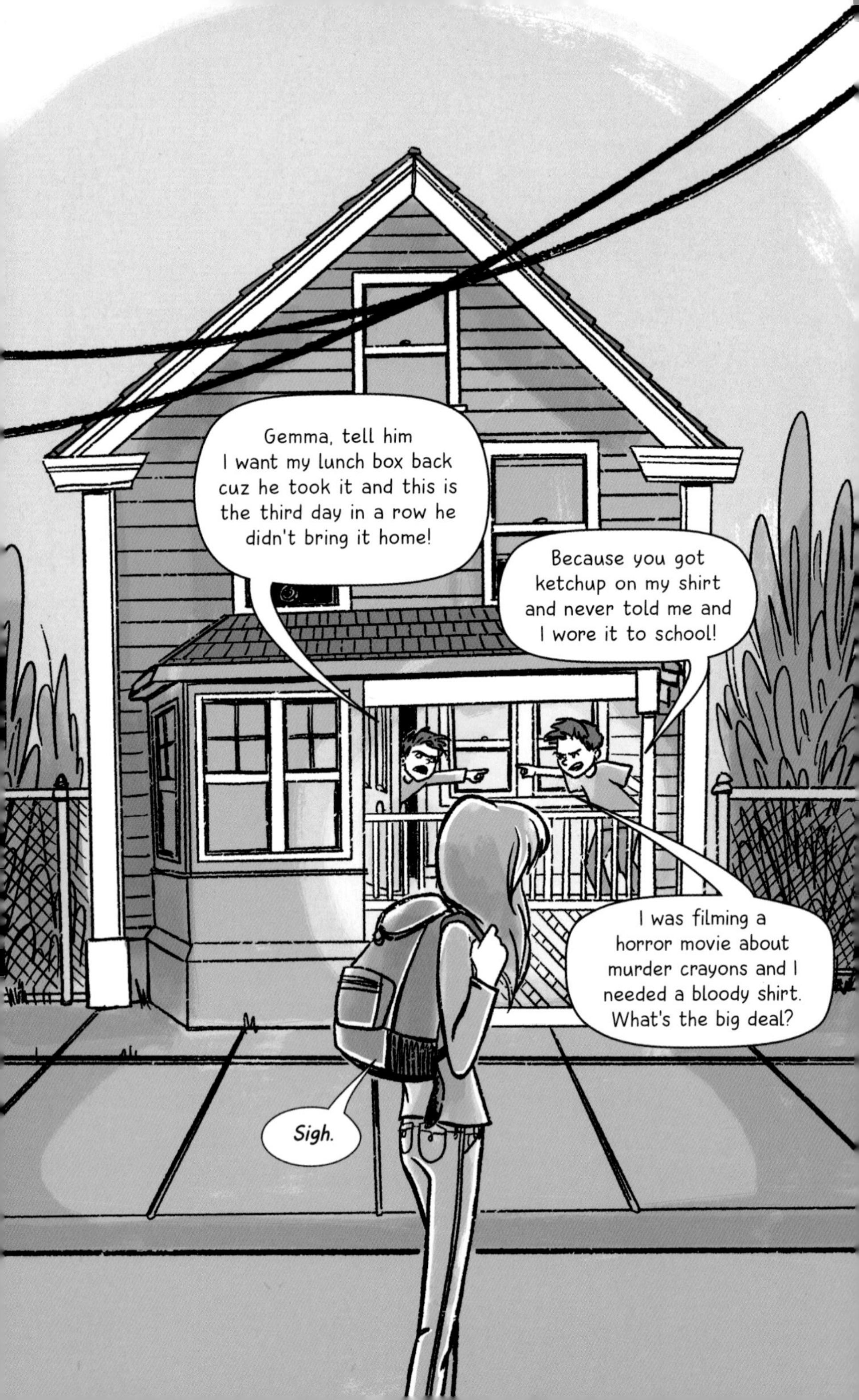
Gemma, tell him I want my lunch box back cuz he took it and this is the third day in a row he didn't bring it home!
Because you got ketchup on my shirt and never told me and I wore it to school!
I was filming a horror movie about murder crayons and I needed a bloody shirt. What's the big deal?
Sigh.

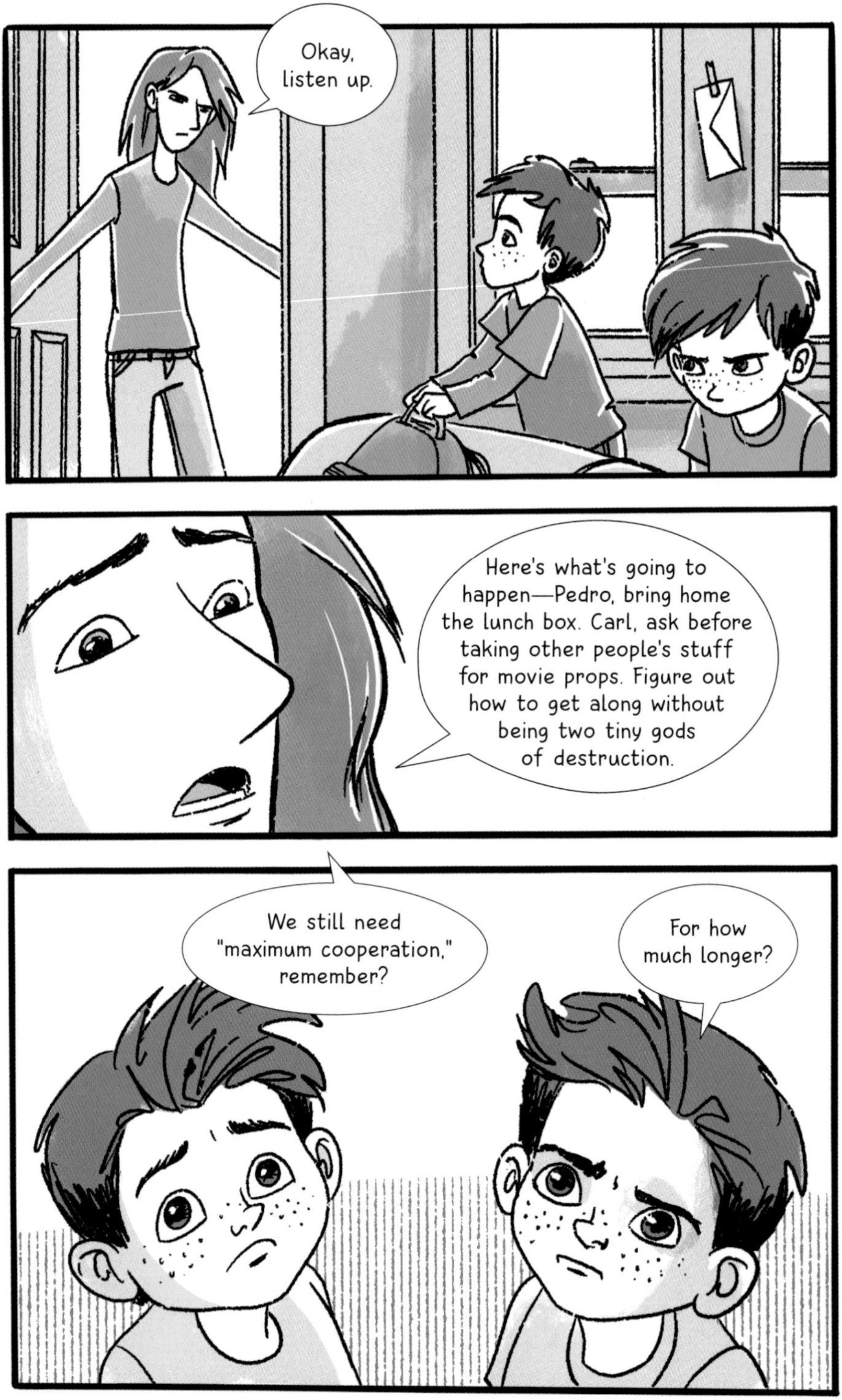
Okay, listen up.
Here's what's going to happen—Pedro, bring home the lunch box. Carl, ask before taking other people's stuff for movie props. Figure out how to get along without being two tiny gods of destruction.
We still need "maximum cooperation," remember?
For how much longer?

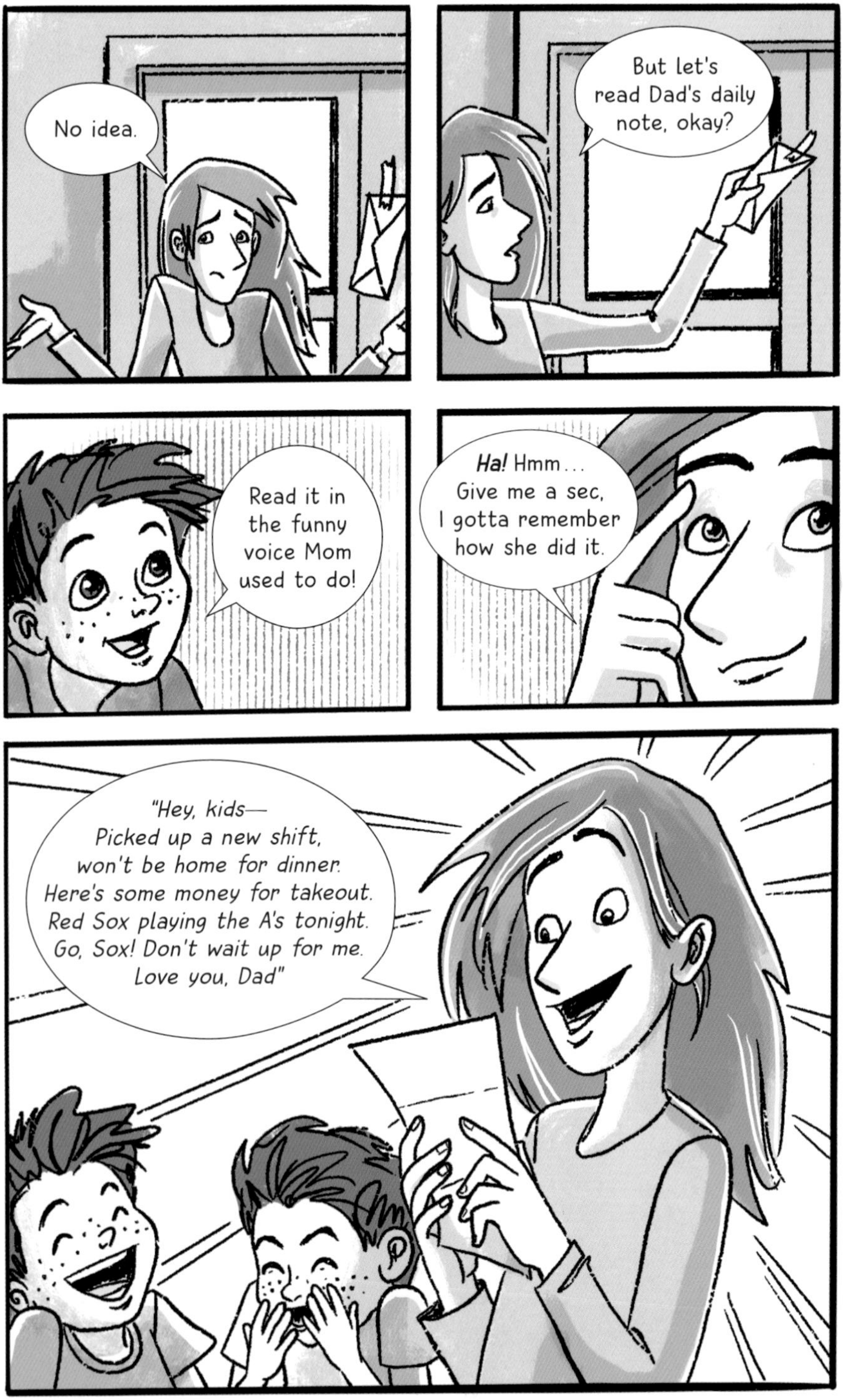
No idea.
But let's read Dad's daily note, okay?
Read it in the funny voice Mom used to do!
Ha! Hmm... Give me a sec, I gotta remember how she did it.
"Hey, kids— Picked up a new shift, won't be home for dinner. Here's some money for takeout. Red Sox playing the A's tonight. Go, Sox! Don't wait up for me. Love you, Dad"

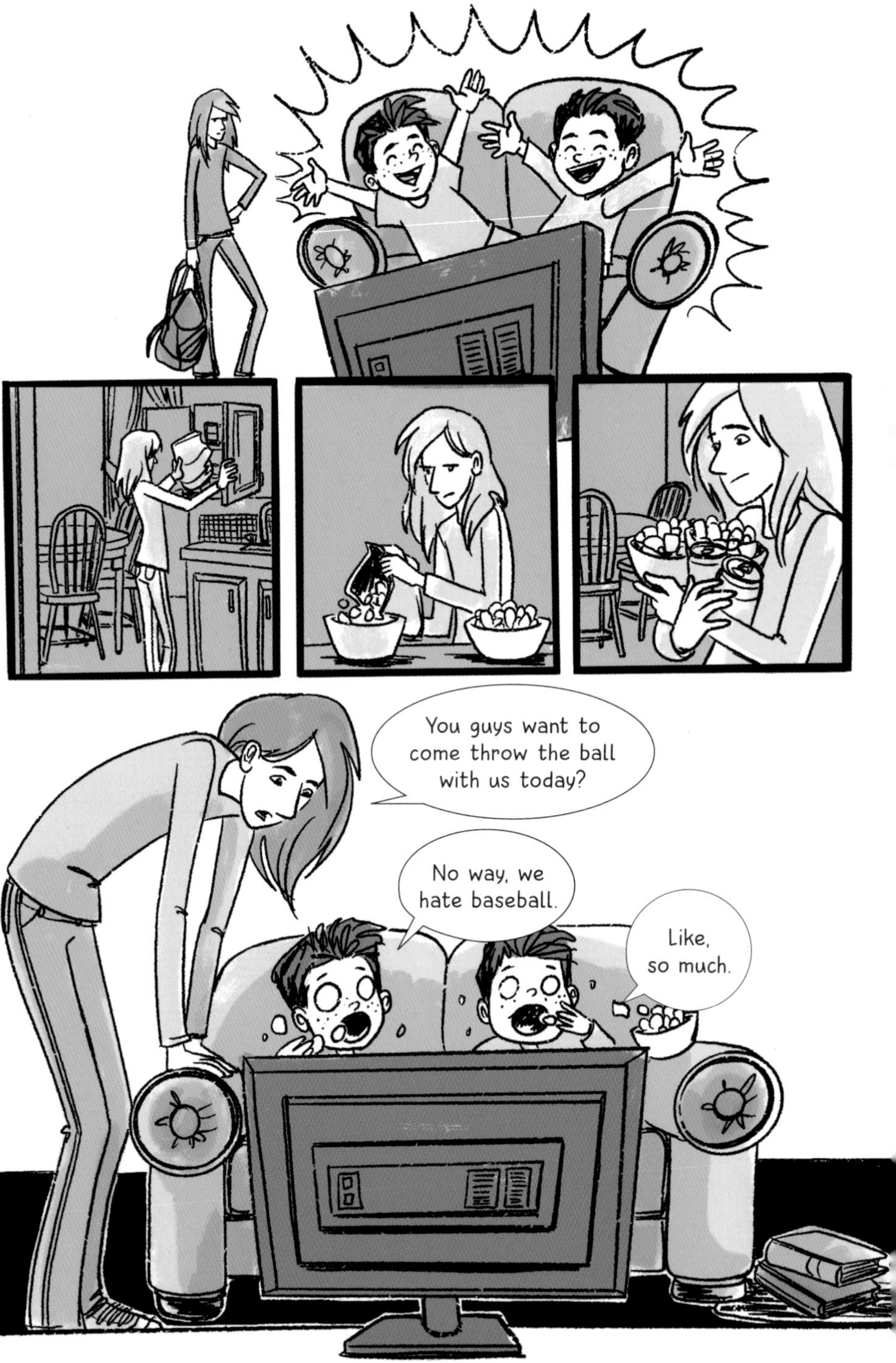
You guys want to come throw the ball with us today?
No way, we hate baseball.
Like, so much.

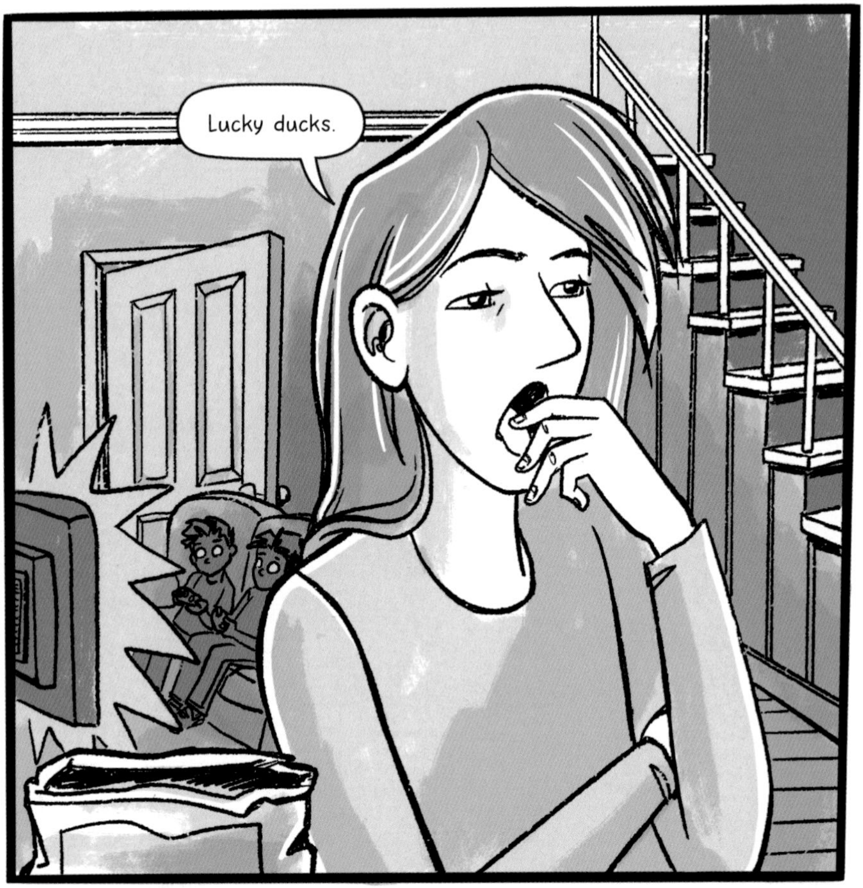
Lucky ducks.

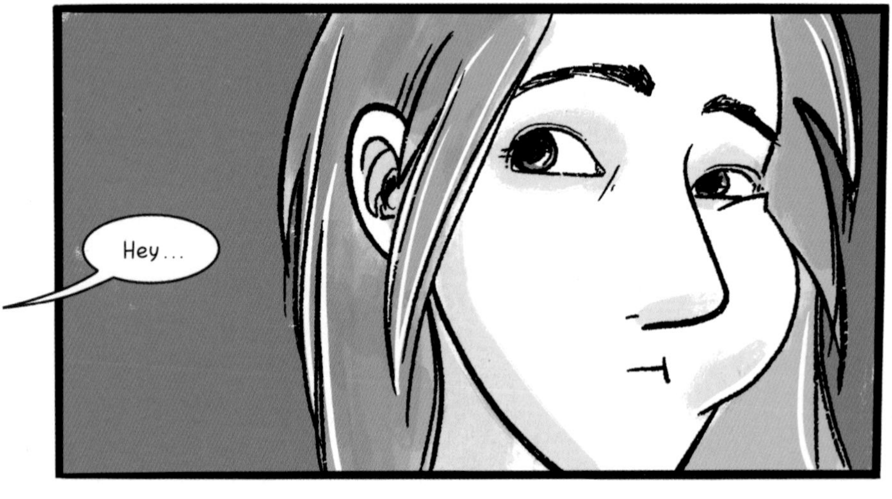
Hey...

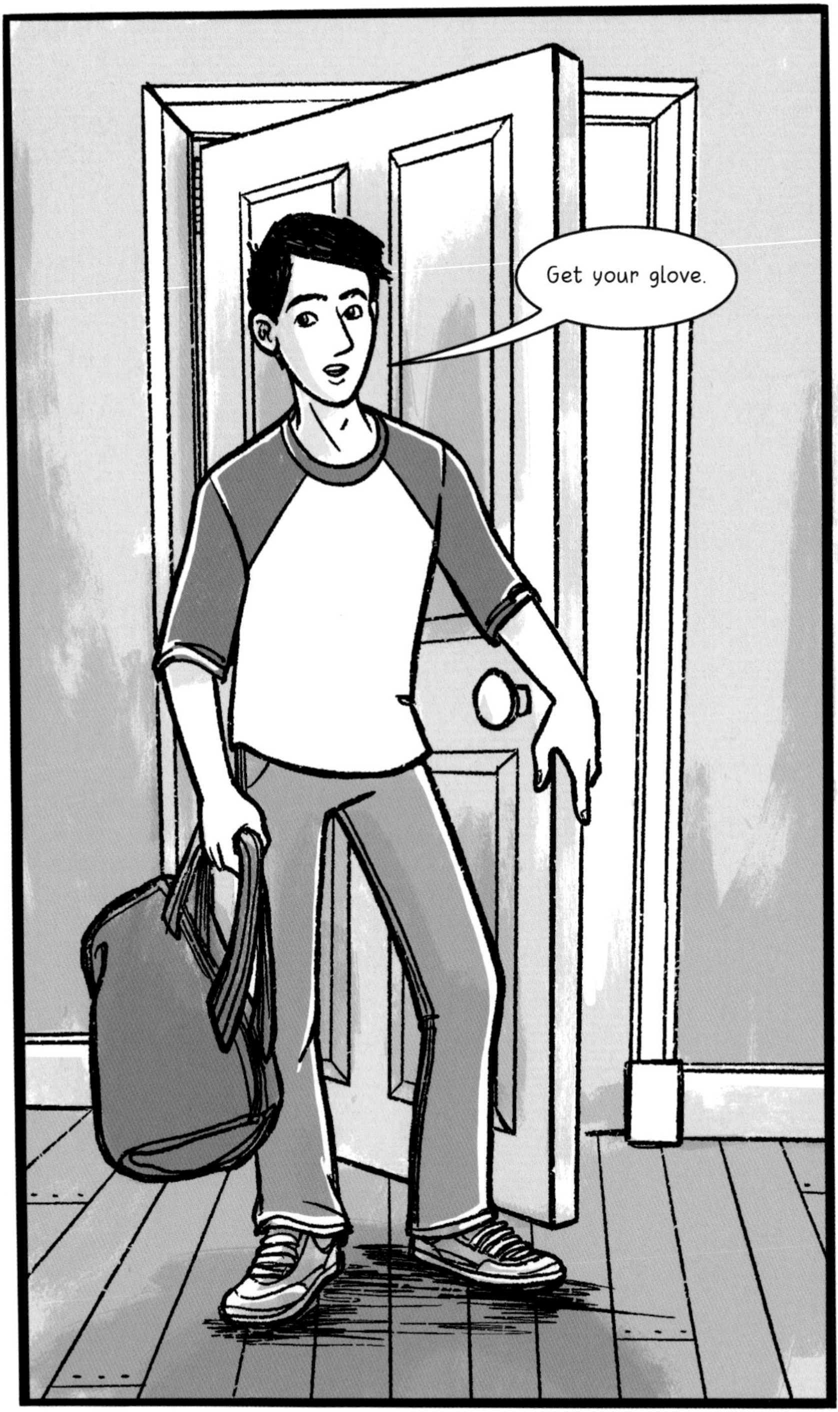
Get your glove.

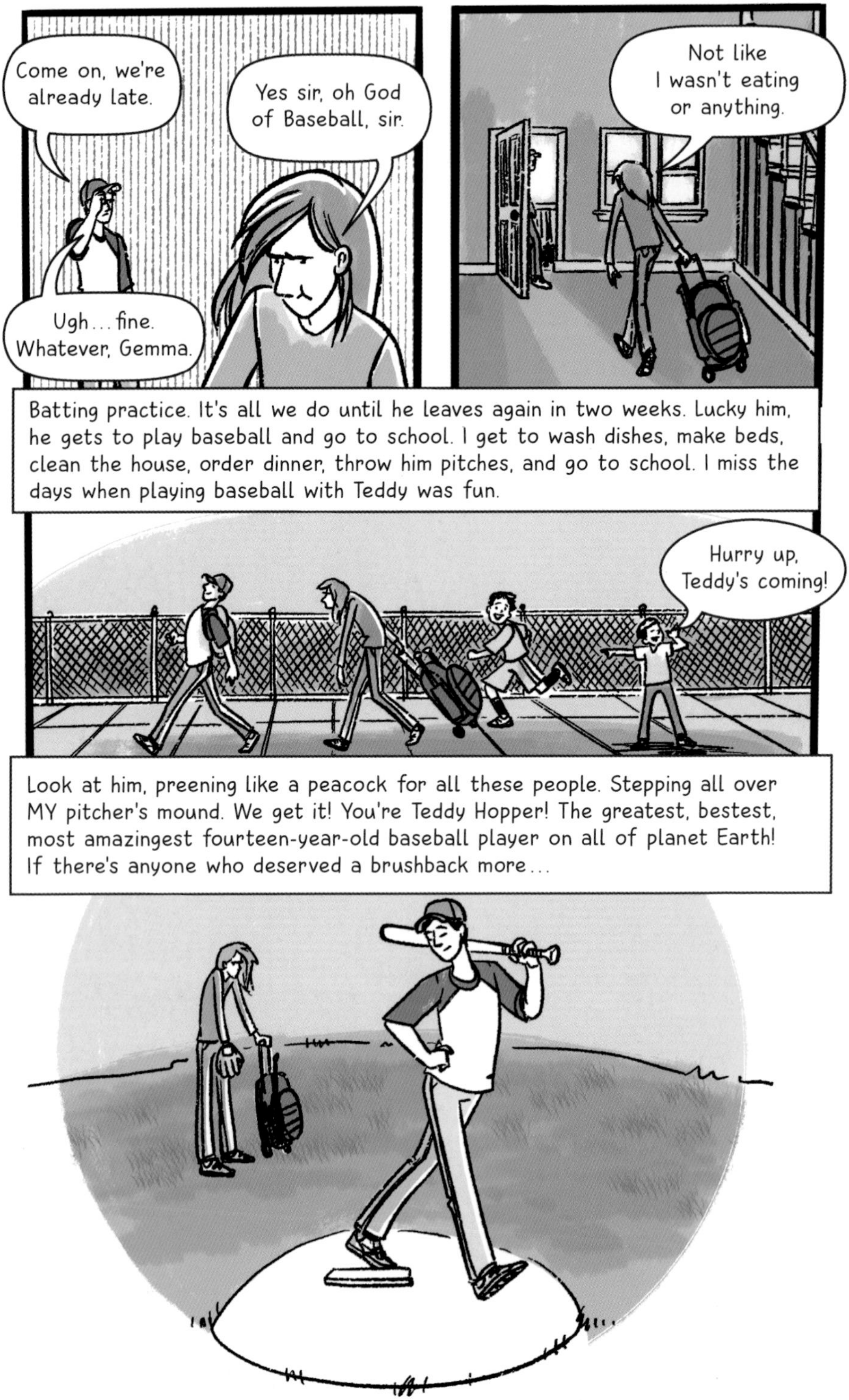
Come on, we're already late.
Yes sir, oh God of Baseball, sir.
Ugh... fine. Whatever, Gemma.
Not like I wasn't eating or anything.
Batting practice. It's all we do until he leaves again in two weeks. Lucky him, he gets to play baseball and go to school. I get to wash dishes, make beds, clean the house, order dinner, throw him pitches, and go to school. I miss the days when playing baseball with Teddy was fun.
Hurry up, Teddy's coming!
Look at him, preening like a peacock for all these people. Stepping all over MY pitcher's mound. We get it! You're Teddy Hopper! The greatest, bestest, most amazingest fourteen-year-old baseball player on all of planet Earth! If there's anyone who deserved a brushback more...

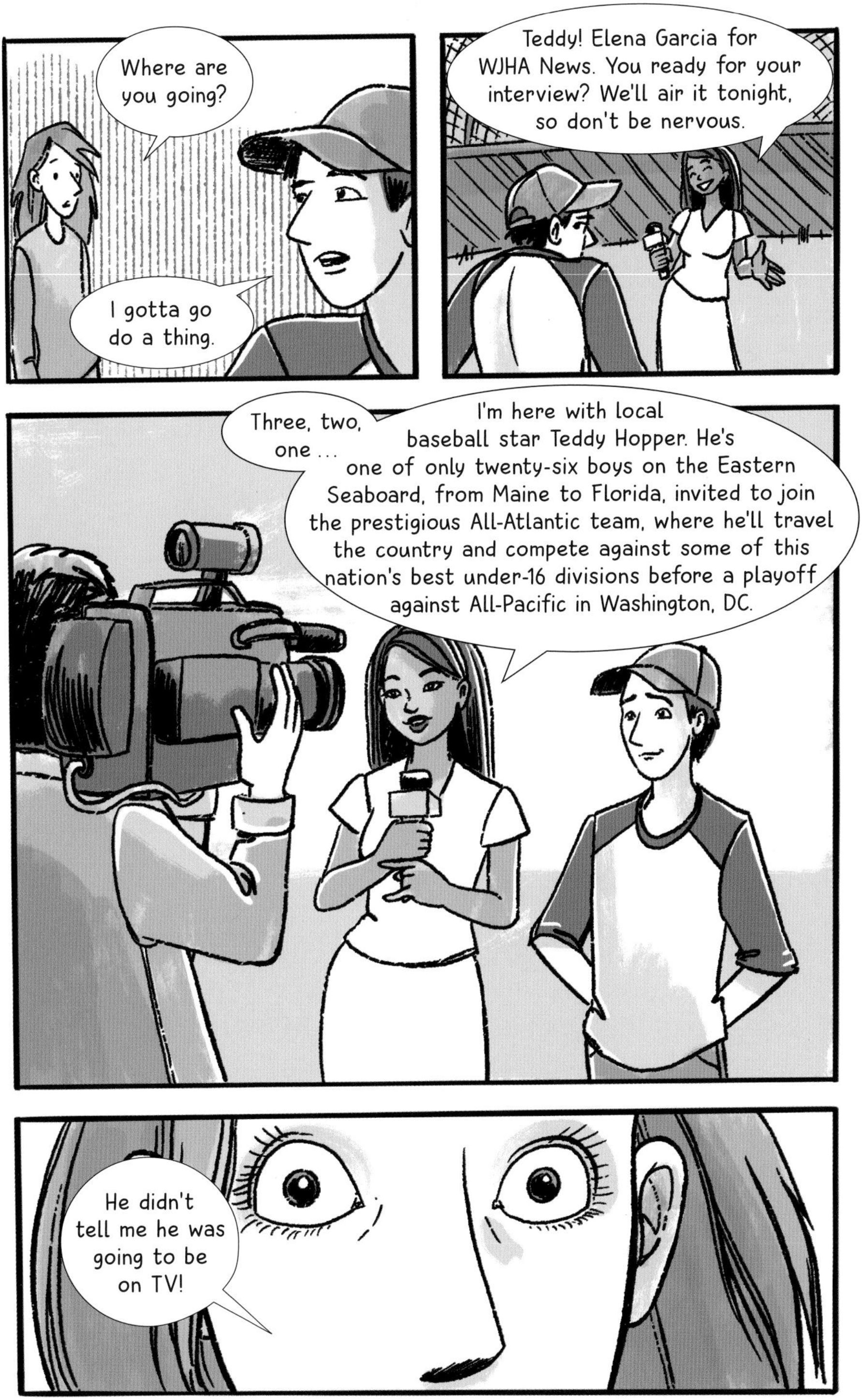
Where are you going?
I gotta go do a thing.
Teddy! Elena Garcia for WJHA News. You ready for your interview? We'll air it tonight, so don't be nervous.
Three, two, one . . .
I'm here with local baseball star Teddy Hopper. He's one of only twenty-six boys on the Eastern Seaboard, from Maine to Florida, invited to join the prestigious All-Atlantic team, where he'll travel the country and compete against some of this nation's best under-16 divisions before a playoff against All-Pacific in Washington, DC.
He didn't tell me he was going to be on TV!

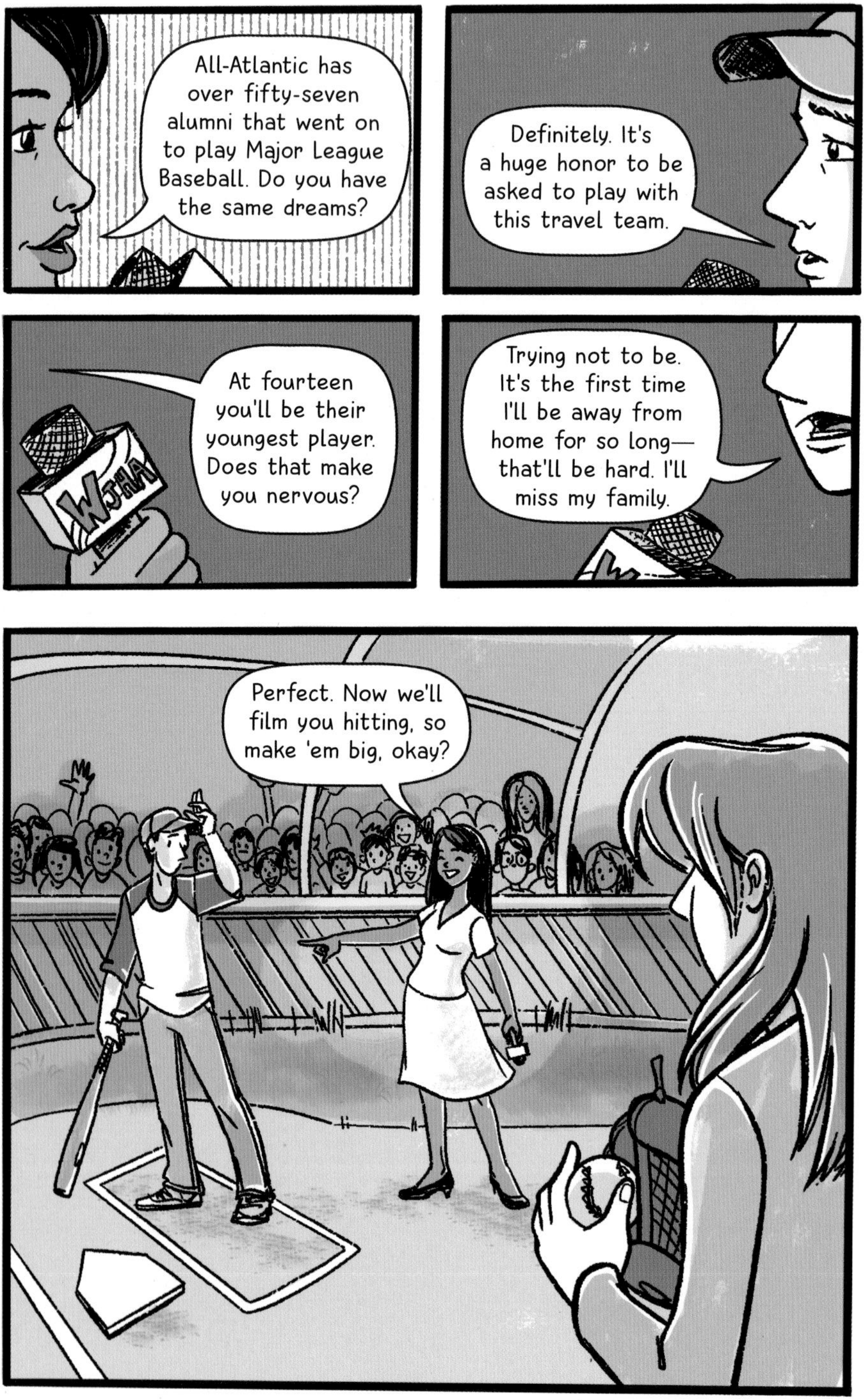
All-Atlantic has over fifty-seven alumni that went on to play Major League Baseball. Do you have the same dreams?
Definitely. It's a huge honor to be asked to play with this travel team.
At fourteen you'll be their youngest player. Does that make you nervous?
WJHA
Trying not to be. It's the first time I'll be away from home for so long— that'll be hard. I'll miss my family.
Perfect. Now we'll film you hitting, so make 'em big, okay?

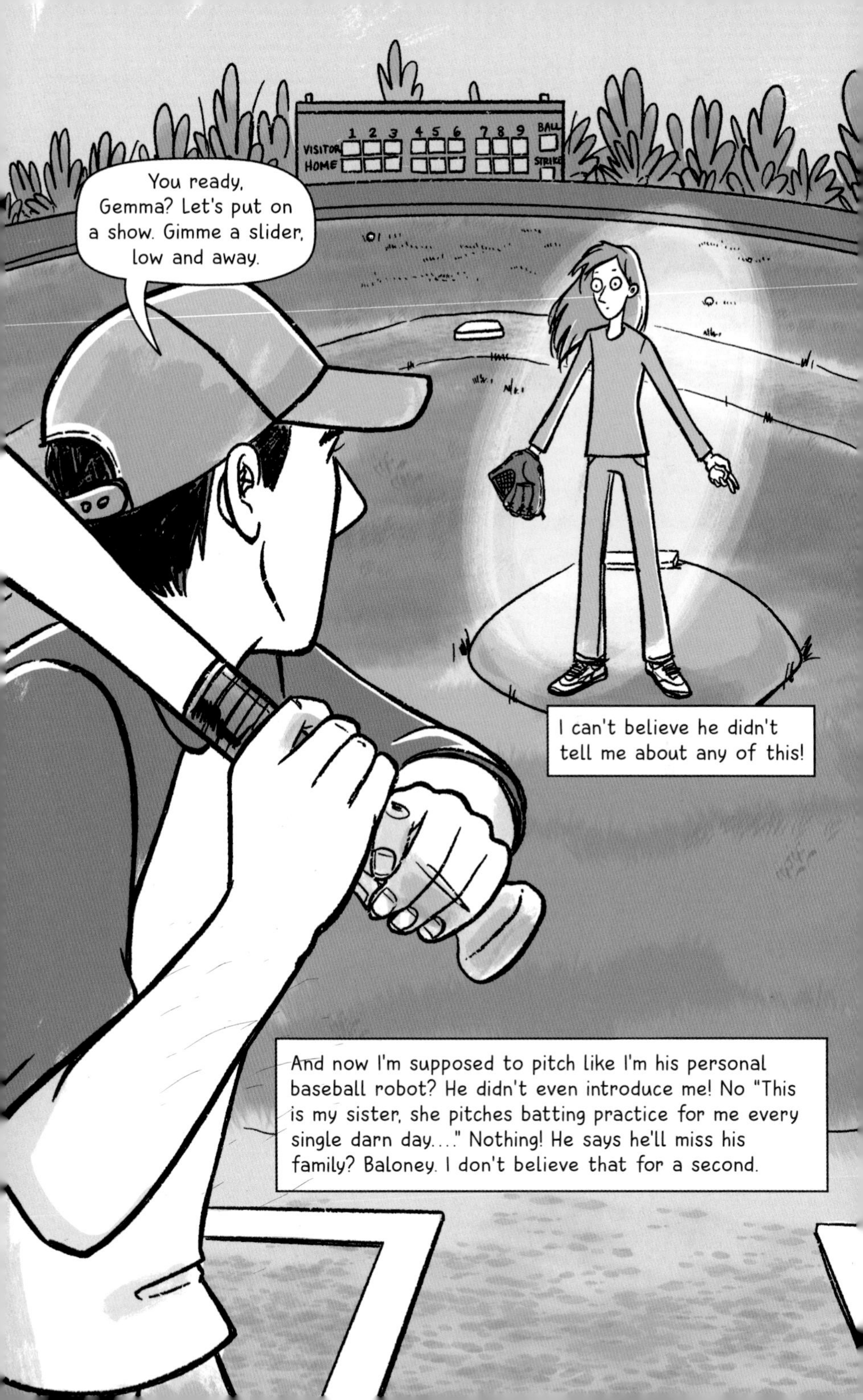

1 2 3 4 5 6 7 8 9
BALL
VISITOR
HOME
STRIKE
You ready, Gemma? Let's put on a show. Gimme a slider, low and away.
I can't believe he didn't tell me about any of this!
And now I'm supposed to pitch like I'm his personal baseball robot? He didn't even introduce me! No "This is my sister, she pitches batting practice for me every single darn day...." Nothing! He says he'll miss his family? Baloney. I don't believe that for a second.

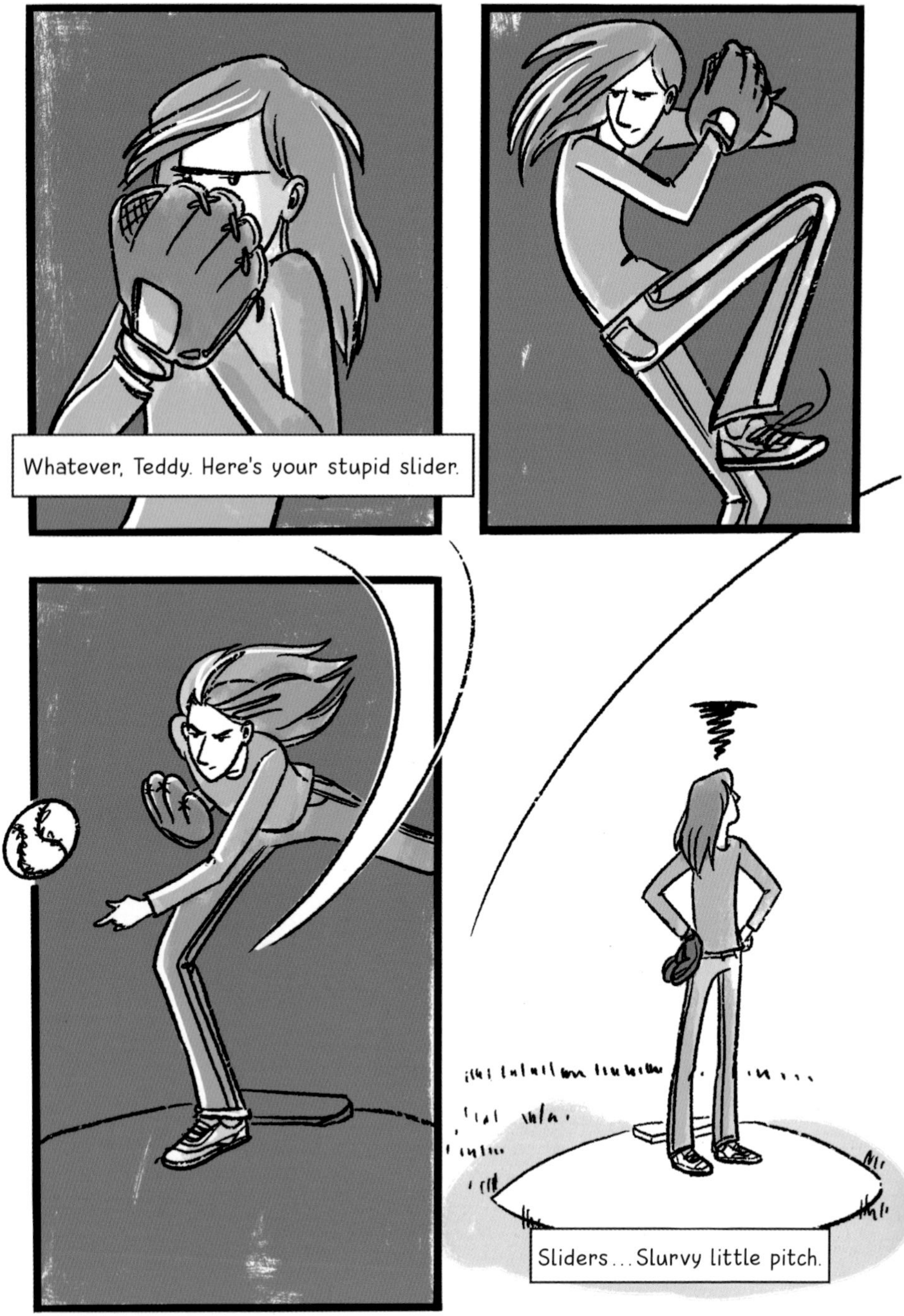
Whatever, Teddy. Here's your stupid slider.
Sliders... Slurvy little pitch.

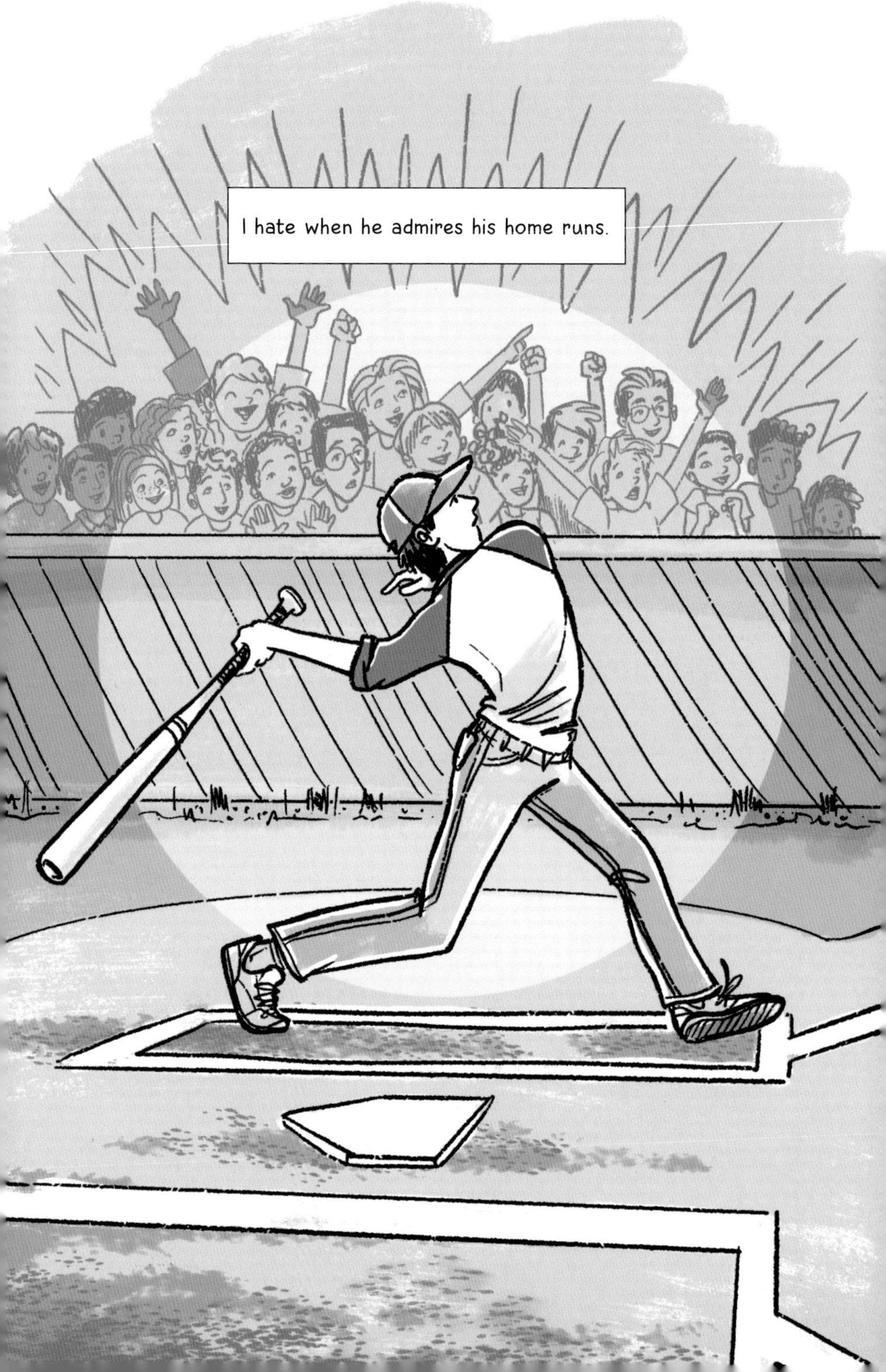
I hate when he admires his home runs.

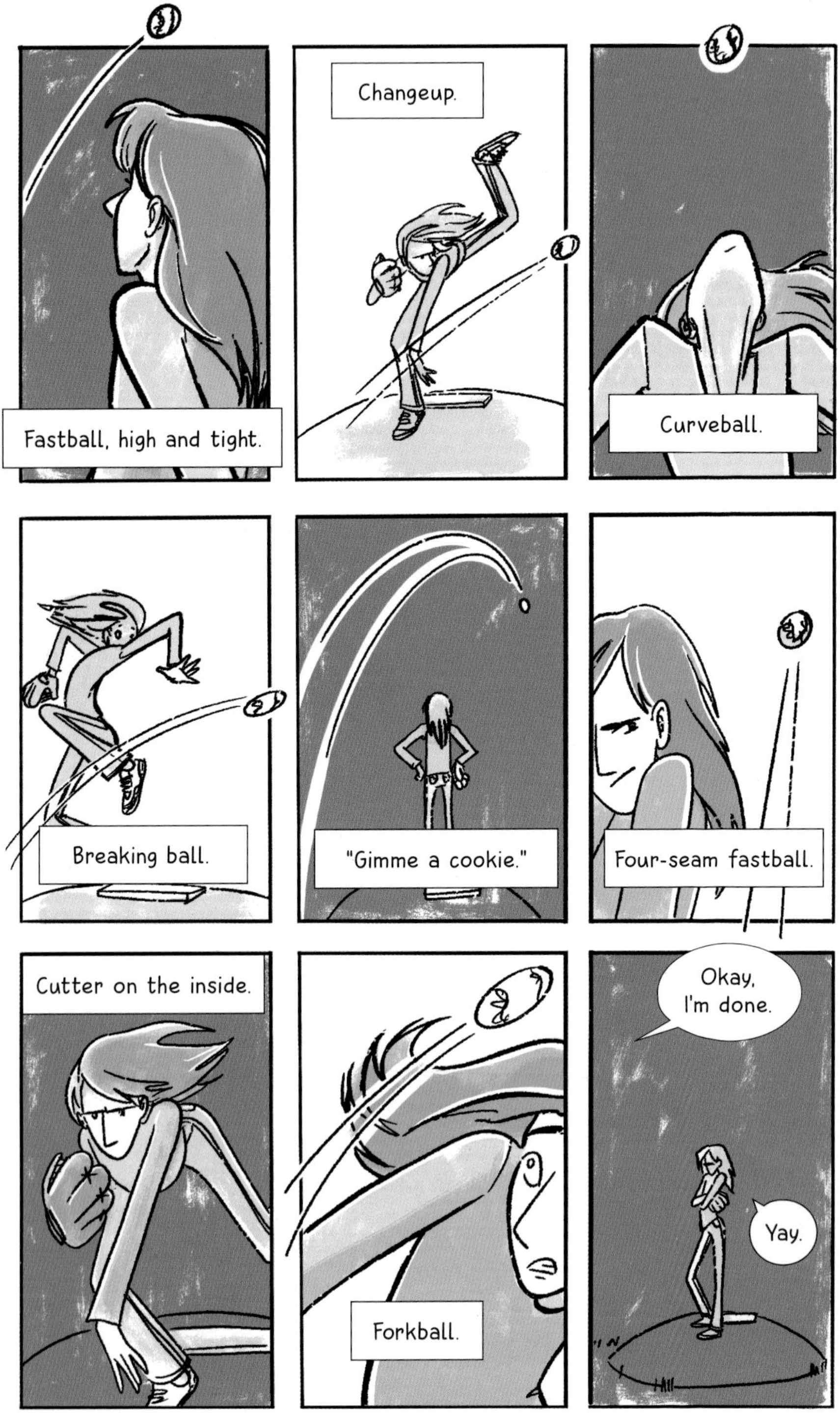

Fastball, high and tight.
Changeup.
Curveball.
Breaking ball.
"Gimme a cookie."
Four-seam fastball.
Cutter on the inside.
Forkball.
Okay, I'm done.
Yay.

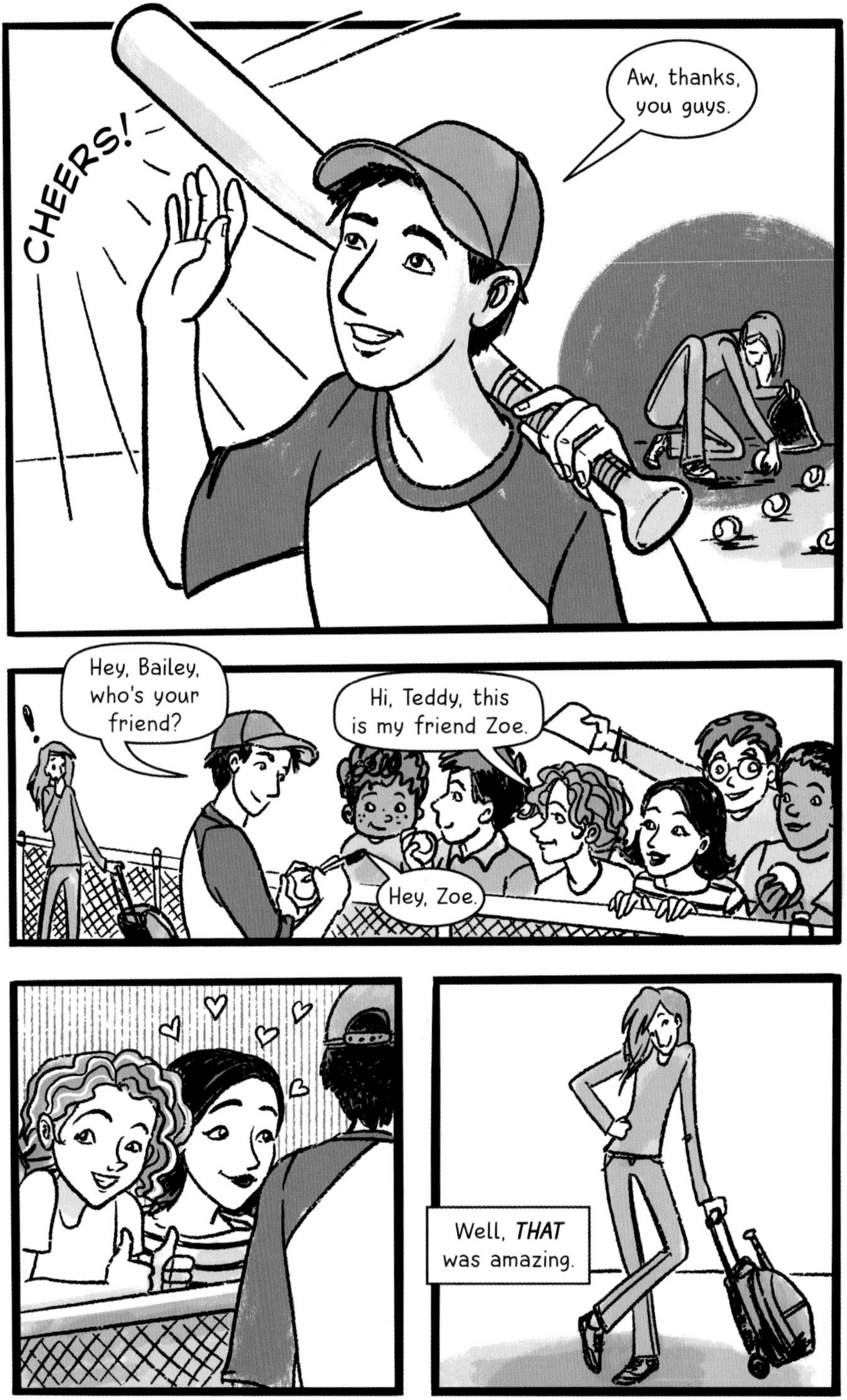
CHEERS!
Aw, thanks, you guys.
Hey, Bailey, who's your friend?
Hi, Teddy, this is my friend Zoe.
Hey, Zoe.
Well, THAT was amazing.

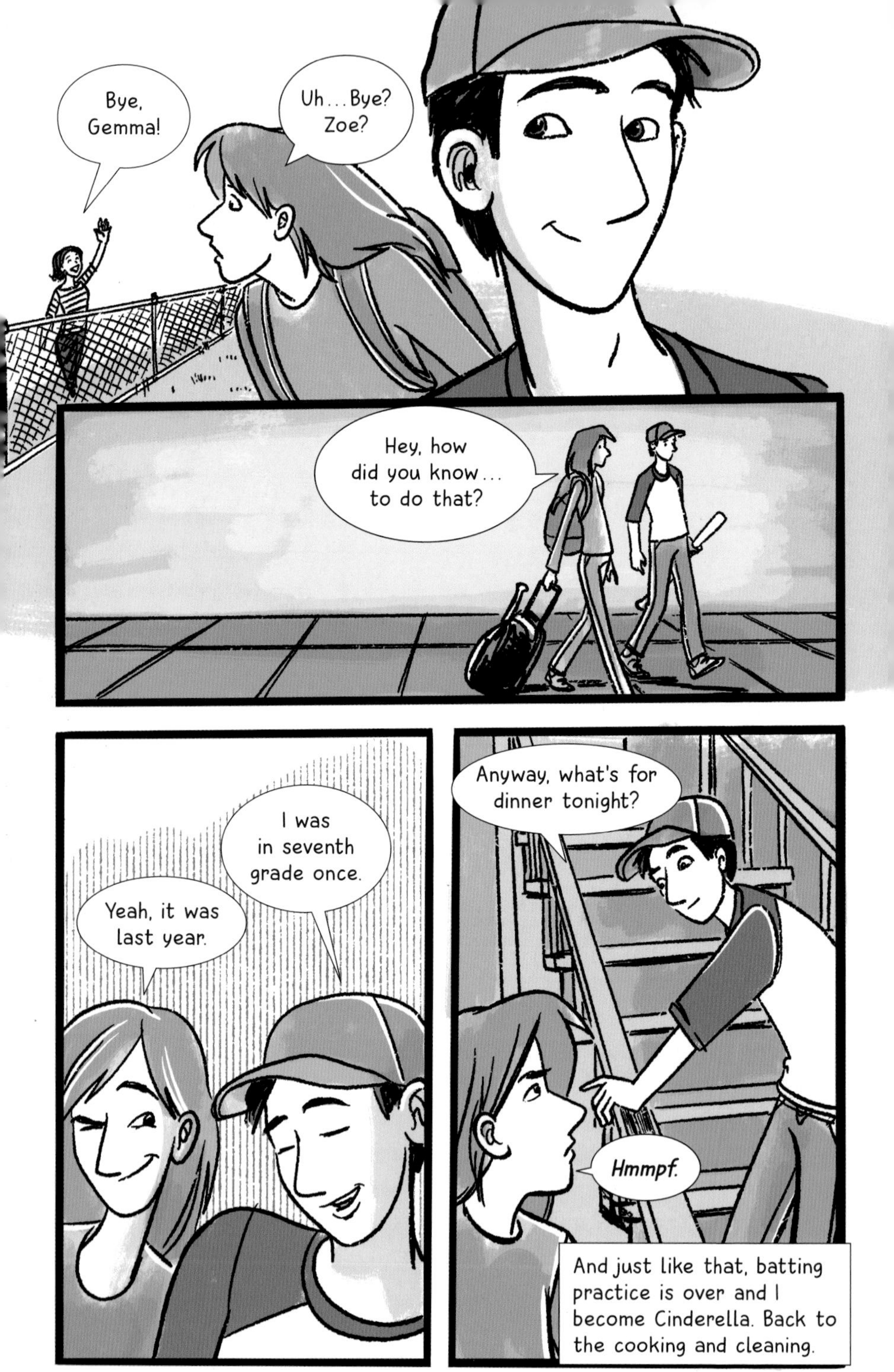
Bye, Gemma!
Uh... Bye? Zoe?
Hey, how did you know... to do that?
I was in seventh grade once.
Yeah, it was last year.
Anyway, what's for dinner tonight?
Hmmpf.
And just like that, batting practice is over and I become Cinderella. Back to the cooking and cleaning.

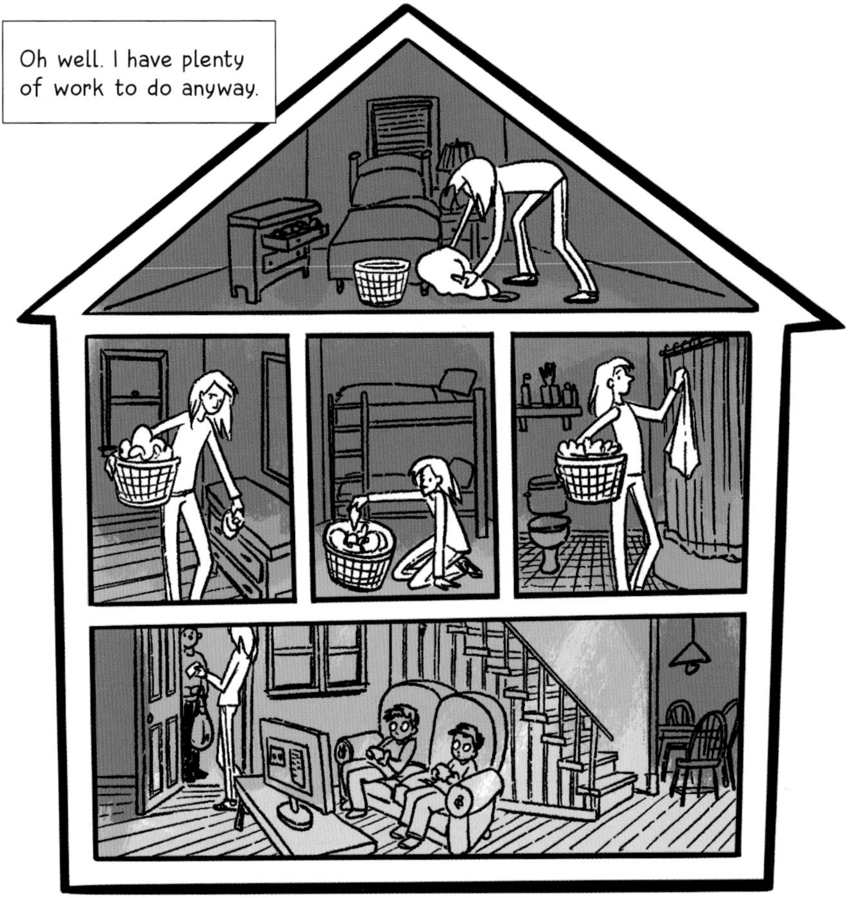
Oh well. I have plenty of work to do anyway.

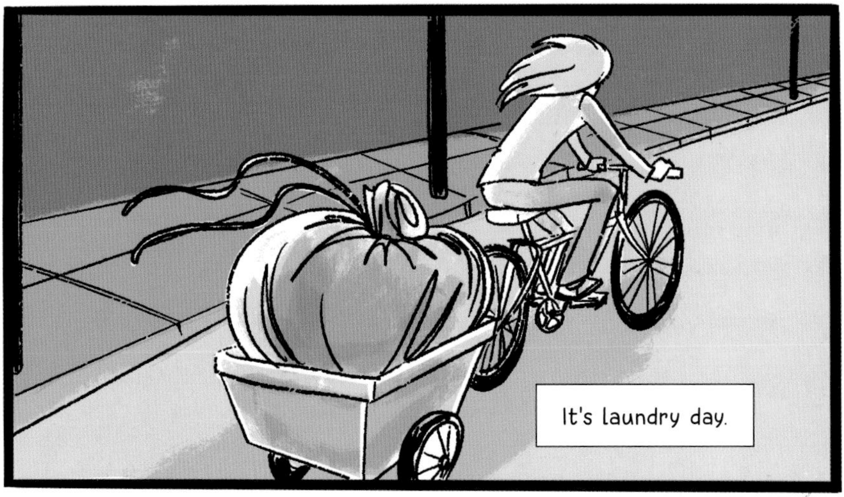
It's laundry day.

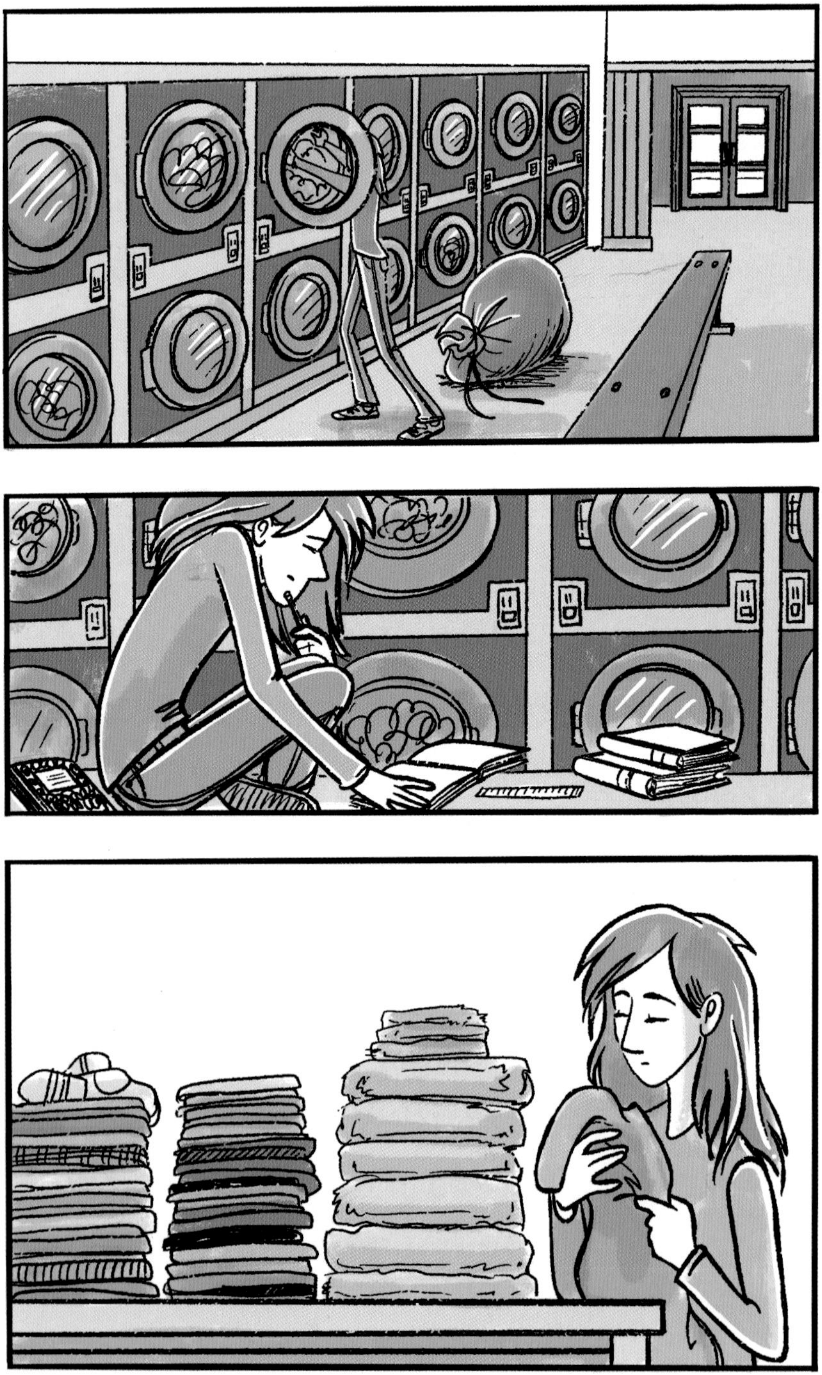

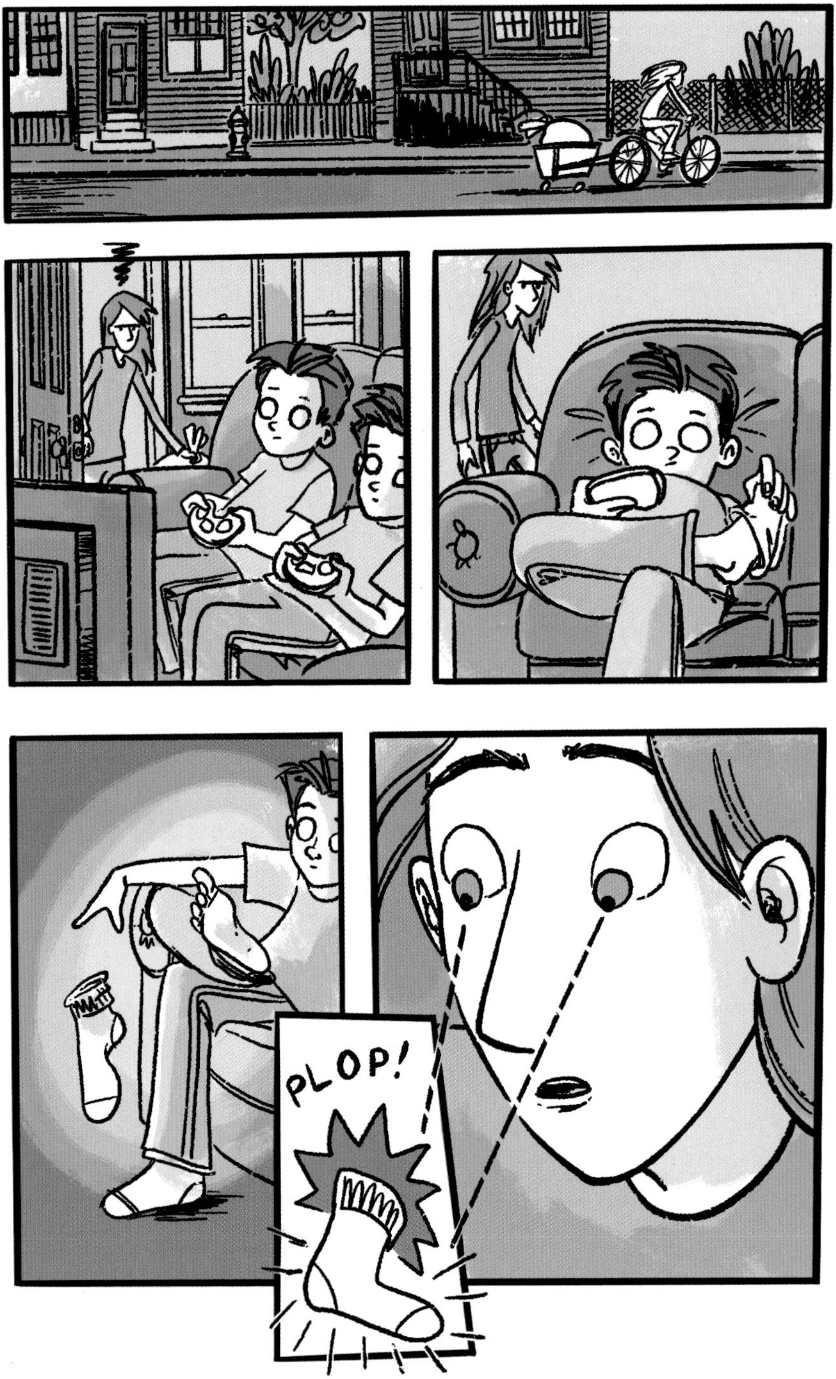
PLOP!

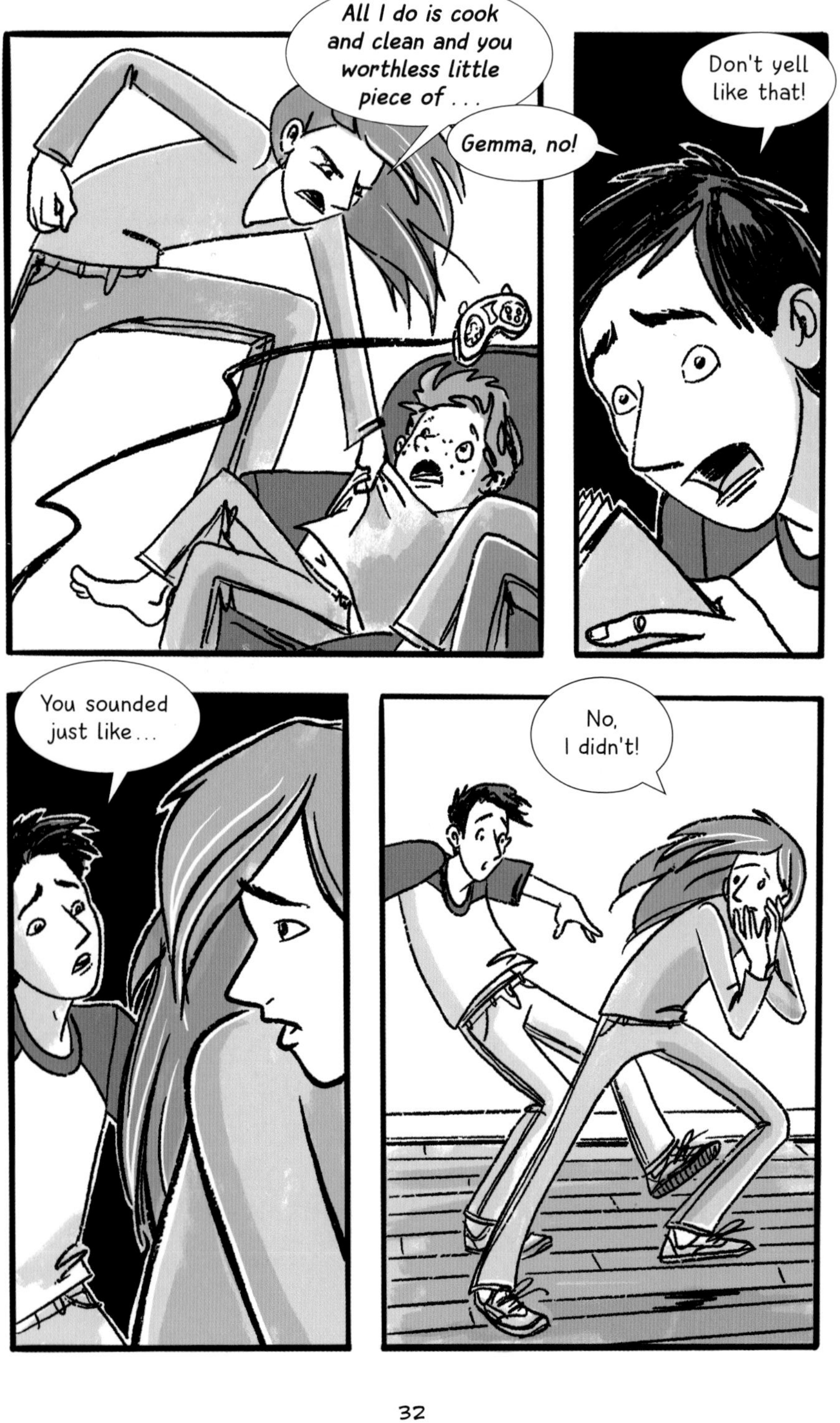
All I do is cook and clean and you worthless little piece of . . .
Gemma, no!
Don't yell like that!
You sounded just like...
No, I didn't!

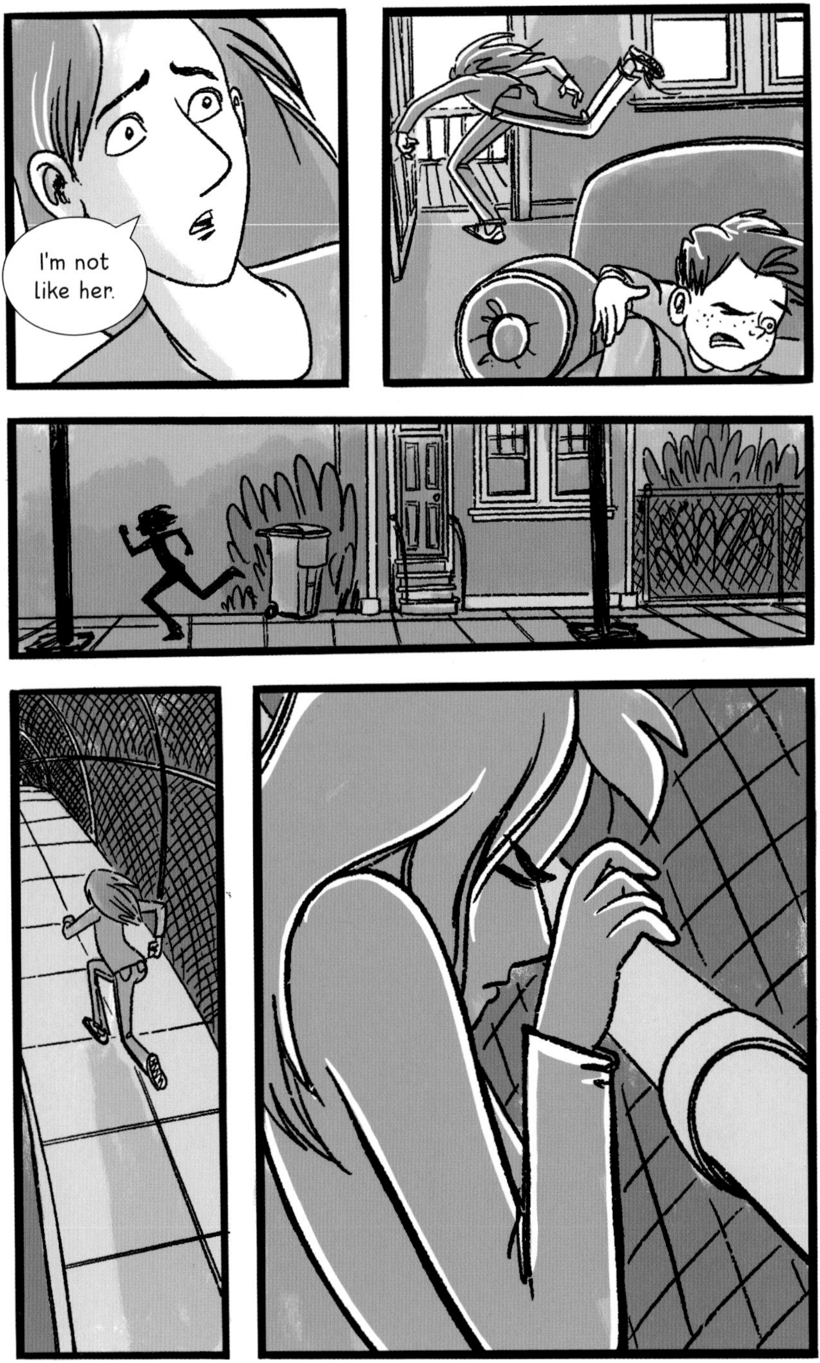
I'm not like her.

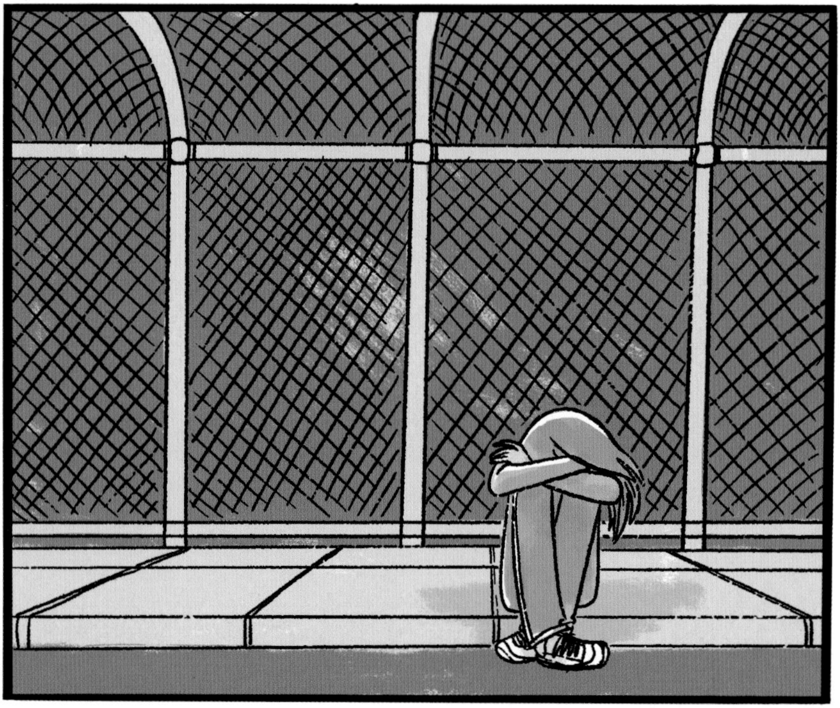

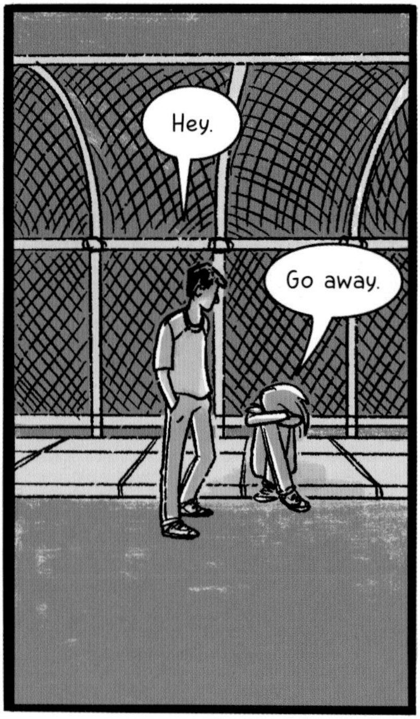
Hey.
Go away.

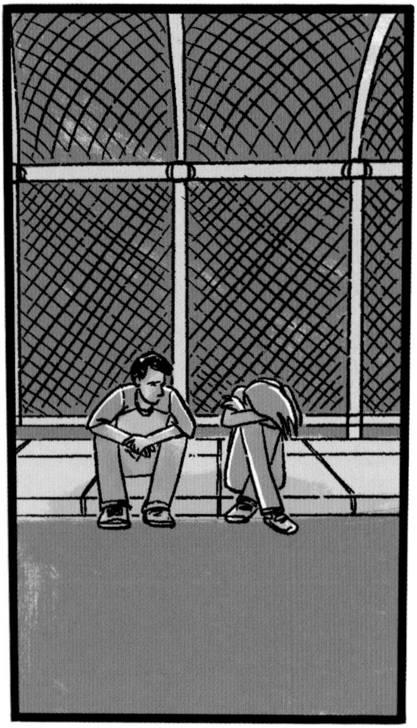

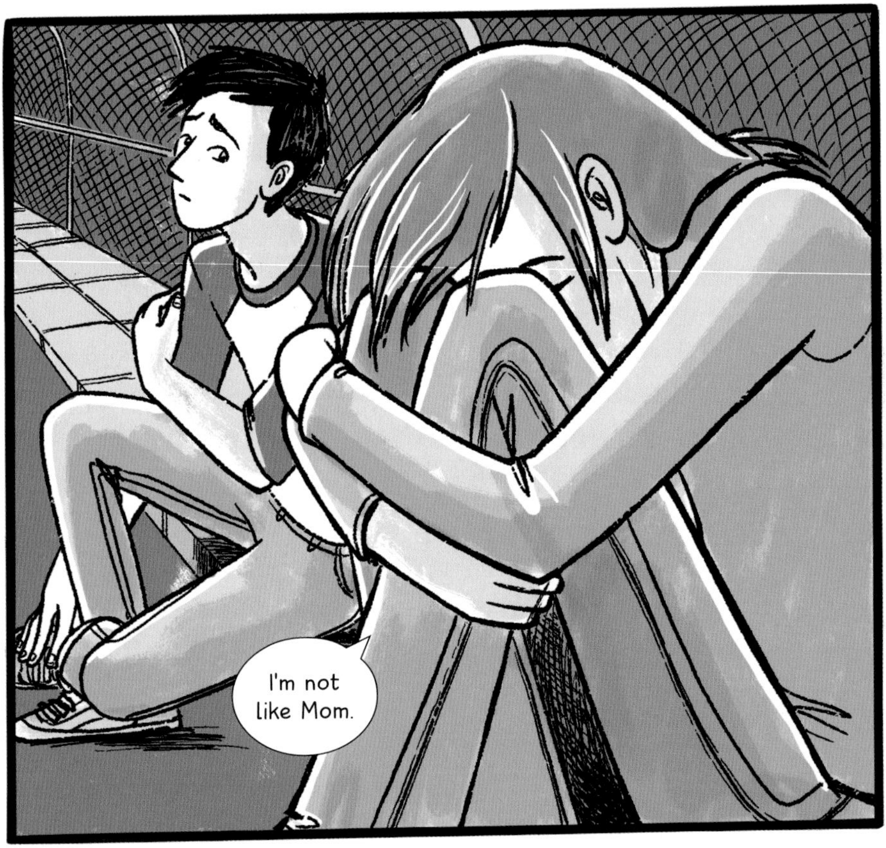
I'm not like Mom.

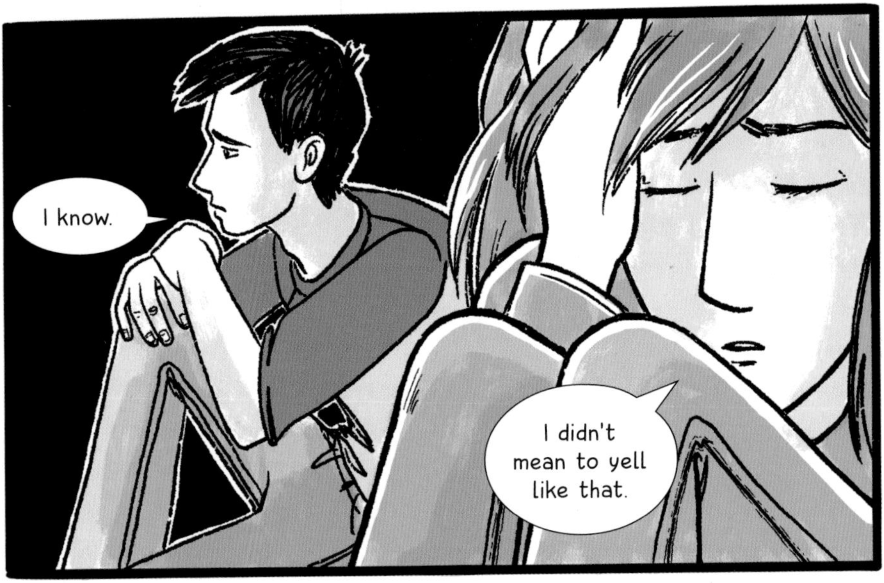
I know.
I didn't mean to yell like that.

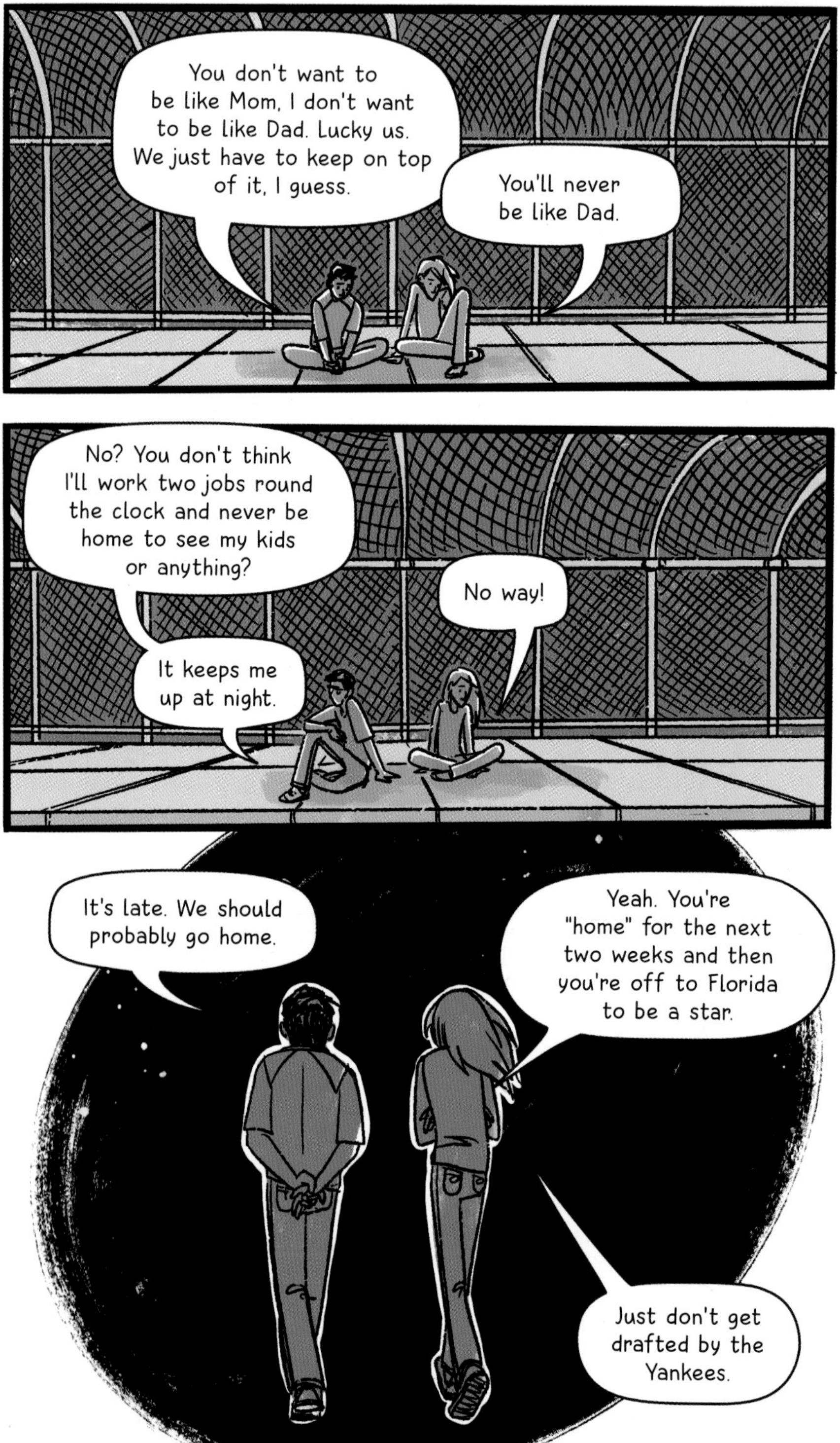
You don't want to be like Mom, I don't want to be like Dad. Lucky us. We just have to keep on top of it, I guess.
You'll never be like Dad.
No? You don't think I'll work two jobs round the clock and never be home to see my kids or anything?
It keeps me up at night.
No way!
It's late. We should probably go home.
Yeah. You're "home" for the next two weeks and then you're off to Florida to be a star.
Just don't get drafted by the Yankees.

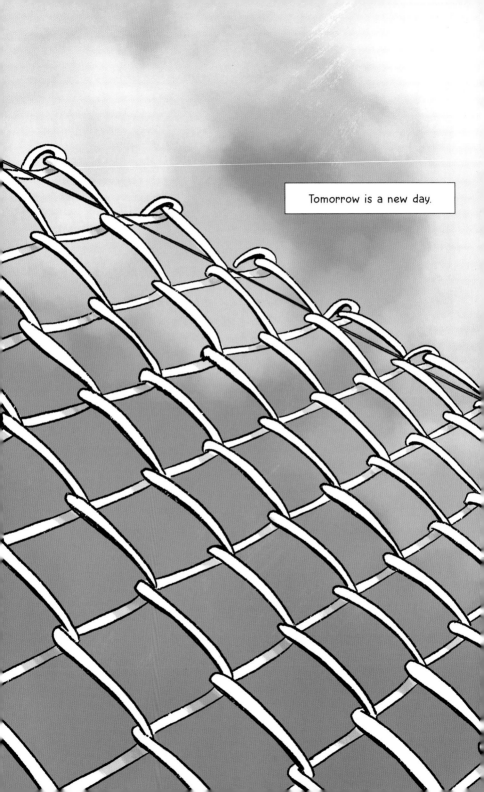

Tomorrow is a new day.

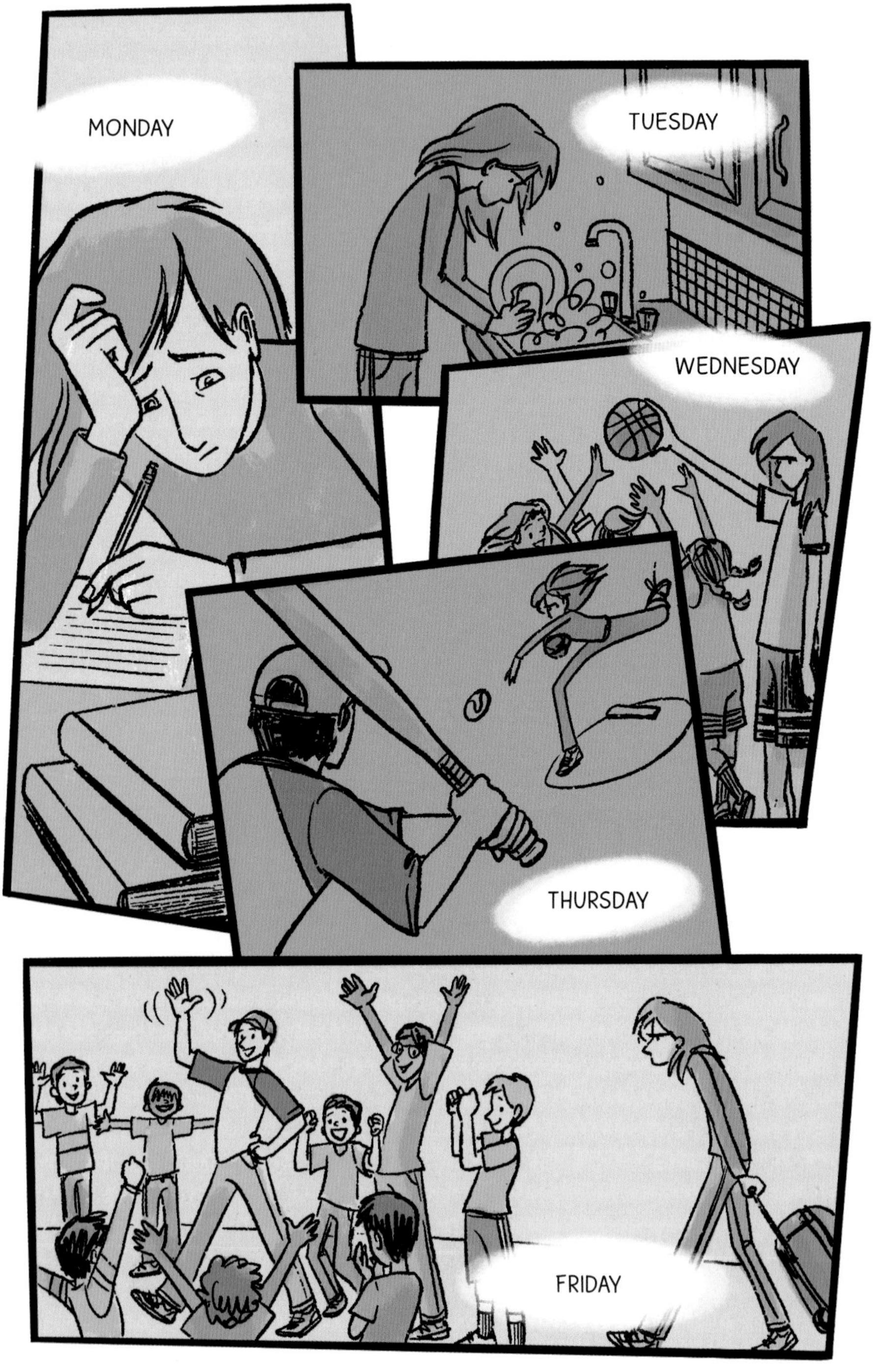
MONDAY
TUESDAY
WEDNESDAY
THURSDAY
FRIDAY

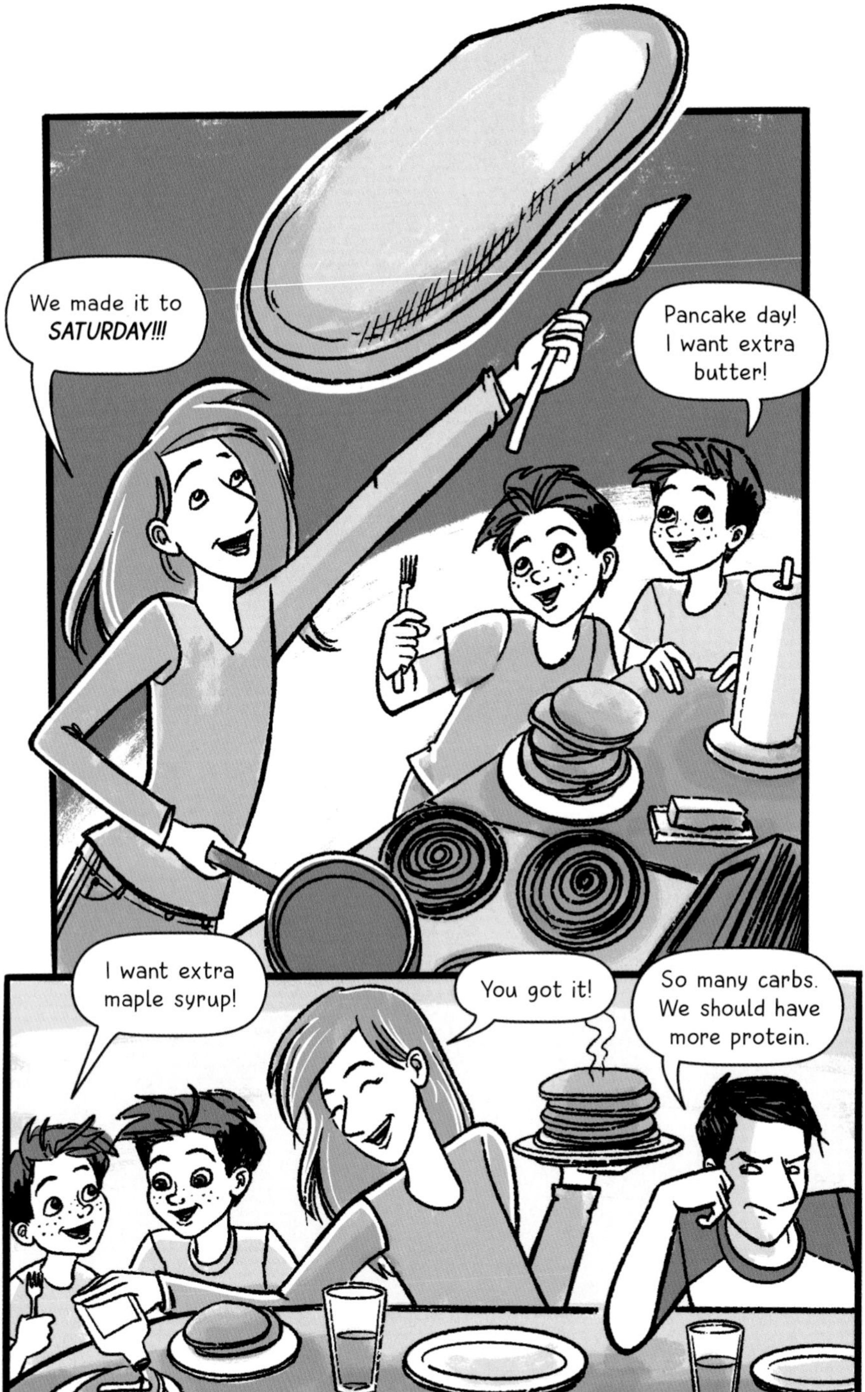
We made it to *SATURDAY!!!*
Pancake day! I want extra butter!
I want extra maple syrup!
You got it!
So many carbs. We should have more protein.

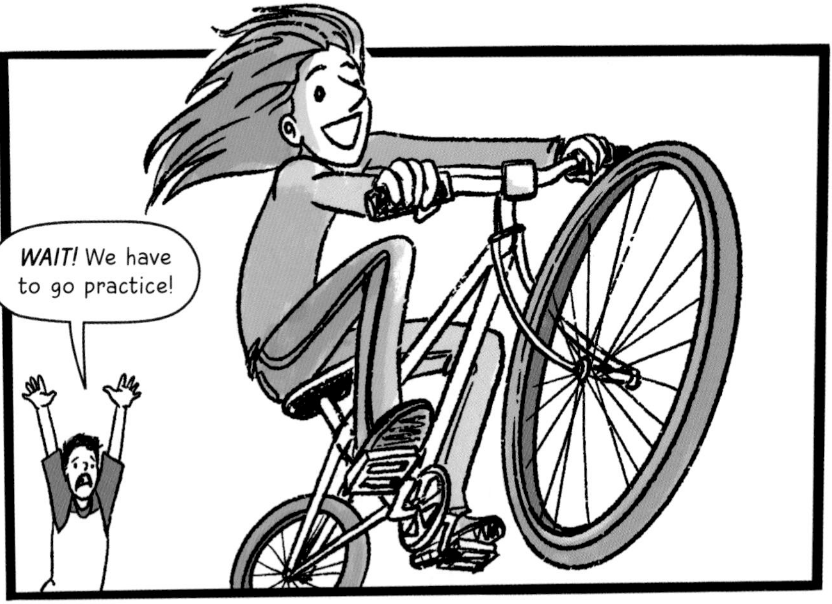
WAIT! We have to go practice!

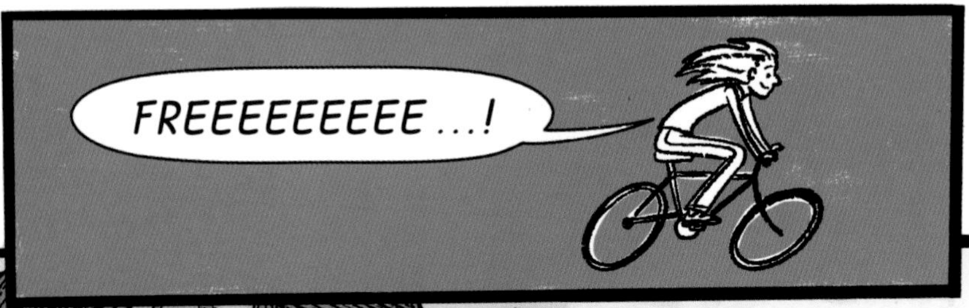
FREEEEEEEEEE . . . !

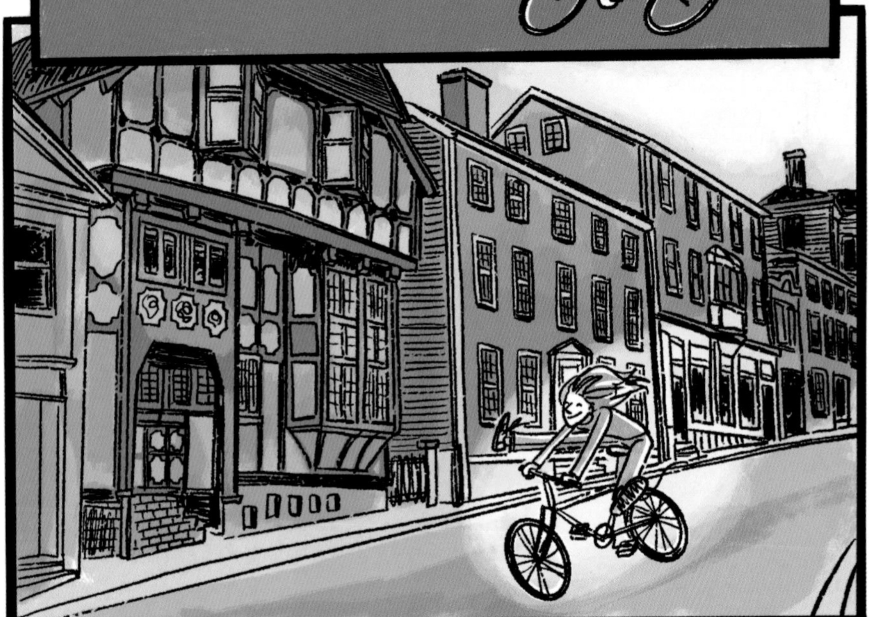

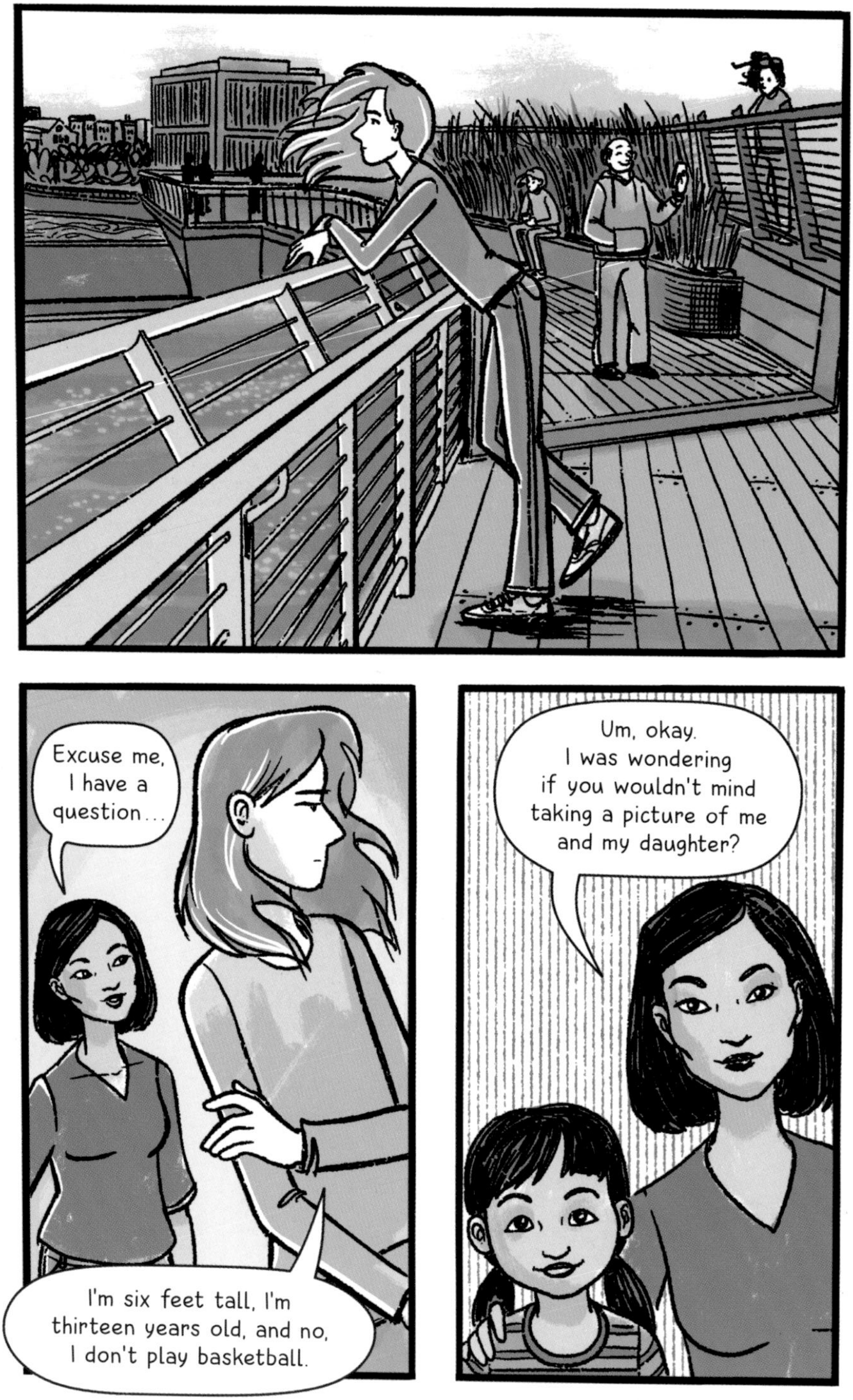
Excuse me, I have a question...
I'm six feet tall, I'm thirteen years old, and no, I don't play basketball.
Um, okay. I was wondering if you wouldn't mind taking a picture of me and my daughter?

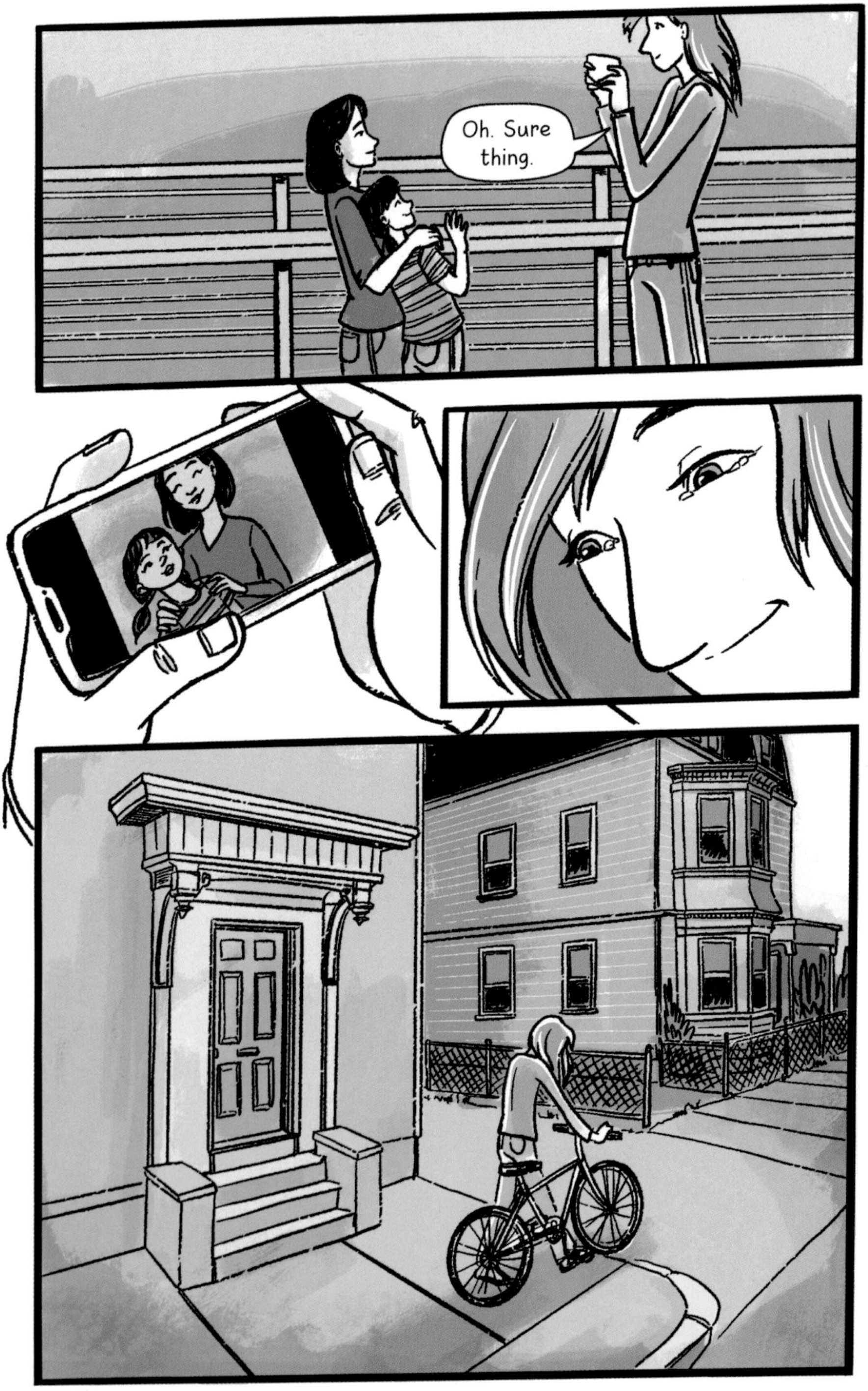
Oh. Sure thing.

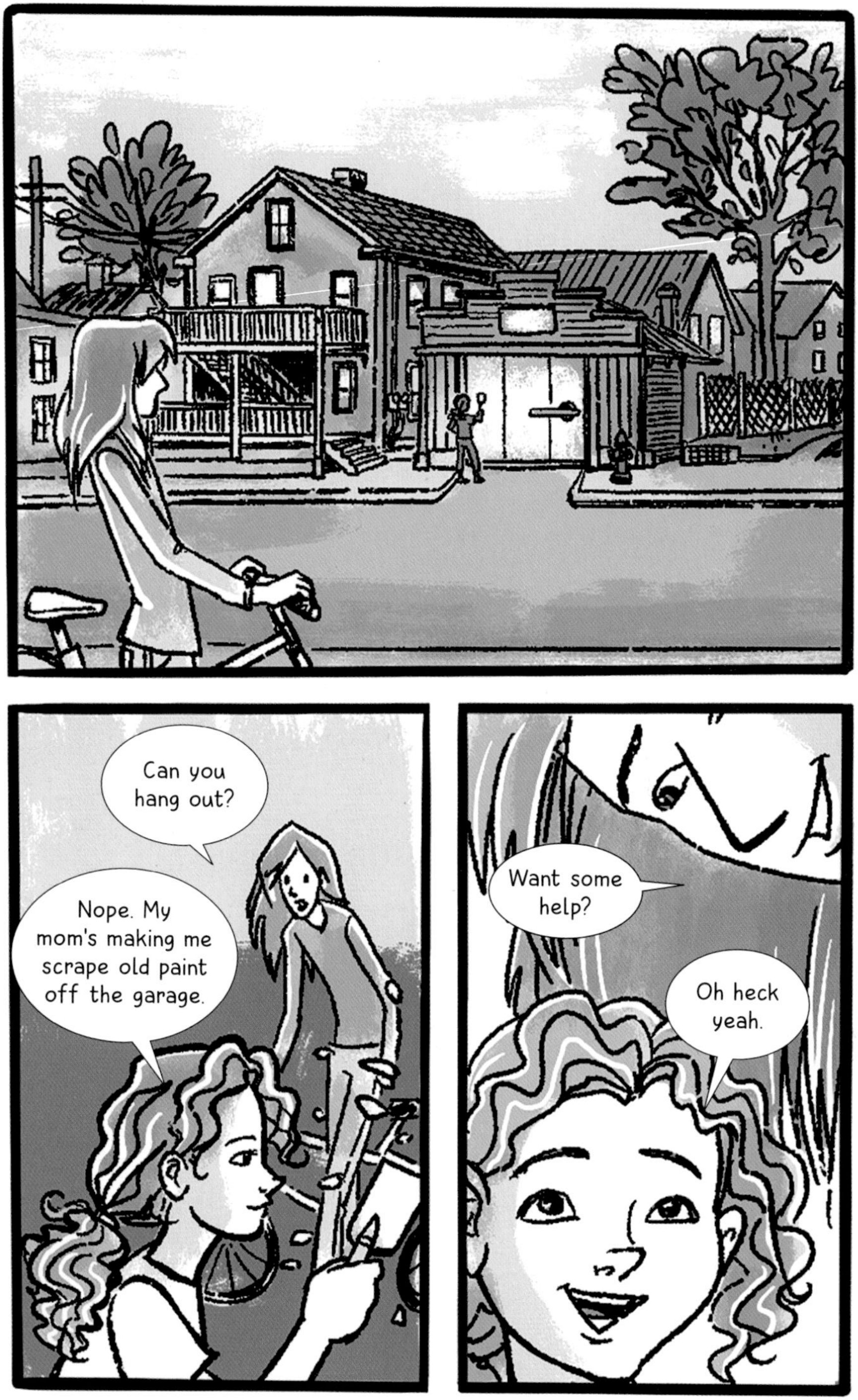
Can you hang out?
Nope. My mom's making me scrape old paint off the garage.
Want some help?
Oh heck yeah.

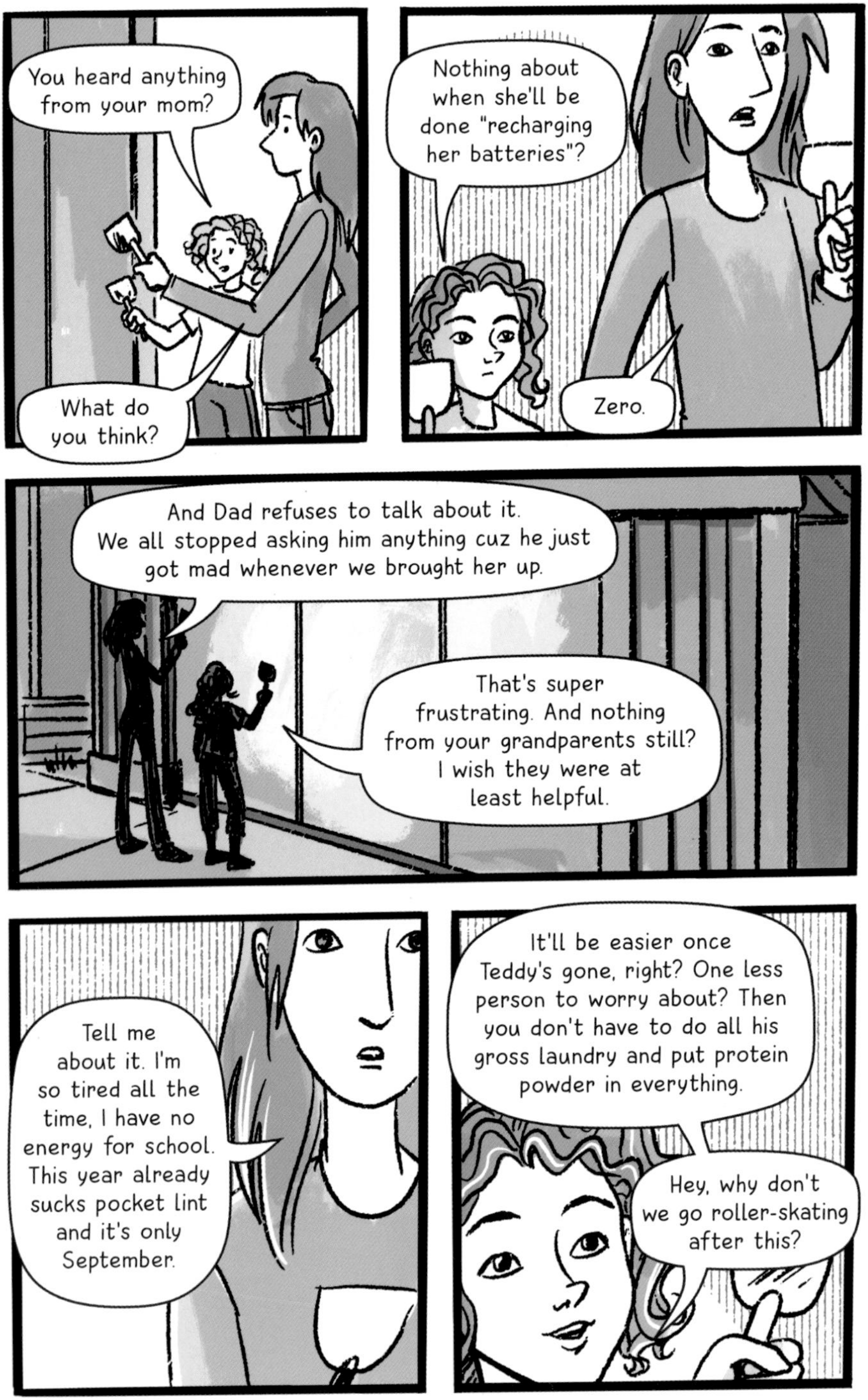
You heard anything from your mom?
What do you think?
Nothing about when she'll be done "recharging her batteries"?
Zero.
And Dad refuses to talk about it. We all stopped asking him anything cuz he just got mad whenever we brought her up.
That's super frustrating. And nothing from your grandparents still? I wish they were at least helpful.
Tell me about it. I'm so tired all the time, I have no energy for school. This year already sucks pocket lint and it's only September.
It'll be easier once Teddy's gone, right? One less person to worry about? Then you don't have to do all his gross laundry and put protein powder in everything.
Hey, why don't we go roller-skating after this?

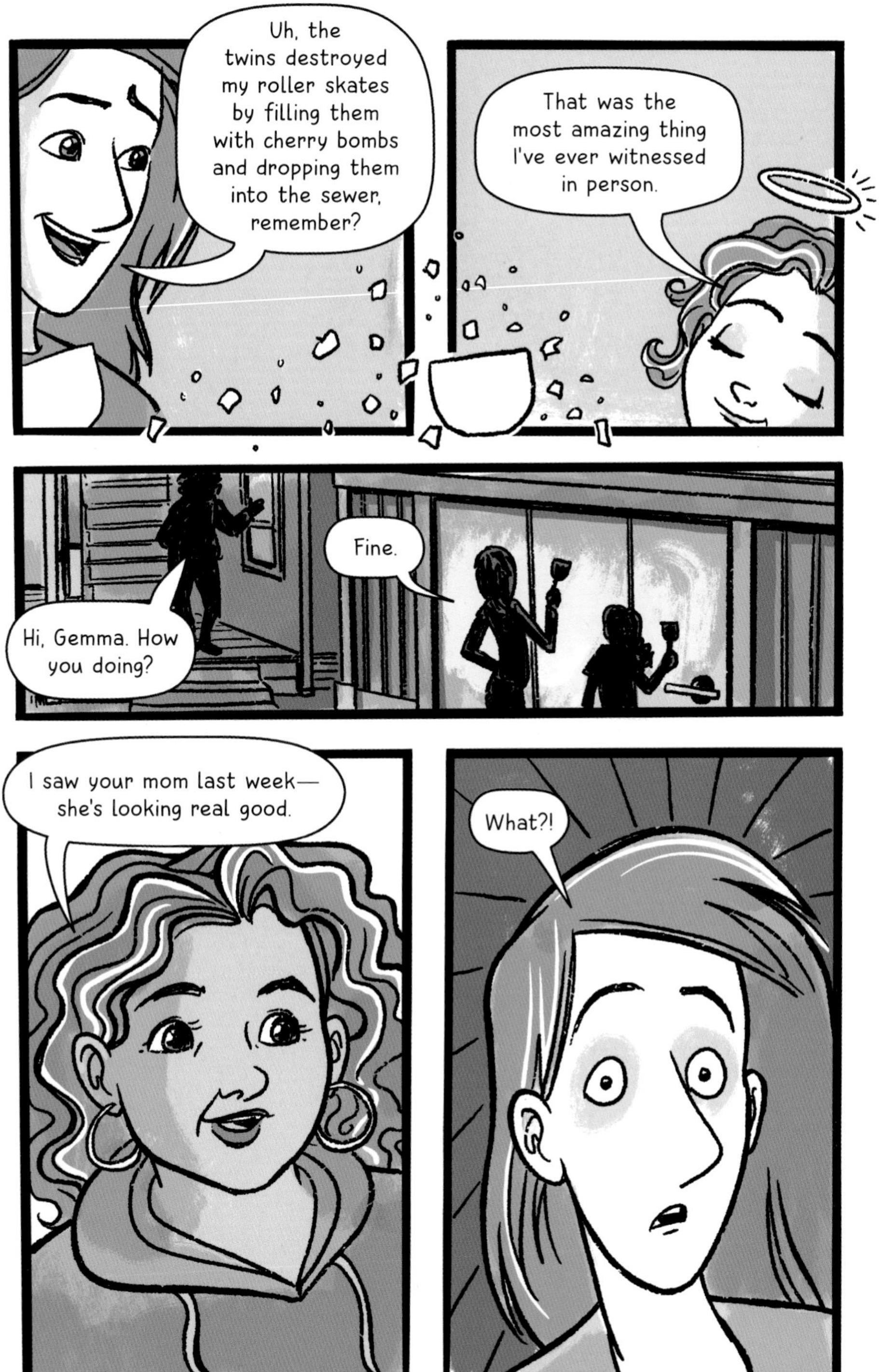
Uh, the twins destroyed my roller skates by filling them with cherry bombs and dropping them into the sewer, remember?
That was the most amazing thing I've ever witnessed in person.
Hi, Gemma. How you doing?
Fine.
I saw your mom last week—she's looking real good.
What?!

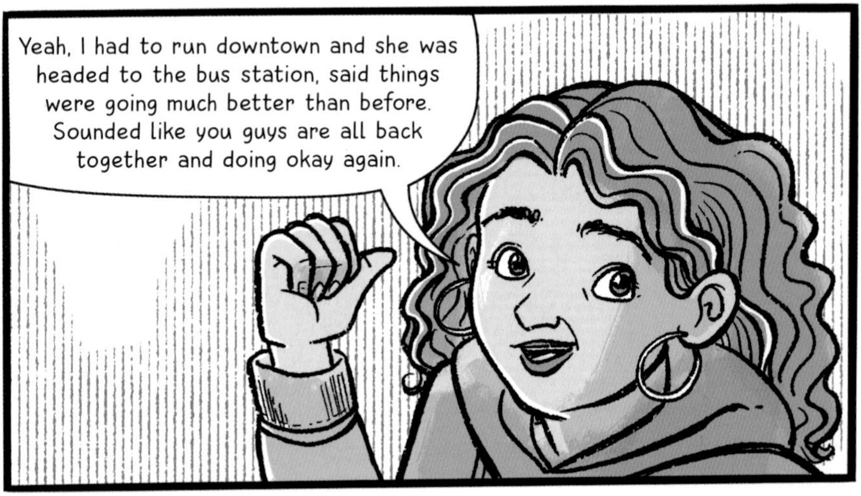
Yeah, I had to run downtown and she was headed to the bus station, said things were going much better than before. Sounded like you guys are all back together and doing okay again.

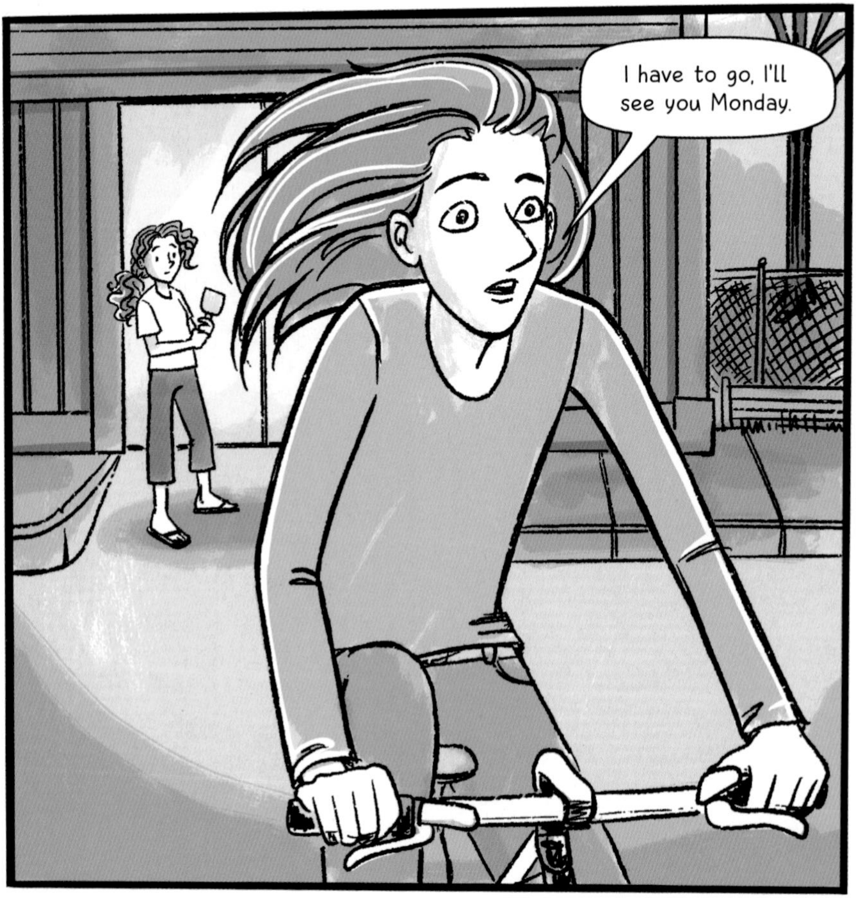
I have to go, I'll see you Monday.

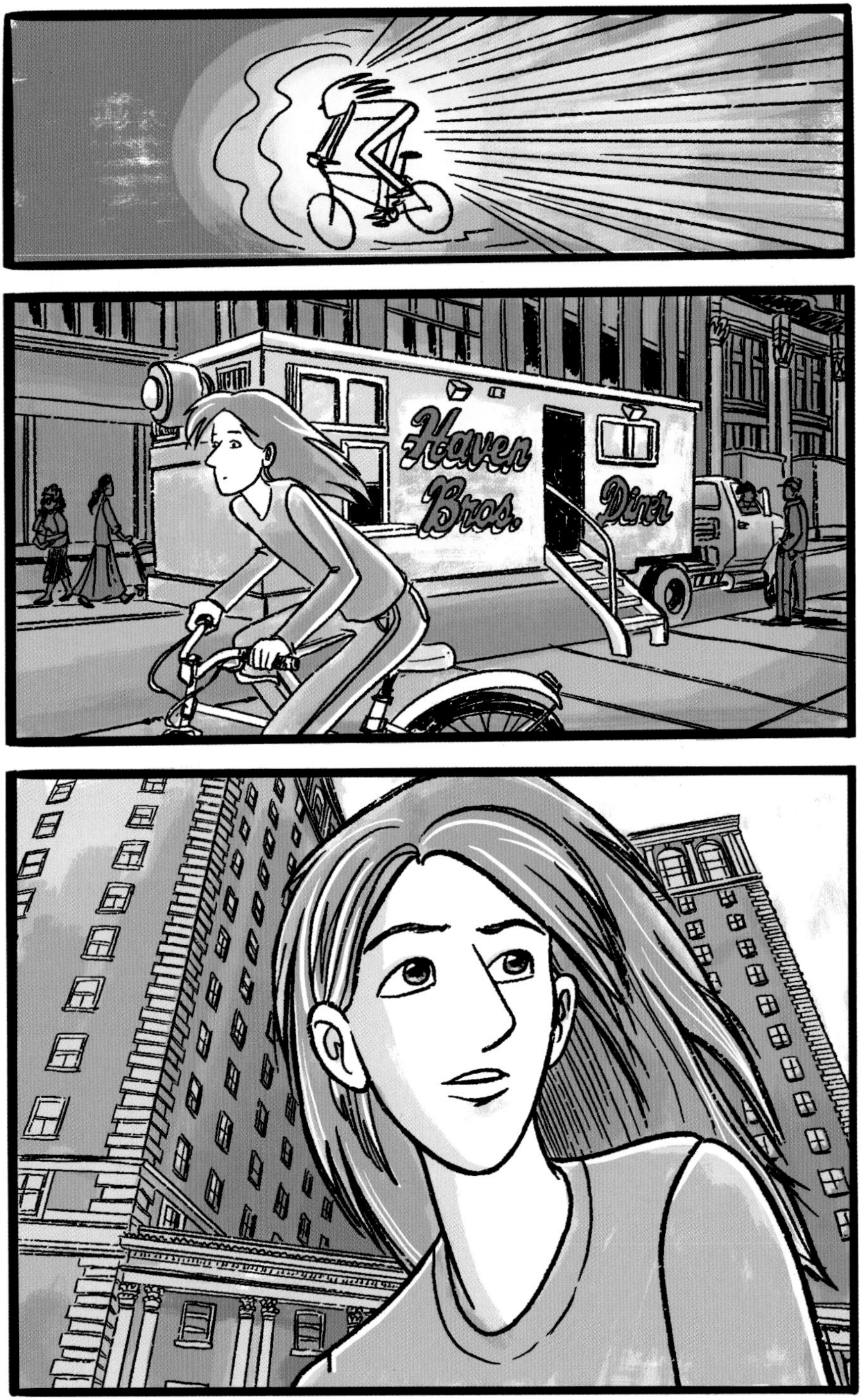
Haven Bros. Diner

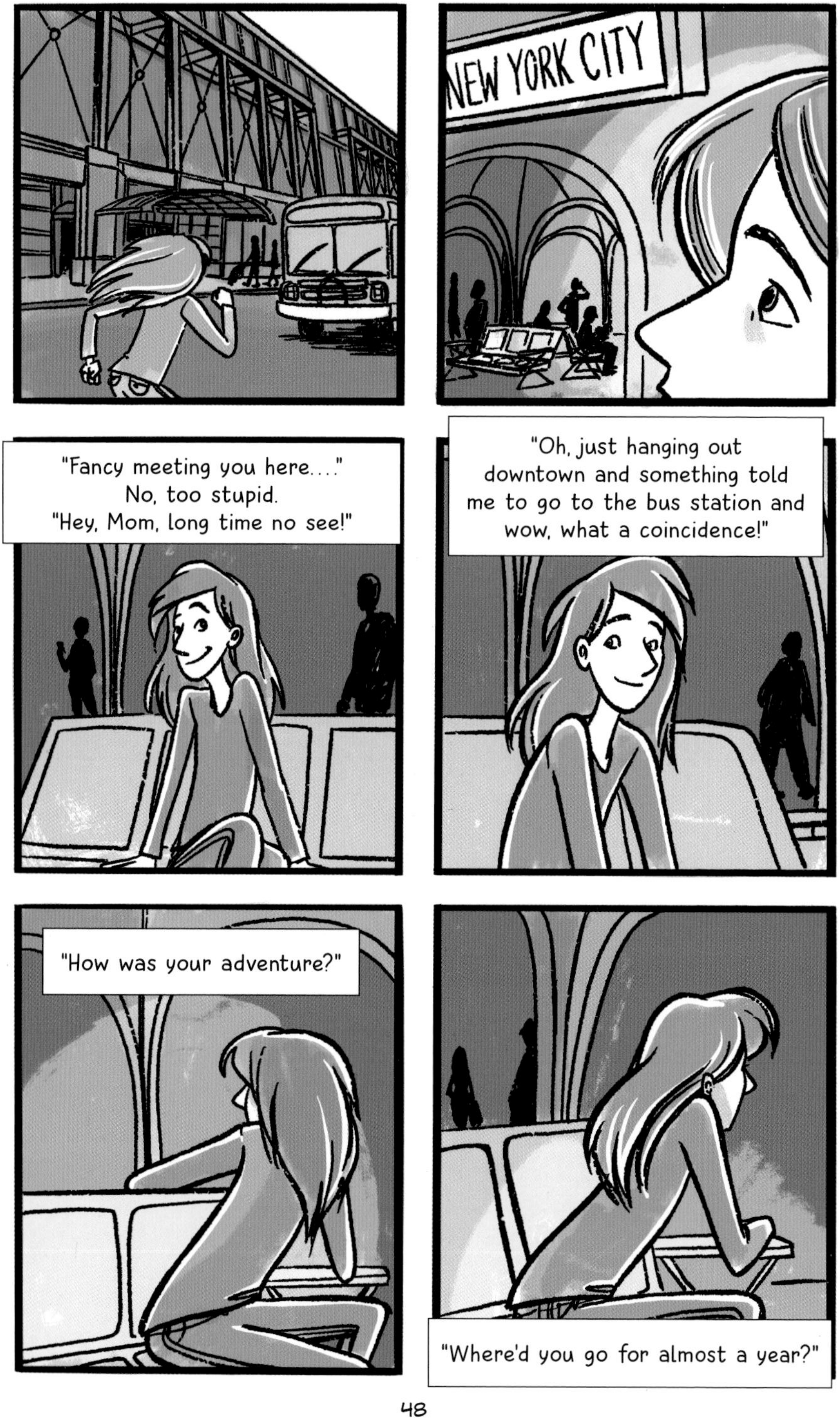
NEW YORK CITY
"Fancy meeting you here...."
No, too stupid.
"Hey, Mom, long time no see!"
"Oh, just hanging out downtown and something told me to go to the bus station and wow, what a coincidence!"
"How was your adventure?"
"Where'd you go for almost a year?"

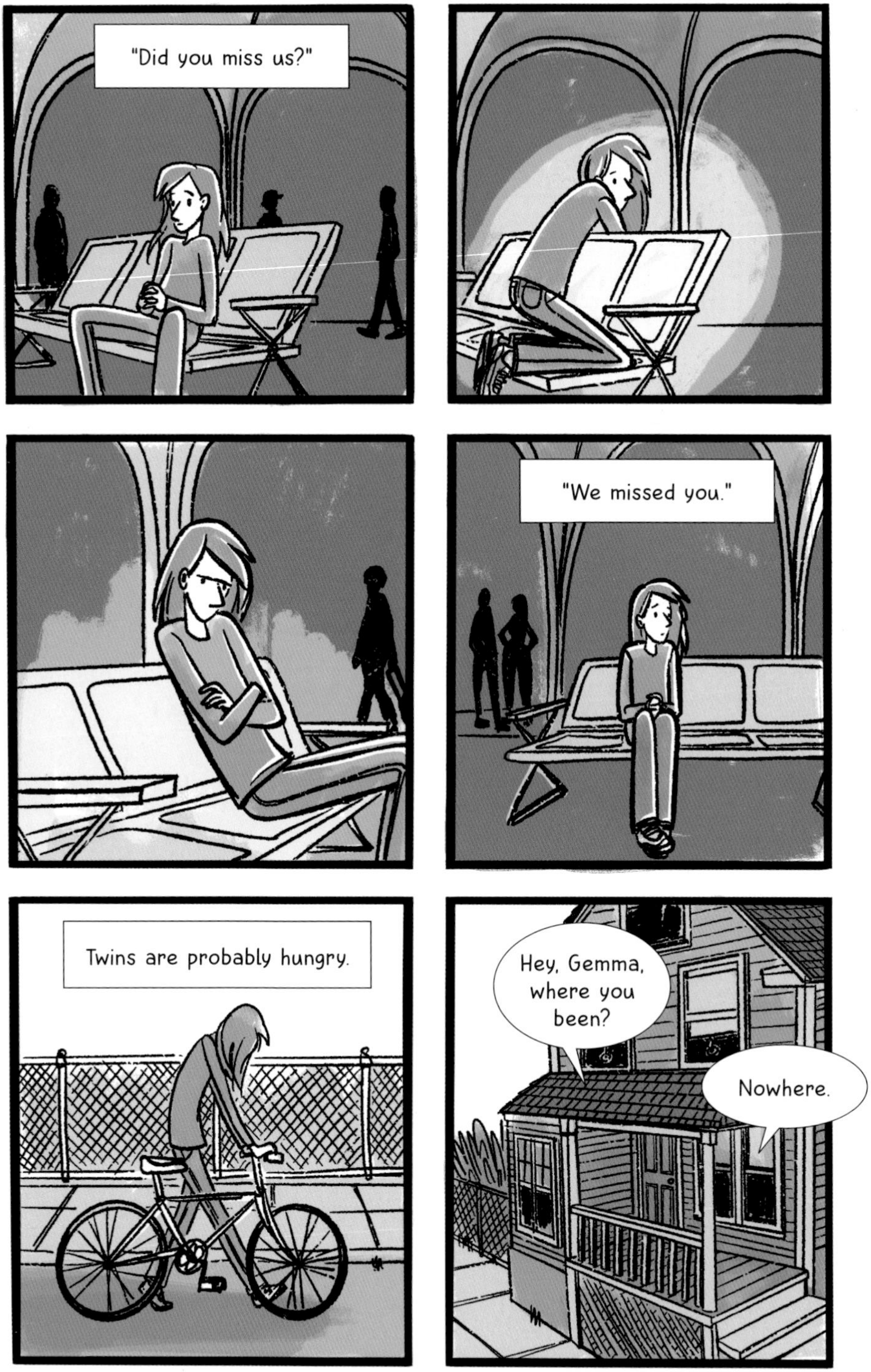
"Did you miss us?"
"We missed you."
Twins are probably hungry.
Hey, Gemma, where you been?
Nowhere.

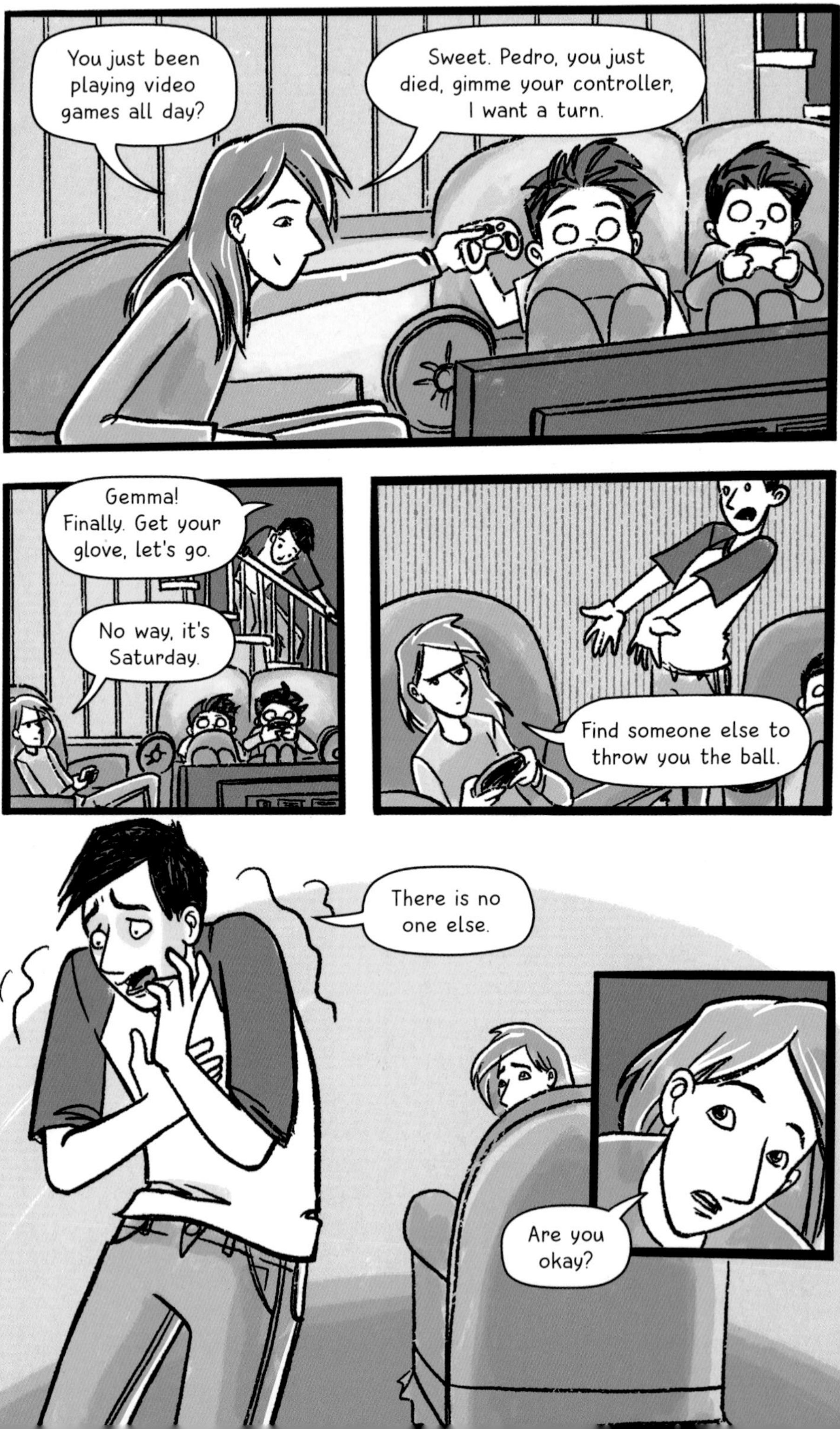
You just been playing video games all day?
Sweet. Pedro, you just died, gimme your controller, I want a turn.
Gemma! Finally. Get your glove, let's go.
No way, it's Saturday.
Find someone else to throw you the ball.
There is no one else.
Are you okay?

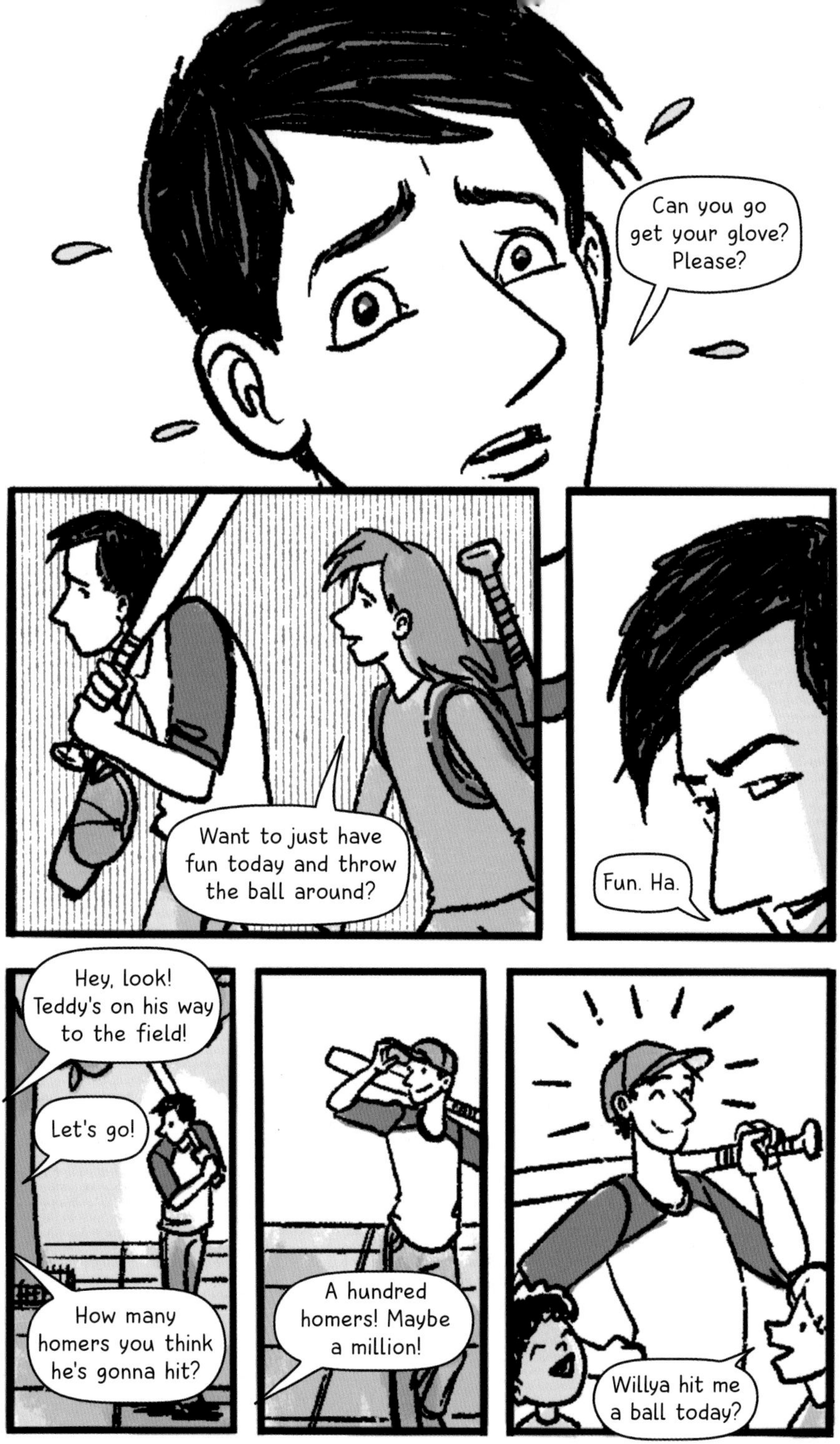
Can you go get your glove? Please?
Want to just have fun today and throw the ball around?
Fun. Ha.
Hey, look! Teddy's on his way to the field!
Let's go!
How many homers you think he's gonna hit?
A hundred homers! Maybe a million!
Willya hit me a ball today?

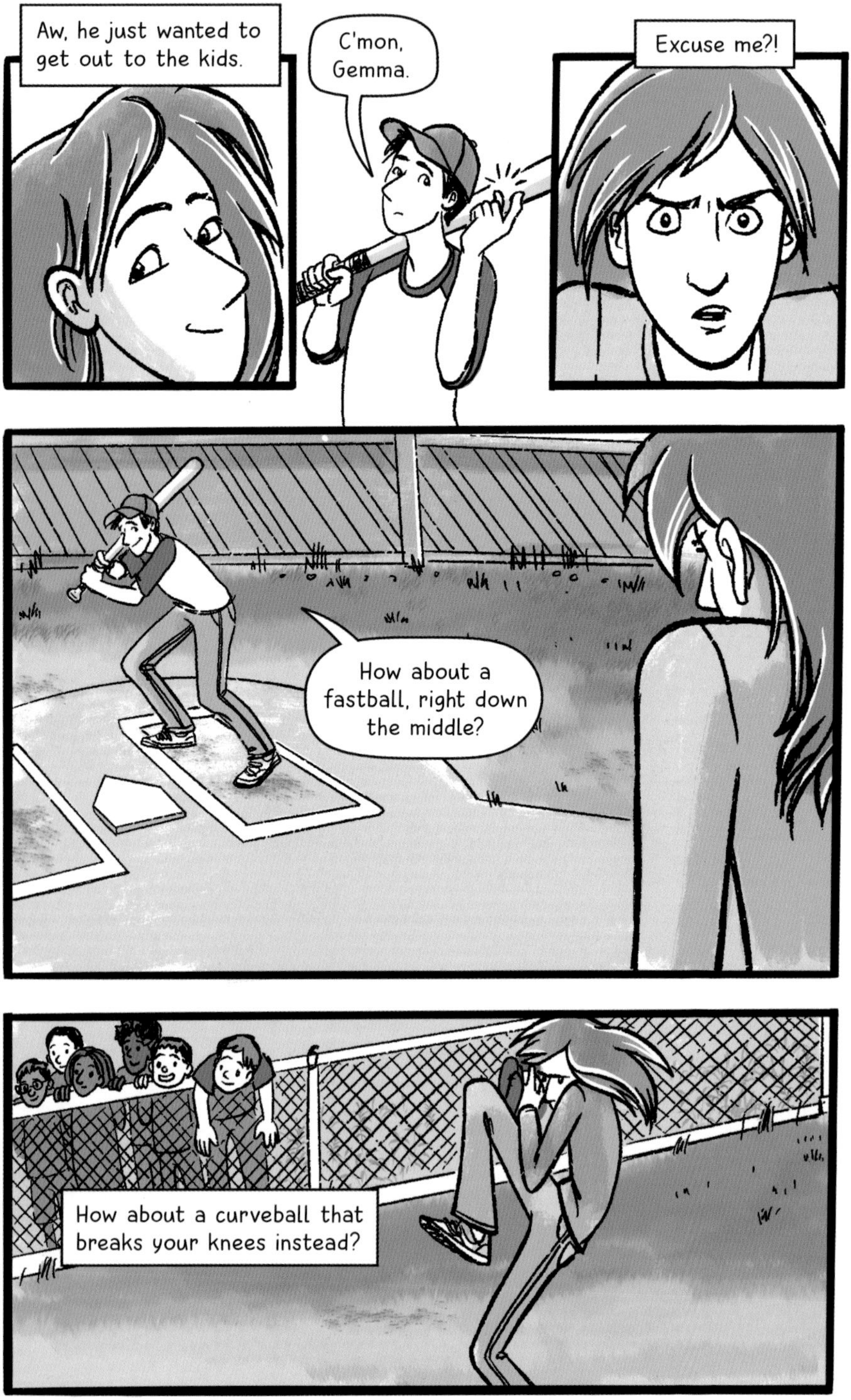

Aw, he just wanted to get out to the kids.
C'mon, Gemma.
Excuse me?!
How about a fastball, right down the middle?
How about a curveball that breaks your knees instead?

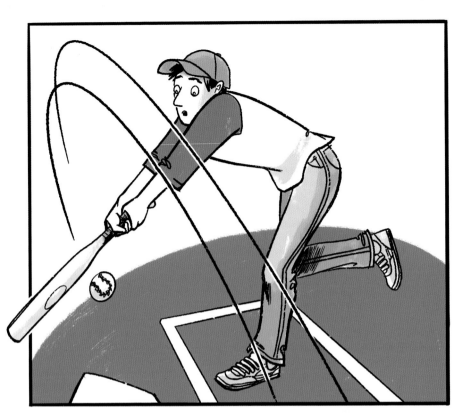

Ha-ha...
Good one.

I shoulda
let her warm
up first. We'll
slow it down.

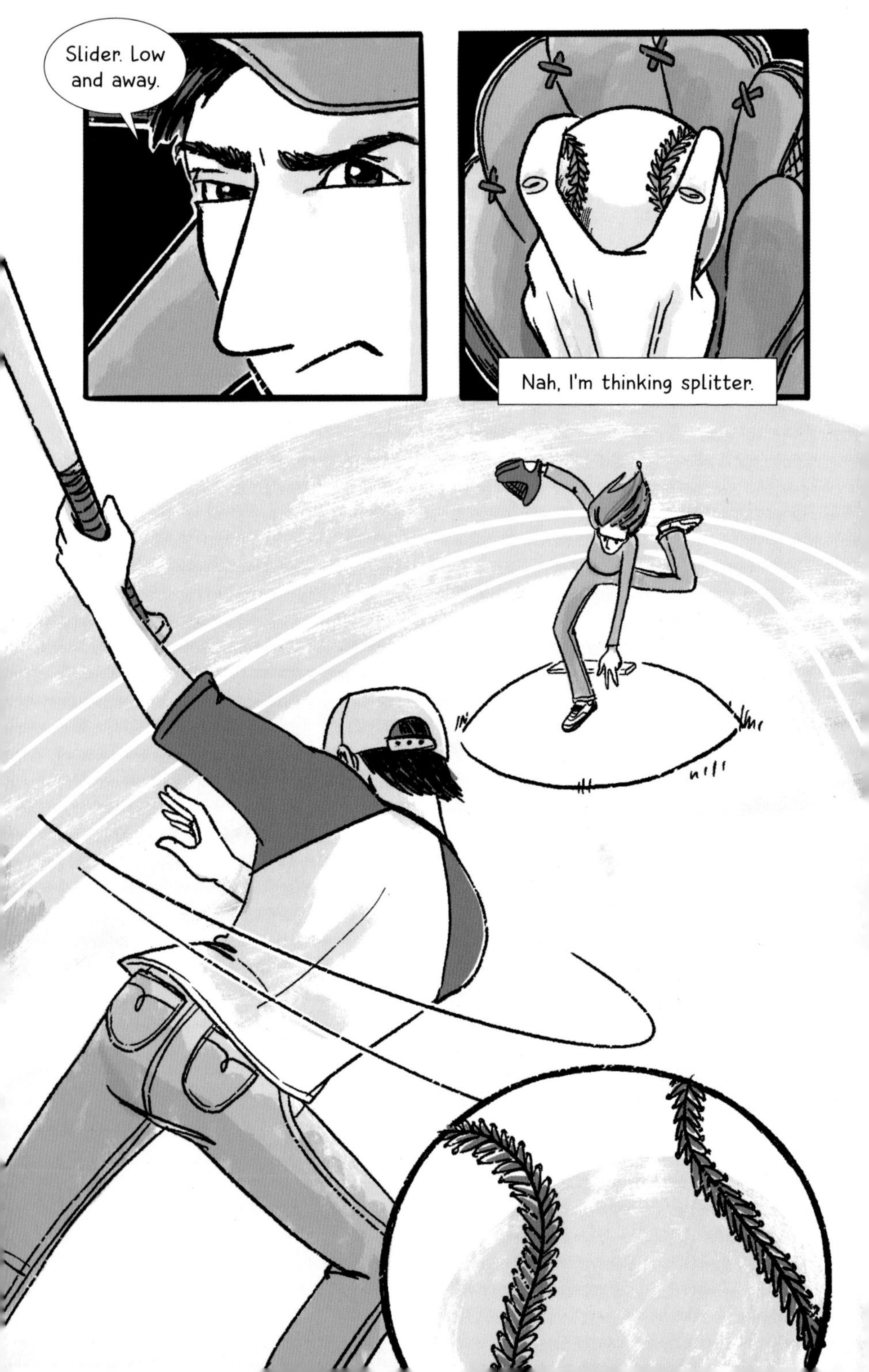
Slider. Low and away.
Nah, I'm thinking splitter.

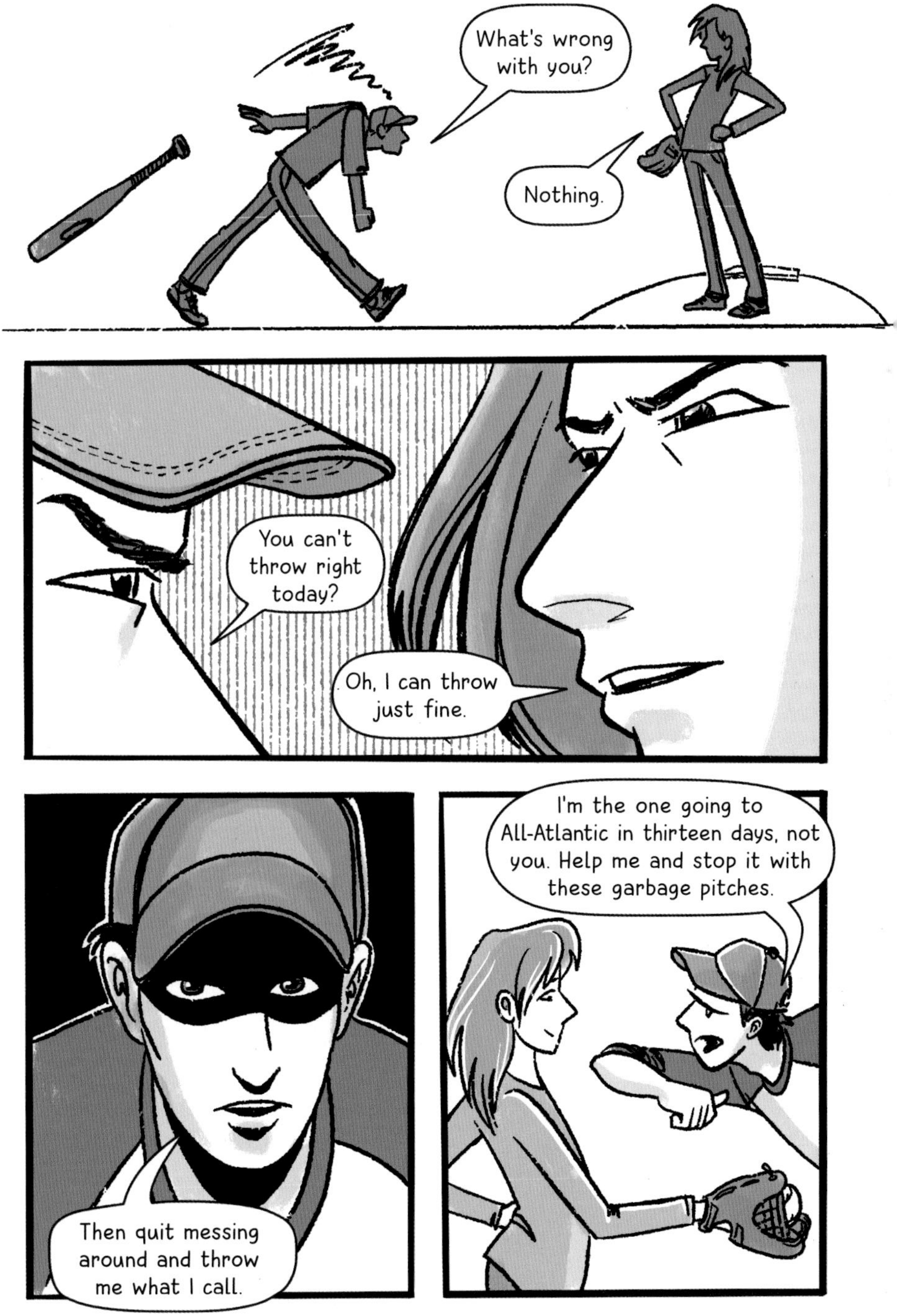
What's wrong with you?
Nothing.
You can't throw right today?
Oh, I can throw just fine.
Then quit messing around and throw me what I call.
I'm the one going to All-Atlantic in thirteen days, not you. Help me and stop it with these garbage pitches.

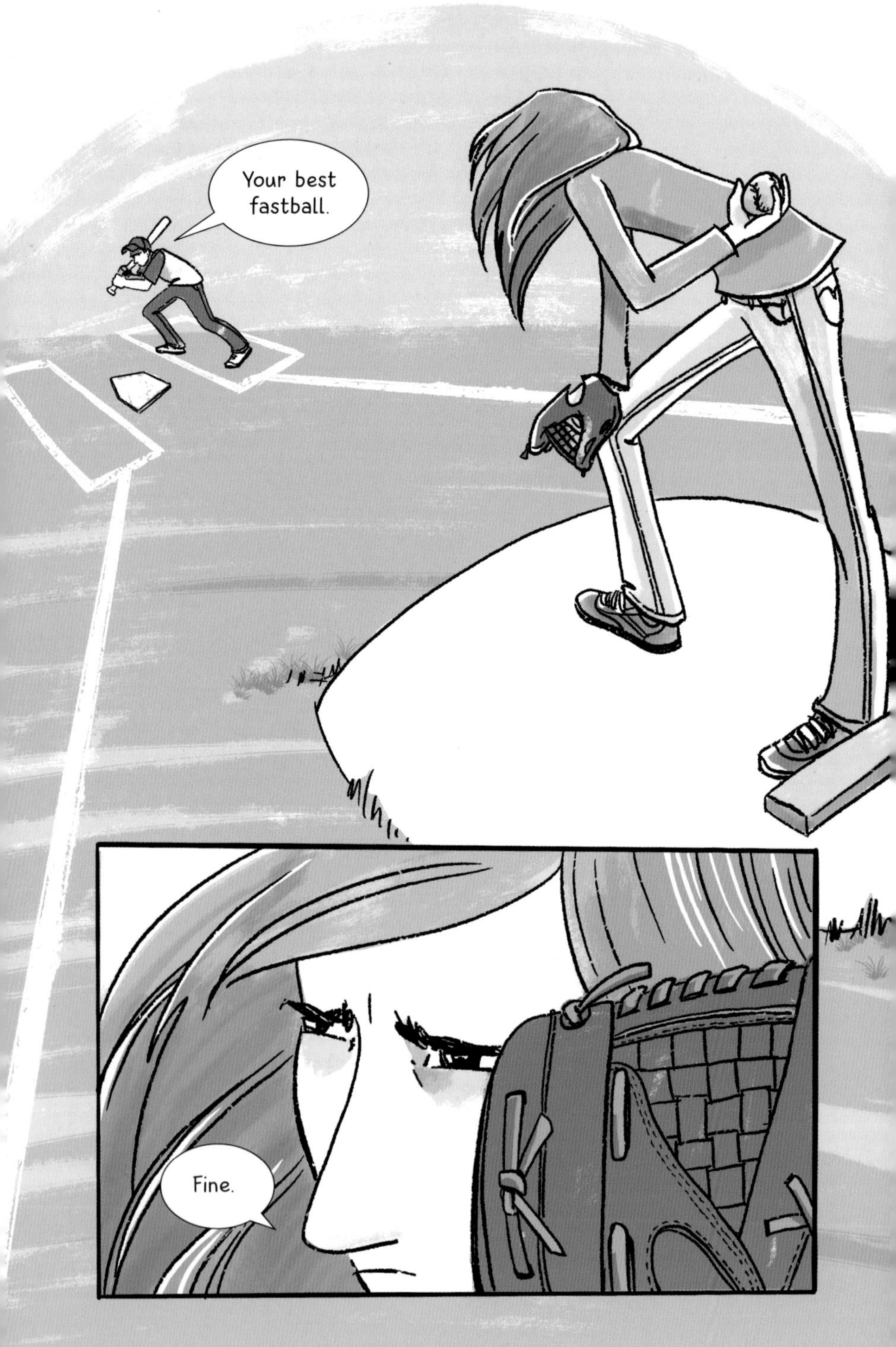
Your best fastball.
Fine.

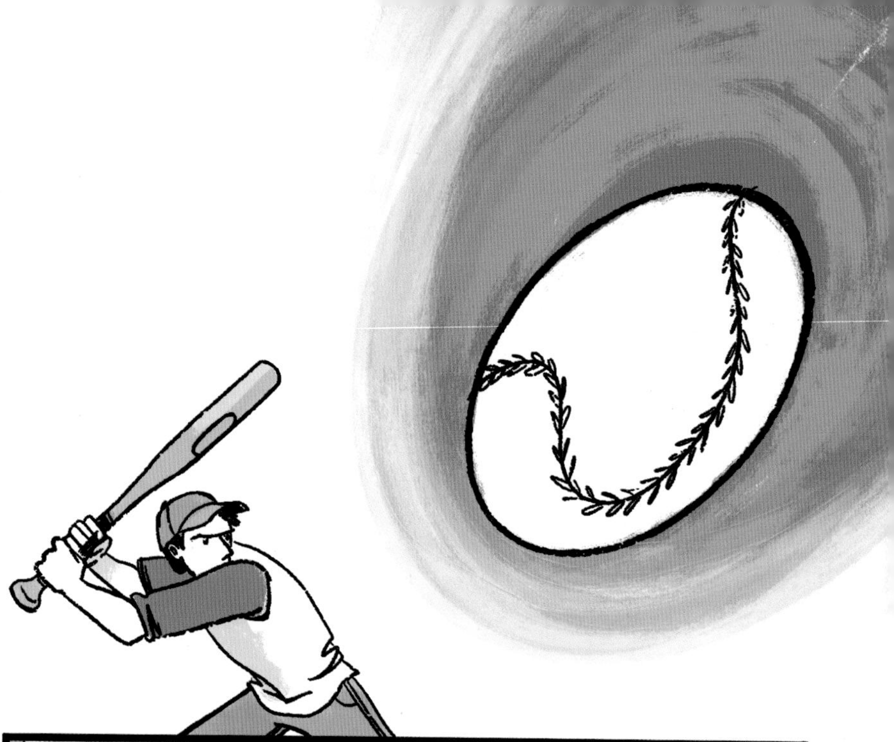

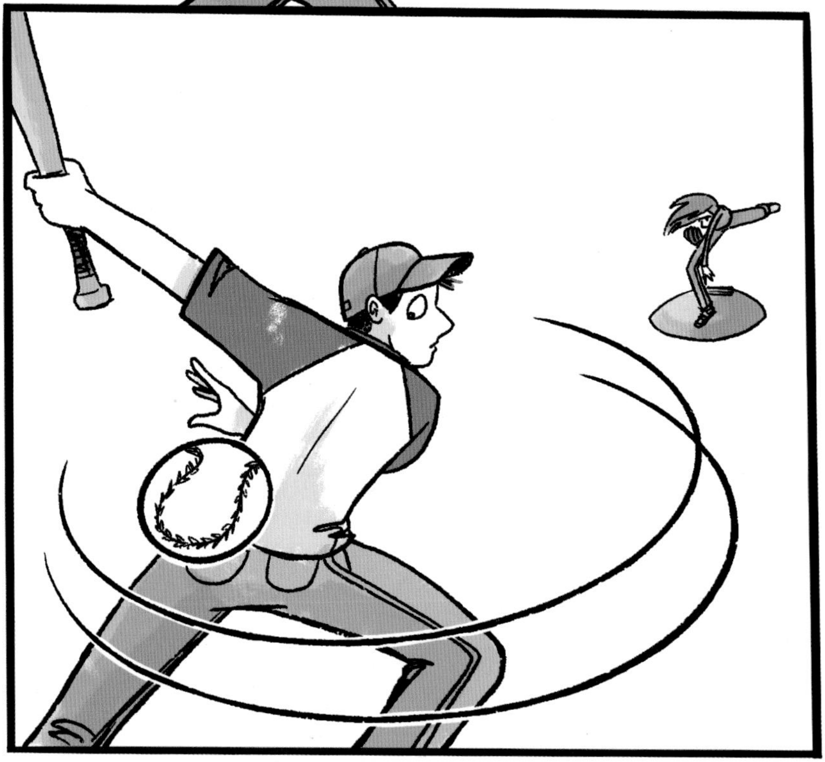

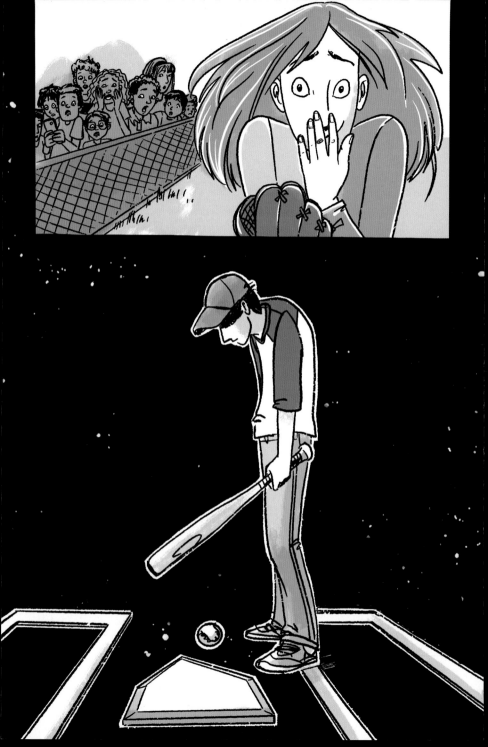

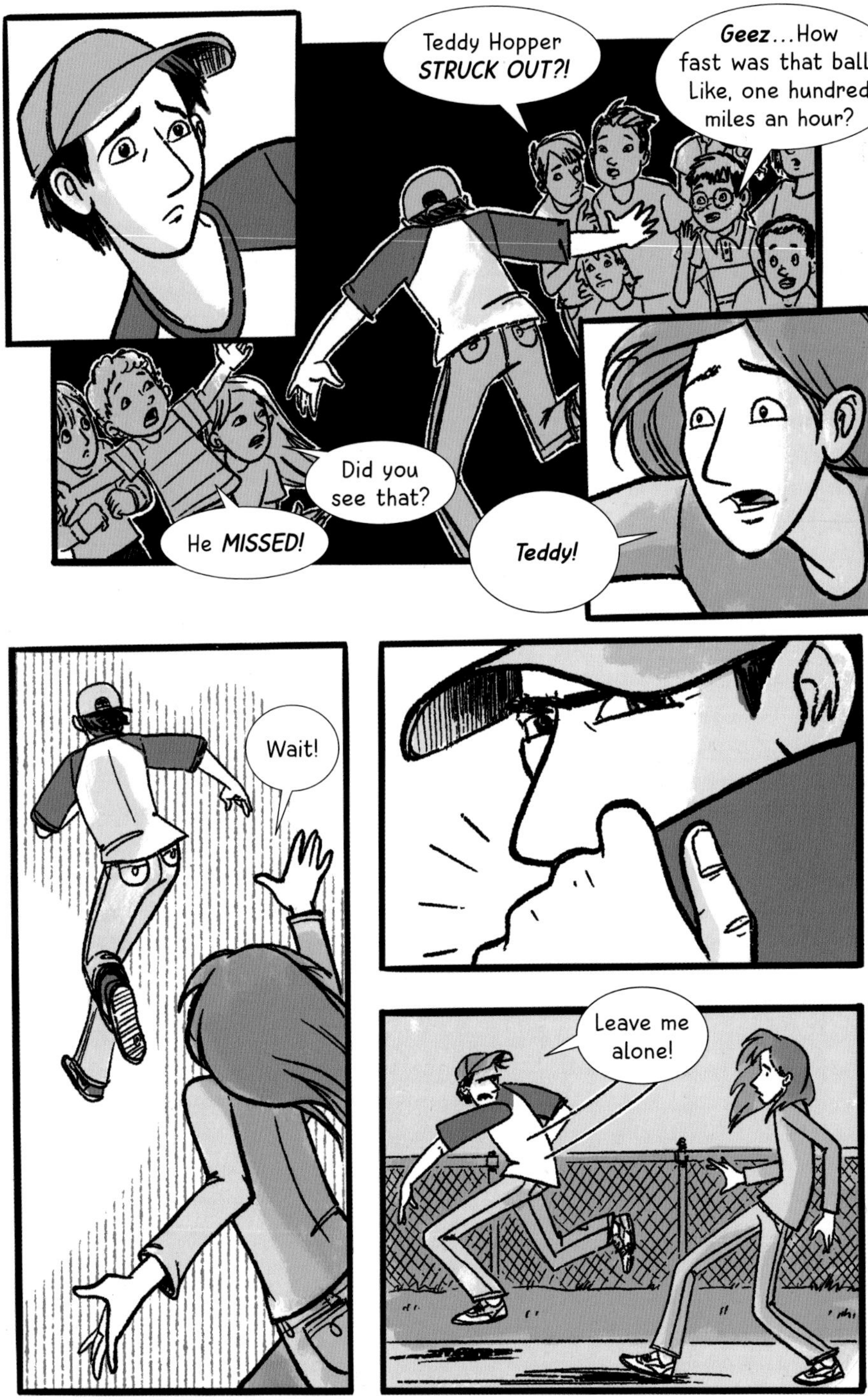
Teddy Hopper
STRUCK OUT?!
Geez...How fast was that ball? Like, one hundred miles an hour?
Did you see that?
He MISSED!
Teddy!
Wait!
Leave me alone!

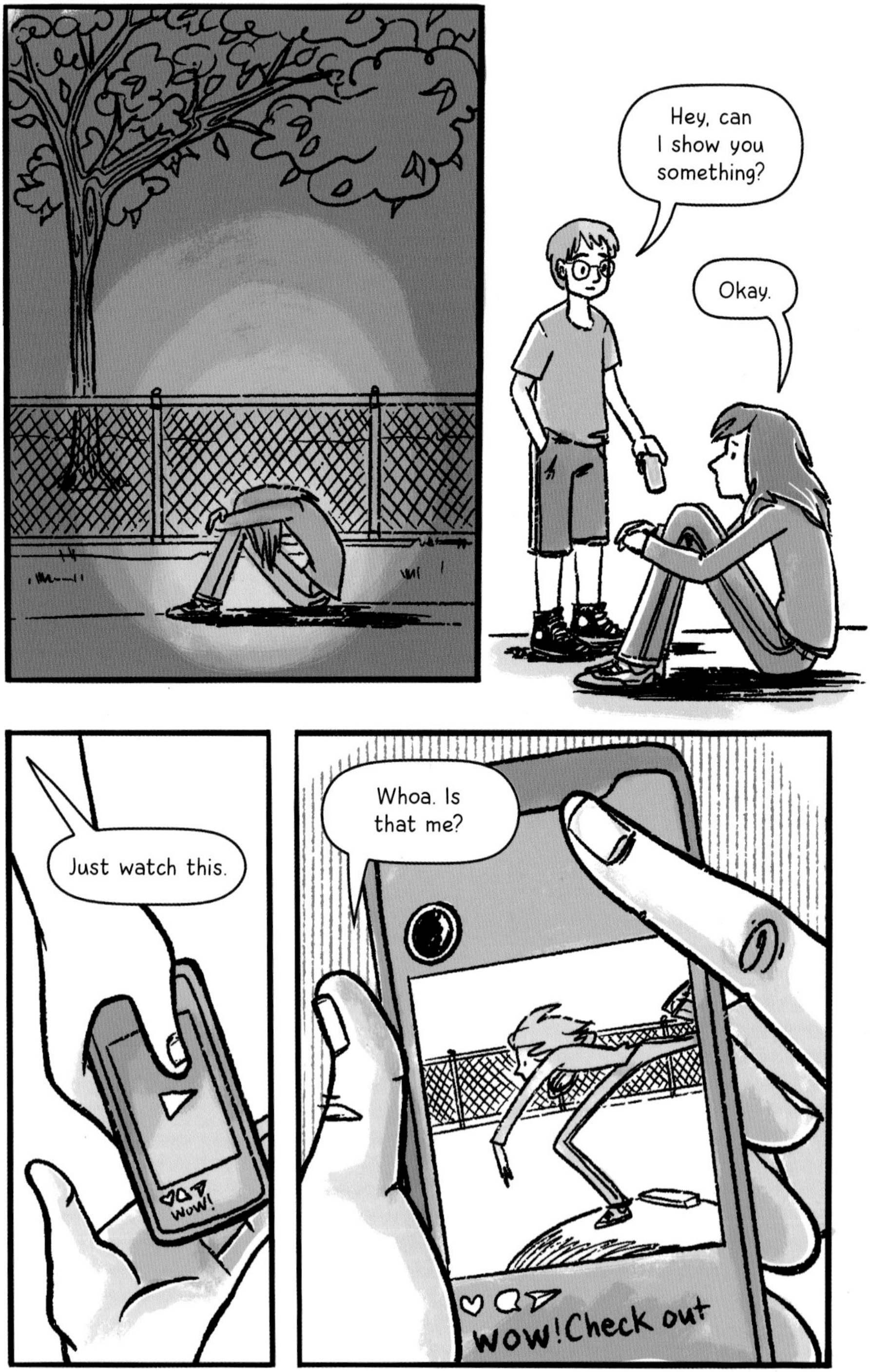
Hey, can I show you something?
Okay.
Just watch this.
WOW!
Whoa. Is that me?
WOW! Check out

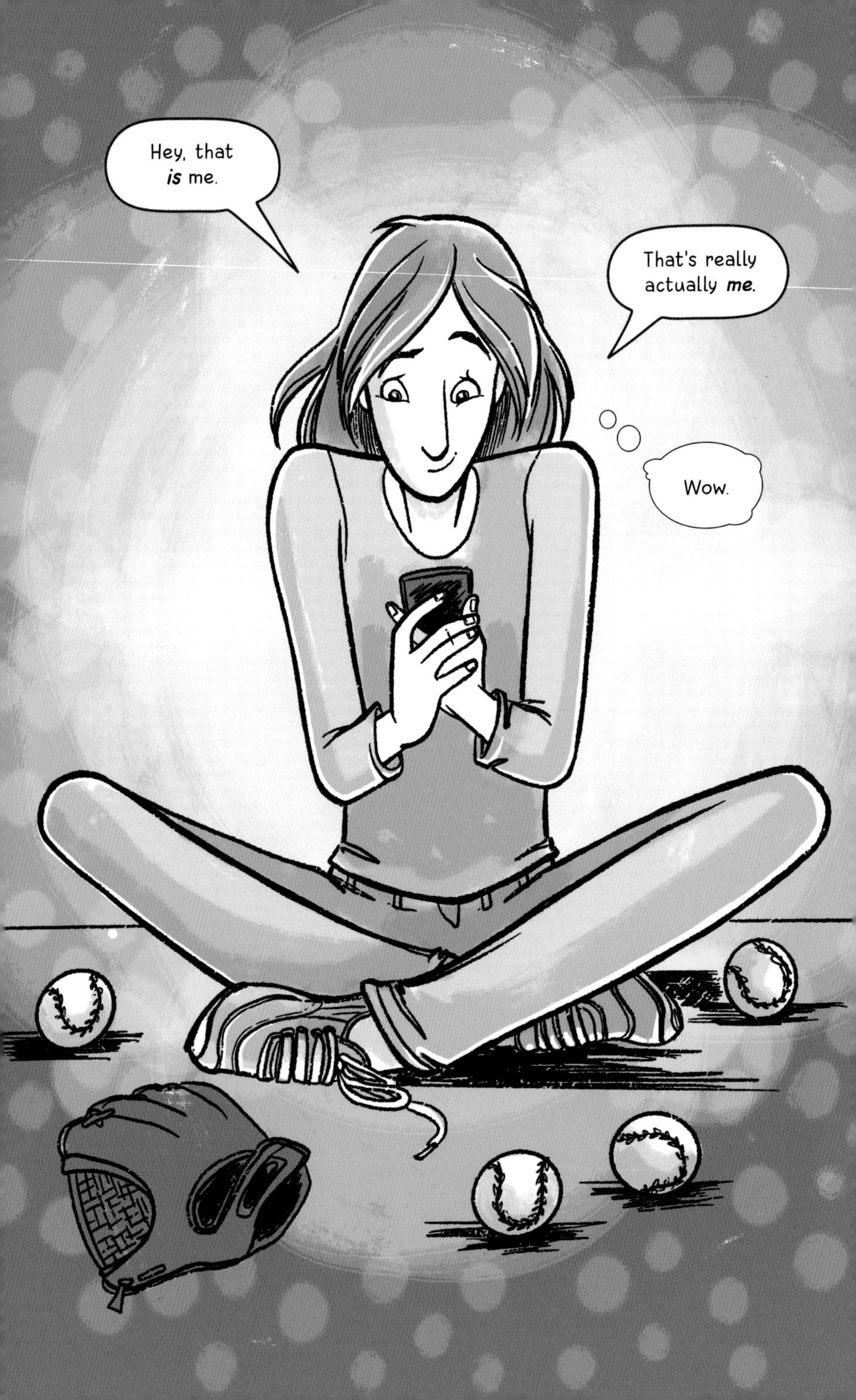
Hey, that *is* me.
That's really actually **me**.
Wow.

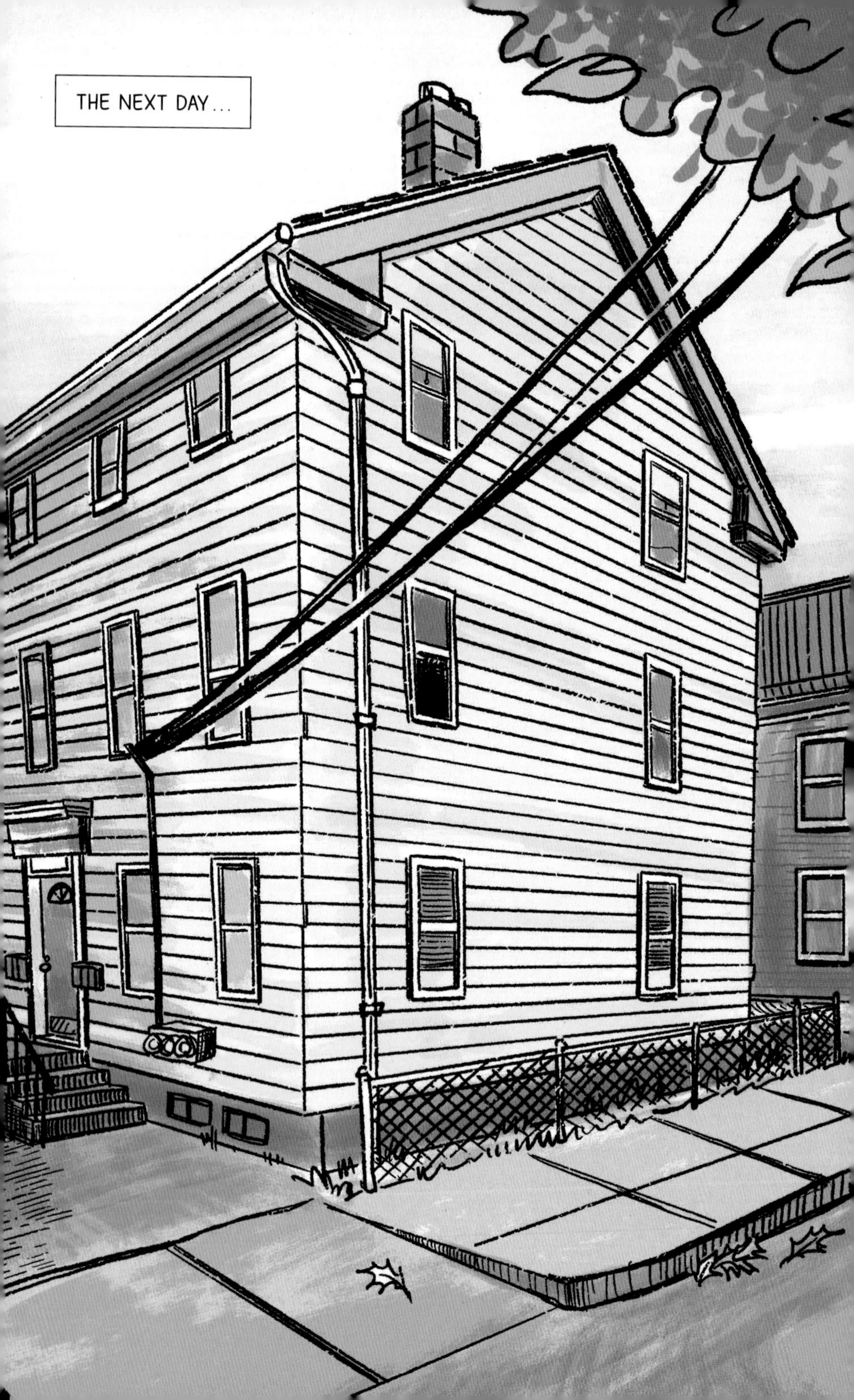
THE NEXT DAY...

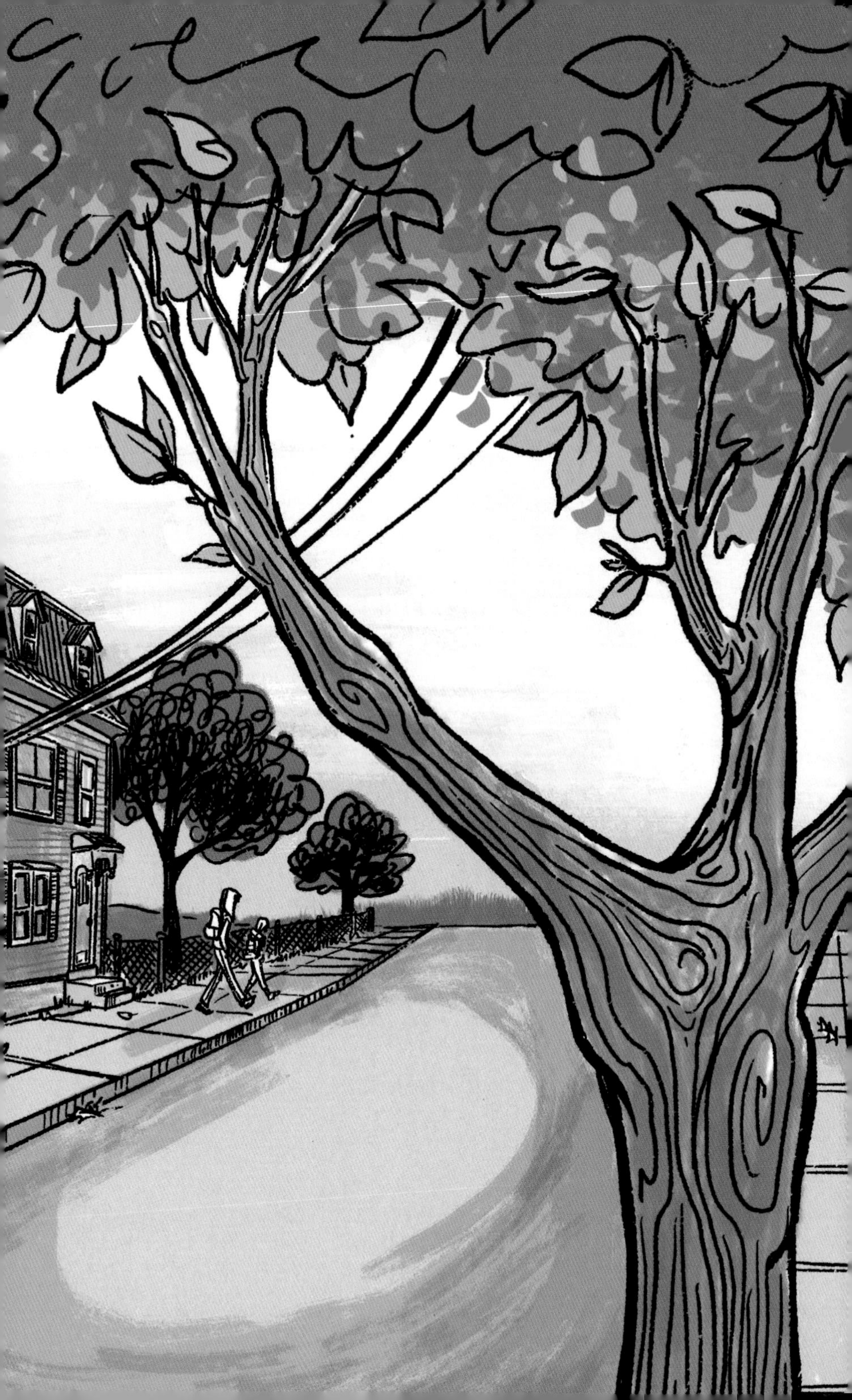

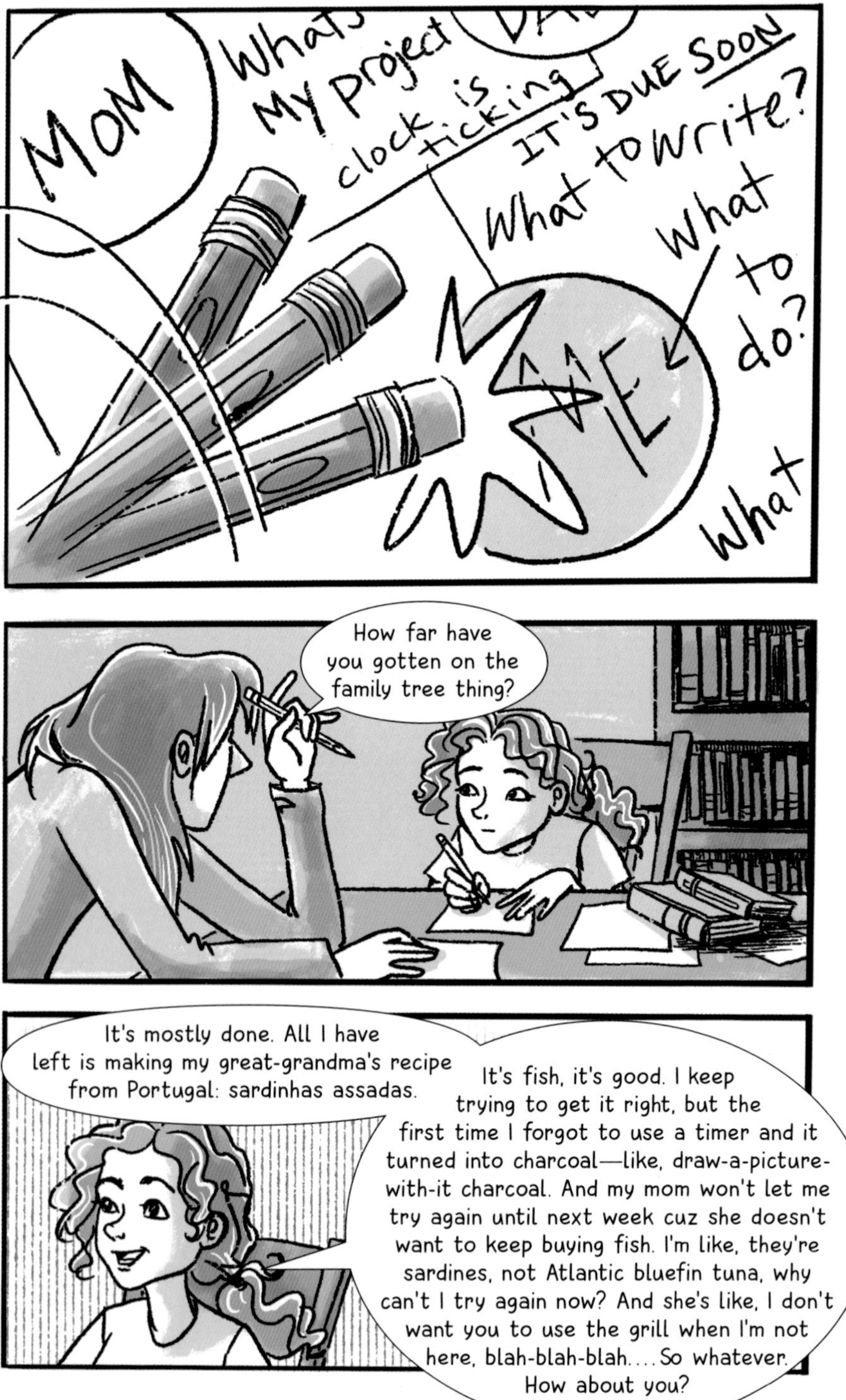
MOM
Whats
My project
clock is ticking
IT'S DUE SOON
What to write?
What to do?
What
How far have you gotten on the family tree thing?
It's mostly done. All I have left is making my great-grandma's recipe from Portugal: sardinhas assadas.
It's fish, it's good. I keep trying to get it right, but the first time I forgot to use a timer and it turned into charcoal—like, draw-a-picture-with-it charcoal. And my mom won't let me try again until next week cuz she doesn't want to keep buying fish. I'm like, they're sardines, not Atlantic bluefin tuna, why can't I try again now? And she's like, I don't want you to use the grill when I'm not here, blah-blah-blah.... So whatever. How about you?

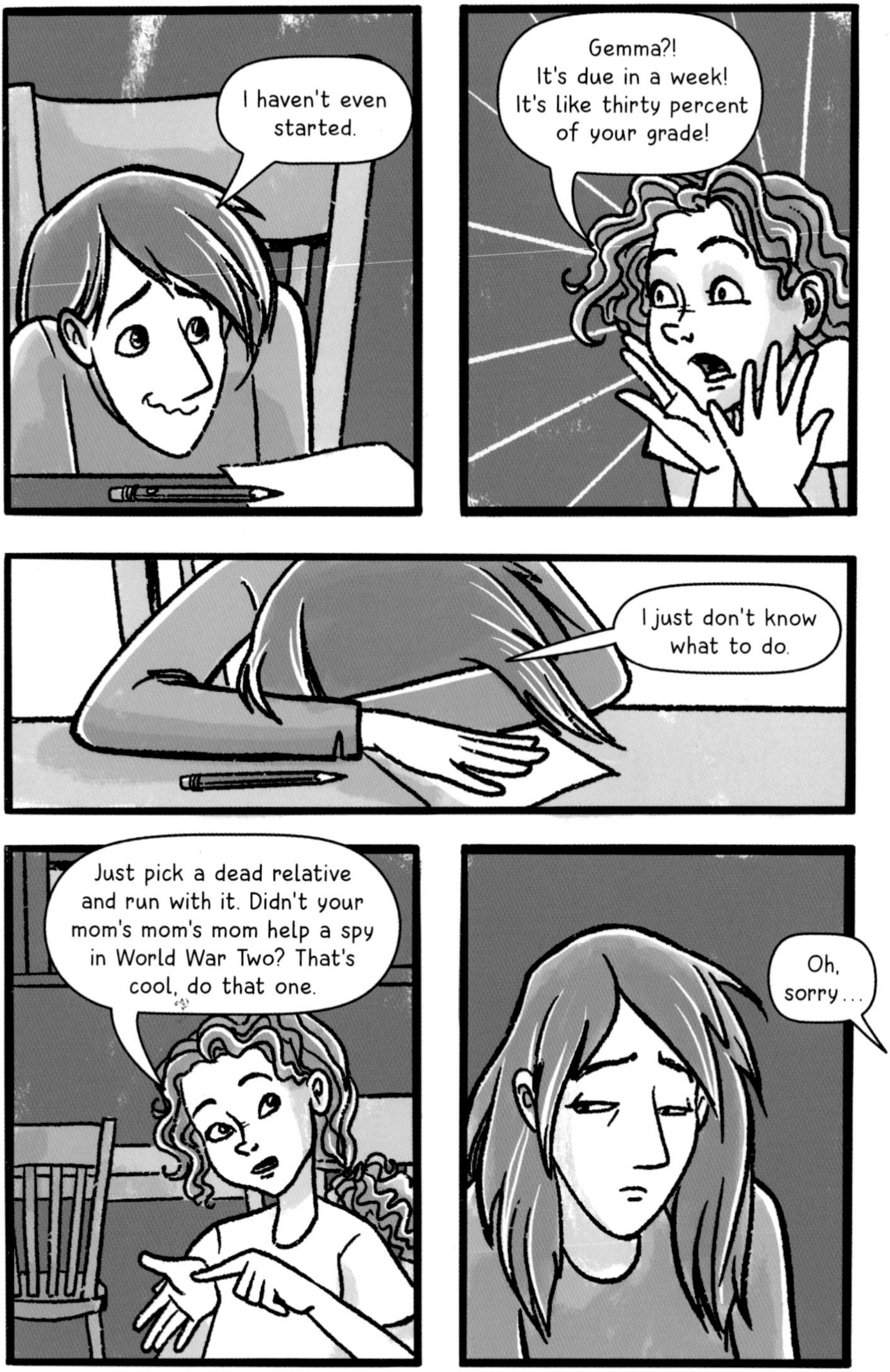
I haven't even started.
Gemma?! It's due in a week! It's like thirty percent of your grade!
I just don't know what to do.
Just pick a dead relative and run with it. Didn't your mom's mom's mom help a spy in World War Two? That's cool, do that one.
Oh, sorry...

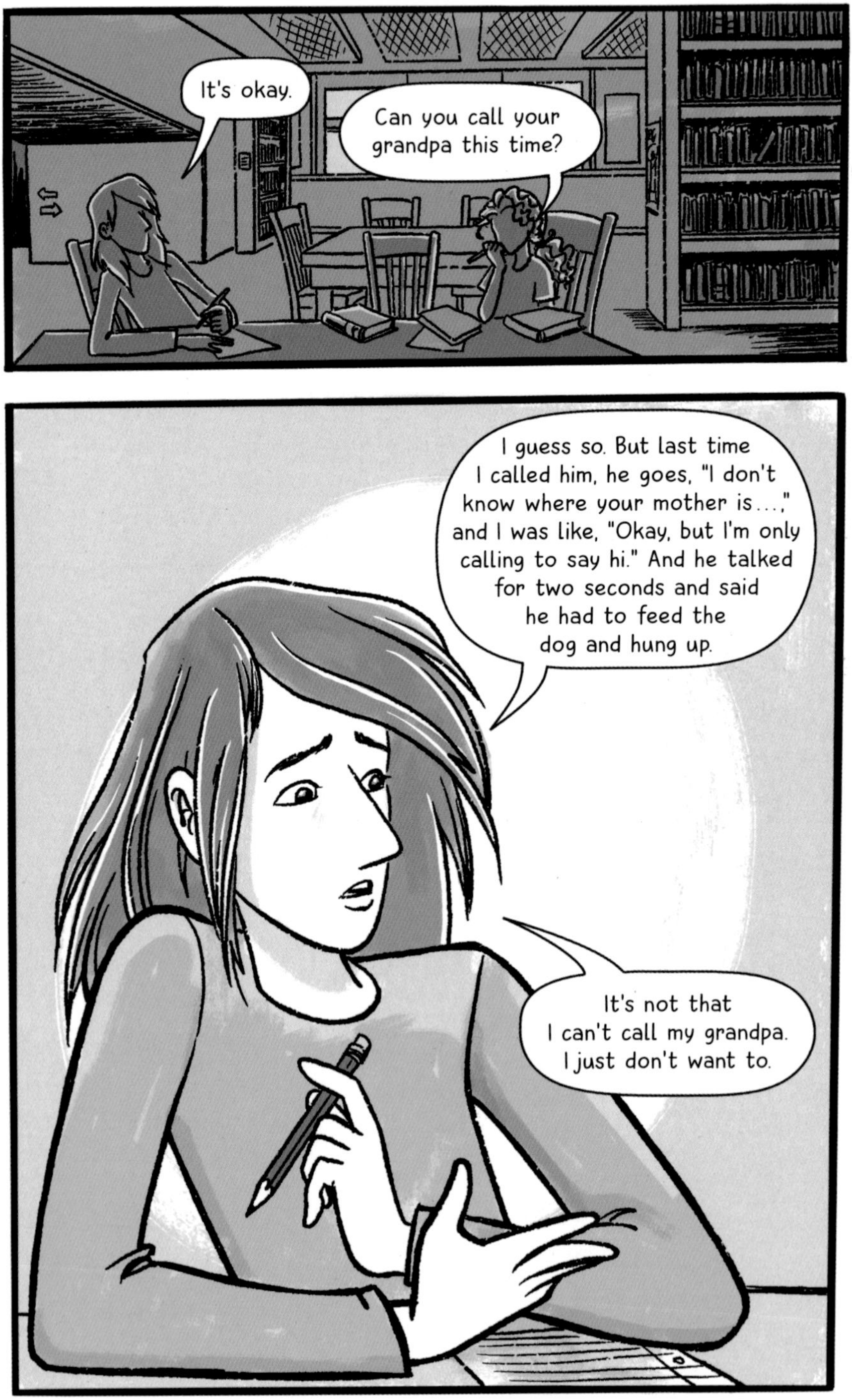
It's okay.
Can you call your grandpa this time?
I guess so. But last time I called him, he goes, "I don't know where your mother is...," and I was like, "Okay, but I'm only calling to say hi." And he talked for two seconds and said he had to feed the dog and hung up.
It's not that I can't call my grandpa. I just don't want to.

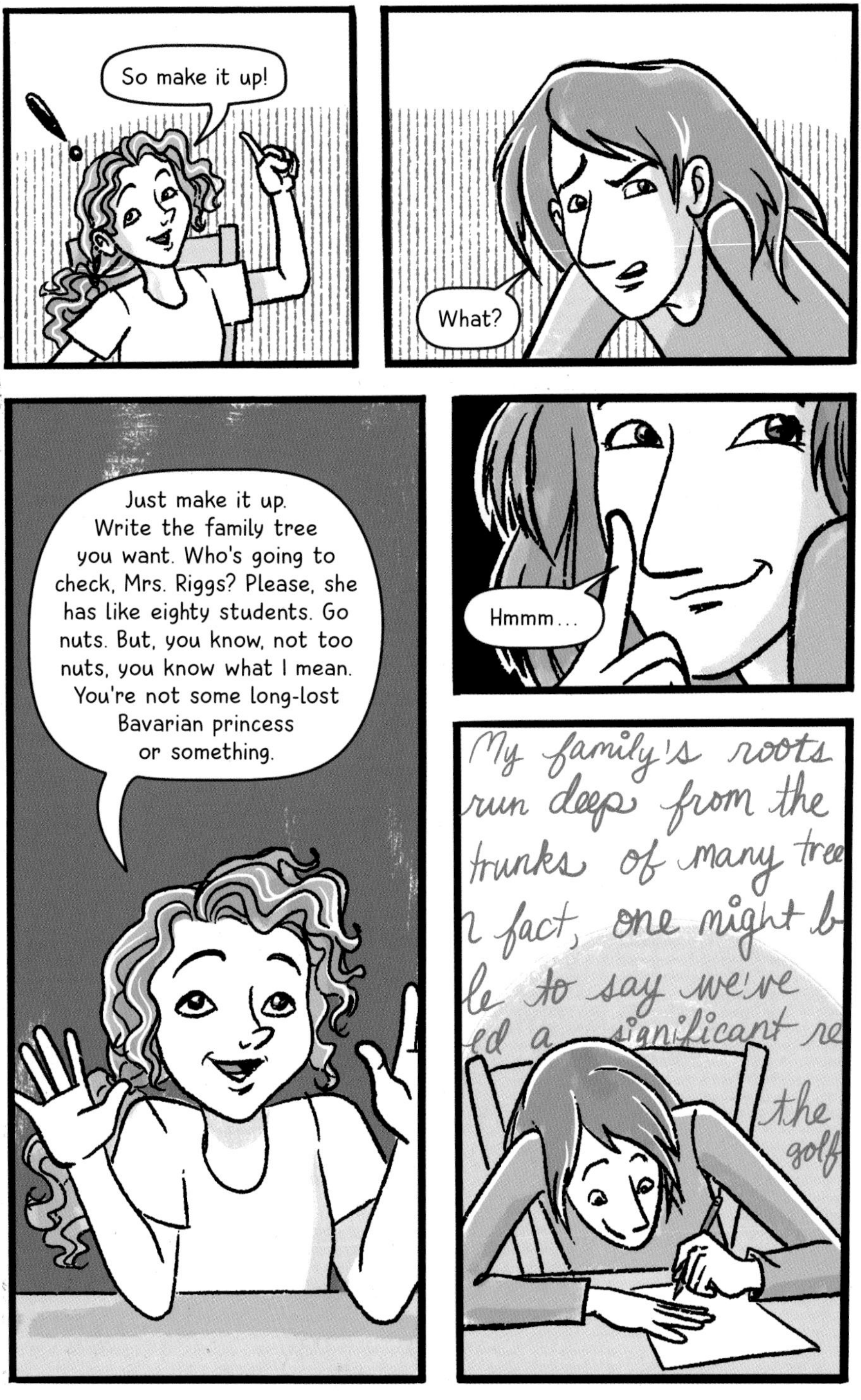
So make it up!
What?
Just make it up. Write the family tree you want. Who's going to check, Mrs. Riggs? Please, she has like eighty students. Go nuts. But, you know, not too nuts, you know what I mean. You're not some long-lost Bavarian princess or something.
Hmmm...
My family's roots
run deep from the
trunks of many tree
n fact, one might b
le to say we've
ed a significant re
the
golf

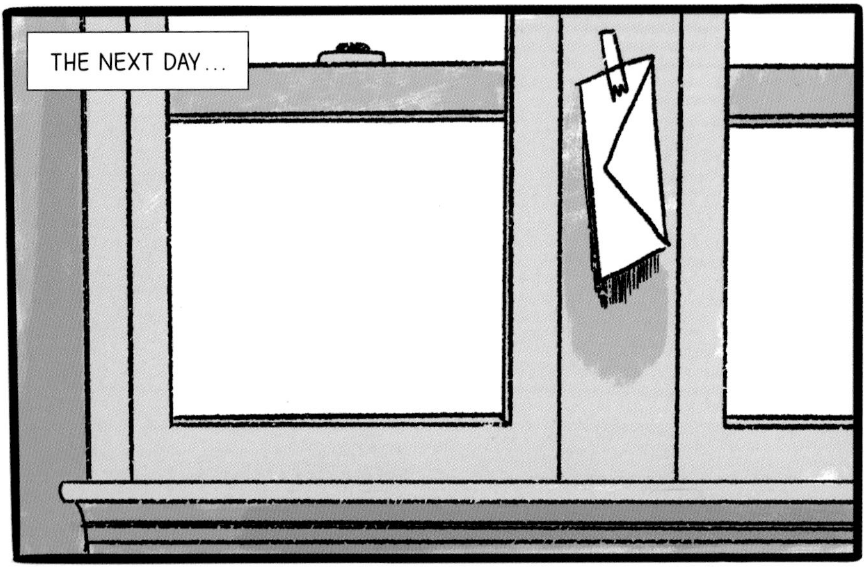
THE NEXT DAY...

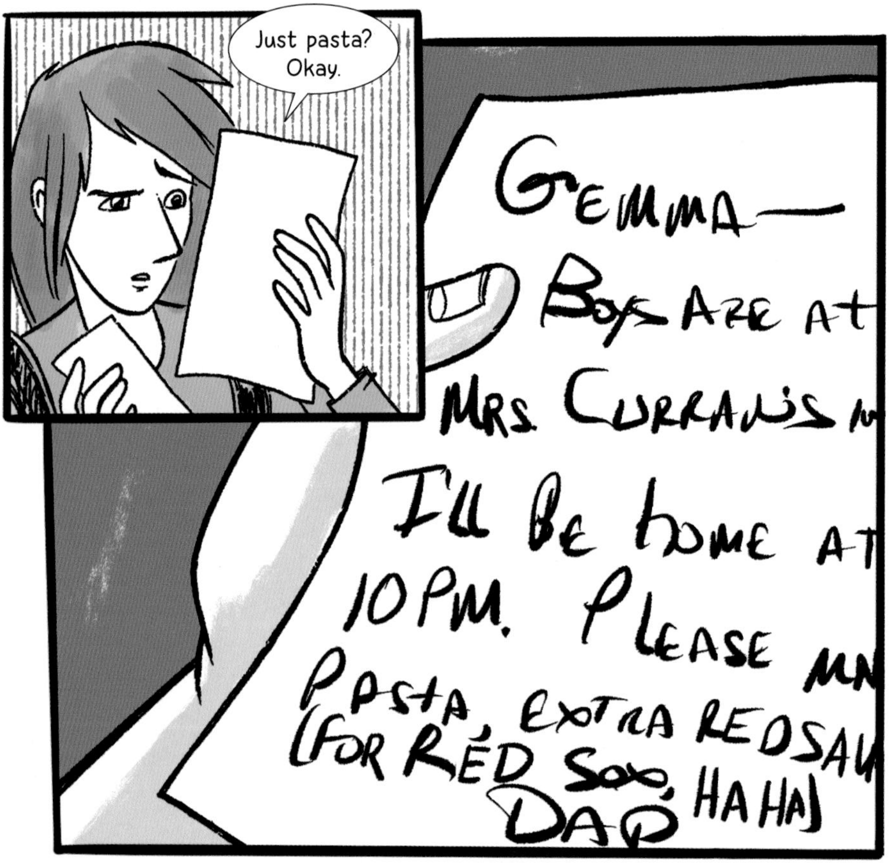
Just pasta? Okay.
GEMMA—
BOYS ARE AT
MRS. CURRAN'S
I'LL BE HOME AT
10 PM. PLEASE
PASTA, EXTRA RED SAU
(FOR RED SOX, HAHA)
DAD

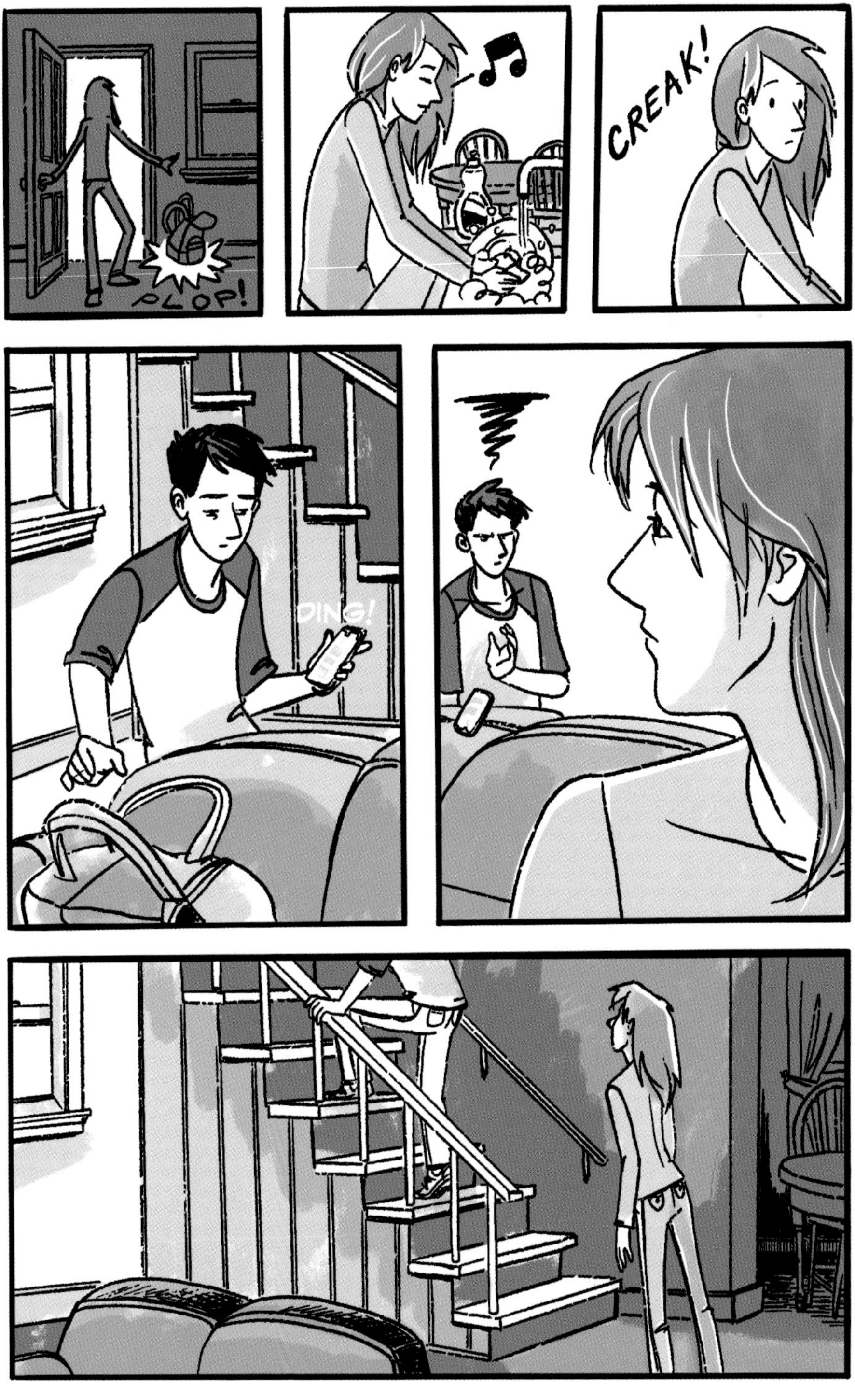
PLOP!
CREAK!
DING!

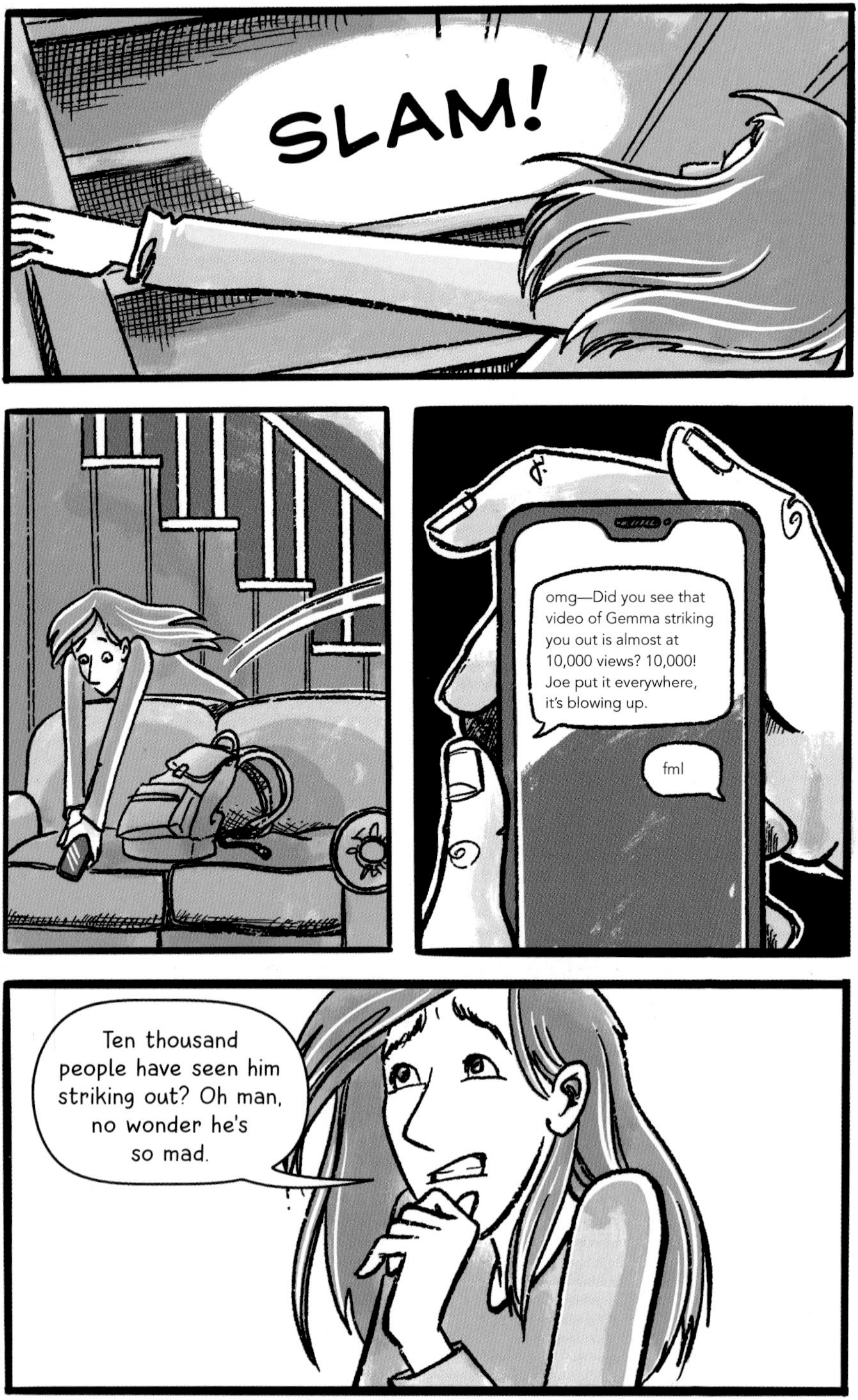
SLAM!
omg—Did you see that video of Gemma striking you out is almost at 10,000 views? 10,000! Joe put it everywhere, it's blowing up.
fml
Ten thousand people have seen him striking out? Oh man, no wonder he's so mad.

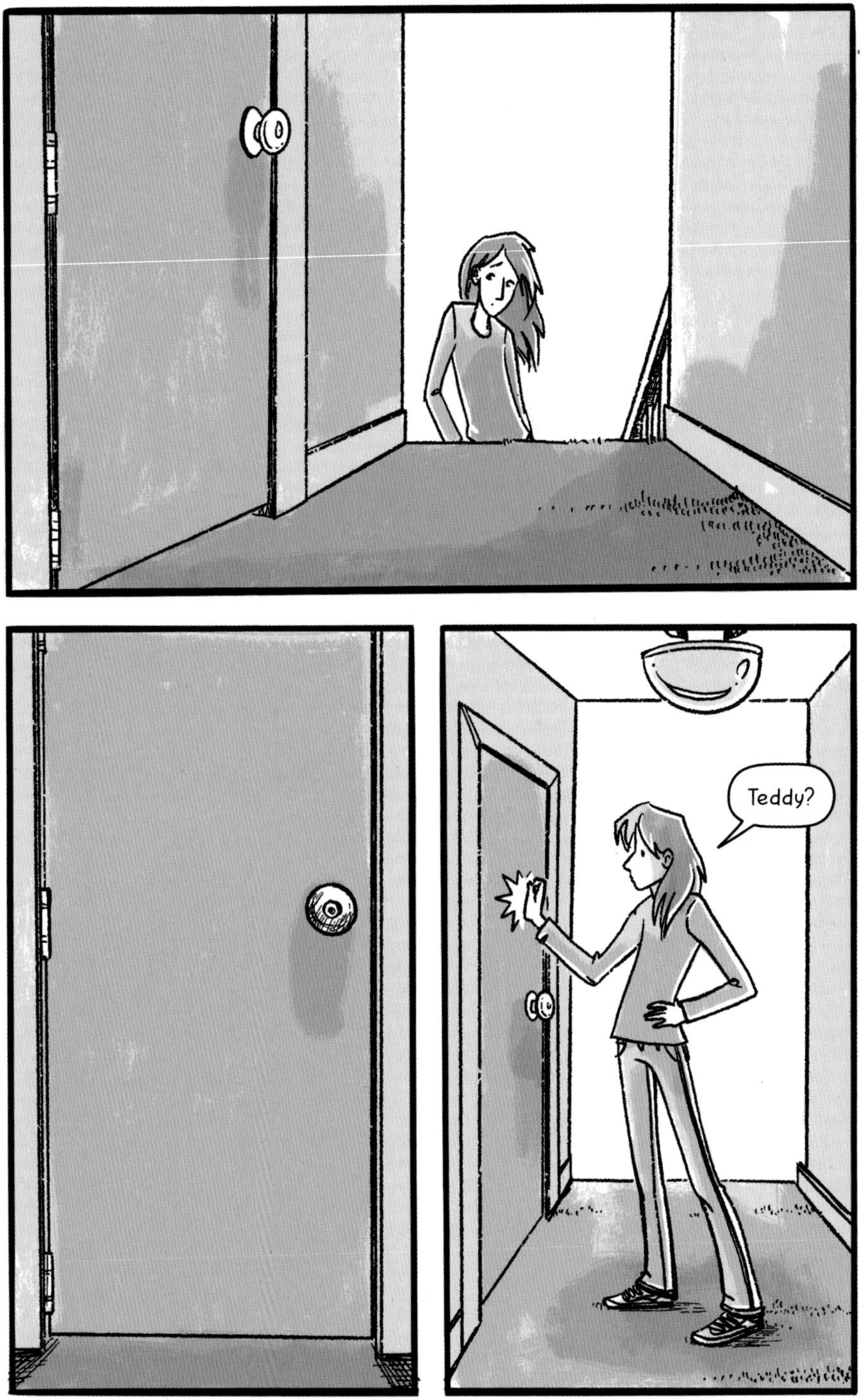
Teddy?

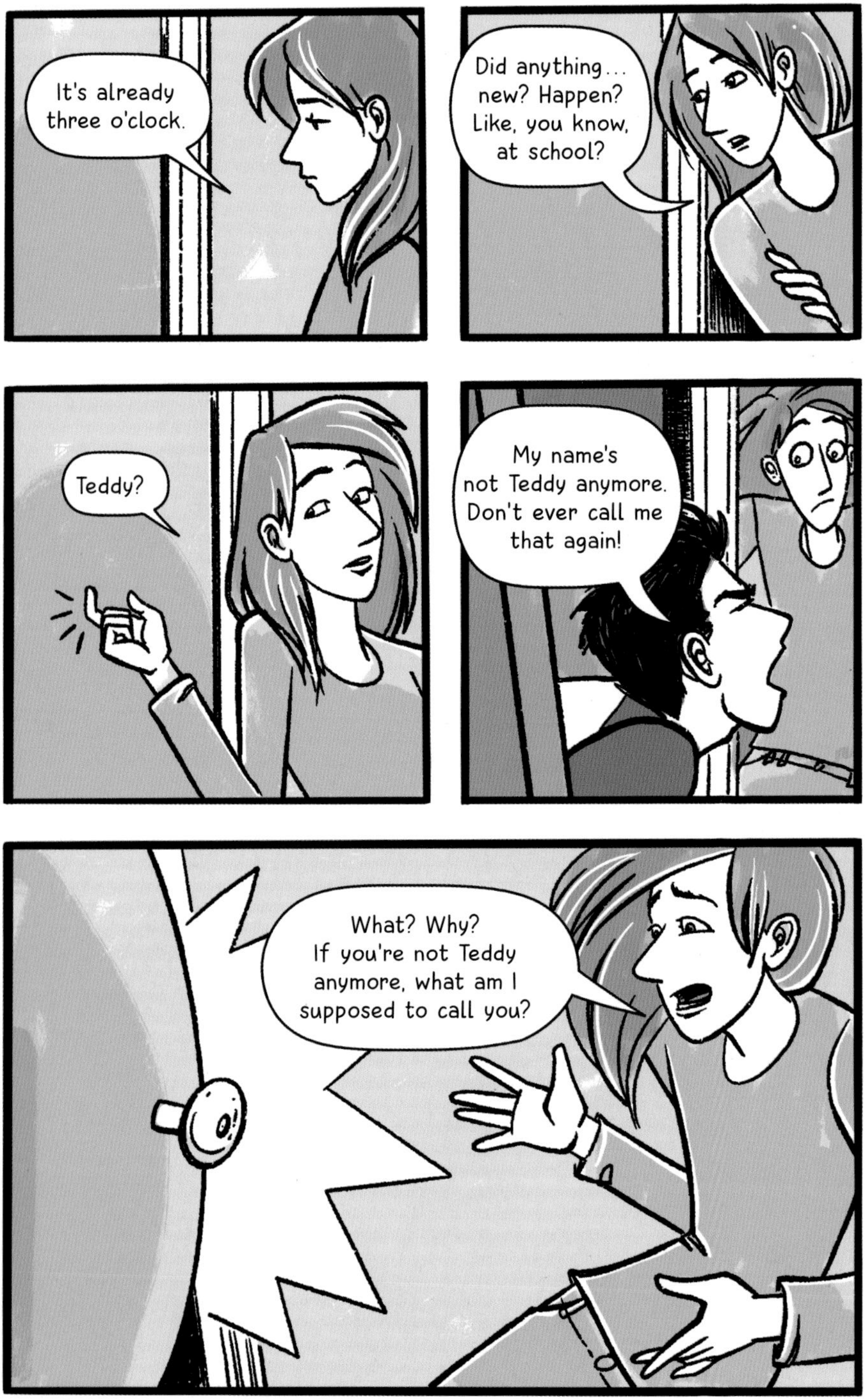
It's already three o'clock.
Did anything... new? Happen? Like, you know, at school?
Teddy?
My name's not Teddy anymore. Don't ever call me that again!
What? Why? If you're not Teddy anymore, what am I supposed to call you?

SHOOM!

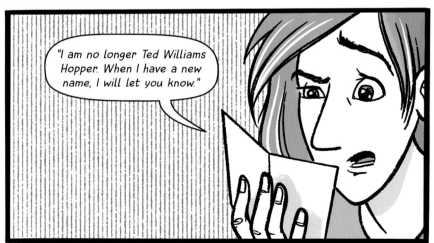

"I am no longer Ted Williams Hopper. When I have a new name, I will let you know."

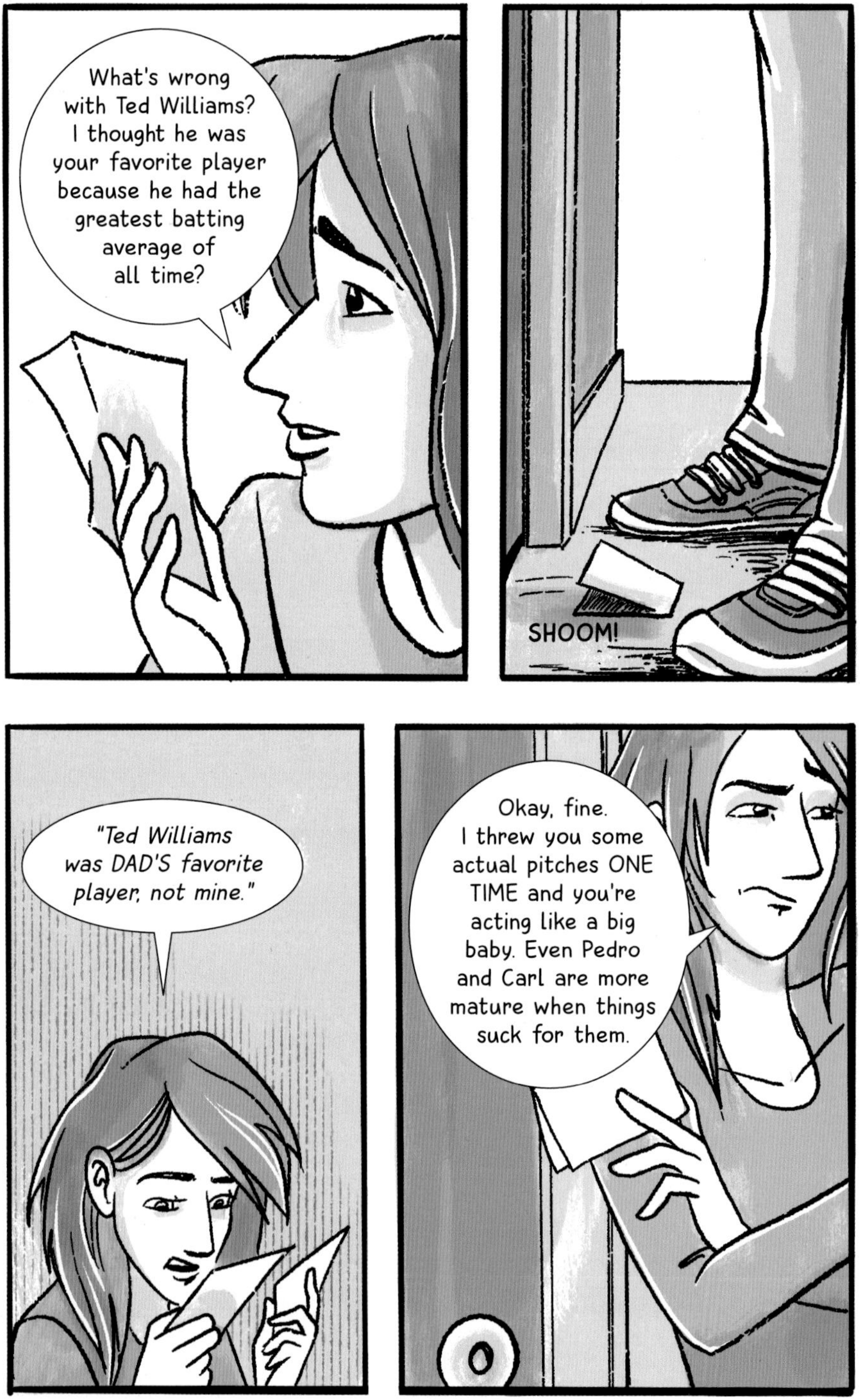
What's wrong with Ted Williams? I thought he was your favorite player because he had the greatest batting average of all time?
SHOOM!
"Ted Williams was DAD'S favorite player, not mine."
Okay, fine. I threw you some actual pitches ONE TIME and you're acting like a big baby. Even Pedro and Carl are more mature when things suck for them.

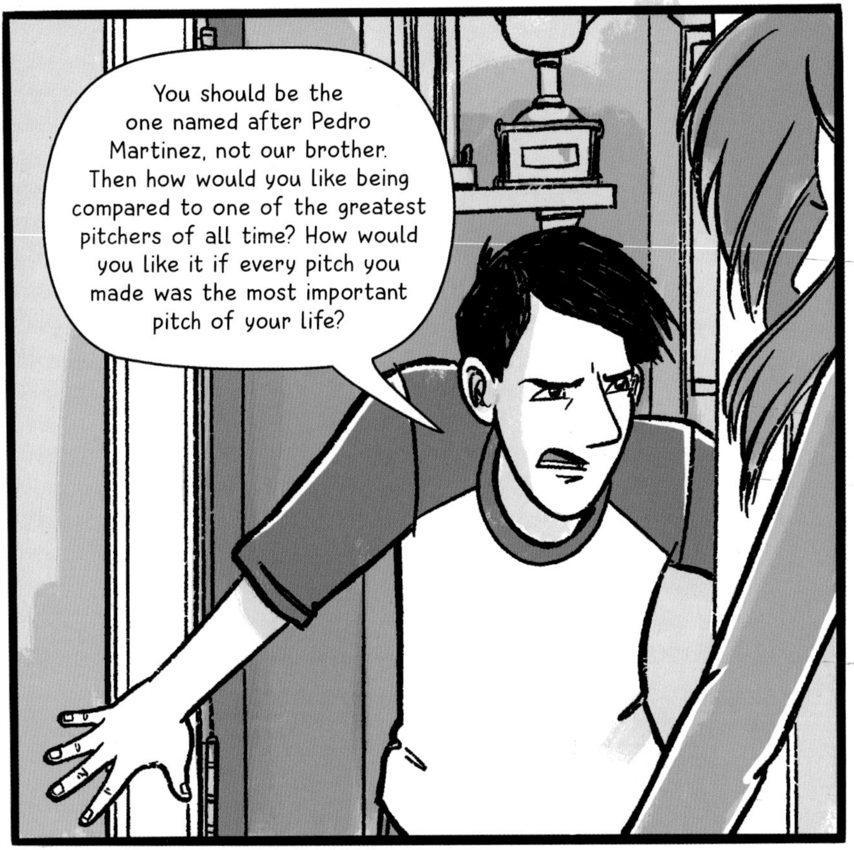
You should be the one named after Pedro Martinez, not our brother. Then how would you like being compared to one of the greatest pitchers of all time? How would you like it if every pitch you made was the most important pitch of your life?

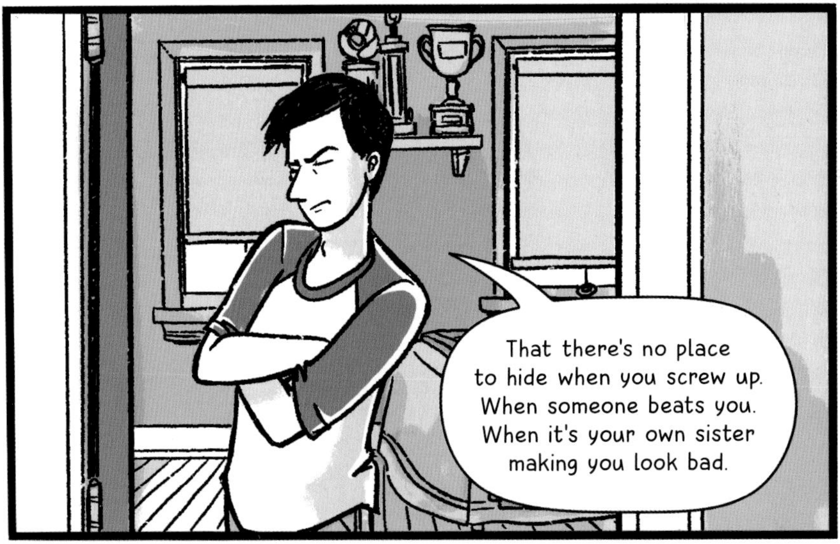
That there's no place to hide when you screw up. When someone beats you. When it's your own sister making you look bad.

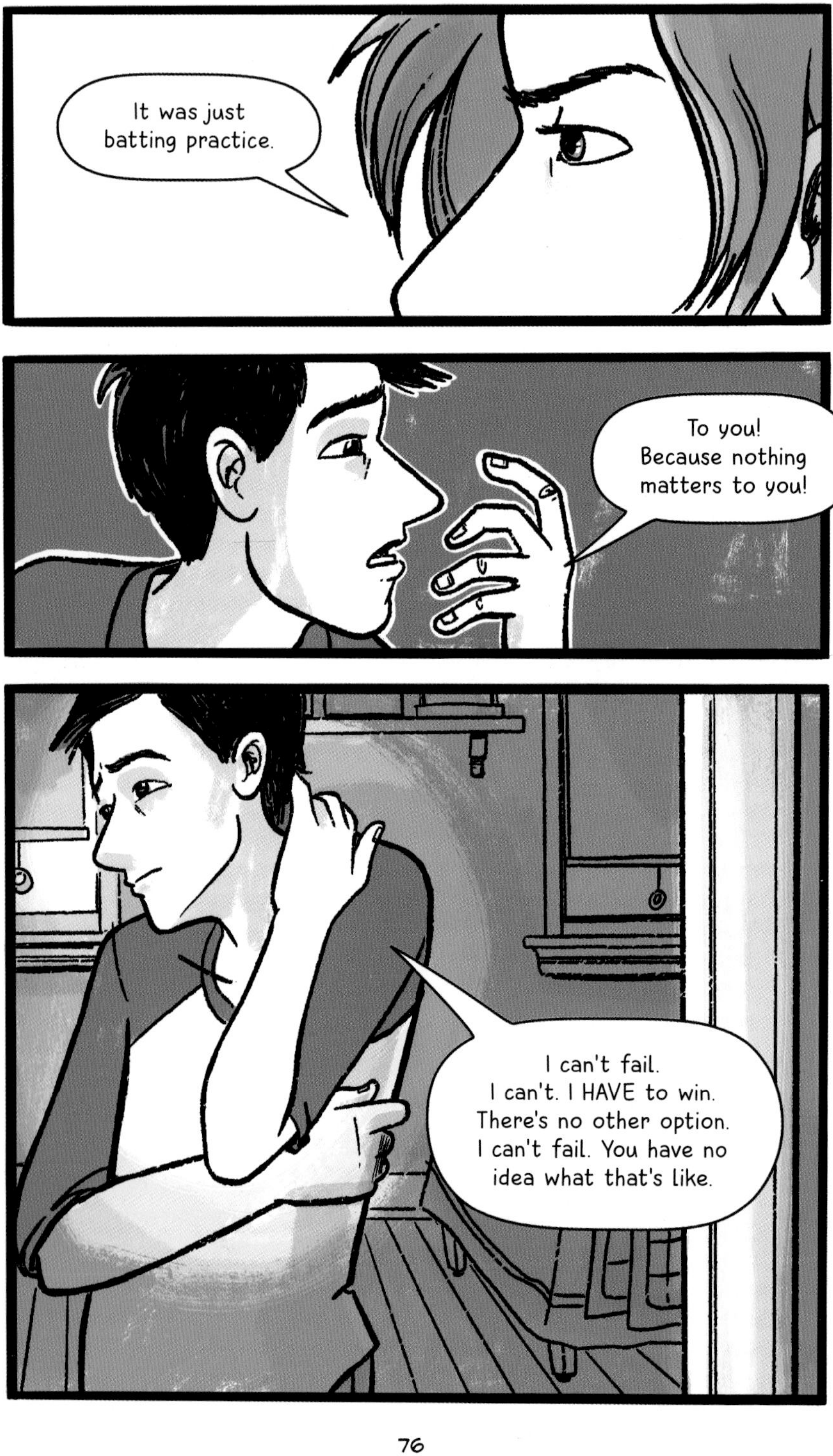
It was just batting practice.
To you! Because nothing matters to you!
I can't fail. I can't. I HAVE to win. There's no other option. I can't fail. You have no idea what that's like.

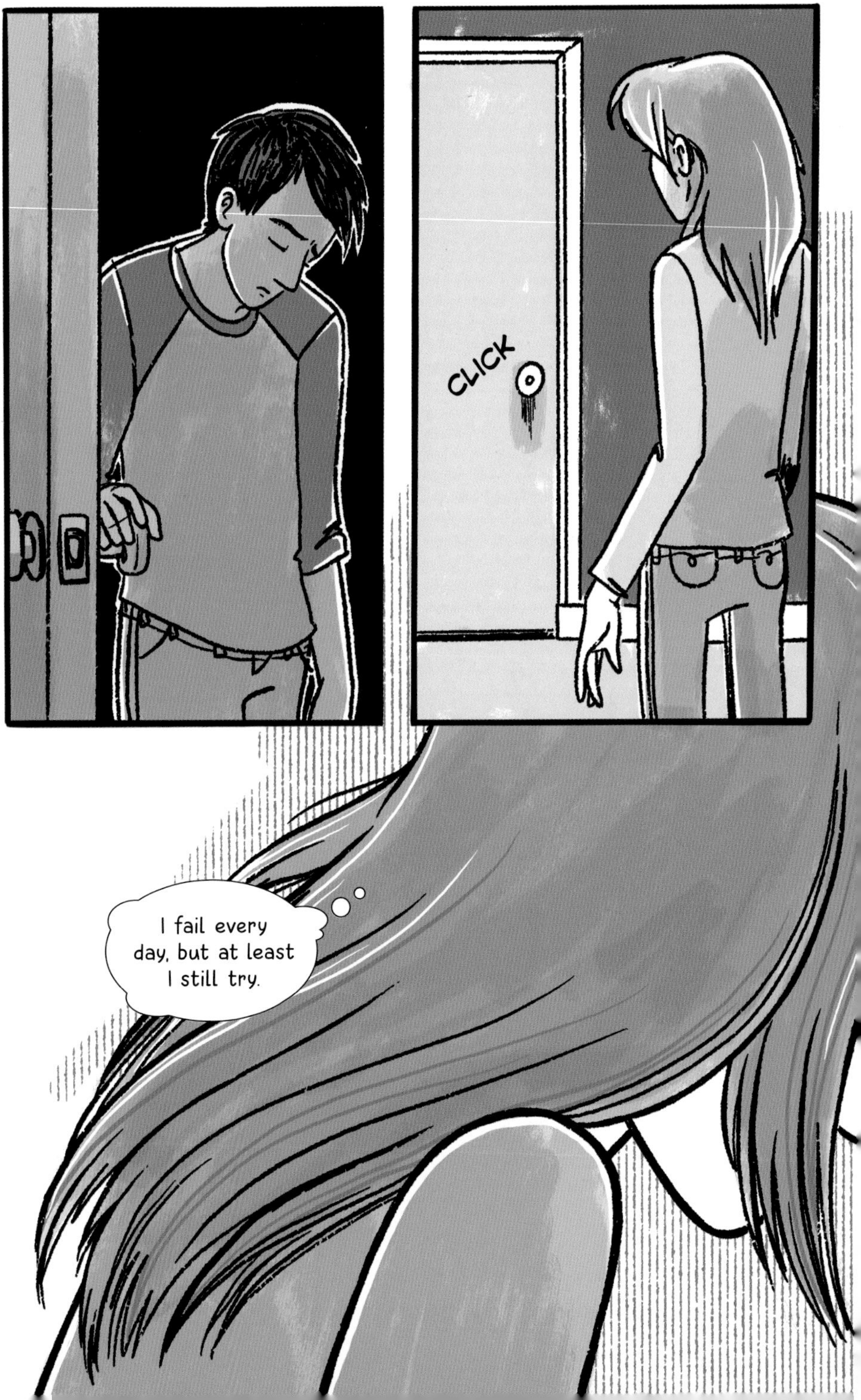
CLICK
I fail every day, but at least I still try.

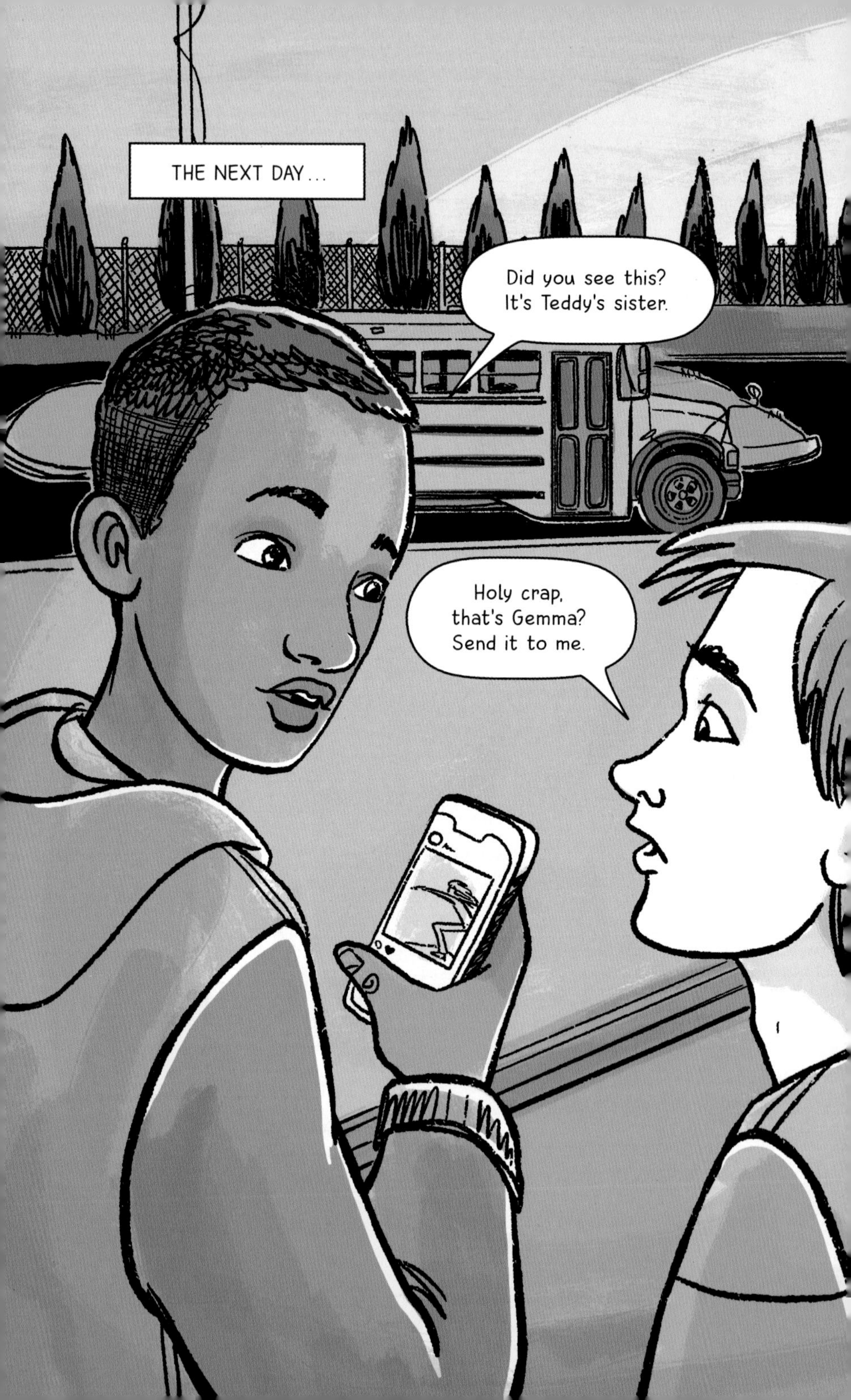
THE NEXT DAY...
Did you see this? It's Teddy's sister.
Holy crap, that's Gemma? Send it to me.

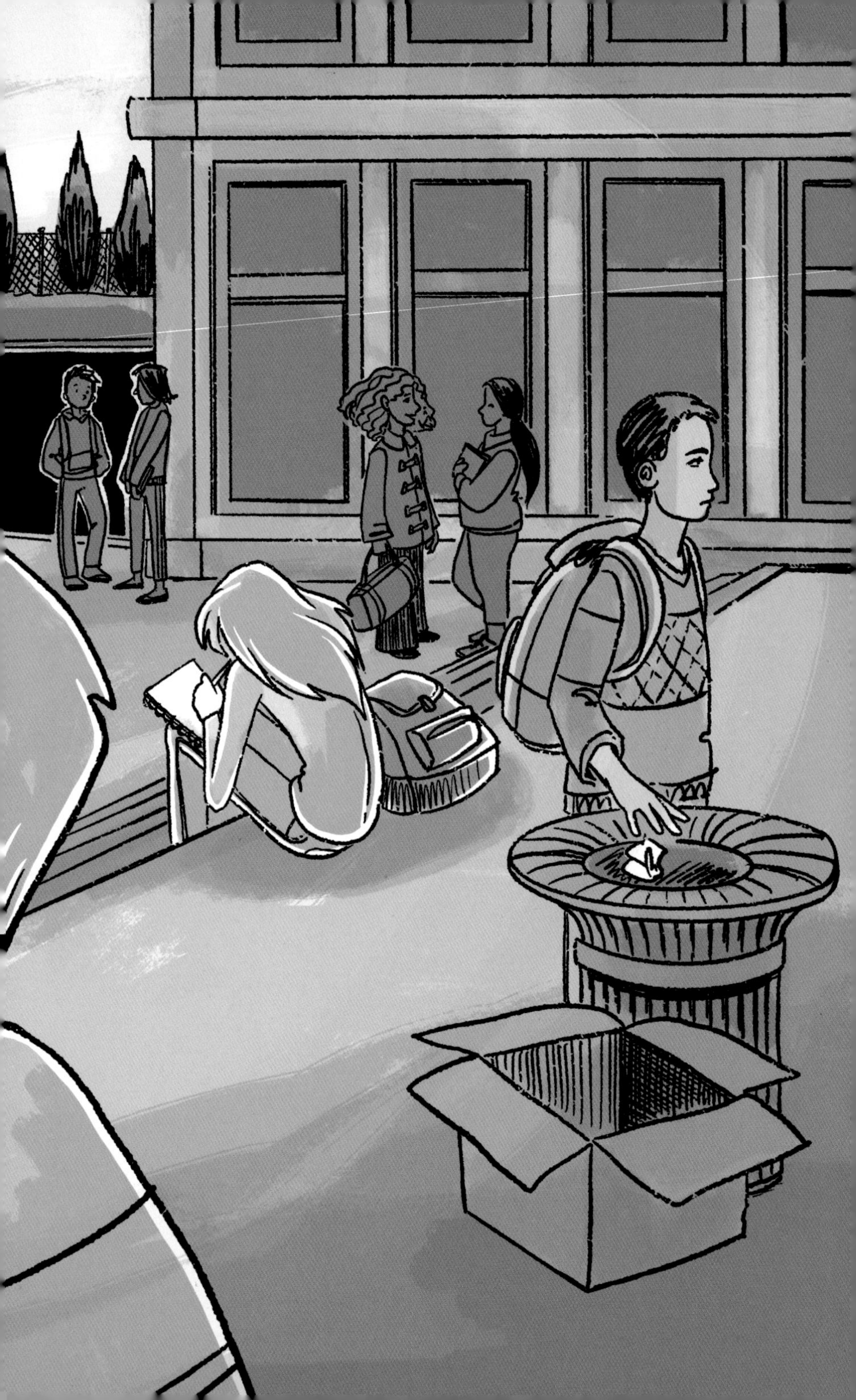

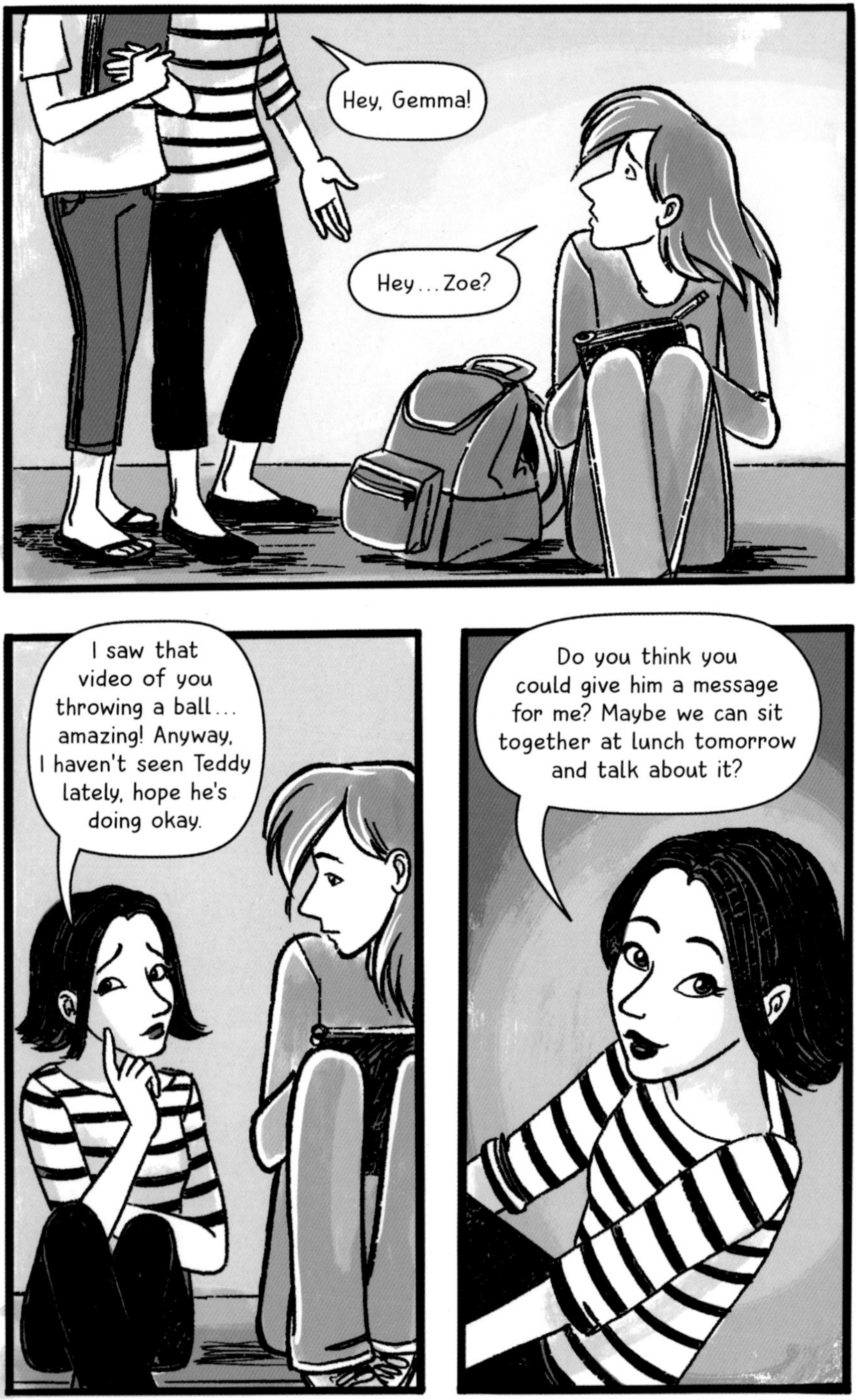
Hey, Gemma!
Hey...Zoe?
I saw that video of you throwing a ball... amazing! Anyway, I haven't seen Teddy lately, hope he's doing okay.
Do you think you could give him a message for me? Maybe we can sit together at lunch tomorrow and talk about it?

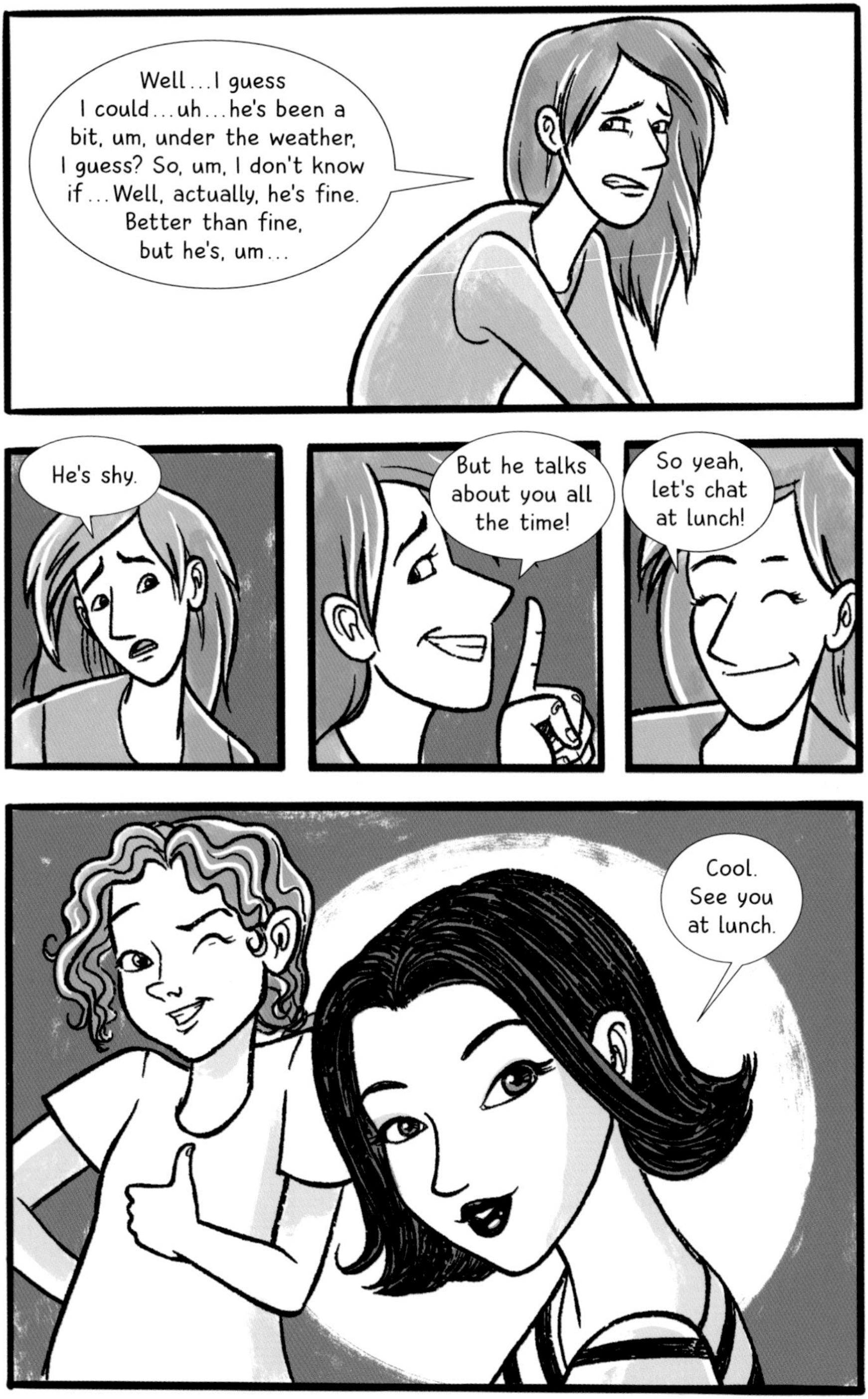
Well...I guess I could...uh...he's been a bit, um, under the weather, I guess? So, um, I don't know if...Well, actually, he's fine. Better than fine, but he's, um...
He's shy.
But he talks about you all the time!
So yeah, let's chat at lunch!
Cool. See you at lunch.

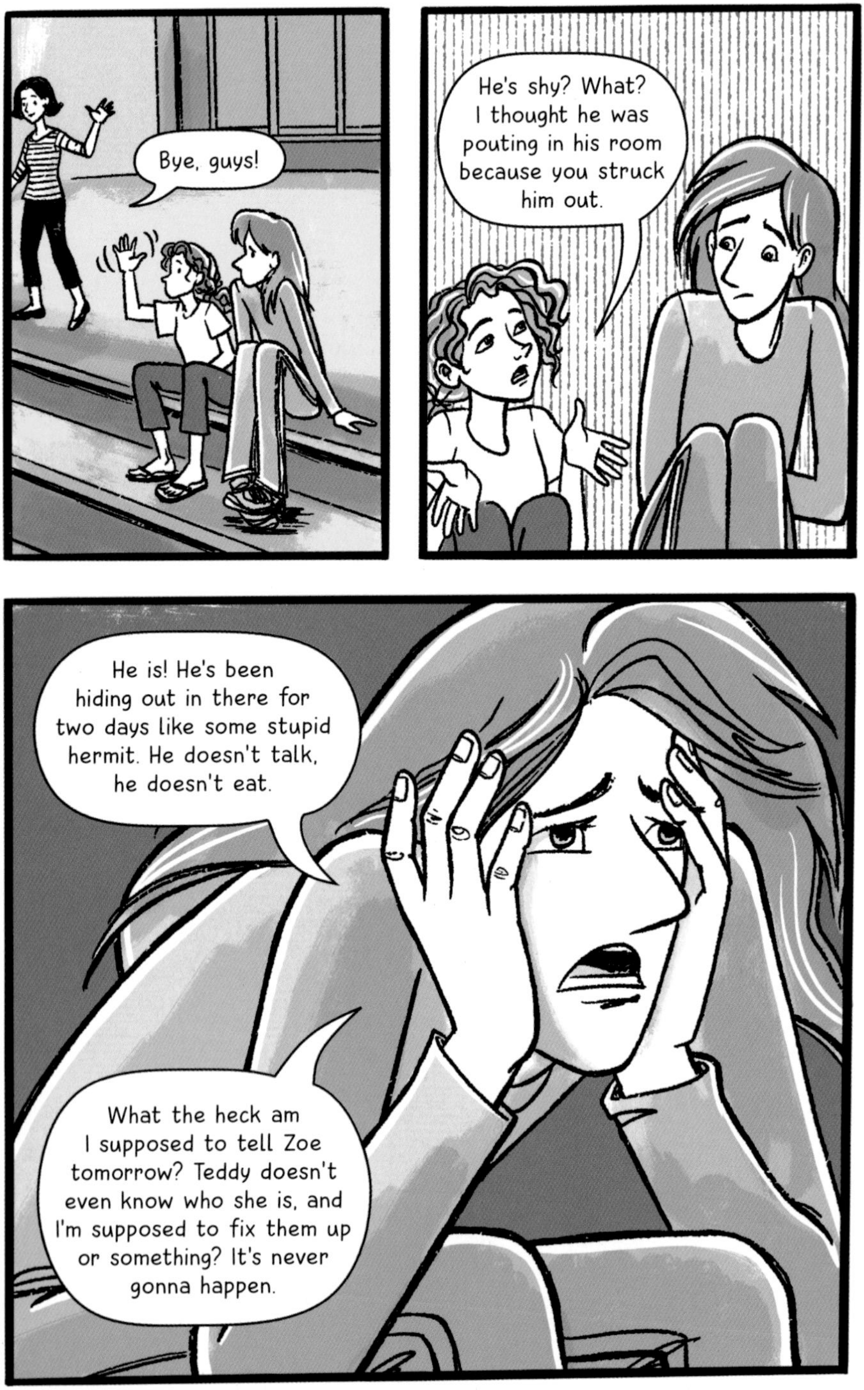
Bye, guys!
He's shy? What? I thought he was pouting in his room because you struck him out.
He is! He's been hiding out in there for two days like some stupid hermit. He doesn't talk, he doesn't eat.
What the heck am I supposed to tell Zoe tomorrow? Teddy doesn't even know who she is, and I'm supposed to fix them up or something? It's never gonna happen.

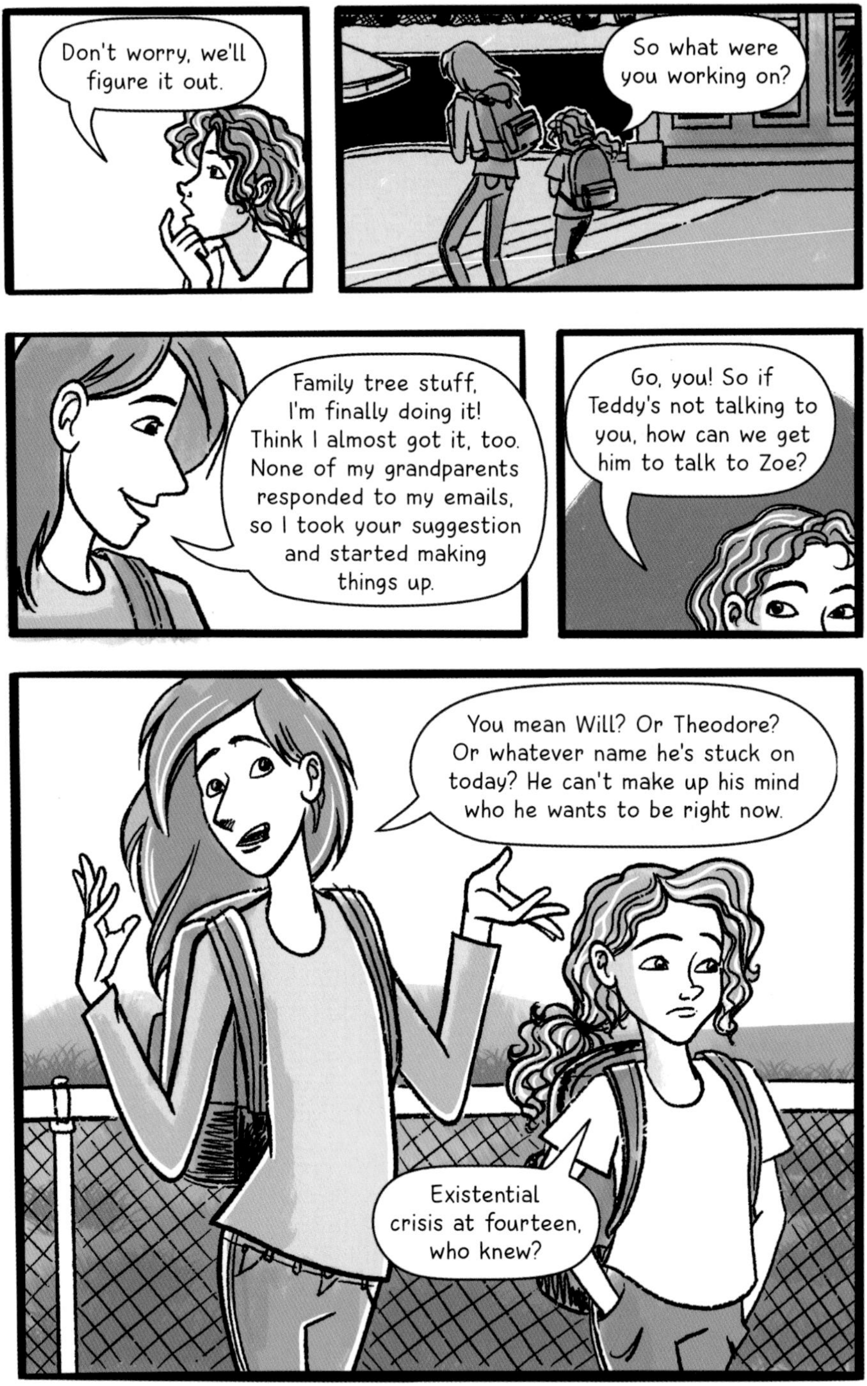
Don't worry, we'll figure it out.
So what were you working on?
Family tree stuff, I'm finally doing it! Think I almost got it, too. None of my grandparents responded to my emails, so I took your suggestion and started making things up.
Go, you! So if Teddy's not talking to you, how can we get him to talk to Zoe?
You mean Will? Or Theodore? Or whatever name he's stuck on today? He can't make up his mind who he wants to be right now.
Existential crisis at fourteen, who knew?

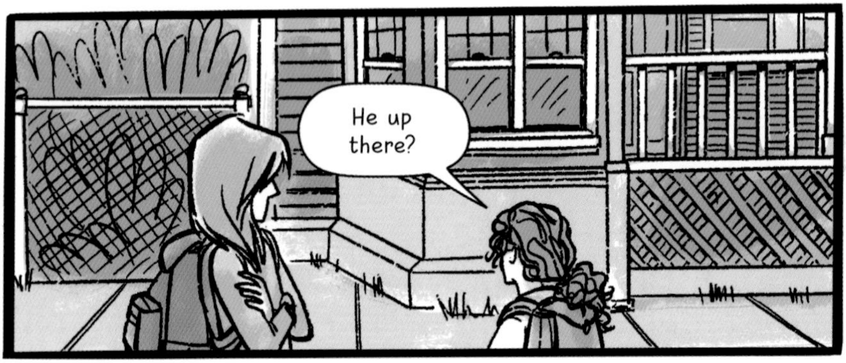
He up there?

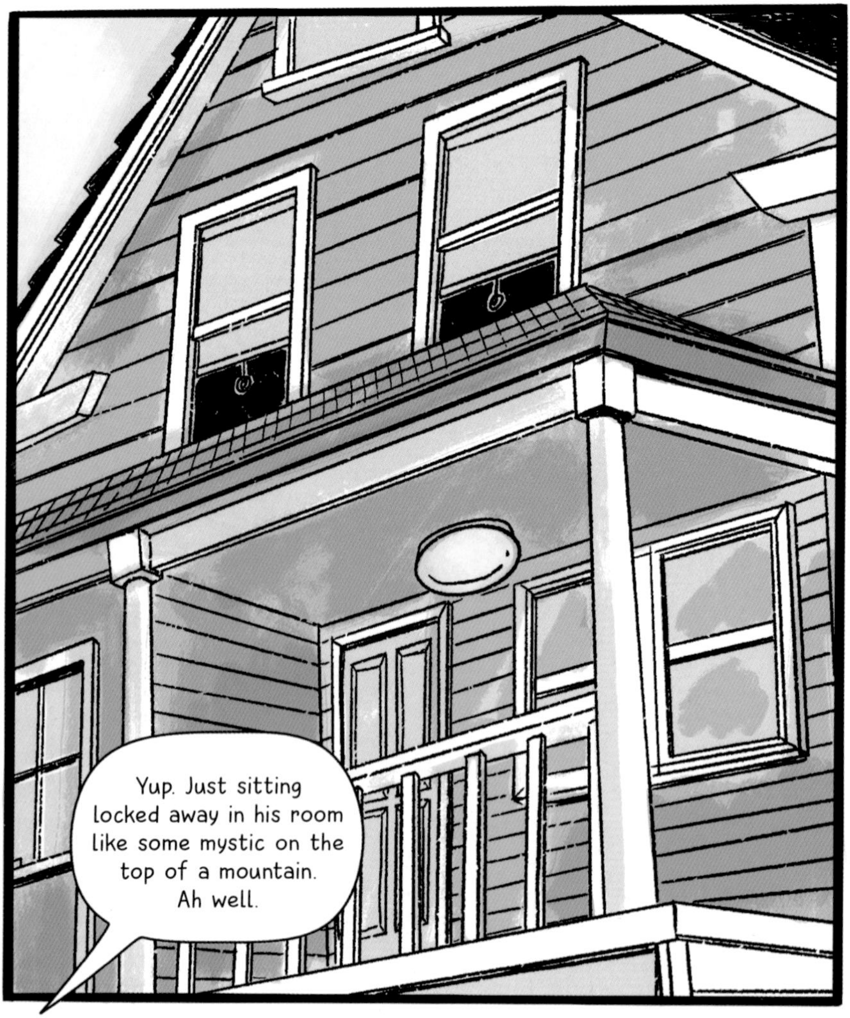
Yup. Just sitting locked away in his room like some mystic on the top of a mountain. Ah well.

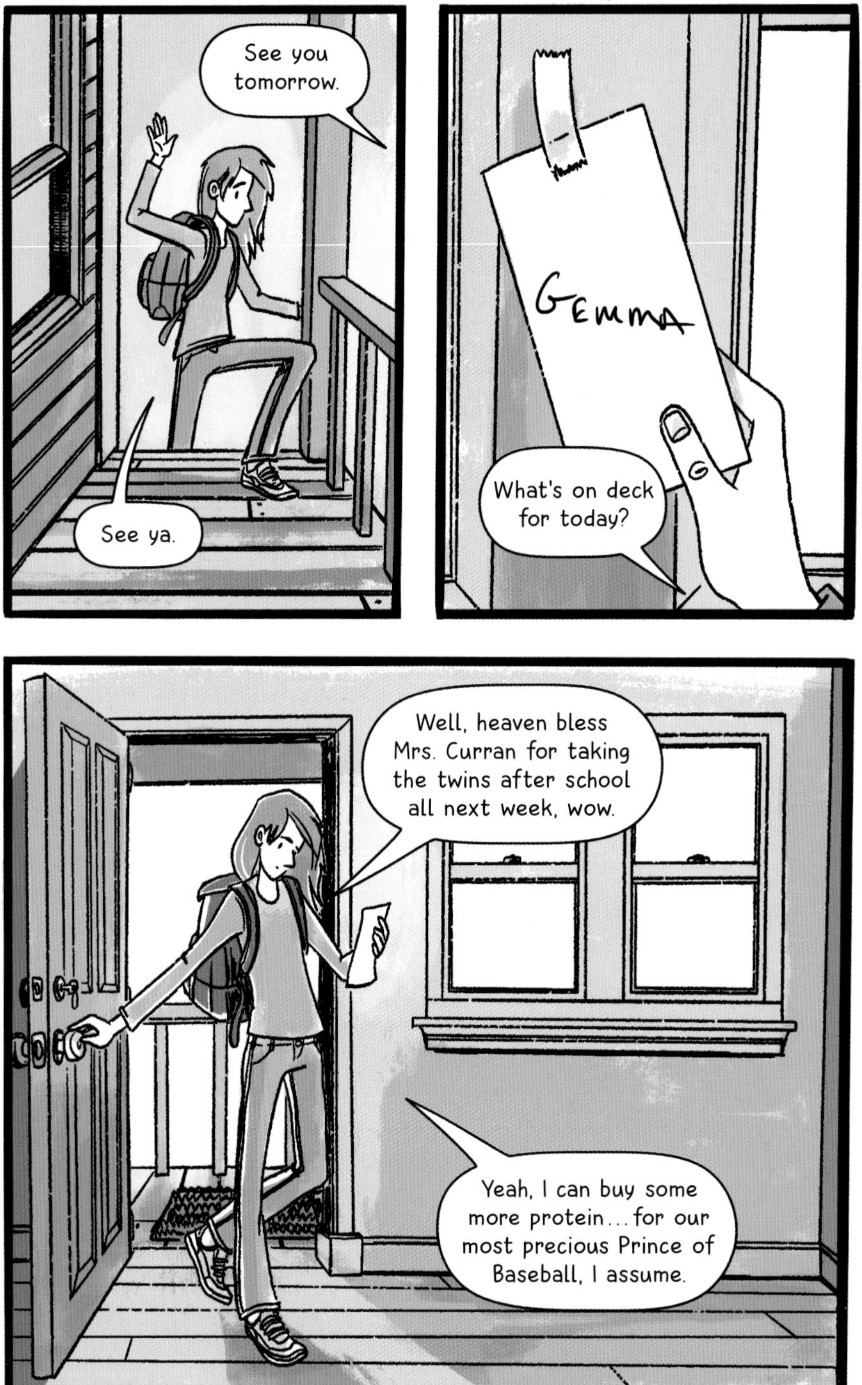
See you tomorrow.
See ya.
GEMMA
What's on deck for today?
Well, heaven bless Mrs. Curran for taking the twins after school all next week, wow.
Yeah, I can buy some more protein... for our most precious Prince of Baseball, I assume.

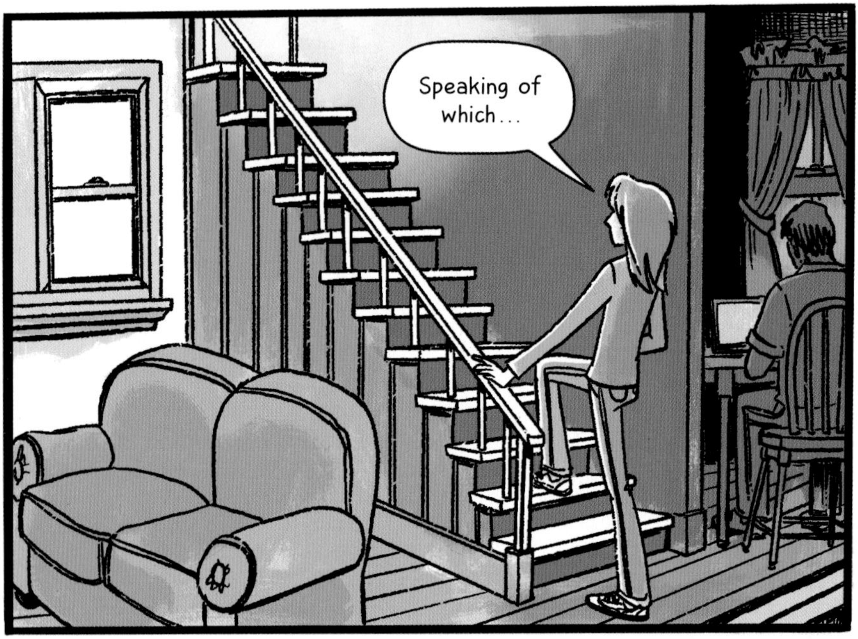
Speaking of which...

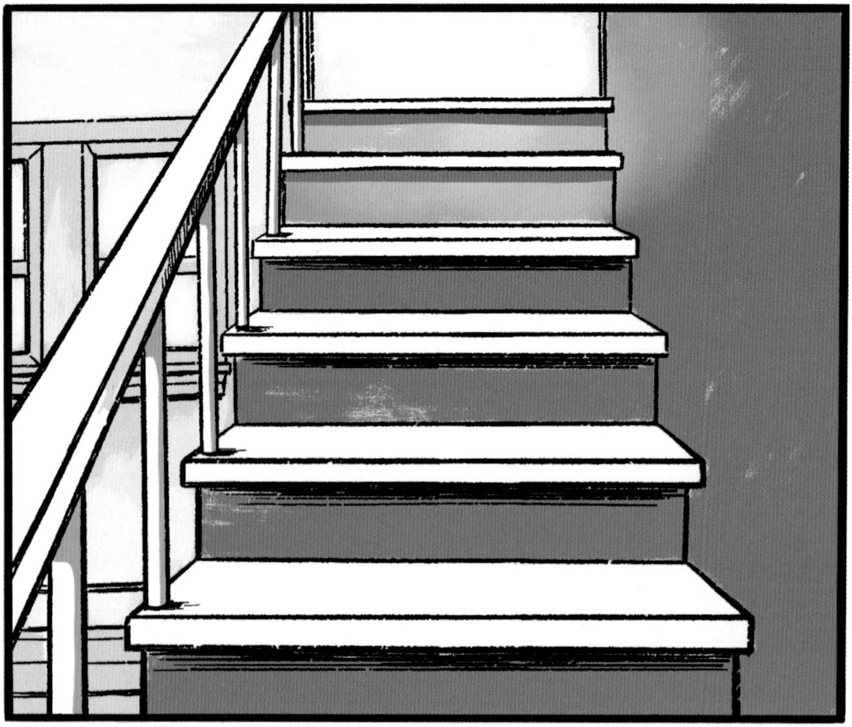

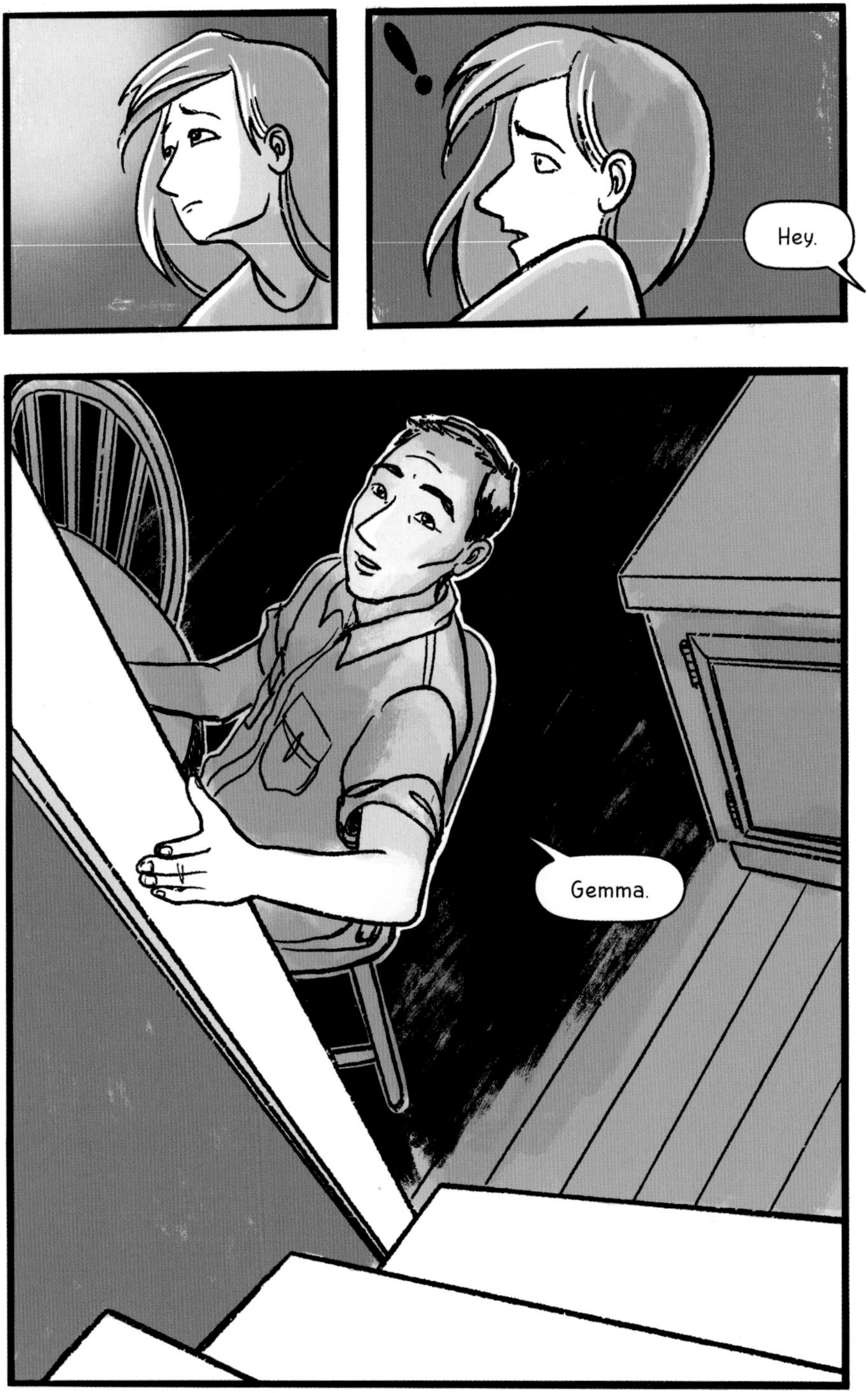
!
Hey.
Gemma.

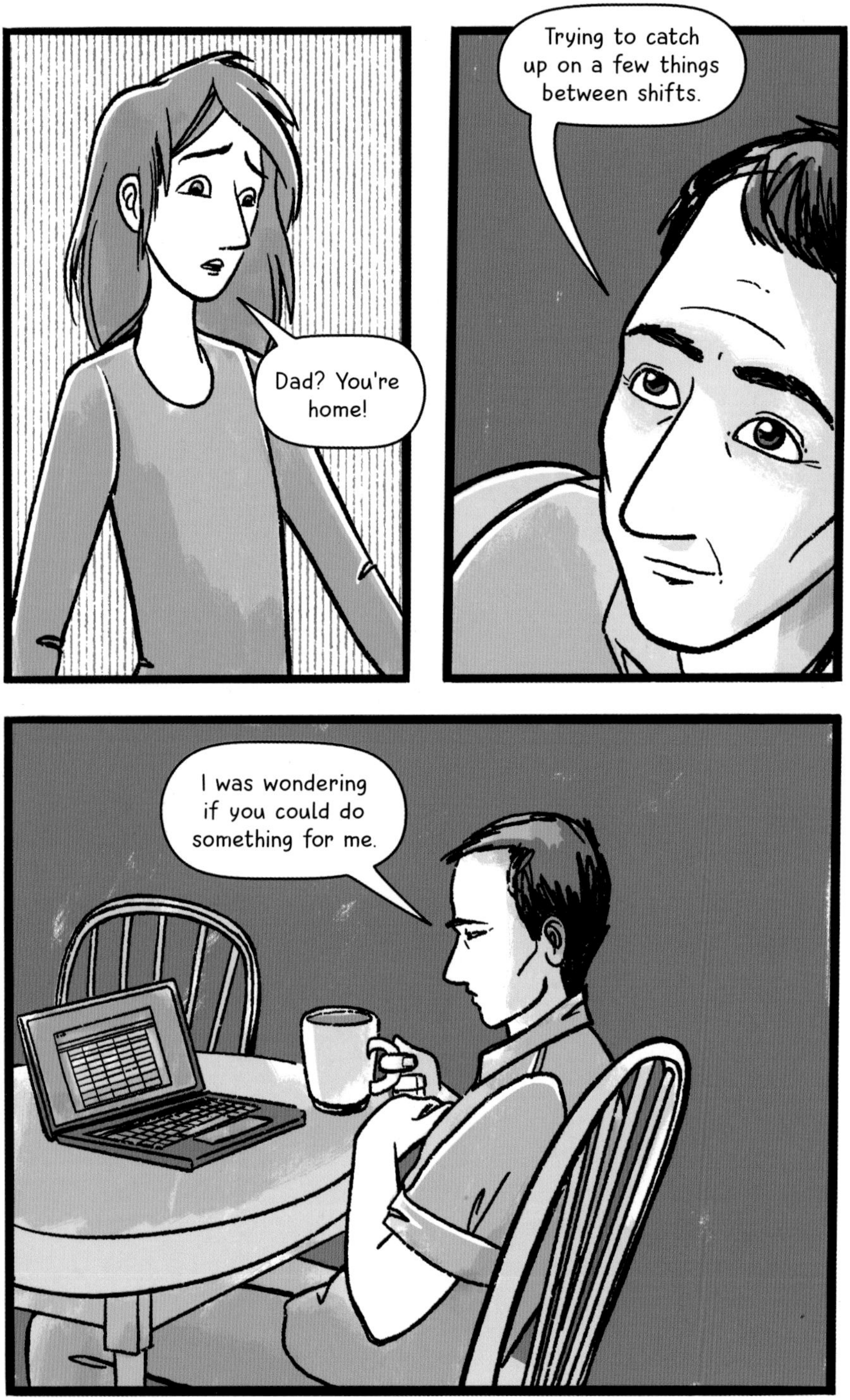
Dad? You're home!
Trying to catch up on a few things between shifts.
I was wondering if you could do something for me.

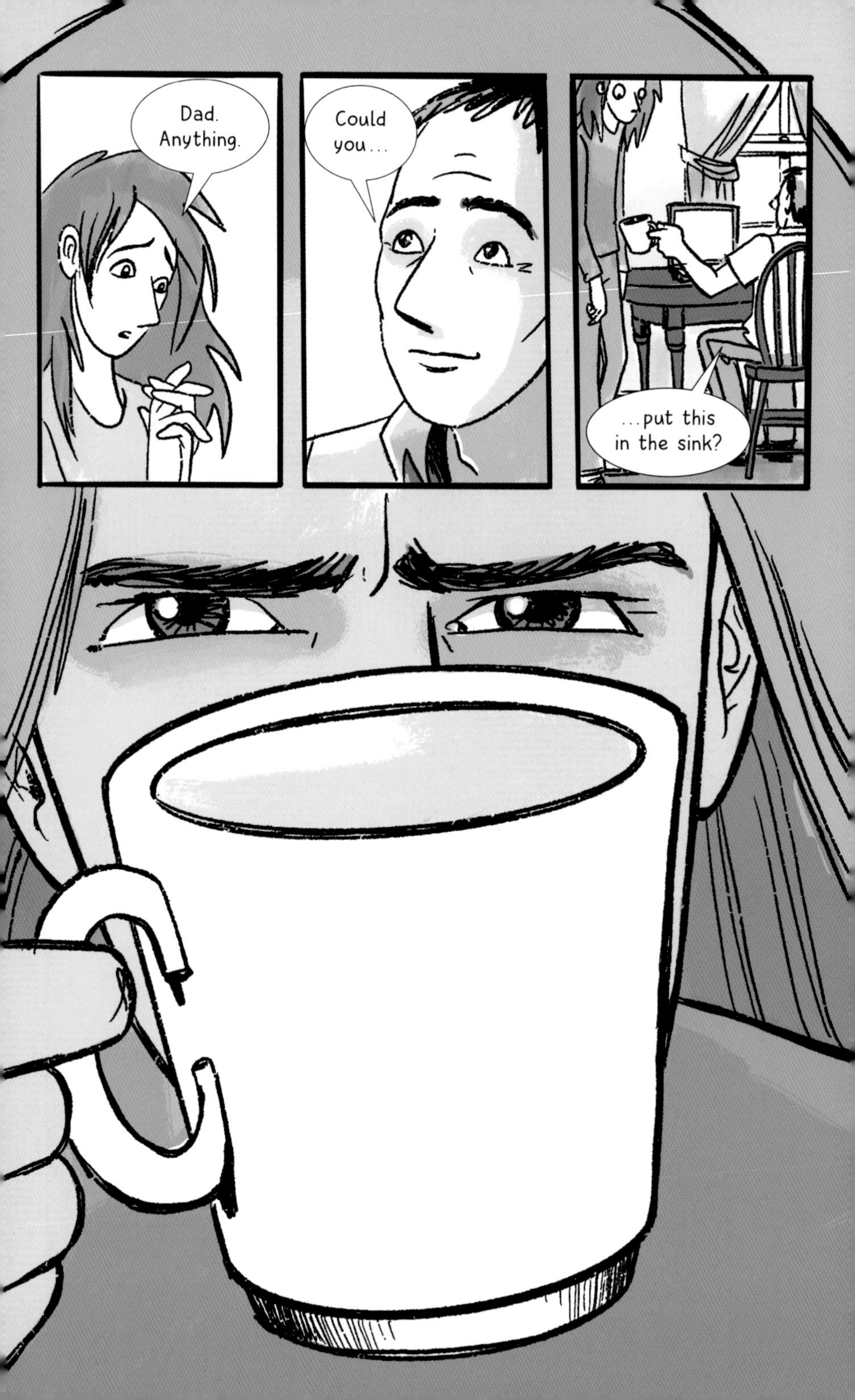
Dad. Anything.
Could you...
...put this in the sink?

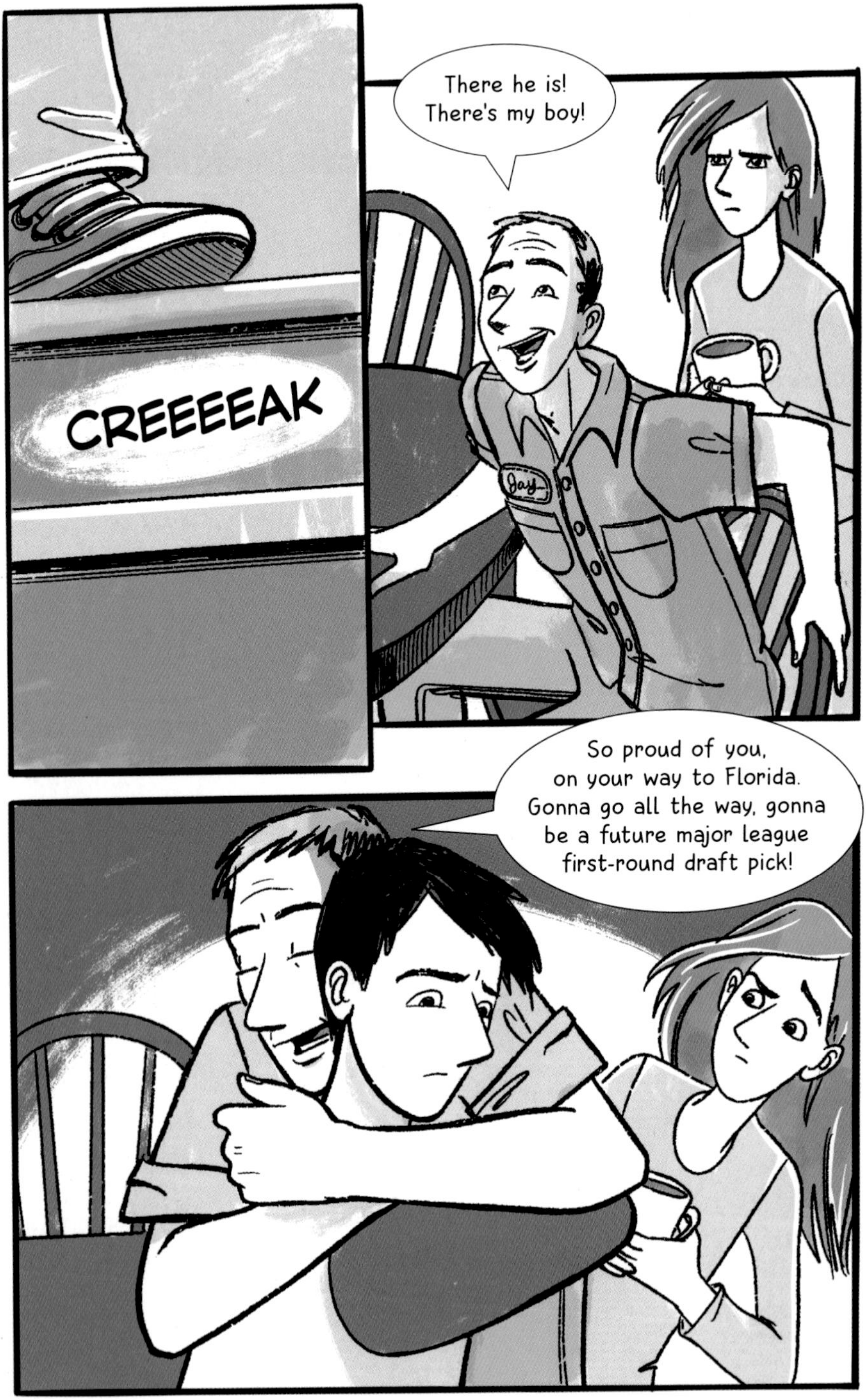
CREEEEAK
There he is! There's my boy!
So proud of you, on your way to Florida. Gonna go all the way, gonna be a future major league first-round draft pick!

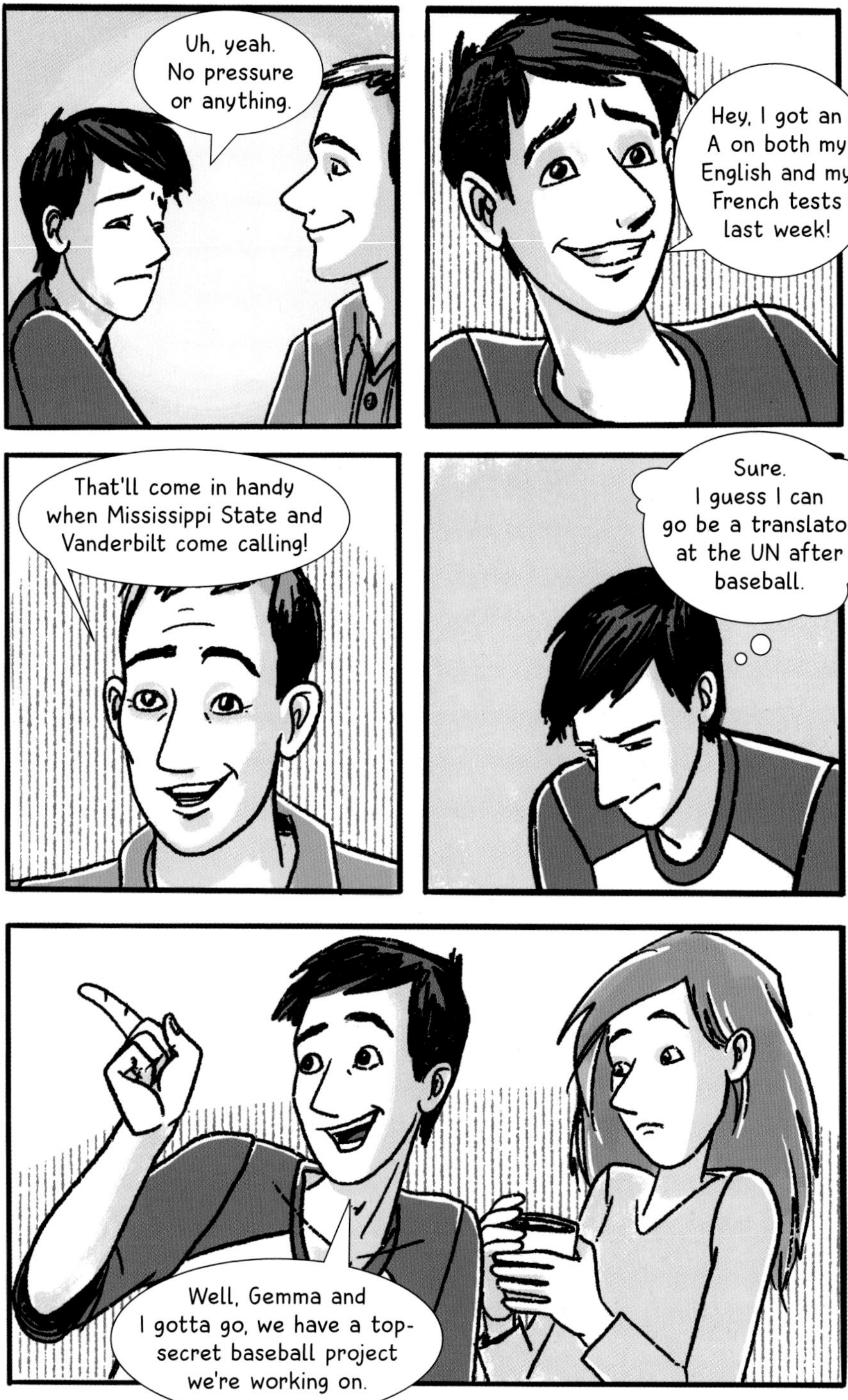
Uh, yeah. No pressure or anything.
Hey, I got an A on both my English and my French tests last week!
That'll come in handy when Mississippi State and Vanderbilt come calling!
Sure. I guess I can go be a translator at the UN after baseball.
Well, Gemma and I gotta go, we have a top-secret baseball project we're working on.

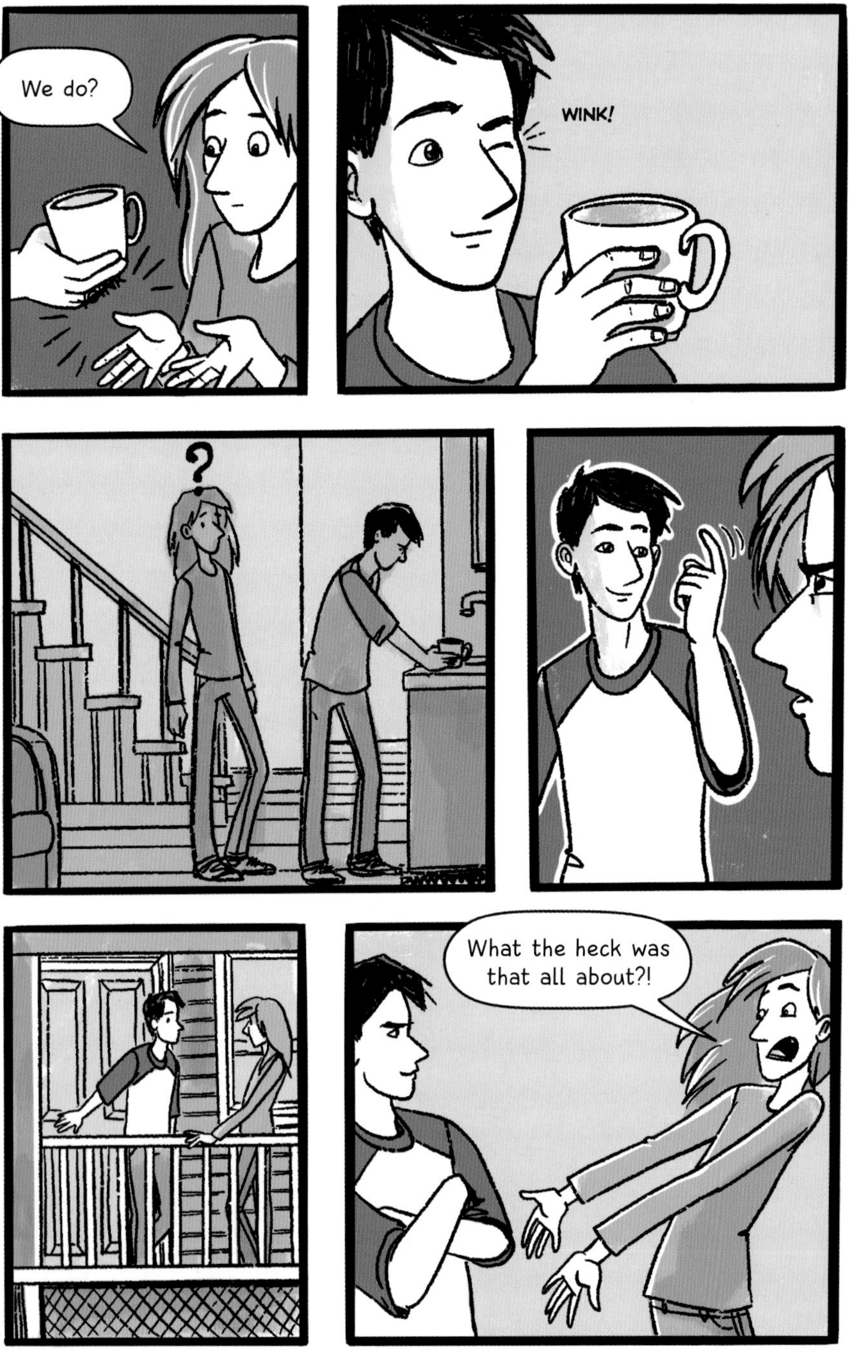

We do?
WINK!
?
What the heck was that all about?!

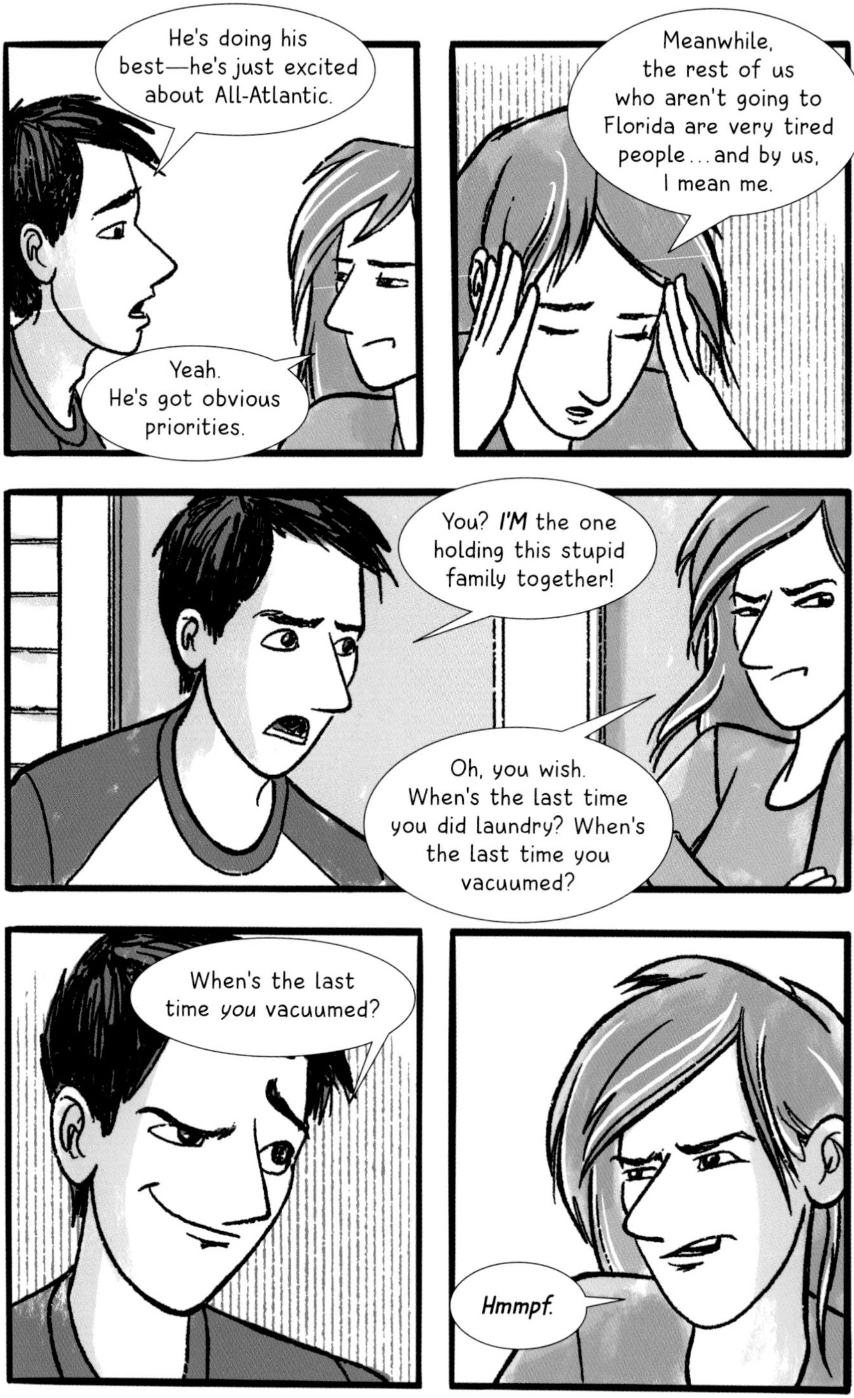
He's doing his best—he's just excited about All-Atlantic.
Yeah. He's got obvious priorities.
Meanwhile, the rest of us who aren't going to Florida are very tired people...and by us, I mean me.
You? *I'M* the one holding this stupid family together!
Oh, you wish. When's the last time you did laundry? When's the last time you vacuumed?
When's the last time *you* vacuumed?
Hmmpf.

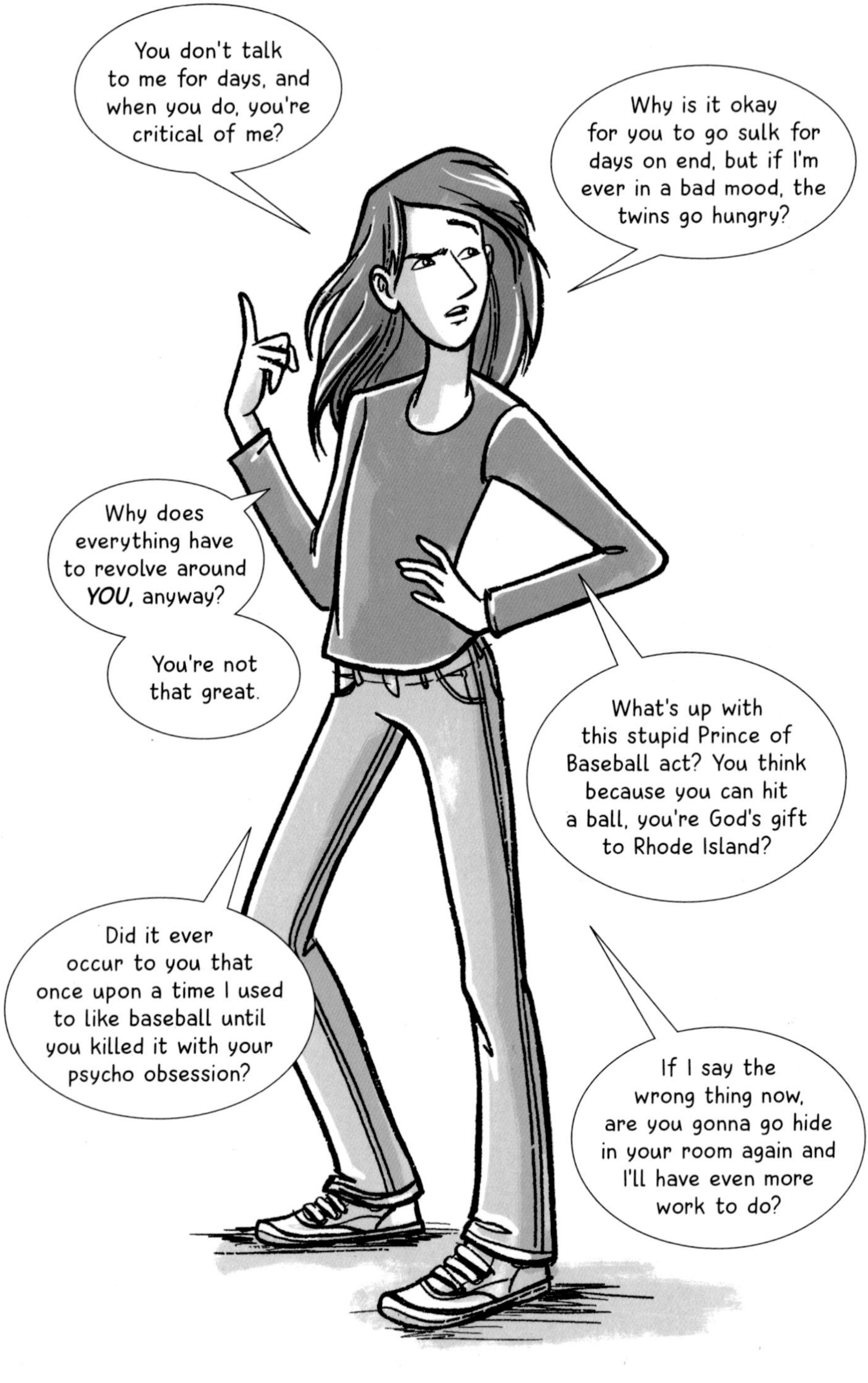
You don't talk to me for days, and when you do, you're critical of me?
Why is it okay for you to go sulk for days on end, but if I'm ever in a bad mood, the twins go hungry?
Why does everything have to revolve around ***YOU,*** anyway?
You're not that great.
What's up with this stupid Prince of Baseball act? You think because you can hit a ball, you're God's gift to Rhode Island?
Did it ever occur to you that once upon a time I used to like baseball until you killed it with your psycho obsession?
If I say the wrong thing now, are you gonna go hide in your room again and I'll have even more work to do?

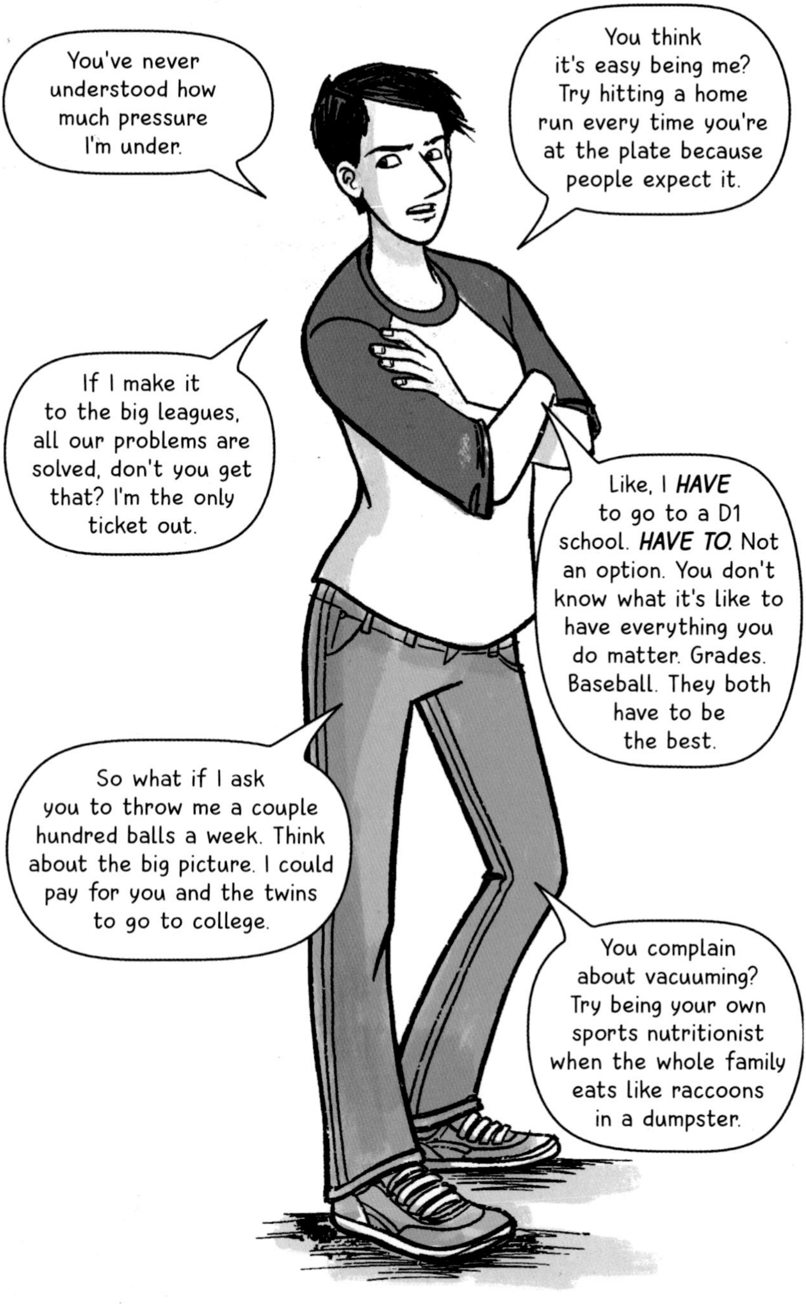
You've never understood how much pressure I'm under.
You think it's easy being me? Try hitting a home run every time you're at the plate because people expect it.
If I make it to the big leagues, all our problems are solved, don't you get that? I'm the only ticket out.
Like, I ***HAVE*** to go to a D1 school. ***HAVE TO.*** Not an option. You don't know what it's like to have everything you do matter. Grades. Baseball. They both have to be the best.
So what if I ask you to throw me a couple hundred balls a week. Think about the big picture. I could pay for you and the twins to go to college.
You complain about vacuuming? Try being your own sports nutritionist when the whole family eats like raccoons in a dumpster.

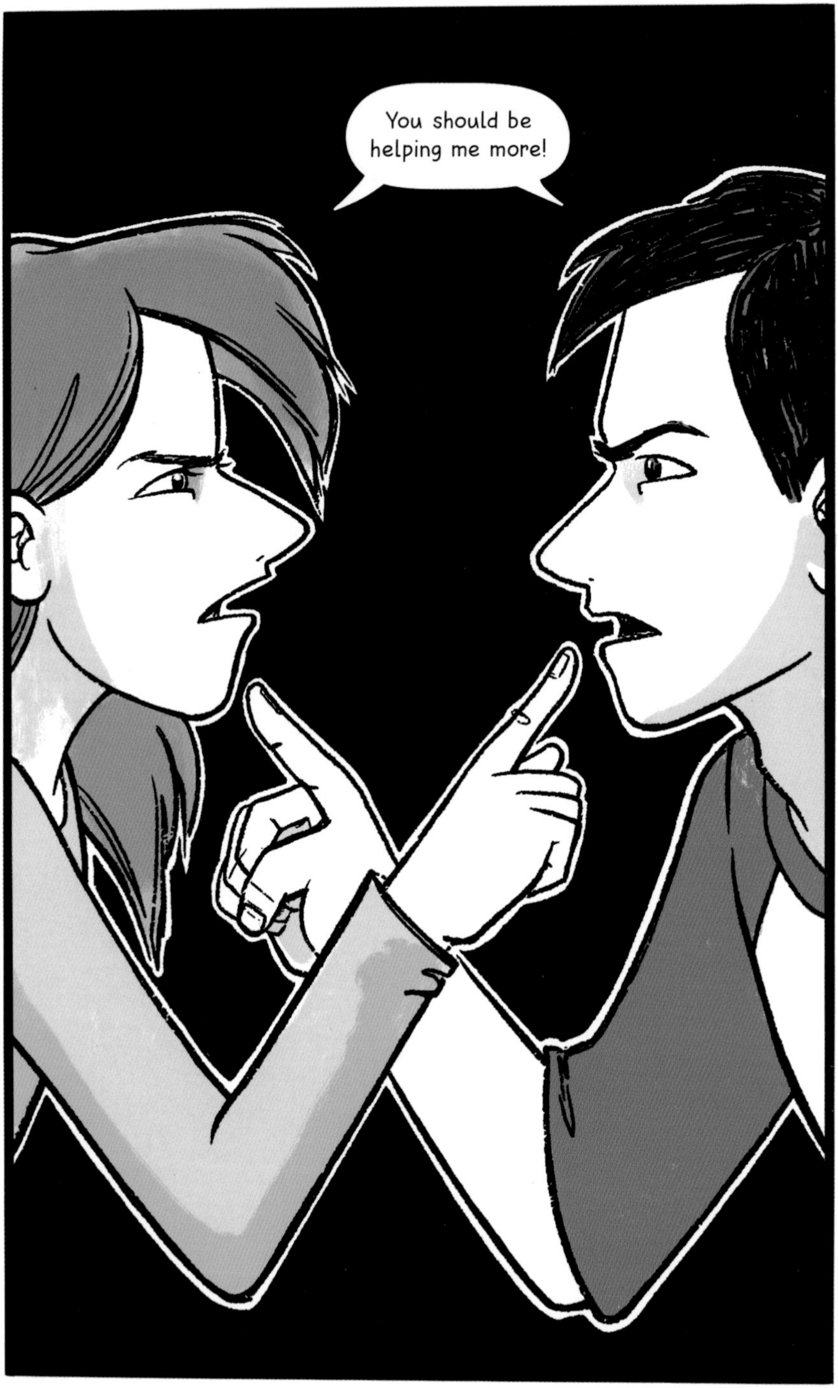
You should be helping me more!

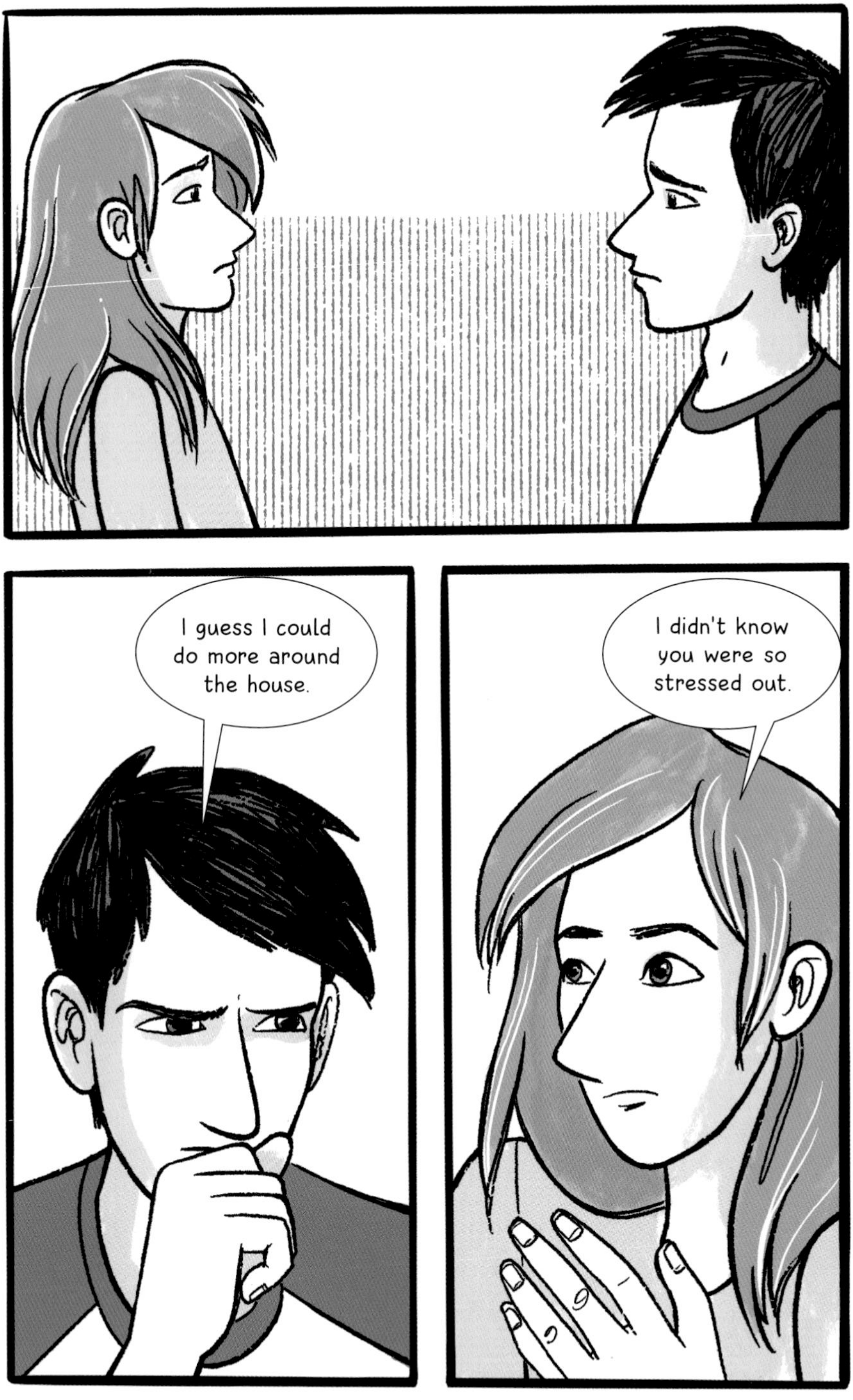
I guess I could do more around the house.
I didn't know you were so stressed out.

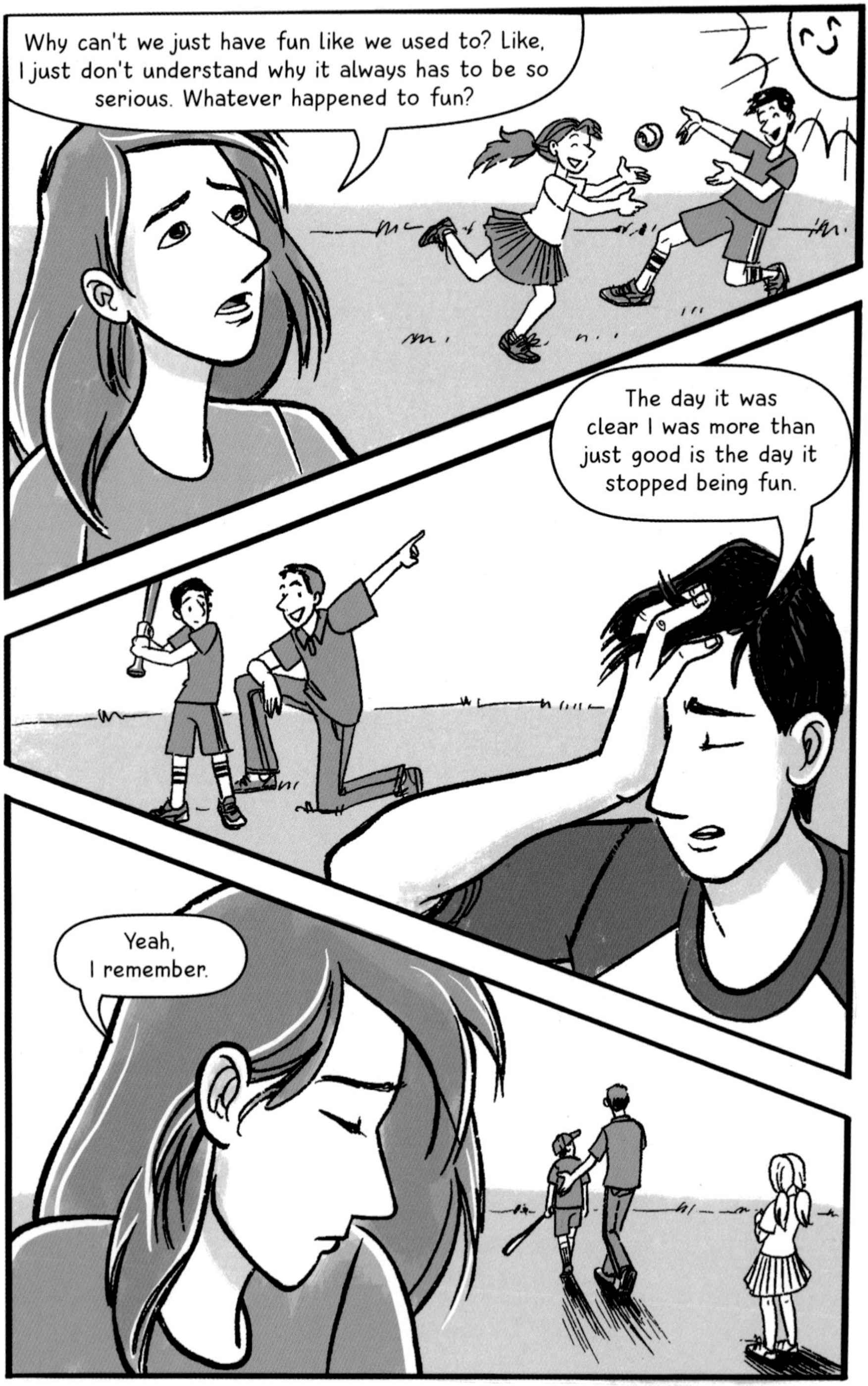

Why can't we just have fun like we used to? Like, I just don't understand why it always has to be so serious. Whatever happened to fun?
The day it was clear I was more than just good is the day it stopped being fun.
Yeah, I remember.

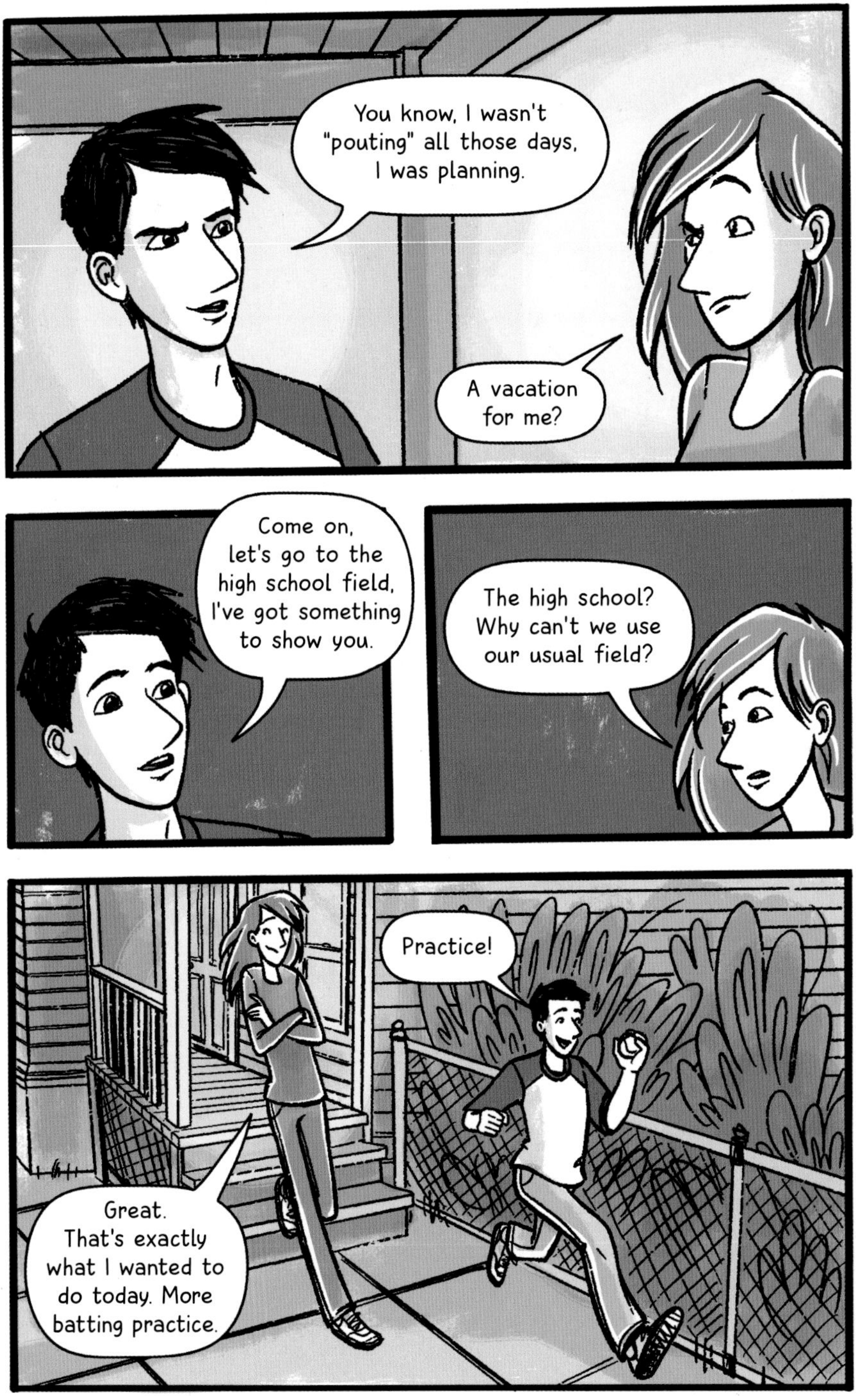
You know, I wasn't "pouting" all those days, I was planning.
A vacation for me?
Come on, let's go to the high school field, I've got something to show you.
The high school? Why can't we use our usual field?
Practice!
Great. That's exactly what I wanted to do today. More batting practice.

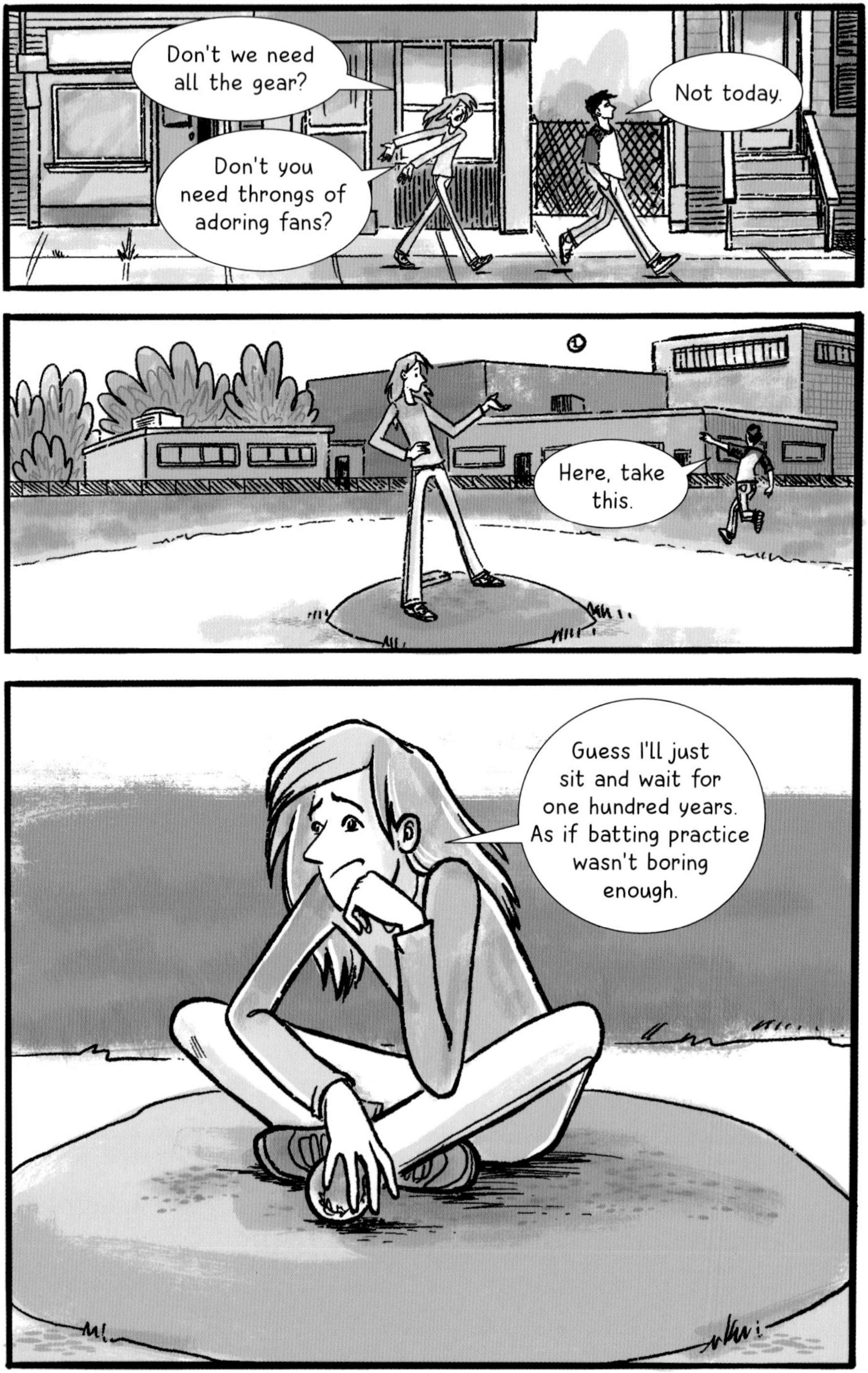
Don't we need all the gear?
Don't you need throngs of adoring fans?
Not today.
Here, take this.
Guess I'll just sit and wait for one hundred years. As if batting practice wasn't boring enough.

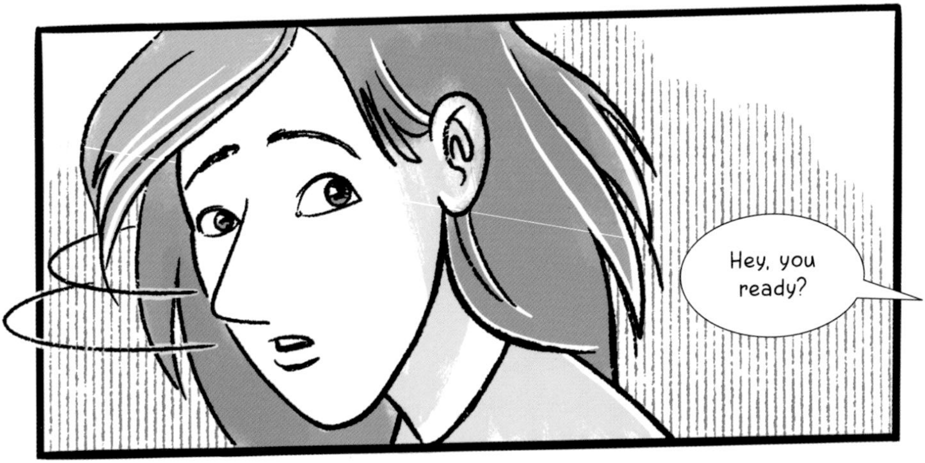
Hey, you ready?

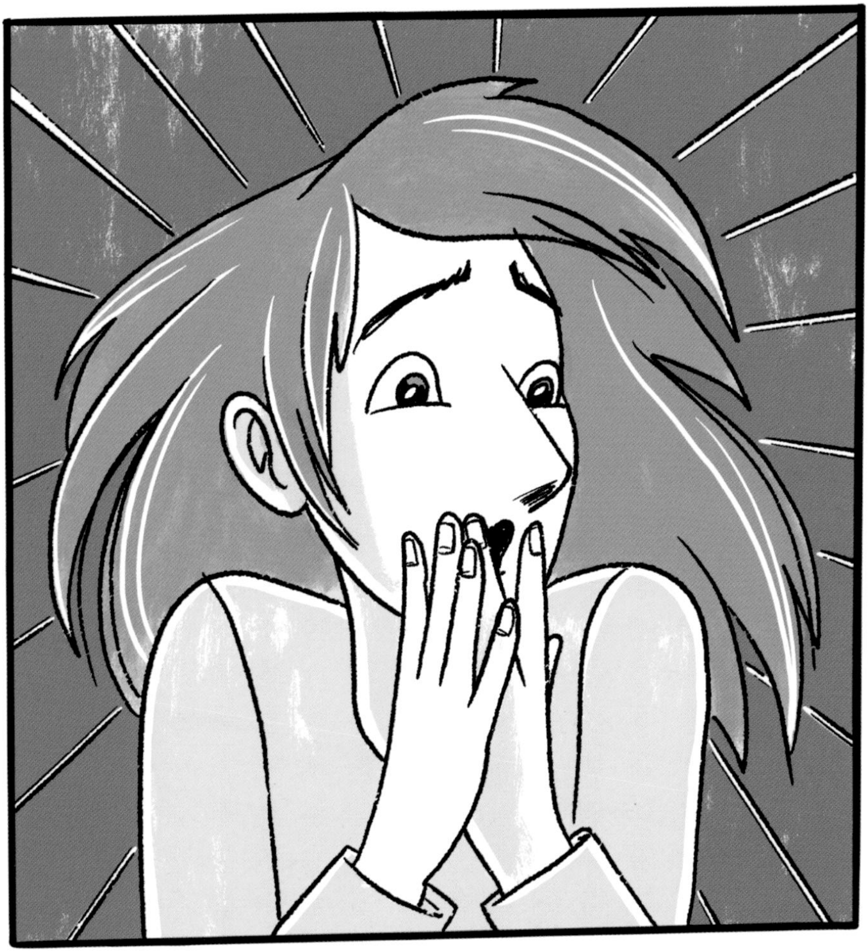

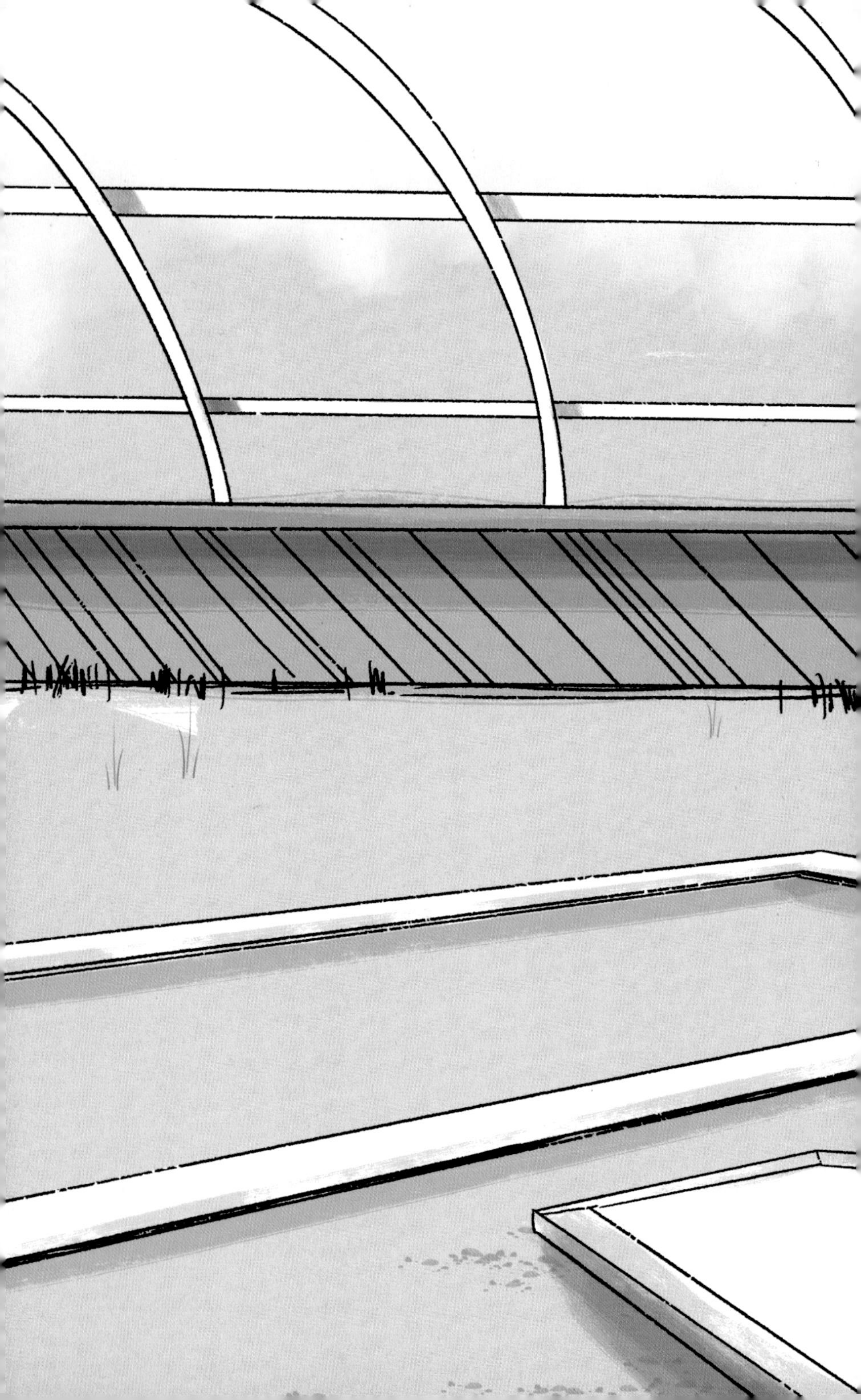

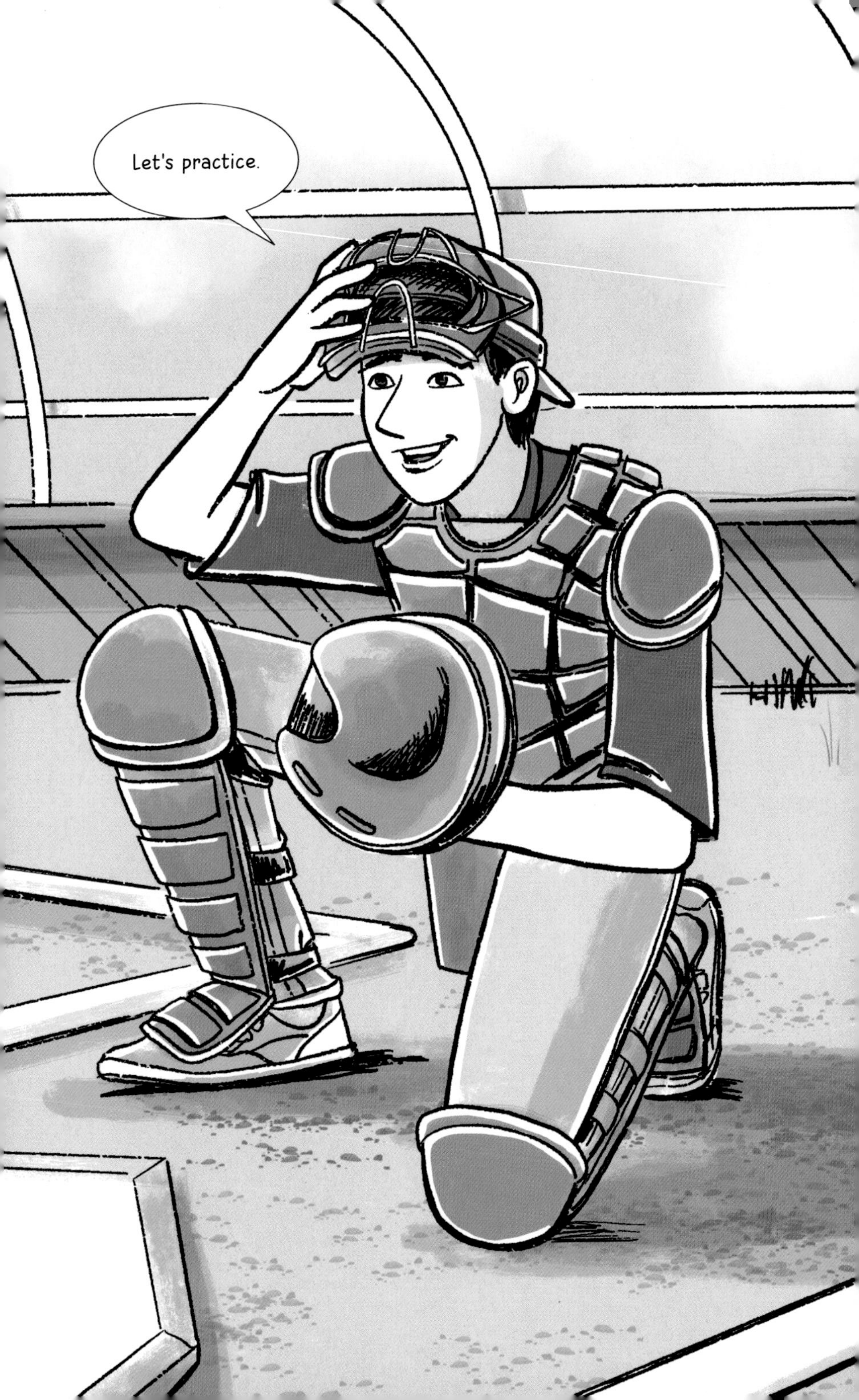
Let's practice.

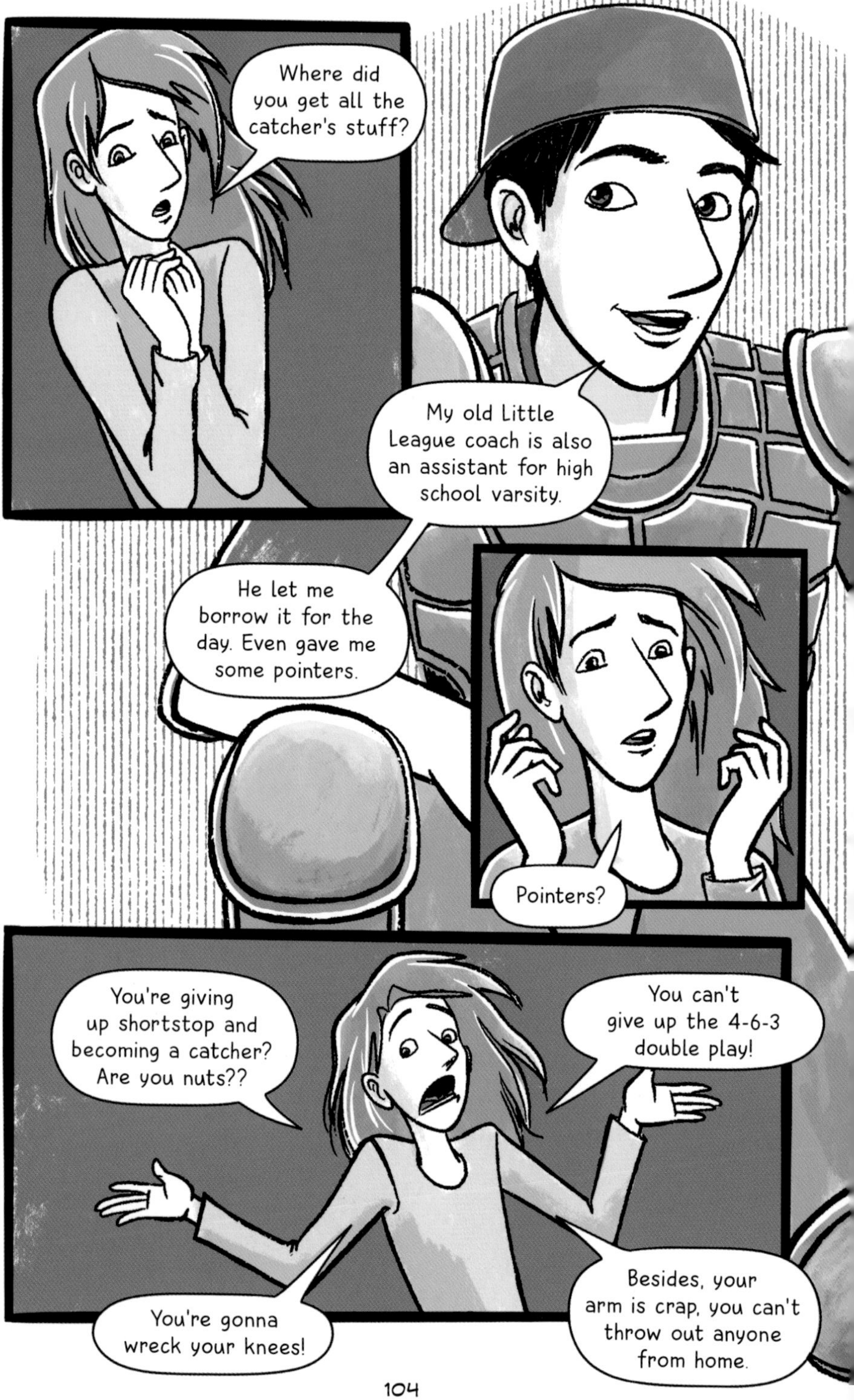
Where did you get all the catcher's stuff?
My old Little League coach is also an assistant for high school varsity.
He let me borrow it for the day. Even gave me some pointers.
Pointers?
You're giving up shortstop and becoming a catcher? Are you nuts??
You can't give up the 4-6-3 double play!
You're gonna wreck your knees!
Besides, your arm is crap, you can't throw out anyone from home.

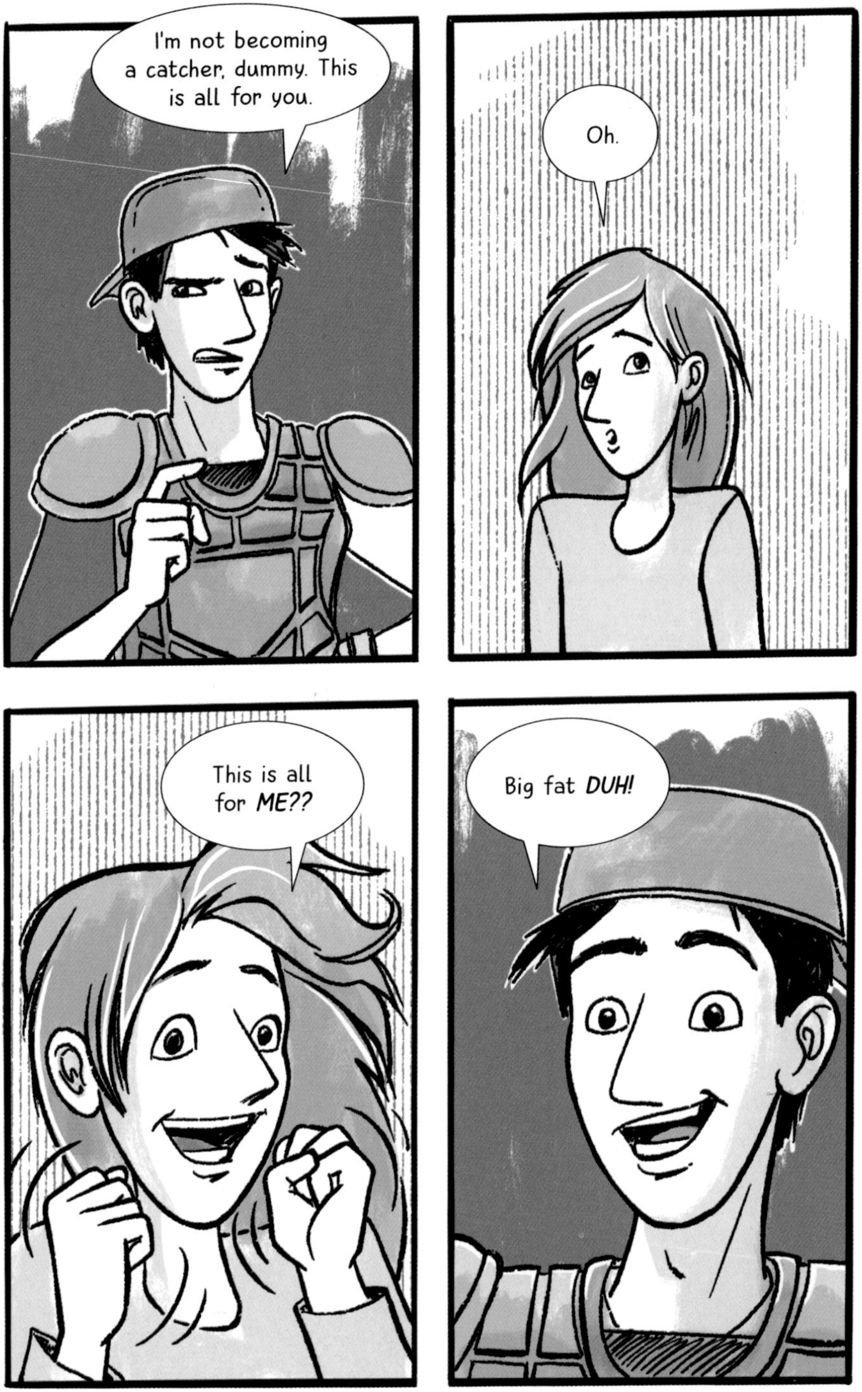
I'm not becoming a catcher, dummy. This is all for you.
Oh.
This is all for *ME??*
Big fat ***DUH!***

Alright, there's a glove behind the mound. Let's go.
PLOP!

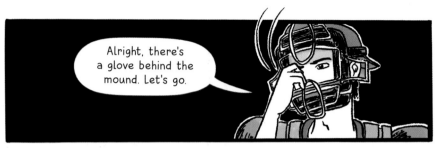

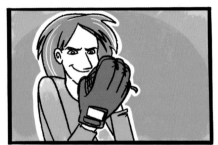

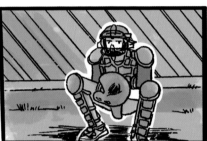

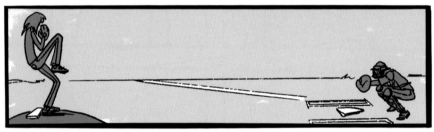

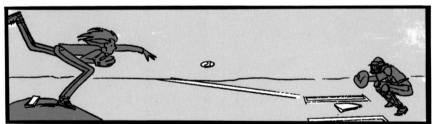

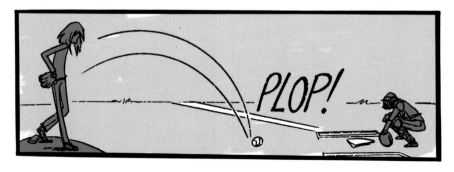

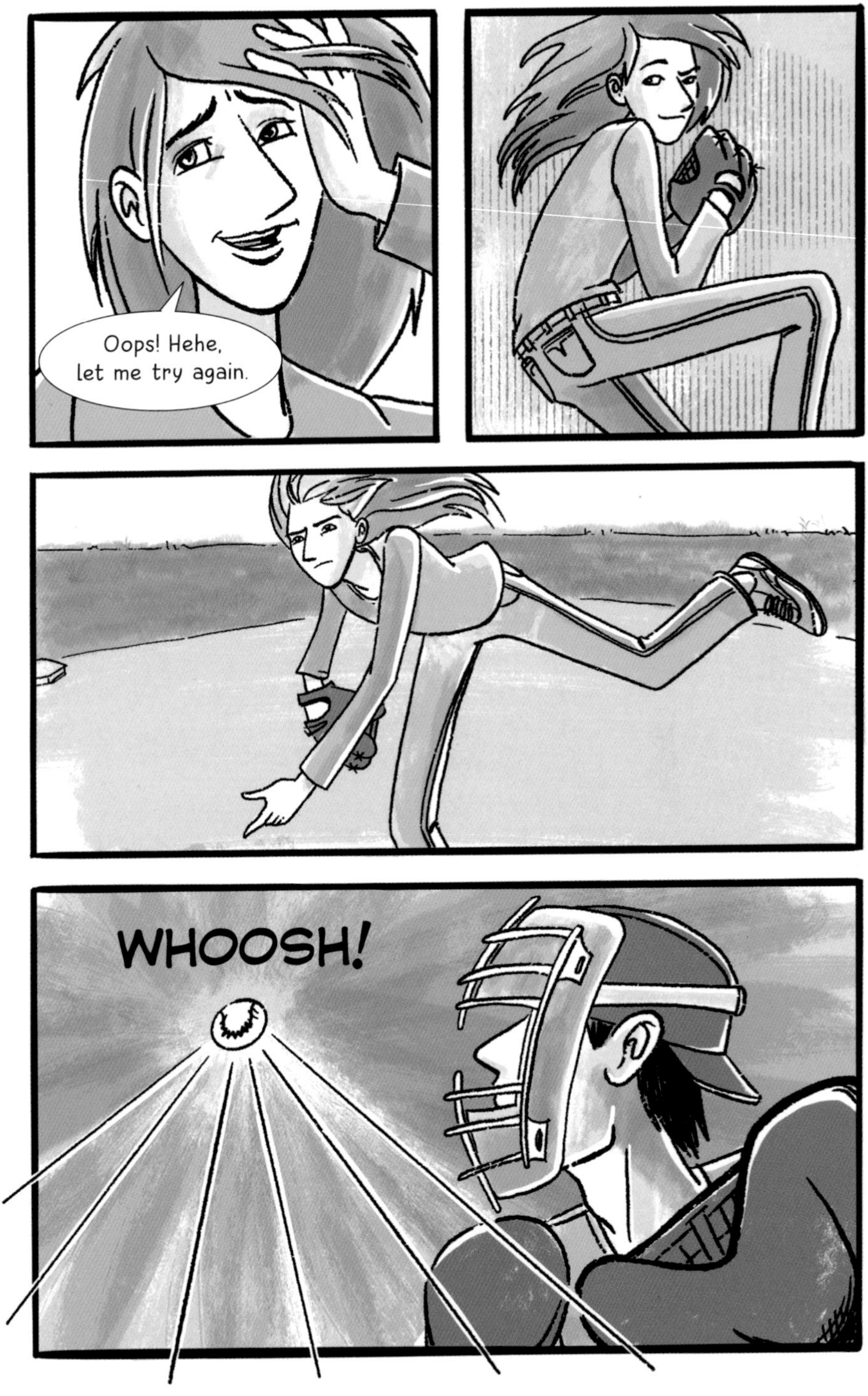
Oops! Hehe, let me try again.
WHOOSH!

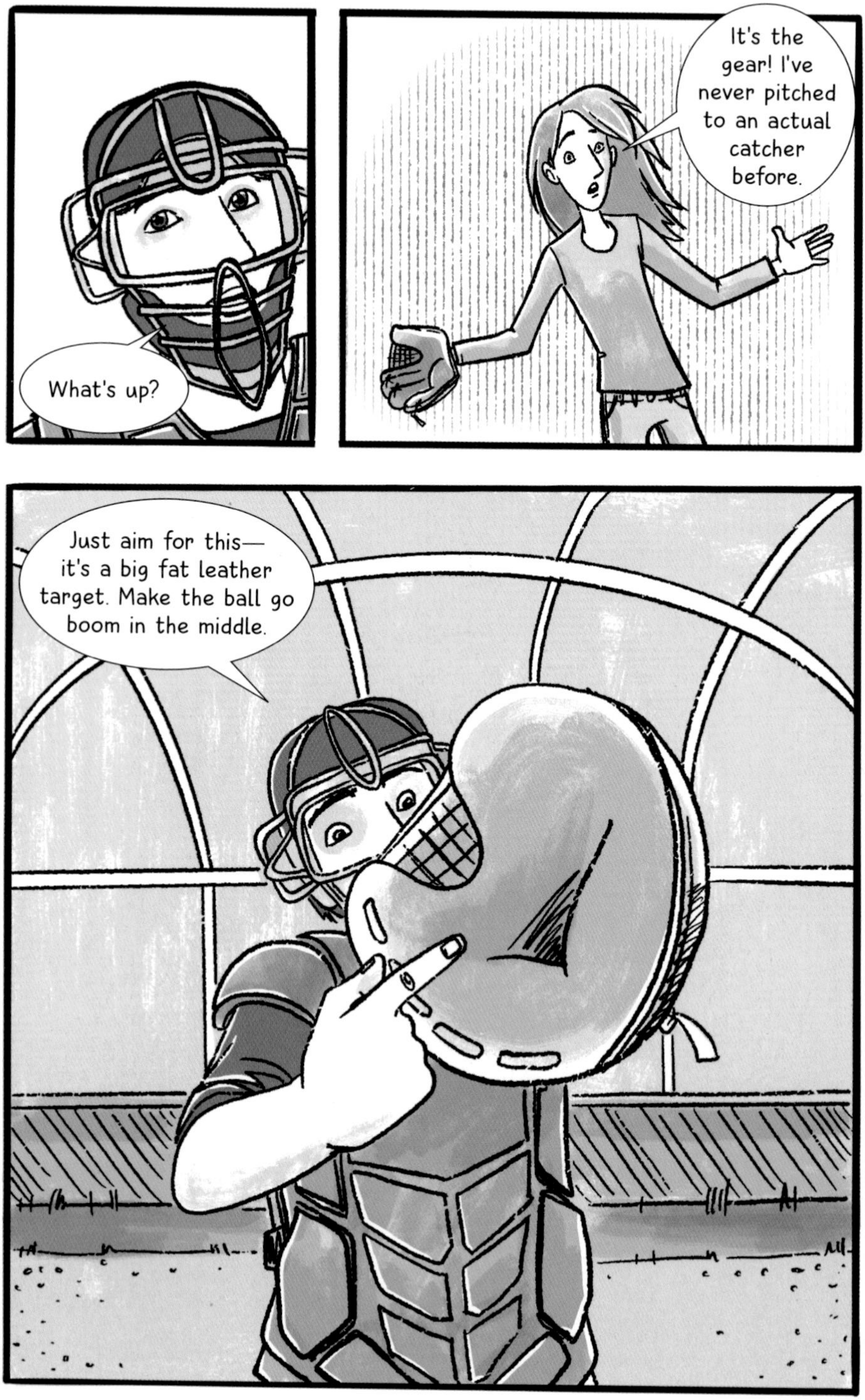
What's up?
It's the gear! I've never pitched to an actual catcher before.
Just aim for this— it's a big fat leather target. Make the ball go boom in the middle.

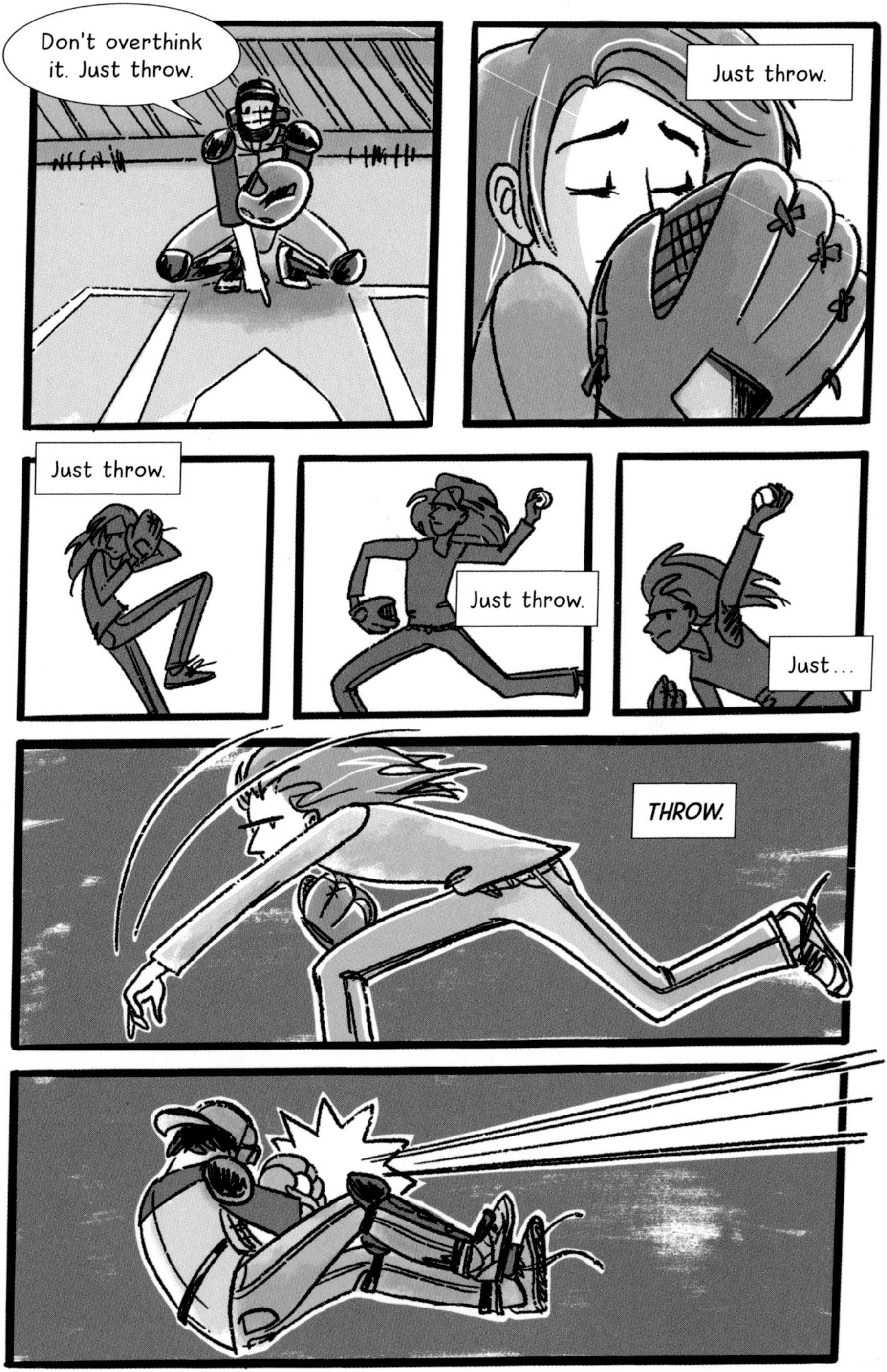
Don't overthink it. Just throw.
Just throw.
Just throw.
Just throw.
Just...
THROW.

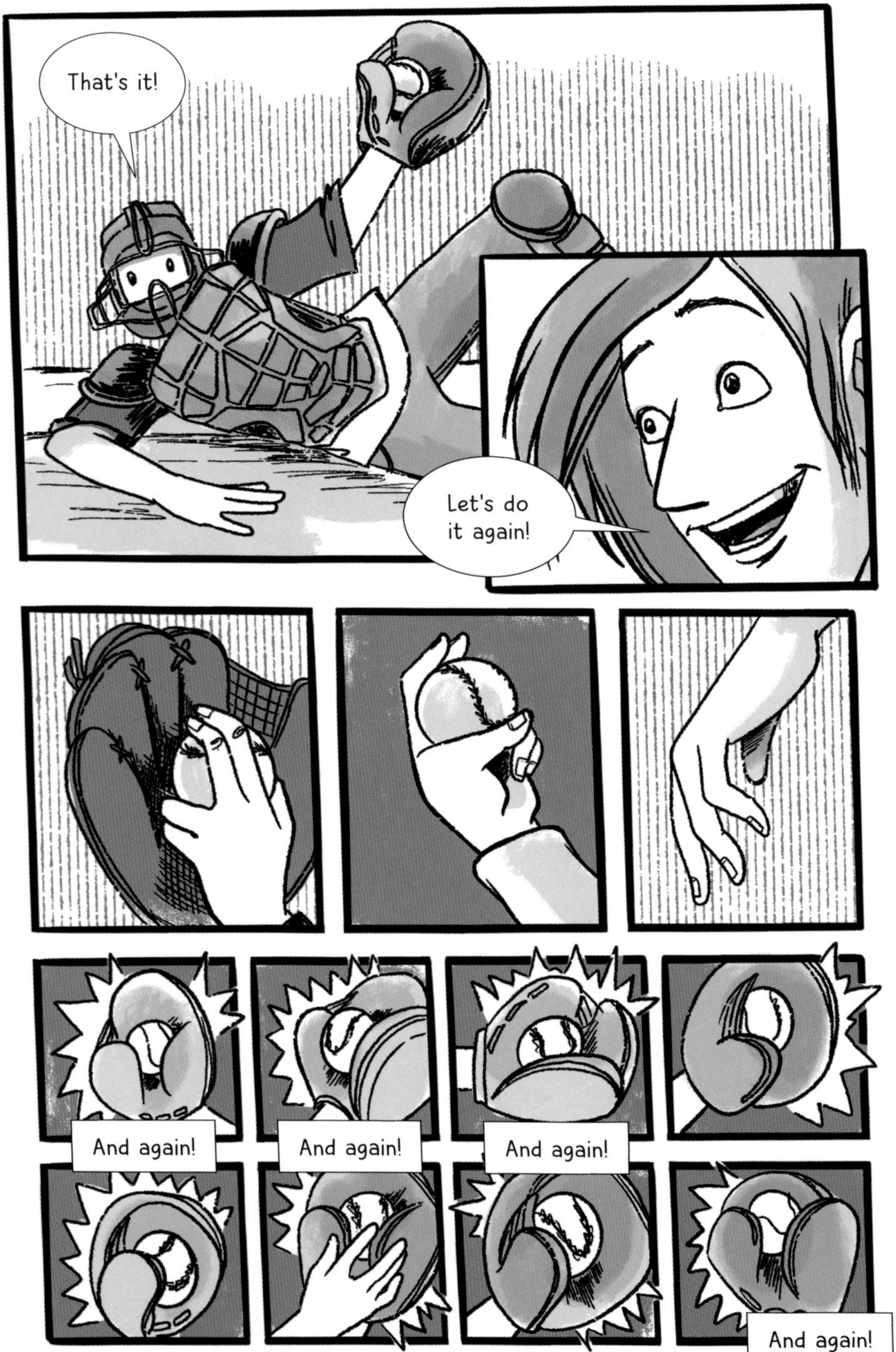
That's it!
Let's do it again!
And again!
And again!
And again!
And again!

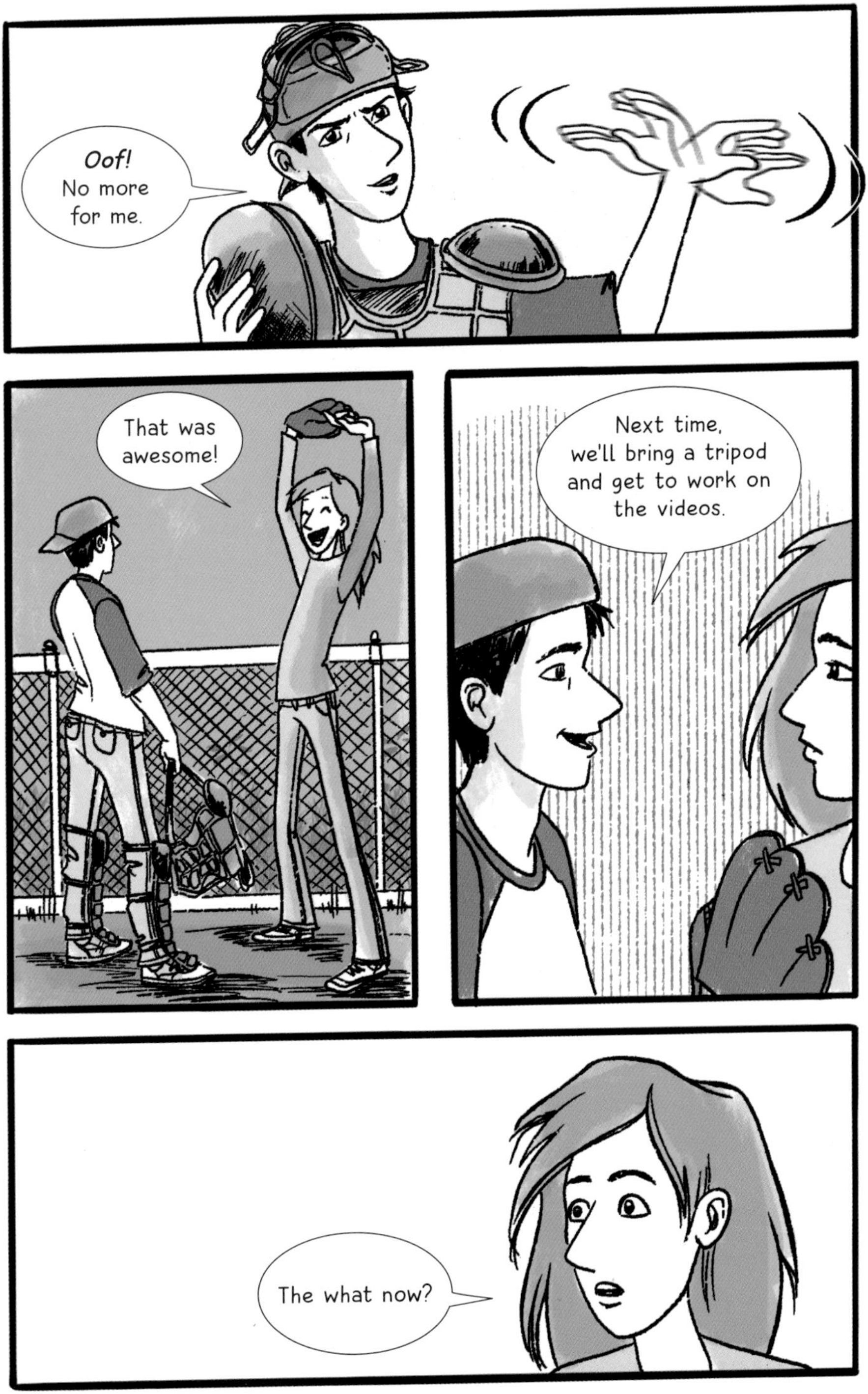
Oof! No more for me.
That was awesome!
Next time, we'll bring a tripod and get to work on the videos.
The what now?

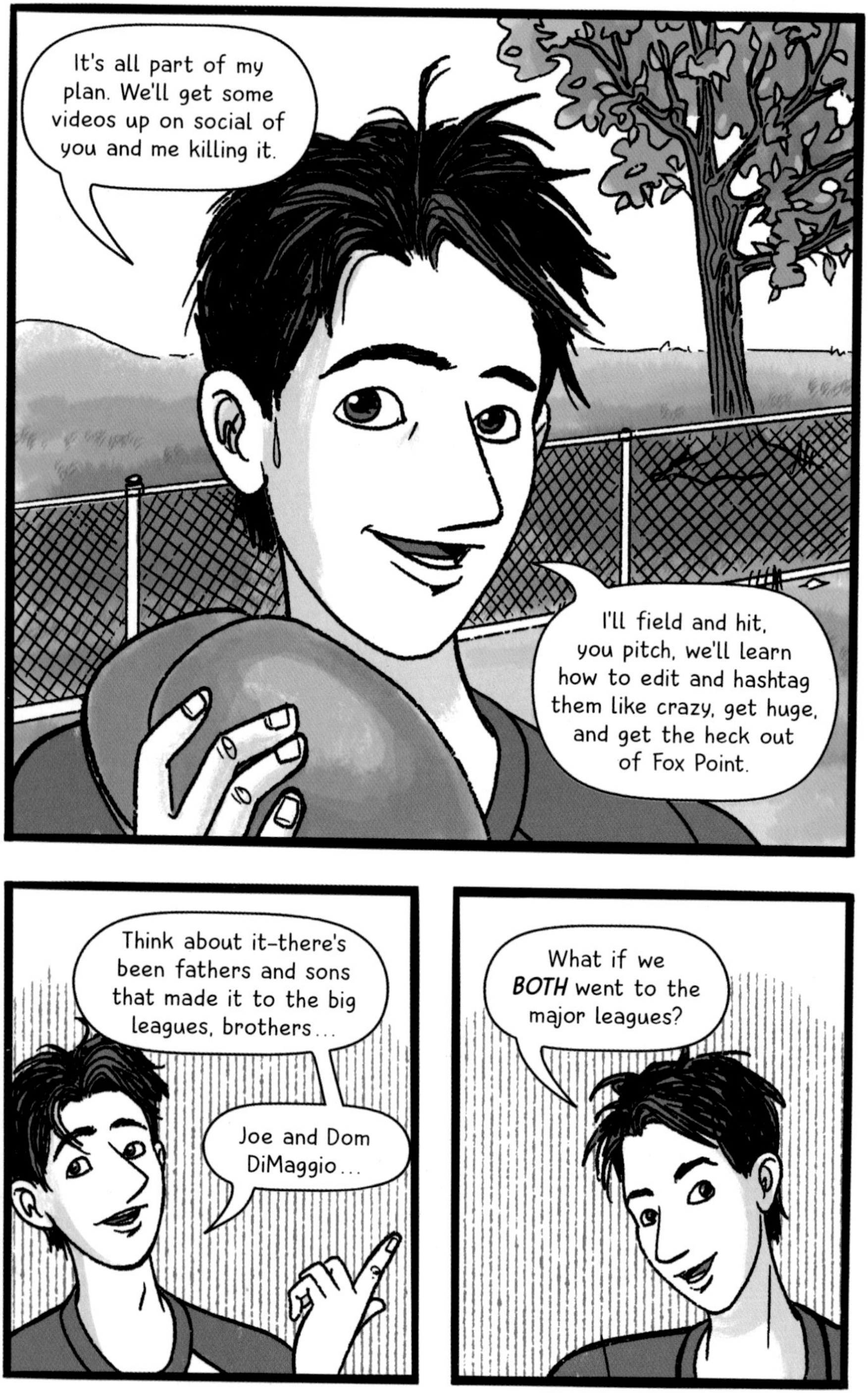
It's all part of my plan. We'll get some videos up on social of you and me killing it.
I'll field and hit, you pitch, we'll learn how to edit and hashtag them like crazy, get huge, and get the heck out of Fox Point.
Think about it–there's been fathers and sons that made it to the big leagues, brothers...
Joe and Dom DiMaggio...
What if we *BOTH* went to the major leagues?

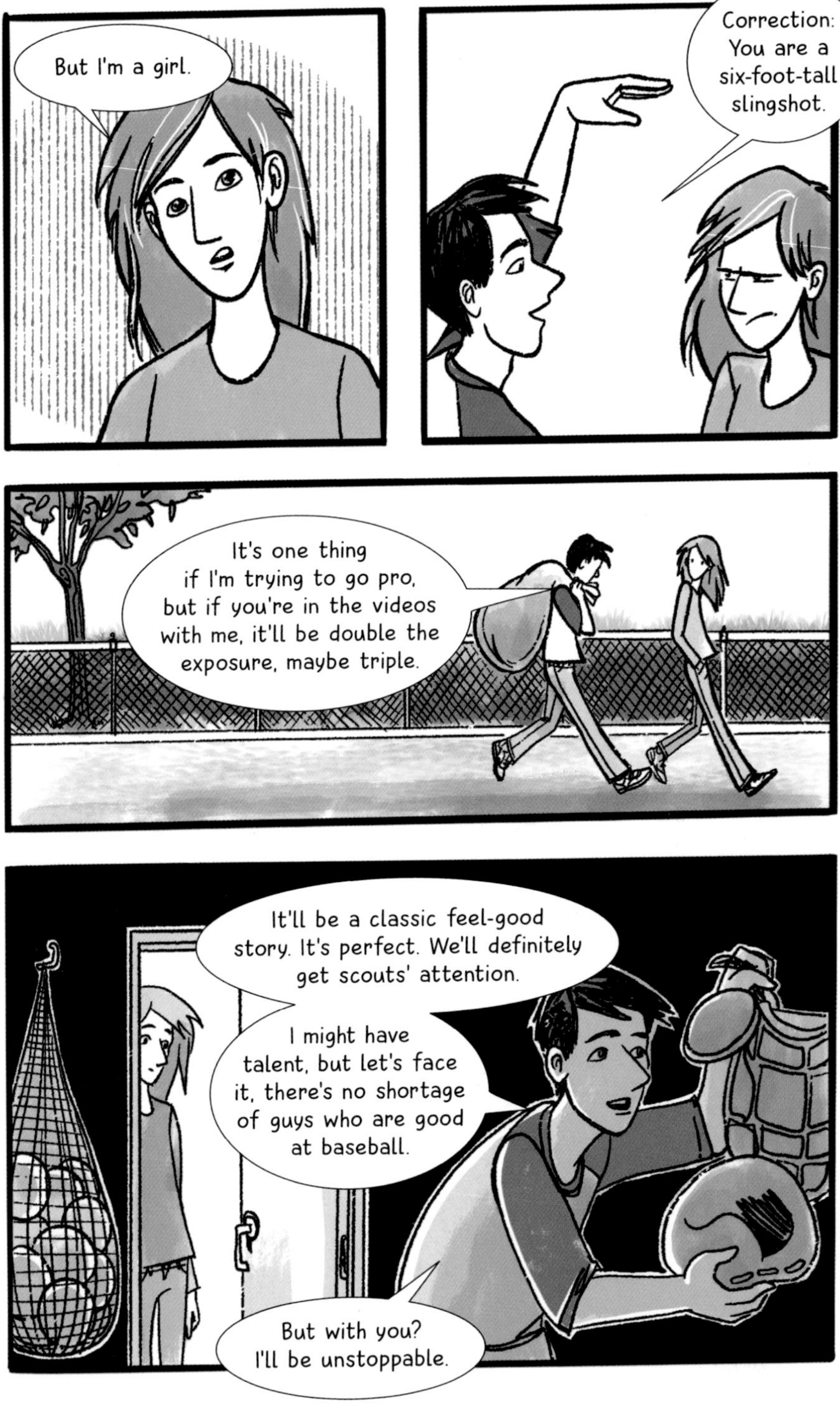
But I'm a girl.
Correction: You are a six-foot-tall slingshot.
It's one thing if I'm trying to go pro, but if you're in the videos with me, it'll be double the exposure, maybe triple.
It'll be a classic feel-good story. It's perfect. We'll definitely get scouts' attention.
I might have talent, but let's face it, there's no shortage of guys who are good at baseball.
But with you? I'll be unstoppable.

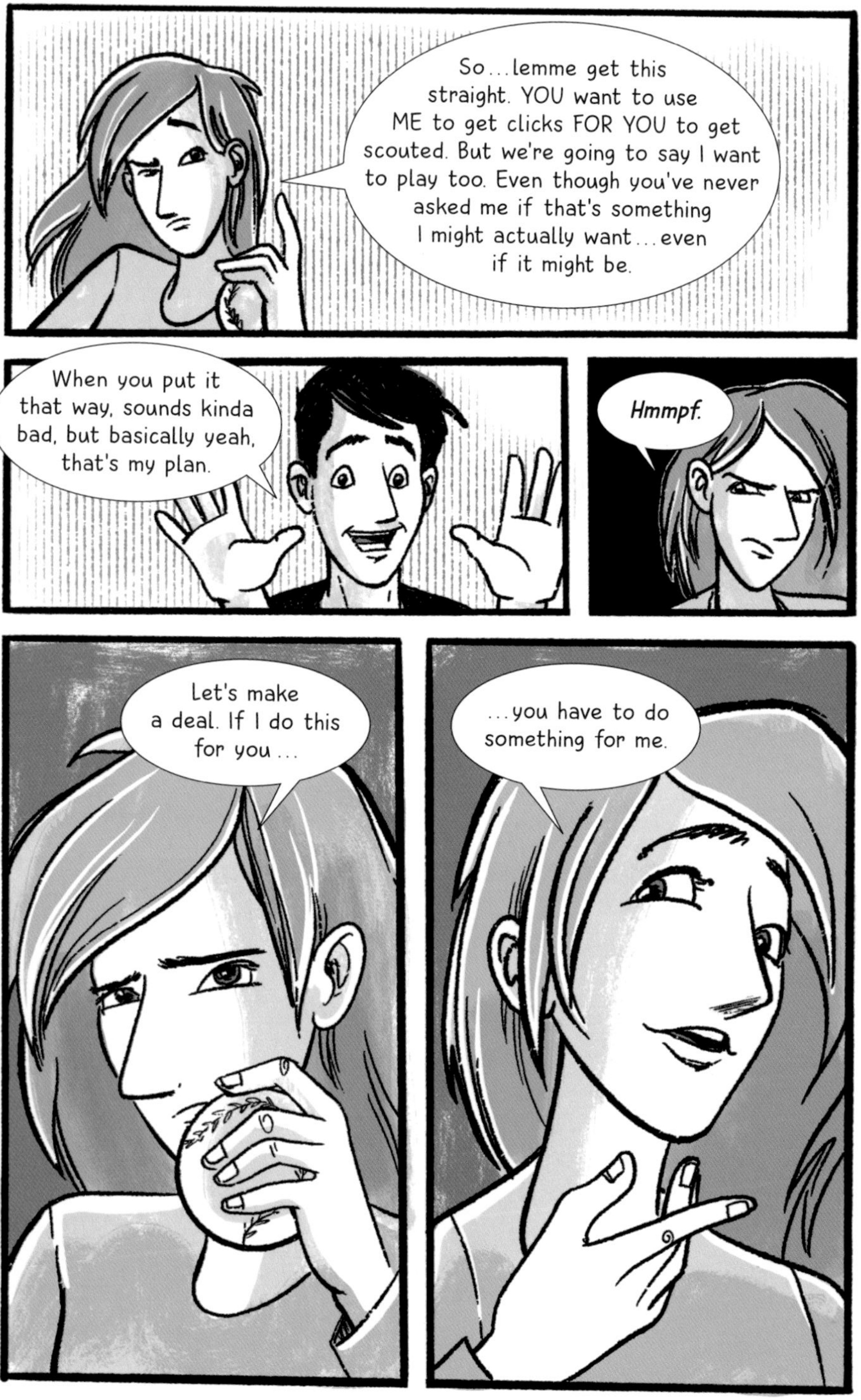
So... lemme get this straight. YOU want to use ME to get clicks FOR YOU to get scouted. But we're going to say I want to play too. Even though you've never asked me if that's something I might actually want... even if it might be.
When you put it that way, sounds kinda bad, but basically yeah, that's my plan.
Hmmpf.
Let's make a deal. If I do this for you...
...you have to do something for me.

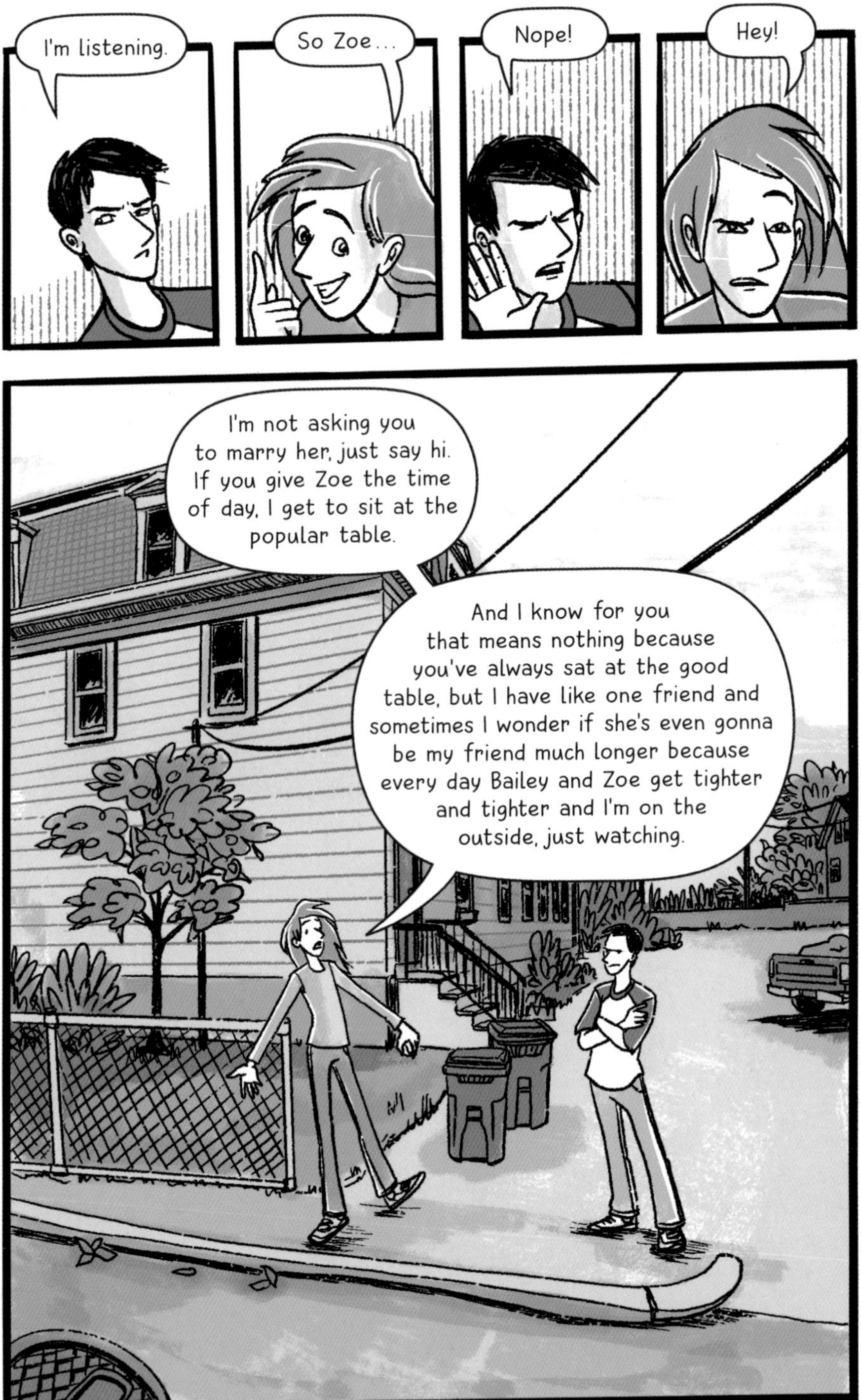

I'm listening.
So Zoe...
Nope!
Hey!
I'm not asking you to marry her, just say hi. If you give Zoe the time of day, I get to sit at the popular table.
And I know for you that means nothing because you've always sat at the good table, but I have like one friend and sometimes I wonder if she's even gonna be my friend much longer because every day Bailey and Zoe get tighter and tighter and I'm on the outside, just watching.

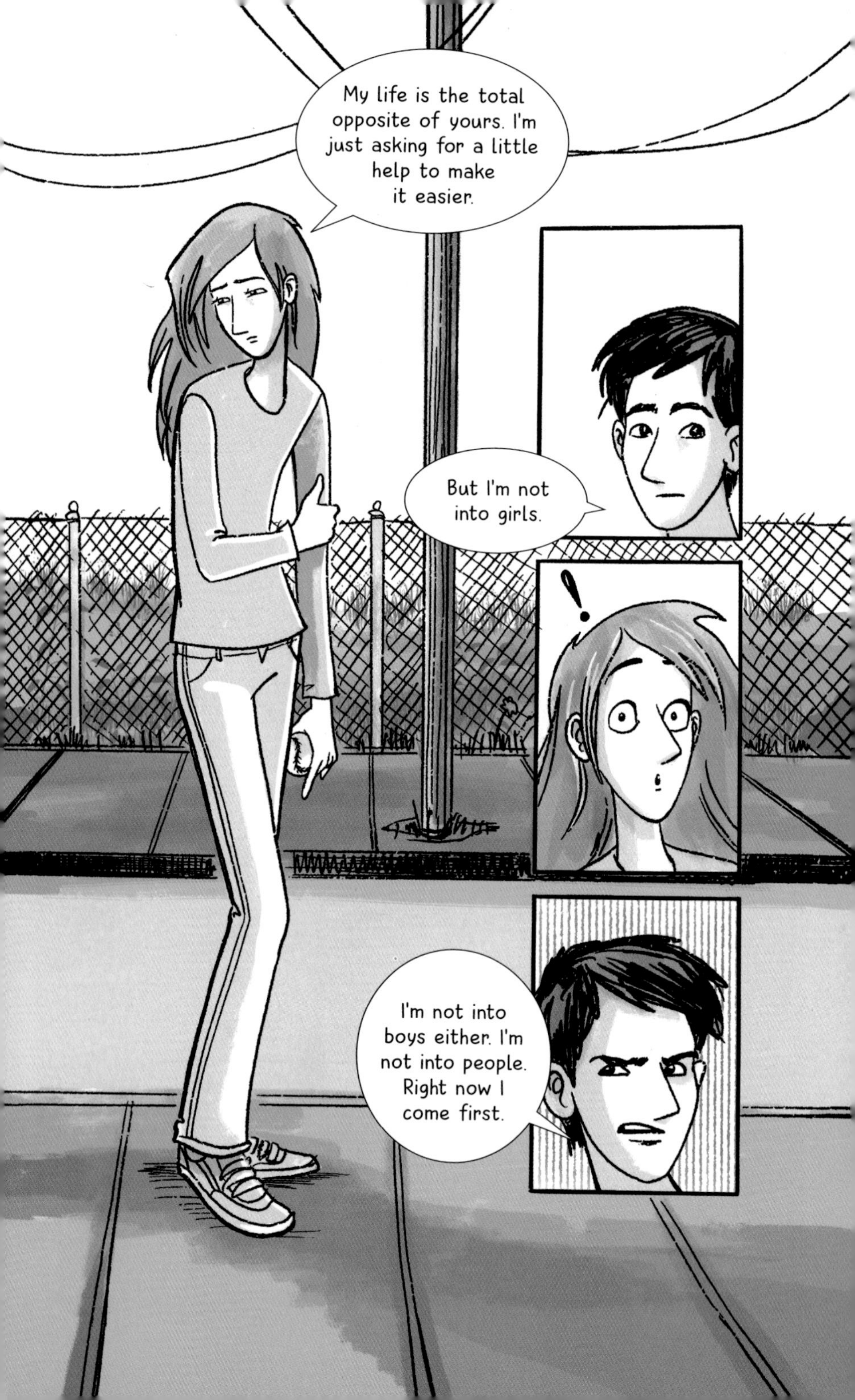
My life is the total opposite of yours. I'm just asking for a little help to make it easier.
But I'm not into girls.
!
I'm not into boys either. I'm not into people. Right now I come first.

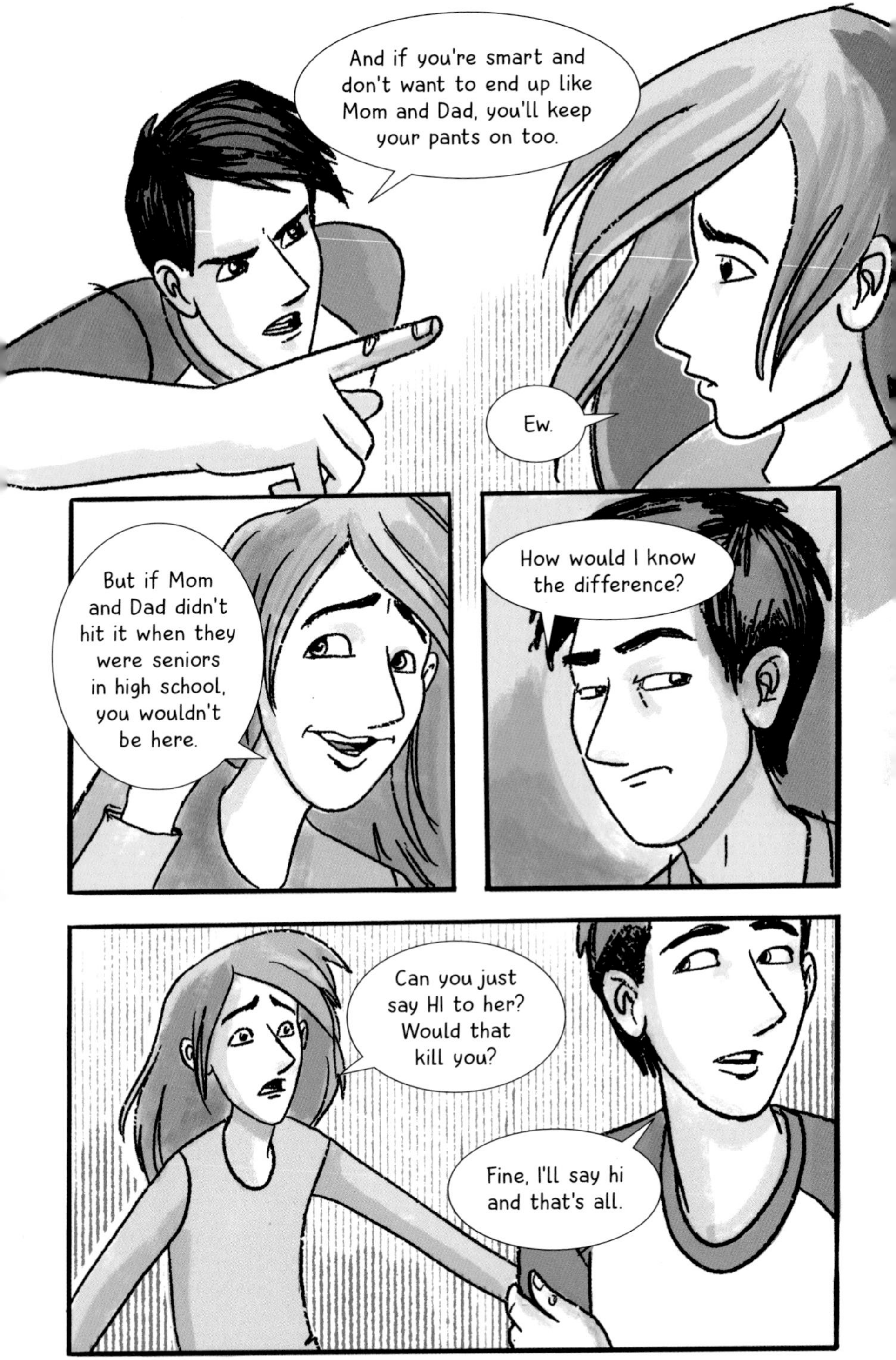
And if you're smart and don't want to end up like Mom and Dad, you'll keep your pants on too.
Ew.
But if Mom and Dad didn't hit it when they were seniors in high school, you wouldn't be here.
How would I know the difference?
Can you just say HI to her? Would that kill you?
Fine, I'll say hi and that's all.

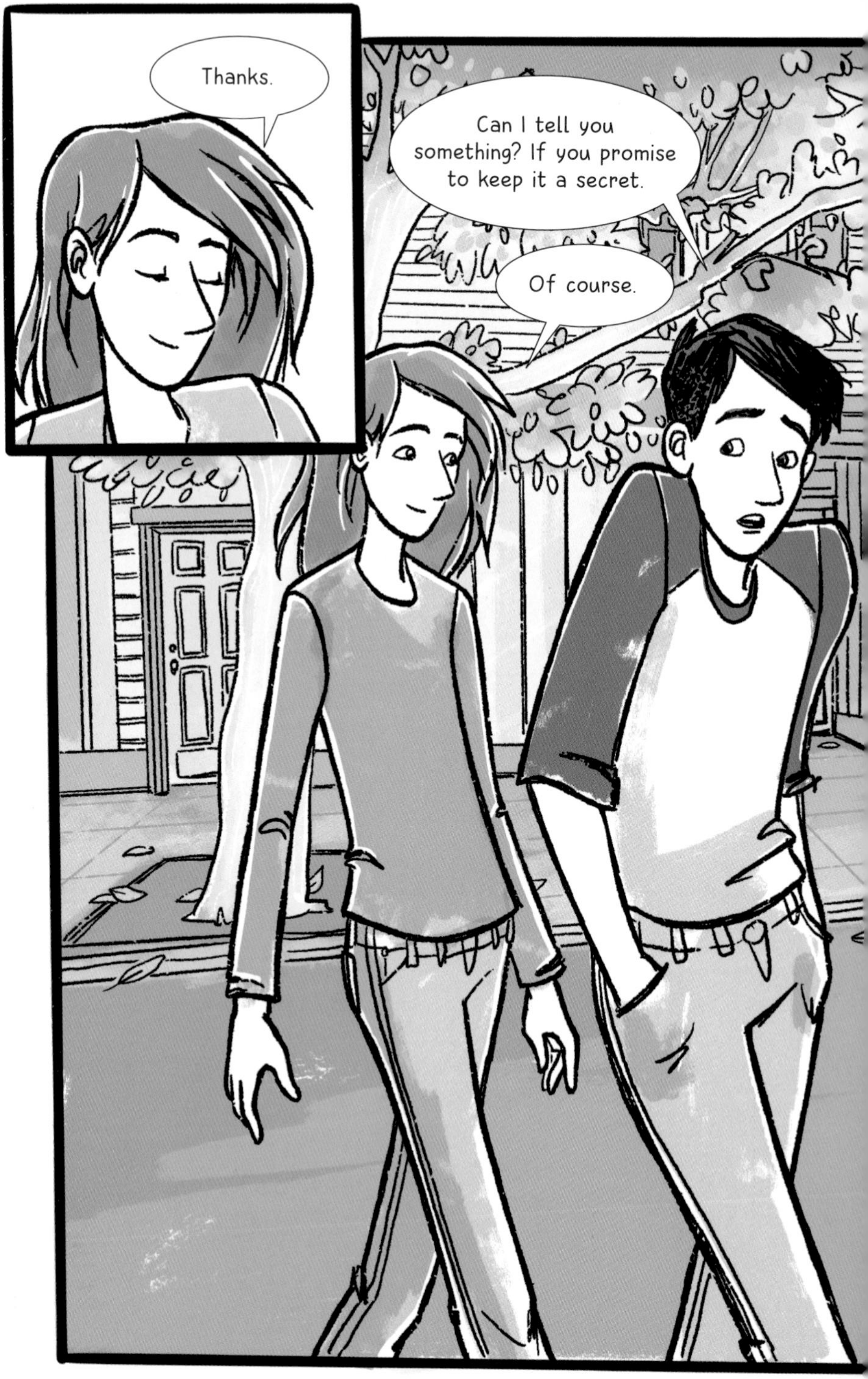
Thanks.
Can I tell you something? If you promise to keep it a secret.
Of course.

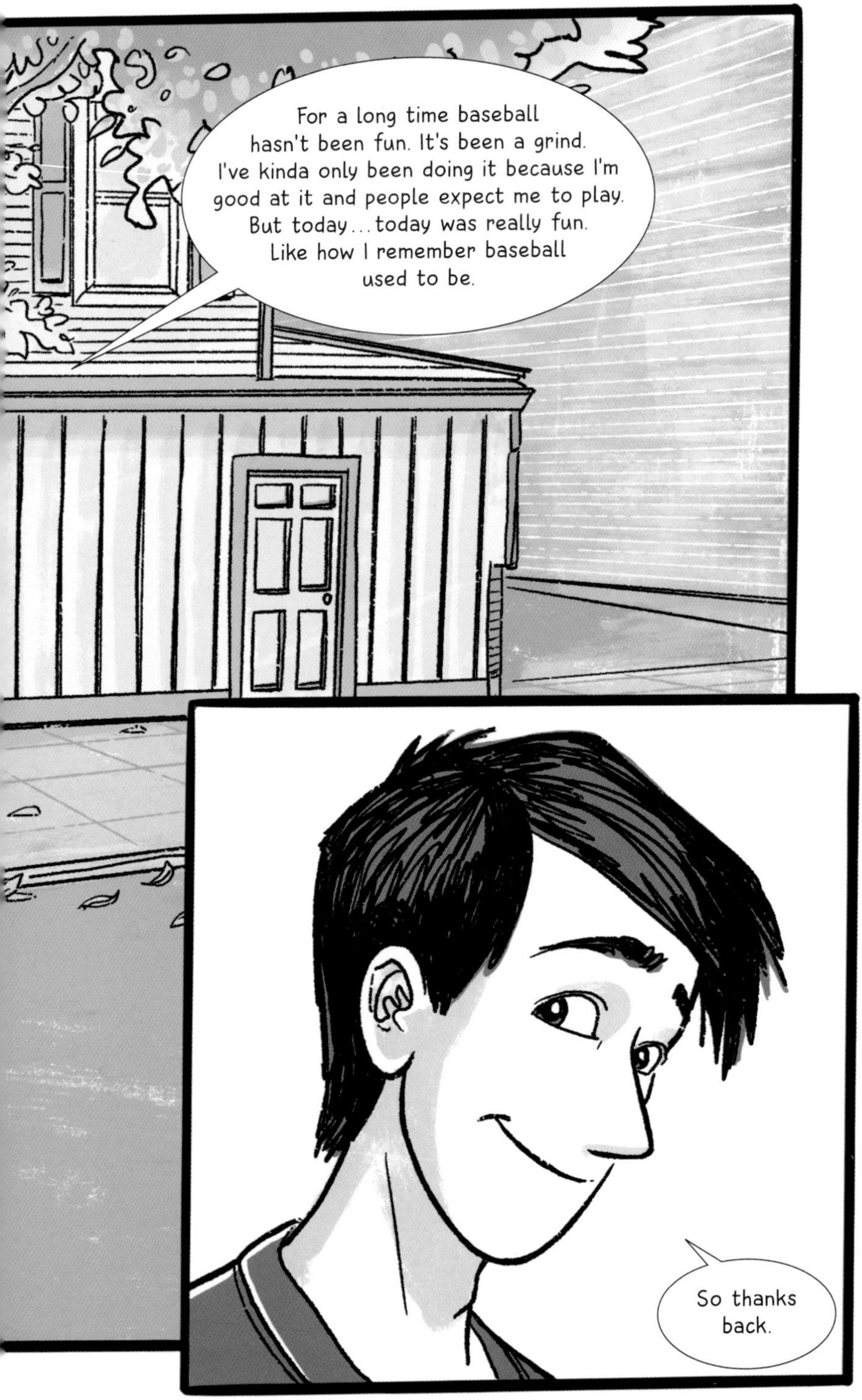
For a long time baseball hasn't been fun. It's been a grind. I've kinda only been doing it because I'm good at it and people expect me to play. But today... today was really fun. Like how I remember baseball used to be.
So thanks back.

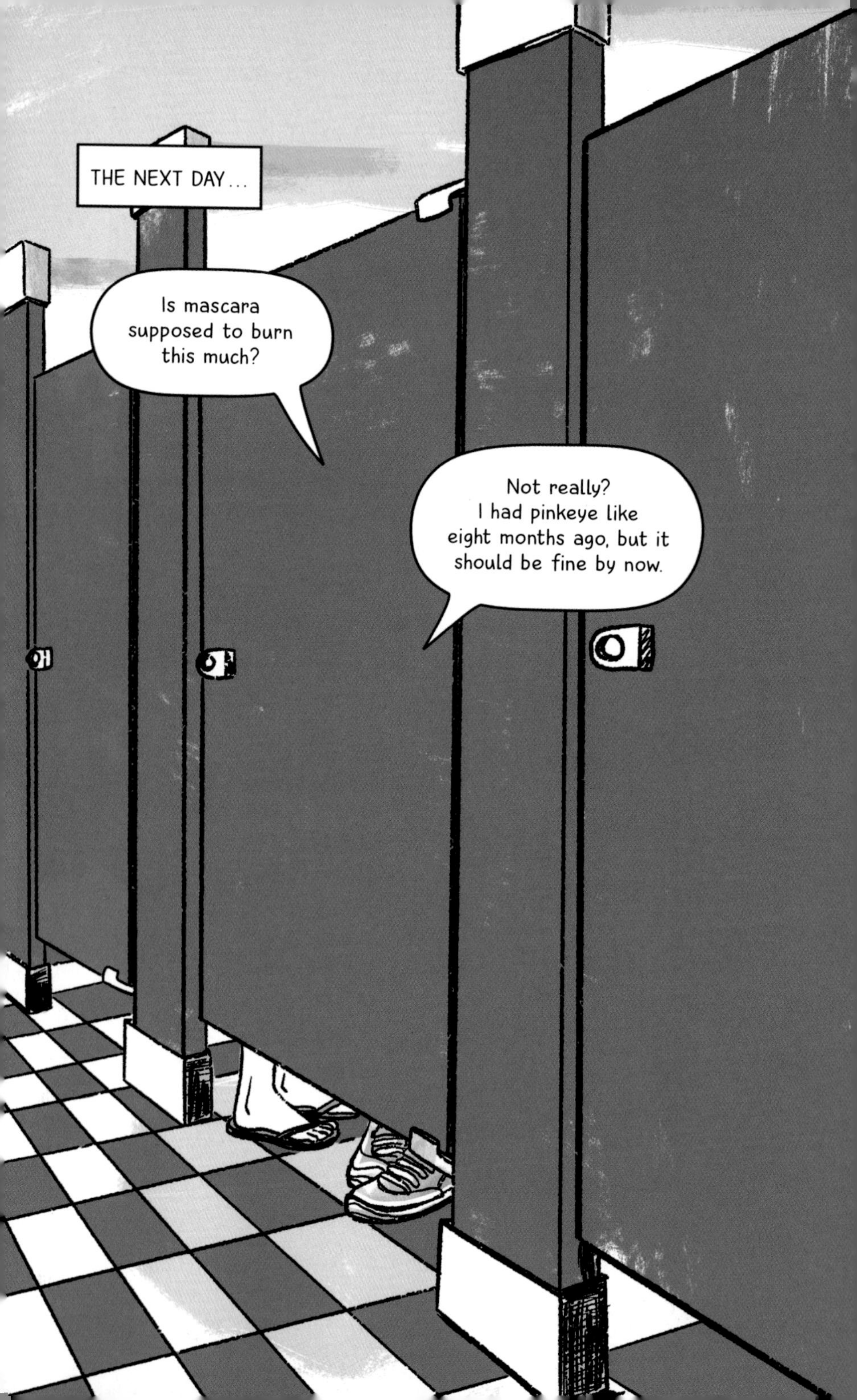
THE NEXT DAY...
Is mascara supposed to burn this much?
Not really? I had pinkeye like eight months ago, but it should be fine by now.

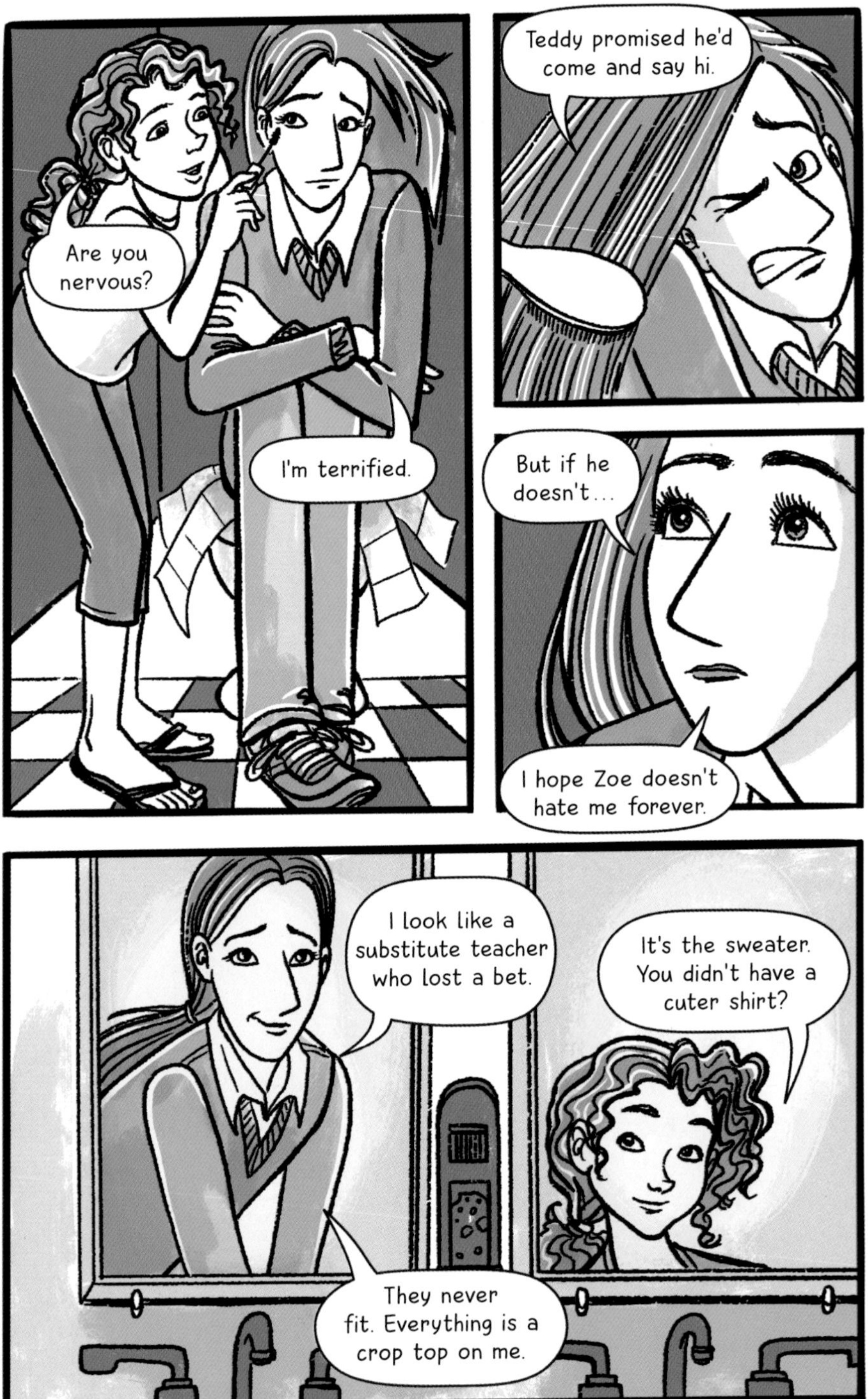
Are you nervous?
I'm terrified.
Teddy promised he'd come and say hi.
But if he doesn't...
I hope Zoe doesn't hate me forever.
I look like a substitute teacher who lost a bet.
It's the sweater. You didn't have a cuter shirt?
They never fit. Everything is a crop top on me.

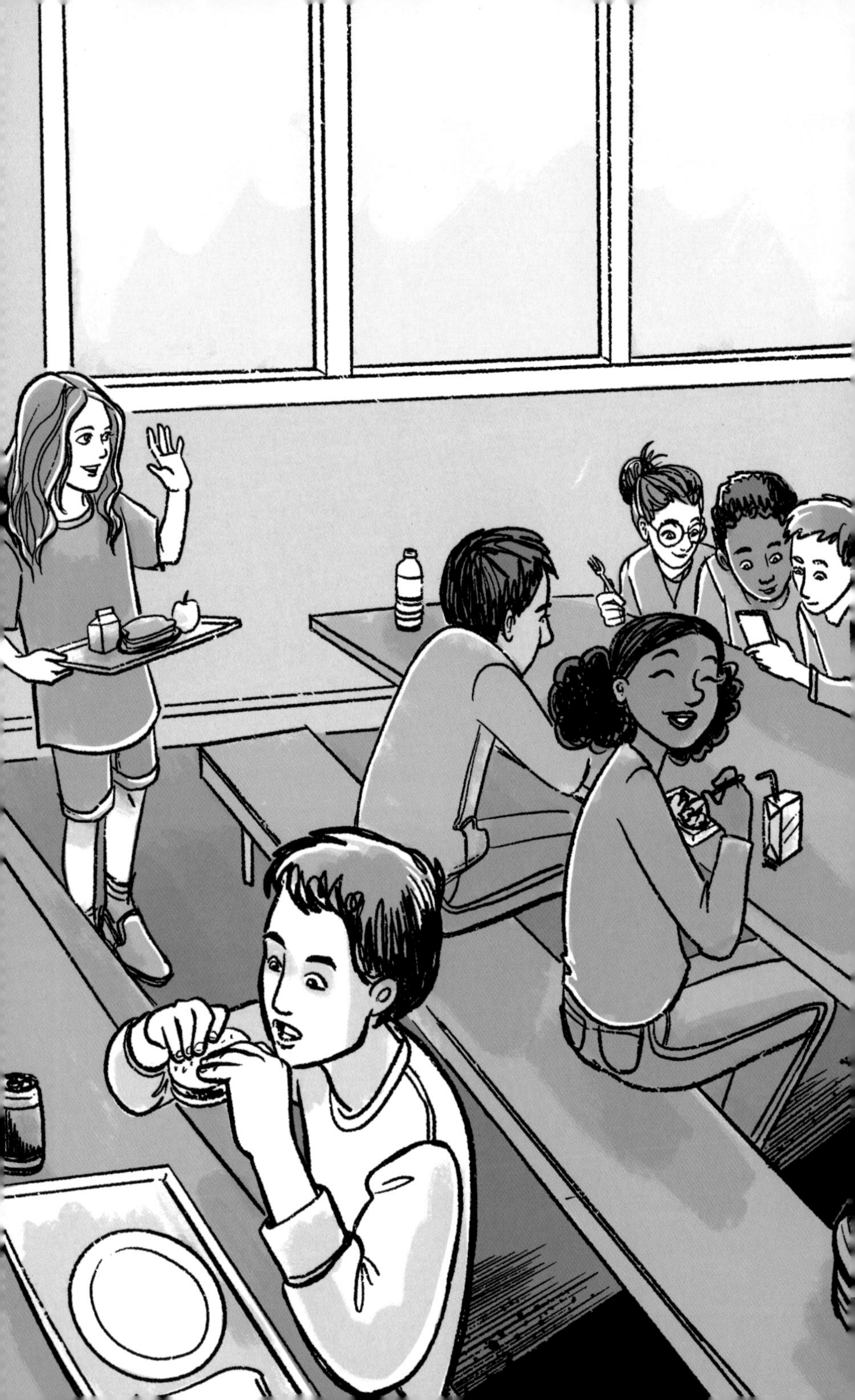

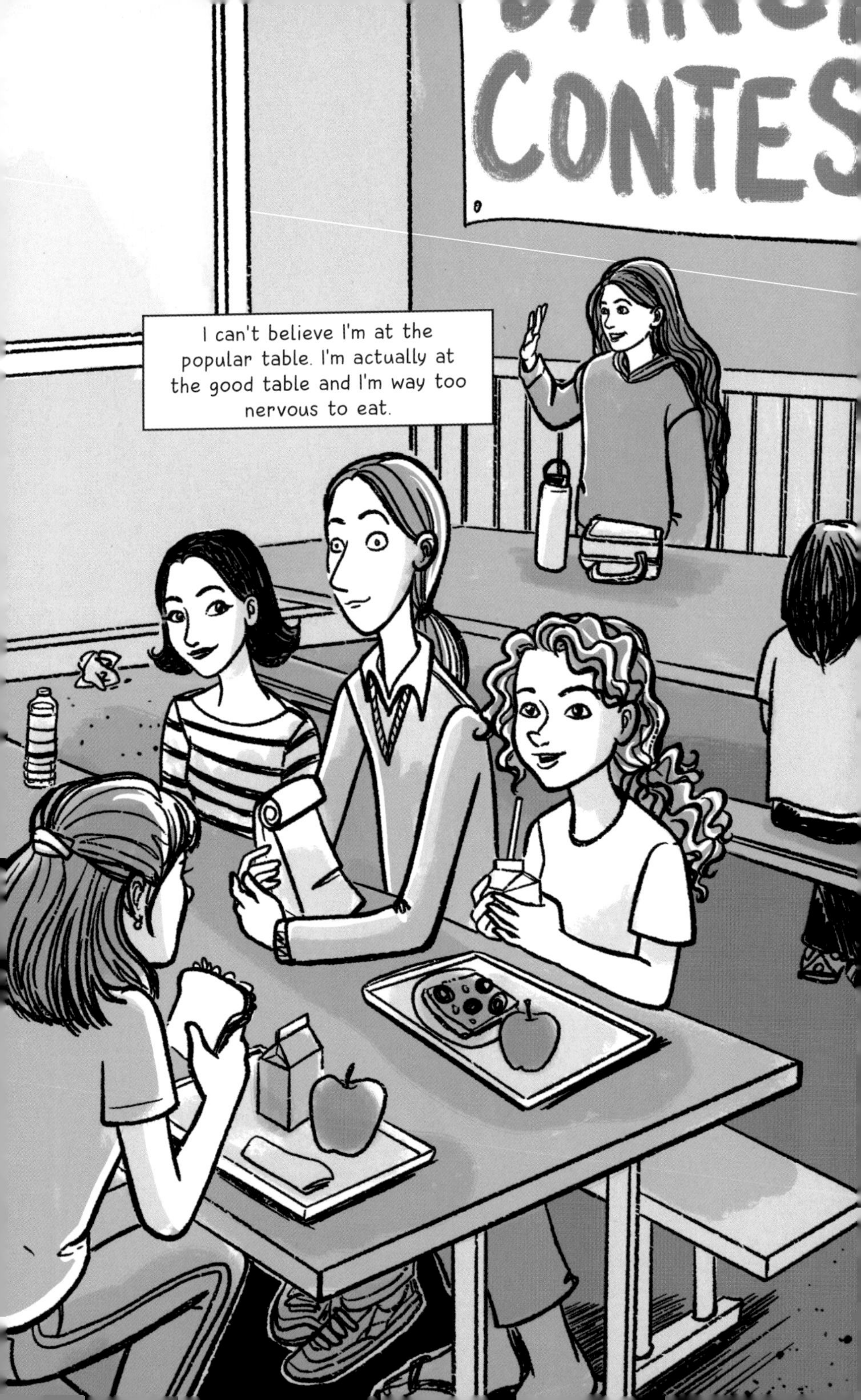
CONTES
I can't believe I'm at the popular table. I'm actually at the good table and I'm way too nervous to eat.

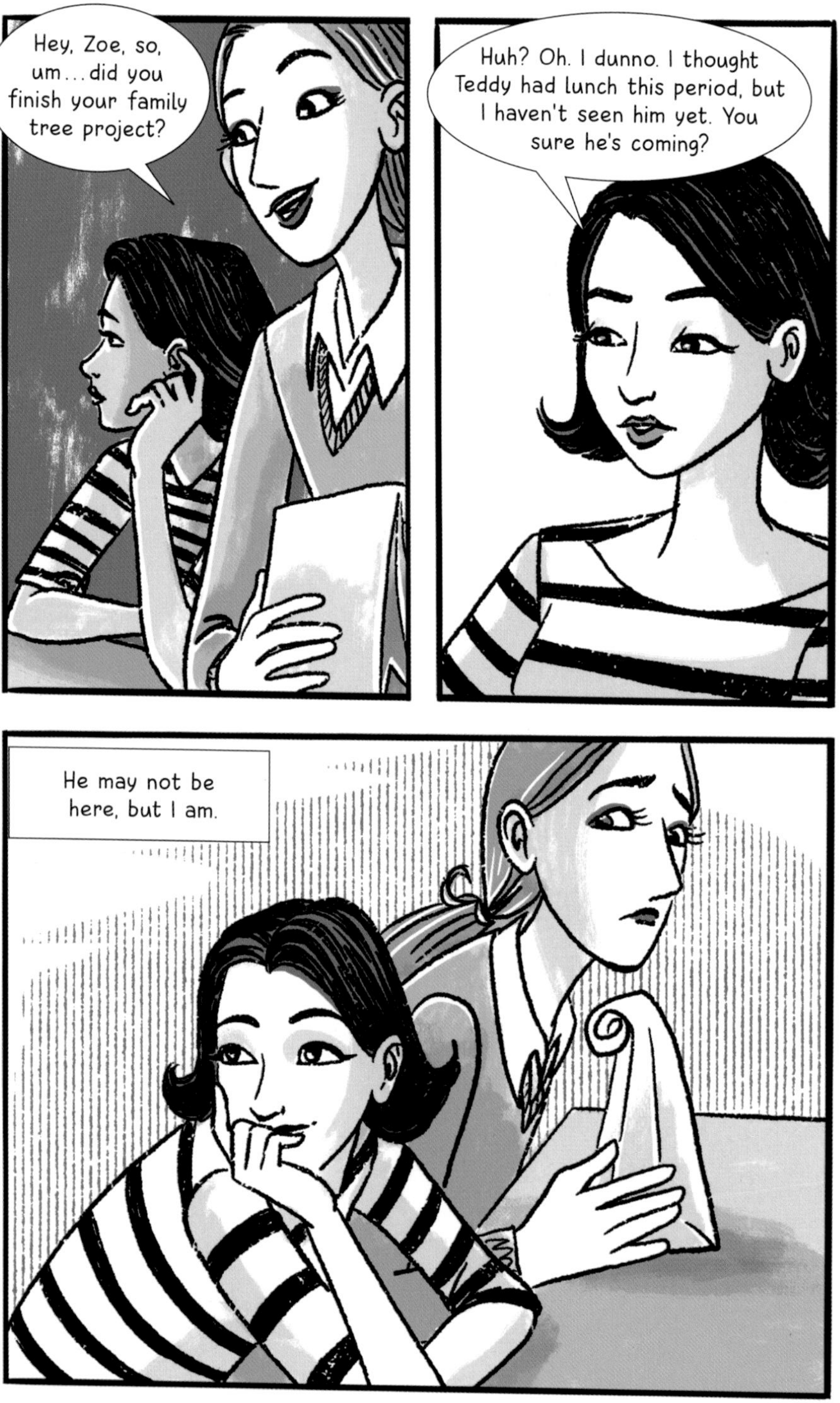
Hey, Zoe, so, um...did you finish your family tree project?
Huh? Oh. I dunno. I thought Teddy had lunch this period, but I haven't seen him yet. You sure he's coming?
He may not be here, but I am.

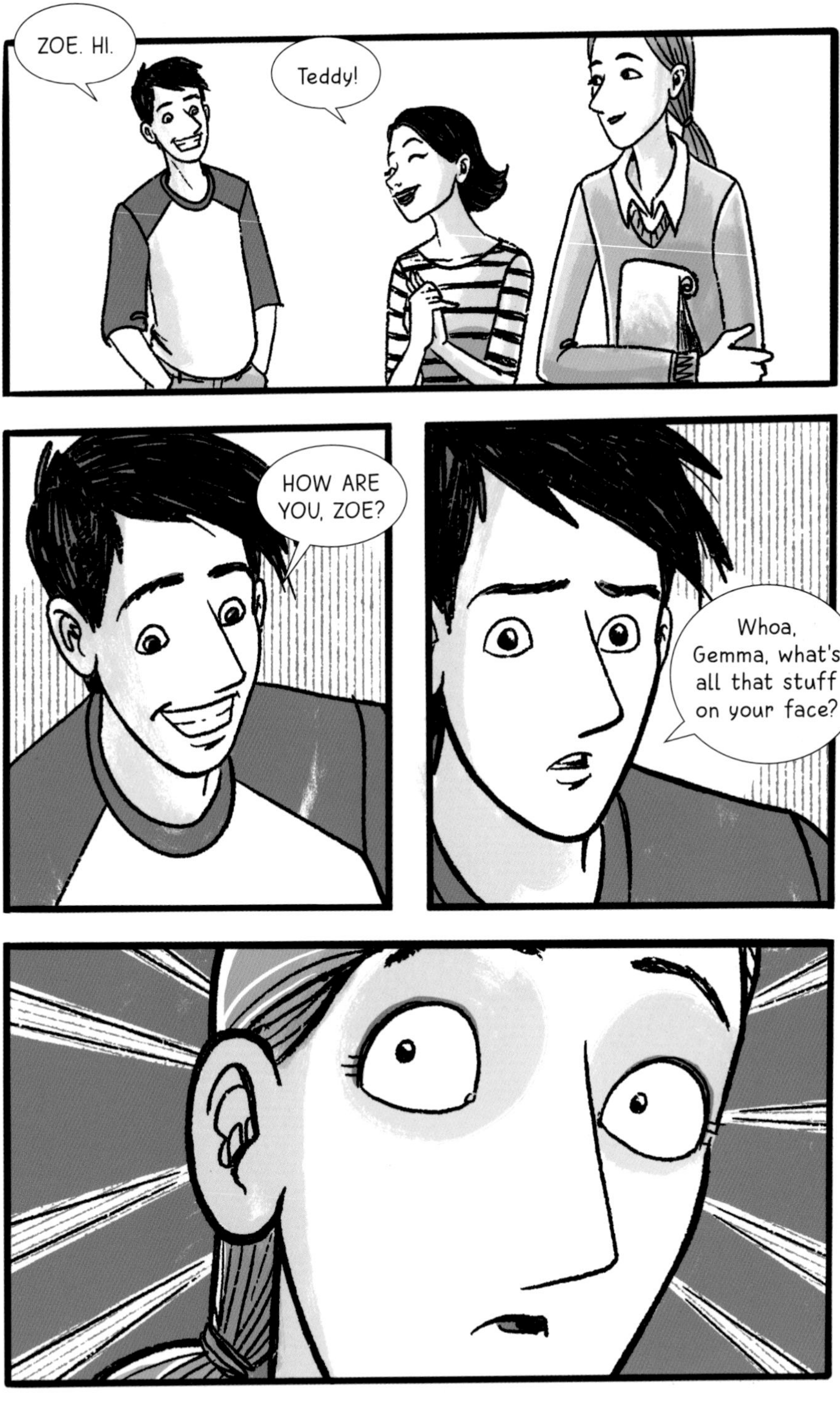
ZOE. HI.
Teddy!
HOW ARE YOU, ZOE?
Whoa, Gemma, what's all that stuff on your face?

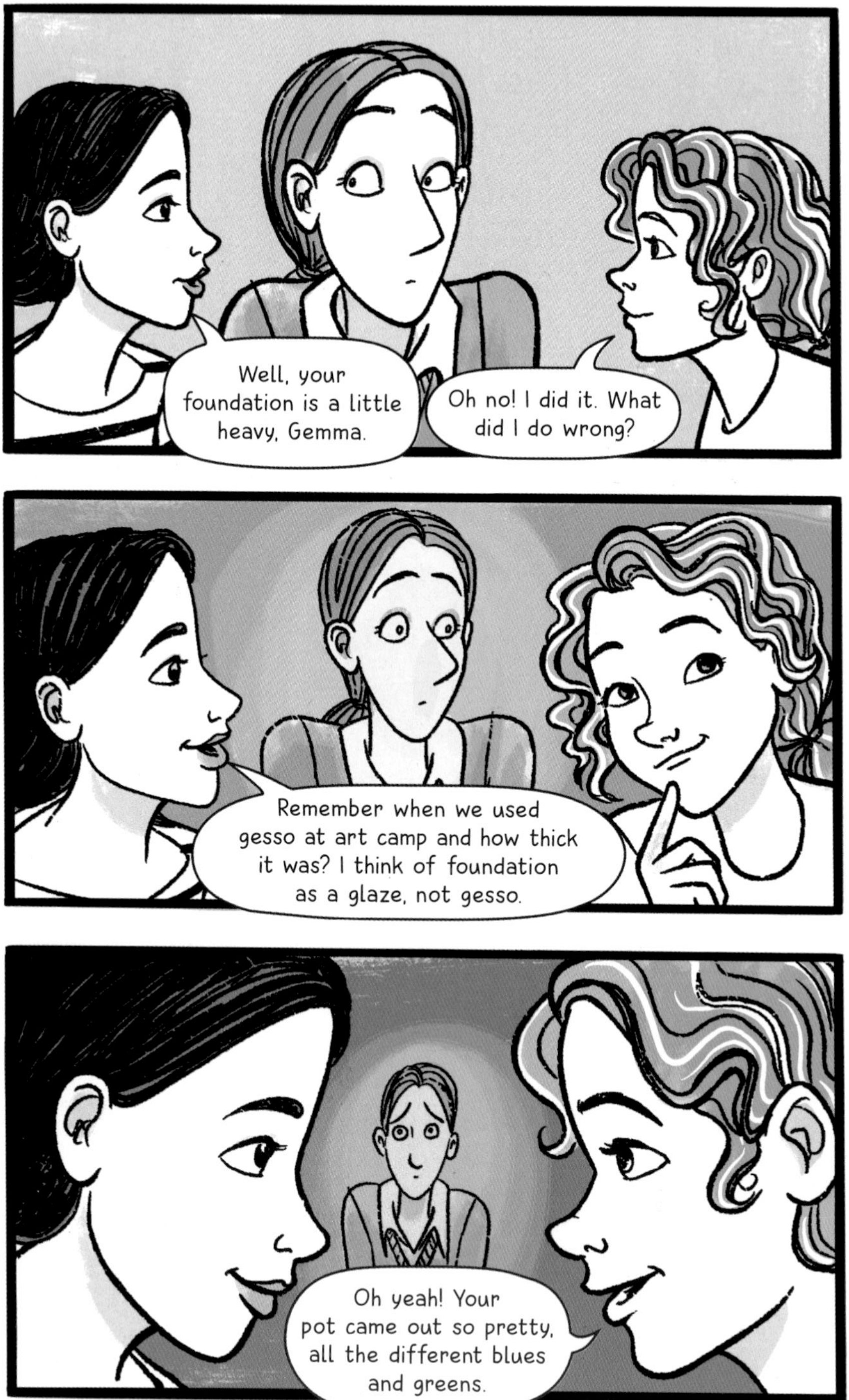
Well, your foundation is a little heavy, Gemma.
Oh no! I did it. What did I do wrong?
Remember when we used gesso at art camp and how thick it was? I think of foundation as a glaze, not gesso.
Oh yeah! Your pot came out so pretty, all the different blues and greens.

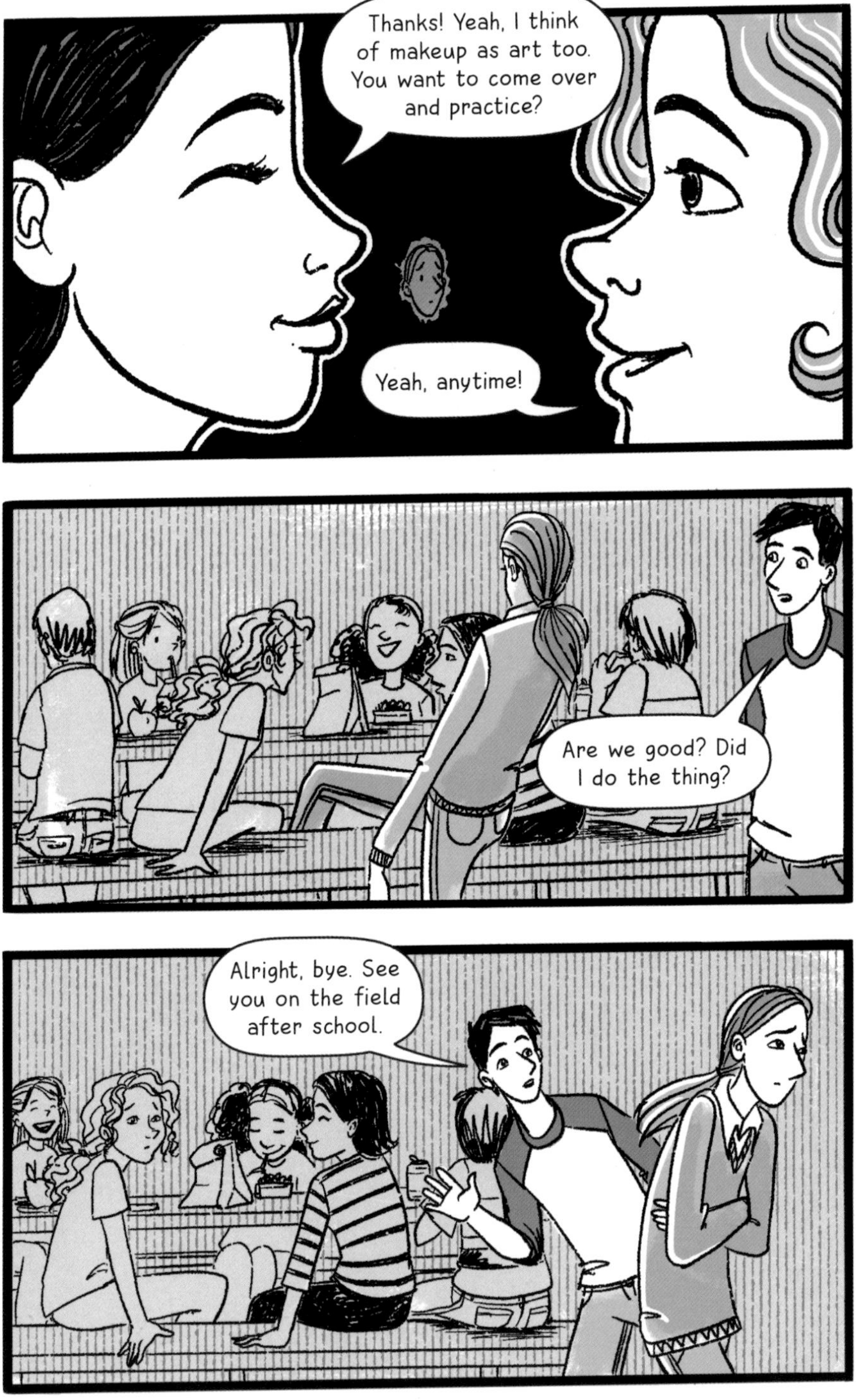
Thanks! Yeah, I think of makeup as art too. You want to come over and practice?
Yeah, anytime!
Are we good? Did I do the thing?
Alright, bye. See you on the field after school.

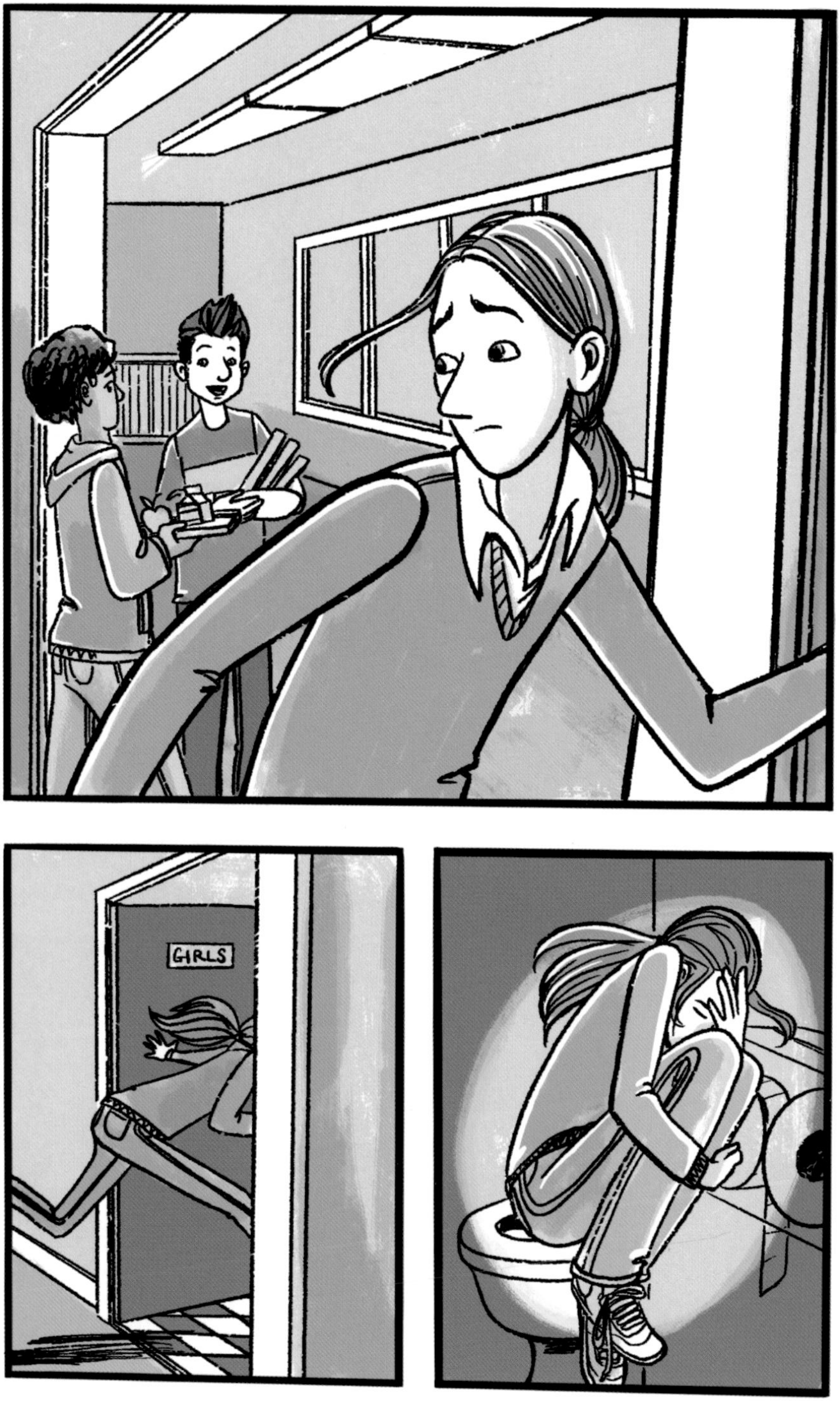
GIRLS

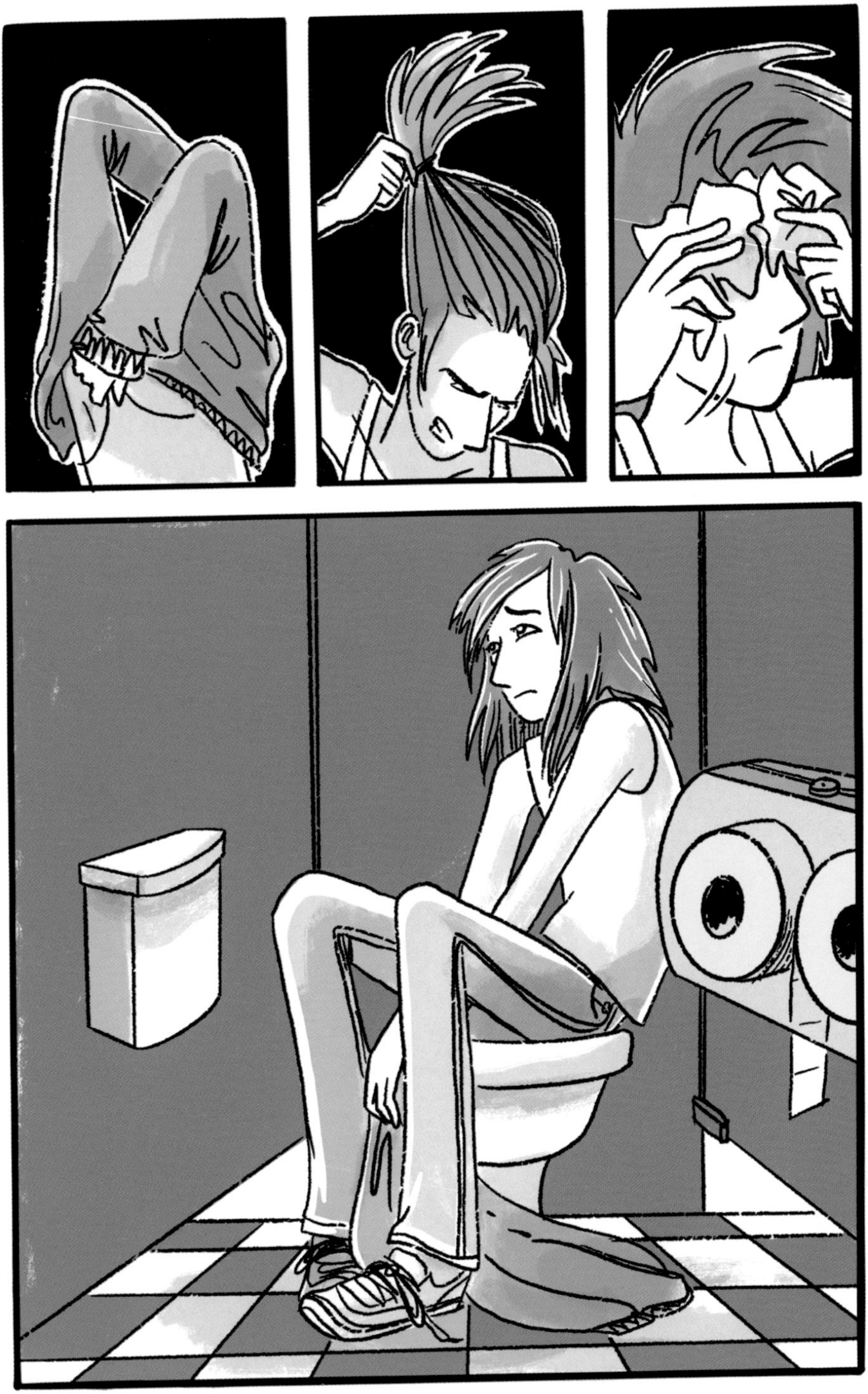

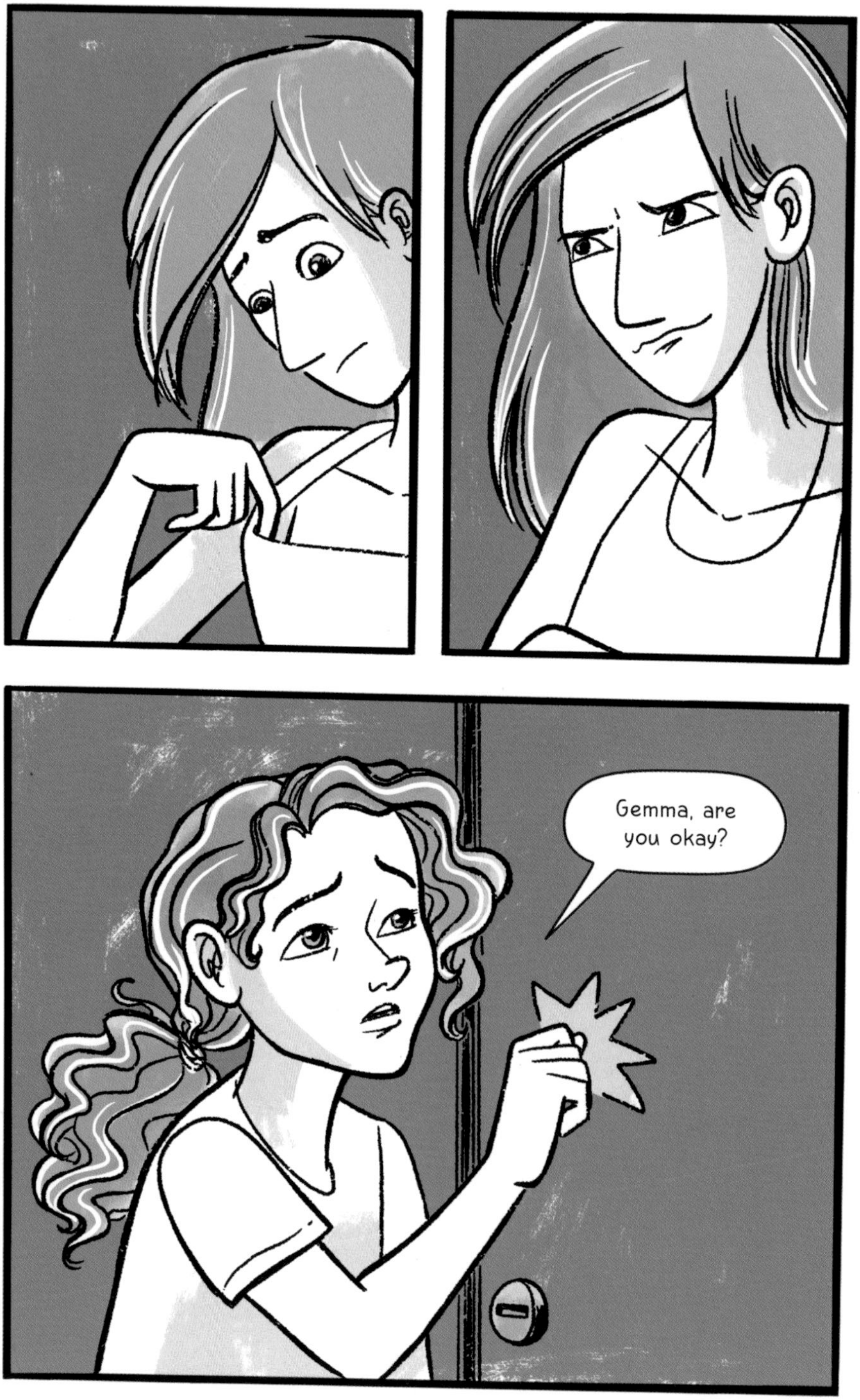
Gemma, are you okay?

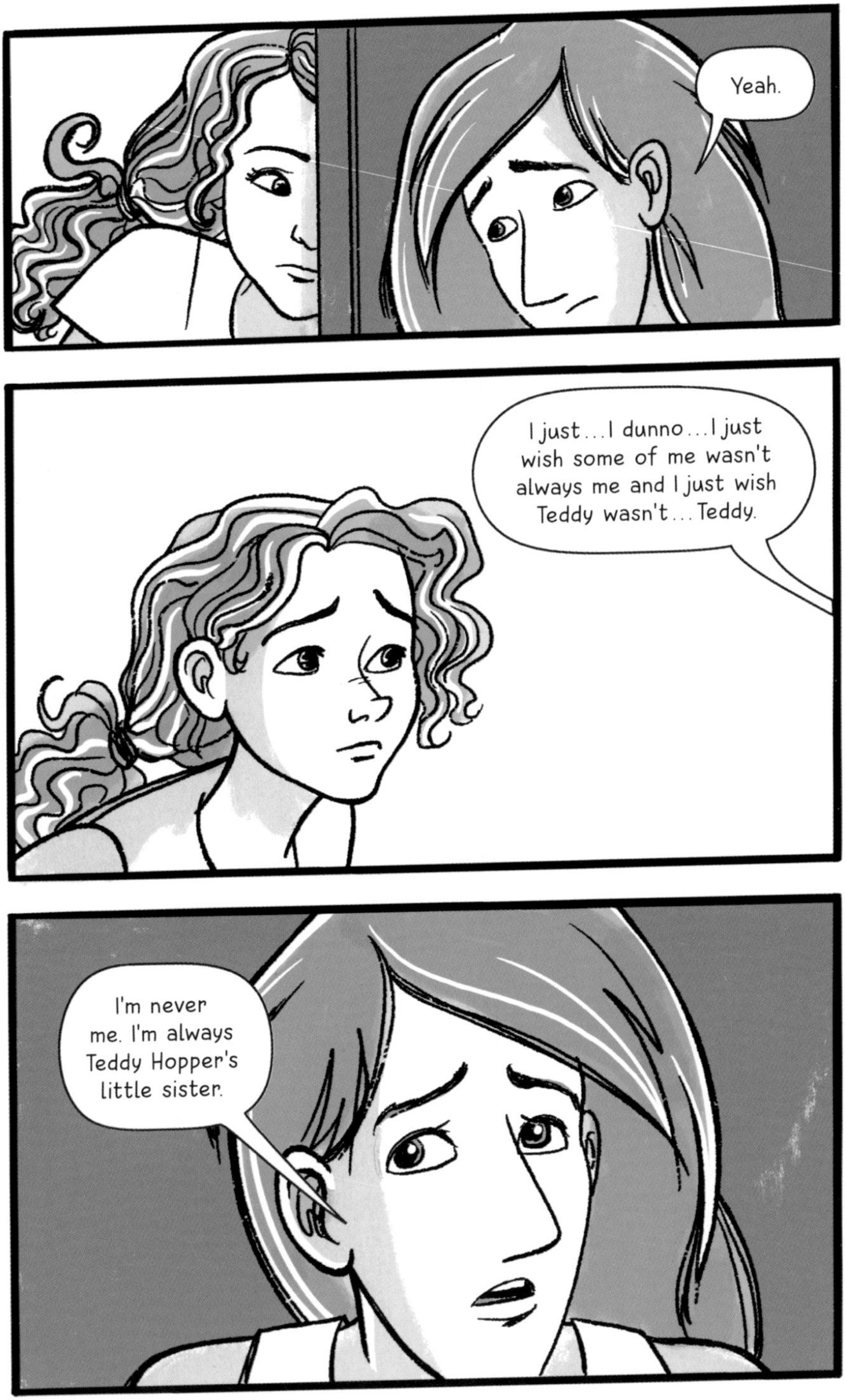
Yeah.
I just...I dunno...I just wish some of me wasn't always me and I just wish Teddy wasn't...Teddy.
I'm never me. I'm always Teddy Hopper's little sister.

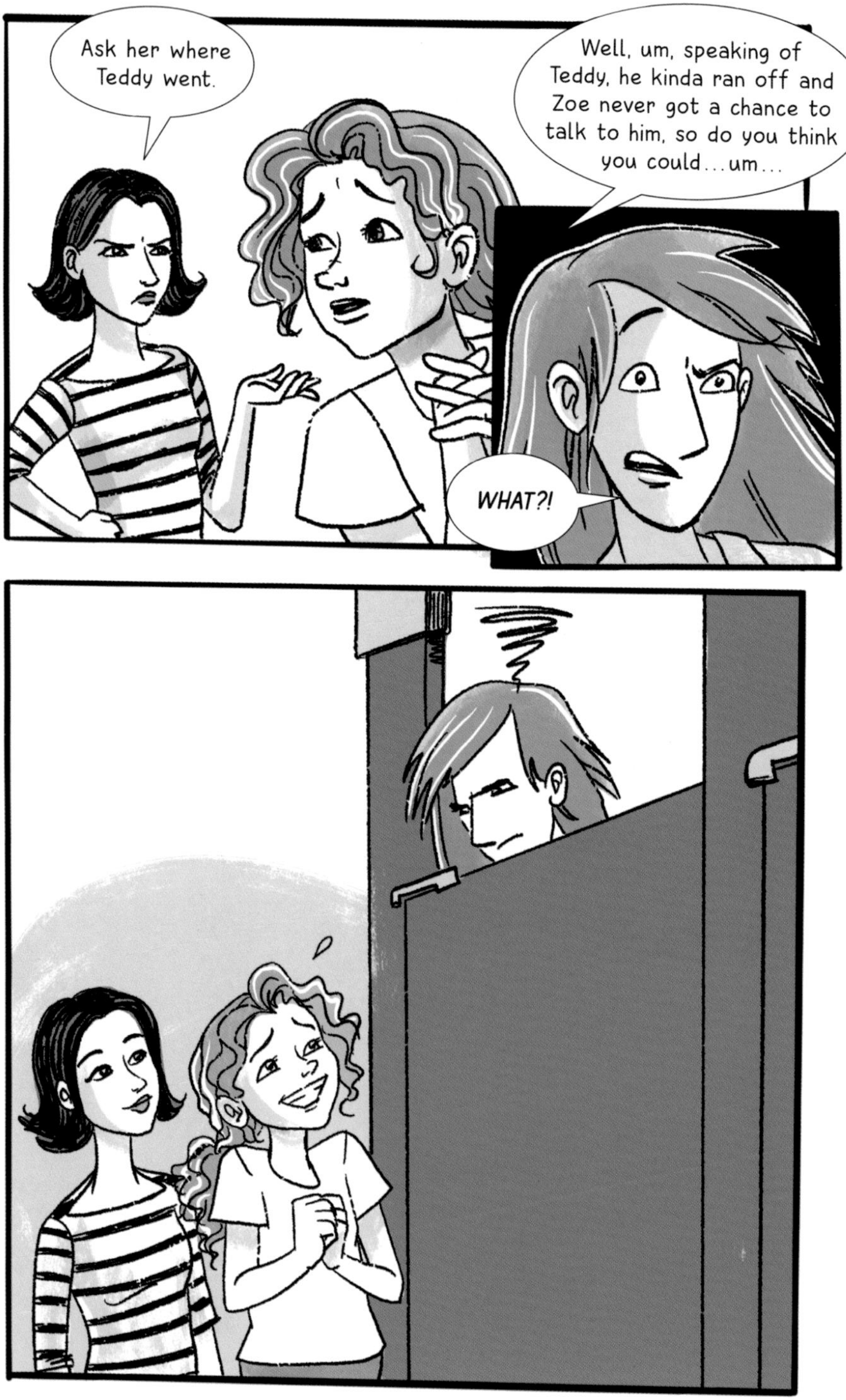
Ask her where Teddy went.
Well, um, speaking of Teddy, he kinda ran off and Zoe never got a chance to talk to him, so do you think you could...um...
WHAT?!

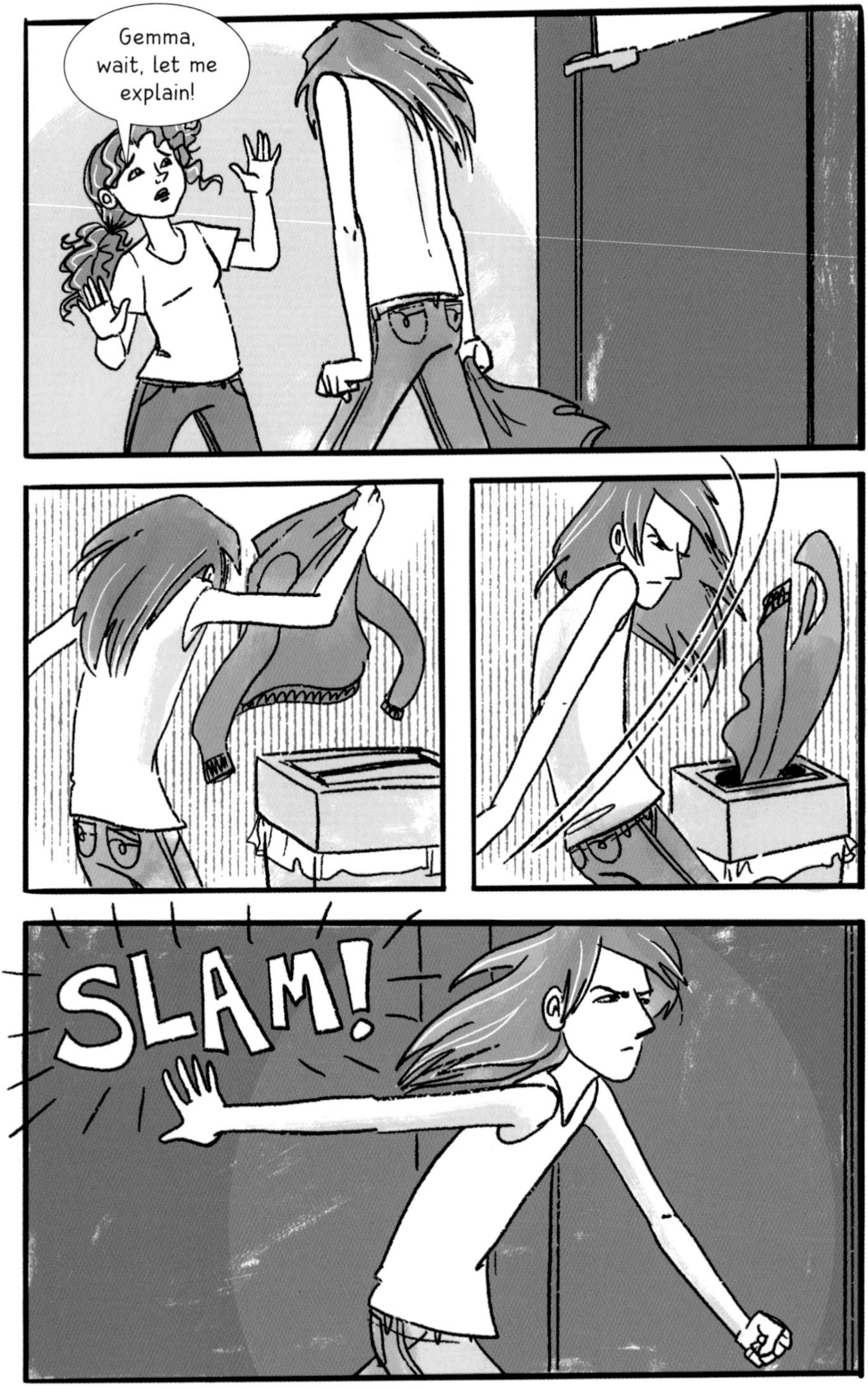
Gemma, wait, let me explain!
SLAM!

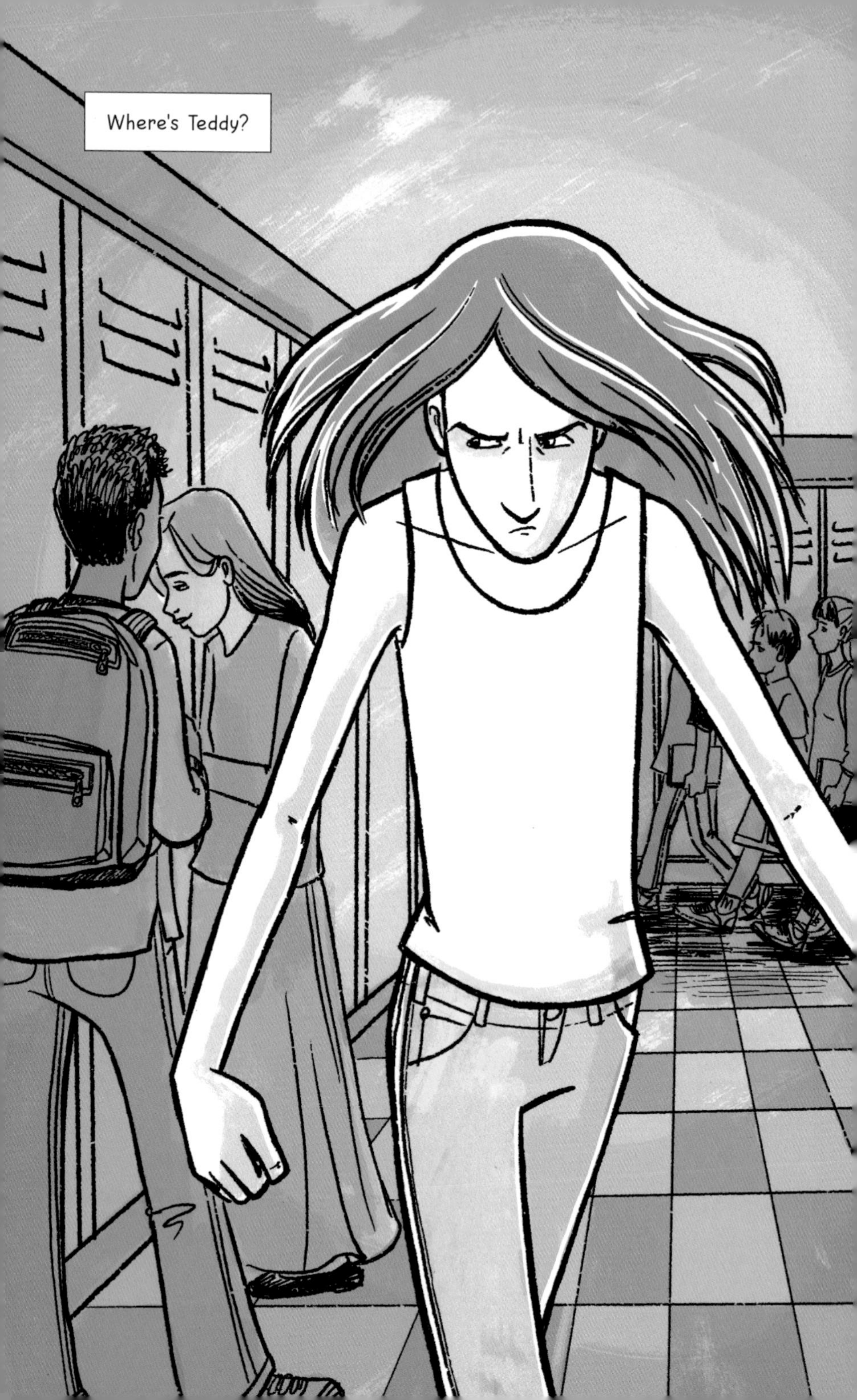
Where's Teddy?

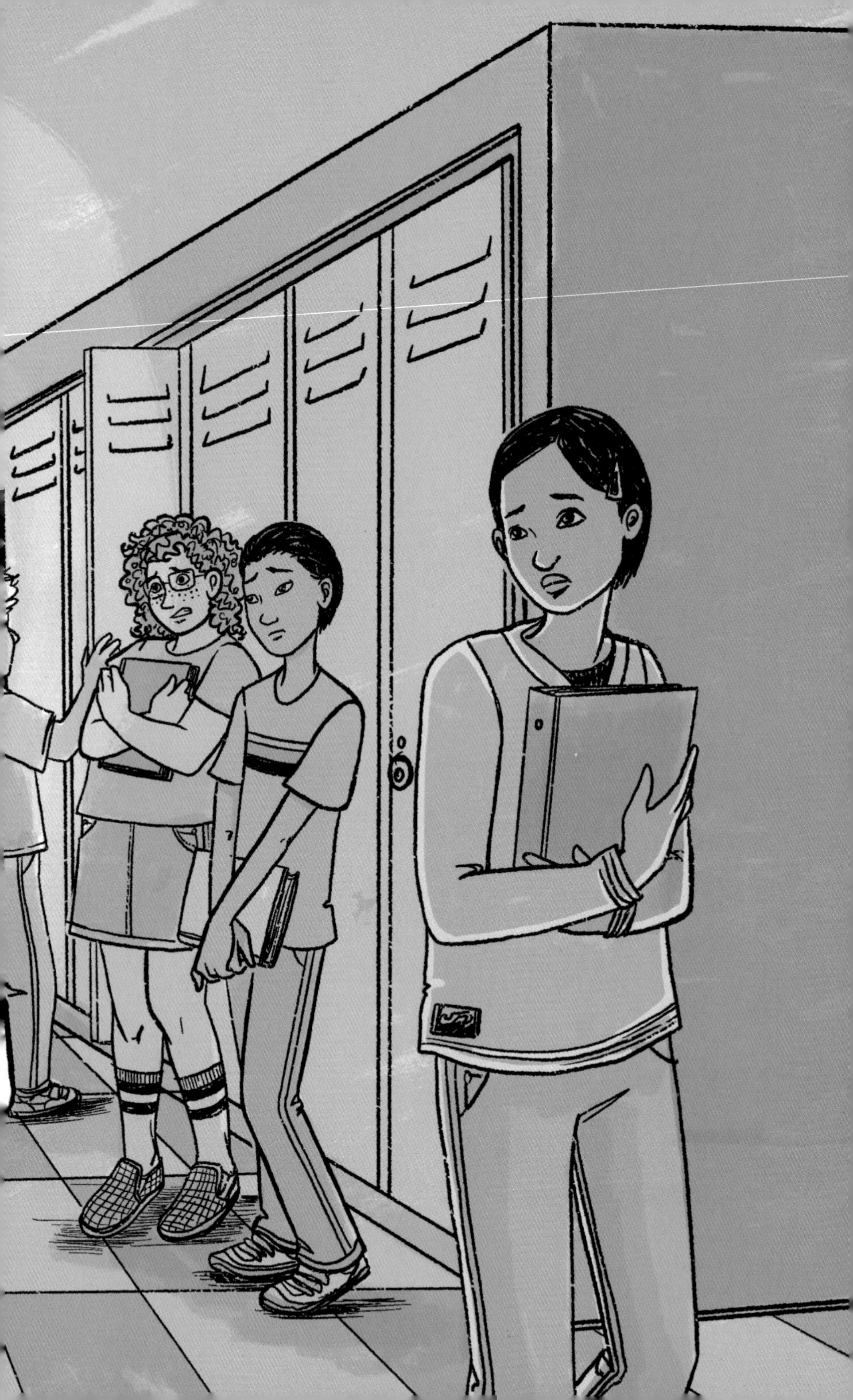

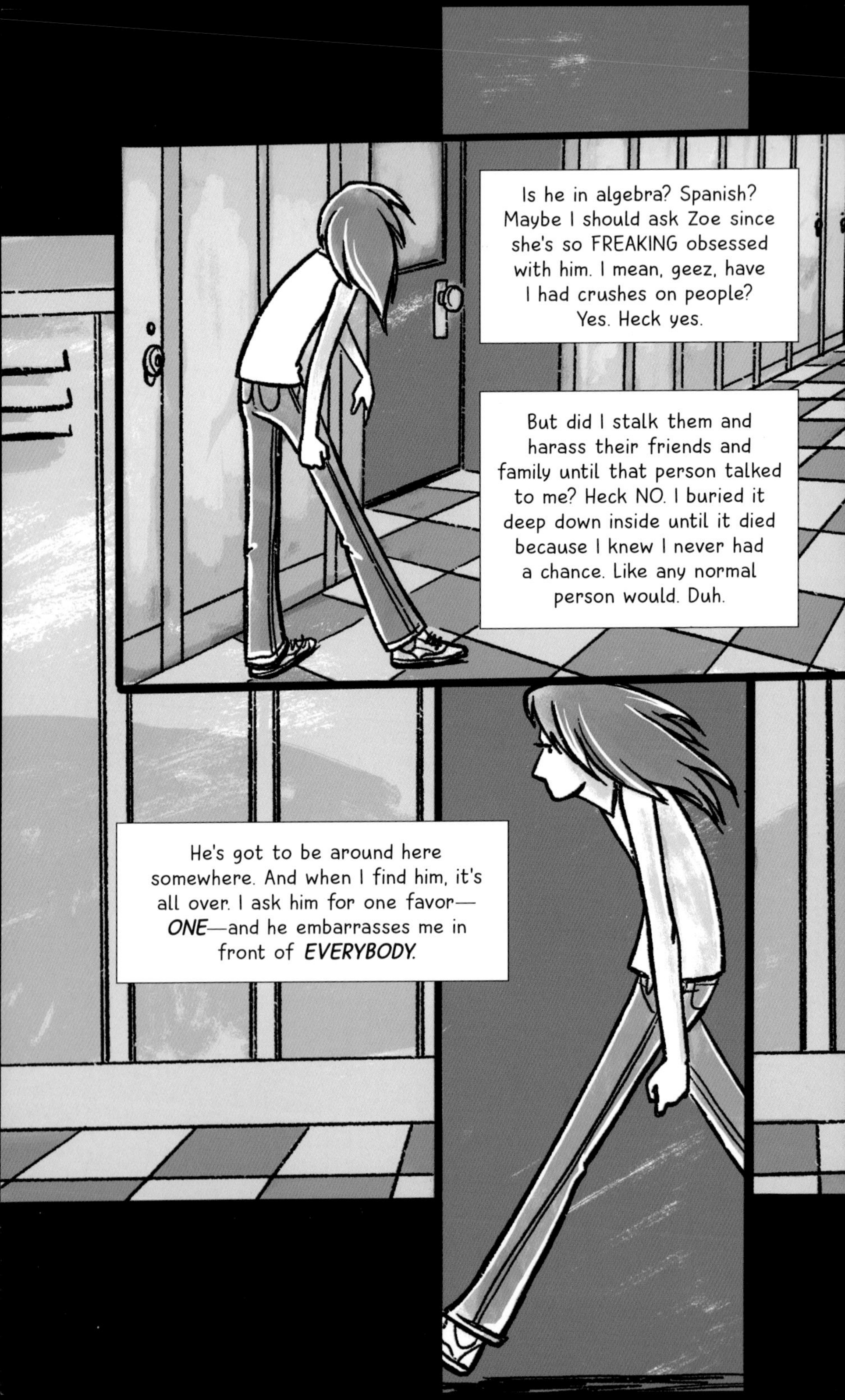
Is he in algebra? Spanish? Maybe I should ask Zoe since she's so FREAKING obsessed with him. I mean, geez, have I had crushes on people? Yes. Heck yes.
But did I stalk them and harass their friends and family until that person talked to me? Heck NO. I buried it deep down inside until it died because I knew I never had a chance. Like any normal person would. Duh.
He's got to be around here somewhere. And when I find him, it's all over. I ask him for one favor—*ONE*—and he embarrasses me in front of ***EVERYBODY.***

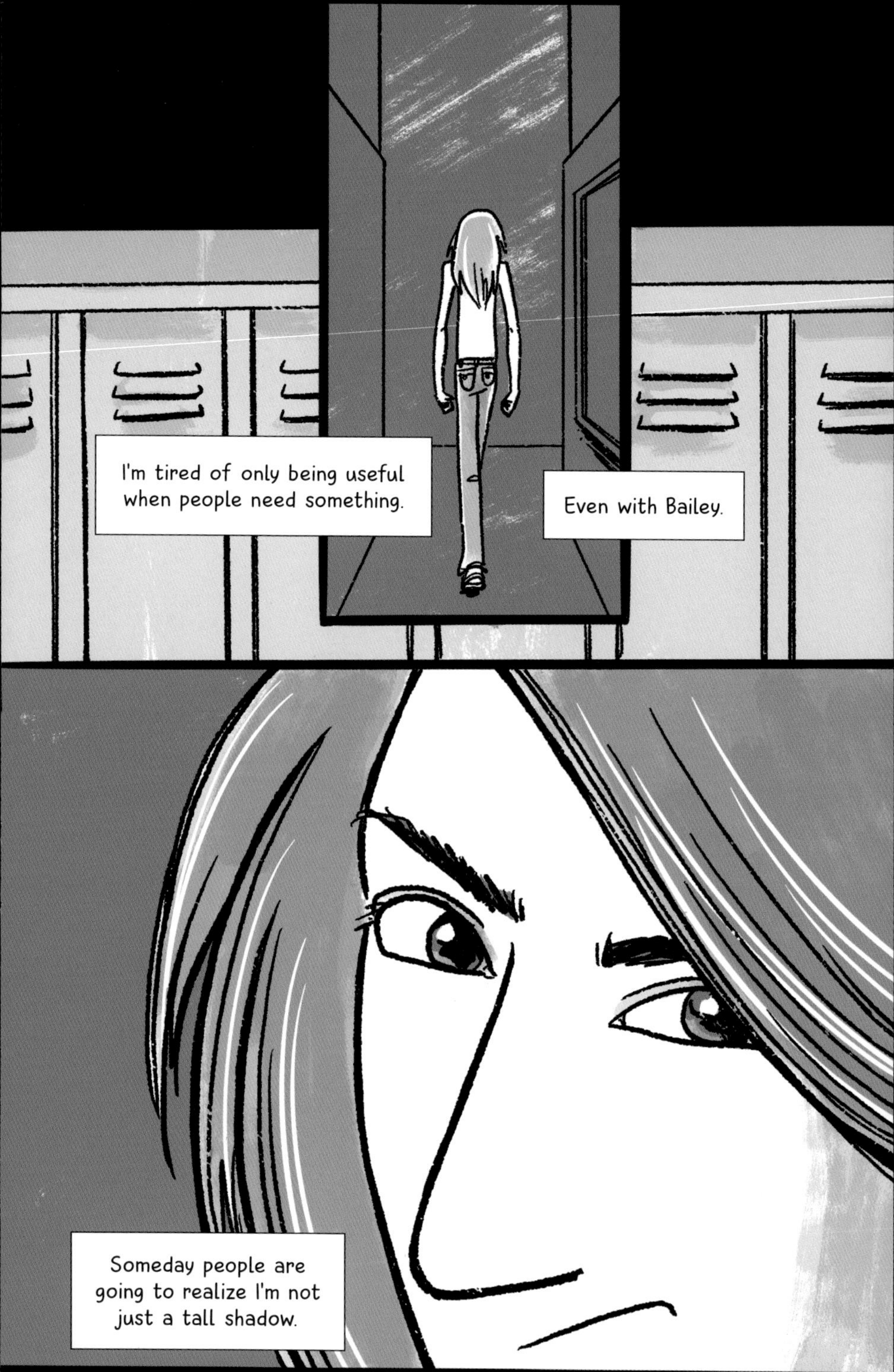
I'm tired of only being useful when people need something.
Even with Bailey.
Someday people are going to realize I'm not just a tall shadow.

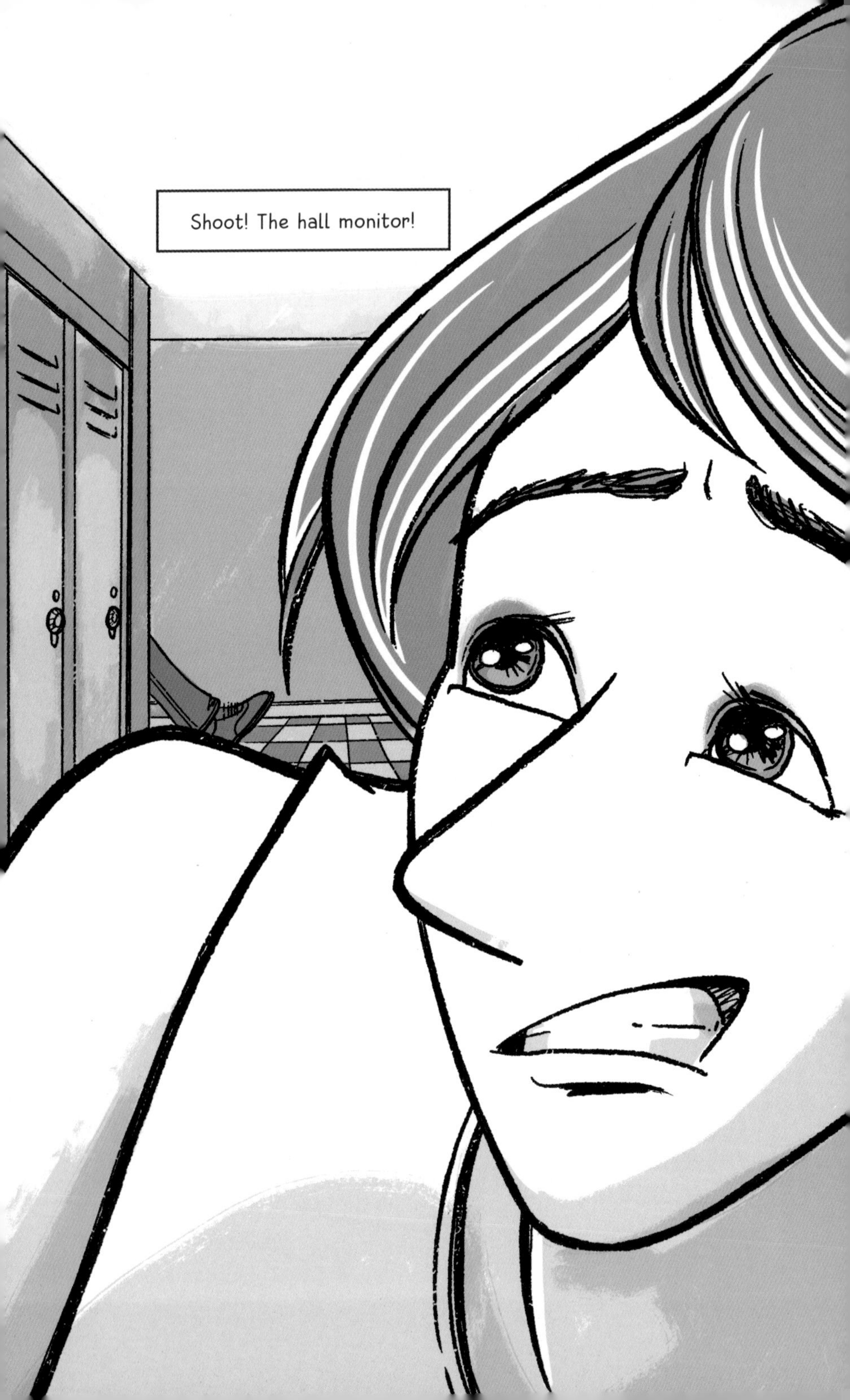
Shoot! The hall monitor!

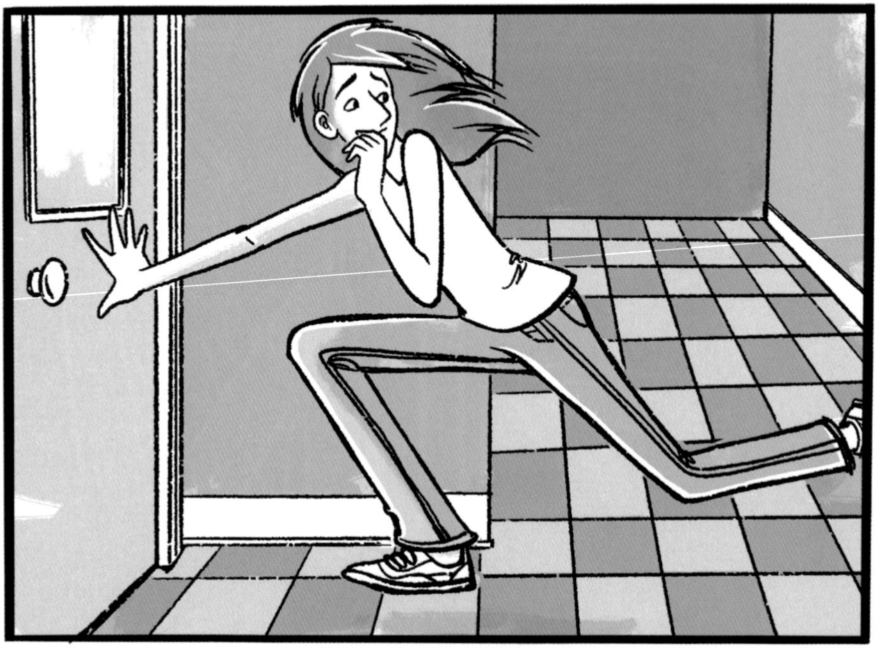

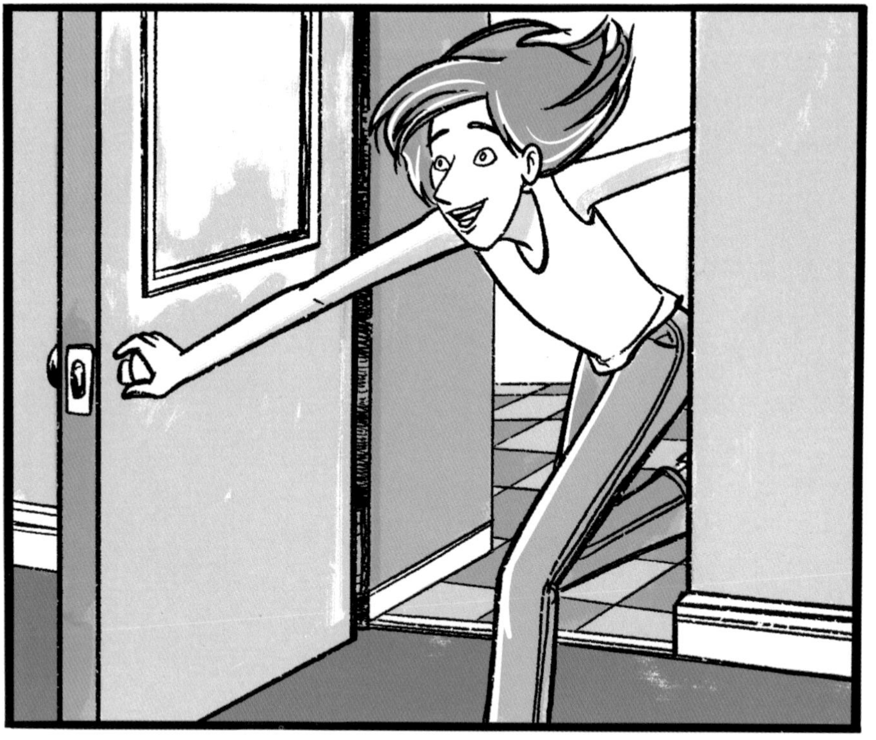

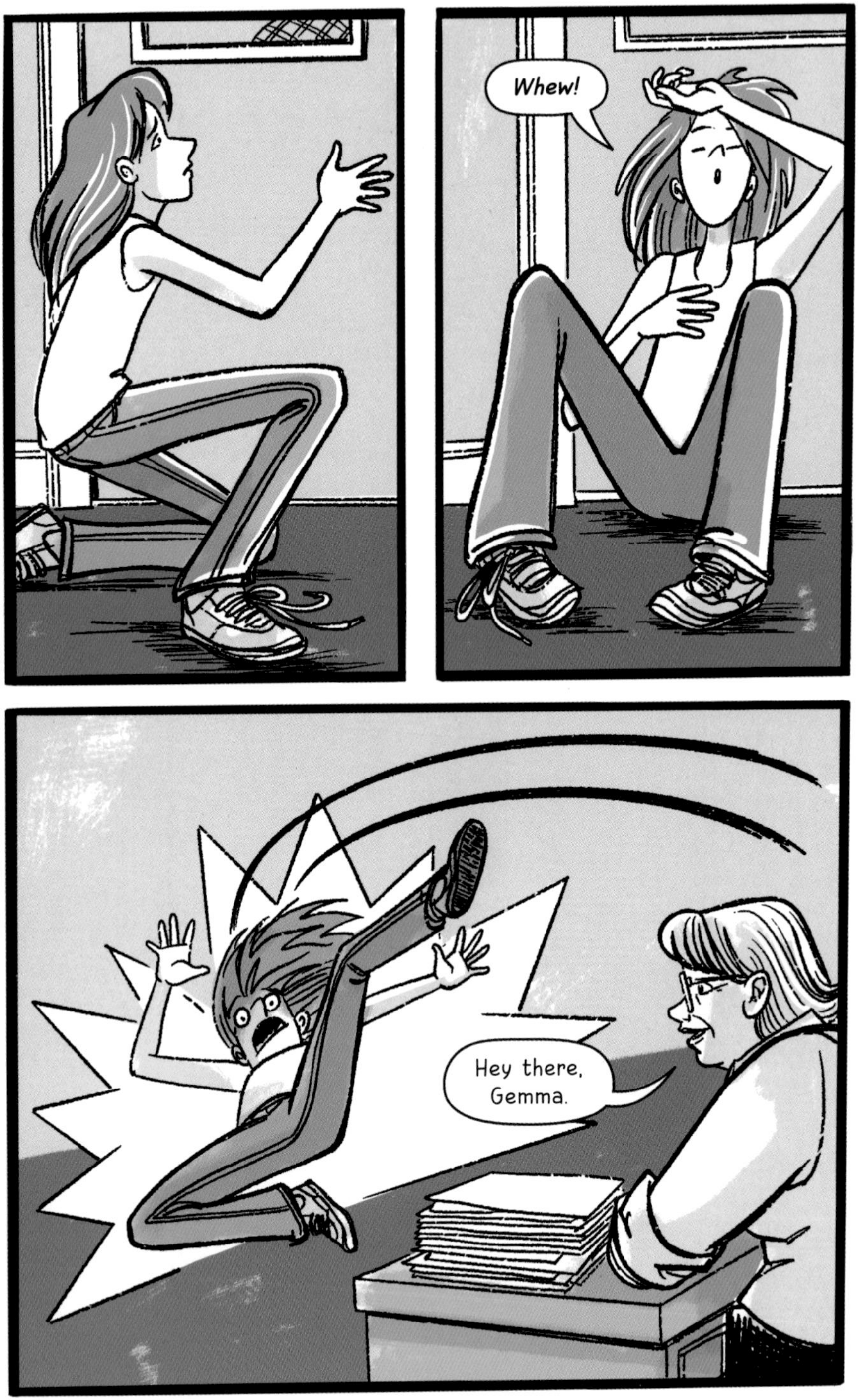
Whew!
Hey there, Gemma.

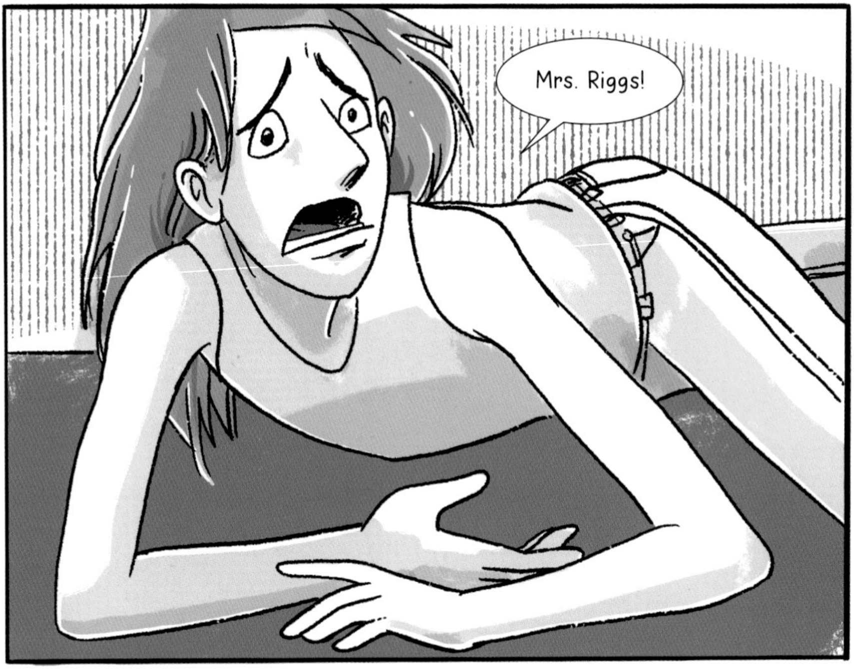
Mrs. Riggs!

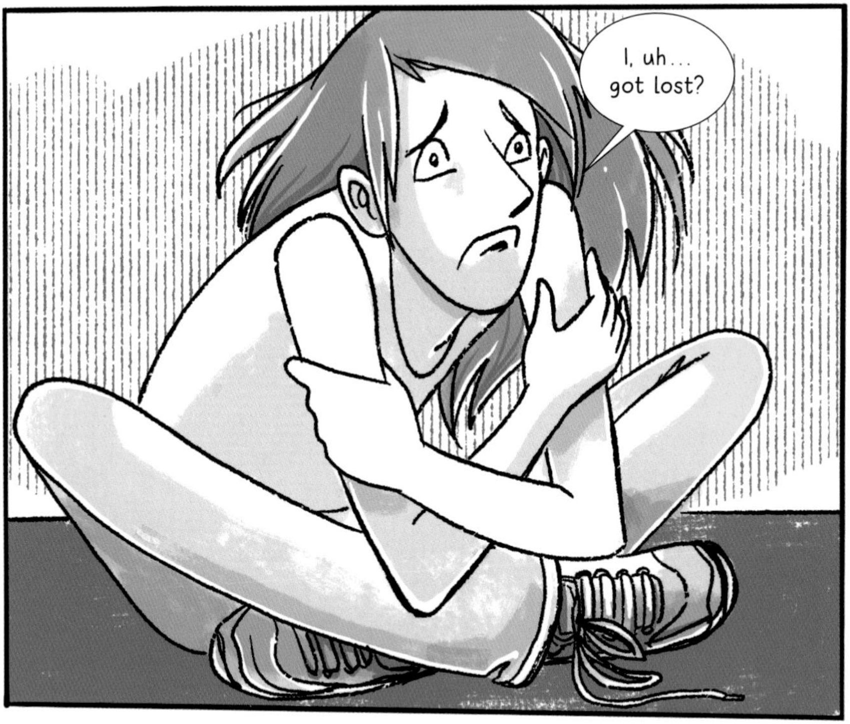
I, uh...
got lost?

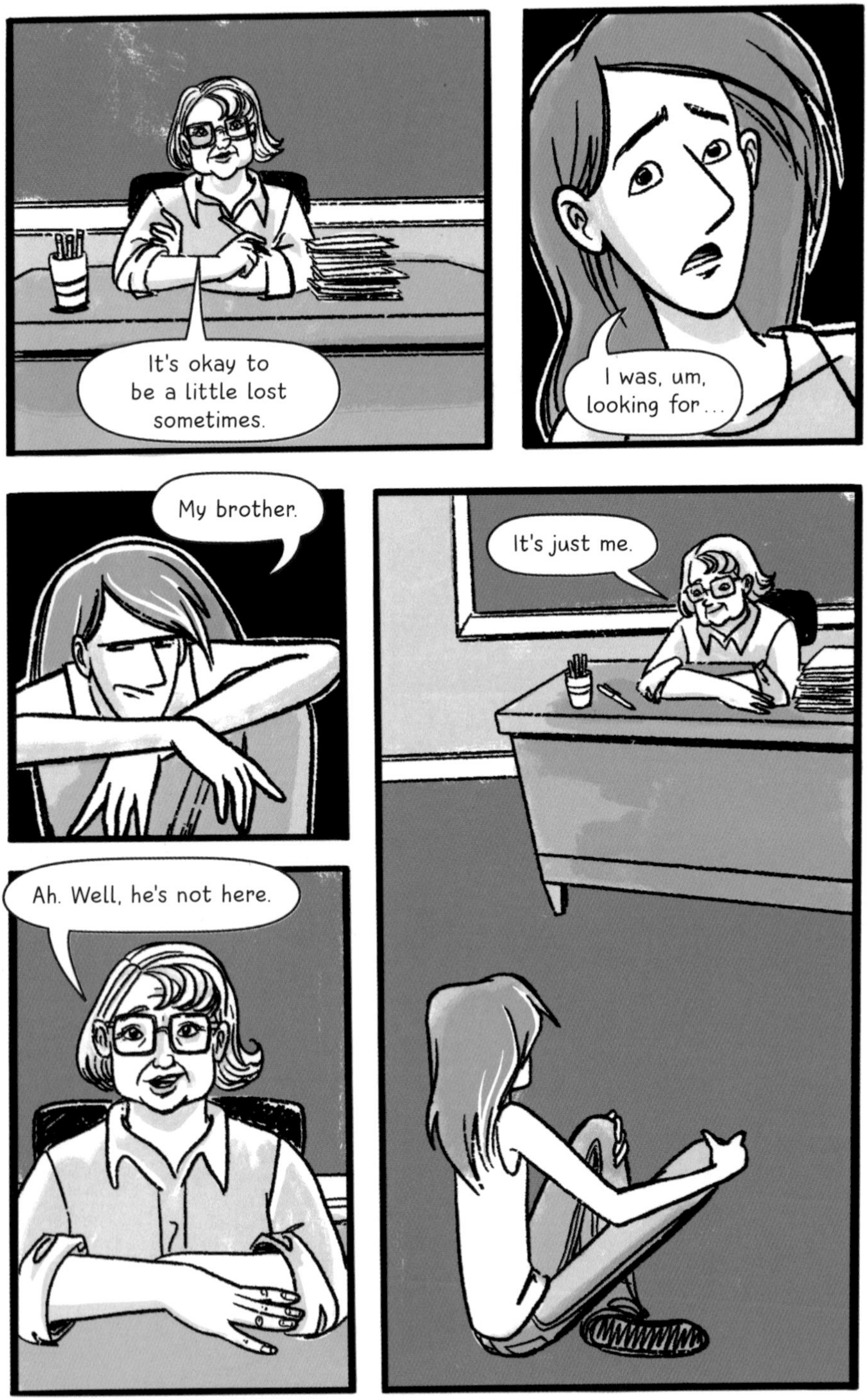
It's okay to be a little lost sometimes.
I was, um, looking for . . .
My brother.
It's just me.
Ah. Well, he's not here.

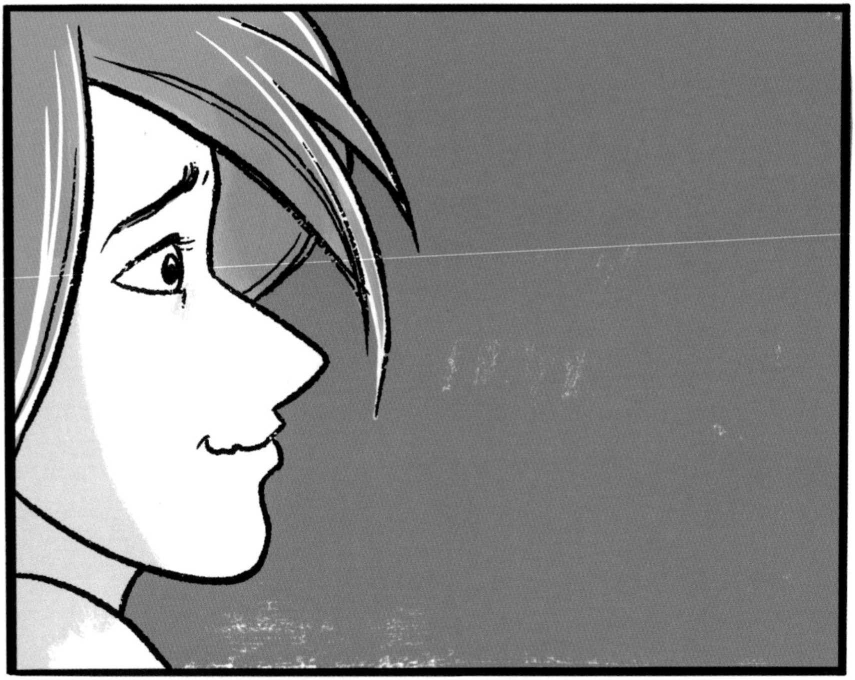

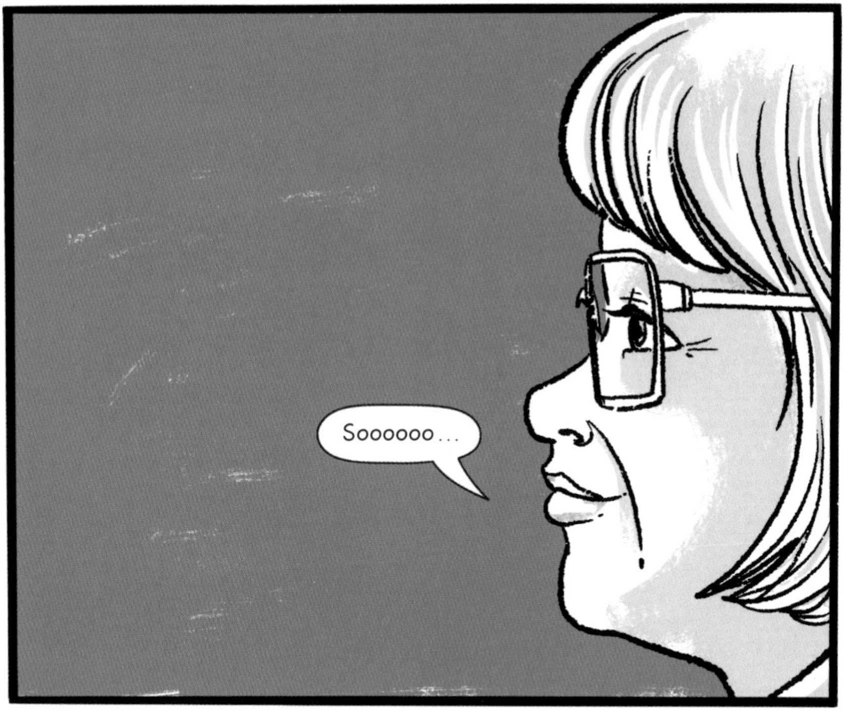
Soooooo...

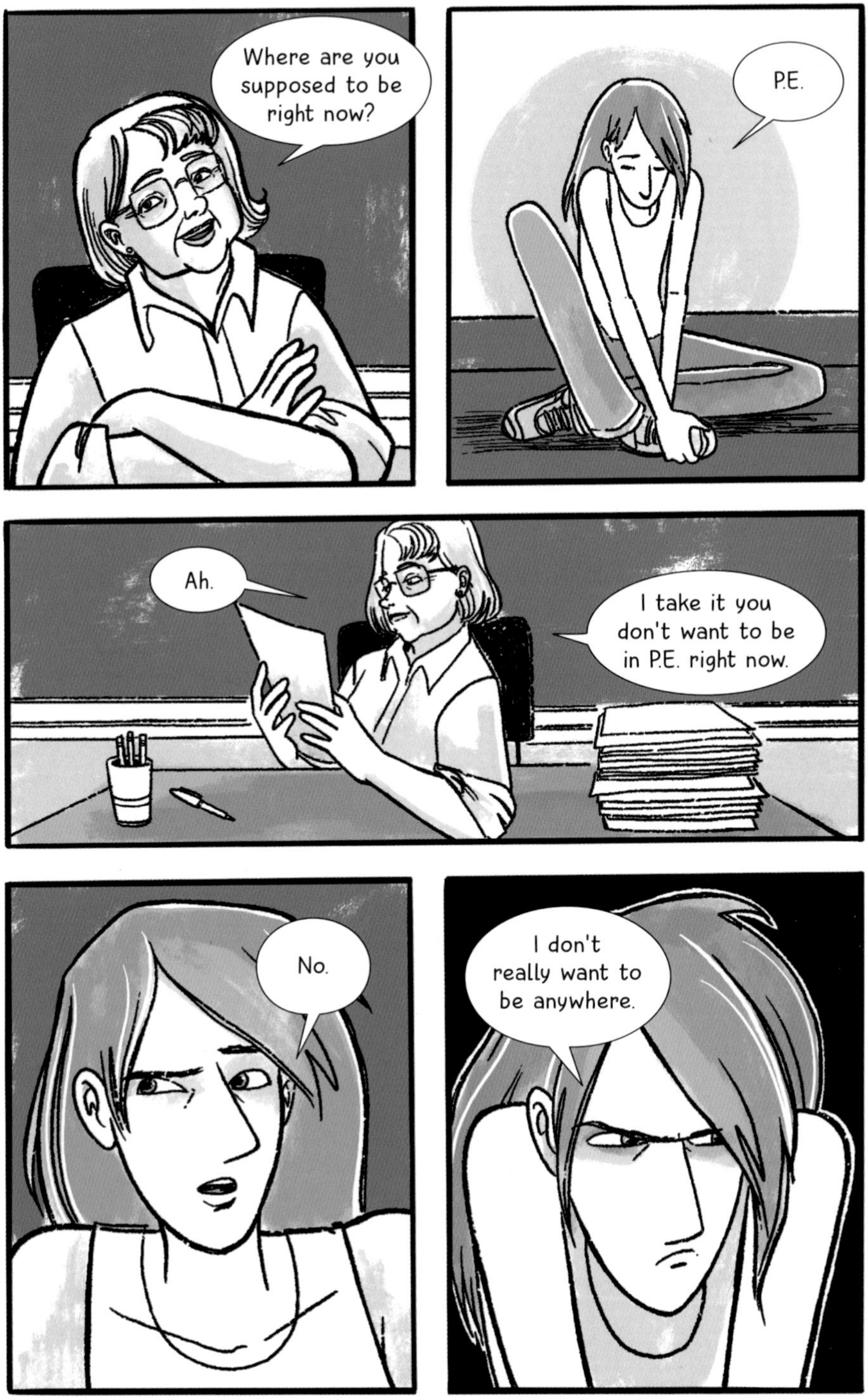
Where are you supposed to be right now?
P.E.
Ah.
I take it you don't want to be in P.E. right now.
No.
I don't really want to be anywhere.

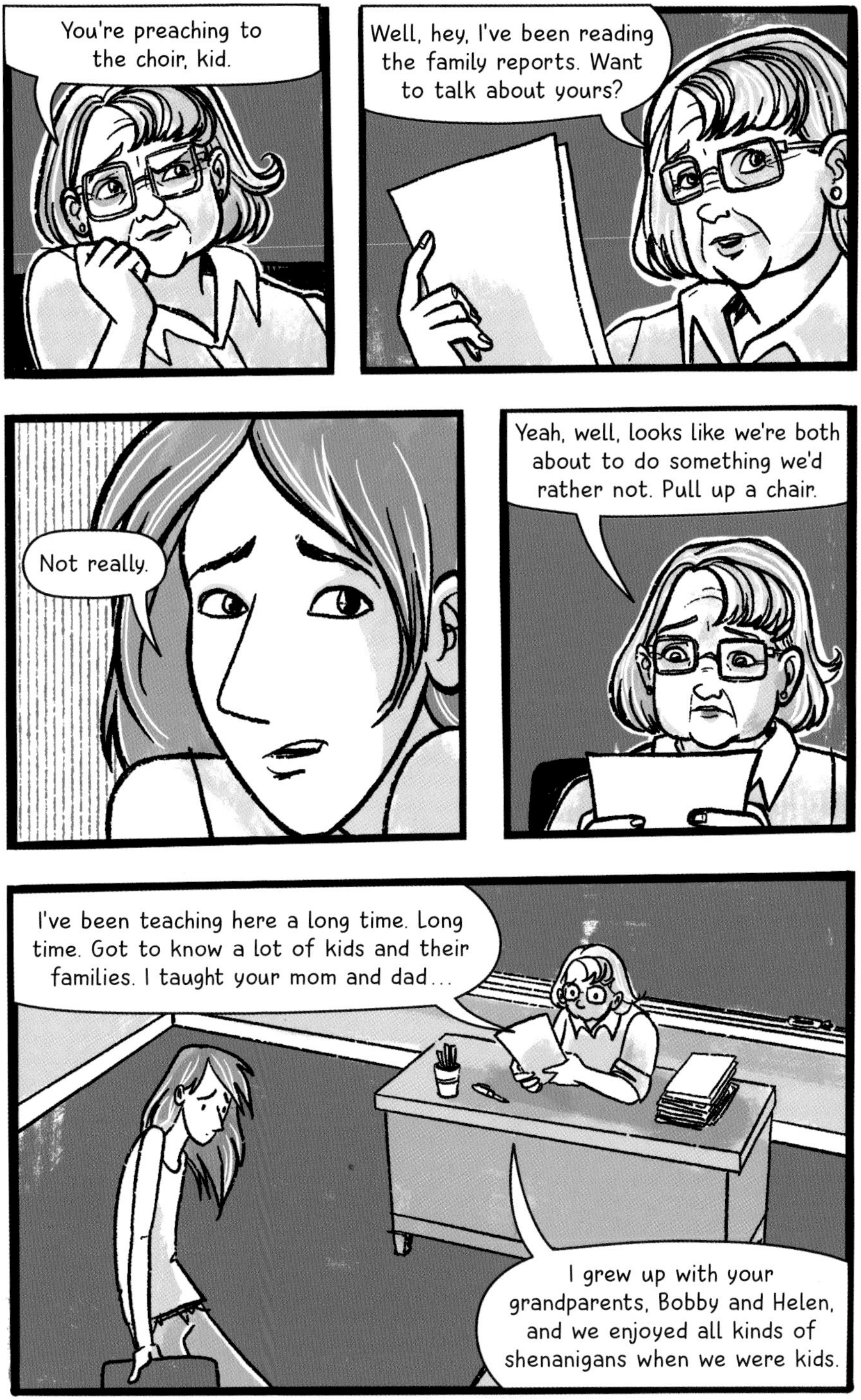
You're preaching to the choir, kid.
Well, hey, I've been reading the family reports. Want to talk about yours?
Not really.
Yeah, well, looks like we're both about to do something we'd rather not. Pull up a chair.
I've been teaching here a long time. Long time. Got to know a lot of kids and their families. I taught your mom and dad...
I grew up with your grandparents, Bobby and Helen, and we enjoyed all kinds of shenanigans when we were kids.

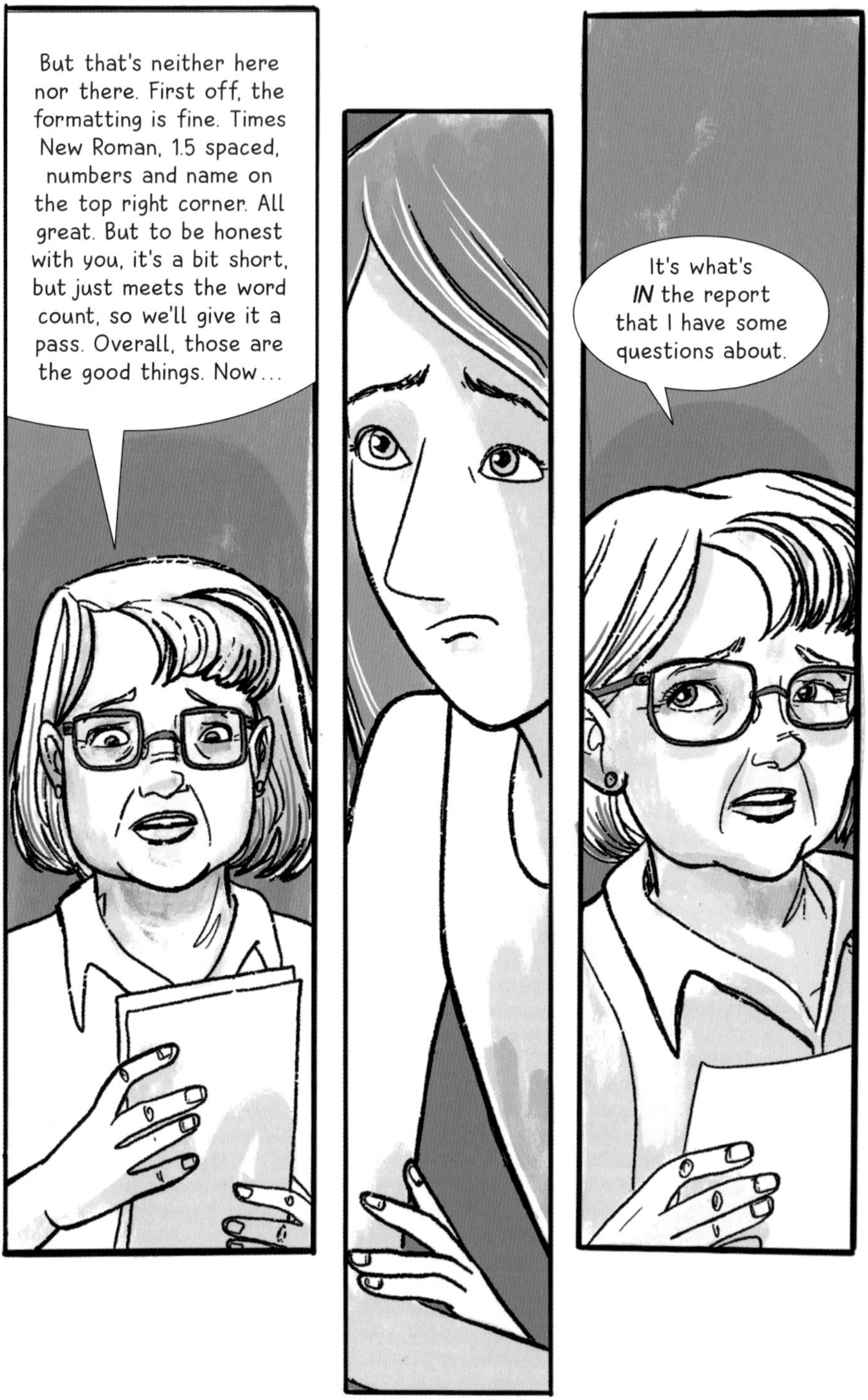
But that's neither here nor there. First off, the formatting is fine. Times New Roman, 1.5 spaced, numbers and name on the top right corner. All great. But to be honest with you, it's a bit short, but just meets the word count, so we'll give it a pass. Overall, those are the good things. Now...
It's what's *IN* the report that I have some questions about.

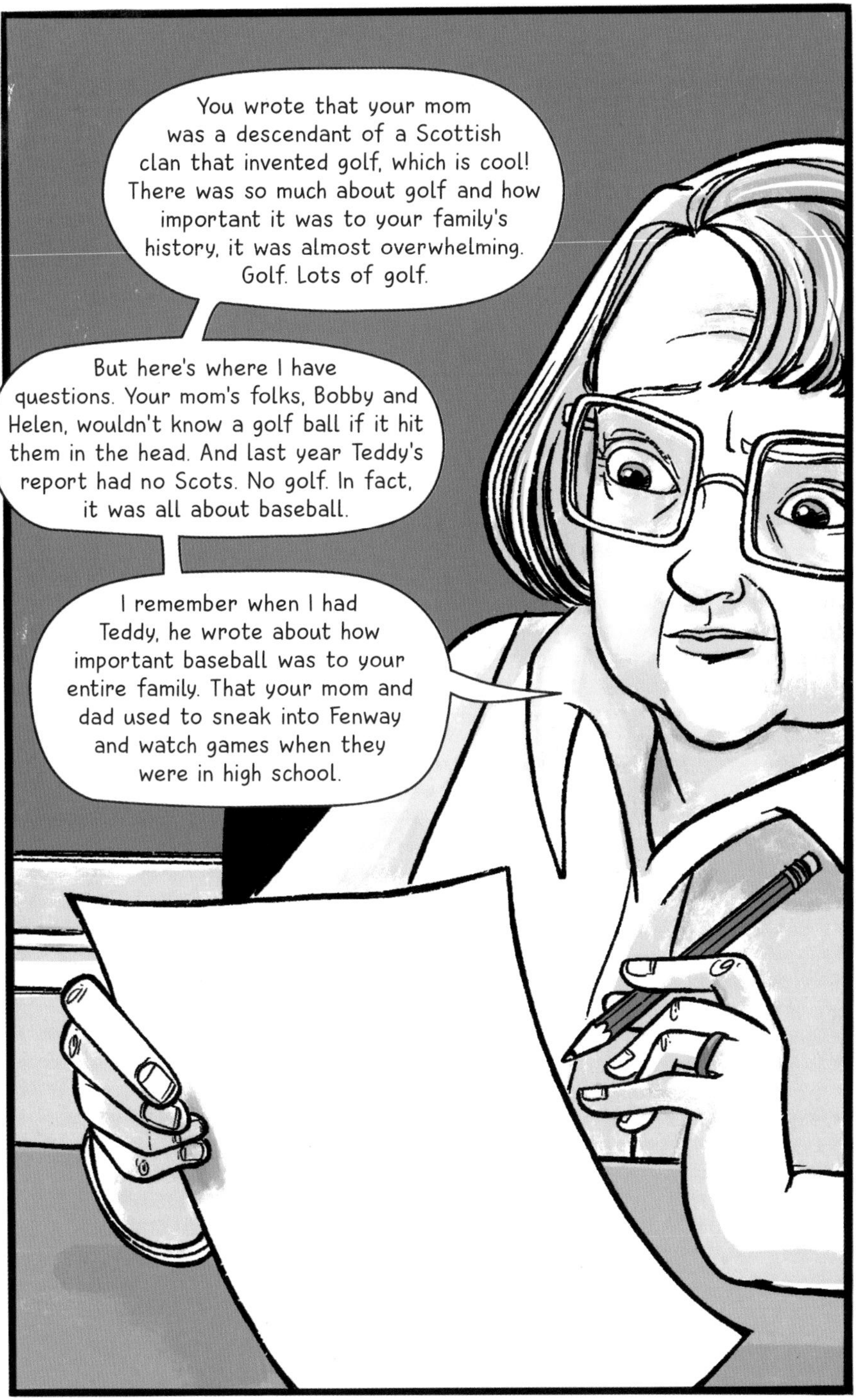
You wrote that your mom was a descendant of a Scottish clan that invented golf, which is cool! There was so much about golf and how important it was to your family's history, it was almost overwhelming. Golf. Lots of golf.
But here's where I have questions. Your mom's folks, Bobby and Helen, wouldn't know a golf ball if it hit them in the head. And last year Teddy's report had no Scots. No golf. In fact, it was all about baseball.
I remember when I had Teddy, he wrote about how important baseball was to your entire family. That your mom and dad used to sneak into Fenway and watch games when they were in high school.

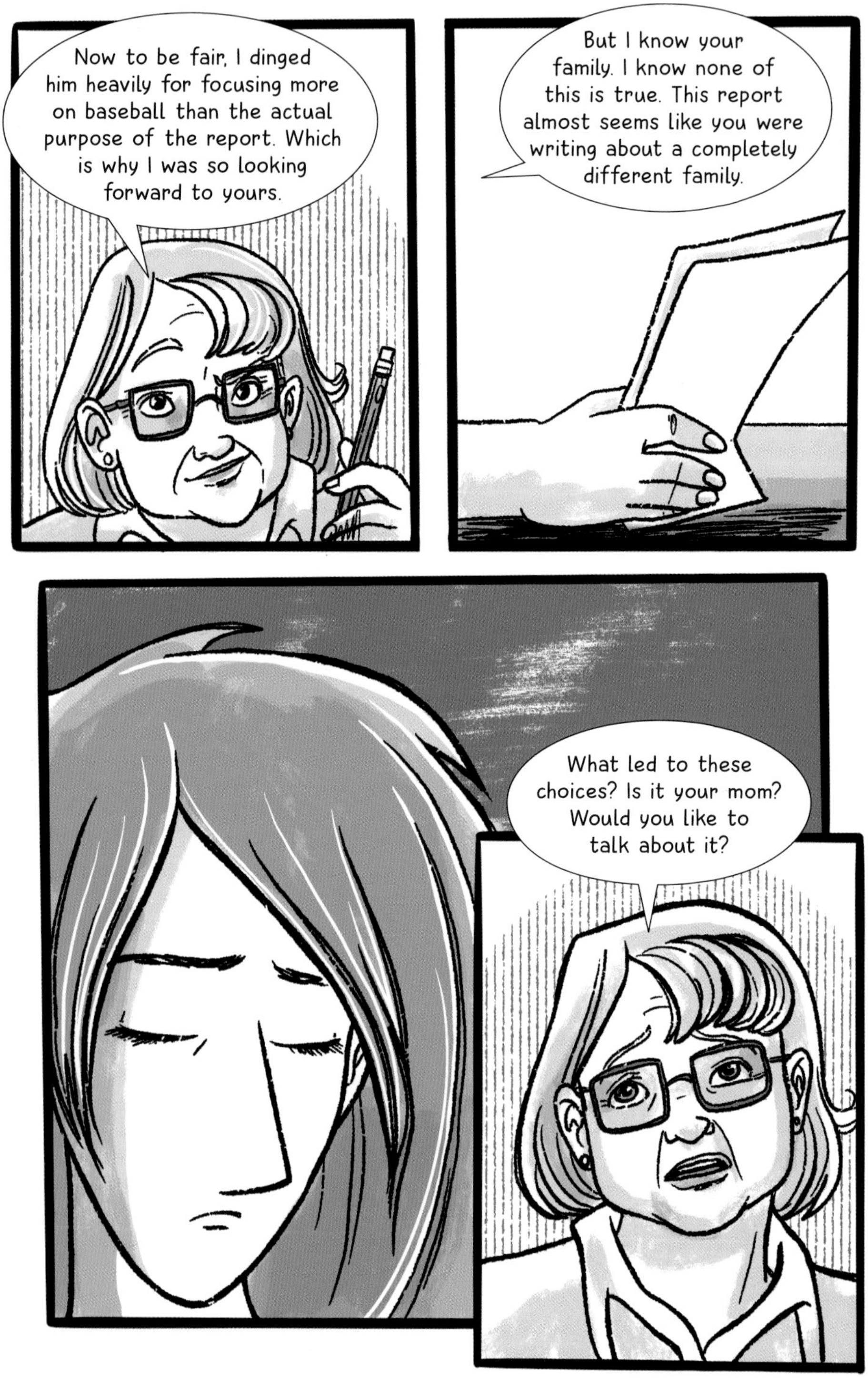
Now to be fair, I dinged him heavily for focusing more on baseball than the actual purpose of the report. Which is why I was so looking forward to yours.
But I know your family. I know none of this is true. This report almost seems like you were writing about a completely different family.
What led to these choices? Is it your mom? Would you like to talk about it?

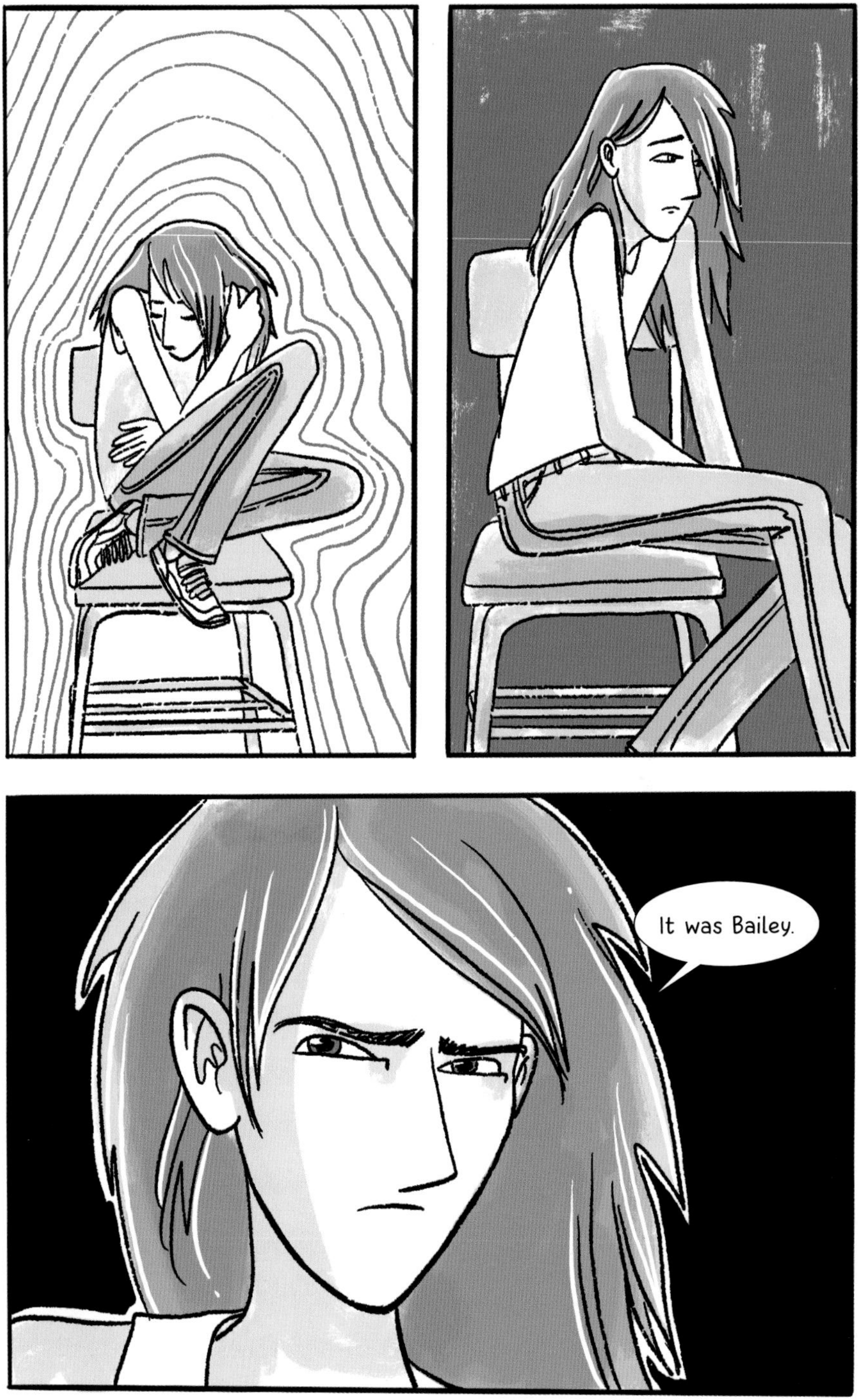
It was Bailey.

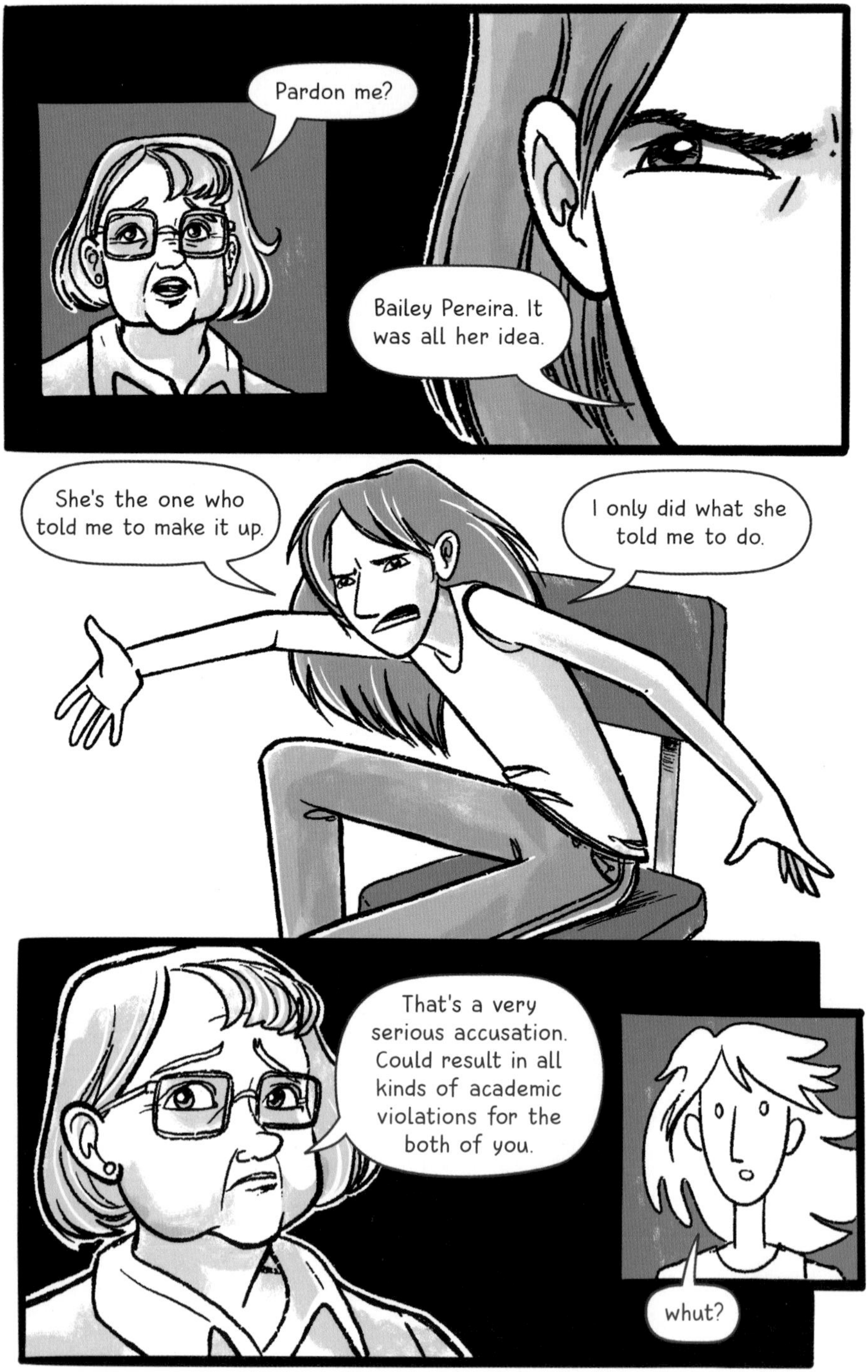
Pardon me?
Bailey Pereira. It was all her idea.
She's the one who told me to make it up.
I only did what she told me to do.
That's a very serious accusation. Could result in all kinds of academic violations for the both of you.
whut?

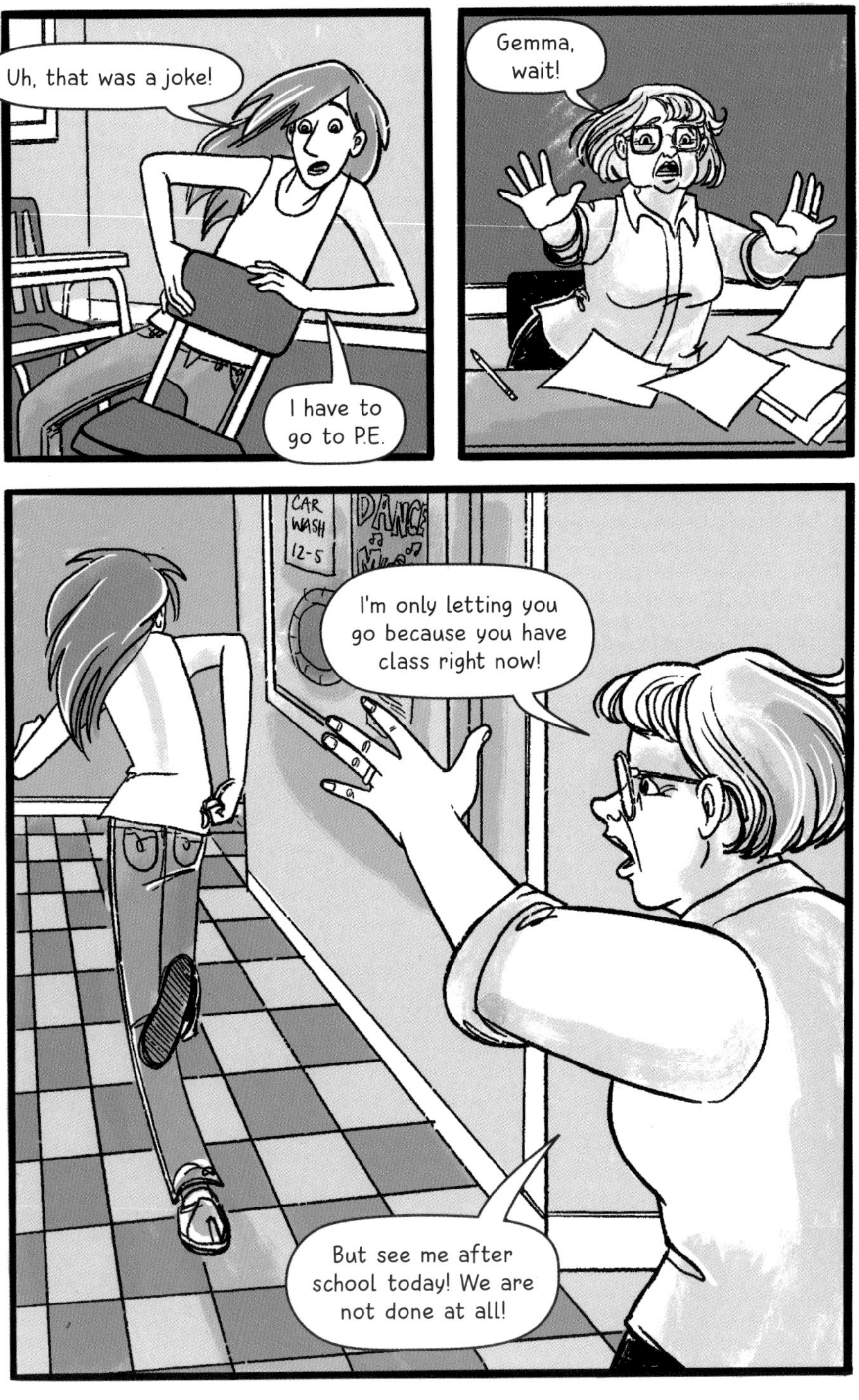
Uh, that was a joke!
I have to go to P.E.
Gemma, wait!
CAR WASH 12-5
I'm only letting you go because you have class right now!
But see me after school today! We are not done at all!

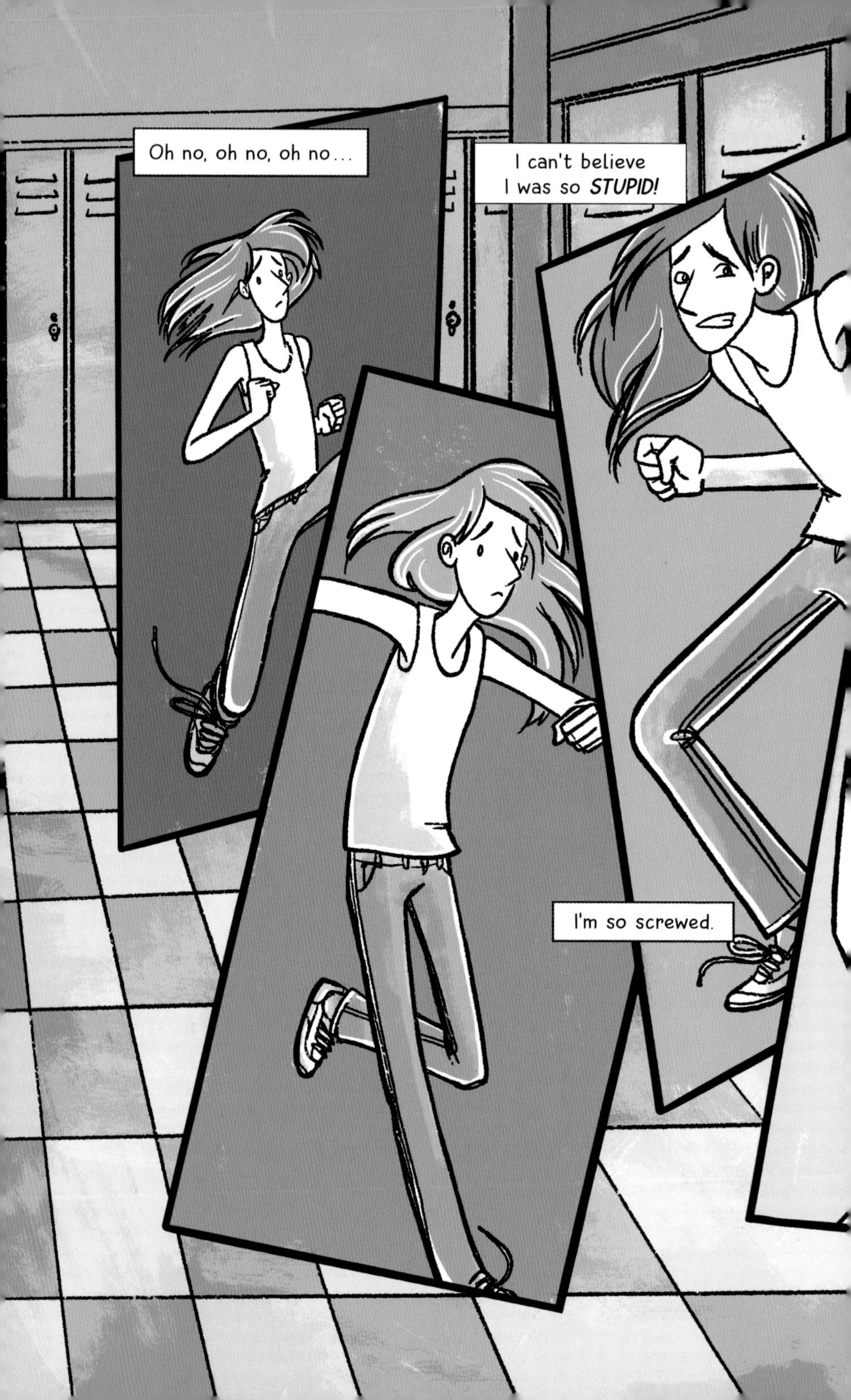
Oh no, oh no, oh no...
I can't believe I was so *STUPID!*
I'm so screwed.

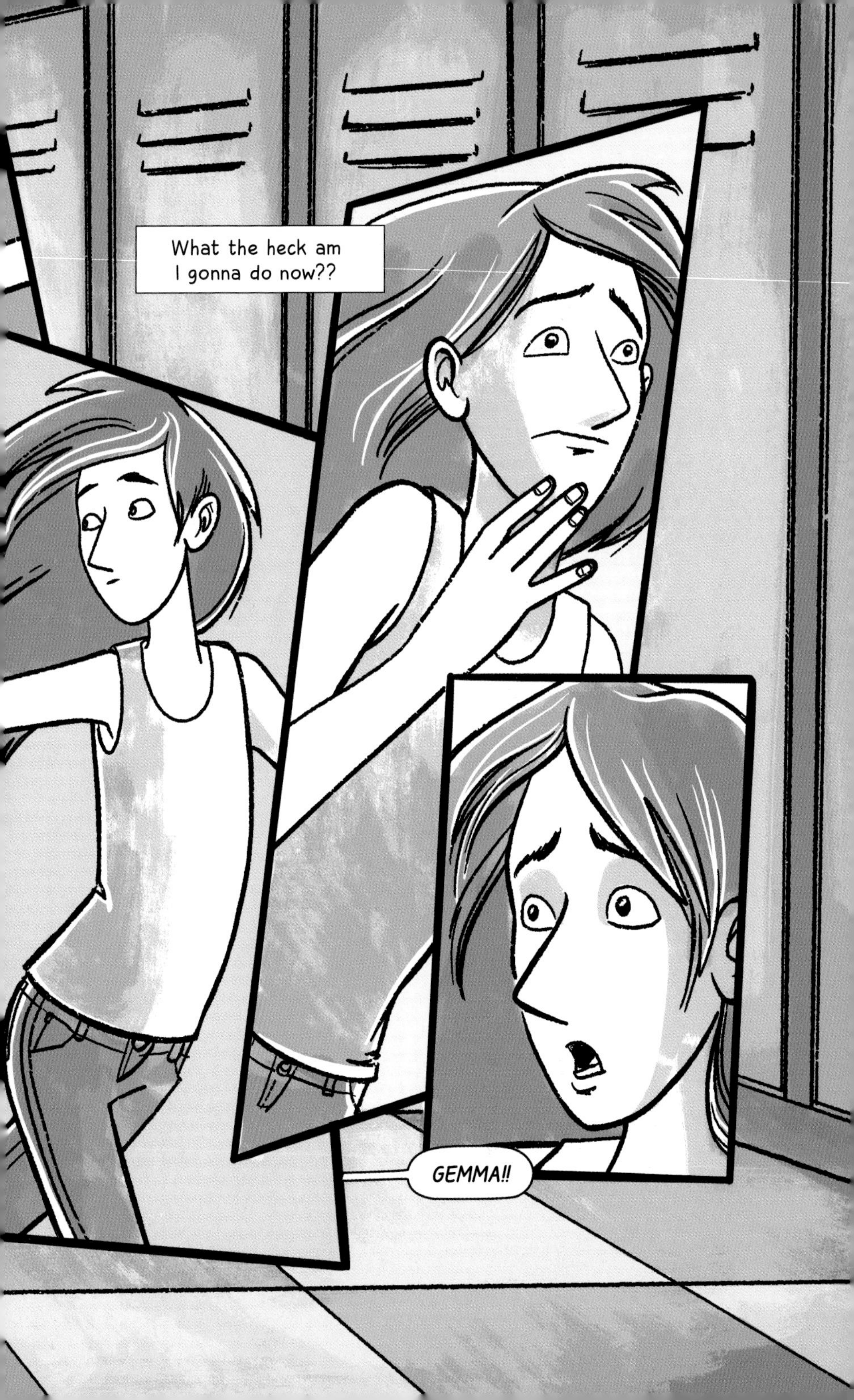
What the heck am I gonna do now??
GEMMA!!

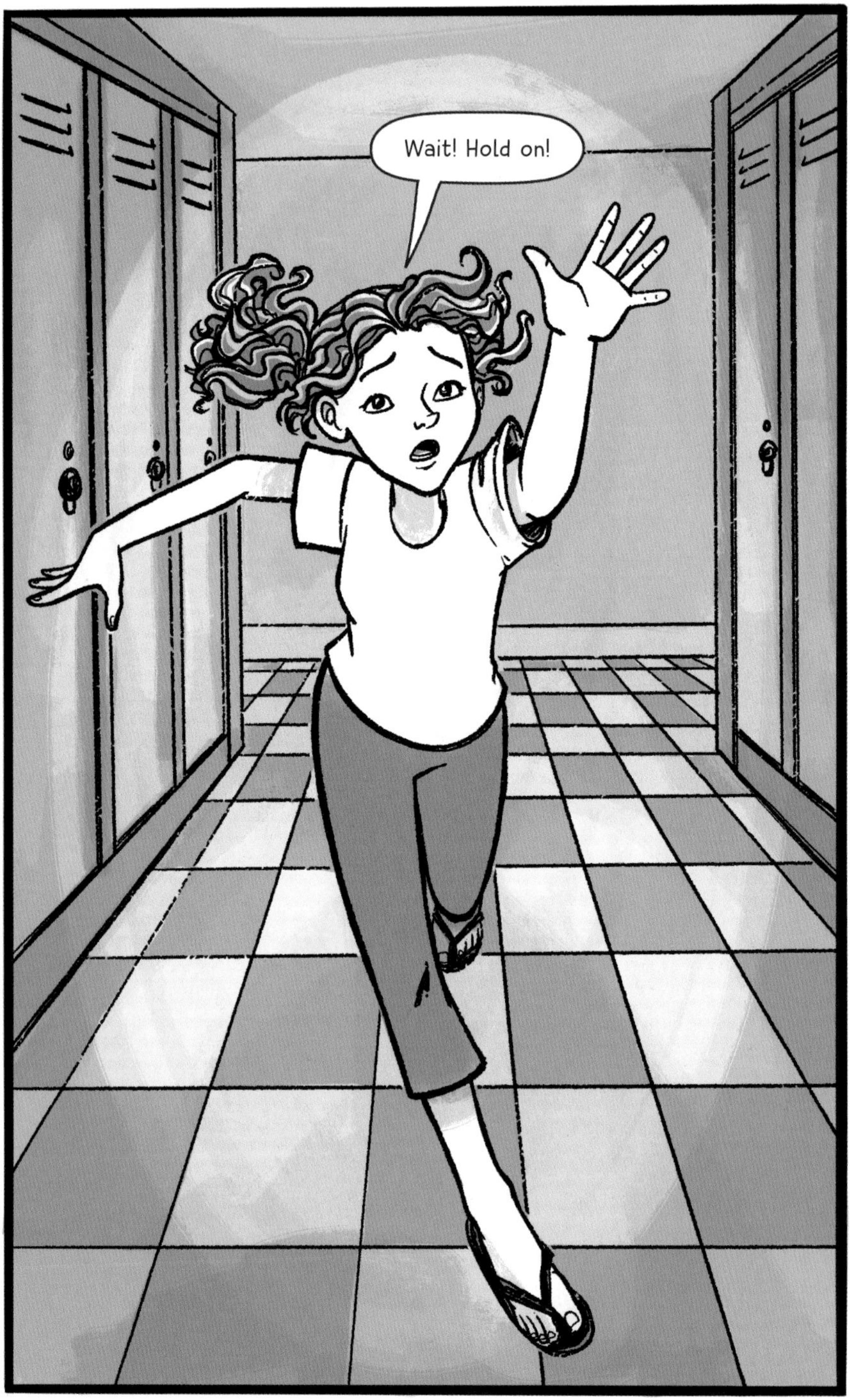
Wait! Hold on!

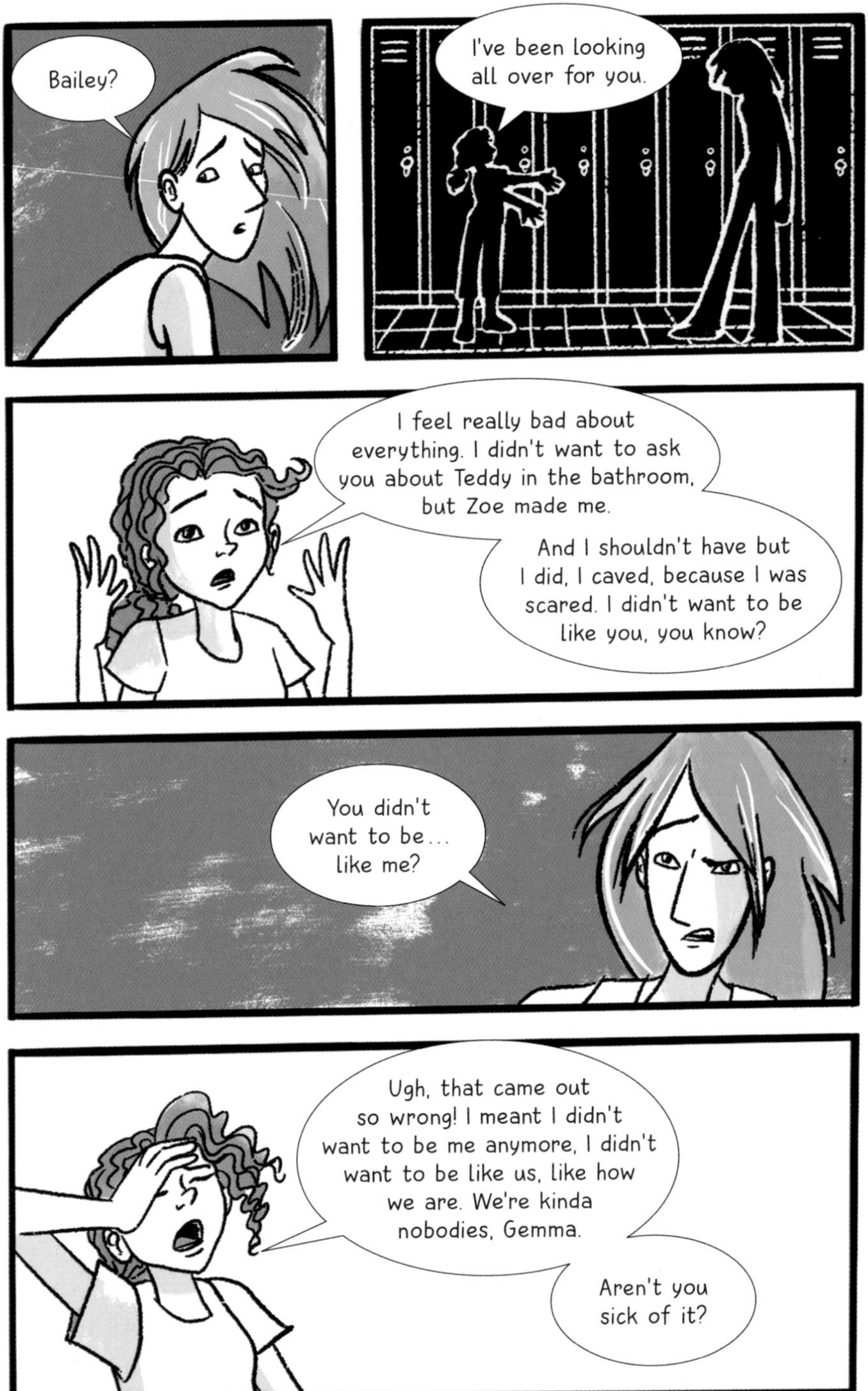
Bailey?
I've been looking all over for you.
I feel really bad about everything. I didn't want to ask you about Teddy in the bathroom, but Zoe made me.
And I shouldn't have but I did, I caved, because I was scared. I didn't want to be like you, you know?
You didn't want to be... like me?
Ugh, that came out so wrong! I meant I didn't want to be me anymore, I didn't want to be like us, like how we are. We're kinda nobodies, Gemma.
Aren't you sick of it?

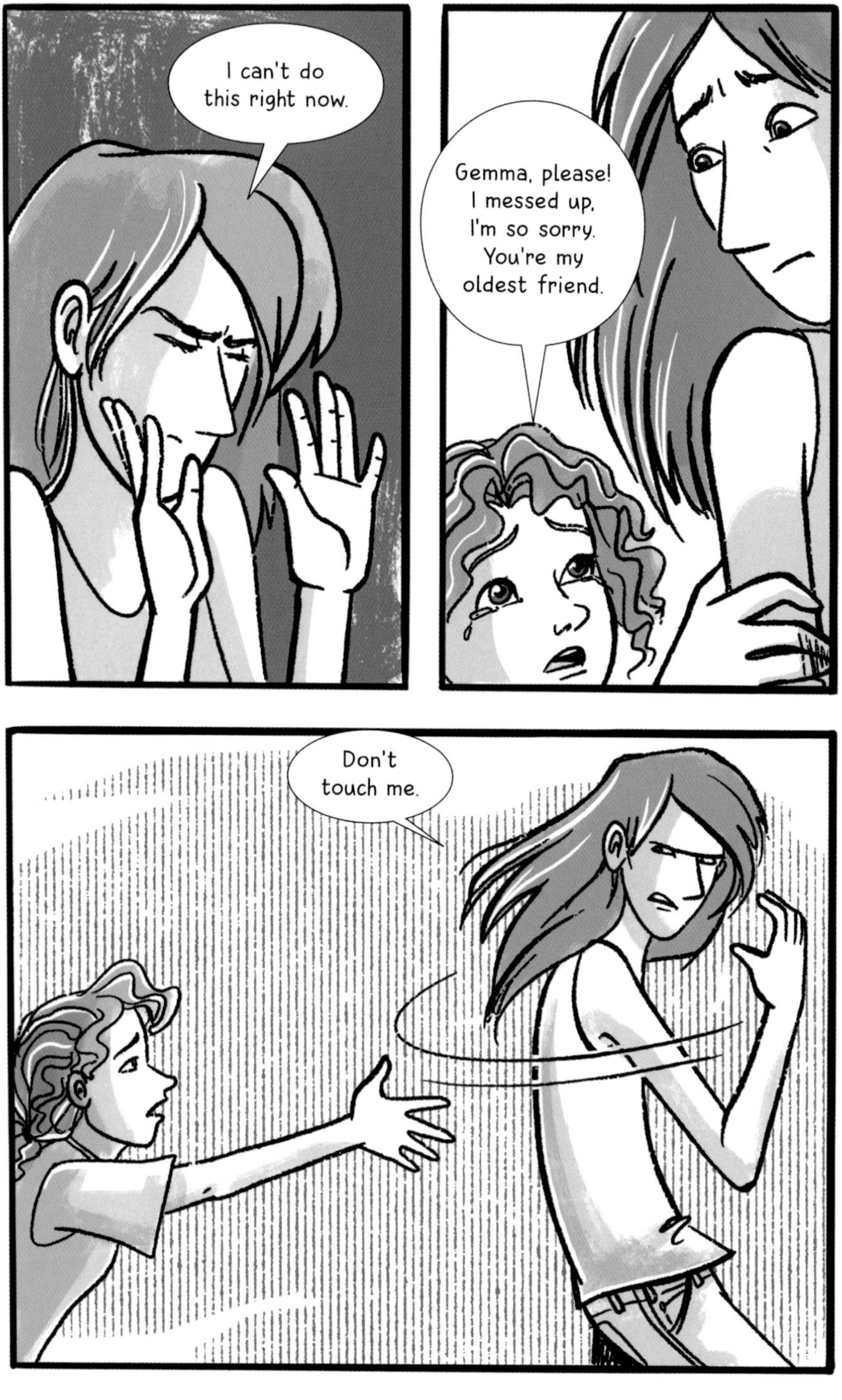
I can't do this right now.
Gemma, please! I messed up, I'm so sorry. You're my oldest friend.
Don't touch me.

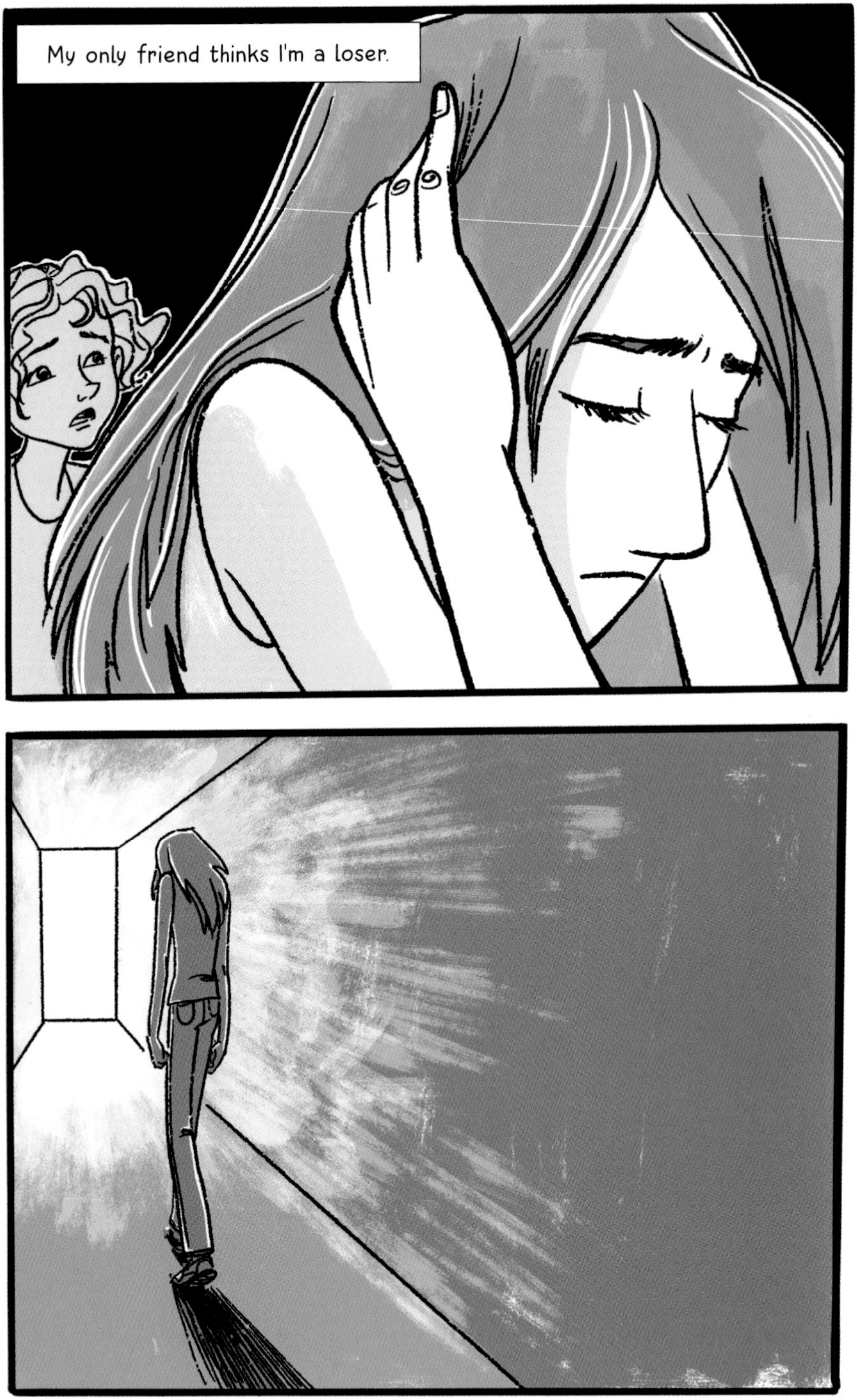

My only friend thinks I'm a loser.

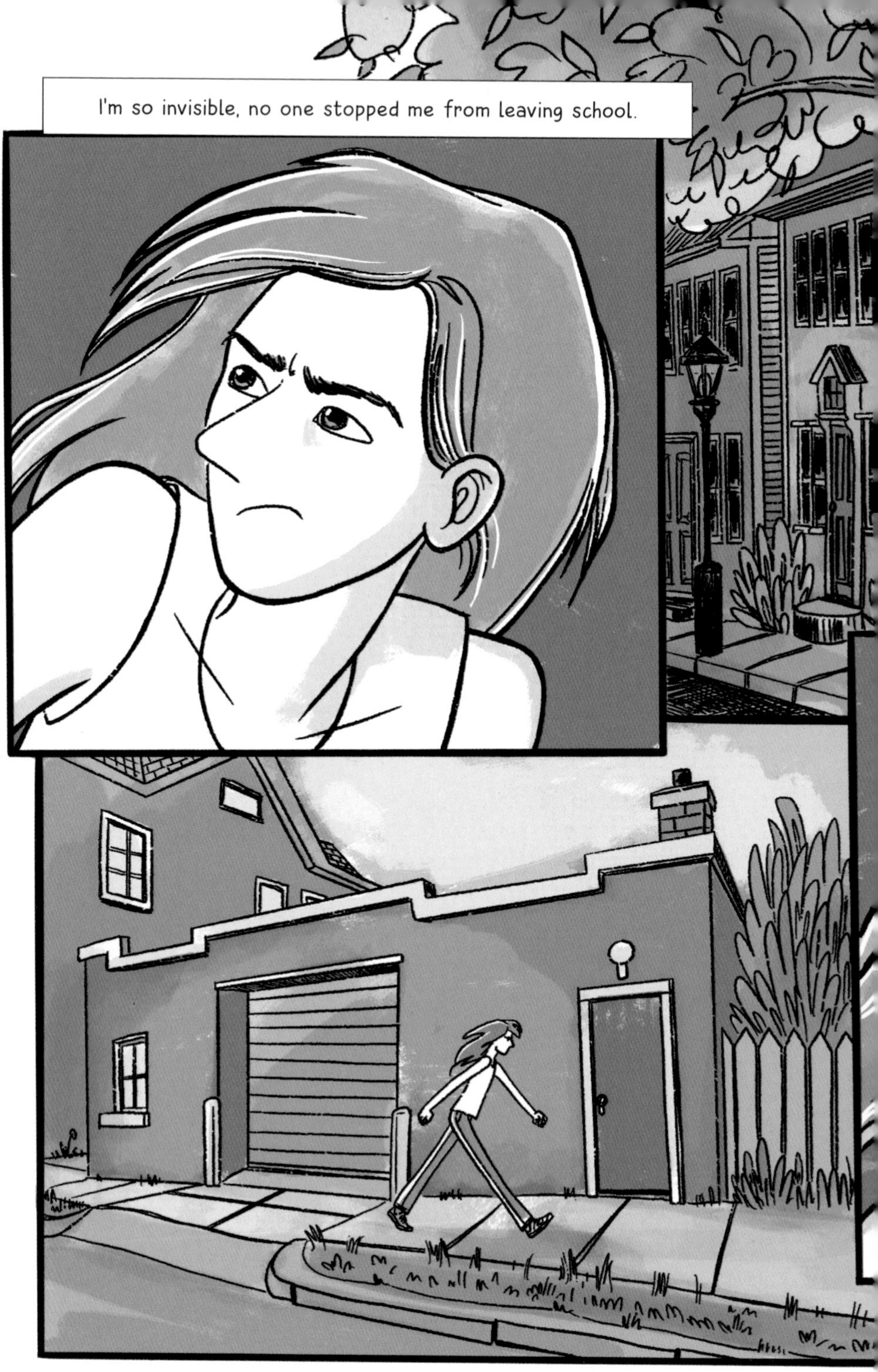
I'm so invisible, no one stopped me from leaving school.

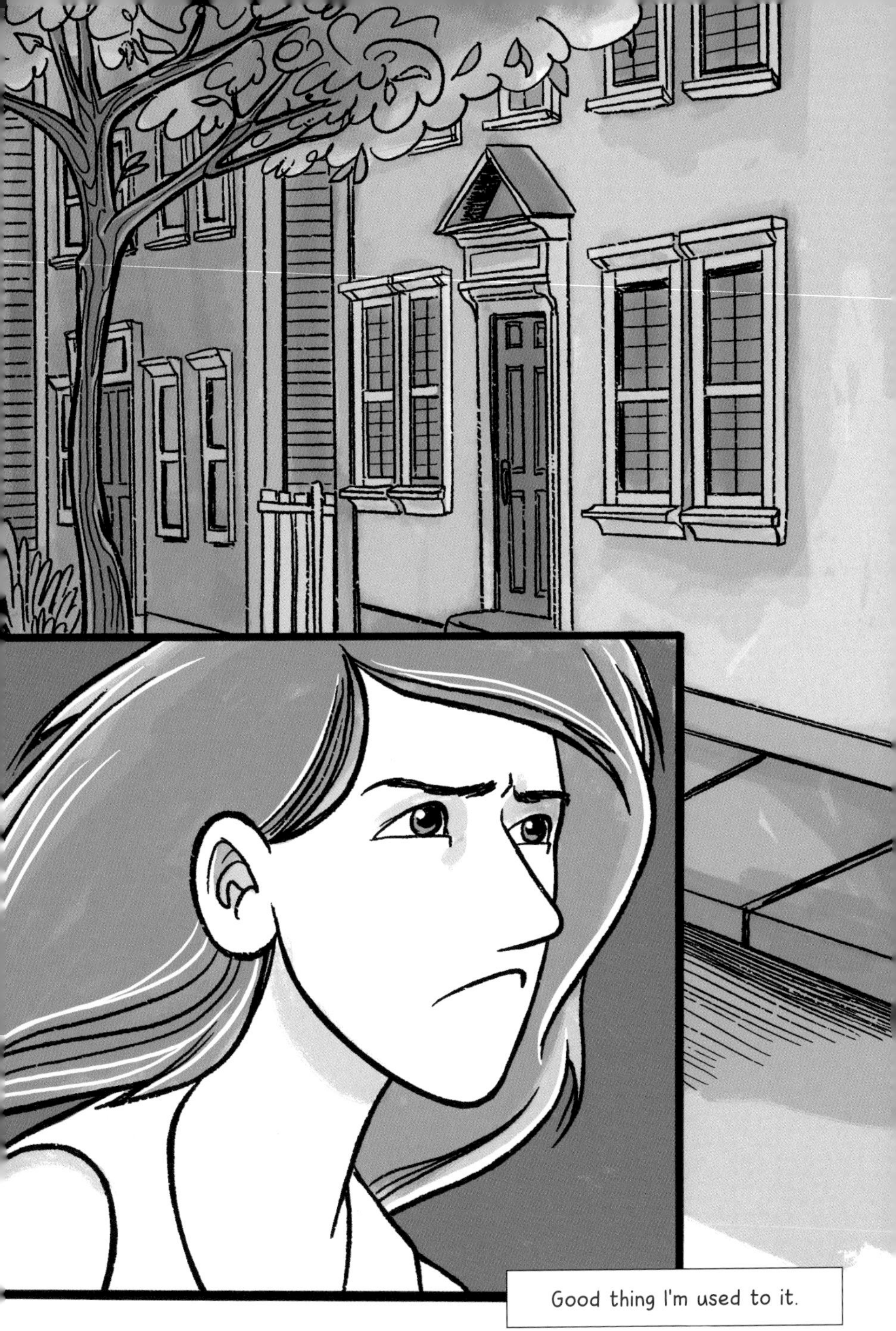
Good thing I'm used to it.

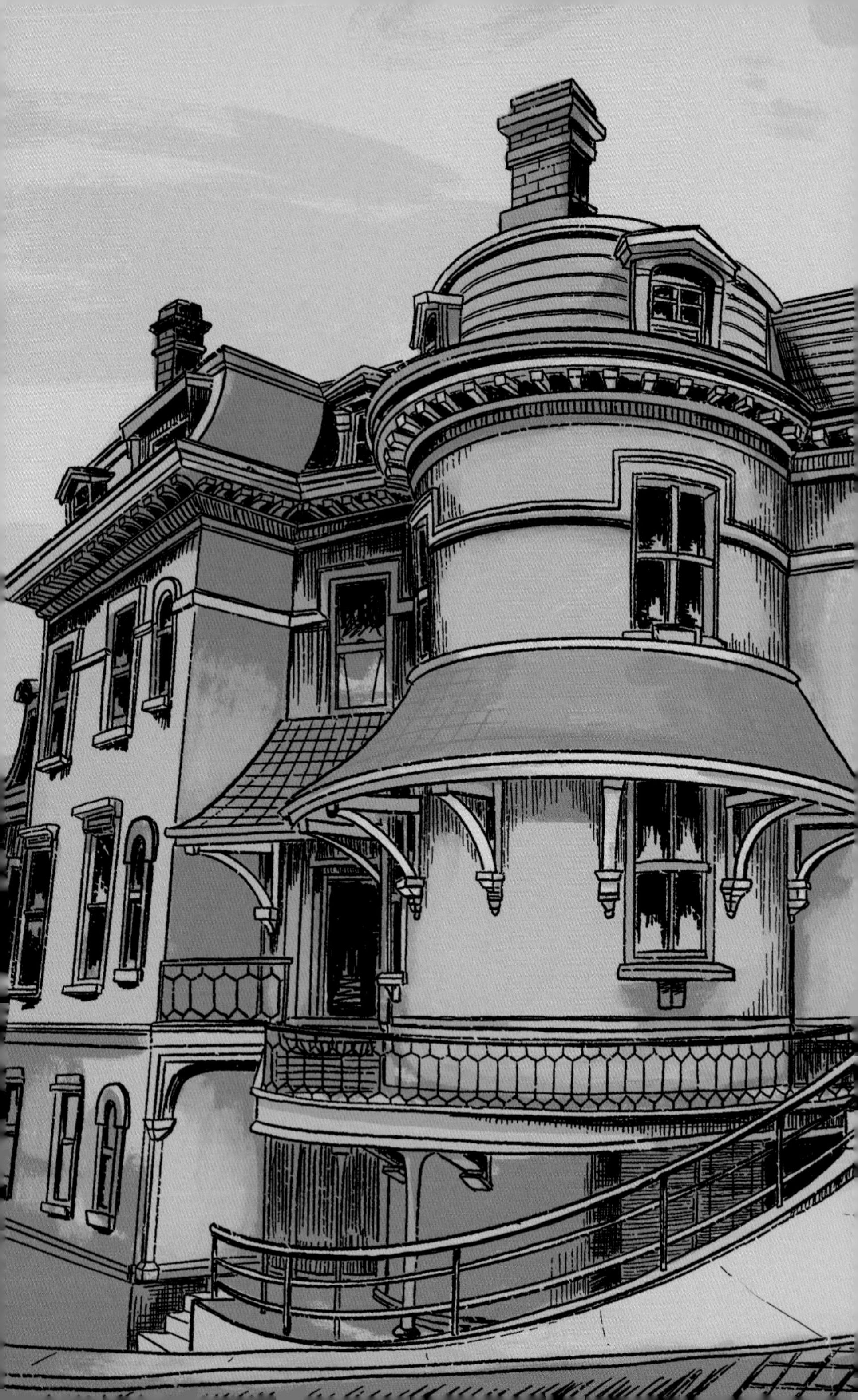

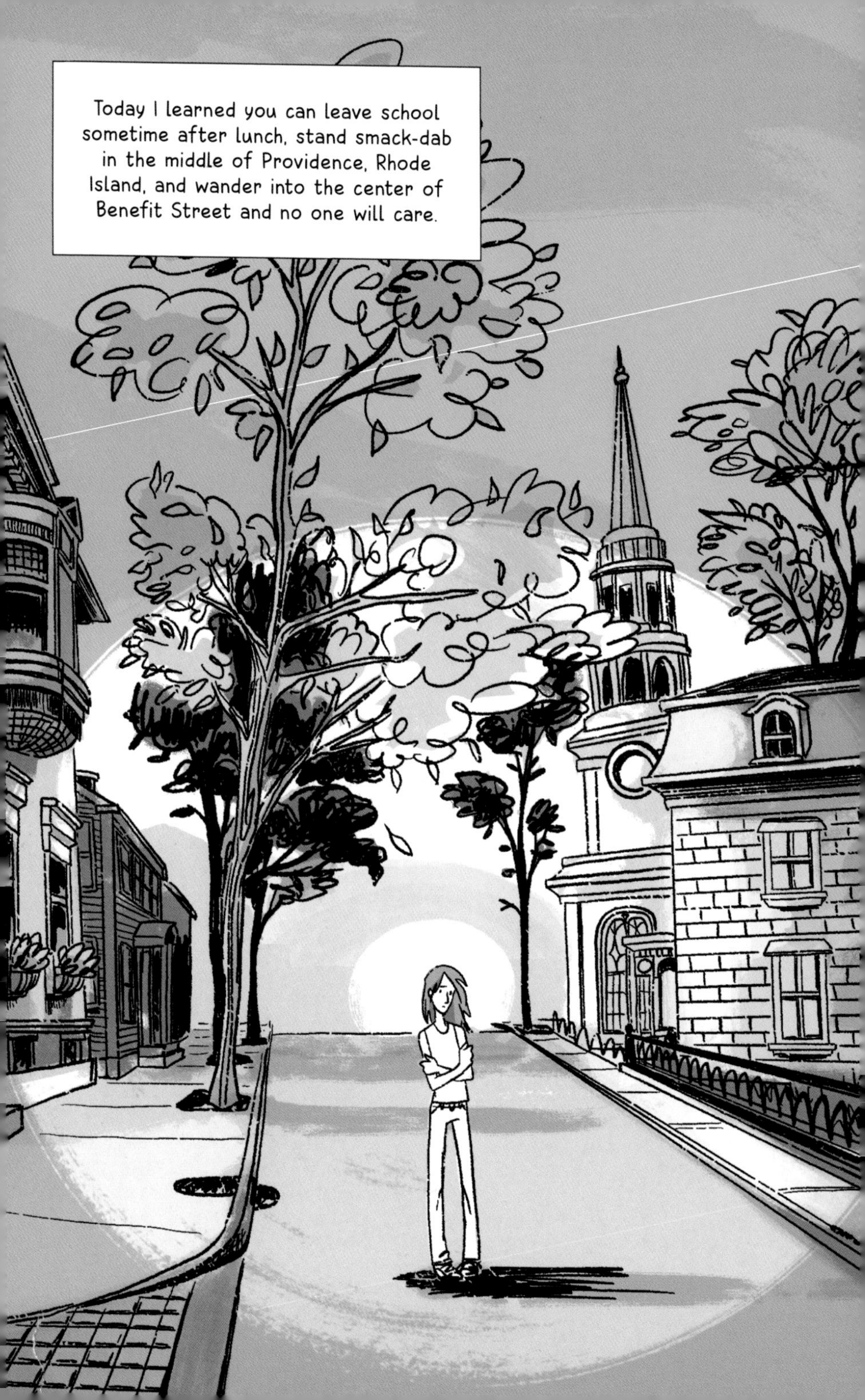
Today I learned you can leave school sometime after lunch, stand smack-dab in the middle of Providence, Rhode Island, and wander into the center of Benefit Street and no one will care.

THE NEXT DAY...

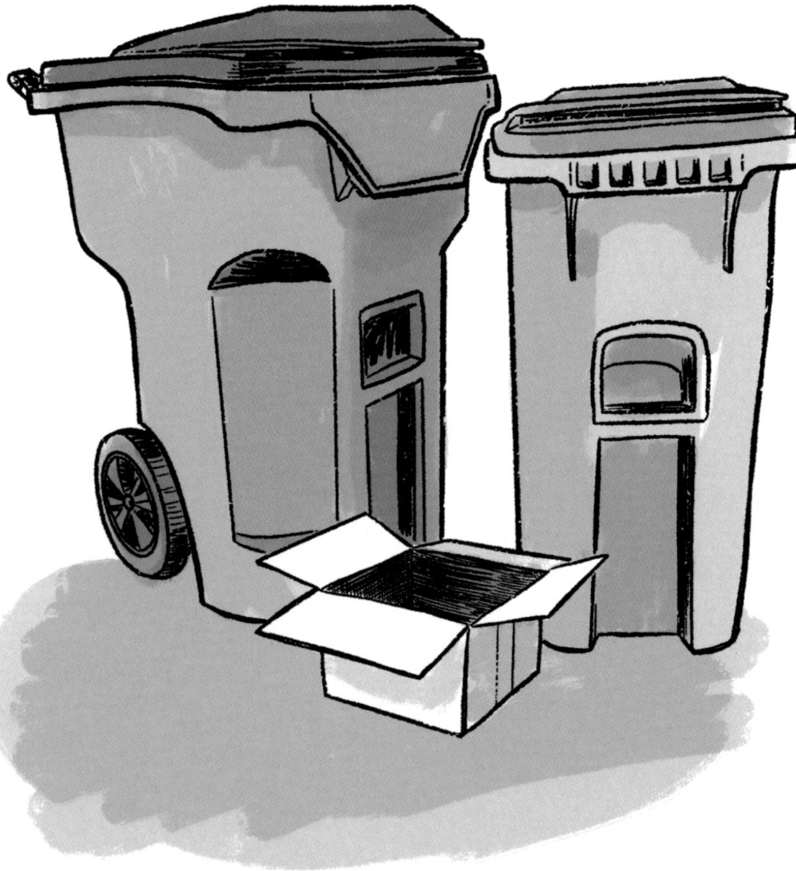

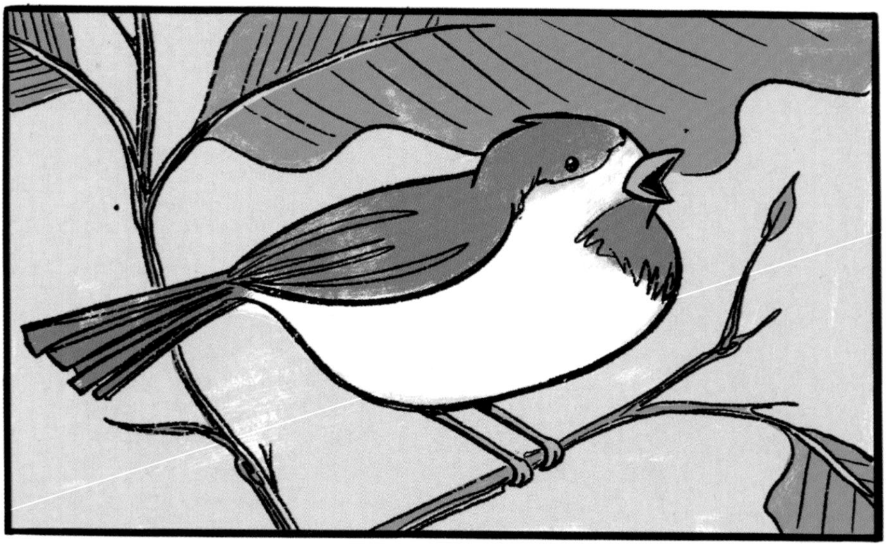

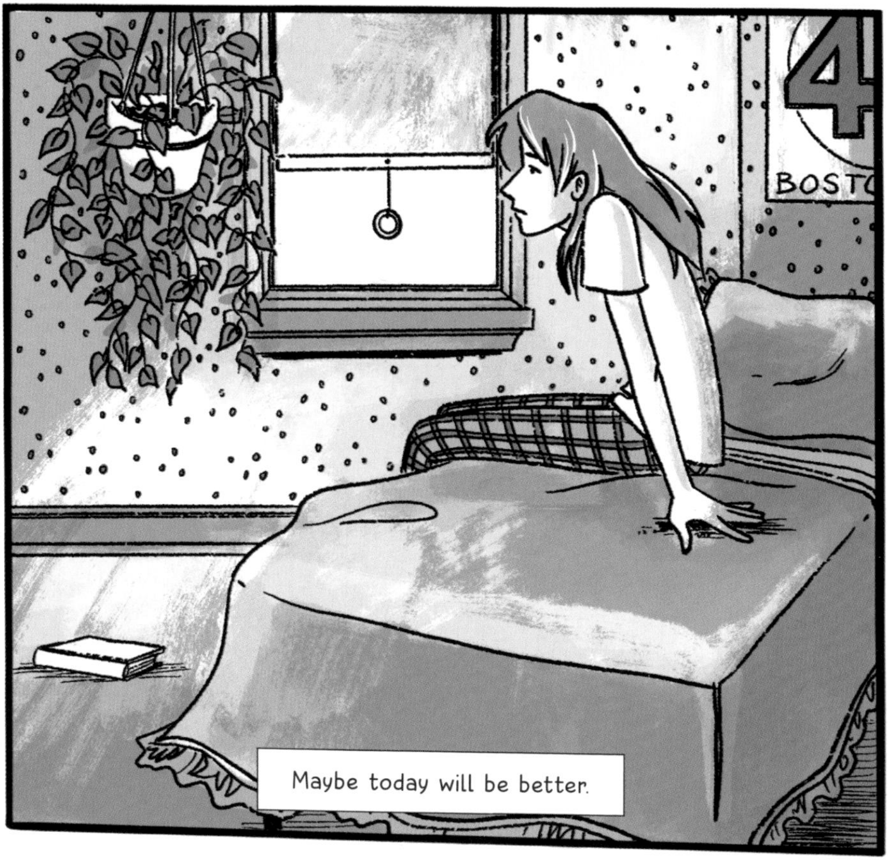
4
BOSTO
Maybe today will be better.

Hey, Gemma, you up yet?

Spoke too soon.

7th GRADE

Are you here to apologize for yesterday, Teddy? Because if you're not, I'm not interested in anything you have to say.

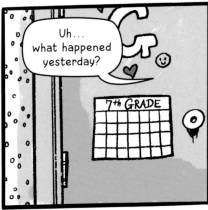

Uh... what happened yesterday?

7th GRADE

If you don't know, then you can forget about me doing anything for you ever again!

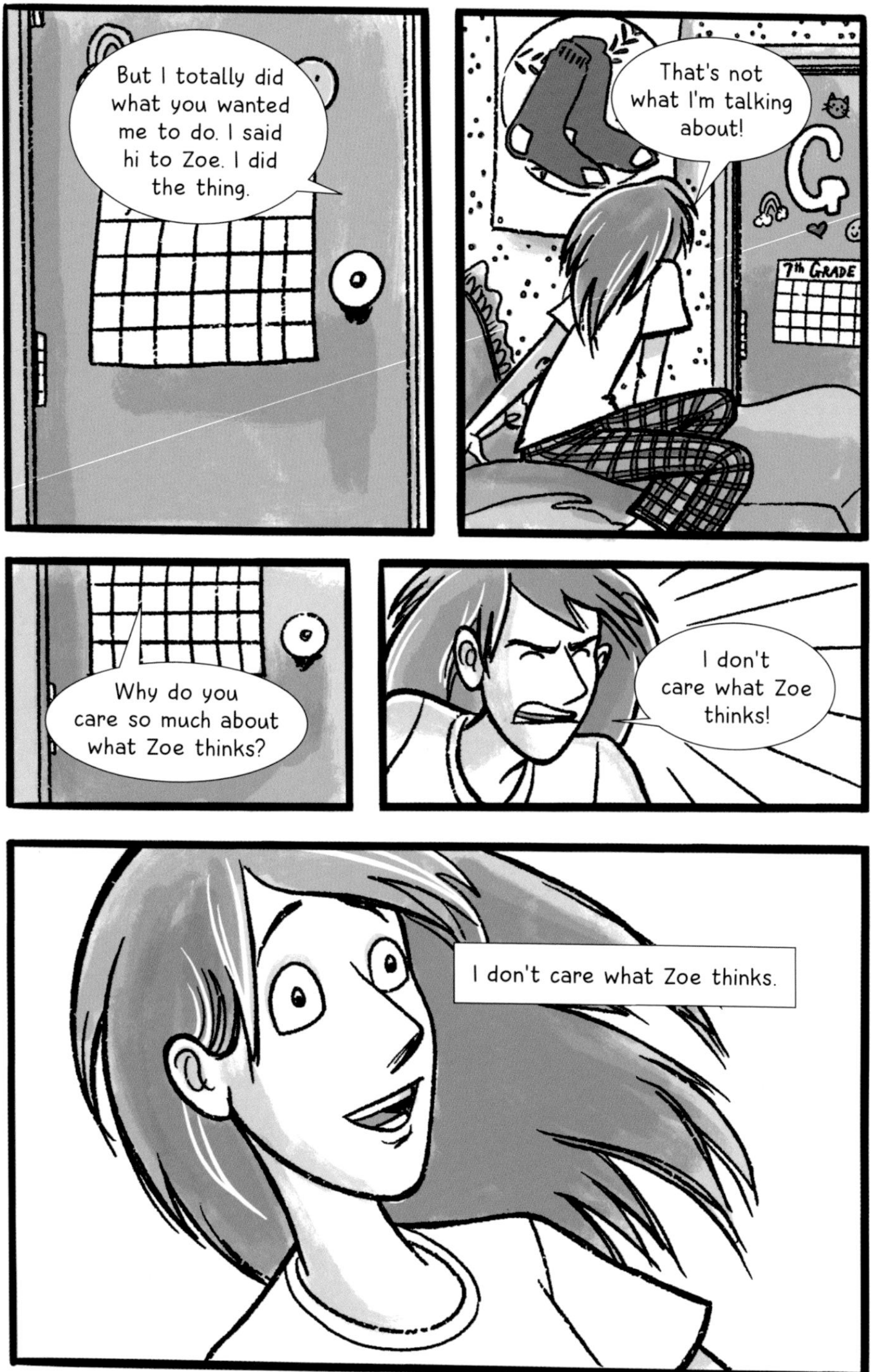
But I totally did what you wanted me to do. I said hi to Zoe. I did the thing.
That's not what I'm talking about!
7th GRADE
Why do you care so much about what Zoe thinks?
I don't care what Zoe thinks!
I don't care what Zoe thinks.

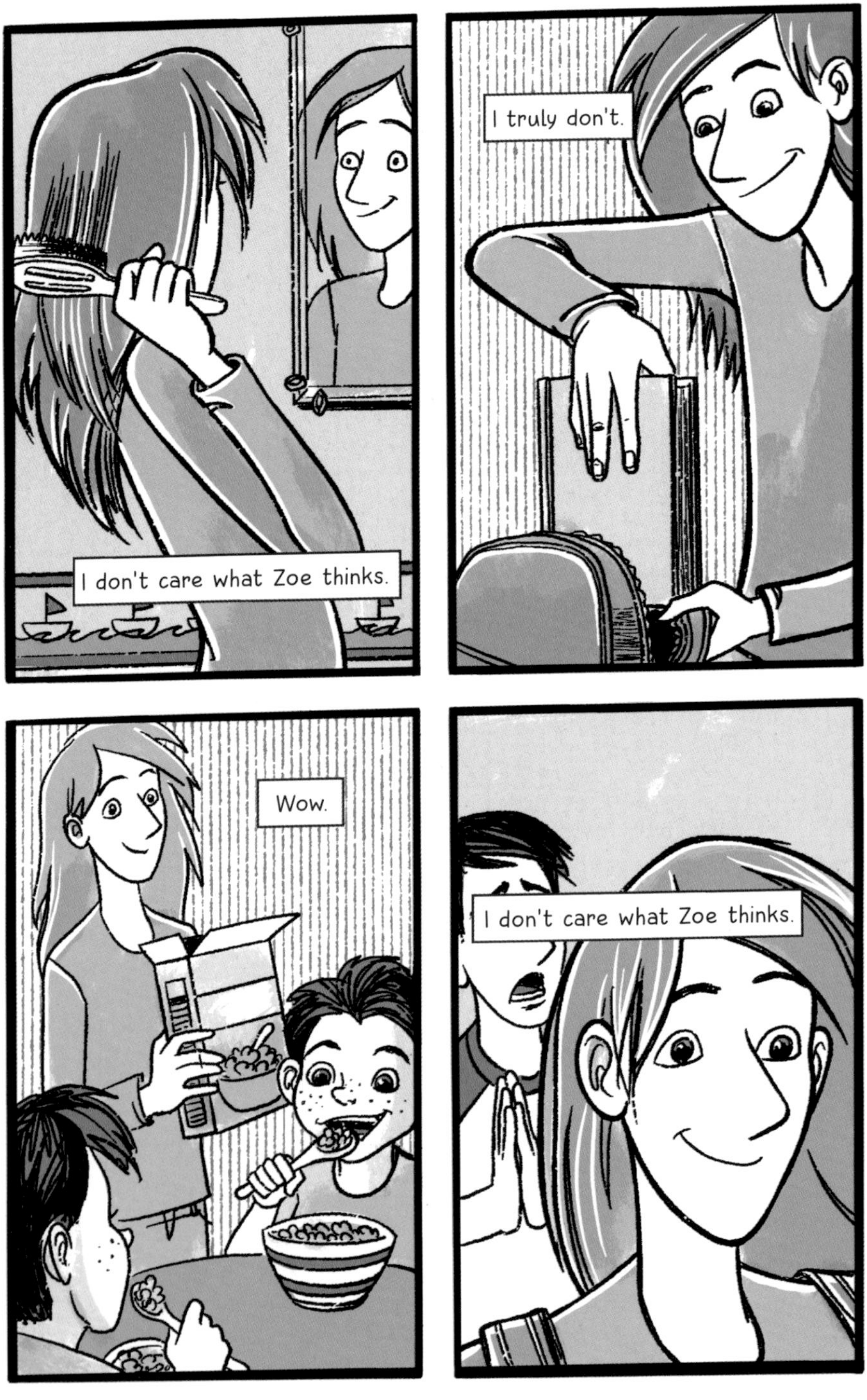
I don't care what Zoe thinks.
I truly don't.
Wow.
I don't care what Zoe thinks.

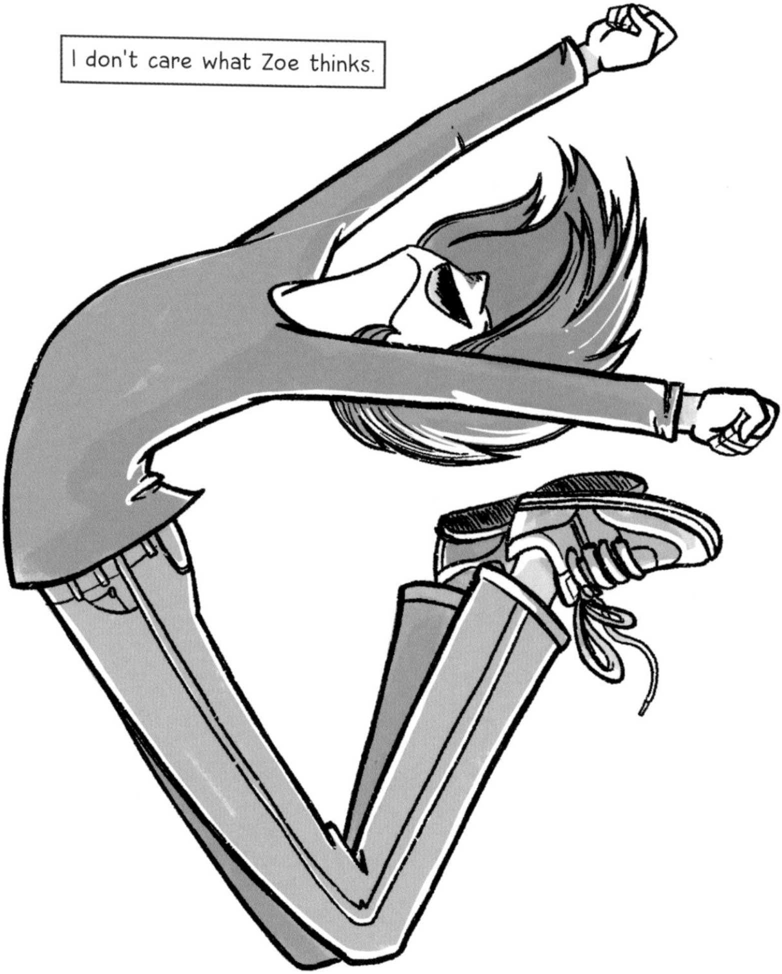
I don't care what Zoe thinks.

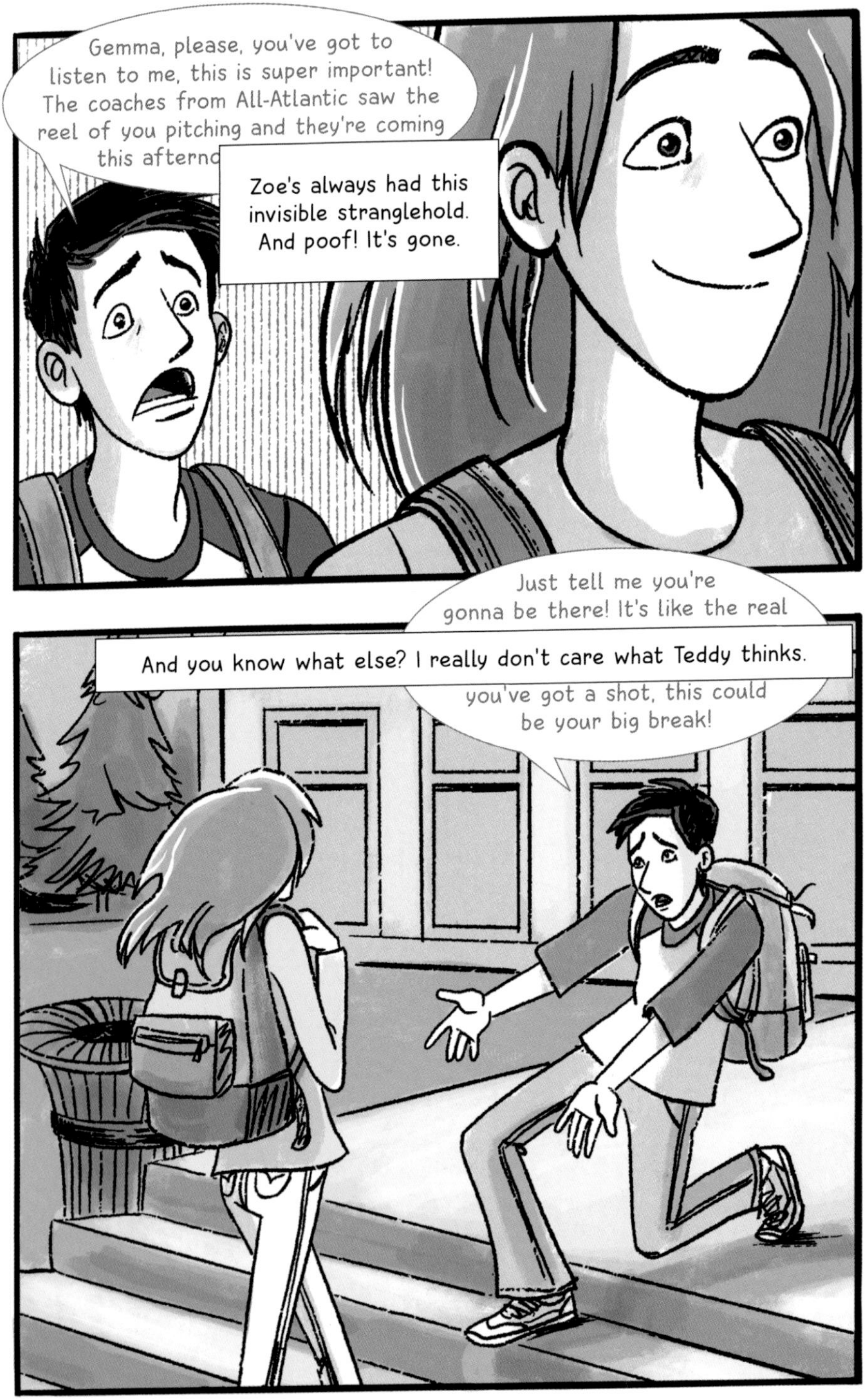
Gemma, please, you've got to listen to me, this is super important! The coaches from All-Atlantic saw the reel of you pitching and they're coming this aftern
Zoe's always had this invisible stranglehold. And poof! It's gone.
Just tell me you're gonna be there! It's like the real
And you know what else? I really don't care what Teddy thinks.
you've got a shot, this could be your big break!

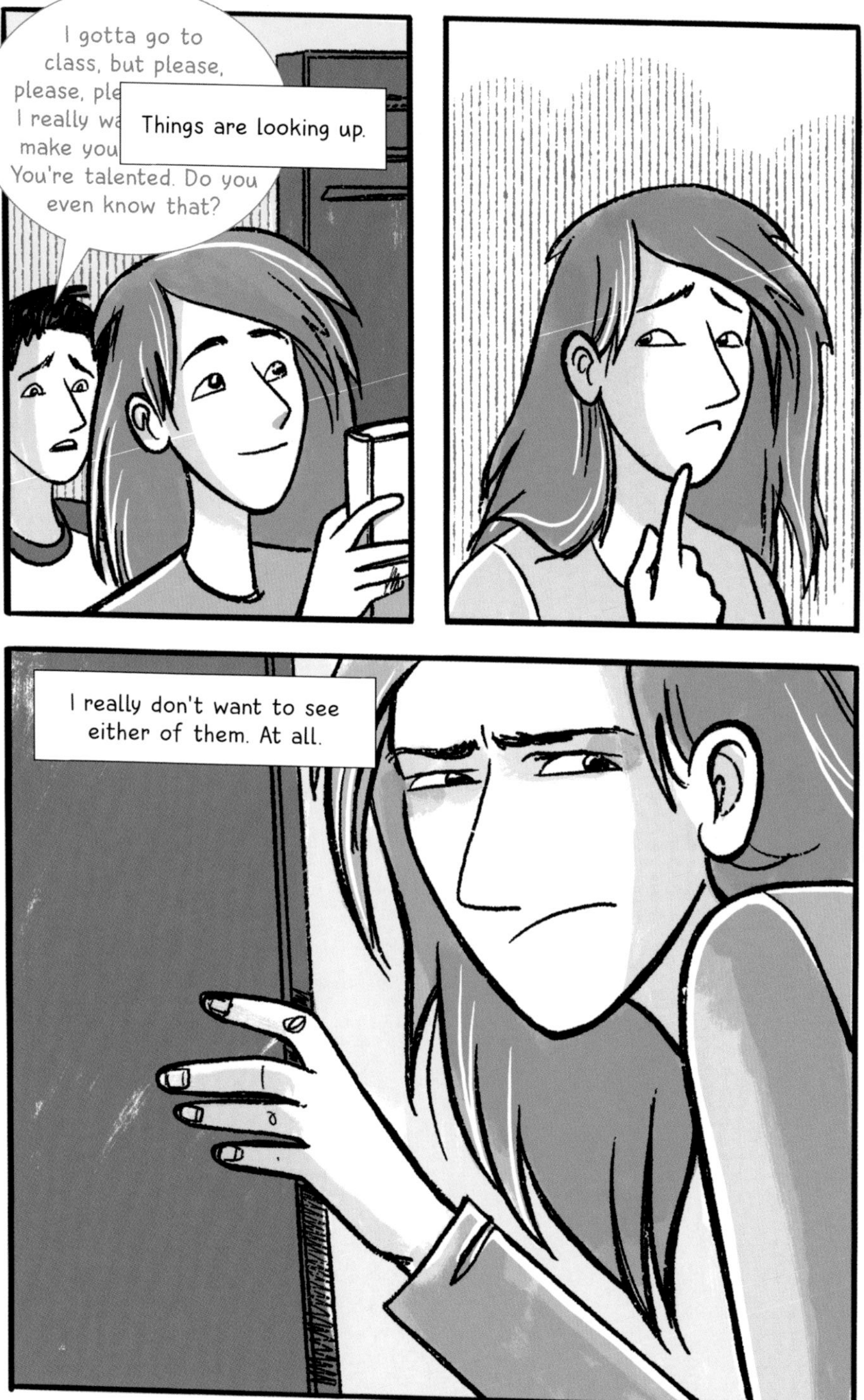

I gotta go to class, but please, please, ple
I really wa
make you
You're talented. Do you even know that?
Things are looking up.
I really don't want to see either of them. At all.

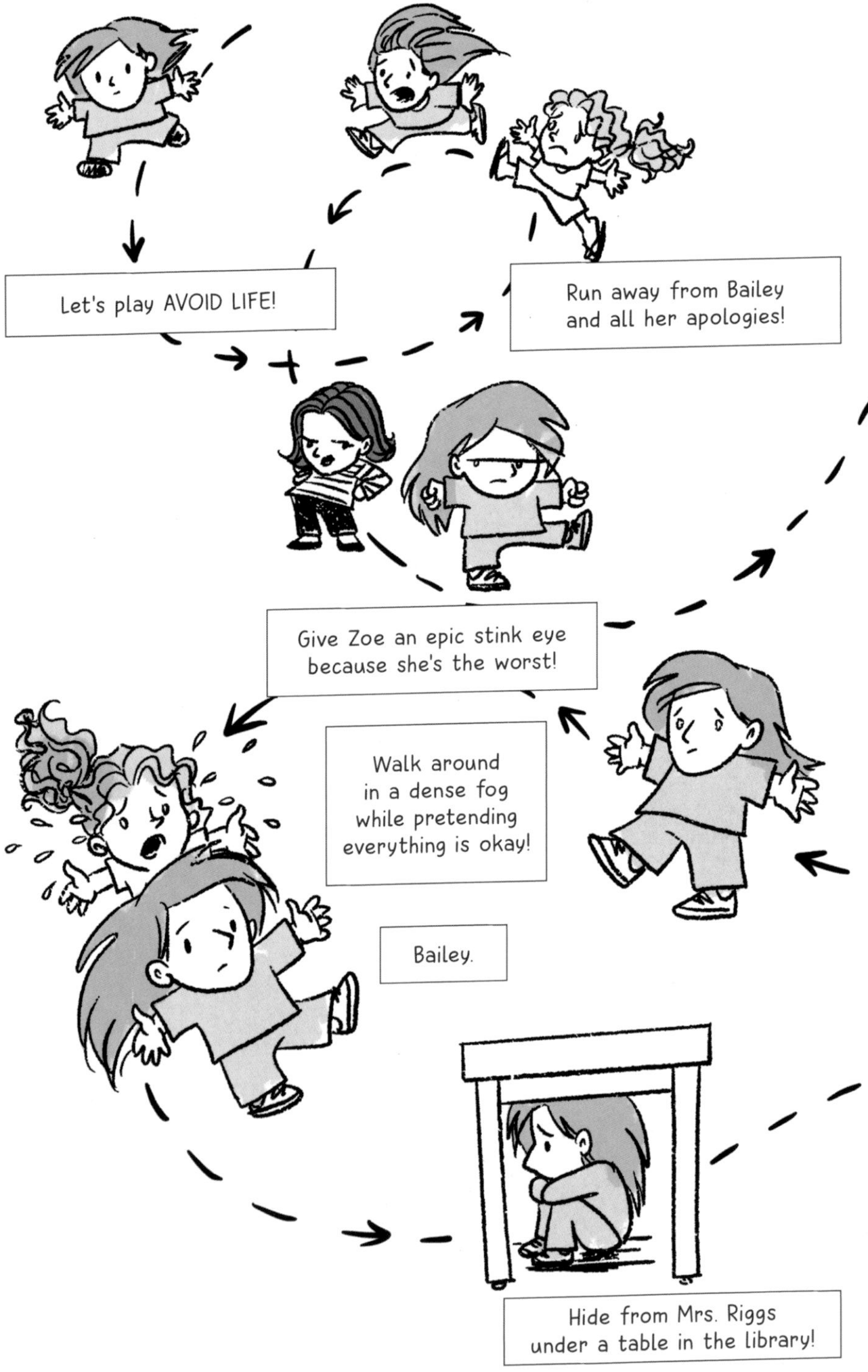
Let's play AVOID LIFE!
Run away from Bailey and all her apologies!
Give Zoe an epic stink eye because she's the worst!
Walk around in a dense fog while pretending everything is okay!
Bailey.
Hide from Mrs. Riggs under a table in the library!

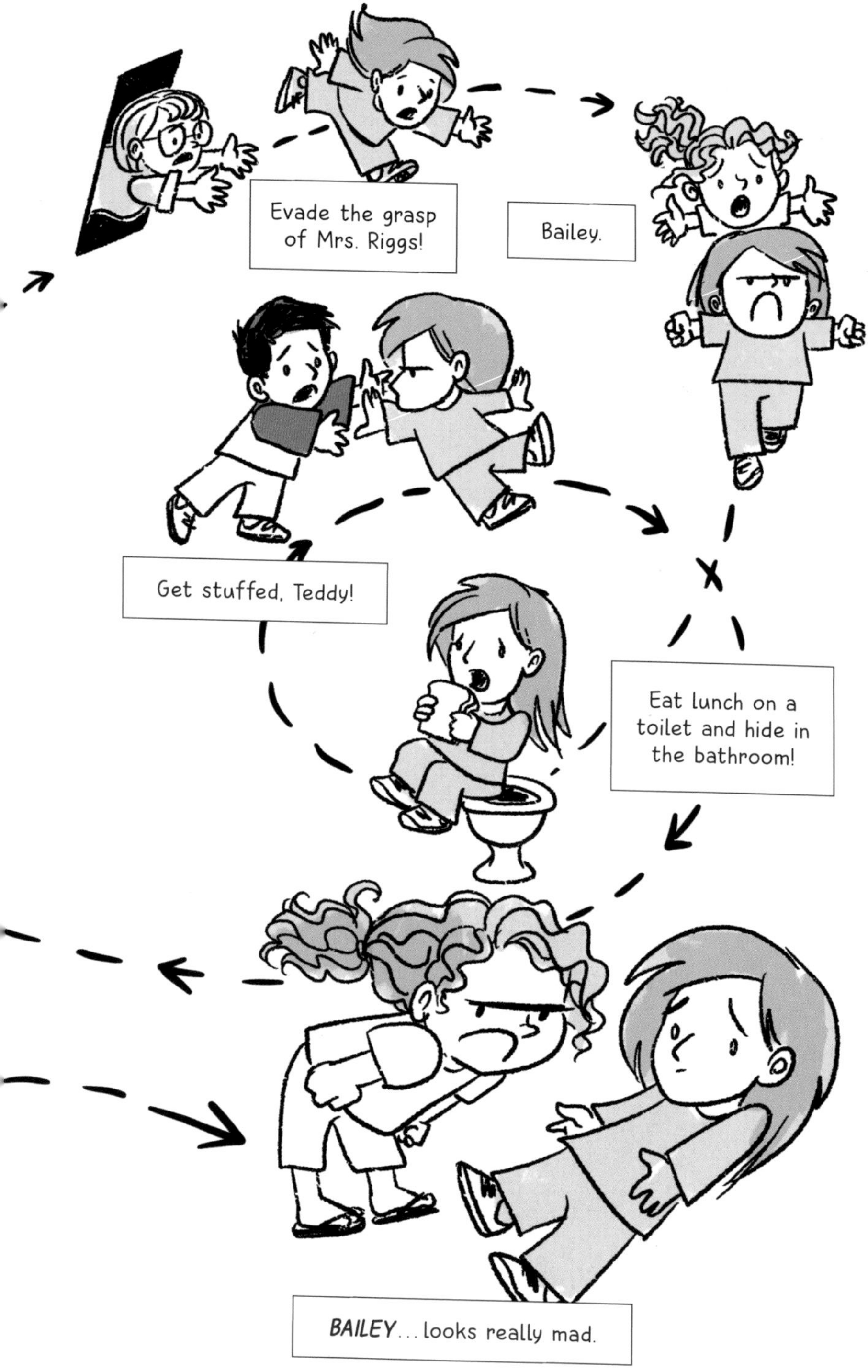
Evade the grasp of Mrs. Riggs!
Bailey.
Get stuffed, Teddy!
Eat lunch on a toilet and hide in the bathroom!
BAILEY... looks really mad.

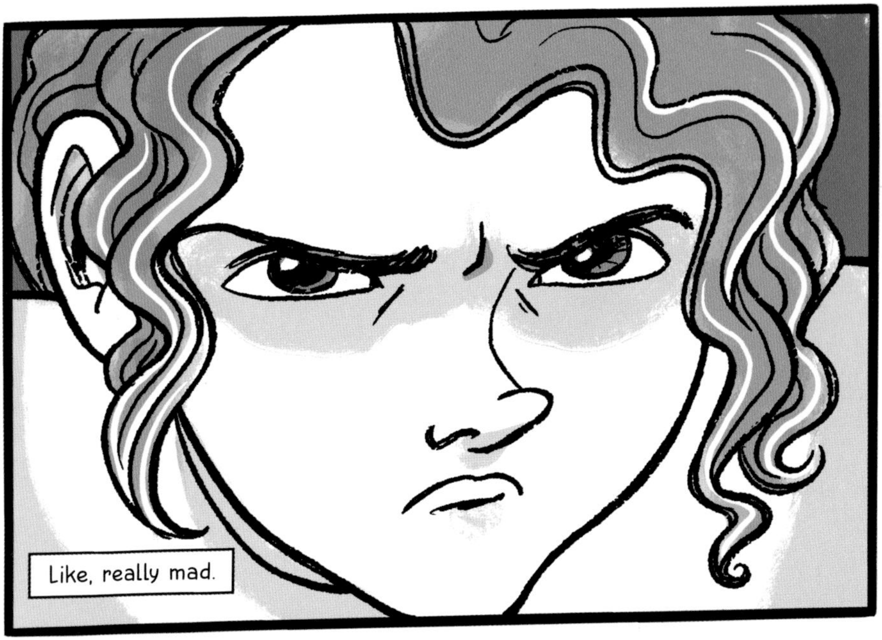
Like, really mad.

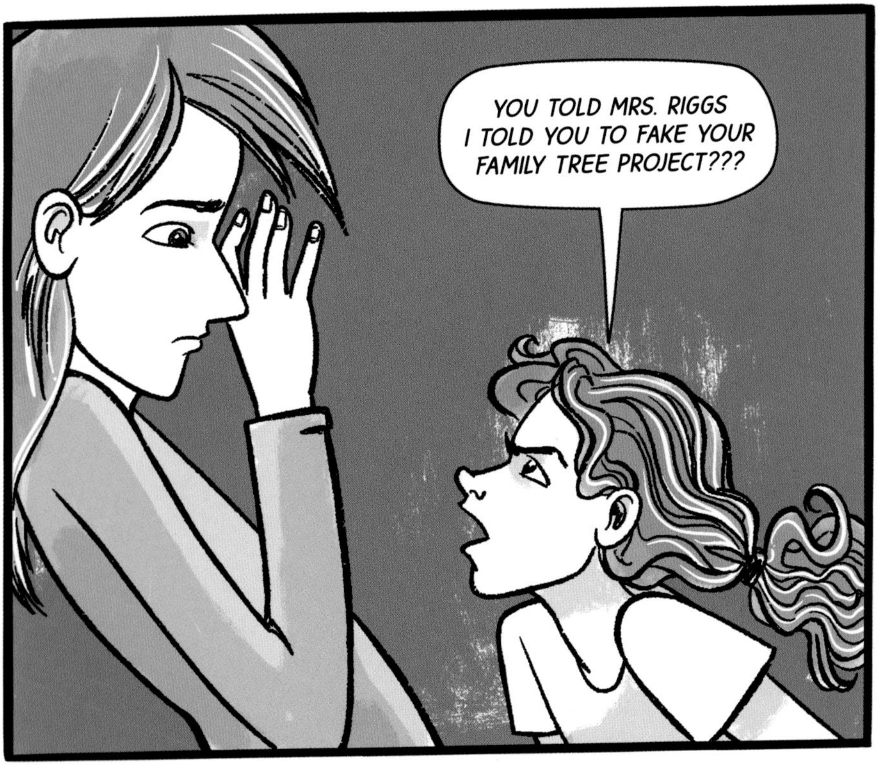
YOU TOLD MRS. RIGGS I TOLD YOU TO FAKE YOUR FAMILY TREE PROJECT???

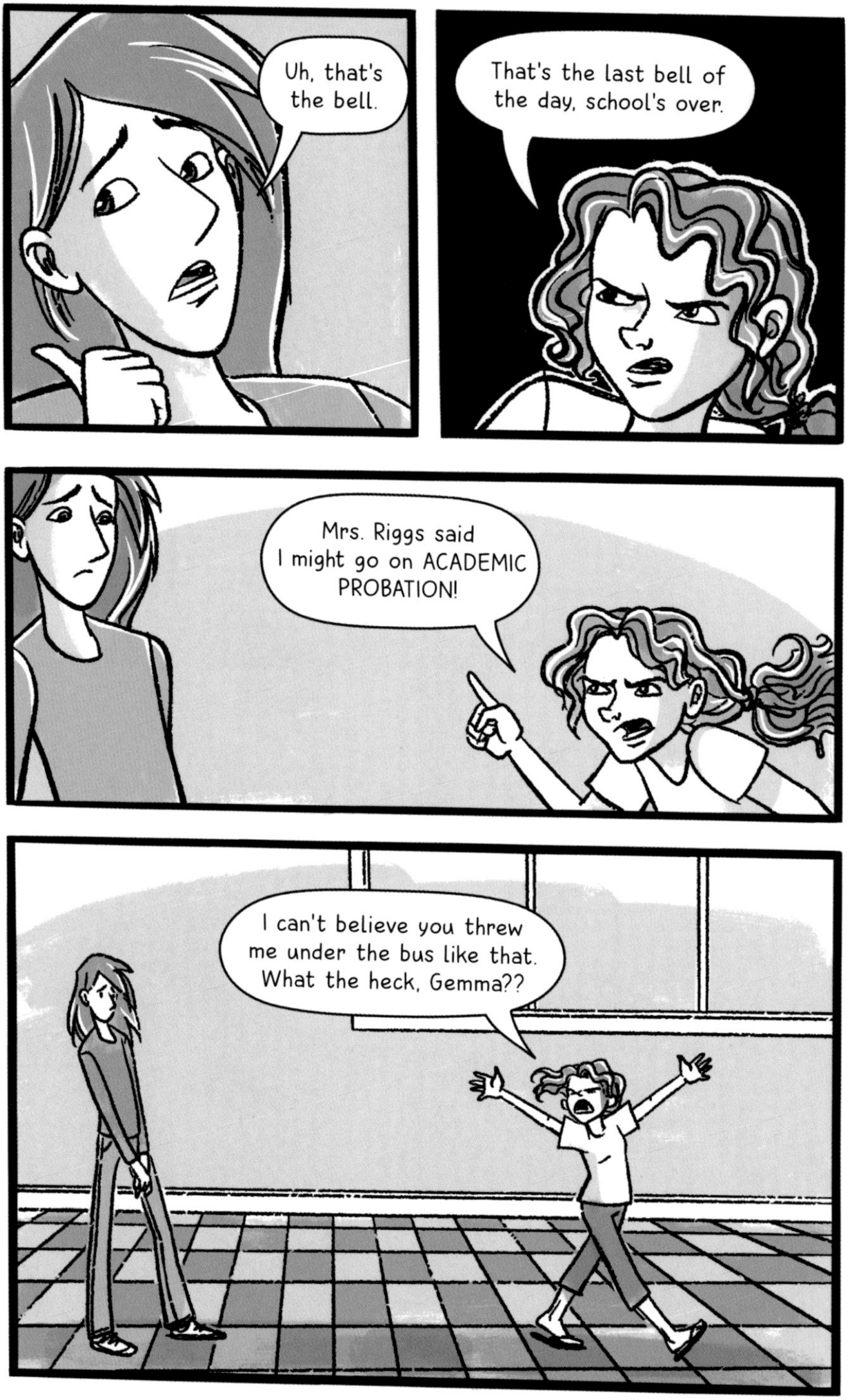
Uh, that's the bell.
That's the last bell of the day, school's over.
Mrs. Riggs said I might go on ACADEMIC PROBATION!
I can't believe you threw me under the bus like that. What the heck, Gemma??

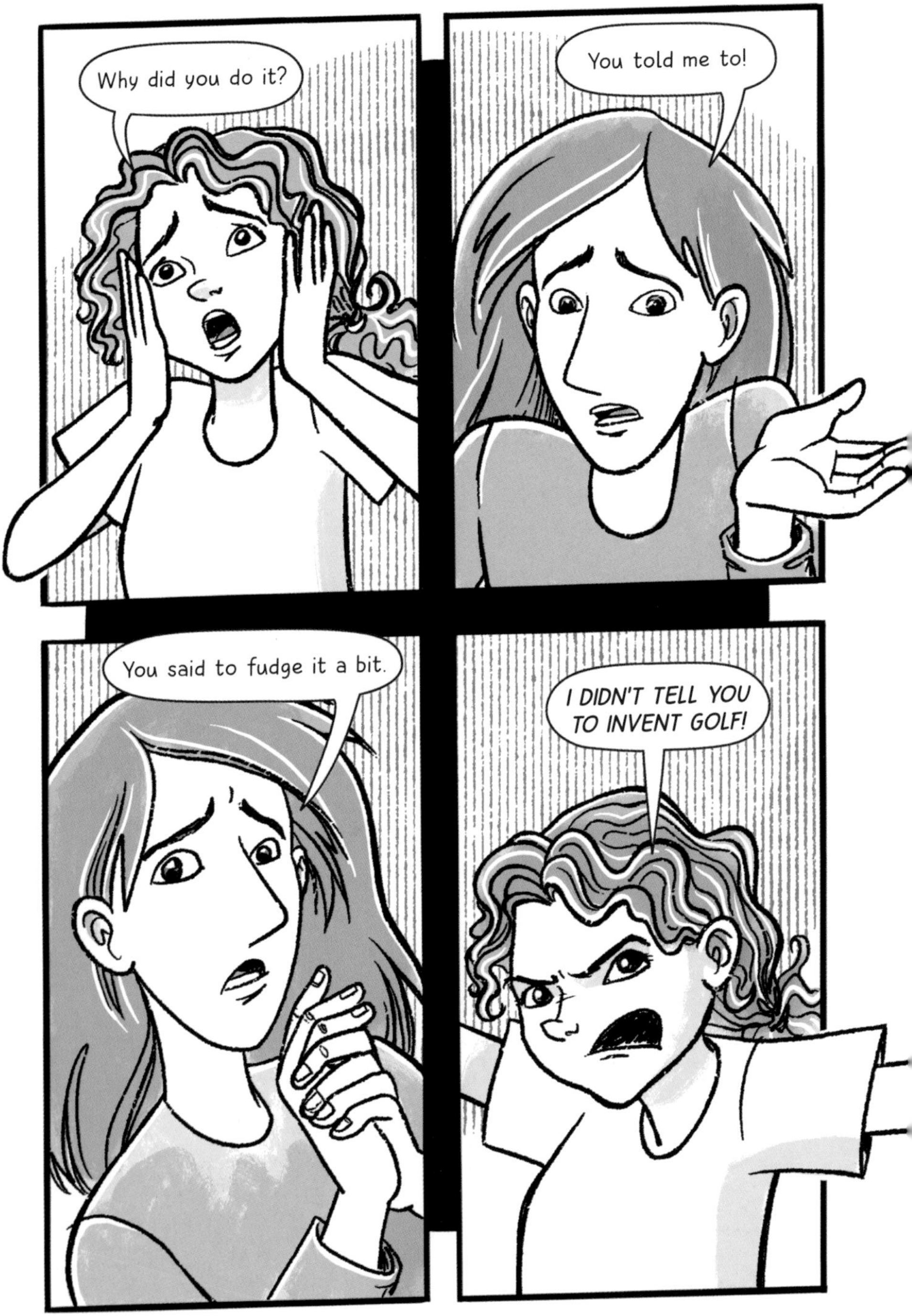

Why did you do it?
You told me to!
You said to fudge it a bit.
I DIDN'T TELL YOU TO INVENT GOLF!

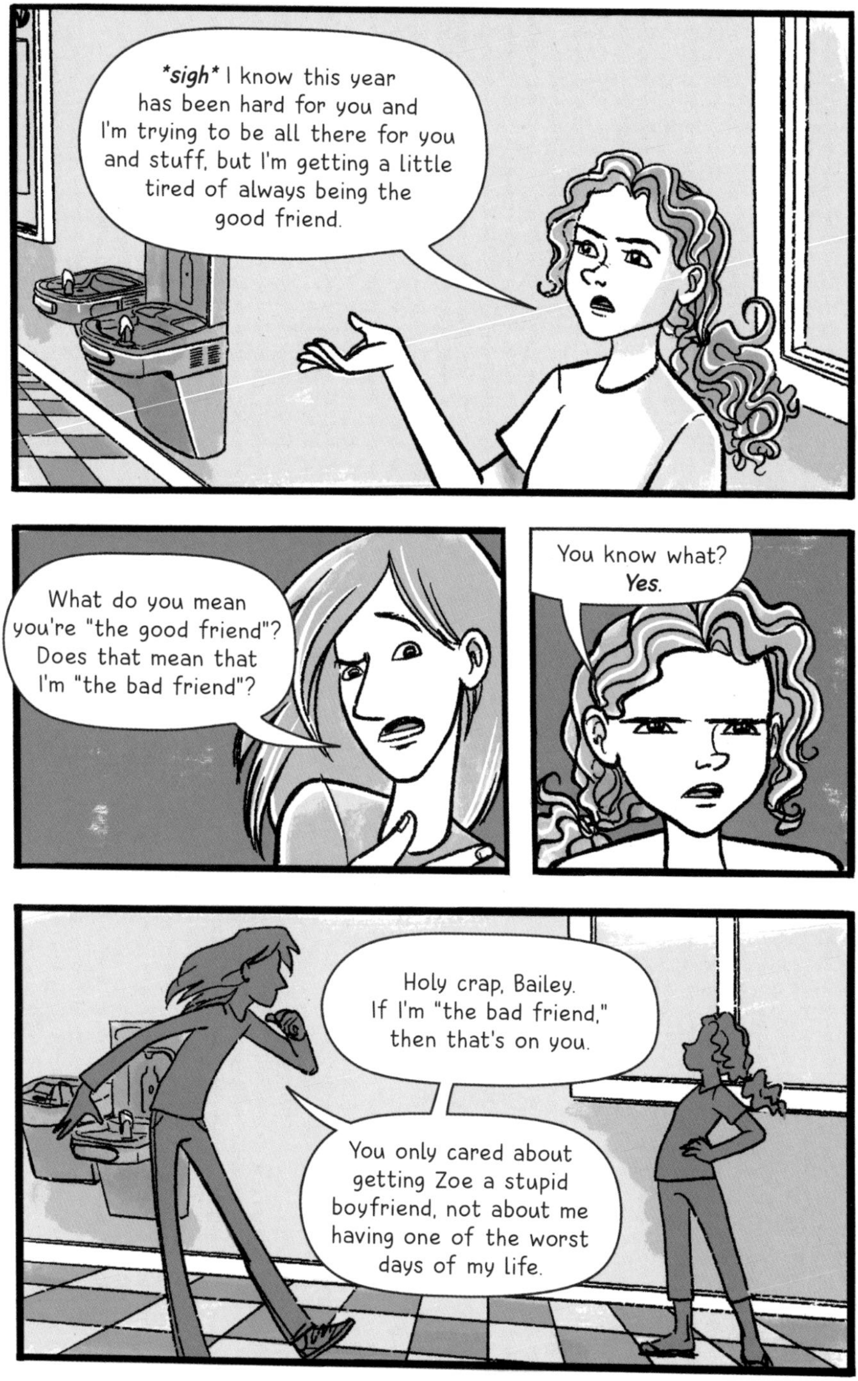
sigh I know this year has been hard for you and I'm trying to be all there for you and stuff, but I'm getting a little tired of always being the good friend.
What do you mean you're "the good friend"? Does that mean that I'm "the bad friend"?
You know what? **Yes.**
Holy crap, Bailey. If I'm "the bad friend," then that's on you.
You only cared about getting Zoe a stupid boyfriend, not about me having one of the worst days of my life.

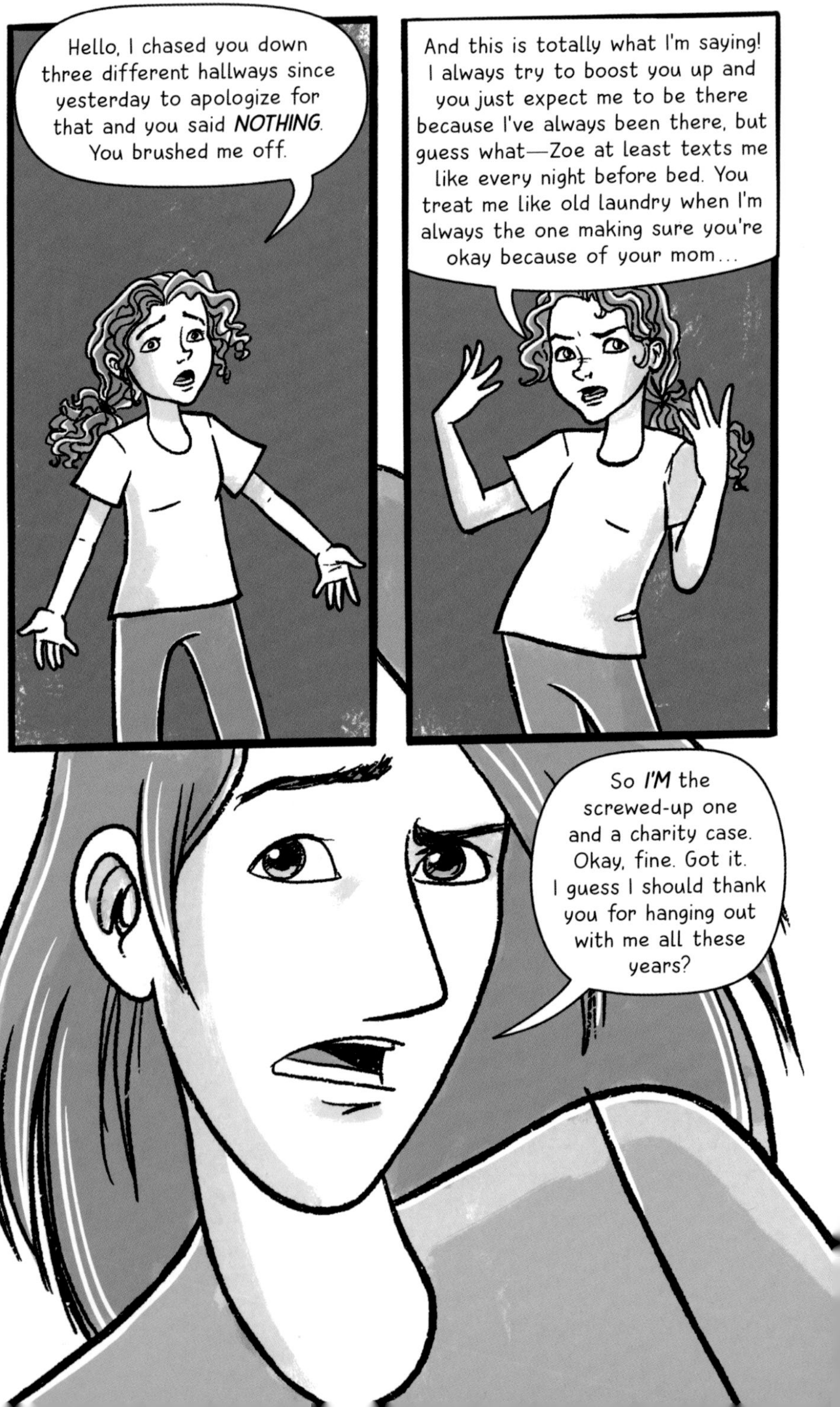
Hello, I chased you down three different hallways since yesterday to apologize for that and you said NOTHING. You brushed me off.
And this is totally what I'm saying! I always try to boost you up and you just expect me to be there because I've always been there, but guess what—Zoe at least texts me like every night before bed. You treat me like old laundry when I'm always the one making sure you're okay because of your mom...
So I'M the screwed-up one and a charity case. Okay, fine. Got it. I guess I should thank you for hanging out with me all these years?

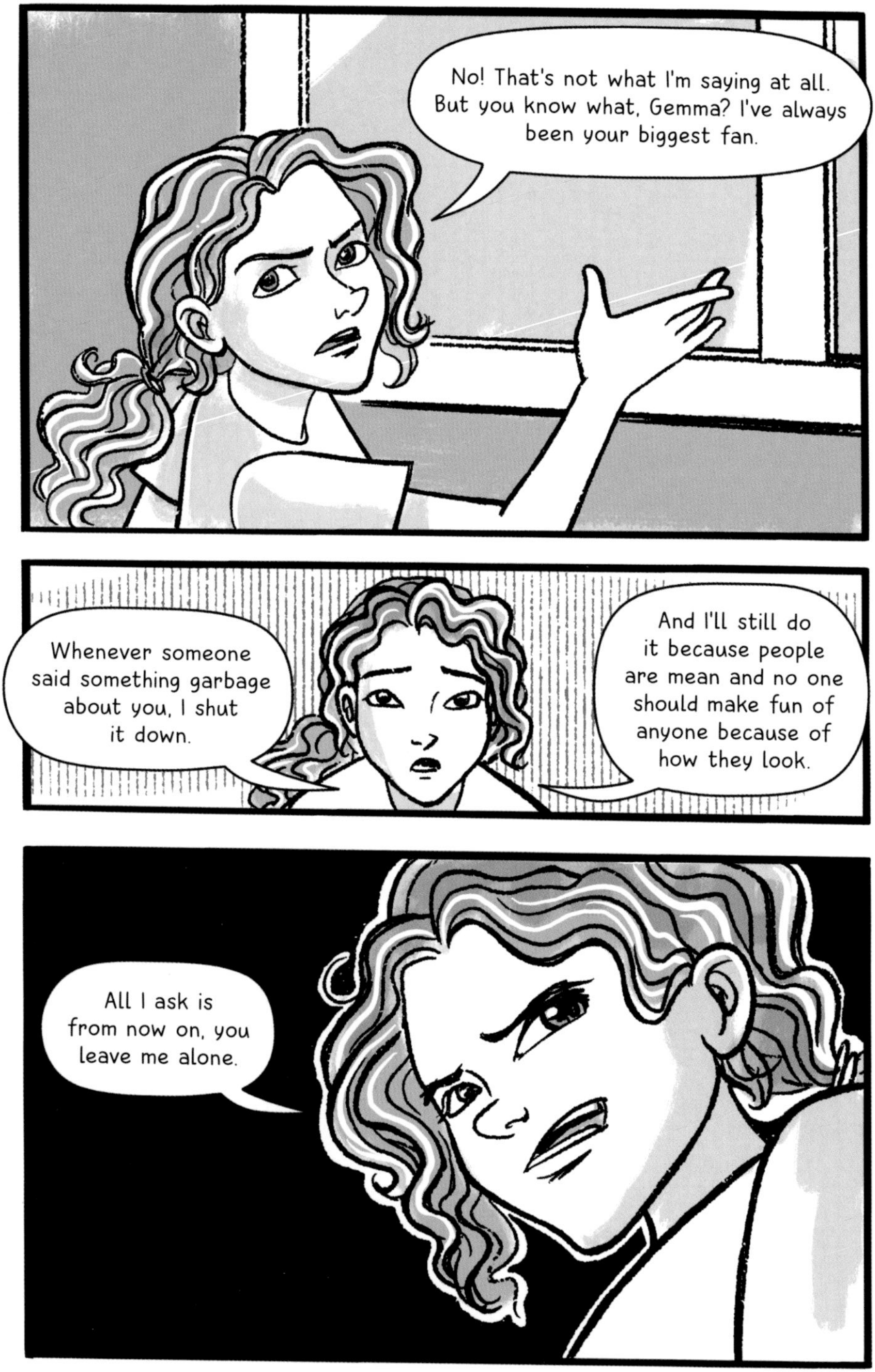
No! That's not what I'm saying at all. But you know what, Gemma? I've always been your biggest fan.
Whenever someone said something garbage about you, I shut it down.
And I'll still do it because people are mean and no one should make fun of anyone because of how they look.
All I ask is from now on, you leave me alone.

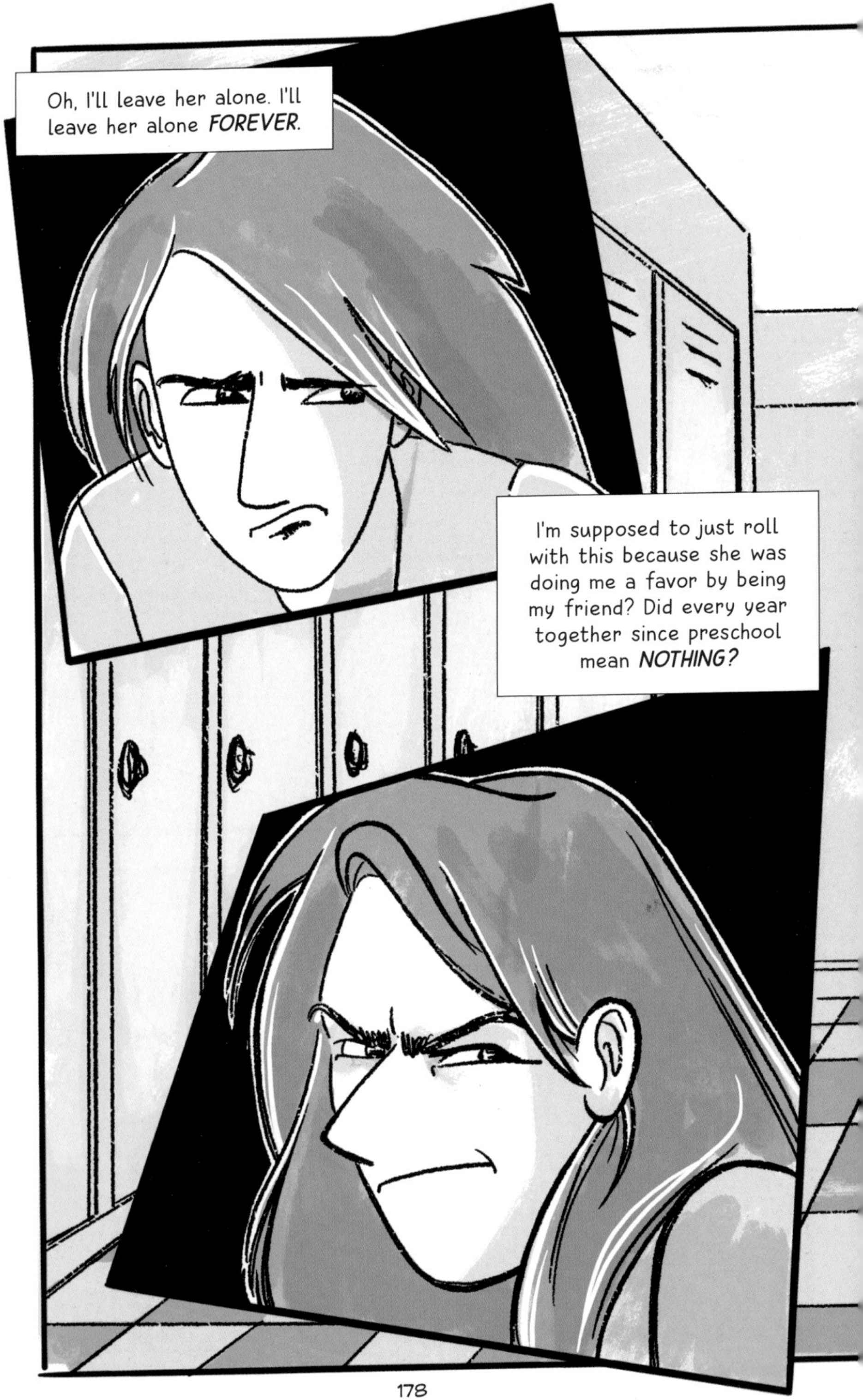
Oh, I'll leave her alone. I'll leave her alone *FOREVER.*
I'm supposed to just roll with this because she was doing me a favor by being my friend? Did every year together since preschool mean *NOTHING?*

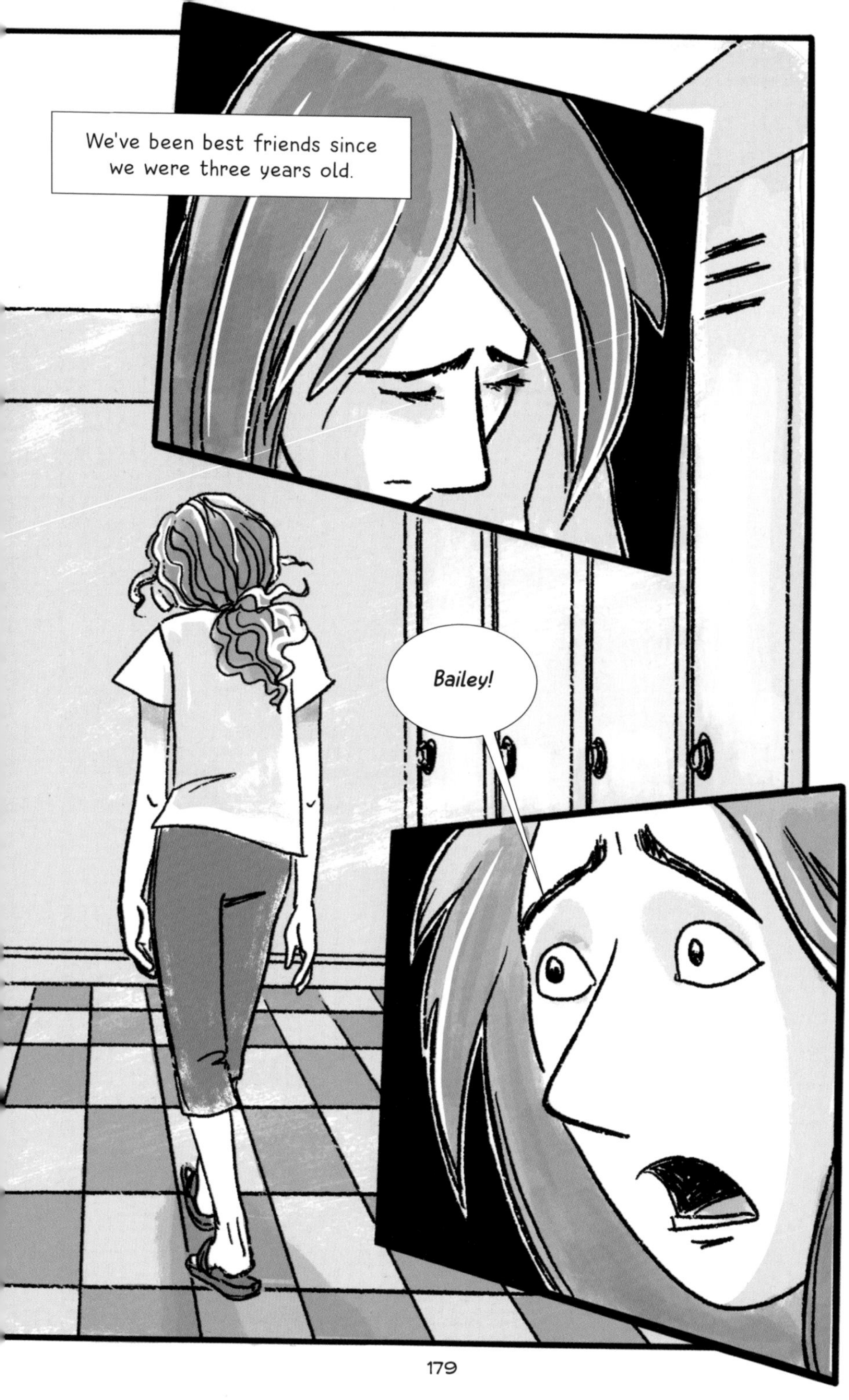
We've been best friends since we were three years old.
Bailey!

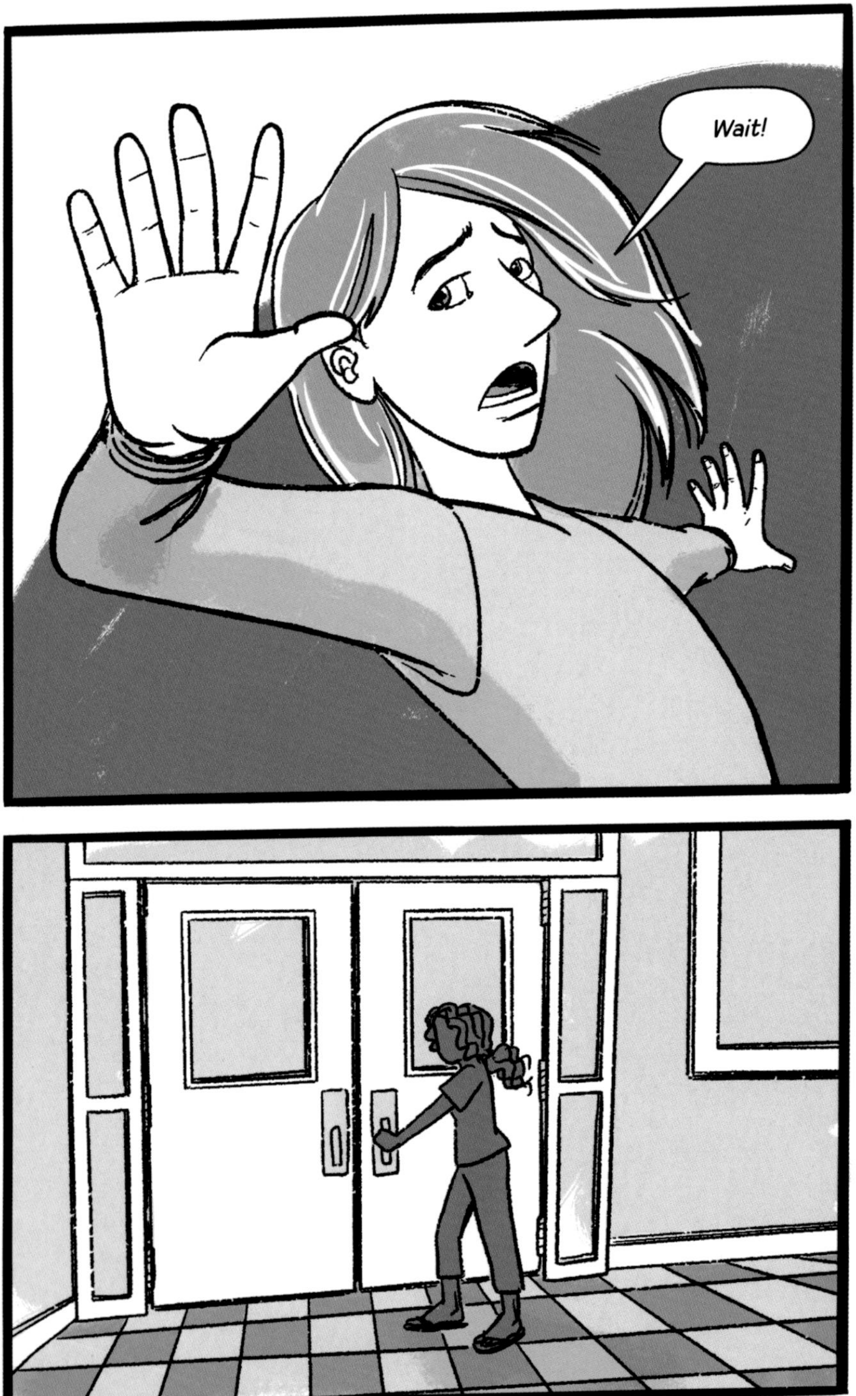
Wait!

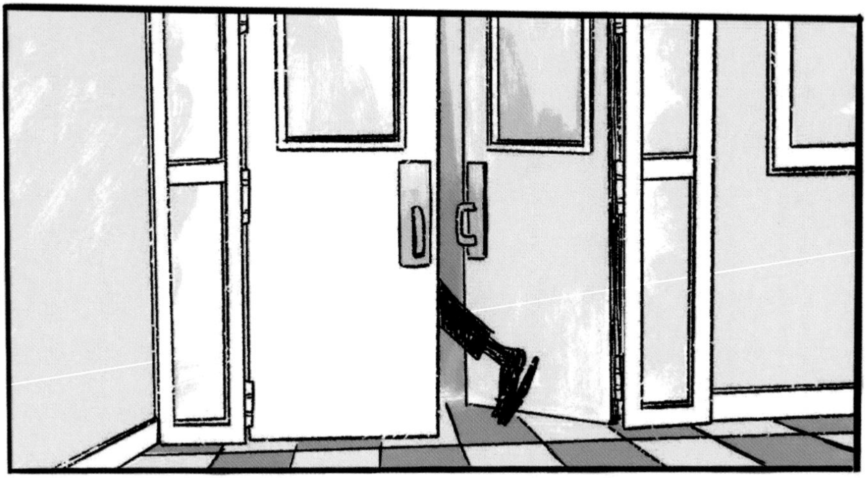

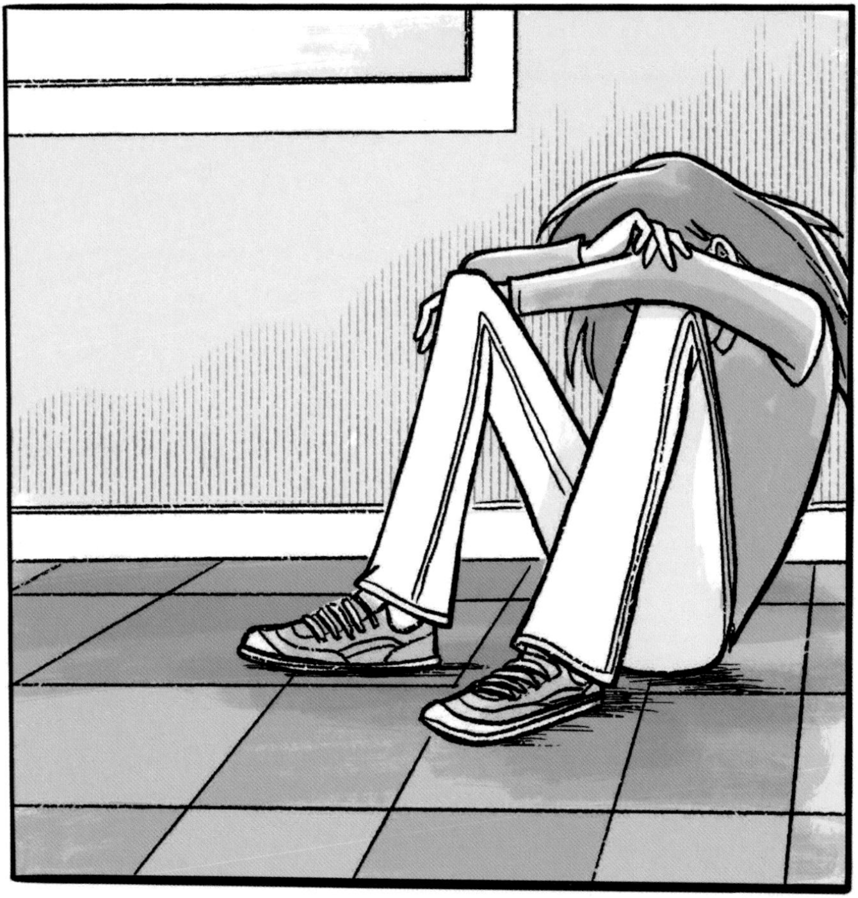

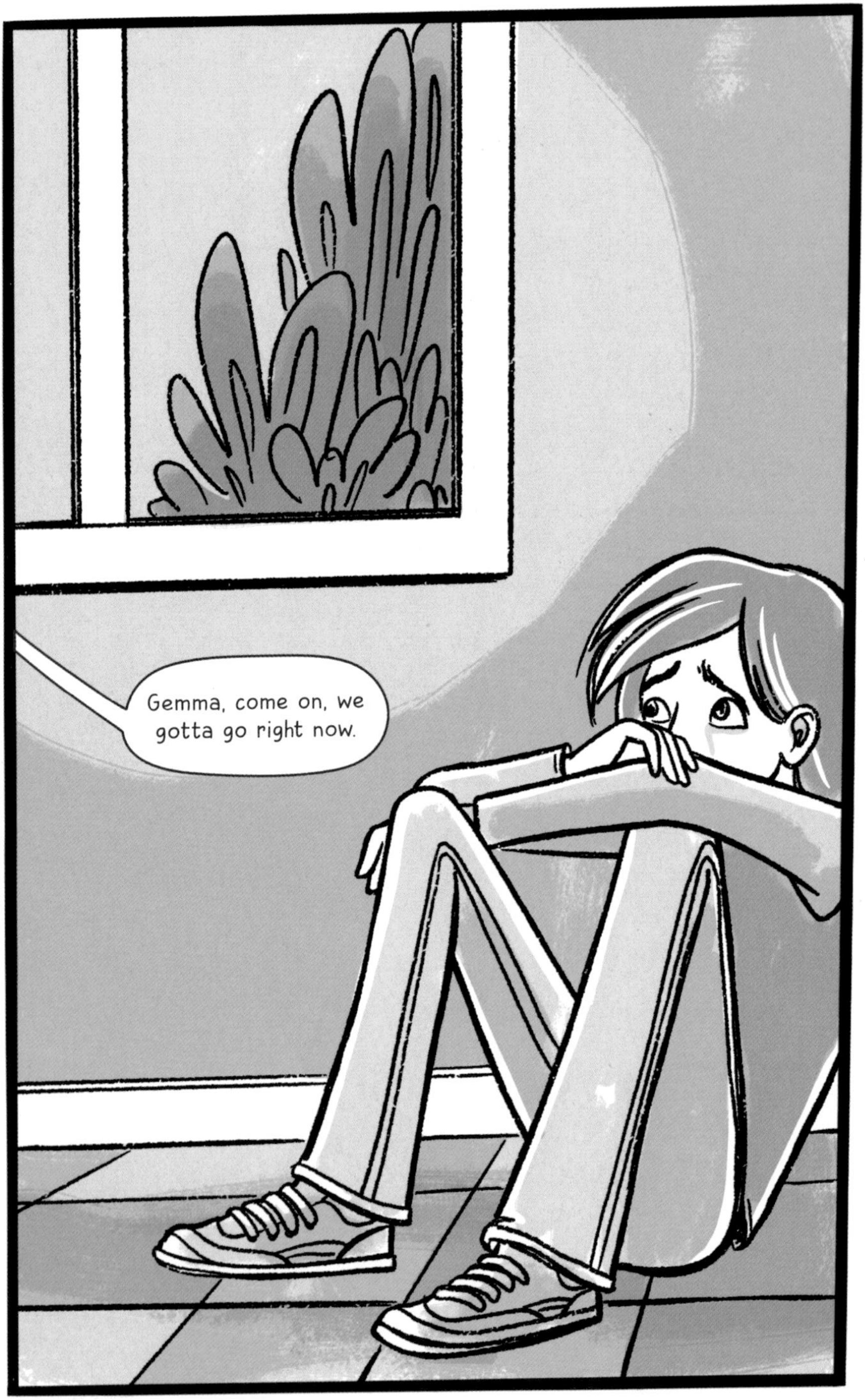
Gemma, come on, we gotta go right now.

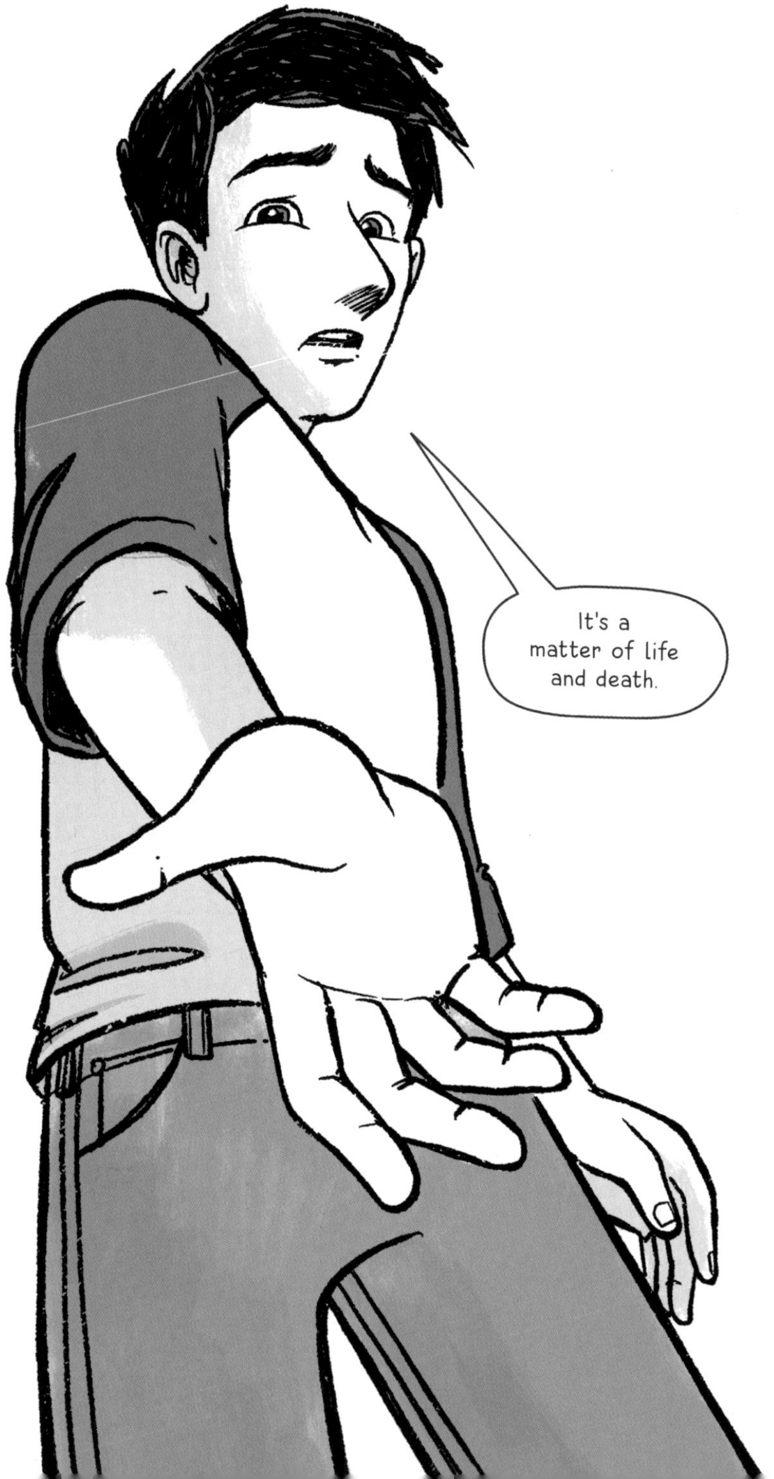
It's a matter of life and death.

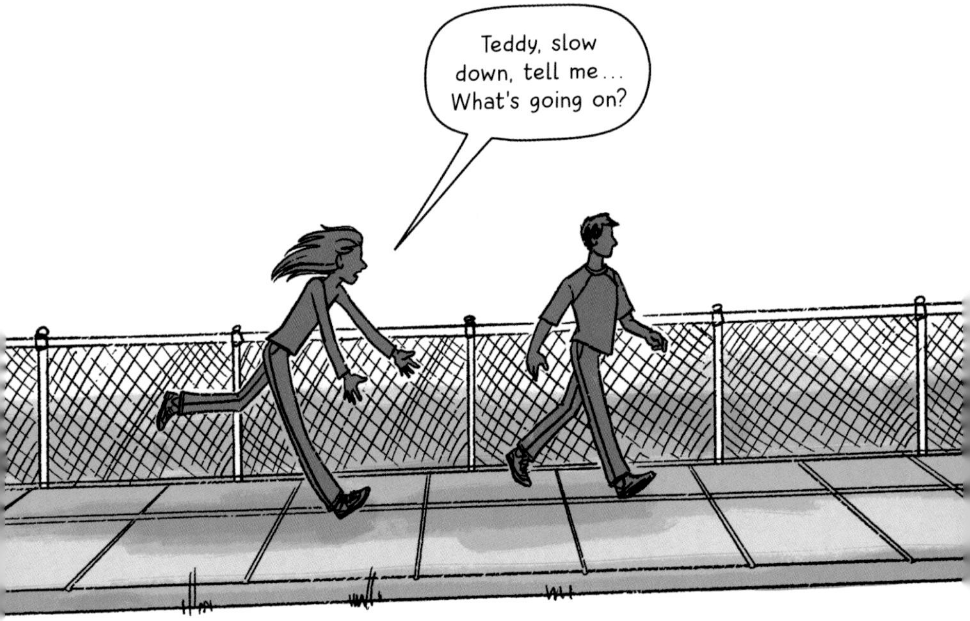
Teddy, slow down, tell me... What's going on?

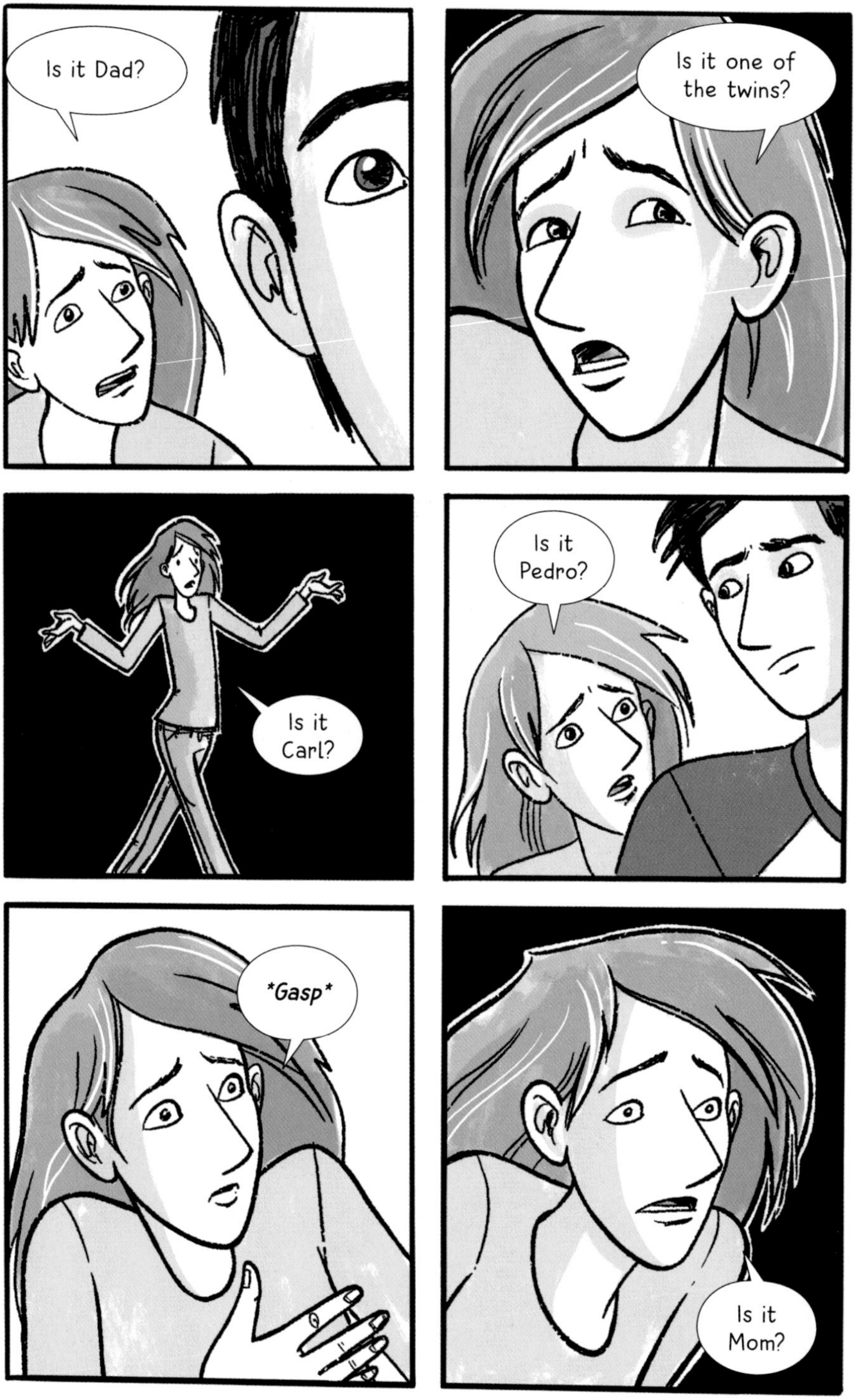
Is it Dad?
Is it one of the twins?
Is it Carl?
Is it Pedro?
Gasp
Is it Mom?

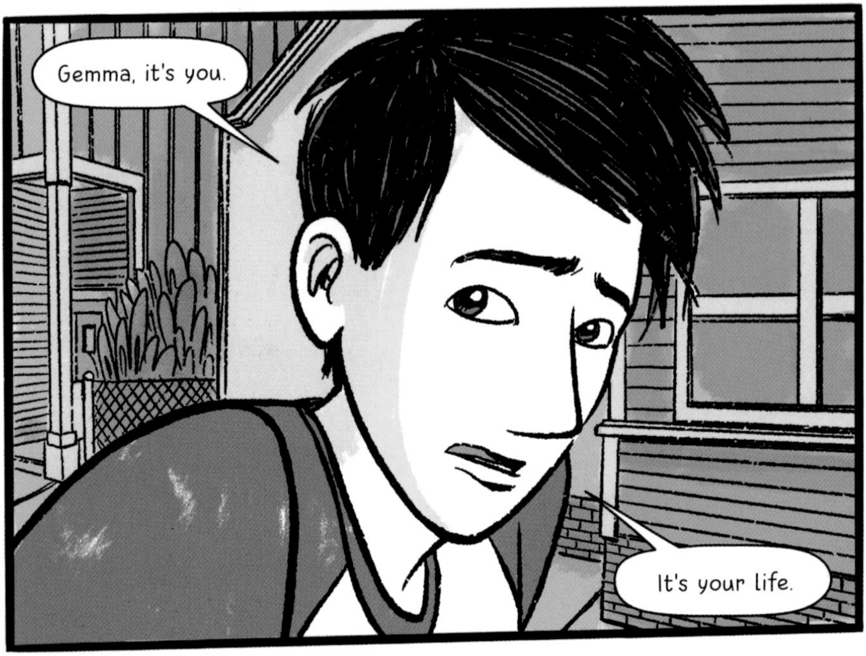
Gemma, it's you.
It's your life.

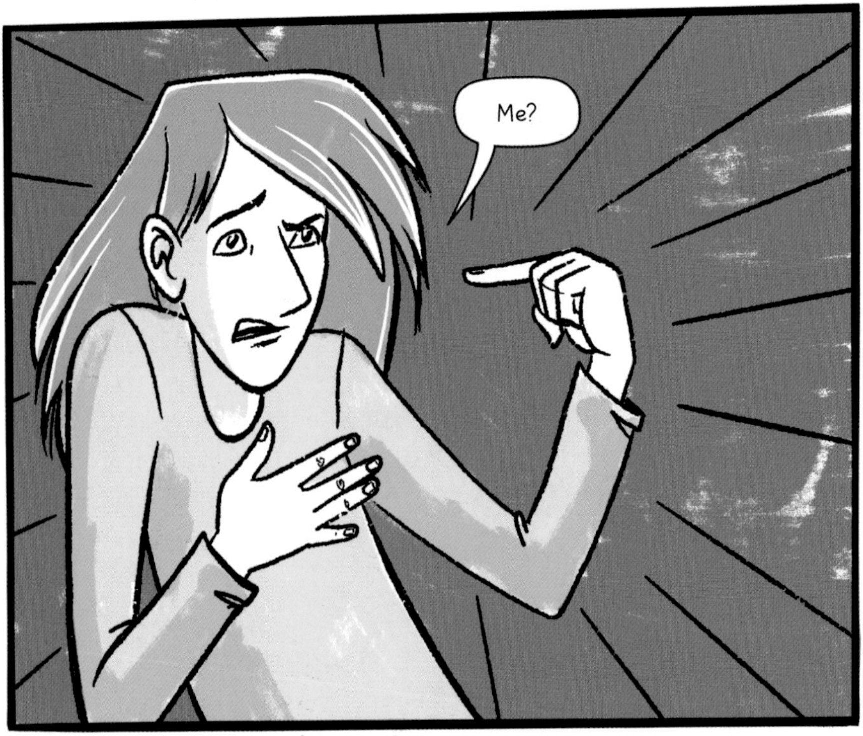
Me?

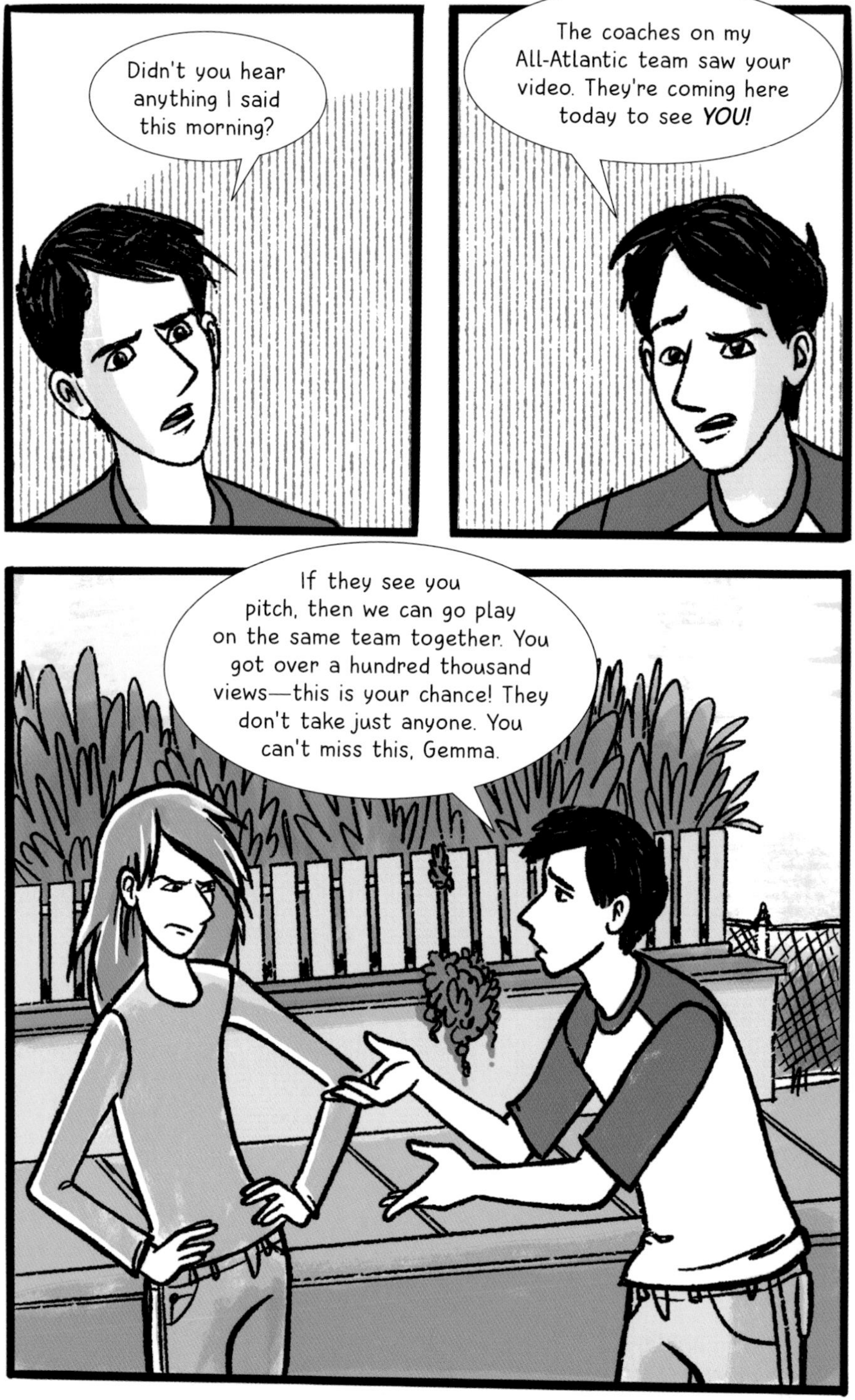
Didn't you hear anything I said this morning?
The coaches on my All-Atlantic team saw your video. They're coming here today to see *YOU!*
If they see you pitch, then we can go play on the same team together. You got over a hundred thousand views—this is your chance! They don't take just anyone. You can't miss this, Gemma.

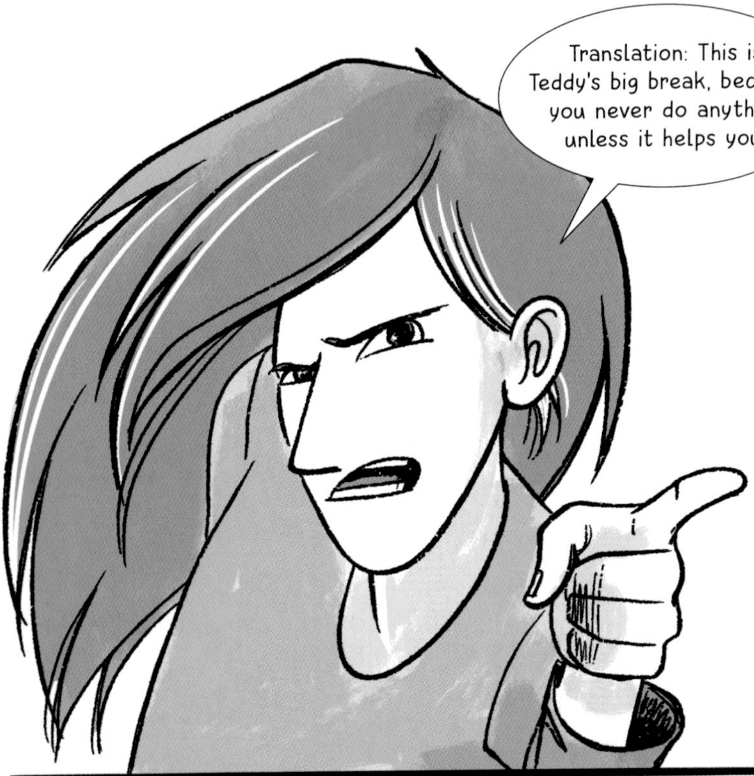
Translation: This is Teddy's big break, because you never do anything unless it helps you.

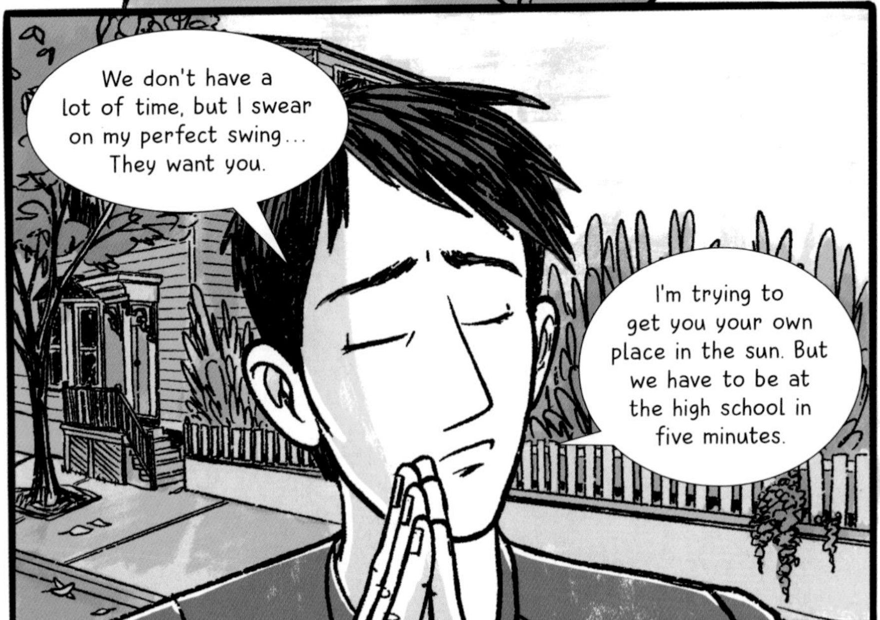
We don't have a lot of time, but I swear on my perfect swing... They want you.
I'm trying to get you your own place in the sun. But we have to be at the high school in five minutes.

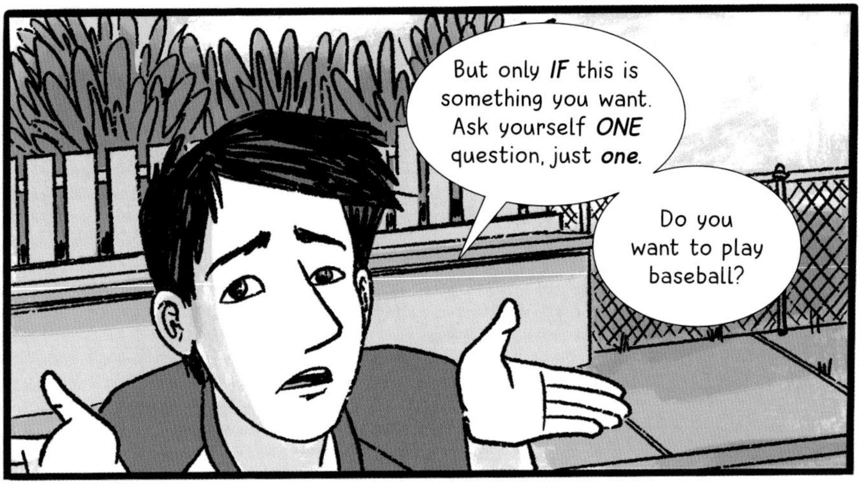
But only IF this is something you want. Ask yourself ONE question, just one.
Do you want to play baseball?

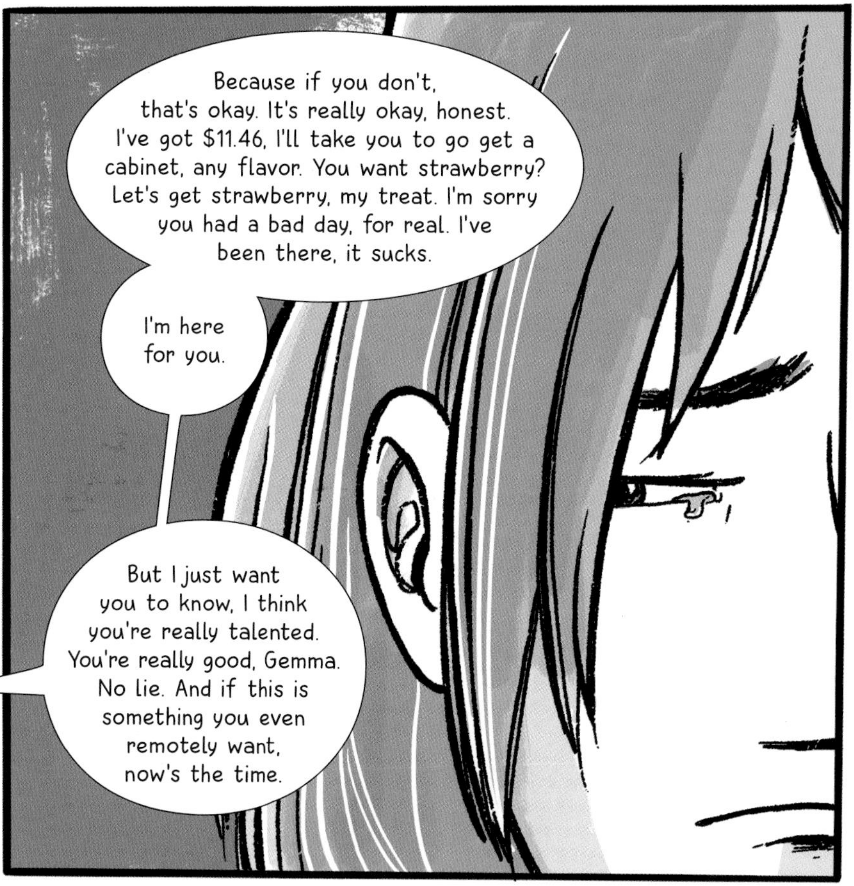
Because if you don't, that's okay. It's really okay, honest. I've got $11.46, I'll take you to go get a cabinet, any flavor. You want strawberry? Let's get strawberry, my treat. I'm sorry you had a bad day, for real. I've been there, it sucks.
I'm here for you.
But I just want you to know, I think you're really talented. You're really good, Gemma. No lie. And if this is something you even remotely want, now's the time.

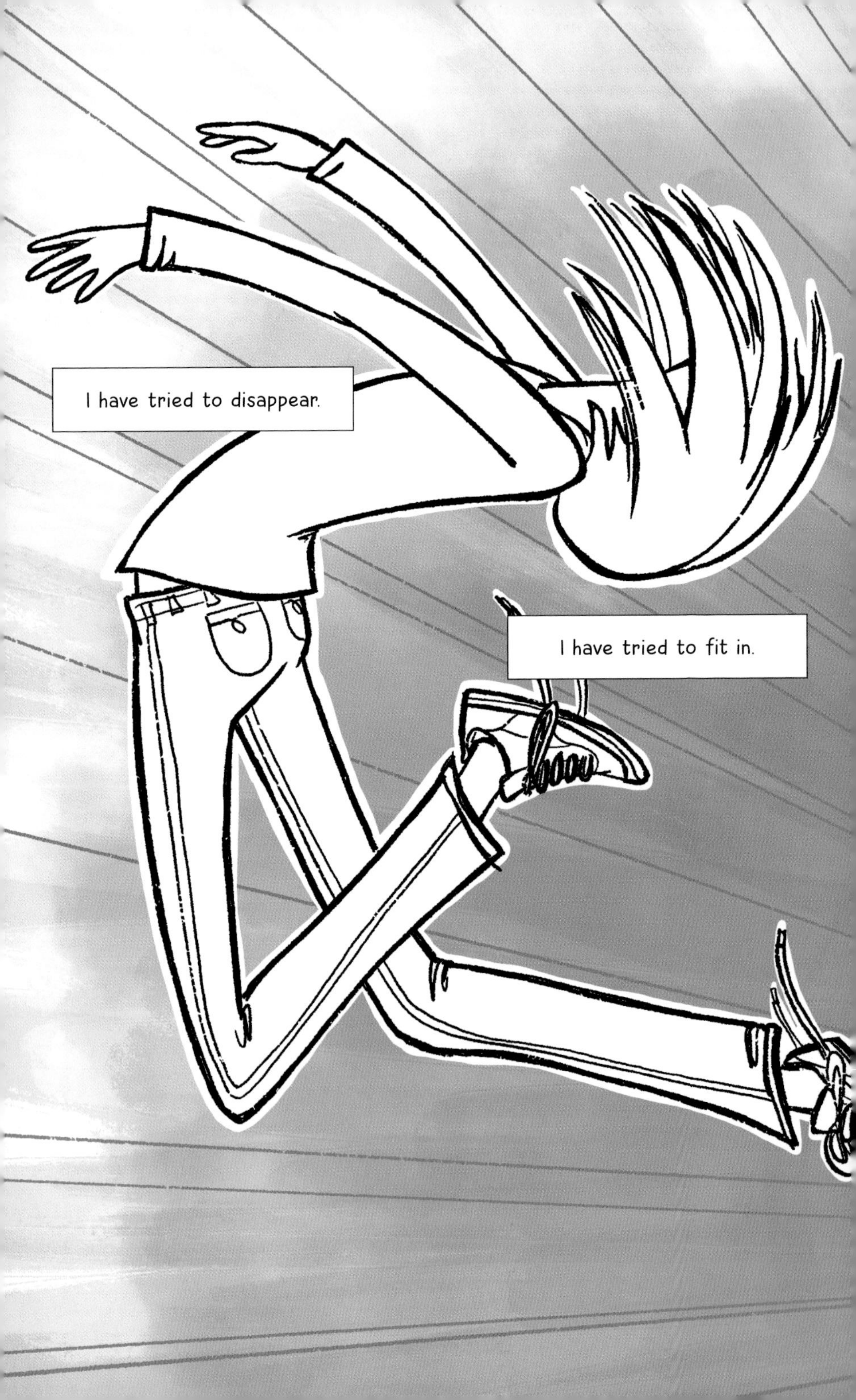
I have tried to disappear.
I have tried to fit in.

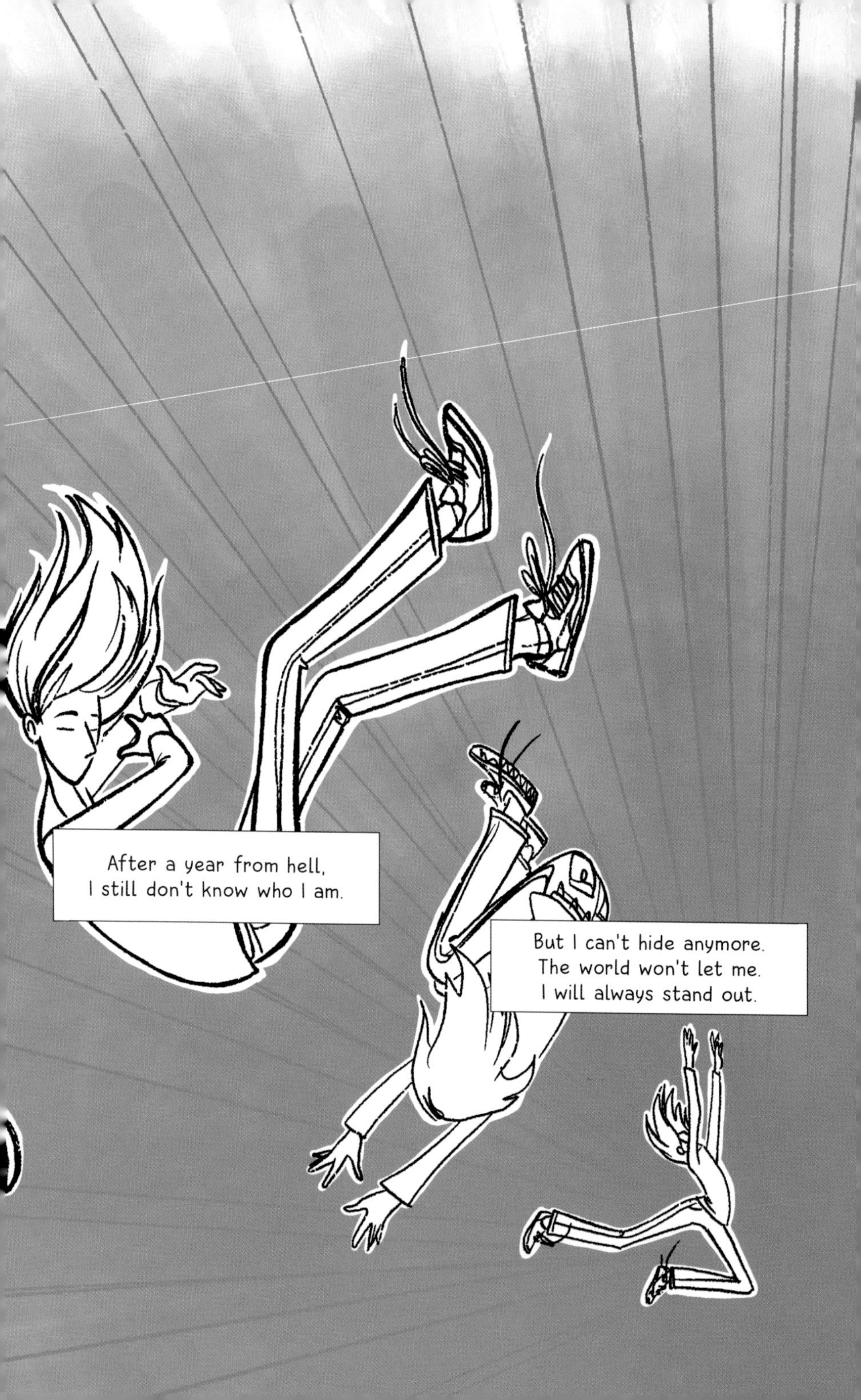
After a year from hell,
I still don't know who I am.
But I can't hide anymore.
The world won't let me.
I will always stand out.

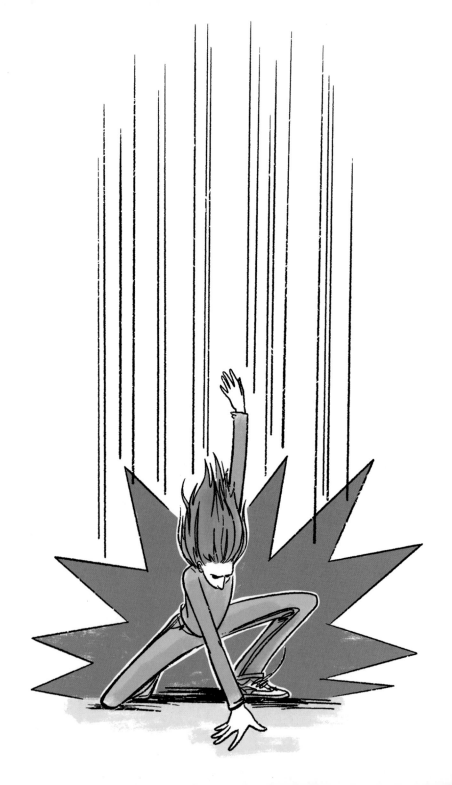

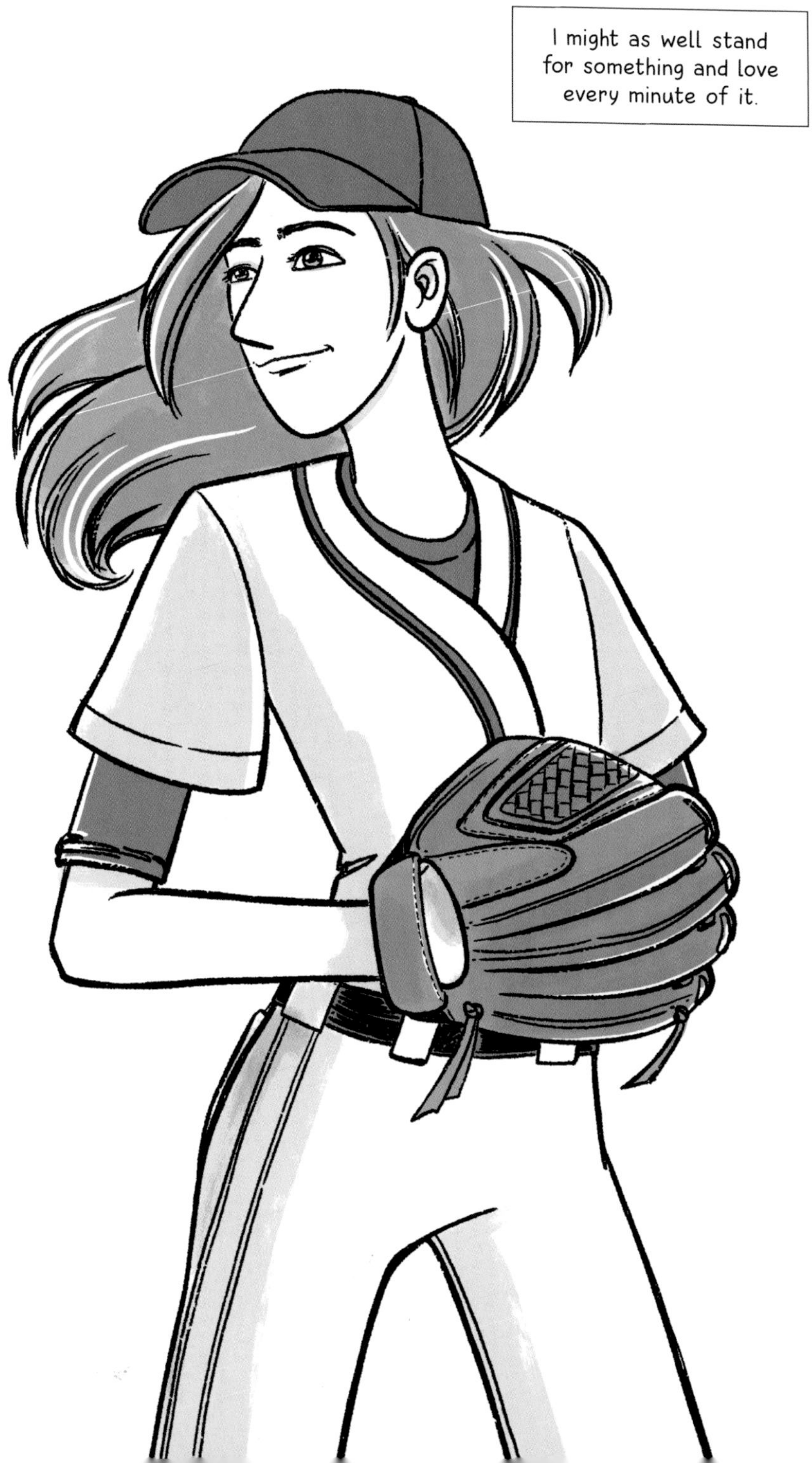
I might as well stand for something and love every minute of it.

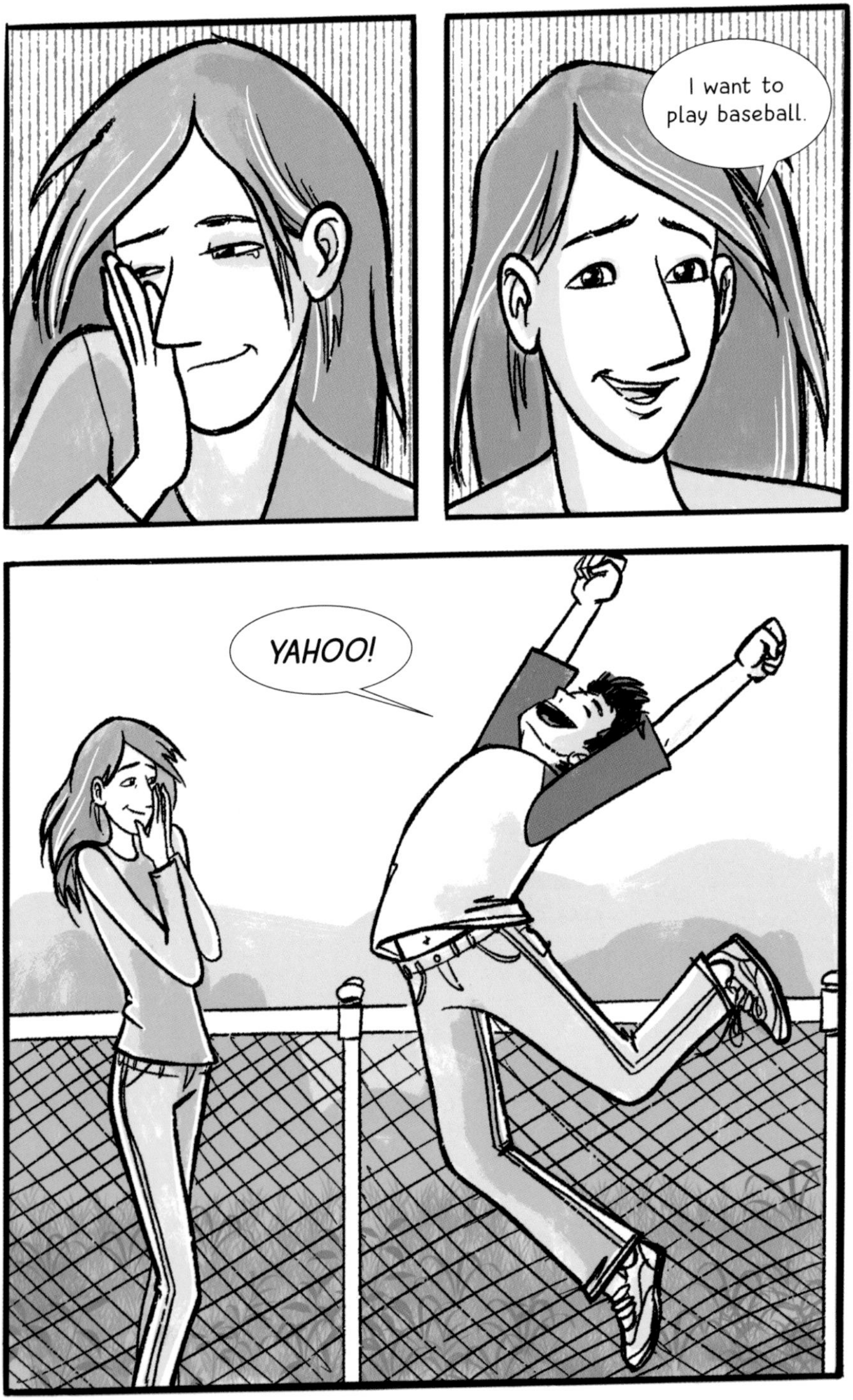
I want to play baseball.
YAHOO!

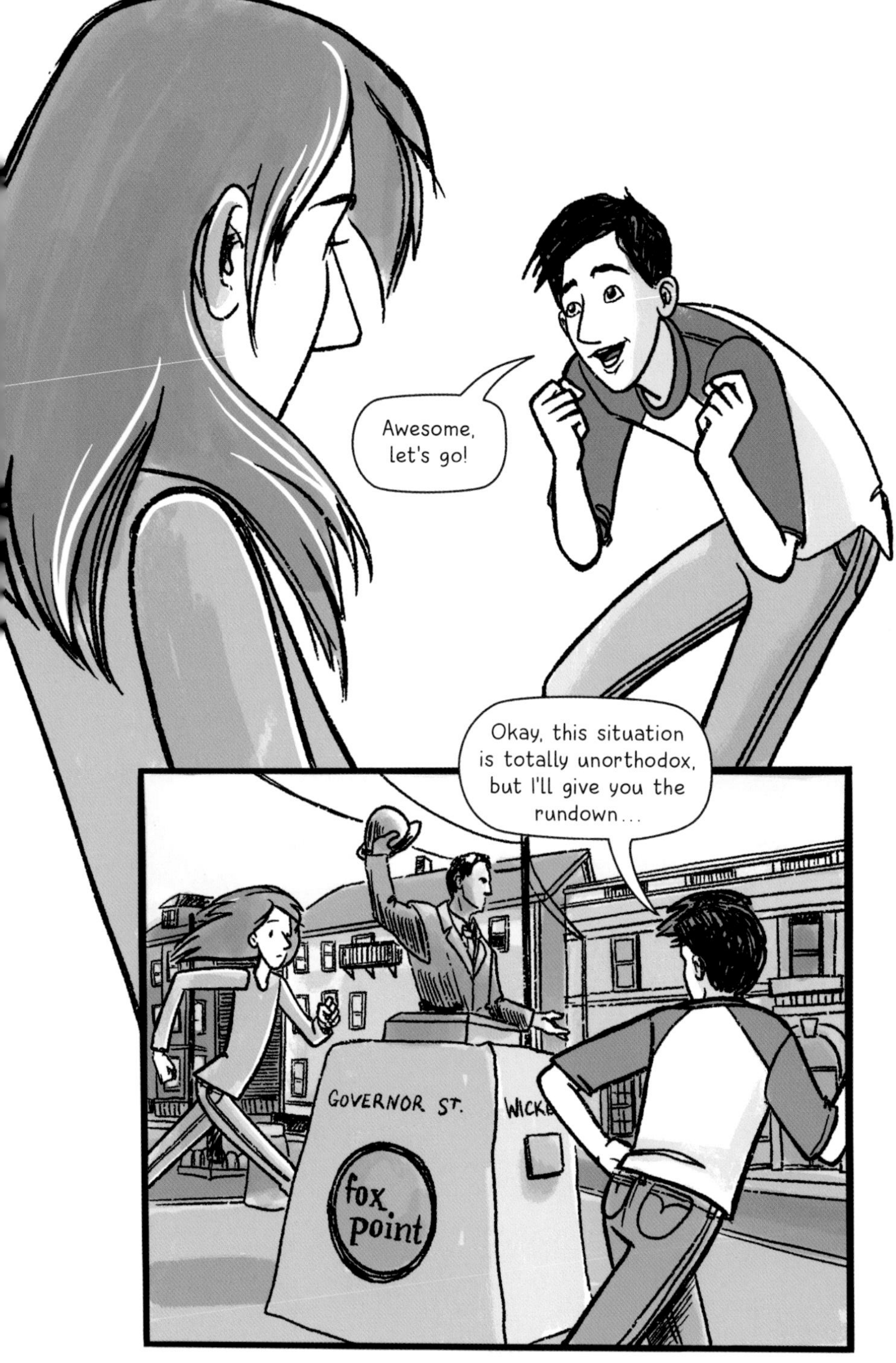
Awesome, let's go!
Okay, this situation is totally unorthodox, but I'll give you the rundown...
GOVERNOR ST.
fox point

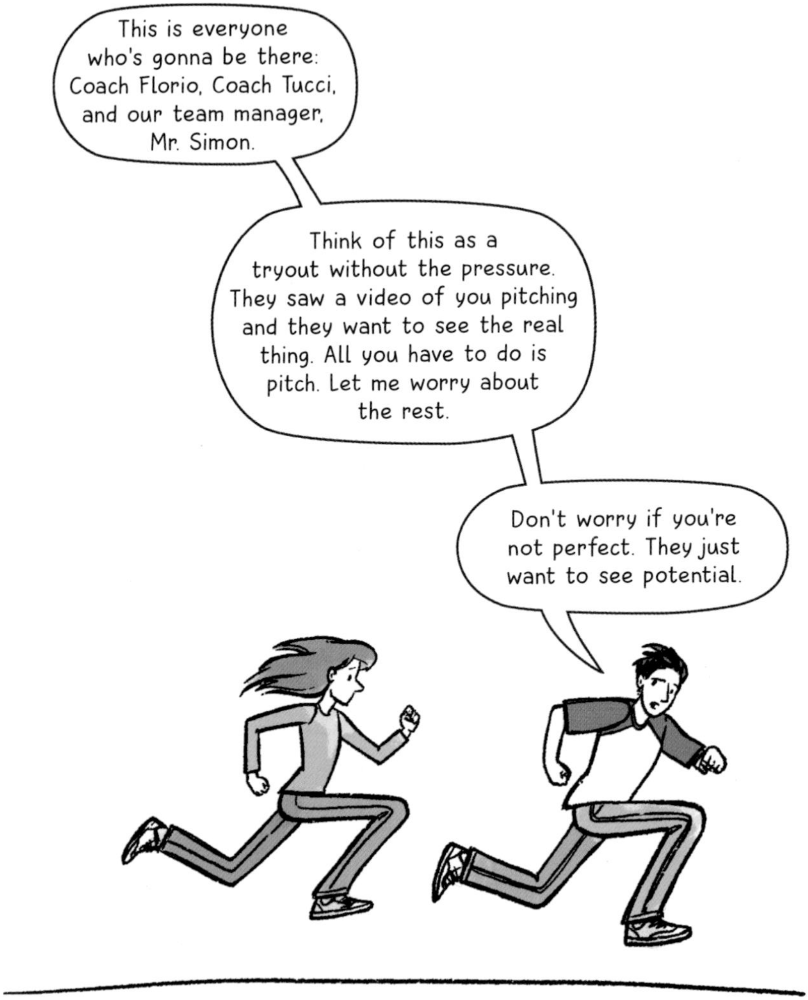
This is everyone who's gonna be there: Coach Florio, Coach Tucci, and our team manager, Mr. Simon.
Think of this as a tryout without the pressure. They saw a video of you pitching and they want to see the real thing. All you have to do is pitch. Let me worry about the rest.
Don't worry if you're not perfect. They just want to see potential.

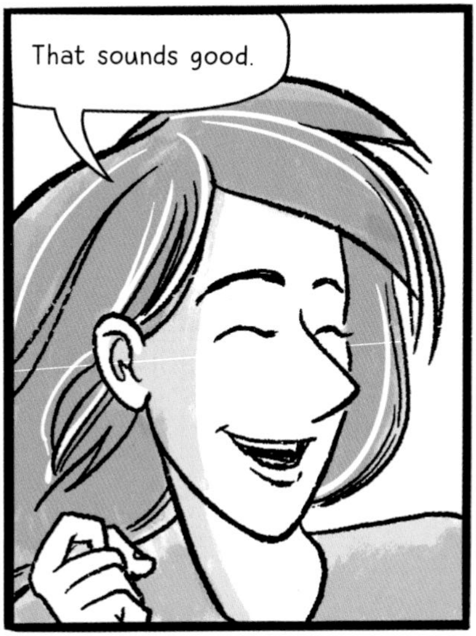
That sounds good.

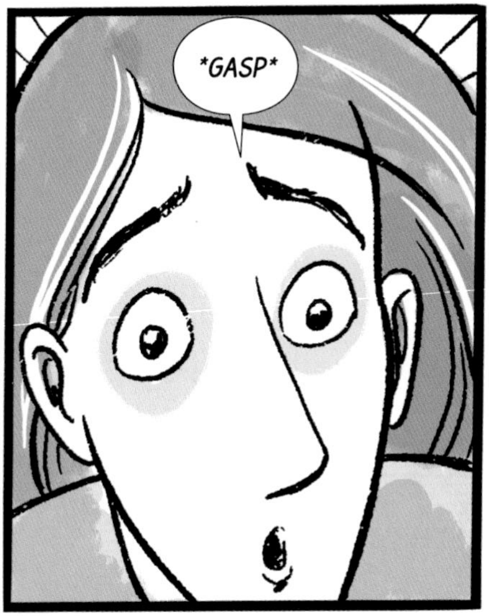
GASP

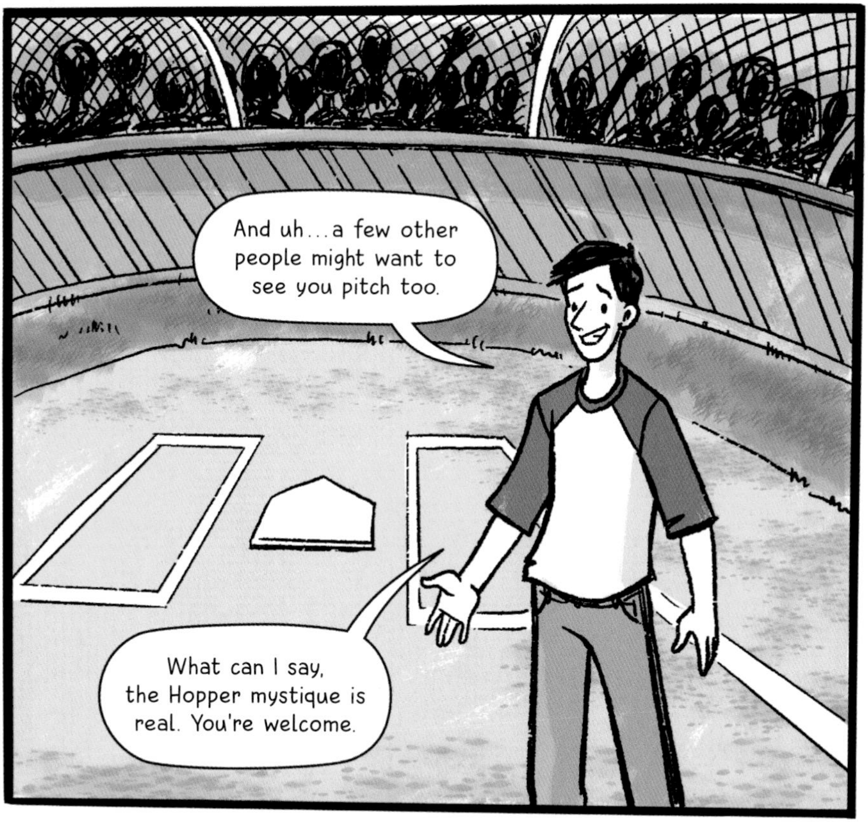
And uh...a few other people might want to see you pitch too.
What can I say, the Hopper mystique is real. You're welcome.

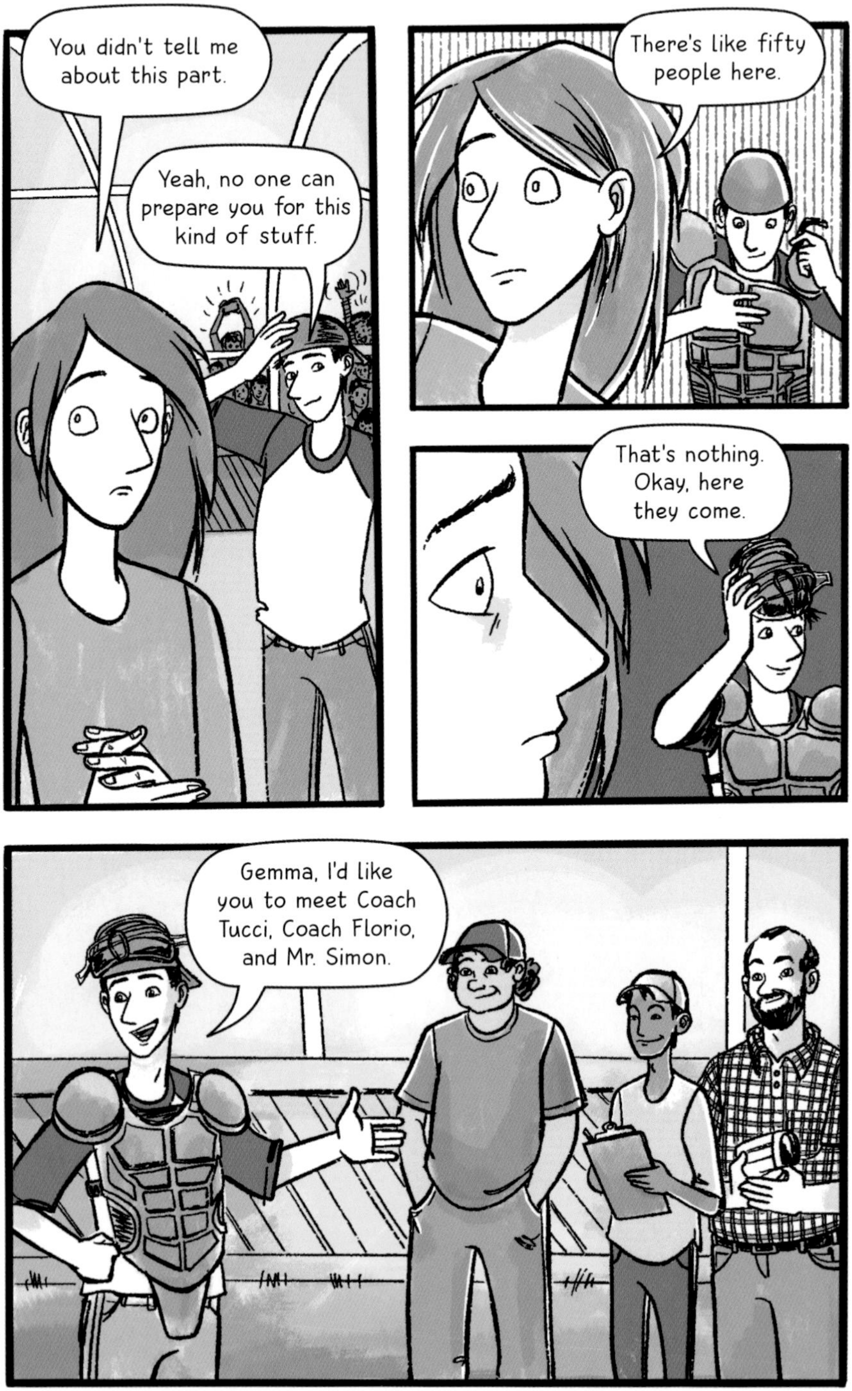
You didn't tell me about this part.
Yeah, no one can prepare you for this kind of stuff.
There's like fifty people here.
That's nothing. Okay, here they come.
Gemma, I'd like you to meet Coach Tucci, Coach Florio, and Mr. Simon.

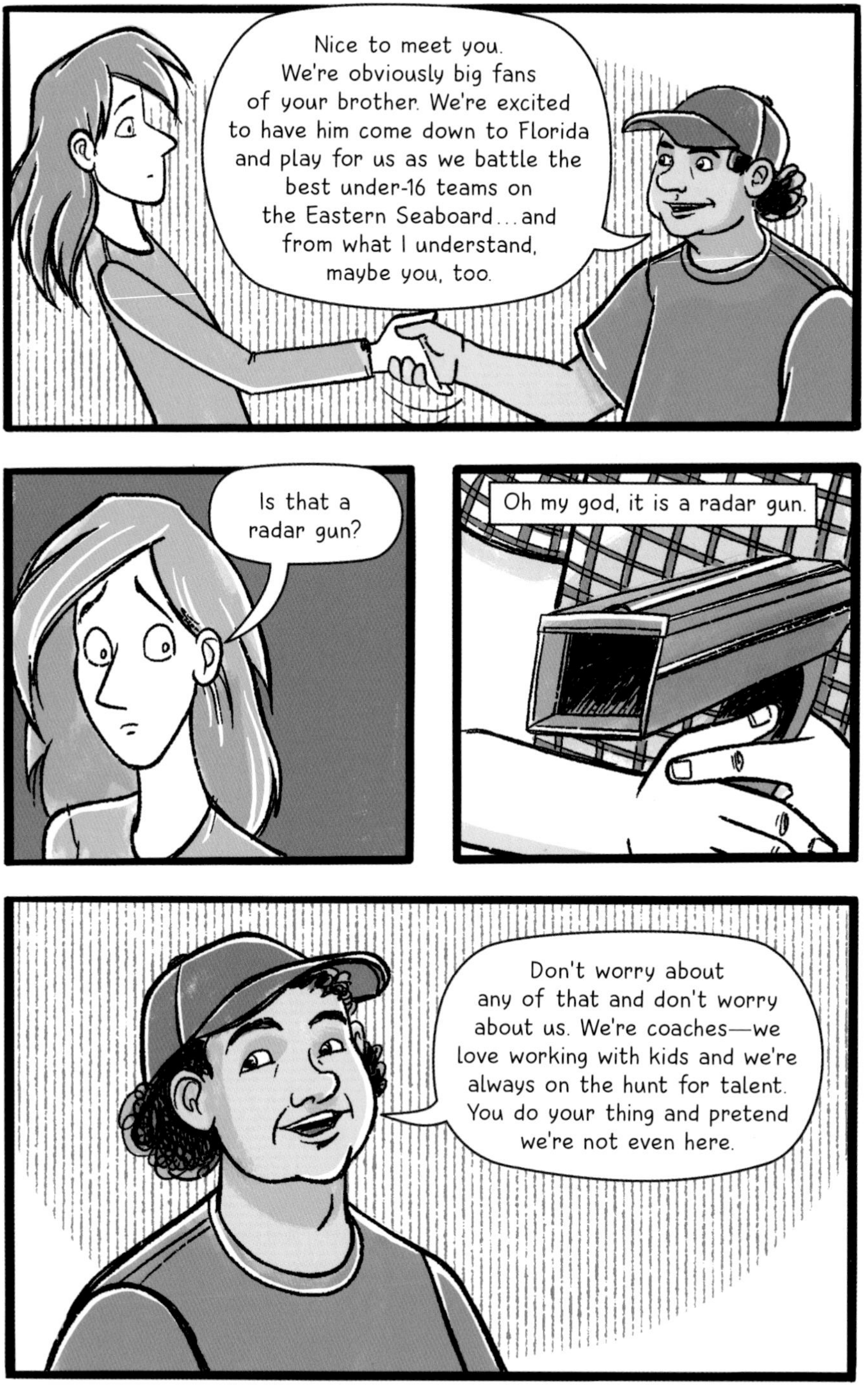

Nice to meet you. We're obviously big fans of your brother. We're excited to have him come down to Florida and play for us as we battle the best under-16 teams on the Eastern Seaboard...and from what I understand, maybe you, too.
Is that a radar gun?
Oh my god, it is a radar gun.
Don't worry about any of that and don't worry about us. We're coaches—we love working with kids and we're always on the hunt for talent. You do your thing and pretend we're not even here.

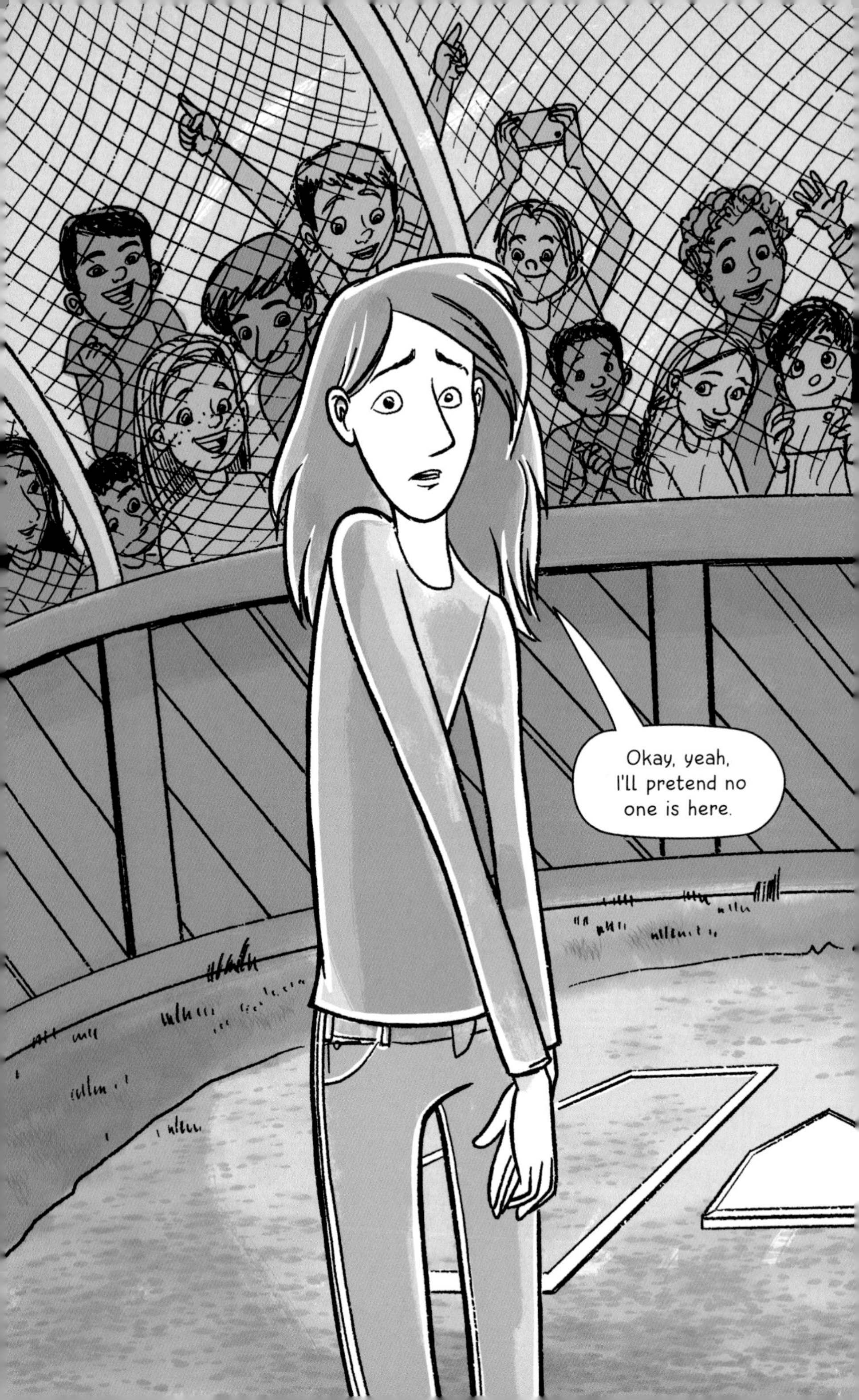
Okay, yeah, I'll pretend no one is here.

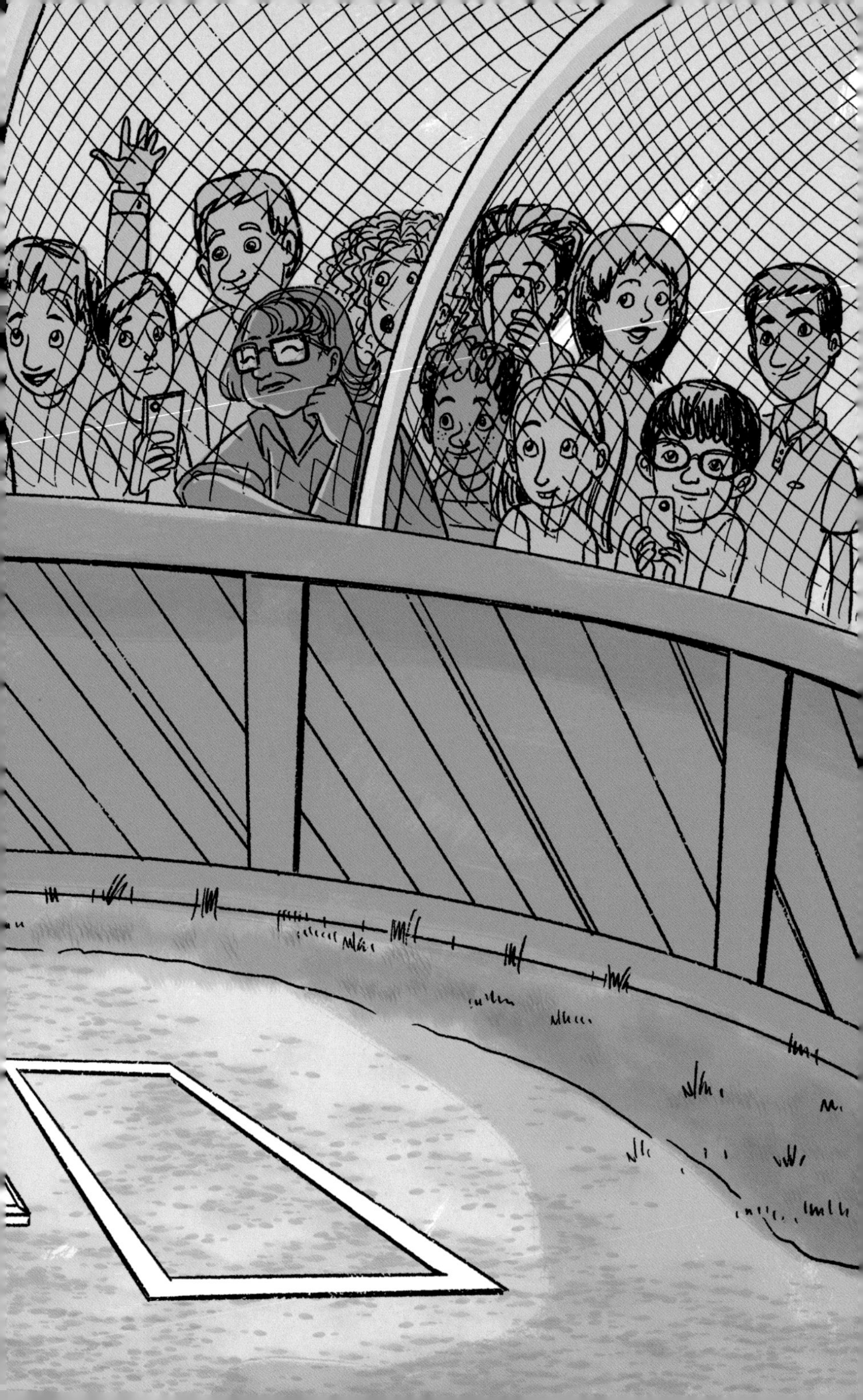

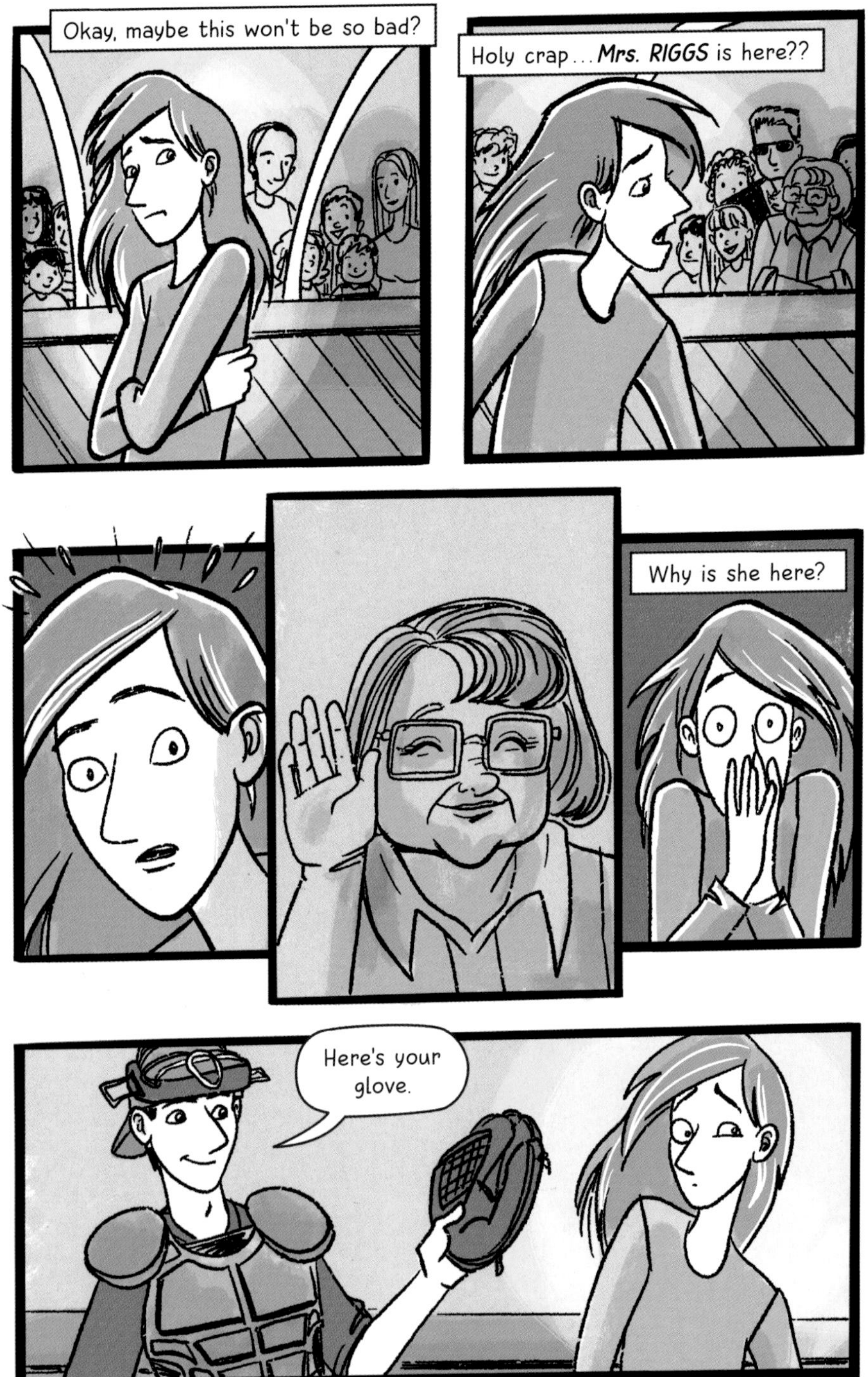
Okay, maybe this won't be so bad?
Holy crap... **Mrs. RIGGS** is here??
Why is she here?
Here's your glove.

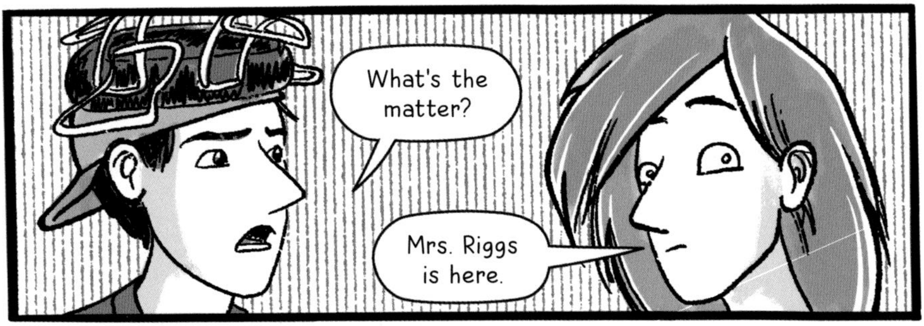
What's the matter?
Mrs. Riggs is here.

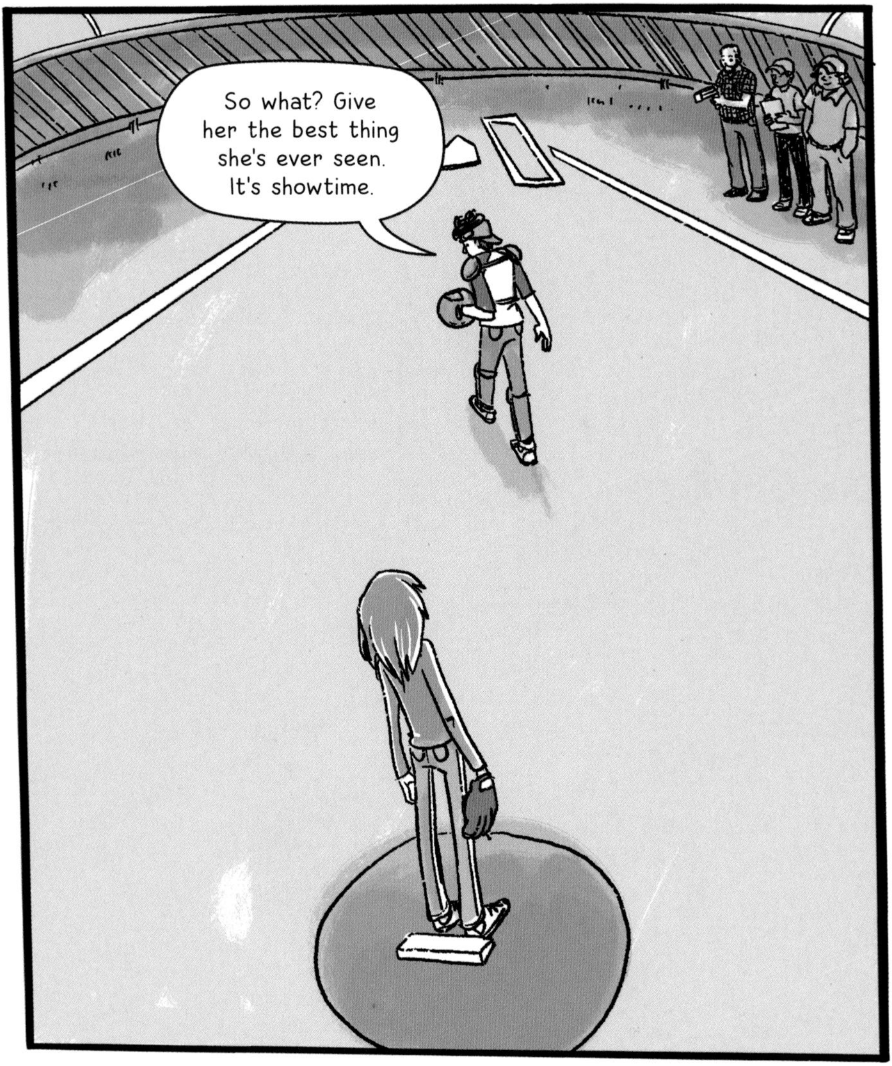
So what? Give her the best thing she's ever seen. It's showtime.

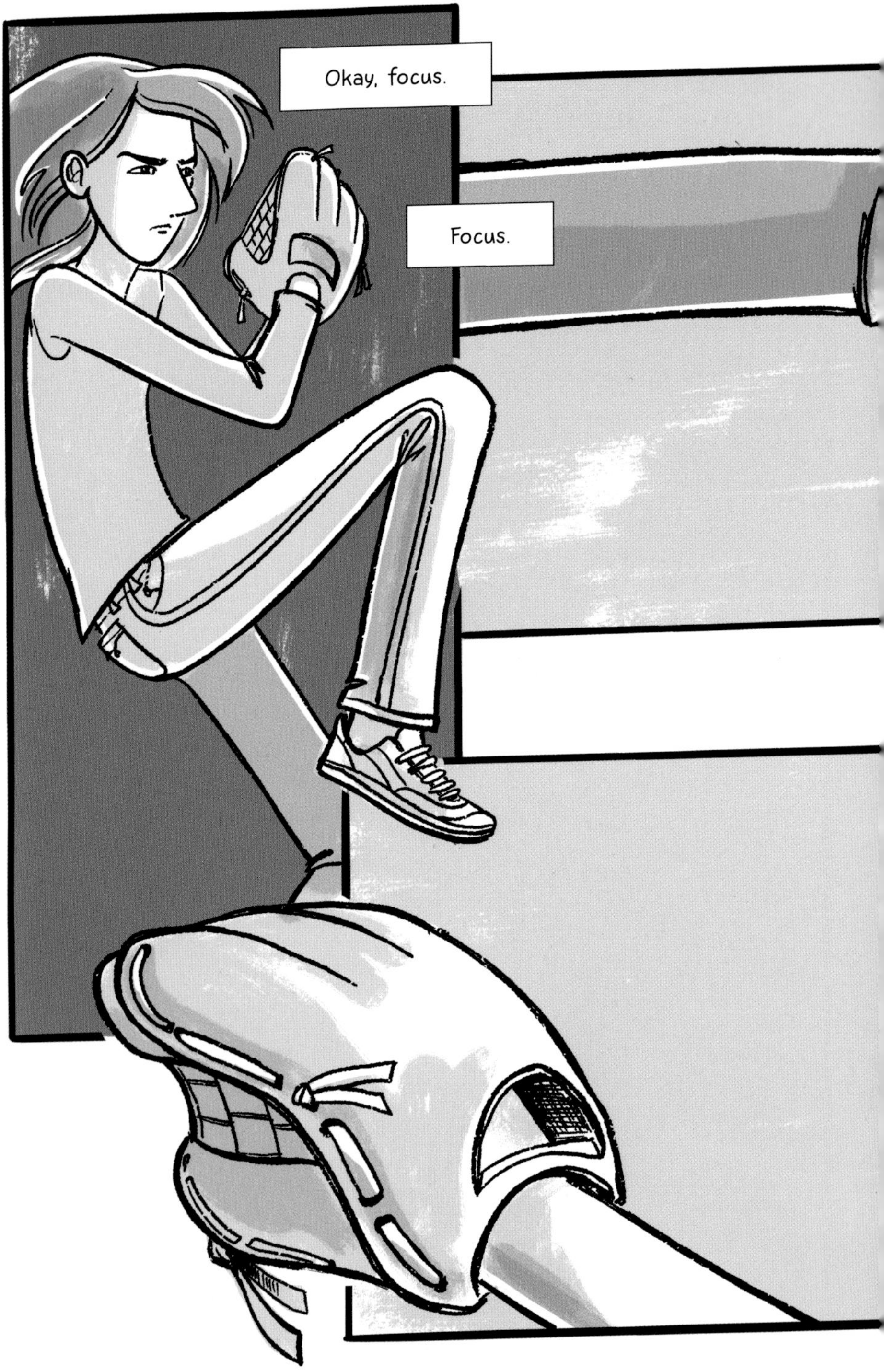
Okay, focus.
Focus.

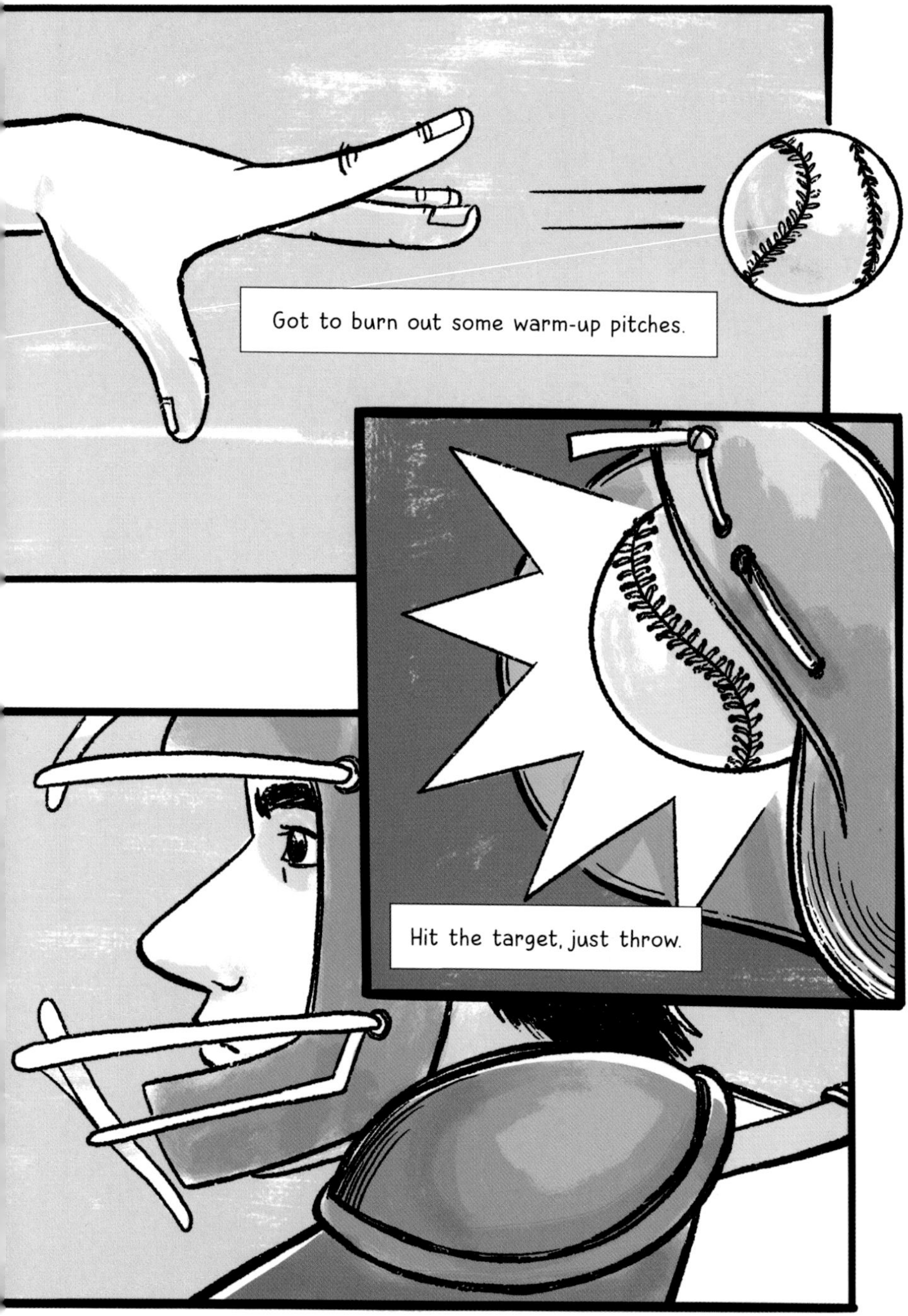
Got to burn out some warm-up pitches.
Hit the target, just throw.

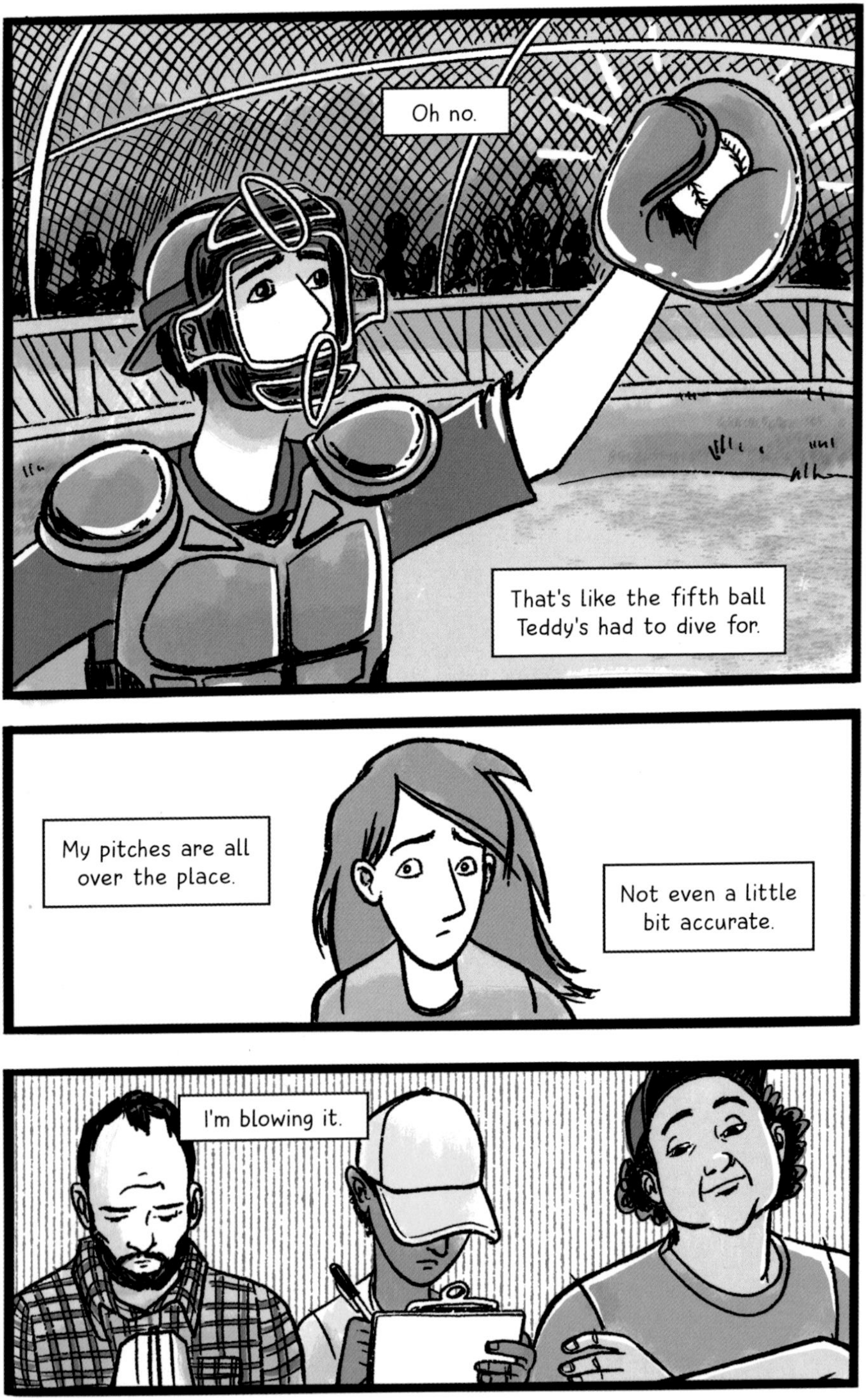
Oh no.
That's like the fifth ball Teddy's had to dive for.
My pitches are all over the place.
Not even a little bit accurate.
I'm blowing it.

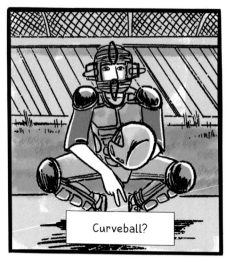

Curveball?

No way.

He's calling for it again.

I can't do it.

Time!

What's the matter?

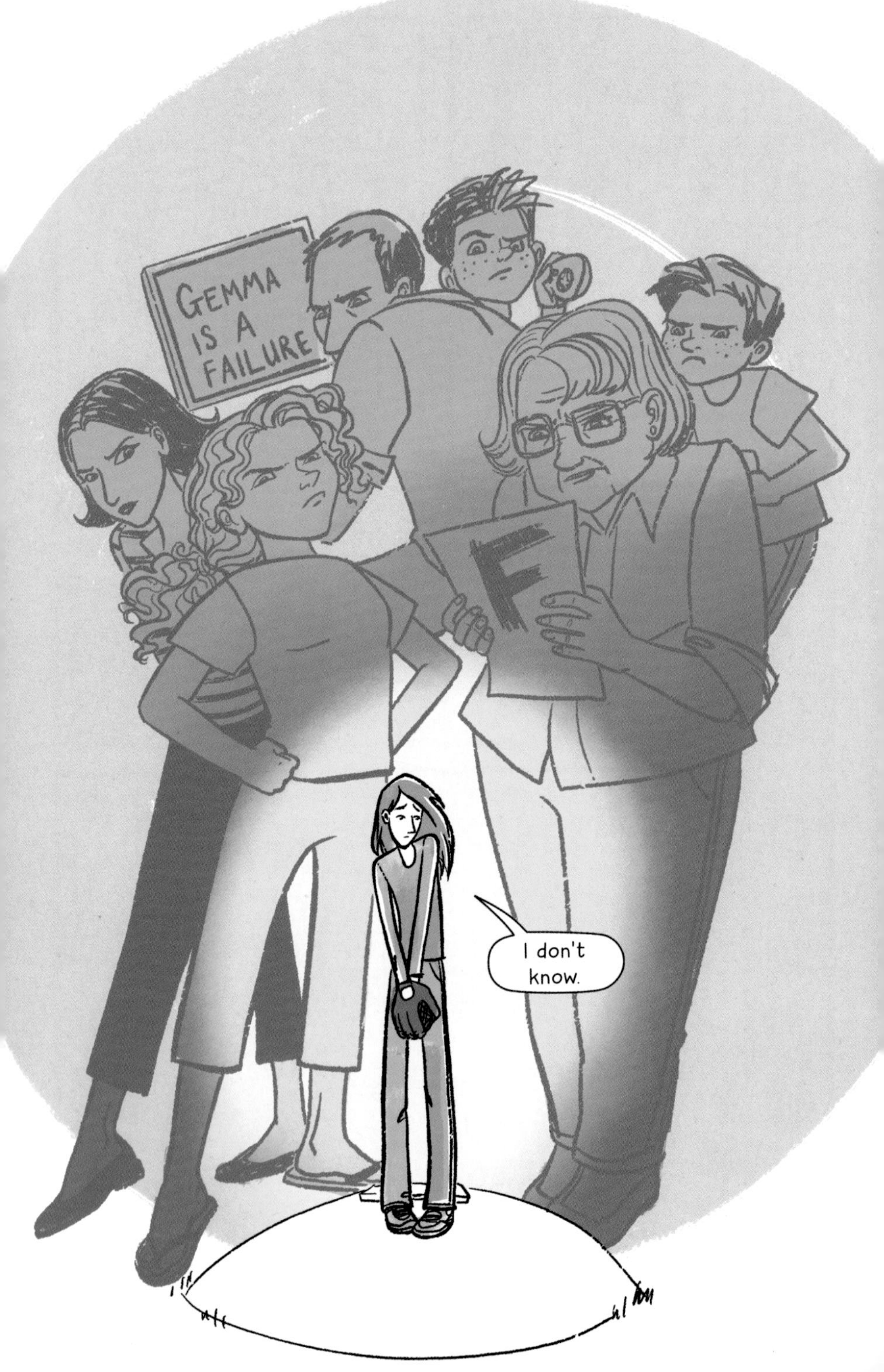
GEMMA IS A FAILURE
F
I don't know.

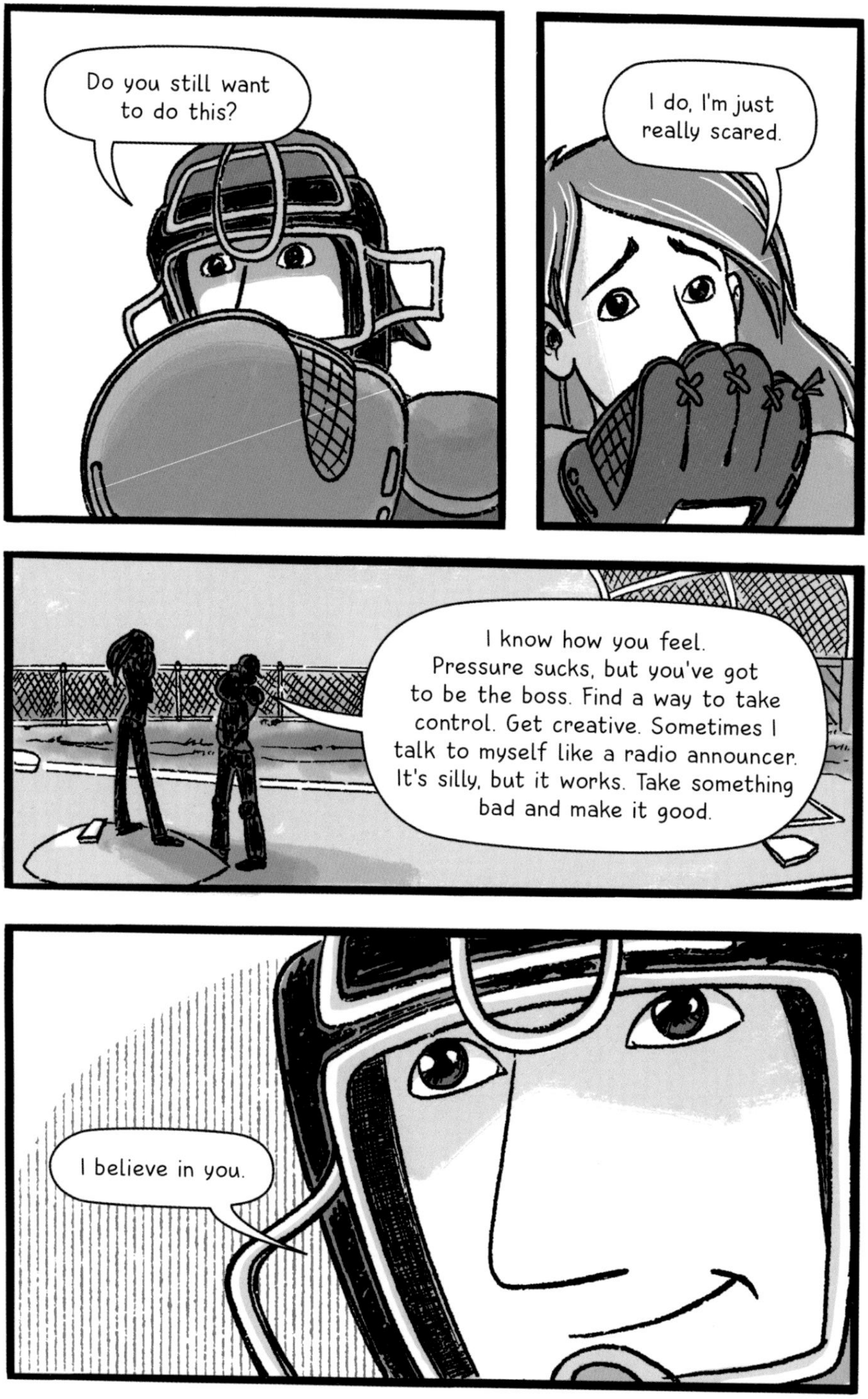
Do you still want to do this?
I do, I'm just really scared.
I know how you feel. Pressure sucks, but you've got to be the boss. Find a way to take control. Get creative. Sometimes I talk to myself like a radio announcer. It's silly, but it works. Take something bad and make it good.
I believe in you.

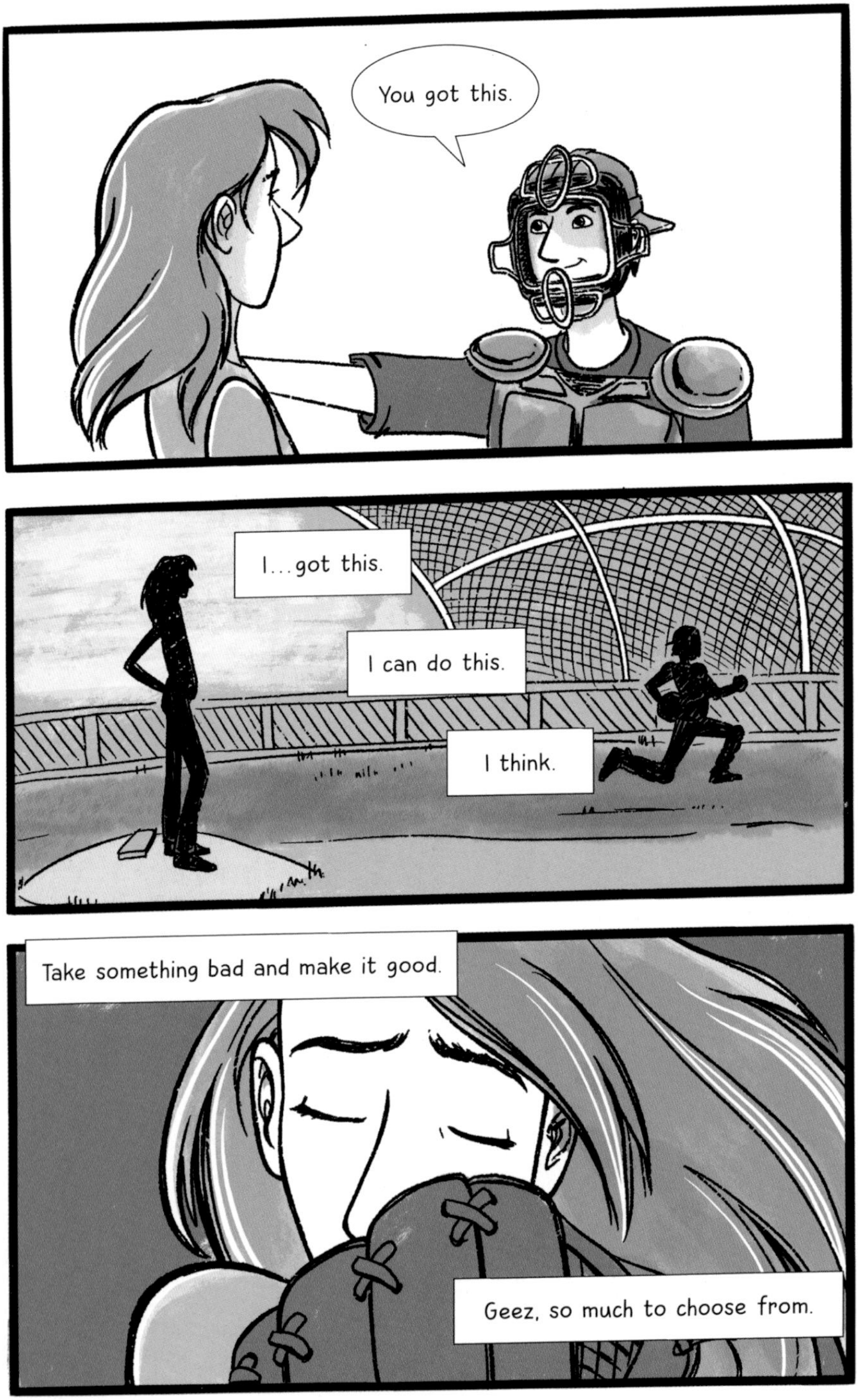
You got this.
I...got this.
I can do this.
I think.
Take something bad and make it good.
Geez, so much to choose from.

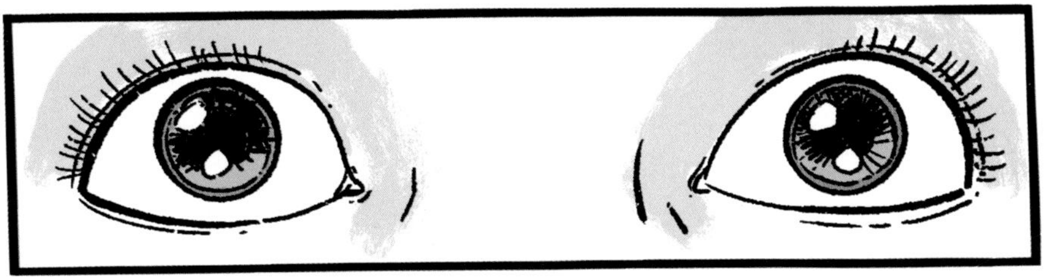

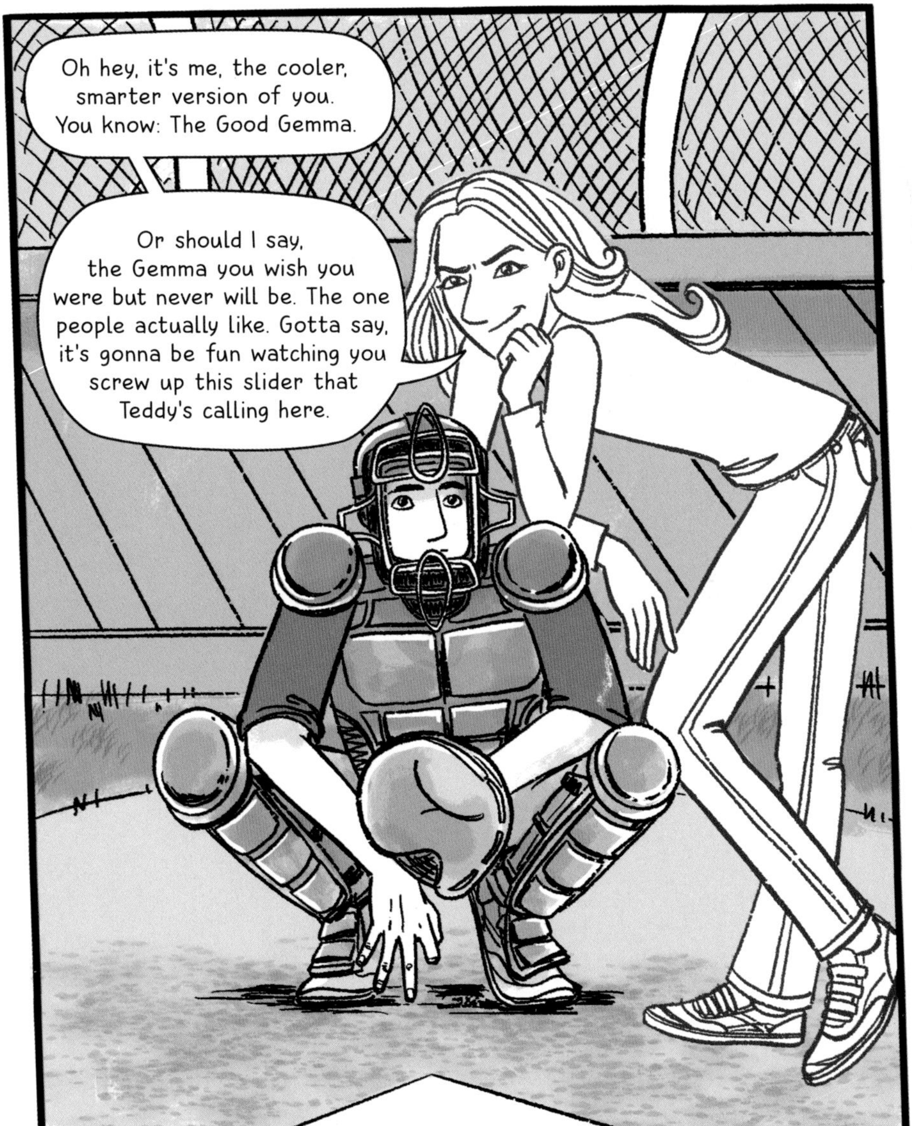
Oh hey, it's me, the cooler, smarter version of you. You know: The Good Gemma.
Or should I say, the Gemma you wish you were but never will be. The one people actually like. Gotta say, it's gonna be fun watching you screw up this slider that Teddy's calling here.

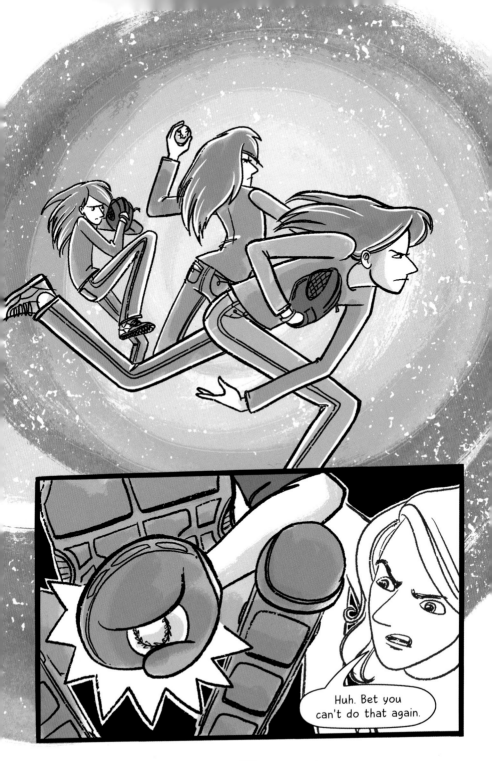

Huh. Bet you
can't do that again.

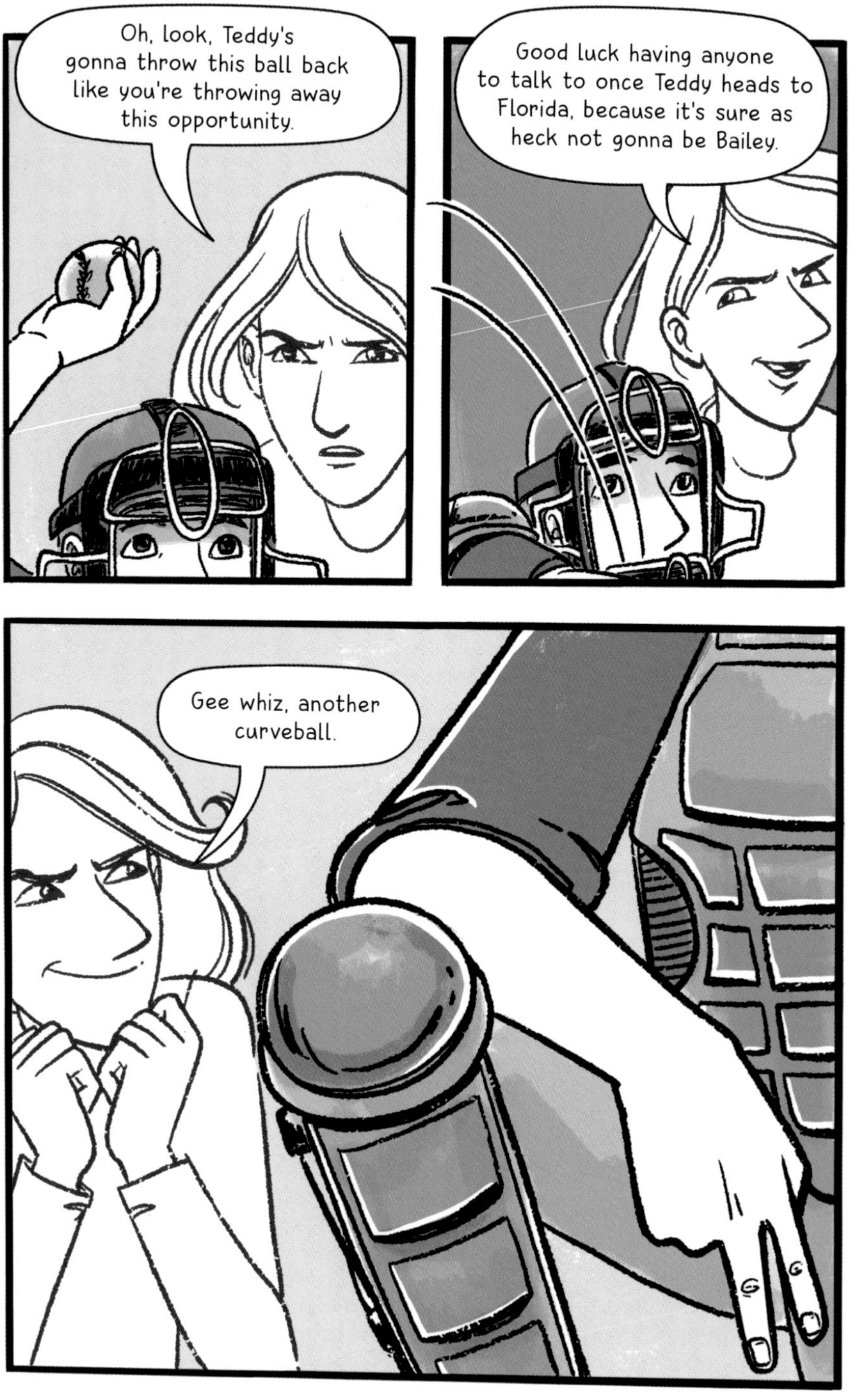
Oh, look, Teddy's gonna throw this ball back like you're throwing away this opportunity.
Good luck having anyone to talk to once Teddy heads to Florida, because it's sure as heck not gonna be Bailey.
Gee whiz, another curveball.

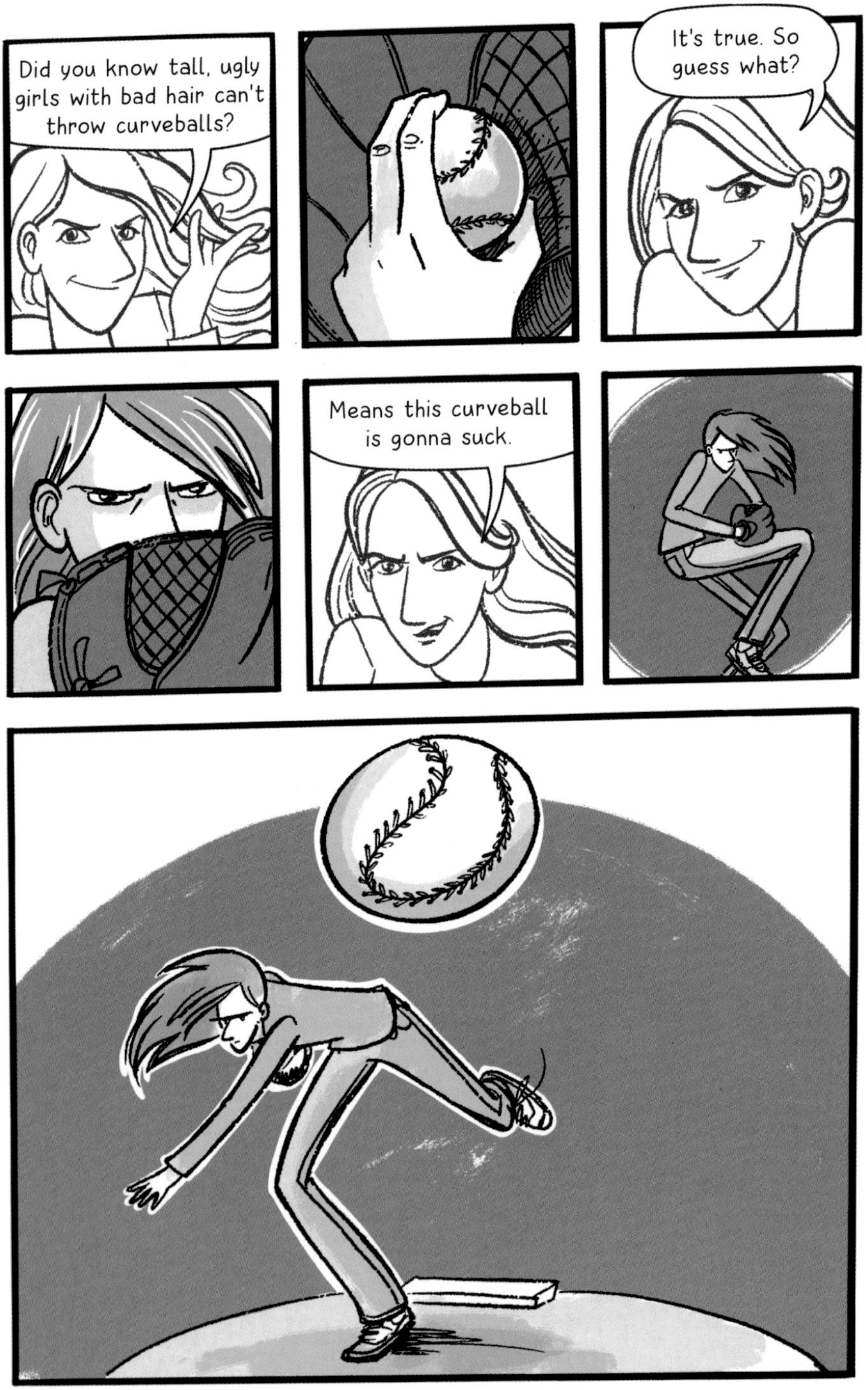
Did you know tall, ugly girls with bad hair can't throw curveballs?
It's true. So guess what?
Means this curveball is gonna suck.

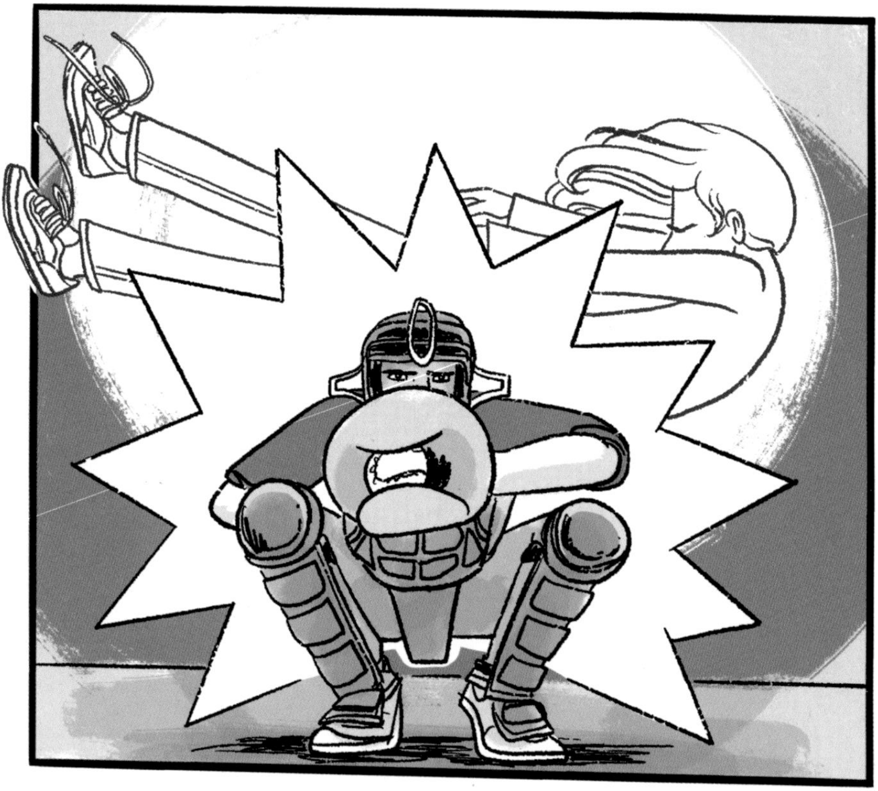

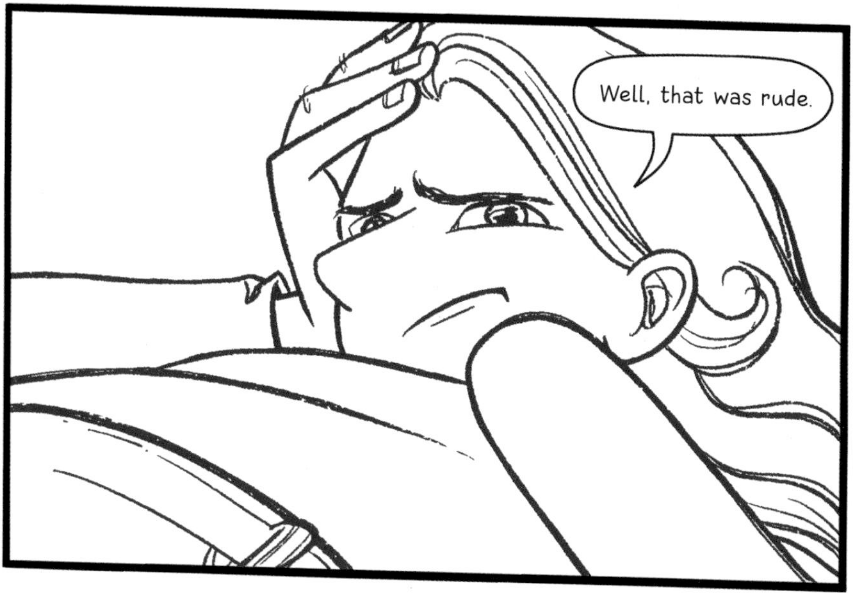
Well, that was rude.

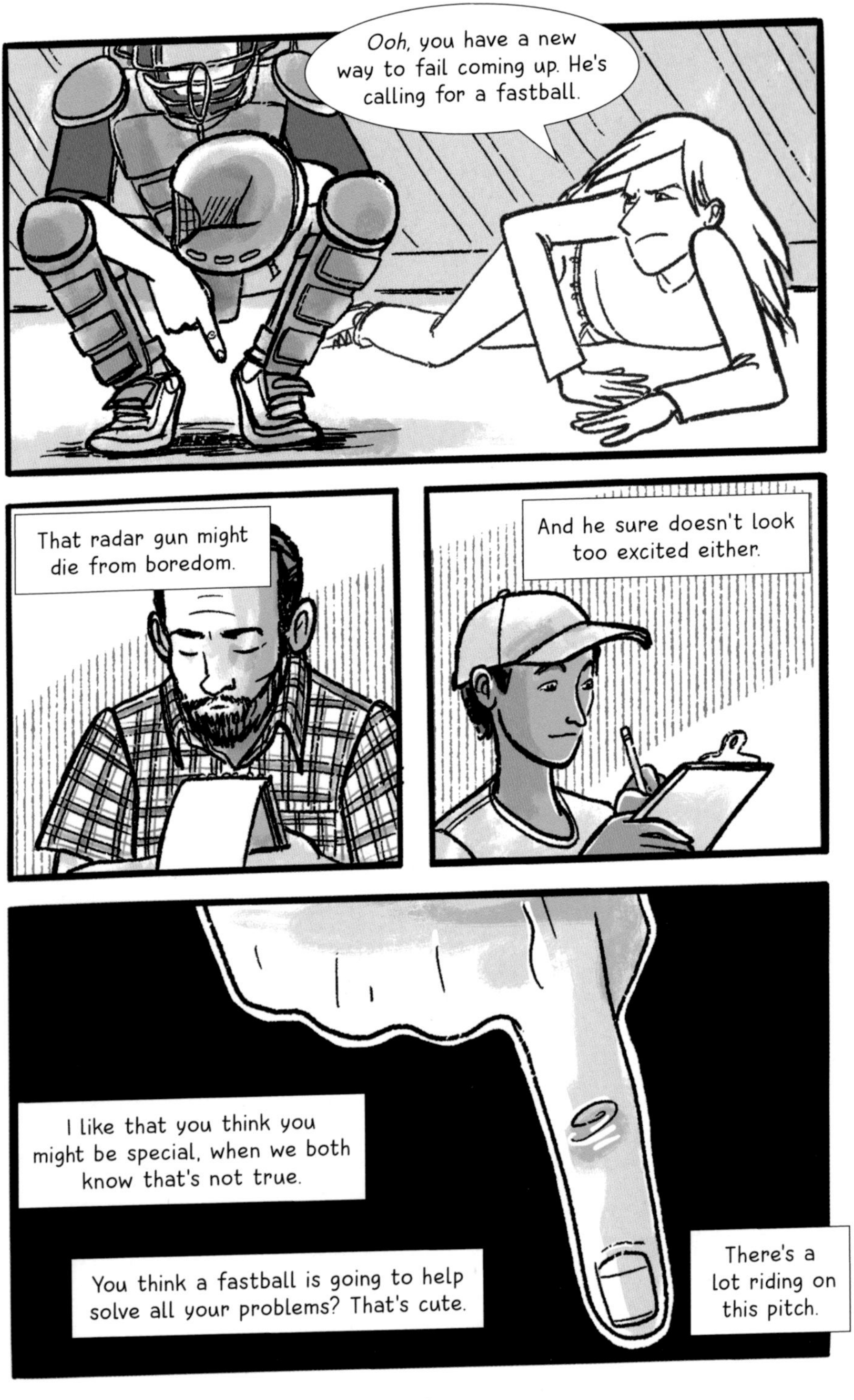
Ooh, you have a new way to fail coming up. He's calling for a fastball.
That radar gun might die from boredom.
And he sure doesn't look too excited either.
I like that you think you might be special, when we both know that's not true.
You think a fastball is going to help solve all your problems? That's cute.
There's a lot riding on this pitch.

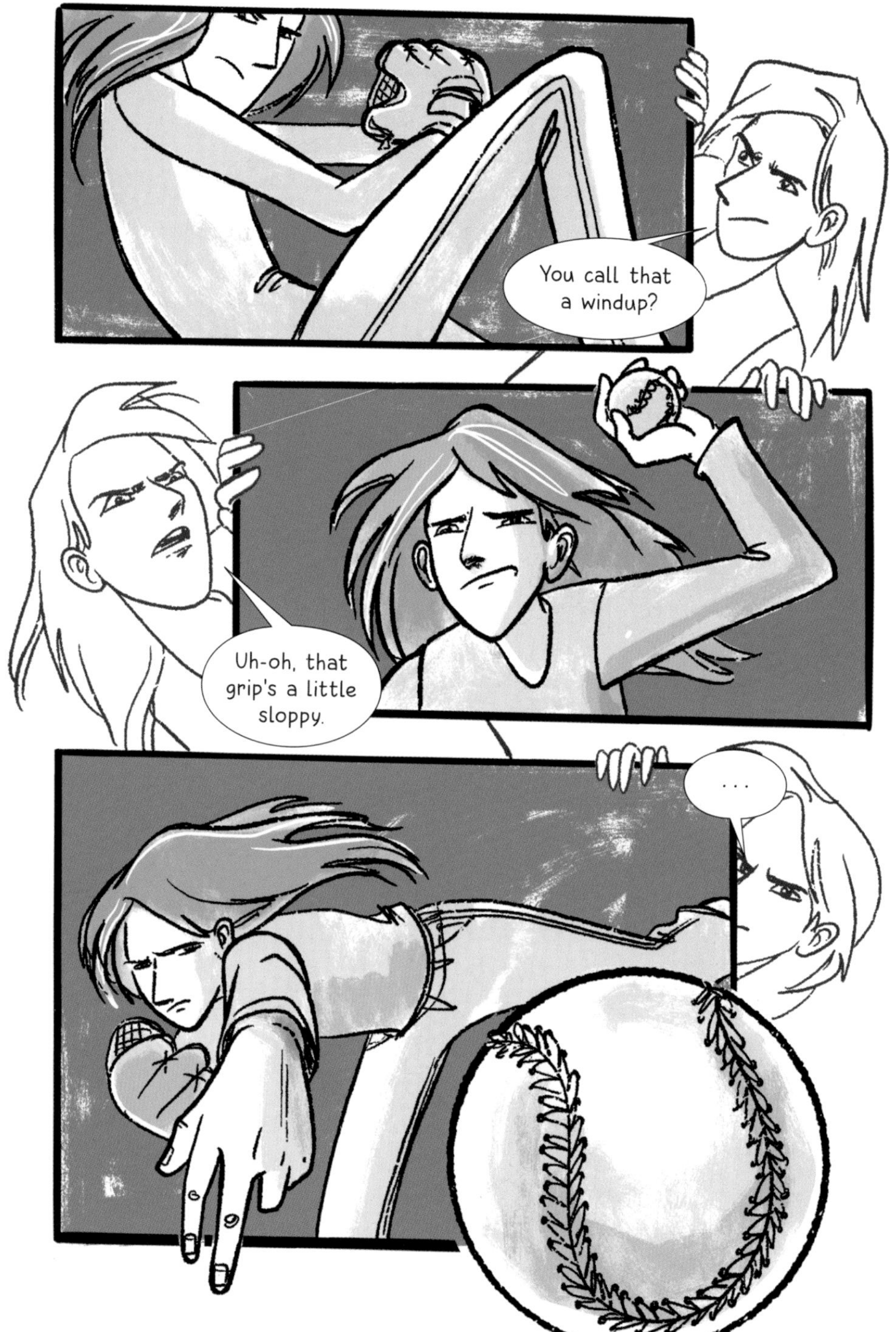
You call that a windup?
Uh-oh, that grip's a little sloppy.
. . .

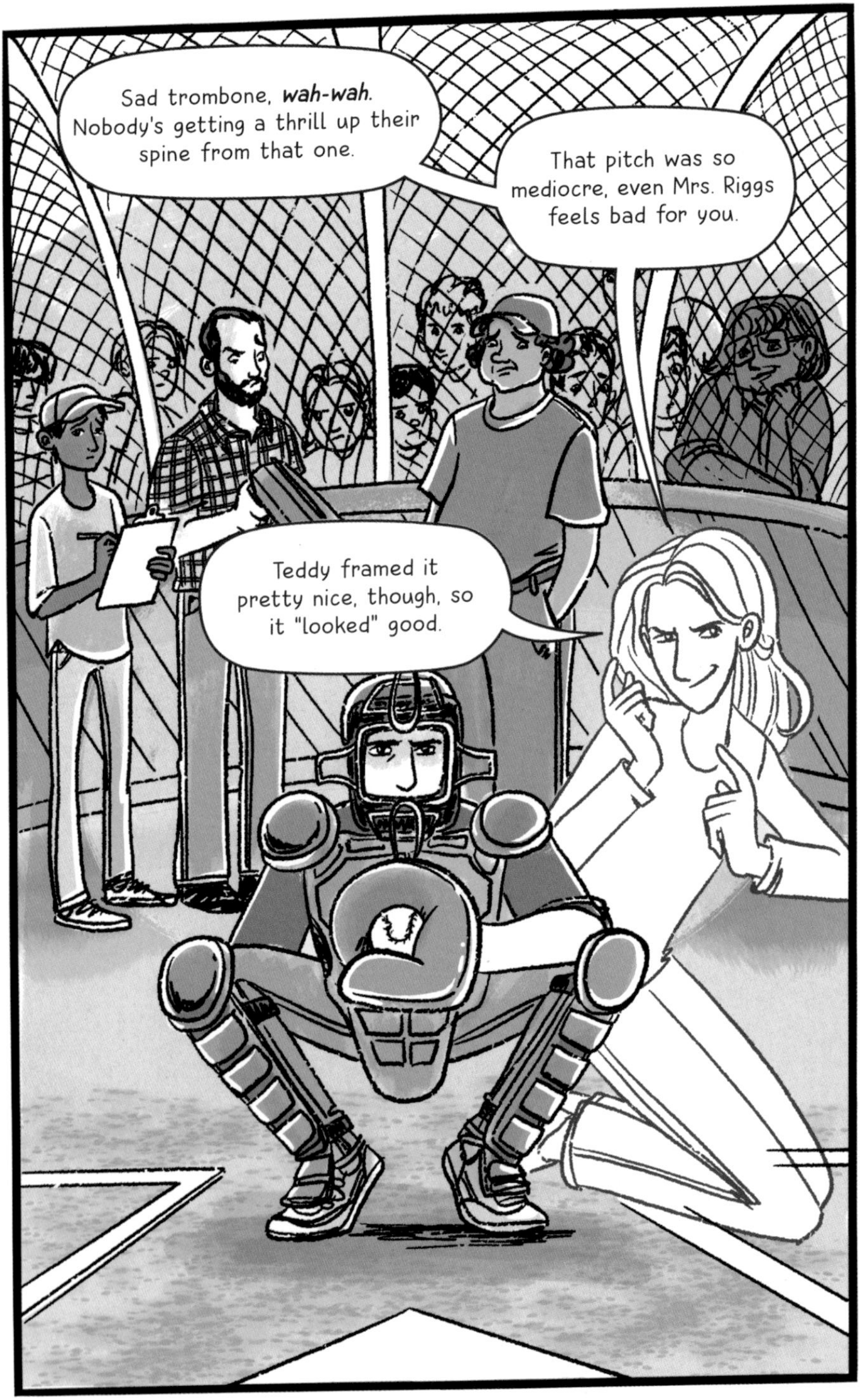
Sad trombone, **wah-wah**. Nobody's getting a thrill up their spine from that one.
That pitch was so mediocre, even Mrs. Riggs feels bad for you.
Teddy framed it pretty nice, though, so it "looked" good.

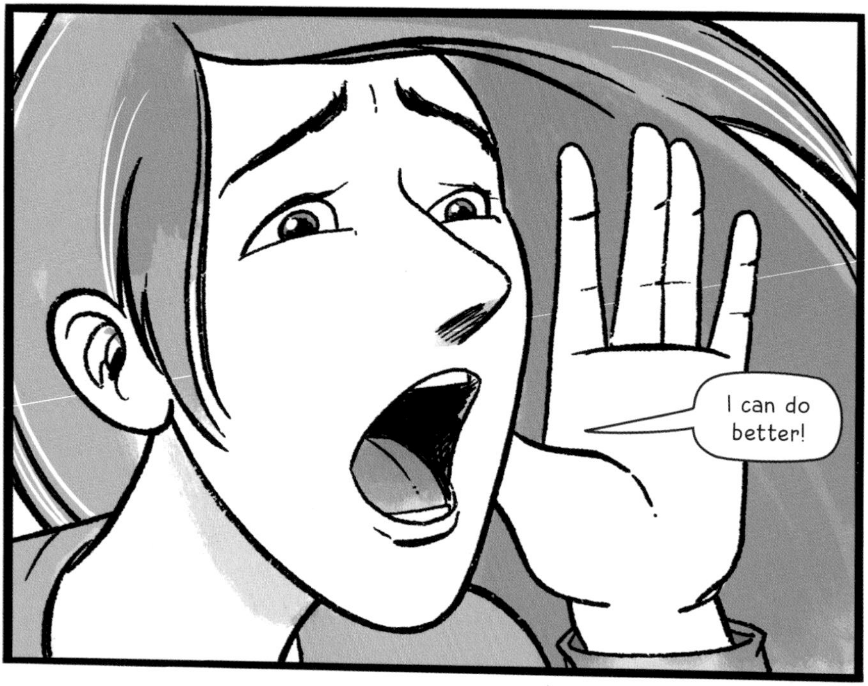
I can do better!

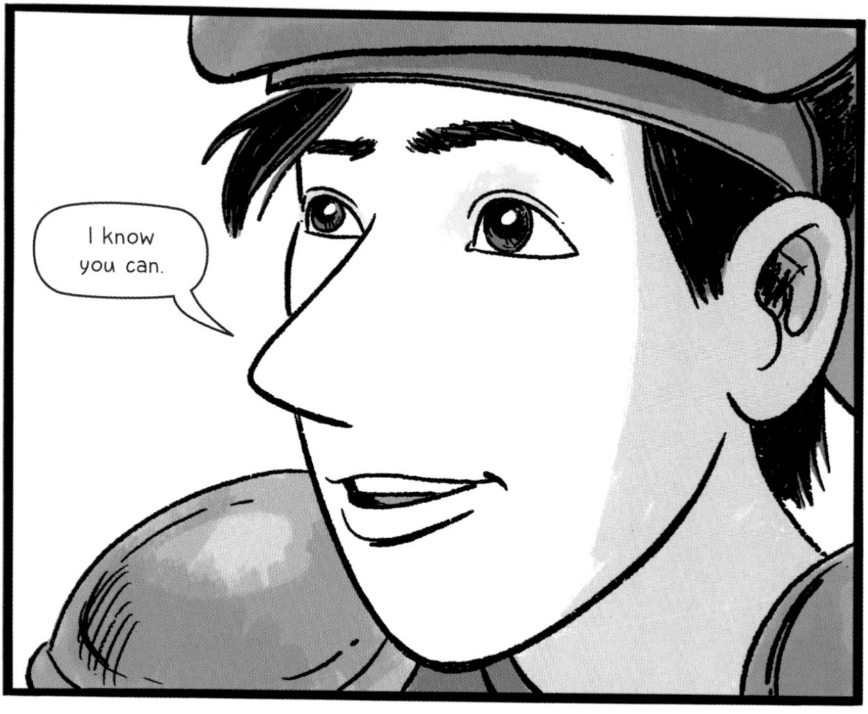
I know you can.

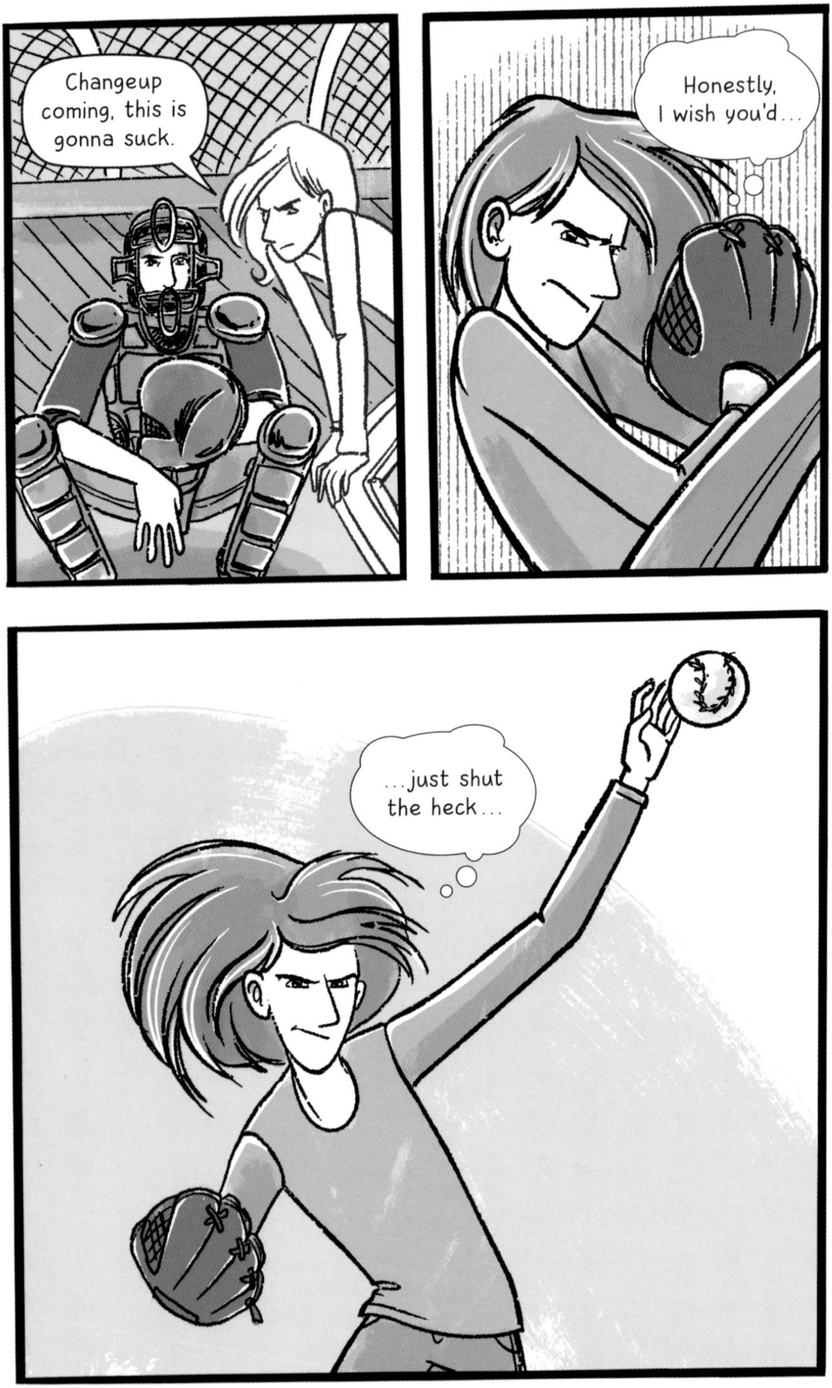
Changeup coming, this is gonna suck.
Honestly, I wish you'd...
...just shut the heck...

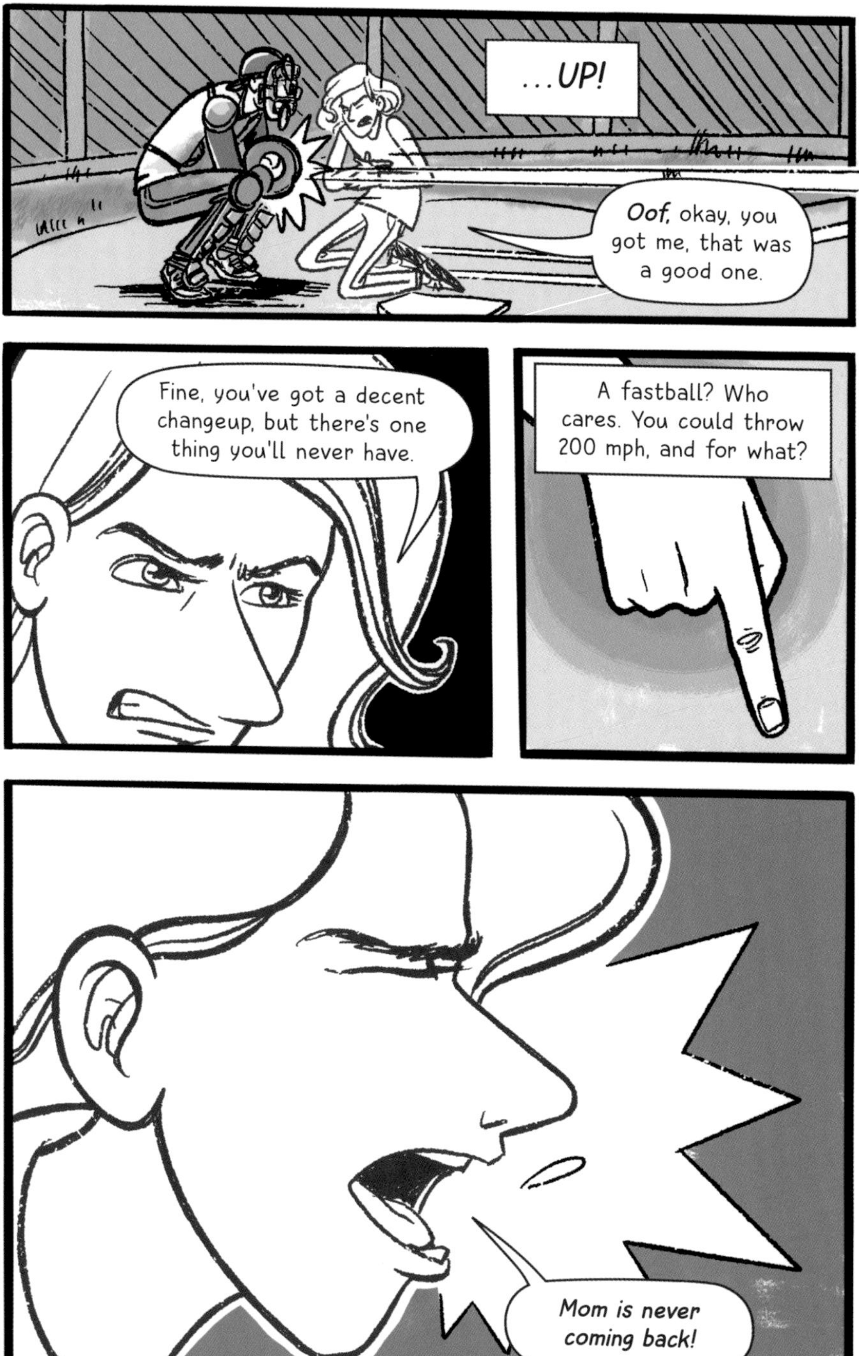

...UP!
Oof, okay, you got me, that was a good one.
Fine, you've got a decent changeup, but there's one thing you'll never have.
A fastball? Who cares. You could throw 200 mph, and for what?
Mom is never coming back!

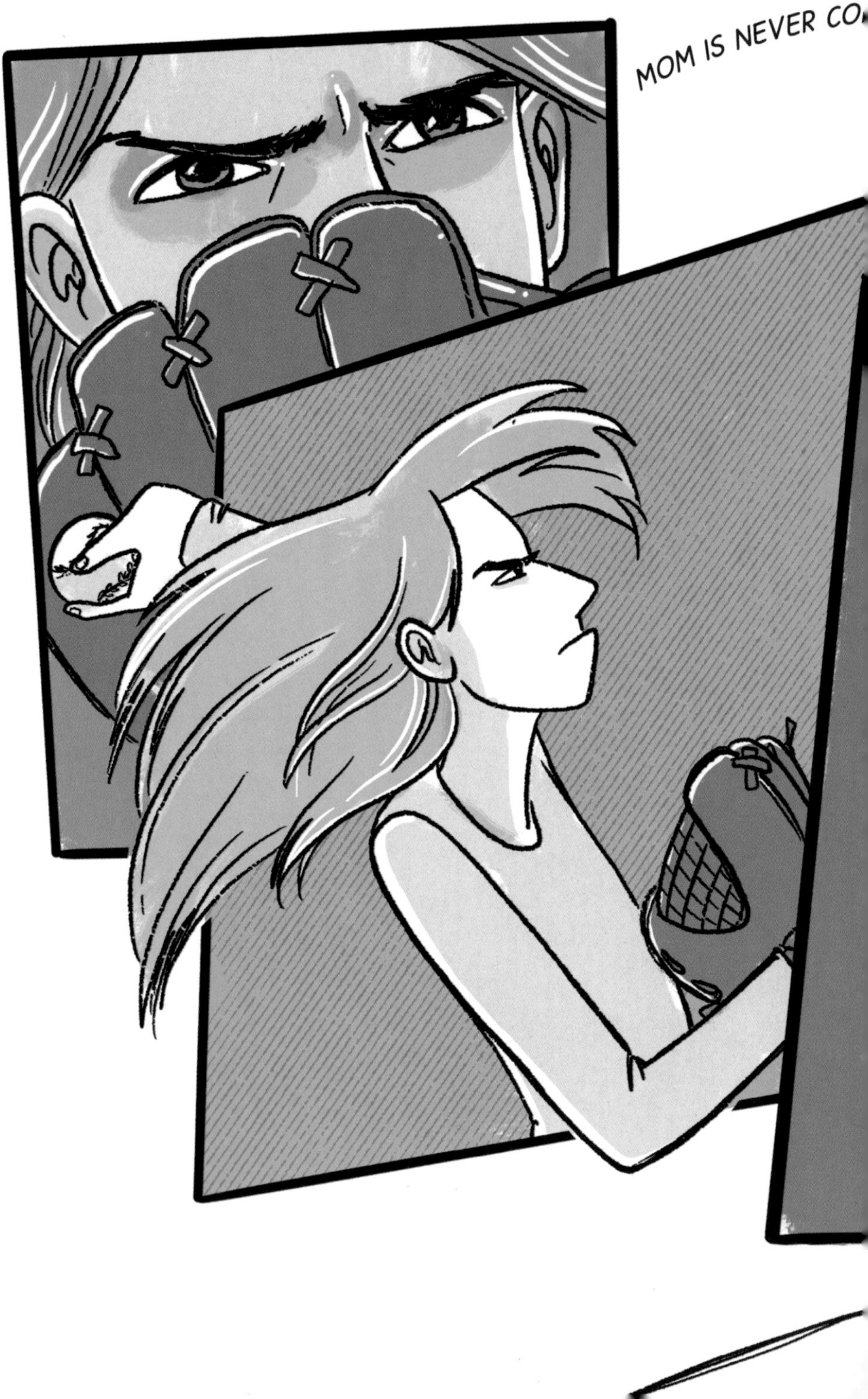
MOM IS NEVER CO

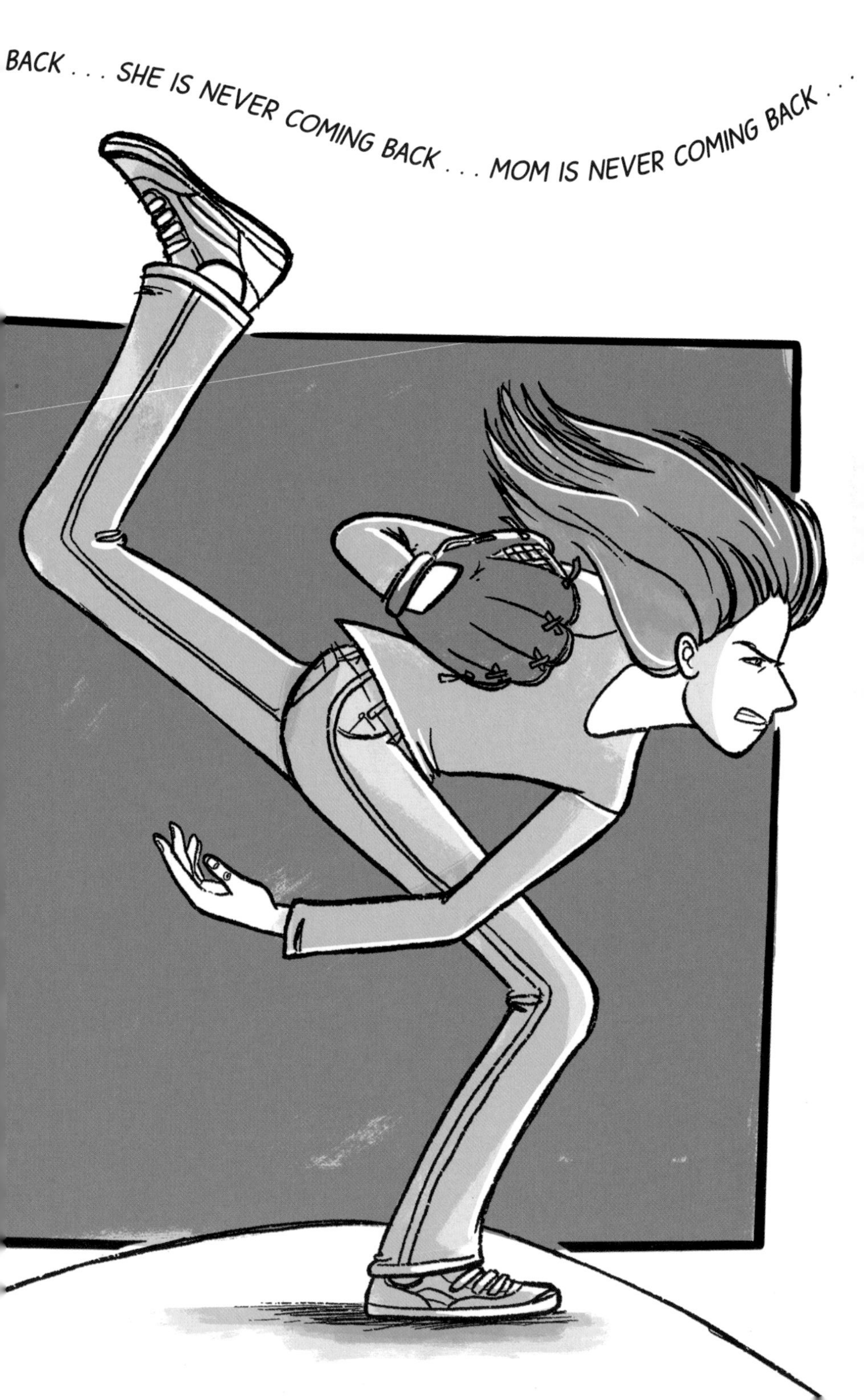
BACK . . . SHE IS NEVER COMING BACK . . . MOM IS NEVER COMING BACK . . .

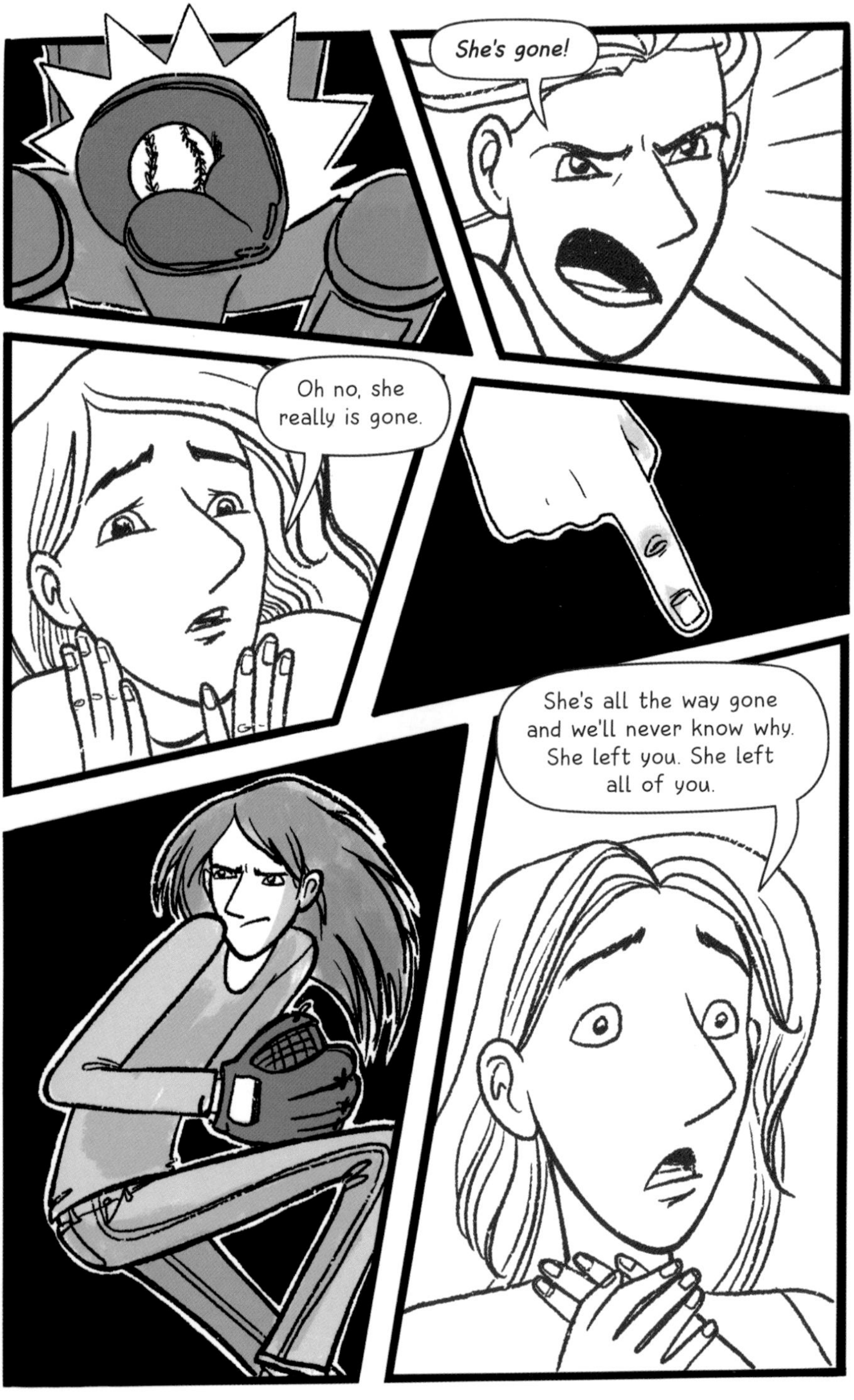
She's gone!
Oh no, she really is gone.
She's all the way gone and we'll never know why. She left you. She left all of you.

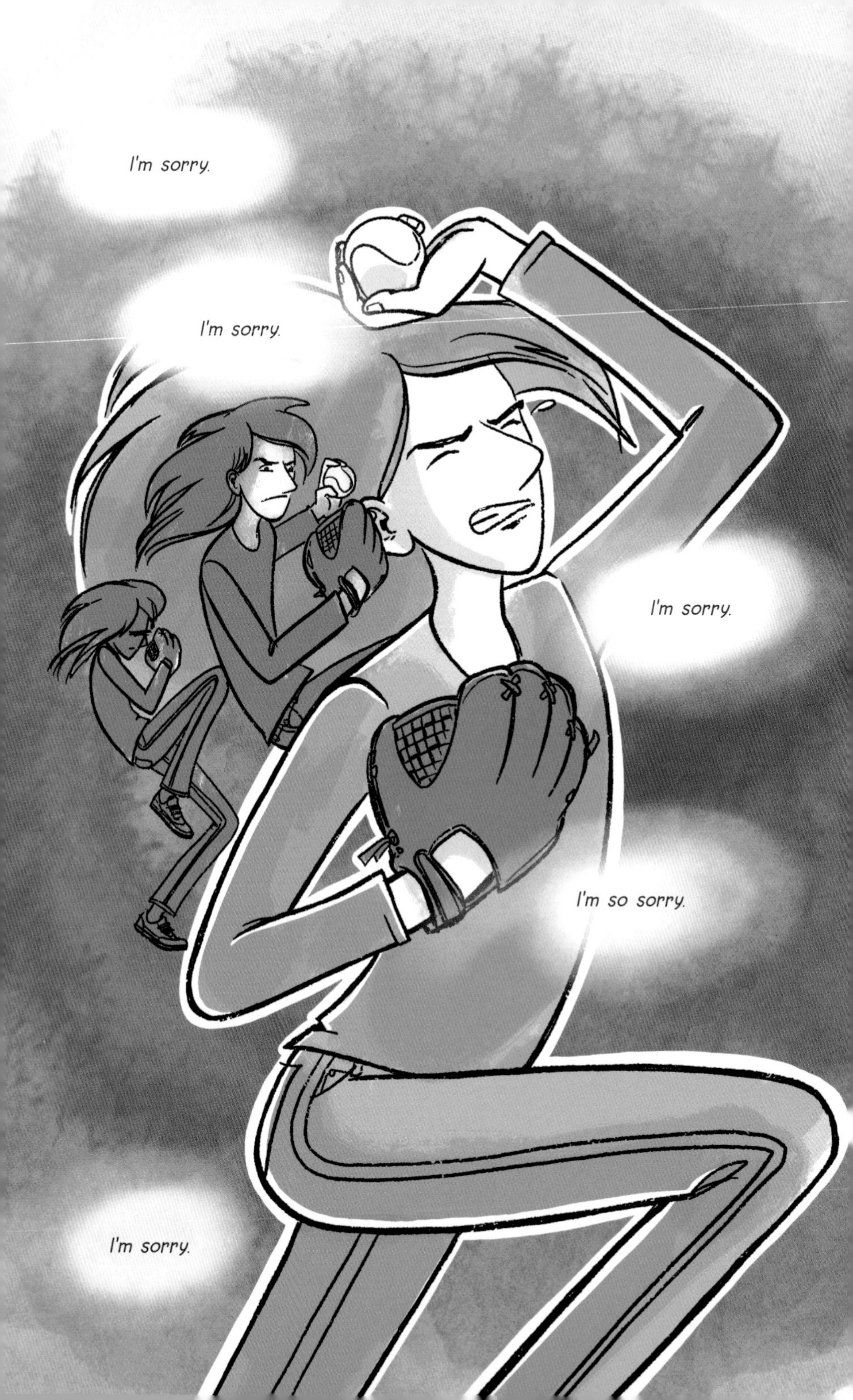
I'm sorry.
I'm sorry.
I'm sorry.
I'm so sorry.
I'm sorry.

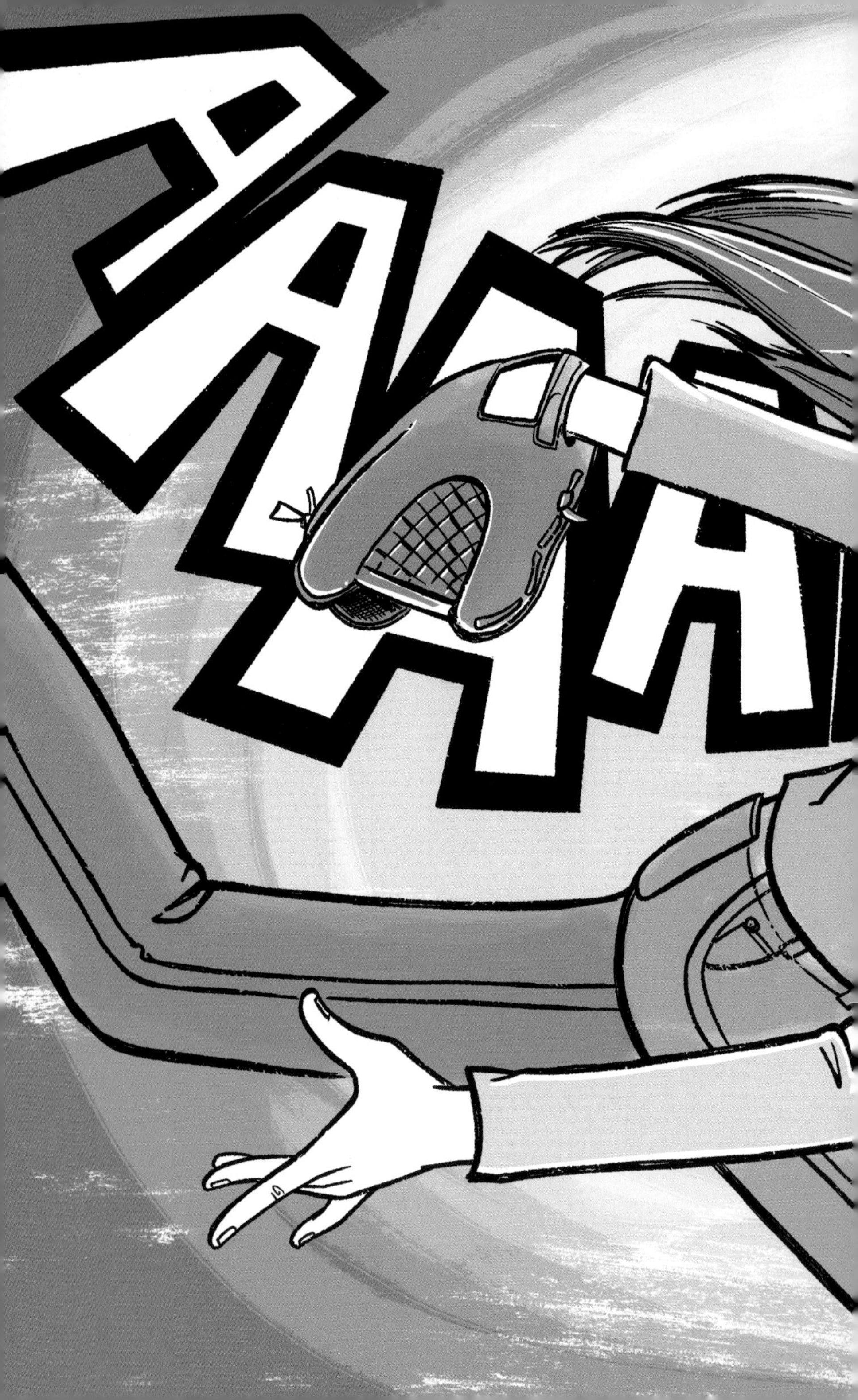
AAAAH

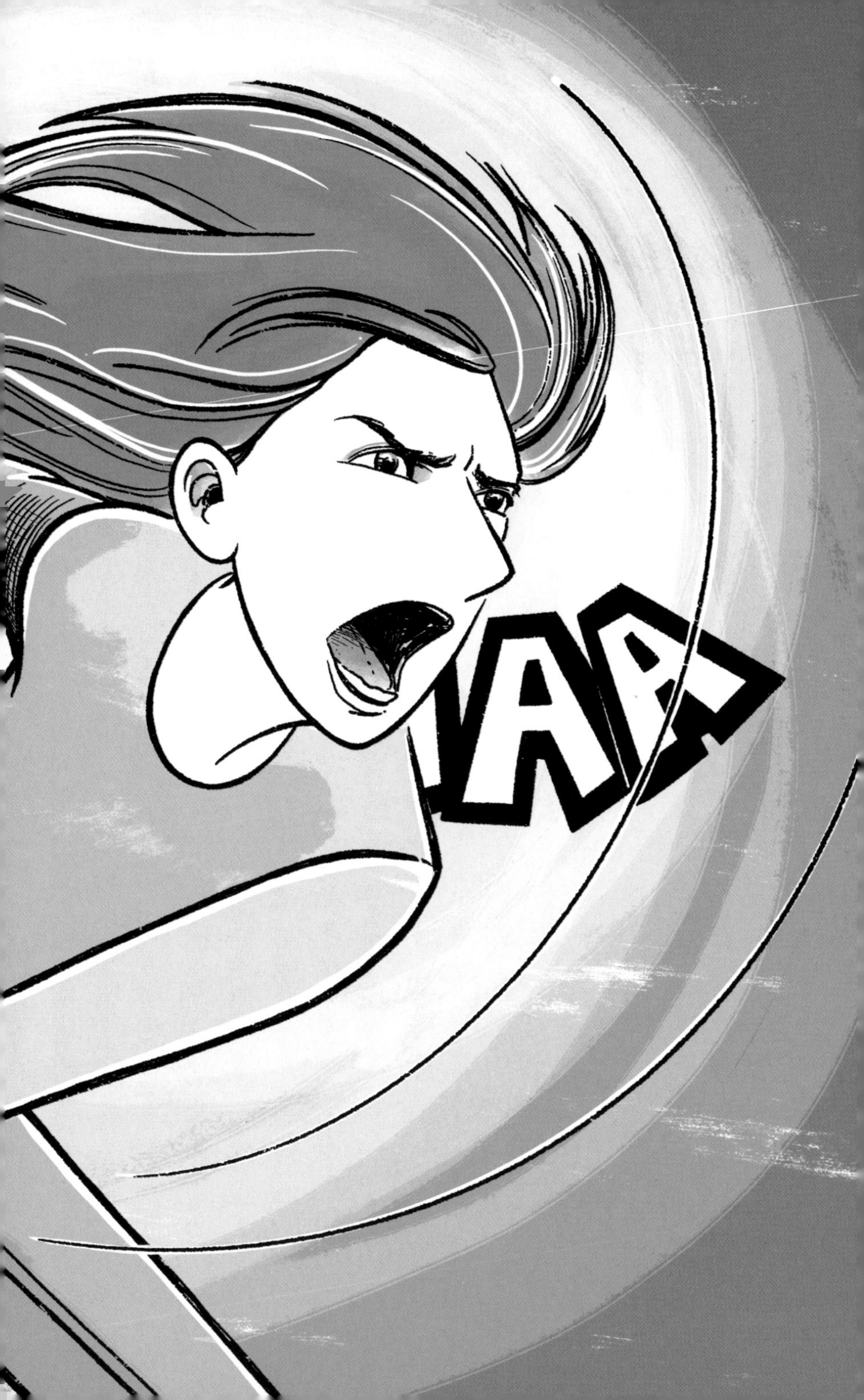
AA

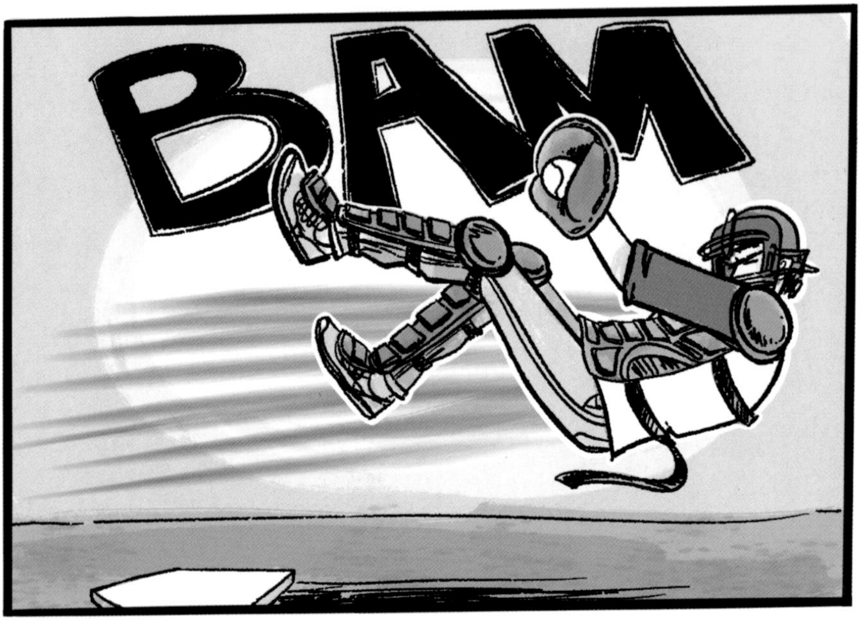
BAM

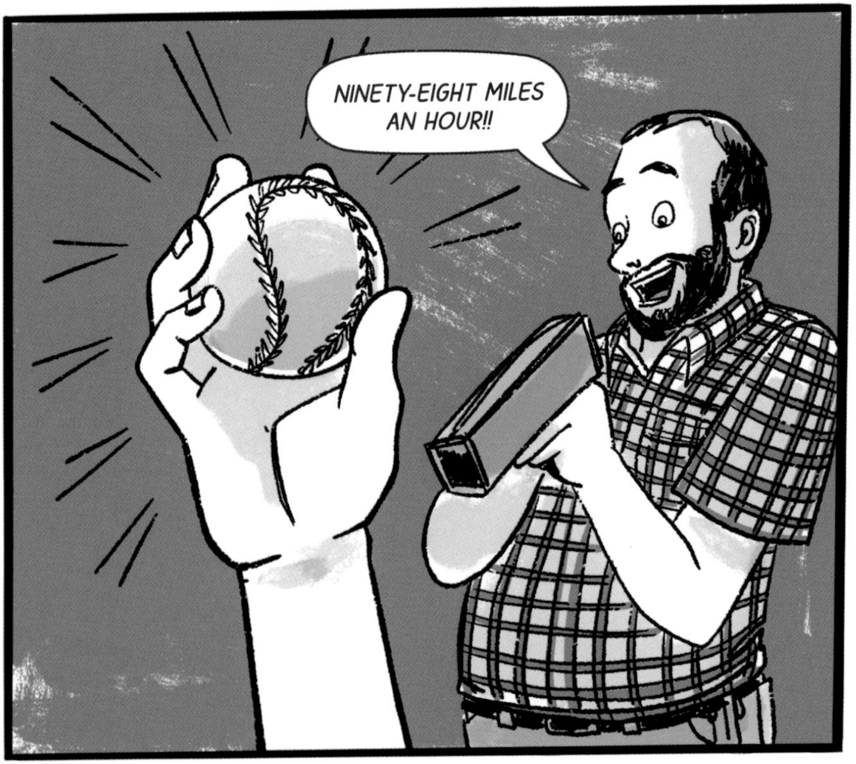
NINETY-EIGHT MILES AN HOUR!!

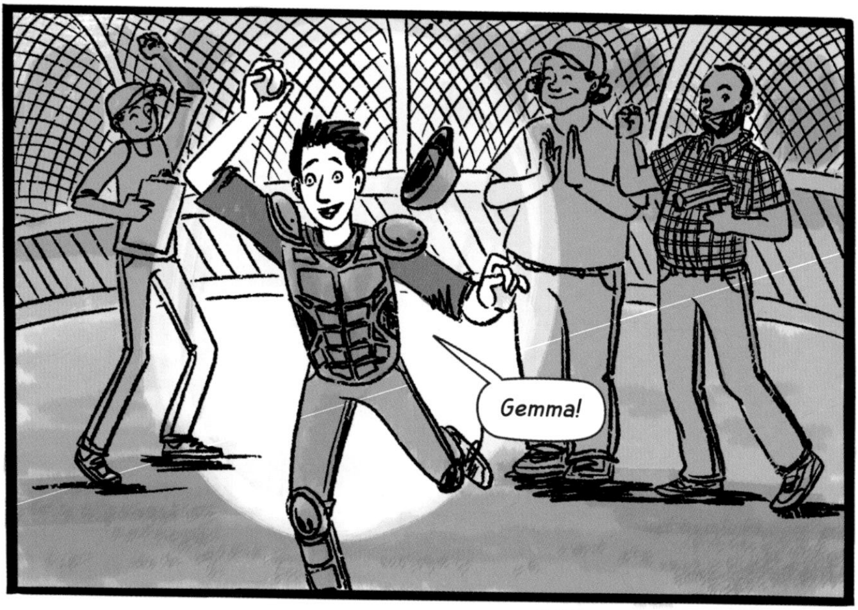
Gemma!

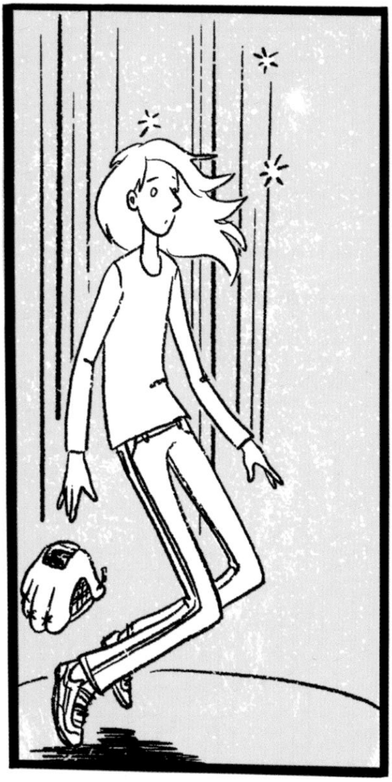

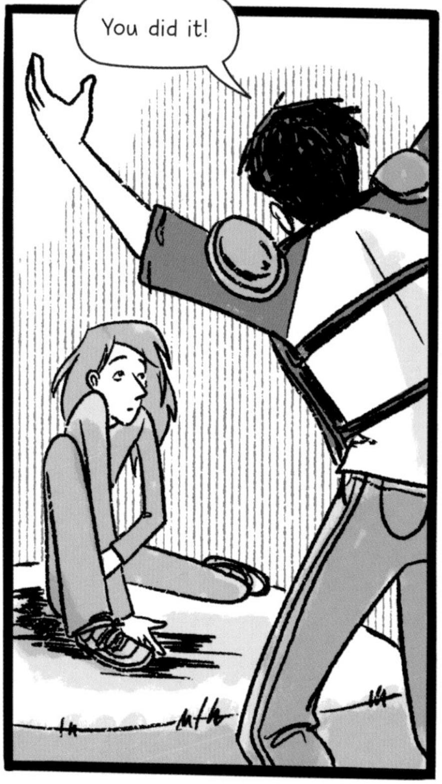
You did it!

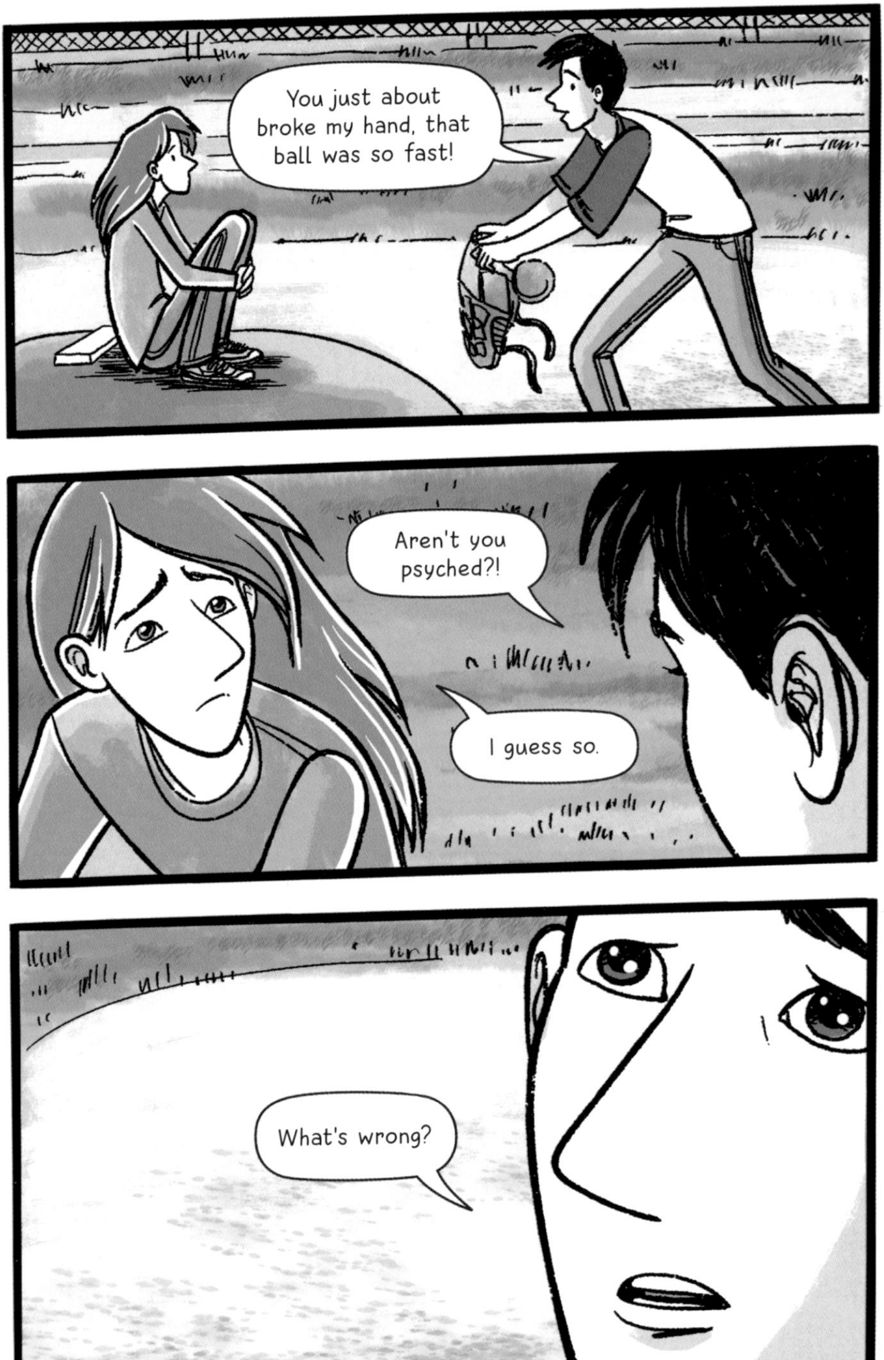
You just about broke my hand, that ball was so fast!
Aren't you psyched?!
I guess so.
What's wrong?

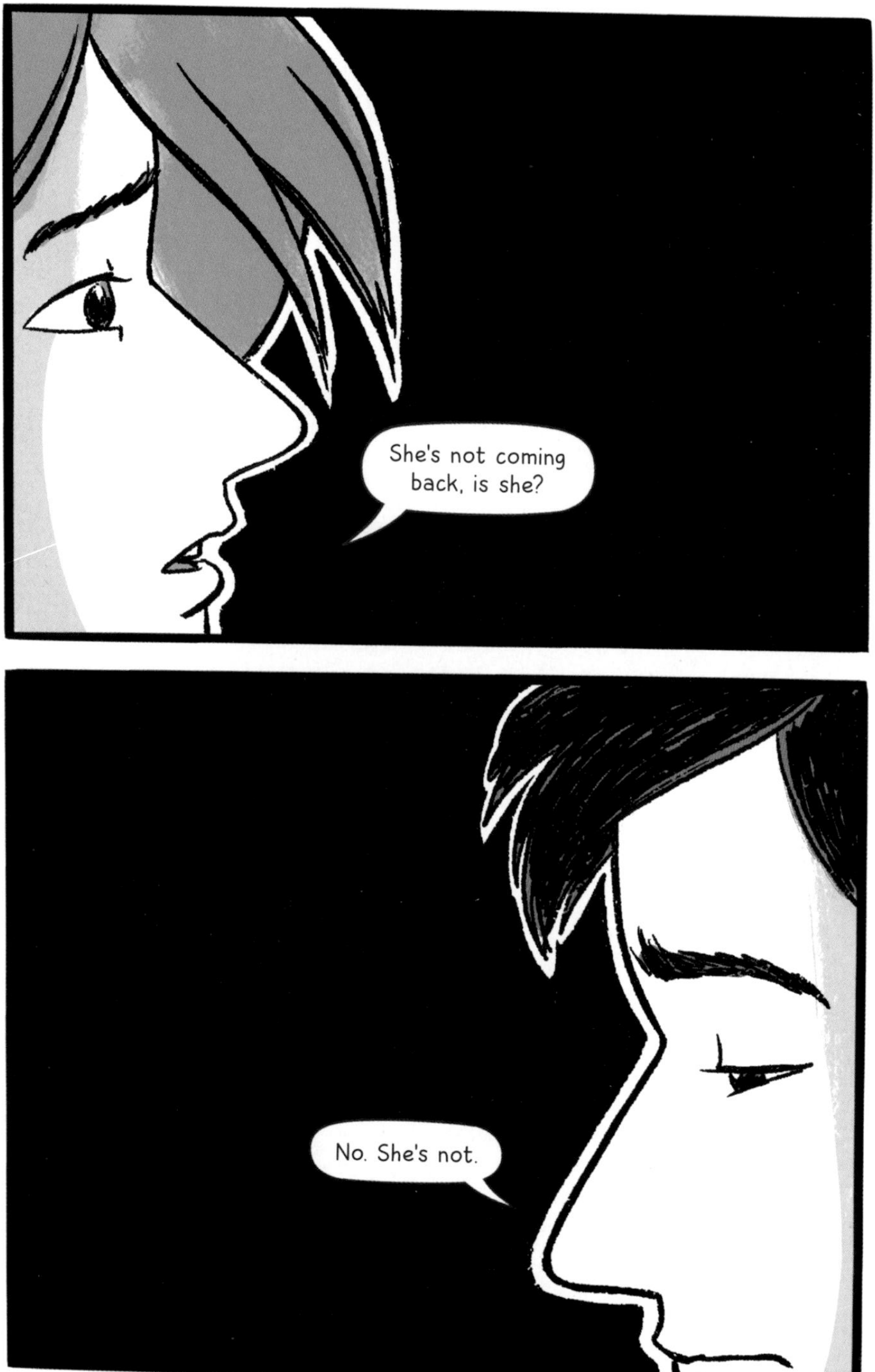
She's not coming back, is she?
No. She's not.

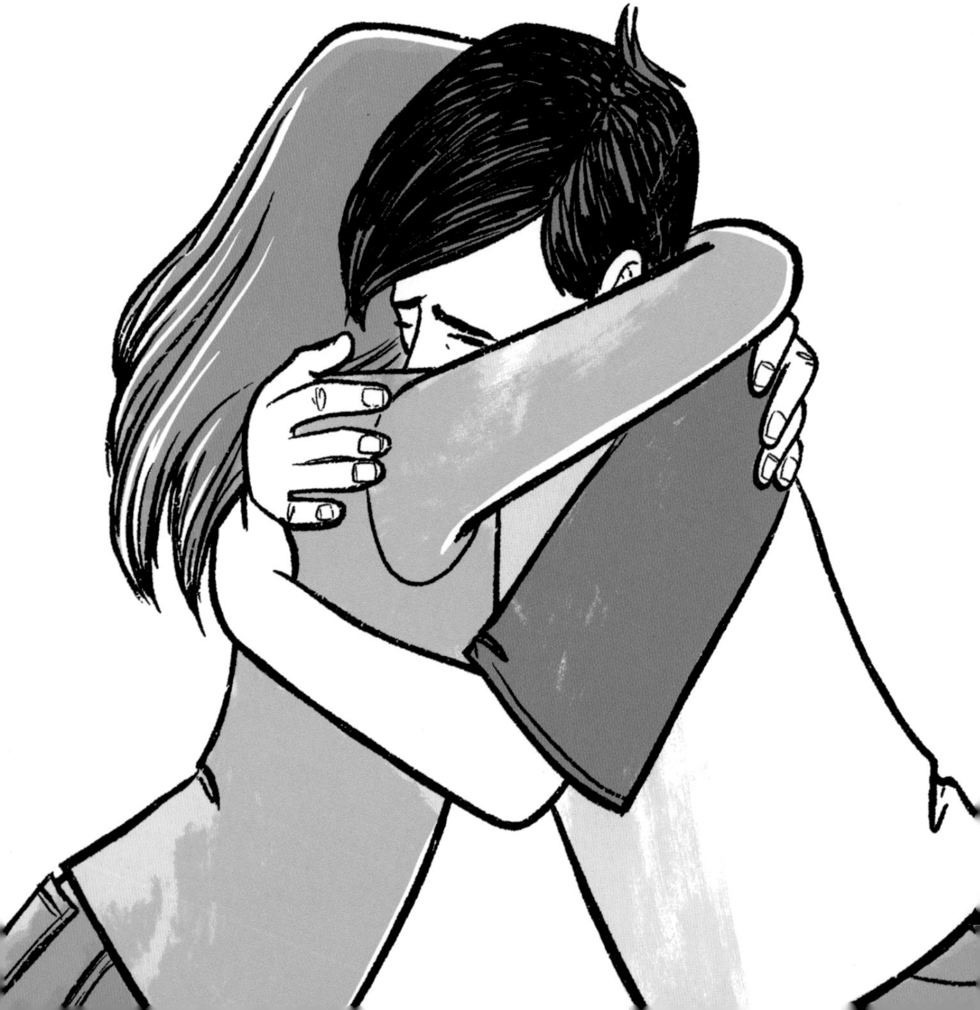

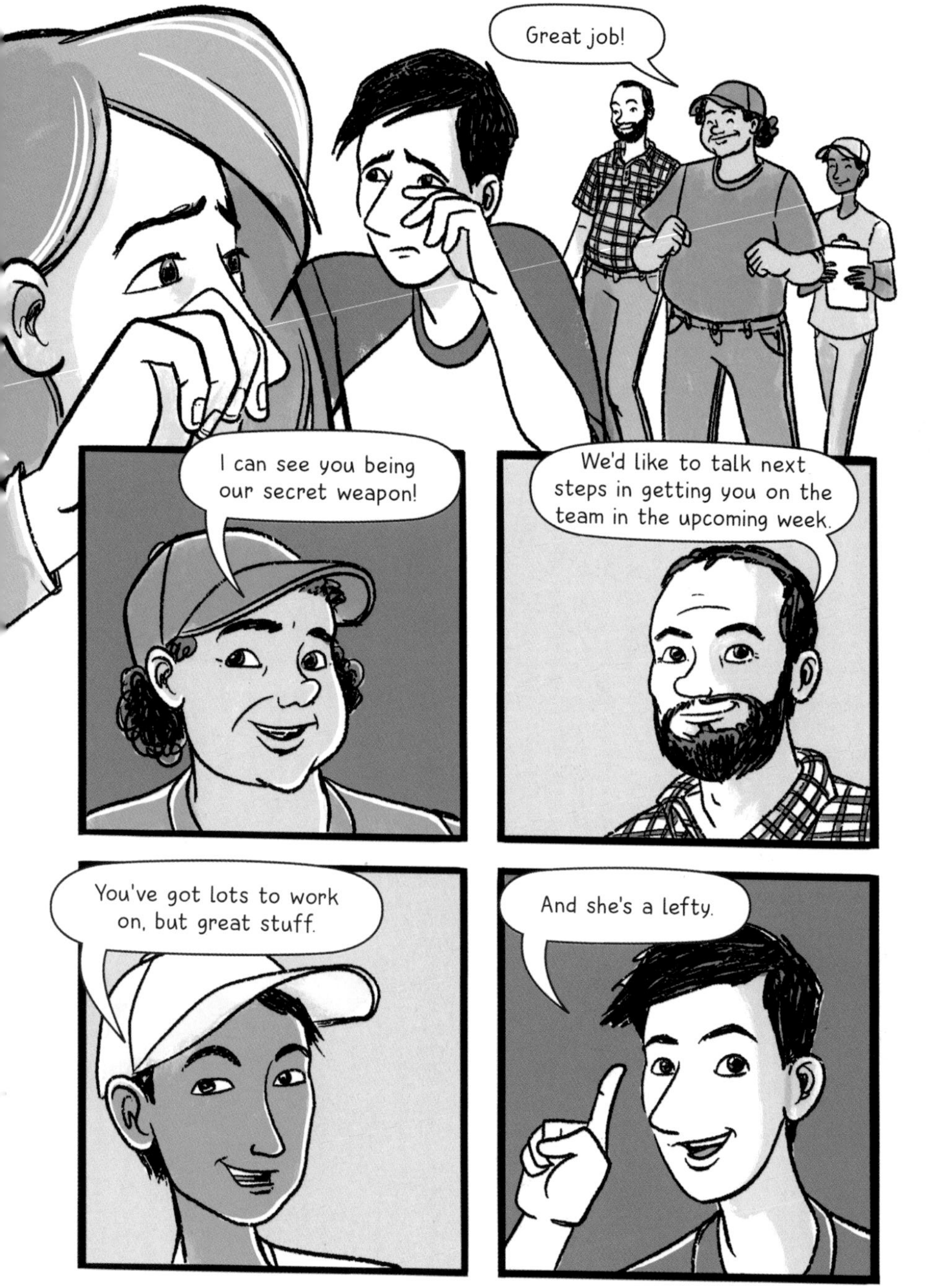
Great job!
I can see you being our secret weapon!
We'd like to talk next steps in getting you on the team in the upcoming week.
You've got lots to work on, but great stuff.
And she's a lefty.

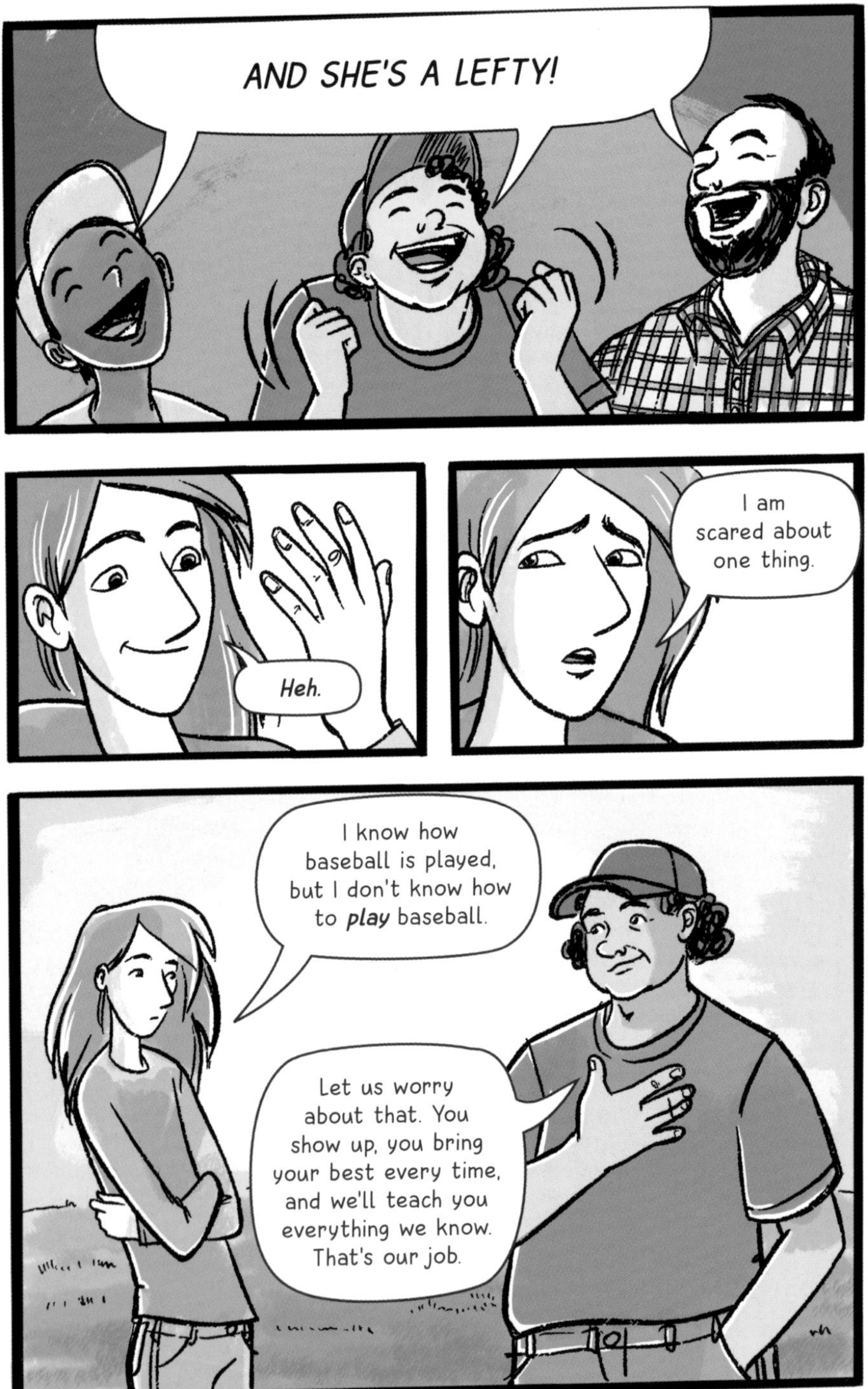
AND SHE'S A LEFTY!
Heh.
I am scared about one thing.
I know how baseball is played, but I don't know how to *play* baseball.
Let us worry about that. You show up, you bring your best every time, and we'll teach you everything we know. That's our job.

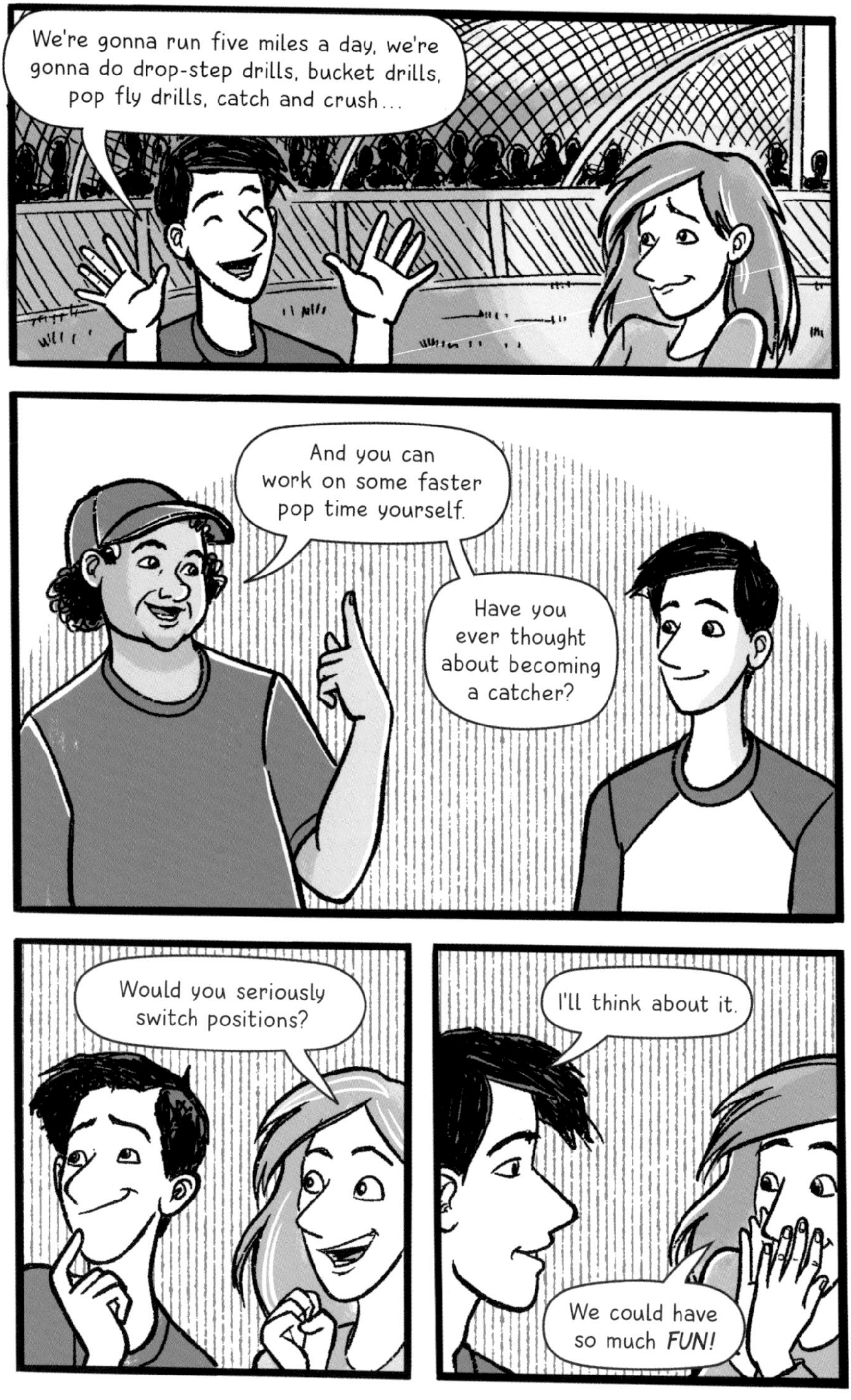
We're gonna run five miles a day, we're gonna do drop-step drills, bucket drills, pop fly drills, catch and crush...
And you can work on some faster pop time yourself.
Have you ever thought about becoming a catcher?
Would you seriously switch positions?
I'll think about it.
We could have so much FUN!

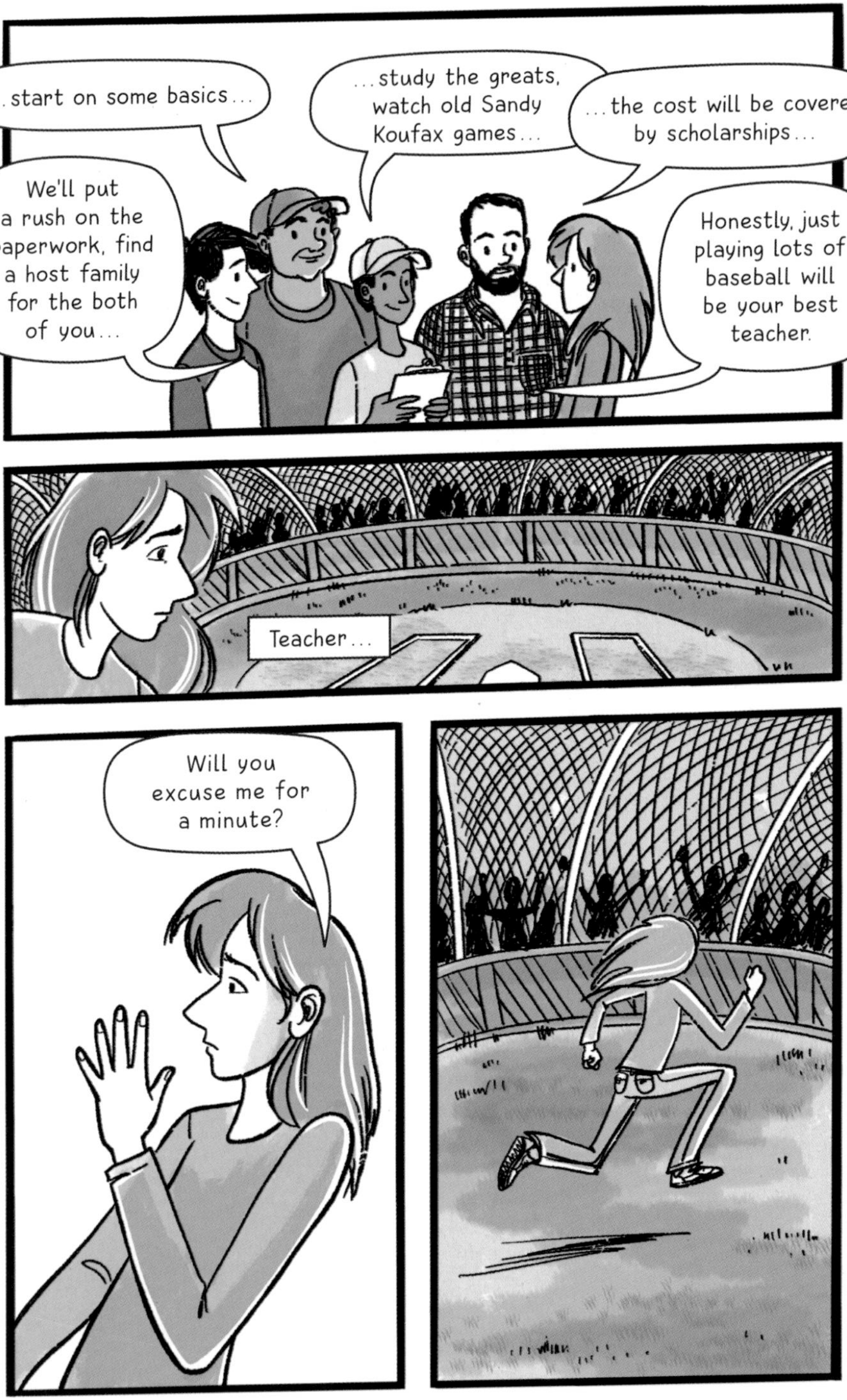
...start on some basics...
...study the greats, watch old Sandy Koufax games...
...the cost will be covered by scholarships...
We'll put a rush on the paperwork, find a host family for the both of you...
Honestly, just playing lots of baseball will be your best teacher.
Teacher...
Will you excuse me for a minute?

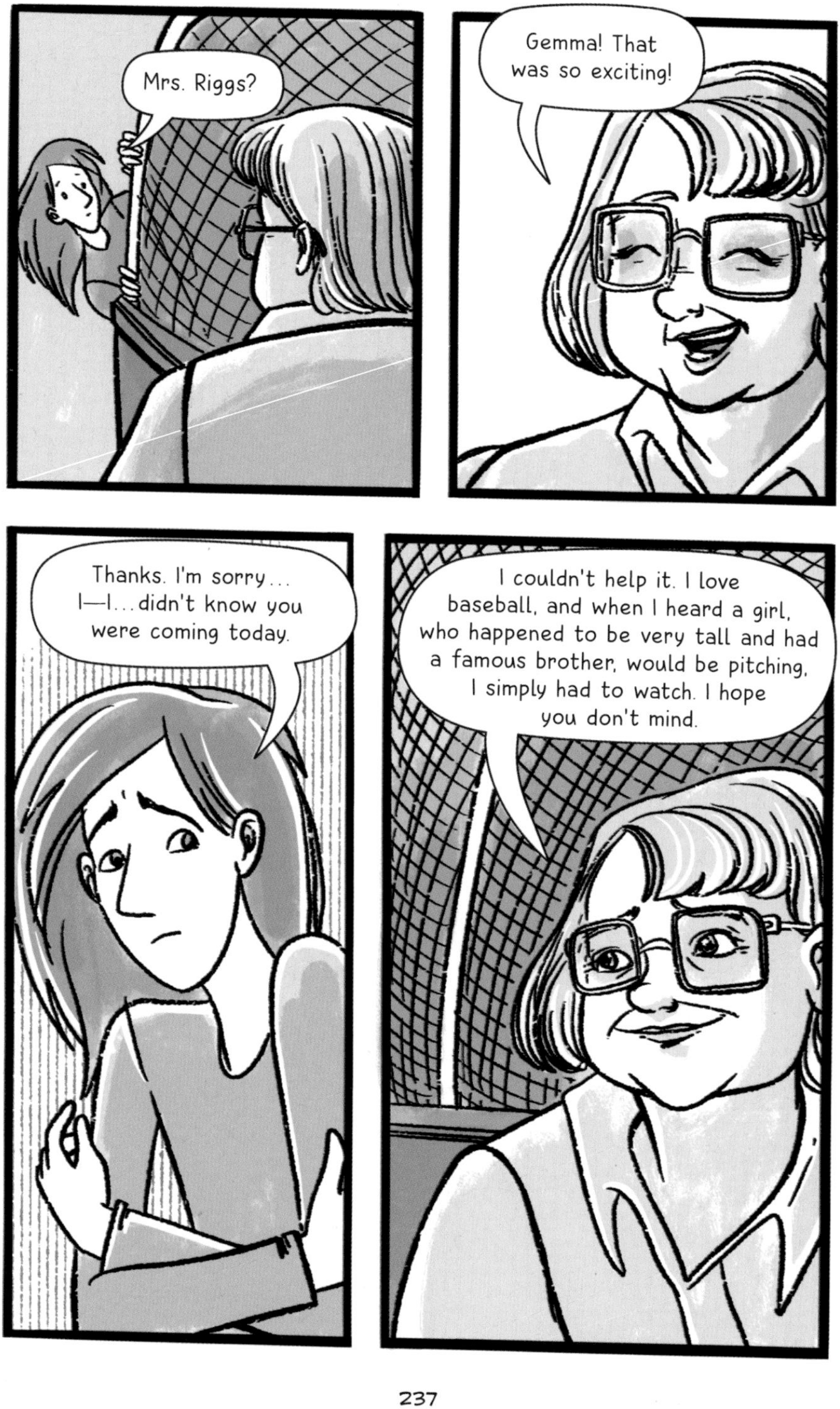
Mrs. Riggs?
Gemma! That was so exciting!
Thanks. I'm sorry... I—I...didn't know you were coming today.
I couldn't help it. I love baseball, and when I heard a girl, who happened to be very tall and had a famous brother, would be pitching, I simply had to watch. I hope you don't mind.

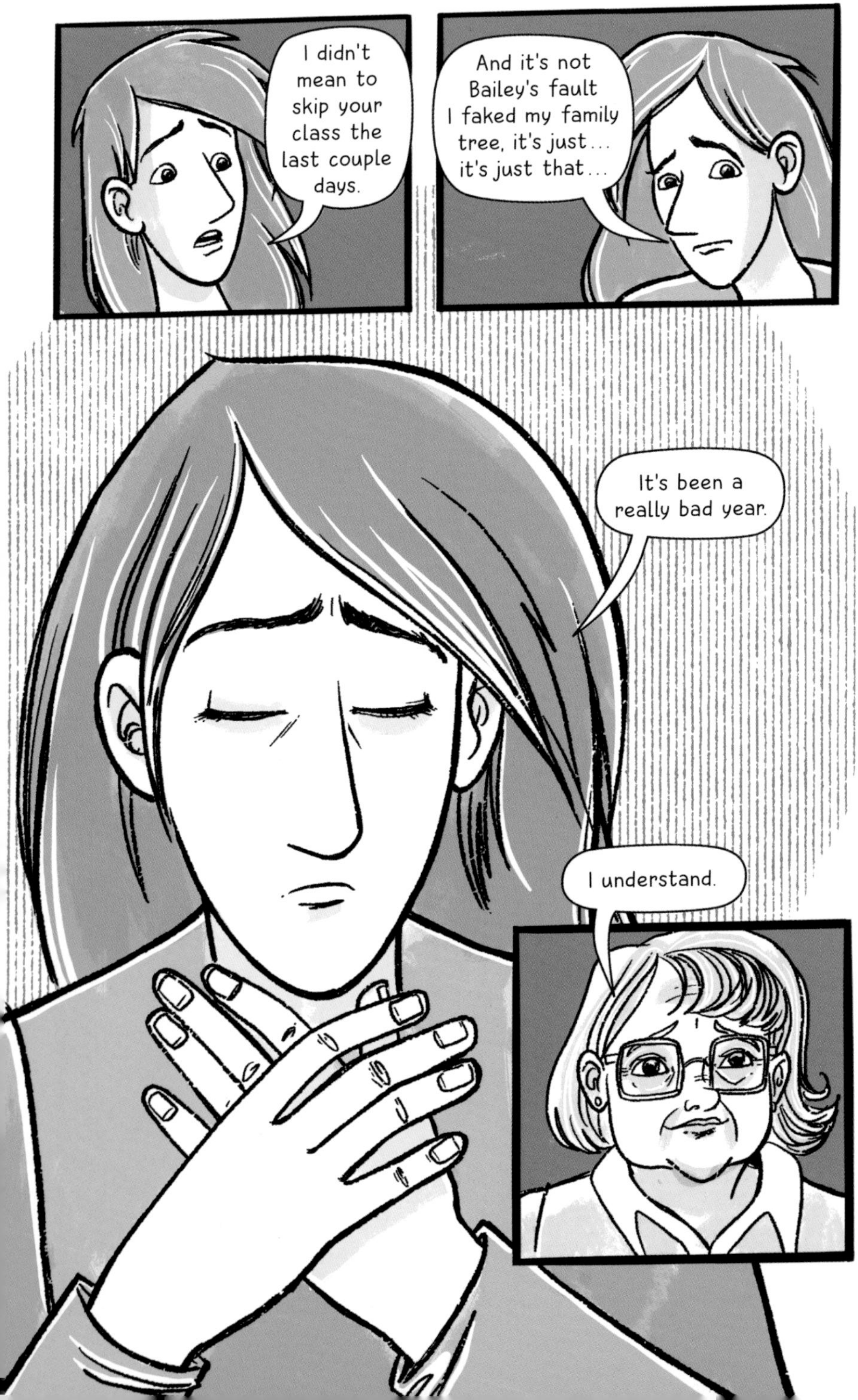
I didn't mean to skip your class the last couple days.
And it's not Bailey's fault I faked my family tree, it's just... it's just that...
It's been a really bad year.
I understand.

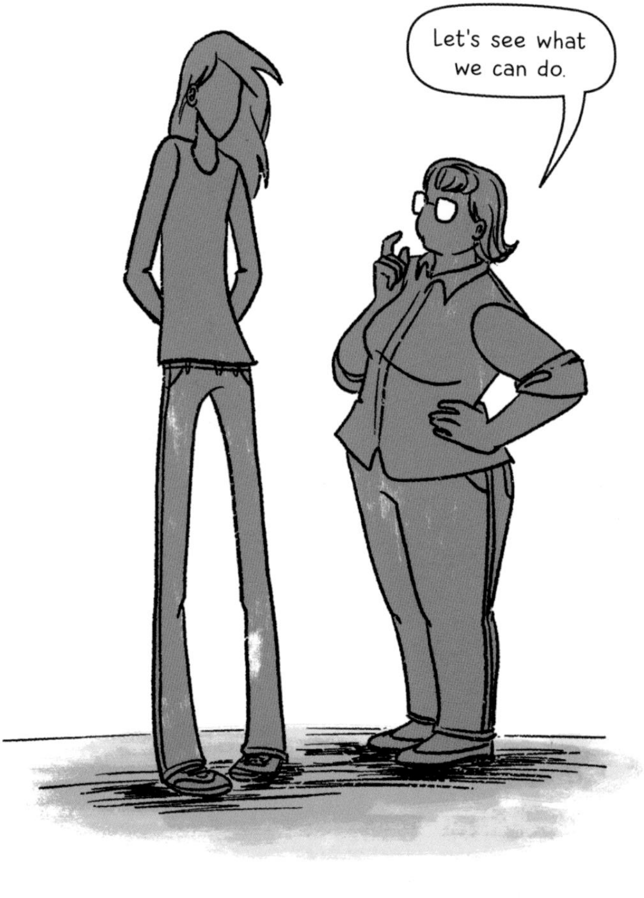
Let's see what we can do.

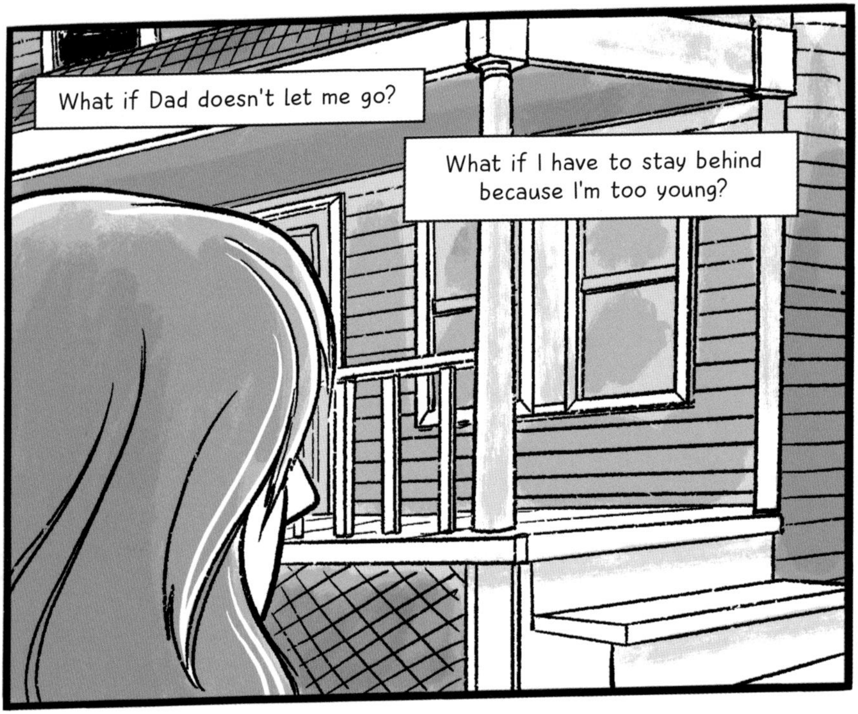
What if Dad doesn't let me go?
What if I have to stay behind because I'm too young?

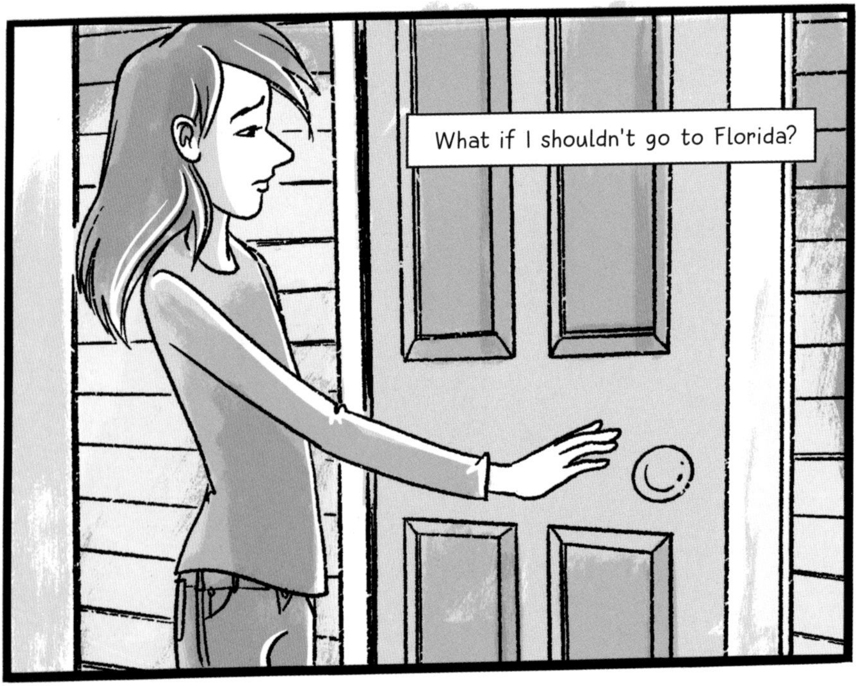
What if I shouldn't go to Florida?

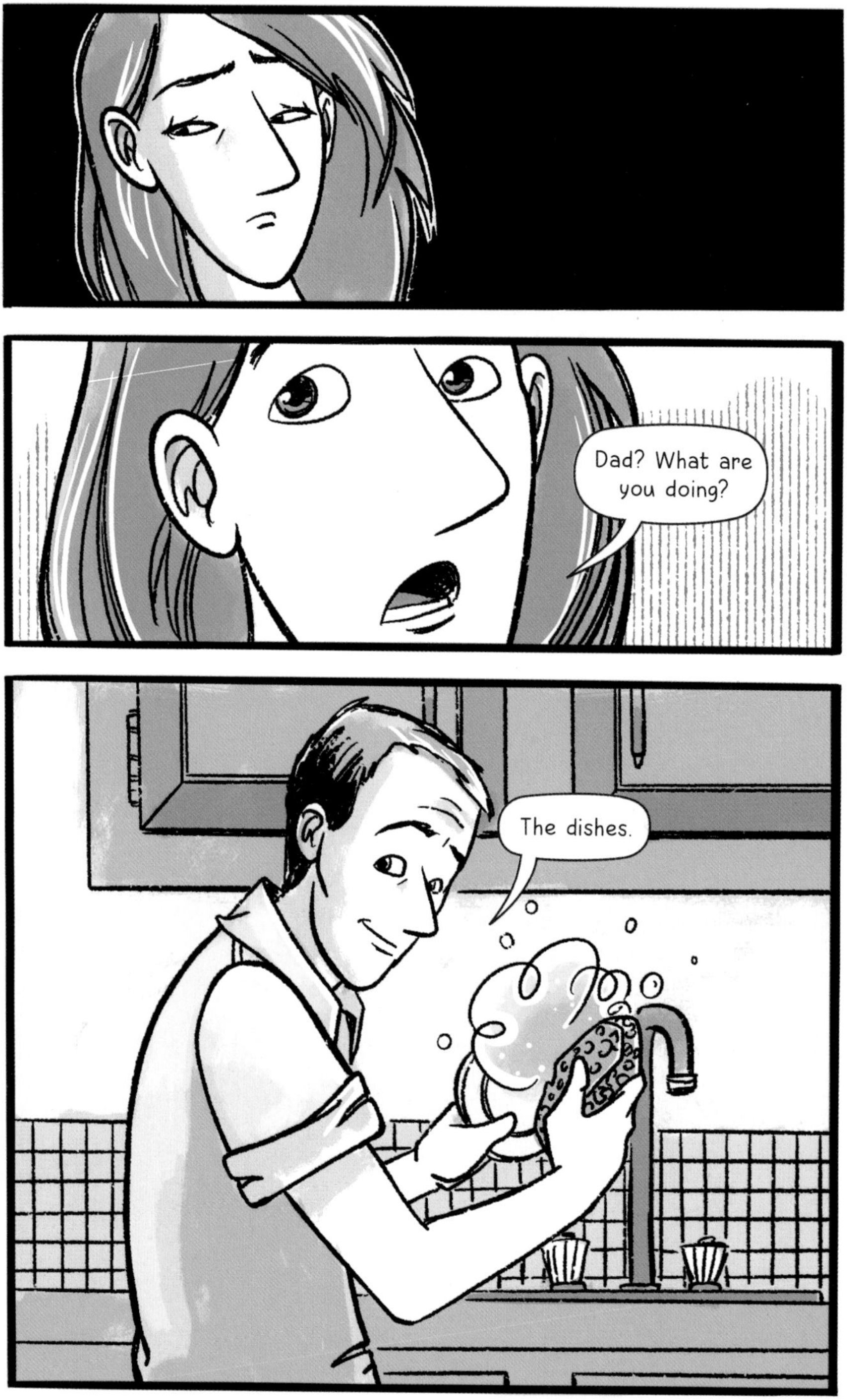
Dad? What are you doing?
The dishes.

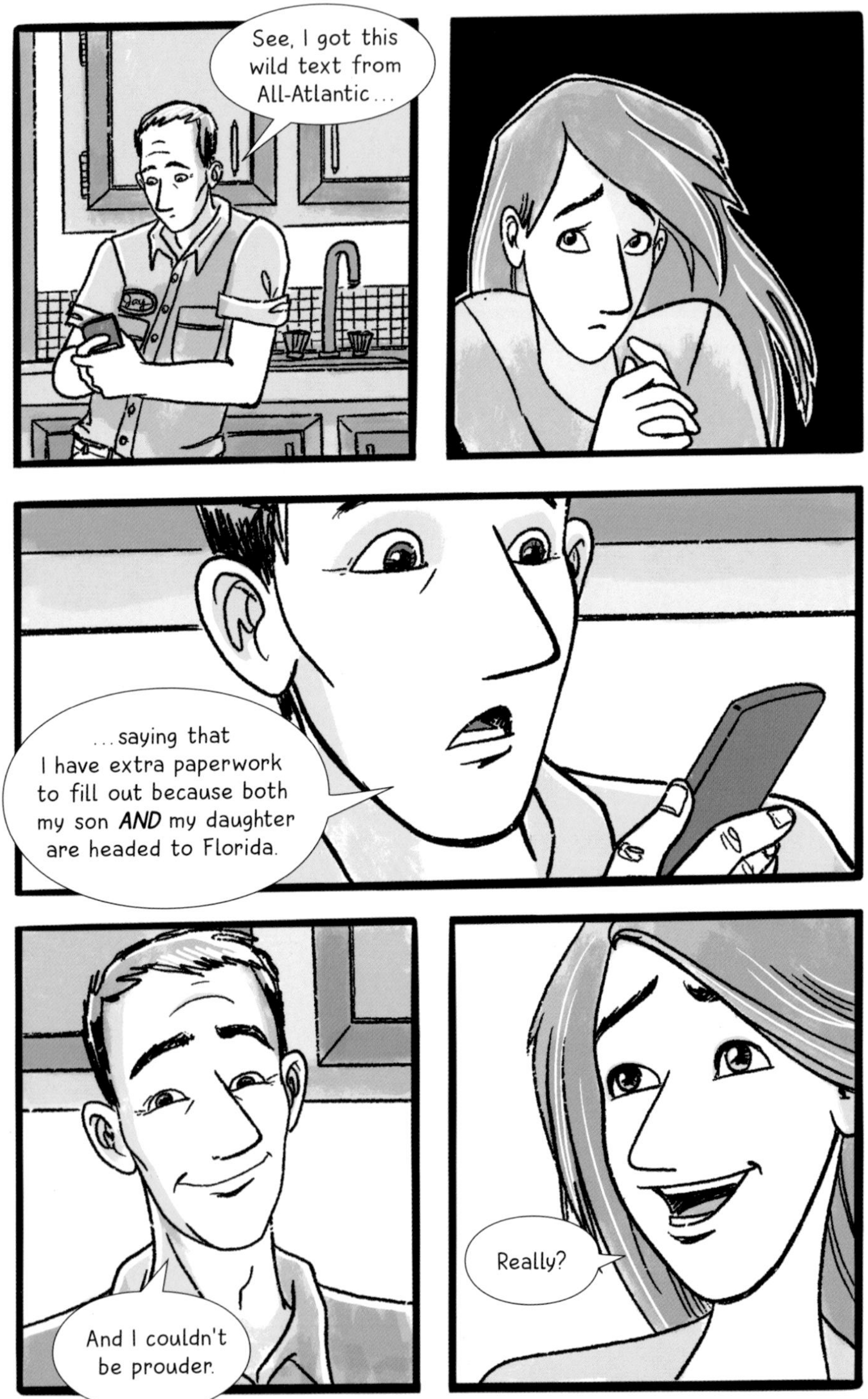
See, I got this wild text from All-Atlantic...
...saying that I have extra paperwork to fill out because both my son AND my daughter are headed to Florida.
And I couldn't be prouder.
Really?

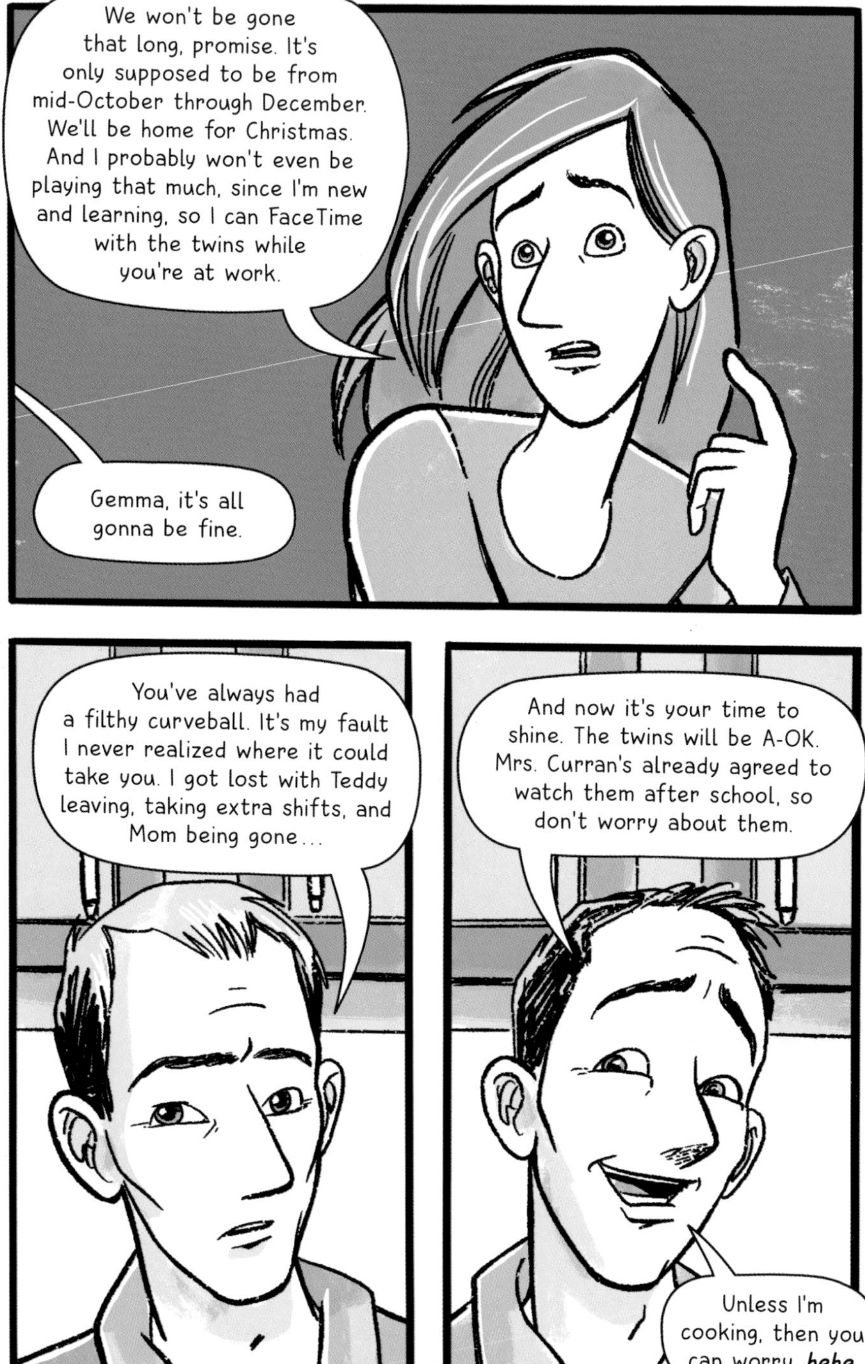
We won't be gone that long, promise. It's only supposed to be from mid-October through December. We'll be home for Christmas. And I probably won't even be playing that much, since I'm new and learning, so I can FaceTime with the twins while you're at work.
Gemma, it's all gonna be fine.
You've always had a filthy curveball. It's my fault I never realized where it could take you. I got lost with Teddy leaving, taking extra shifts, and Mom being gone...
And now it's your time to shine. The twins will be A-OK. Mrs. Curran's already agreed to watch them after school, so don't worry about them.
Unless I'm cooking, then you can worry, ***hehe.***

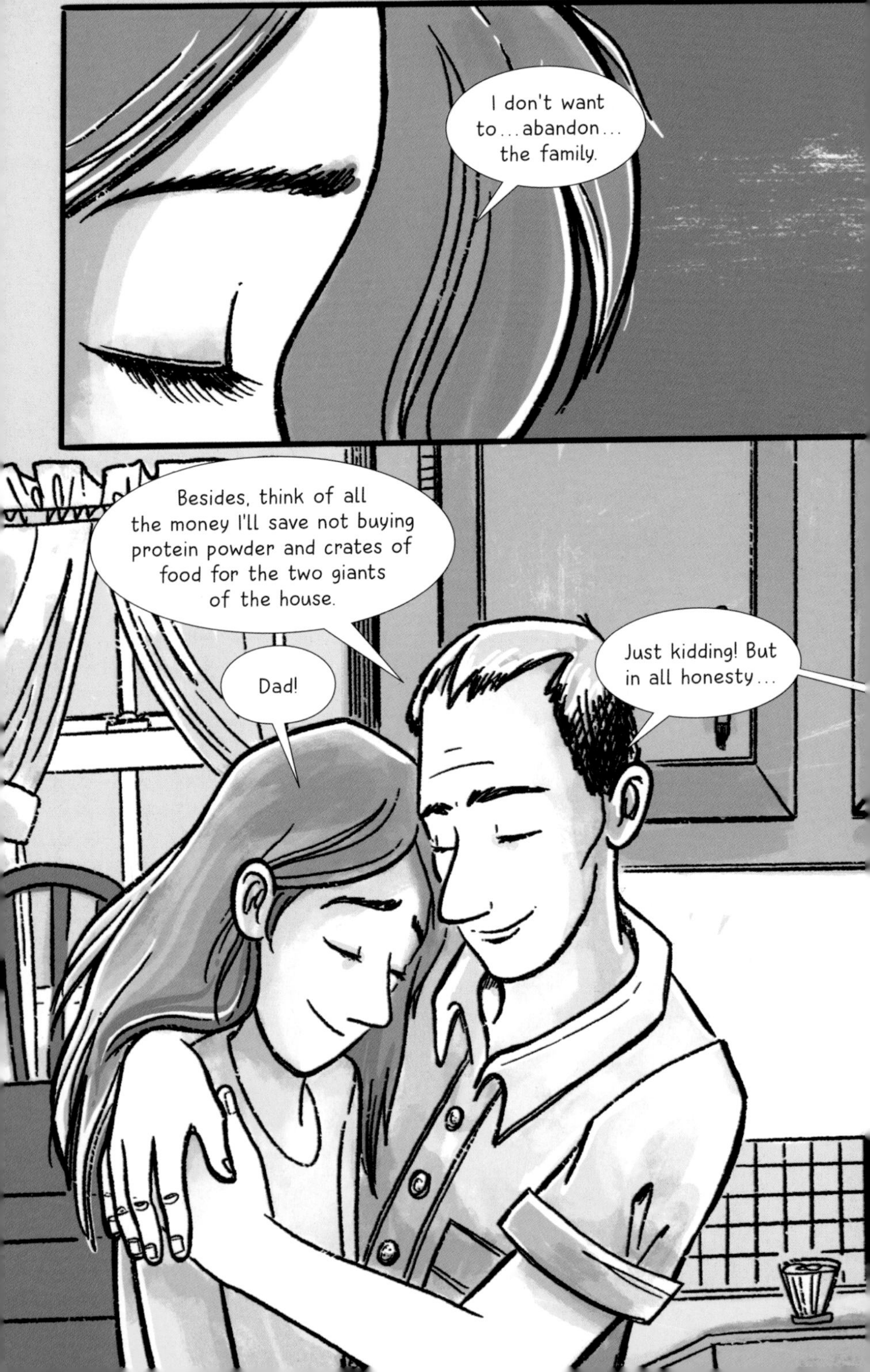
I don't want to... abandon... the family.
Besides, think of all the money I'll save not buying protein powder and crates of food for the two giants of the house.
Dad!
Just kidding! But in all honesty...

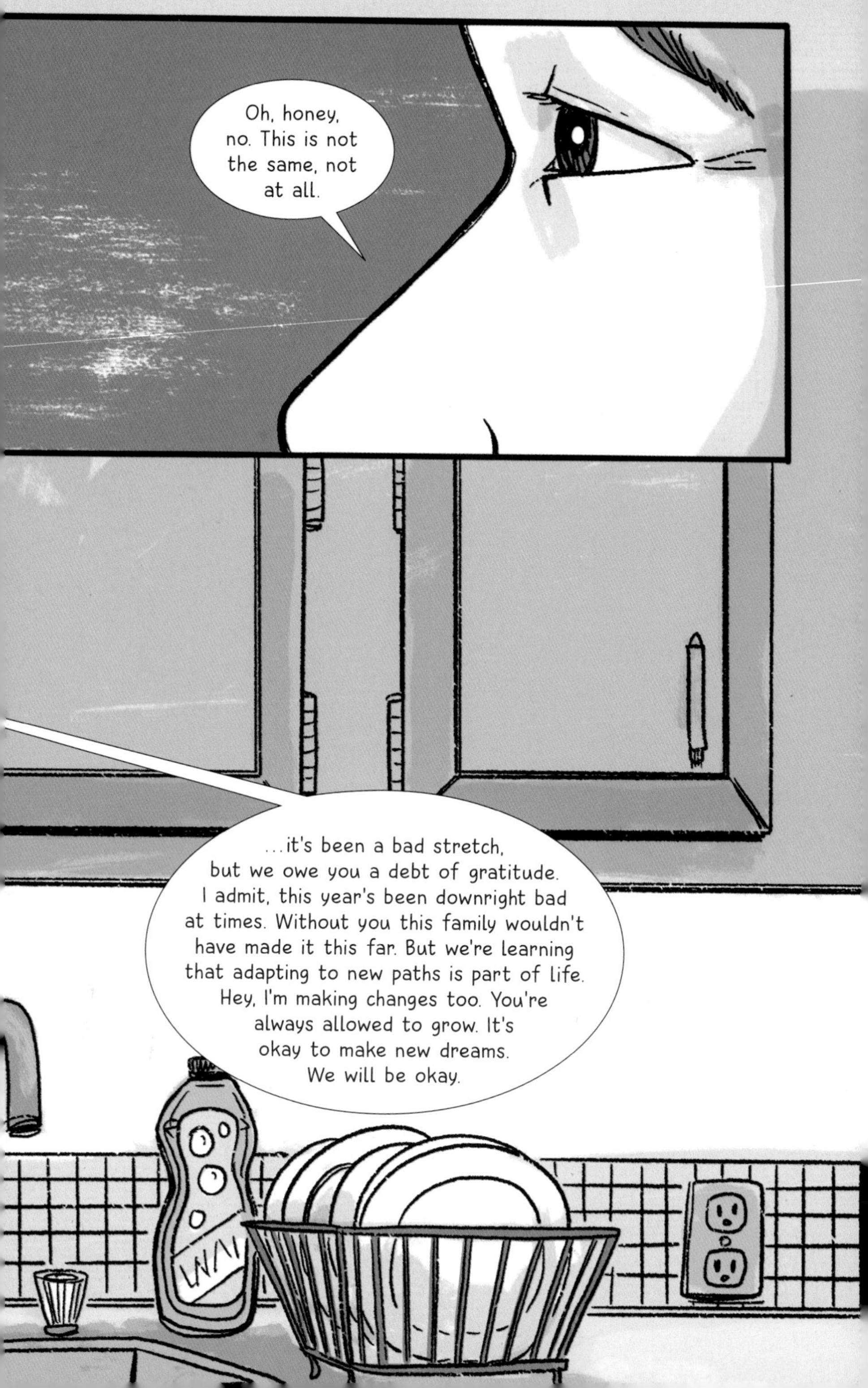
Oh, honey, no. This is not the same, not at all.
...it's been a bad stretch, but we owe you a debt of gratitude. I admit, this year's been downright bad at times. Without you this family wouldn't have made it this far. But we're learning that adapting to new paths is part of life. Hey, I'm making changes too. You're always allowed to grow. It's okay to make new dreams. We will be okay.

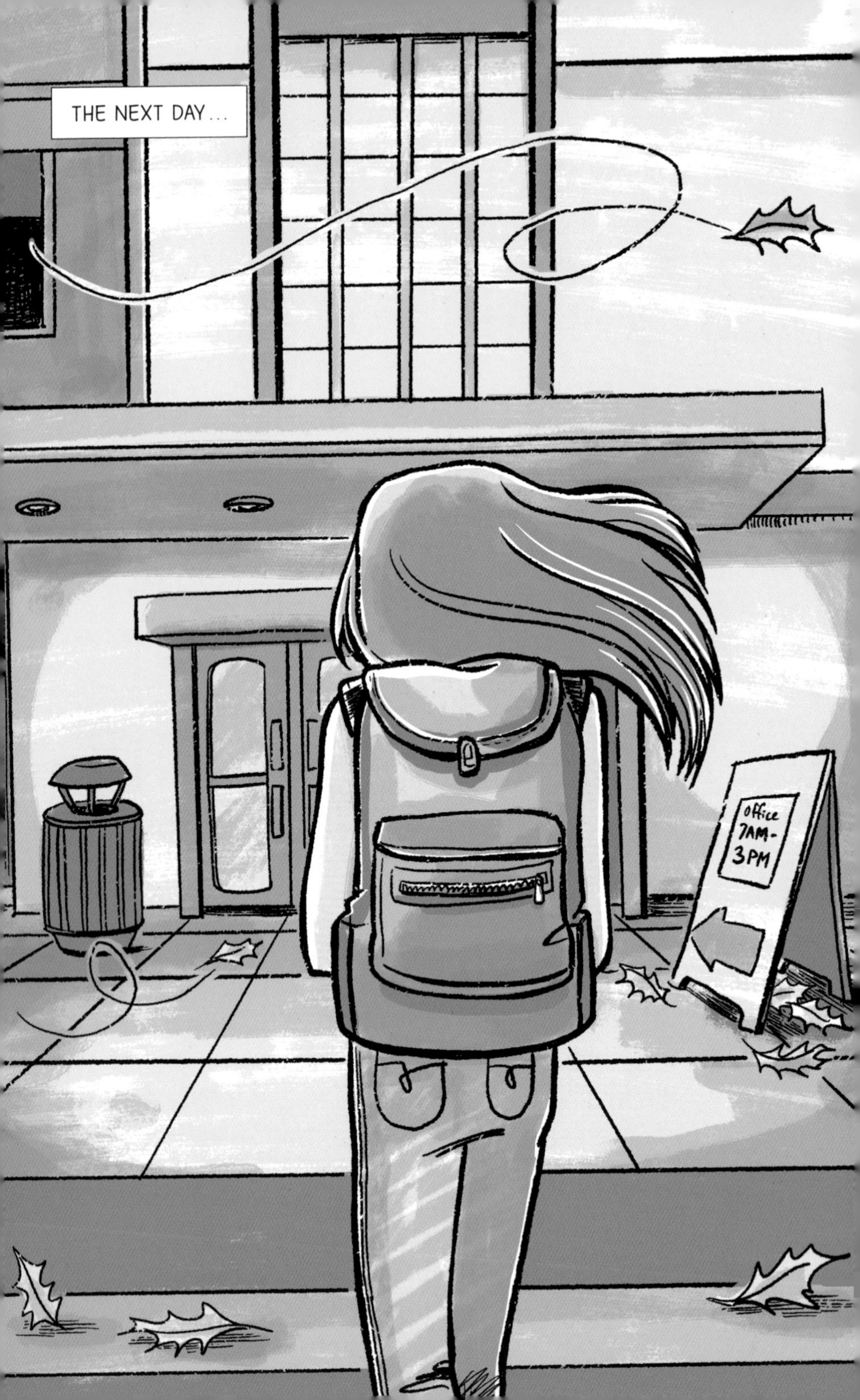
THE NEXT DAY...
Office
7AM-
3PM

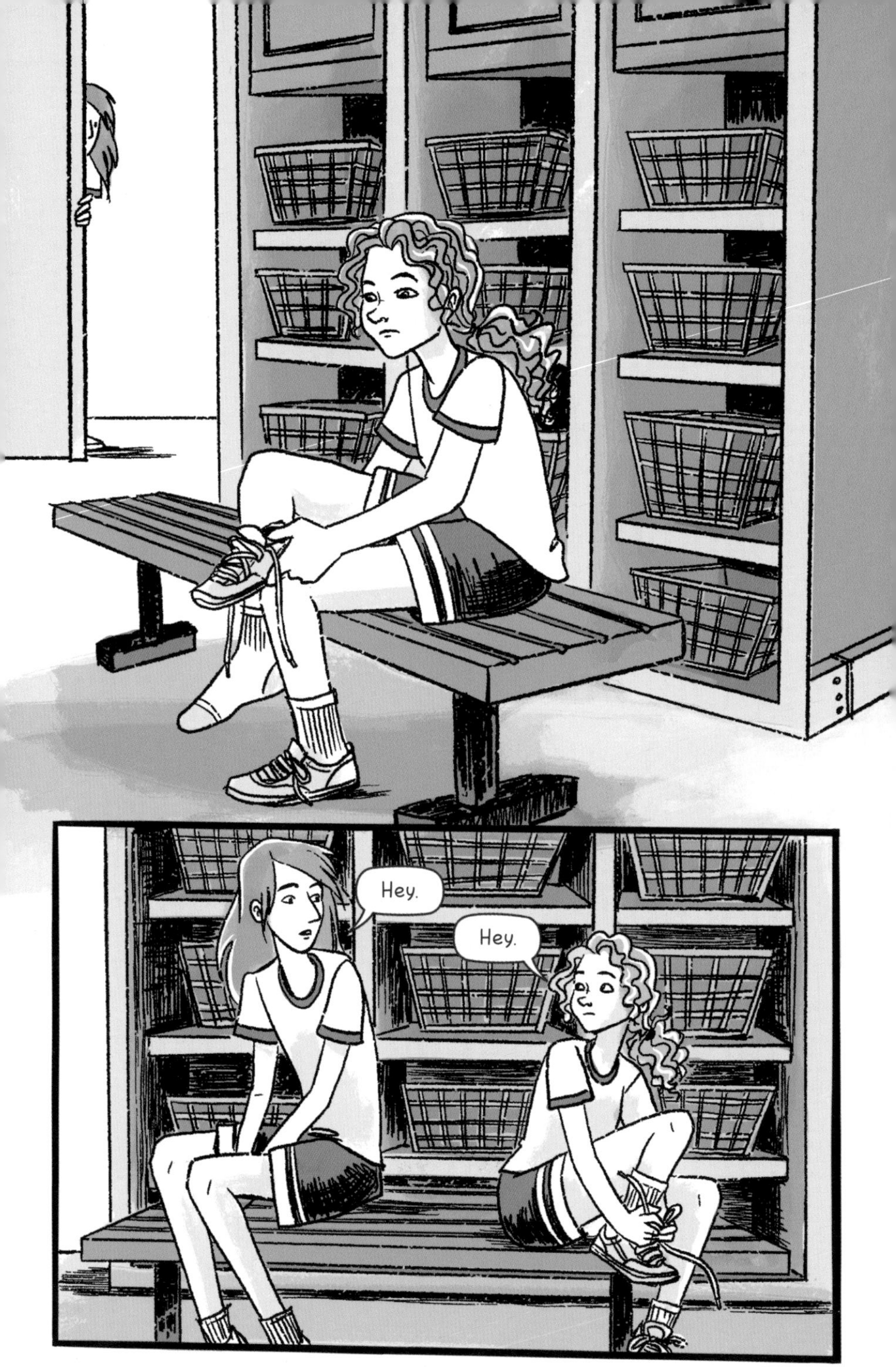
Hey.
Hey.

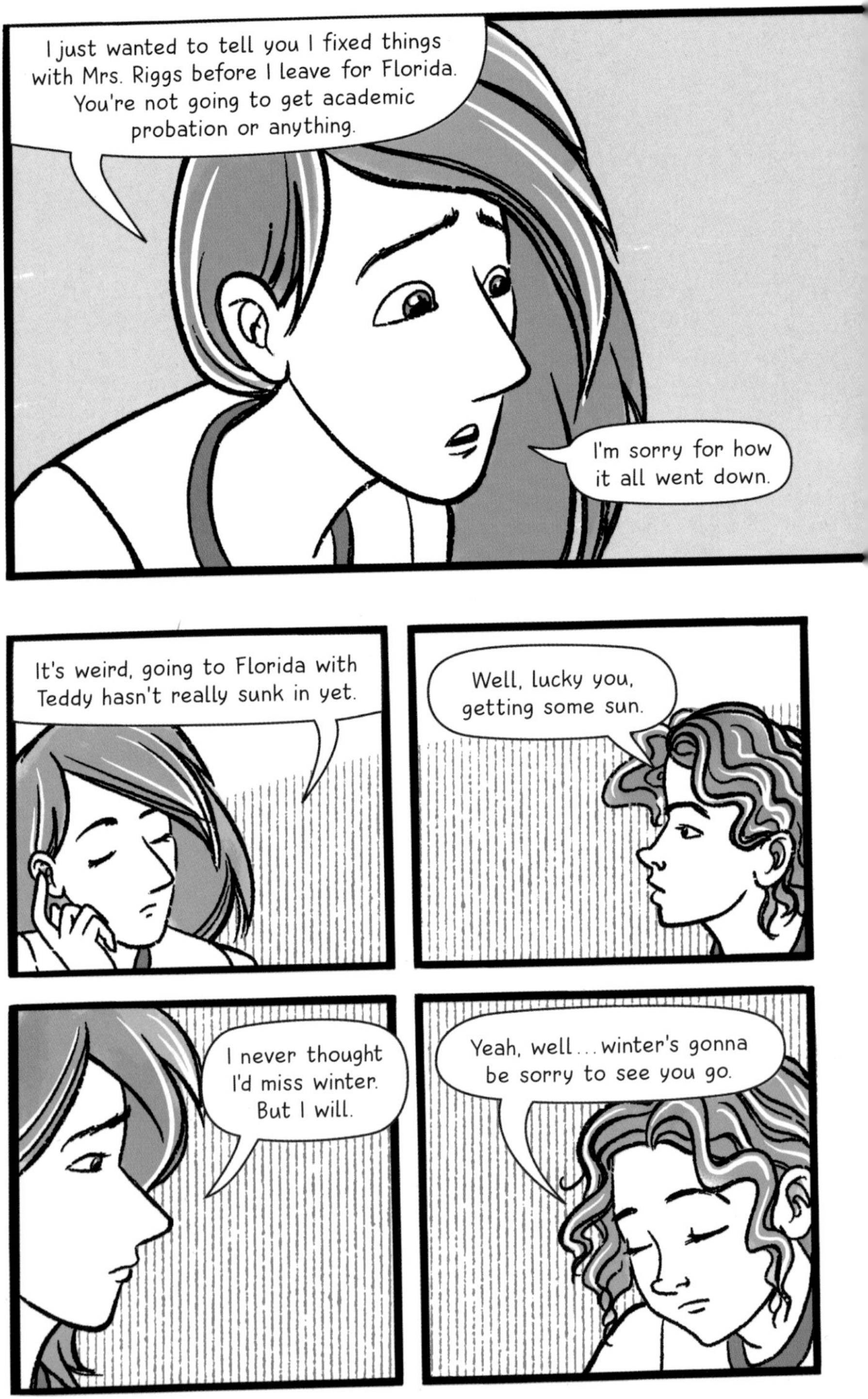
I just wanted to tell you I fixed things with Mrs. Riggs before I leave for Florida. You're not going to get academic probation or anything.
I'm sorry for how it all went down.
It's weird, going to Florida with Teddy hasn't really sunk in yet.
Well, lucky you, getting some sun.
I never thought I'd miss winter. But I will.
Yeah, well...winter's gonna be sorry to see you go.

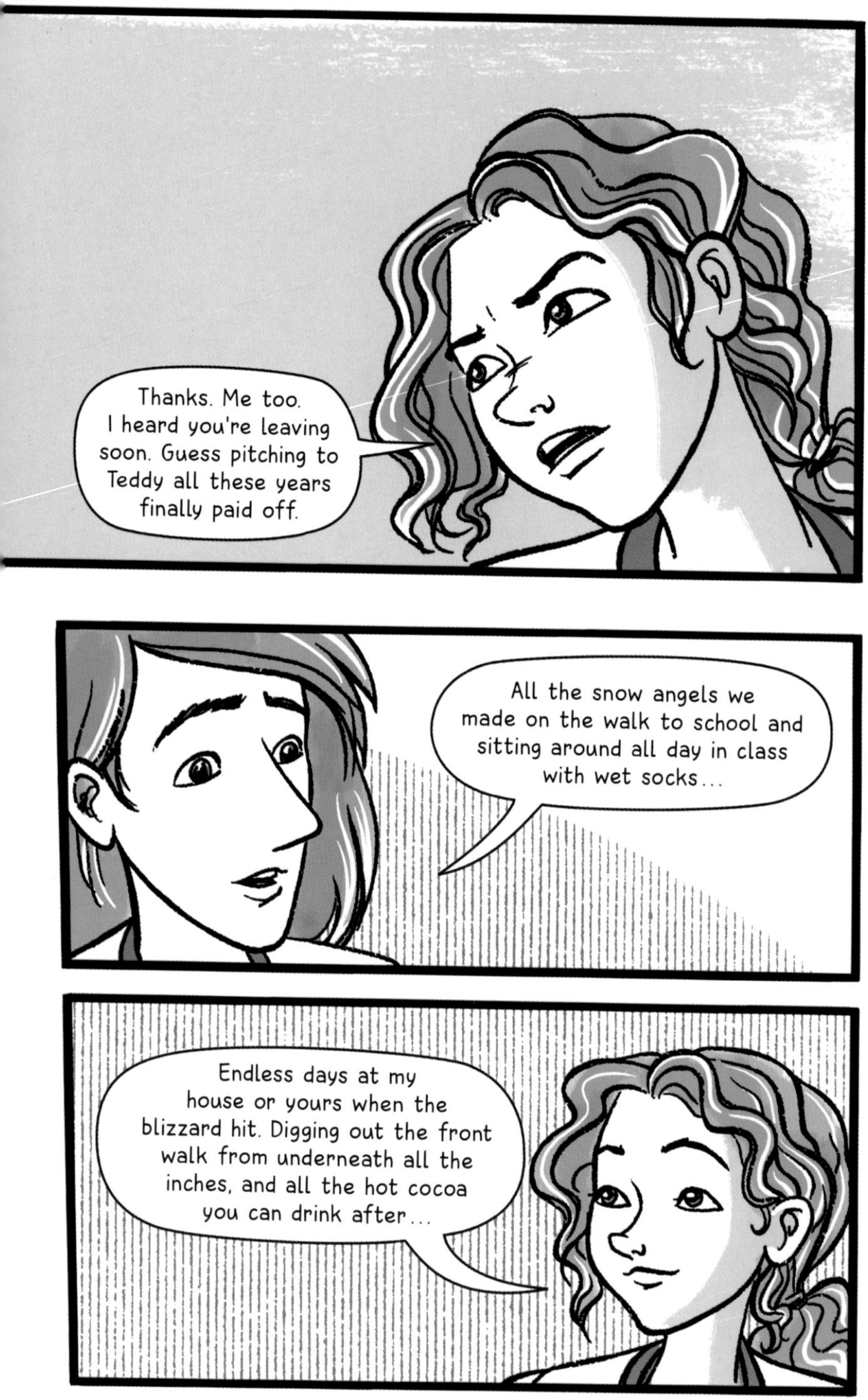
Thanks. Me too. I heard you're leaving soon. Guess pitching to Teddy all these years finally paid off.
All the snow angels we made on the walk to school and sitting around all day in class with wet socks...
Endless days at my house or yours when the blizzard hit. Digging out the front walk from underneath all the inches, and all the hot cocoa you can drink after...

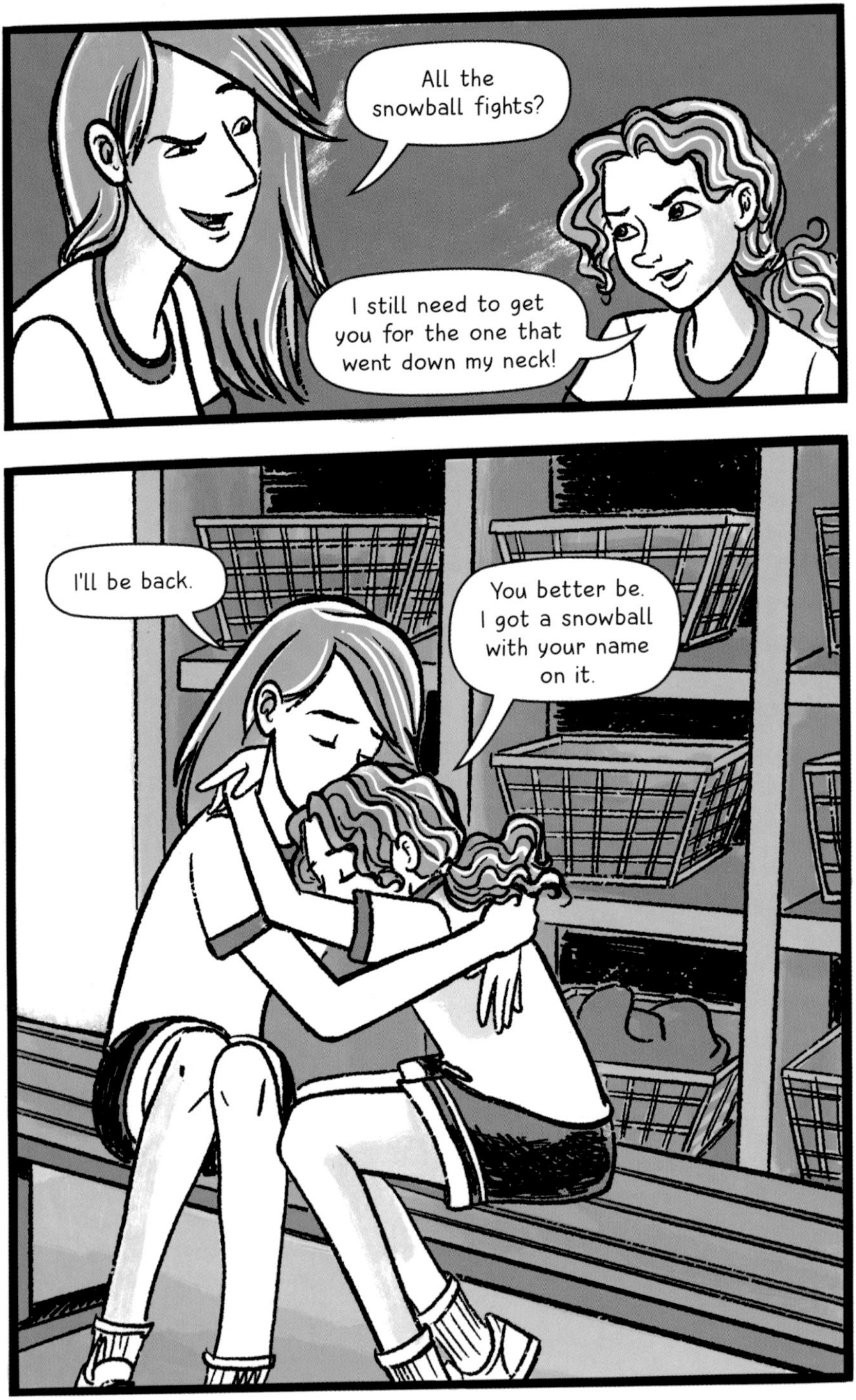
All the snowball fights?
I still need to get you for the one that went down my neck!
I'll be back.
You better be. I got a snowball with your name on it.

THE NEXT DAY...

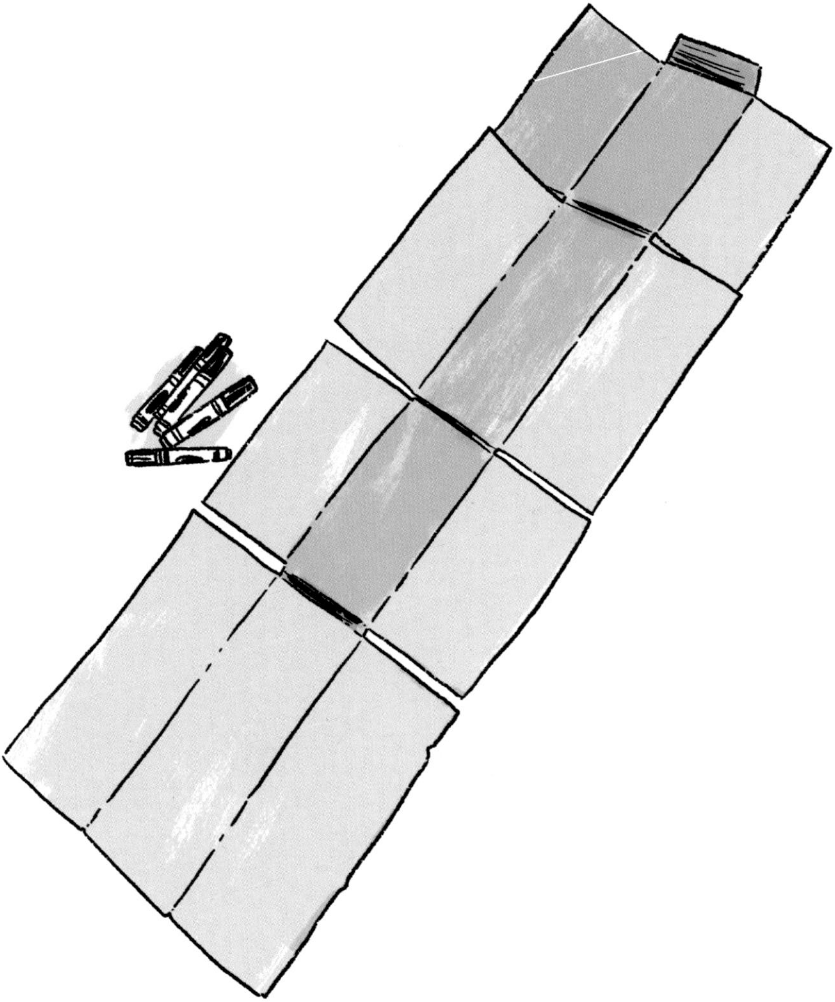

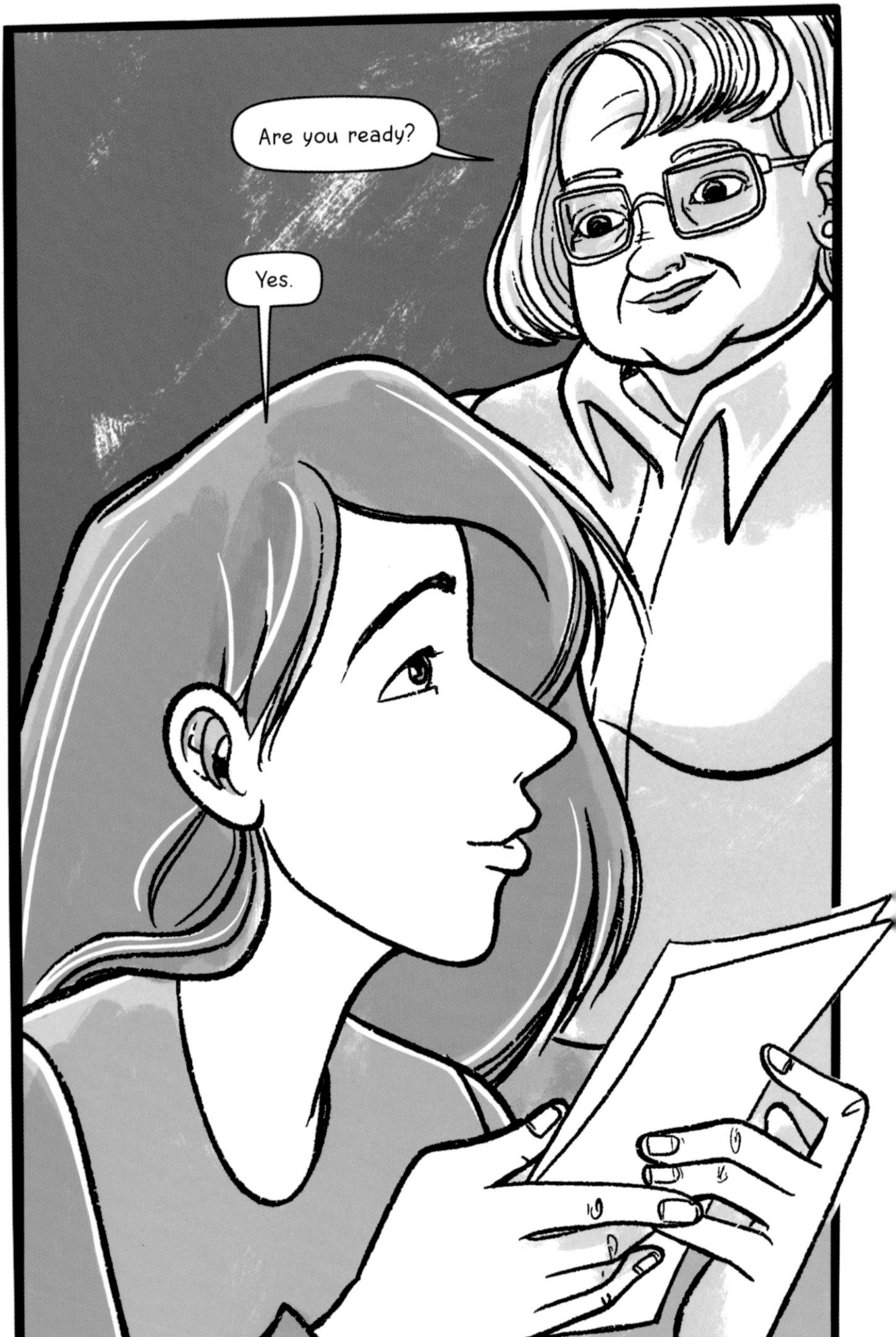
Are you ready?
Yes.

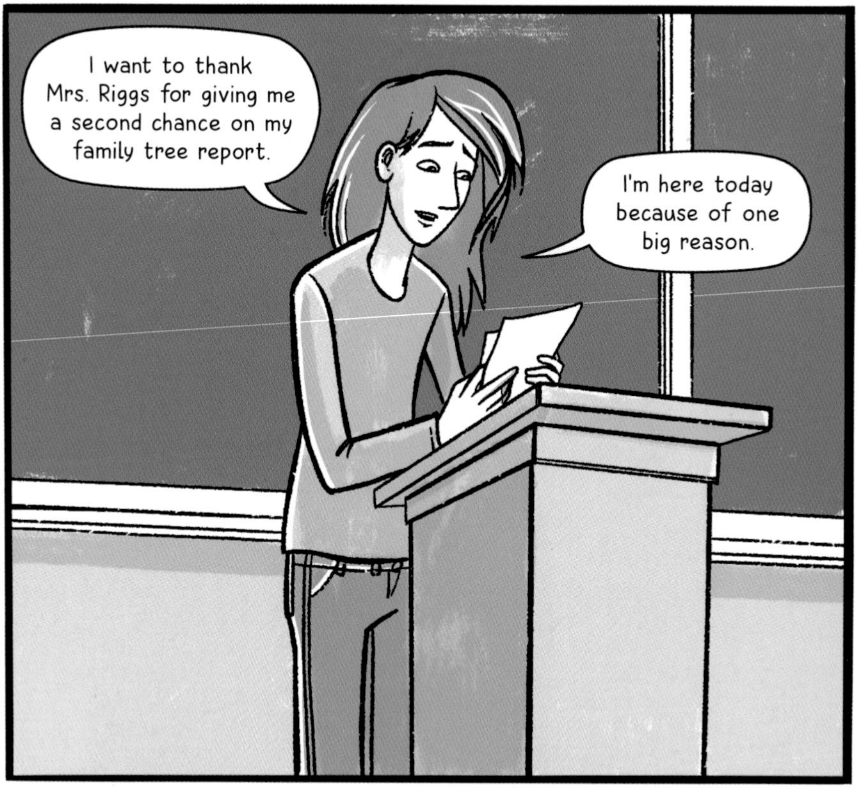
I want to thank Mrs. Riggs for giving me a second chance on my family tree report.
I'm here today because of one big reason.

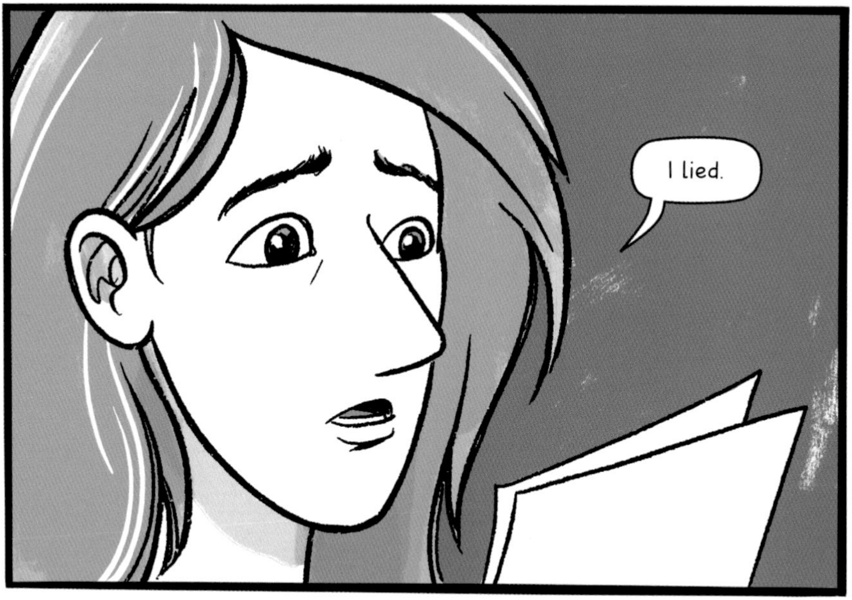
I lied.

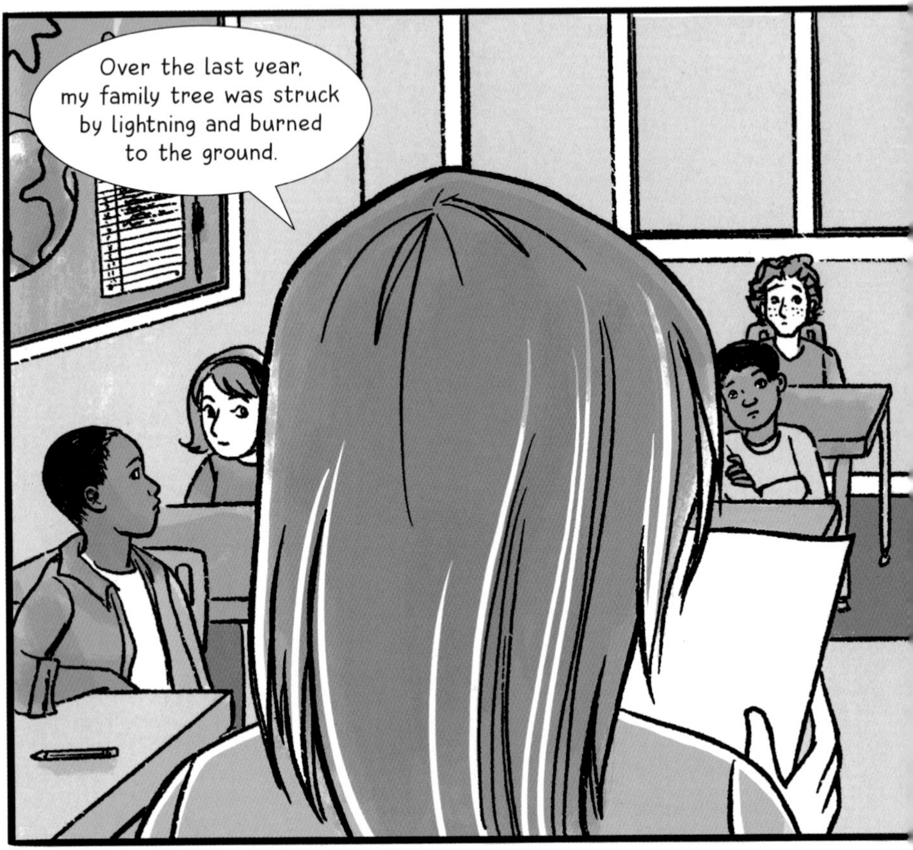
Over the last year, my family tree was struck by lightning and burned to the ground.

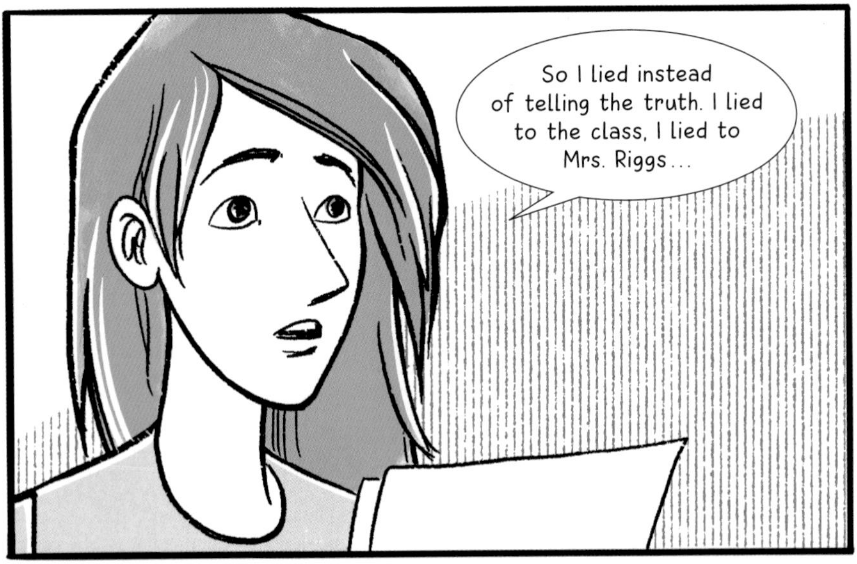
So I lied instead of telling the truth. I lied to the class, I lied to Mrs. Riggs...

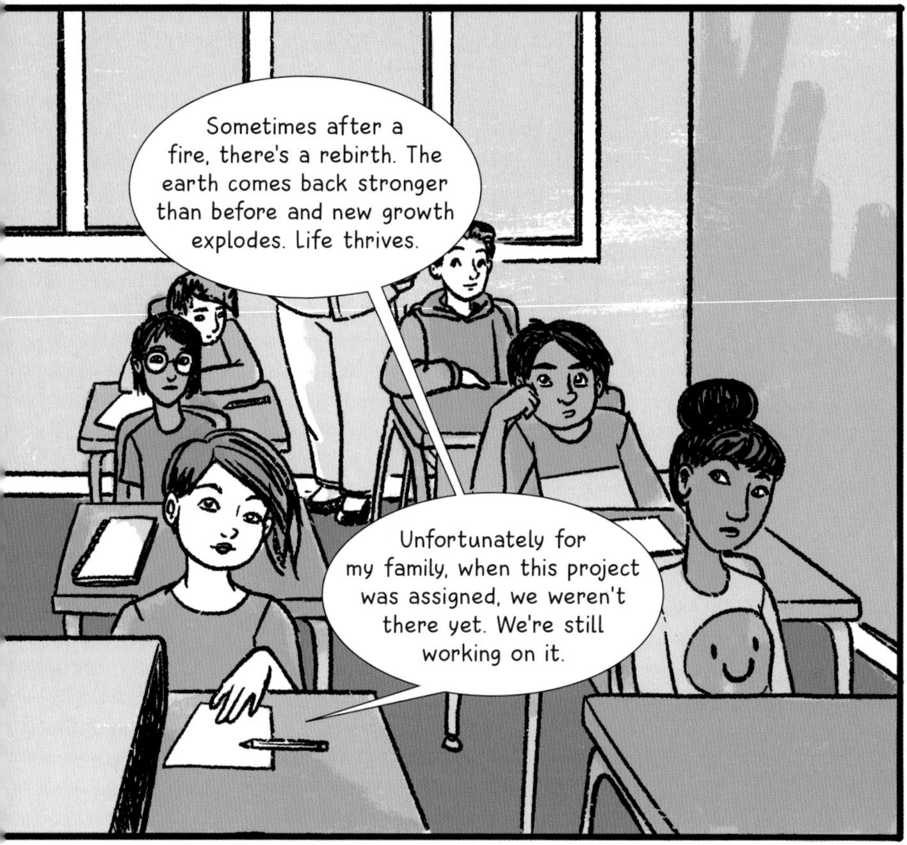
Sometimes after a fire, there's a rebirth. The earth comes back stronger than before and new growth explodes. Life thrives.
Unfortunately for my family, when this project was assigned, we weren't there yet. We're still working on it.

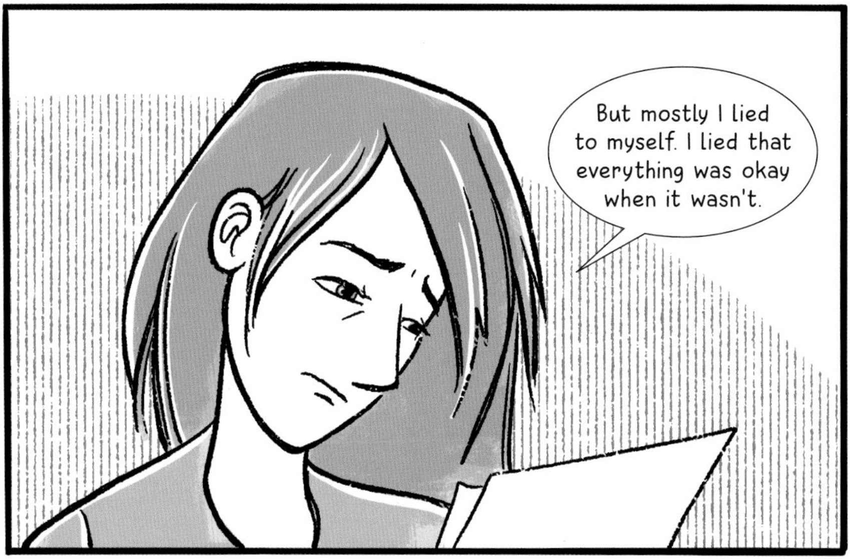
But mostly I lied to myself. I lied that everything was okay when it wasn't.

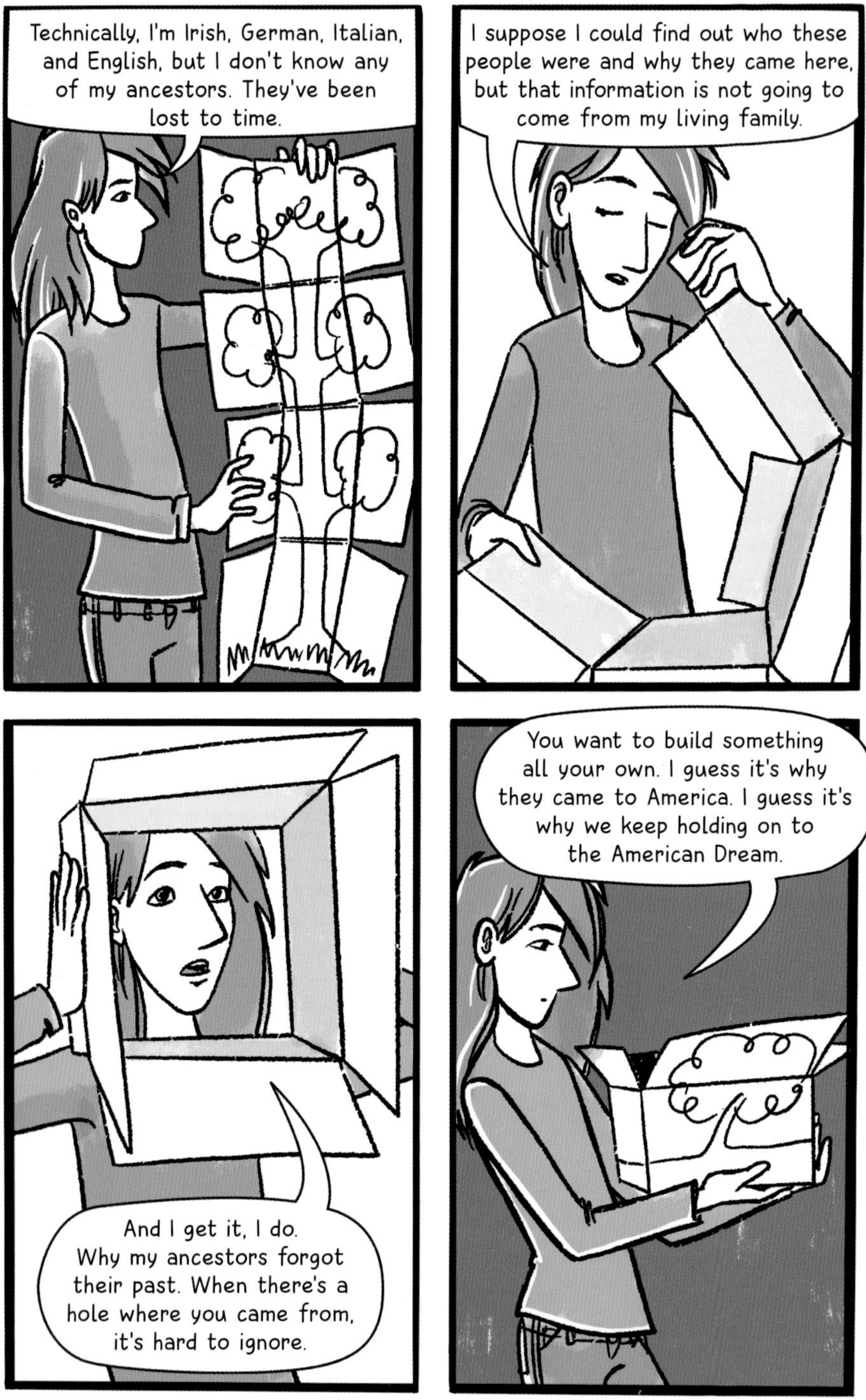
Technically, I'm Irish, German, Italian, and English, but I don't know any of my ancestors. They've been lost to time.
I suppose I could find out who these people were and why they came here, but that information is not going to come from my living family.
And I get it, I do. Why my ancestors forgot their past. When there's a hole where you came from, it's hard to ignore.
You want to build something all your own. I guess it's why they came to America. I guess it's why we keep holding on to the American Dream.

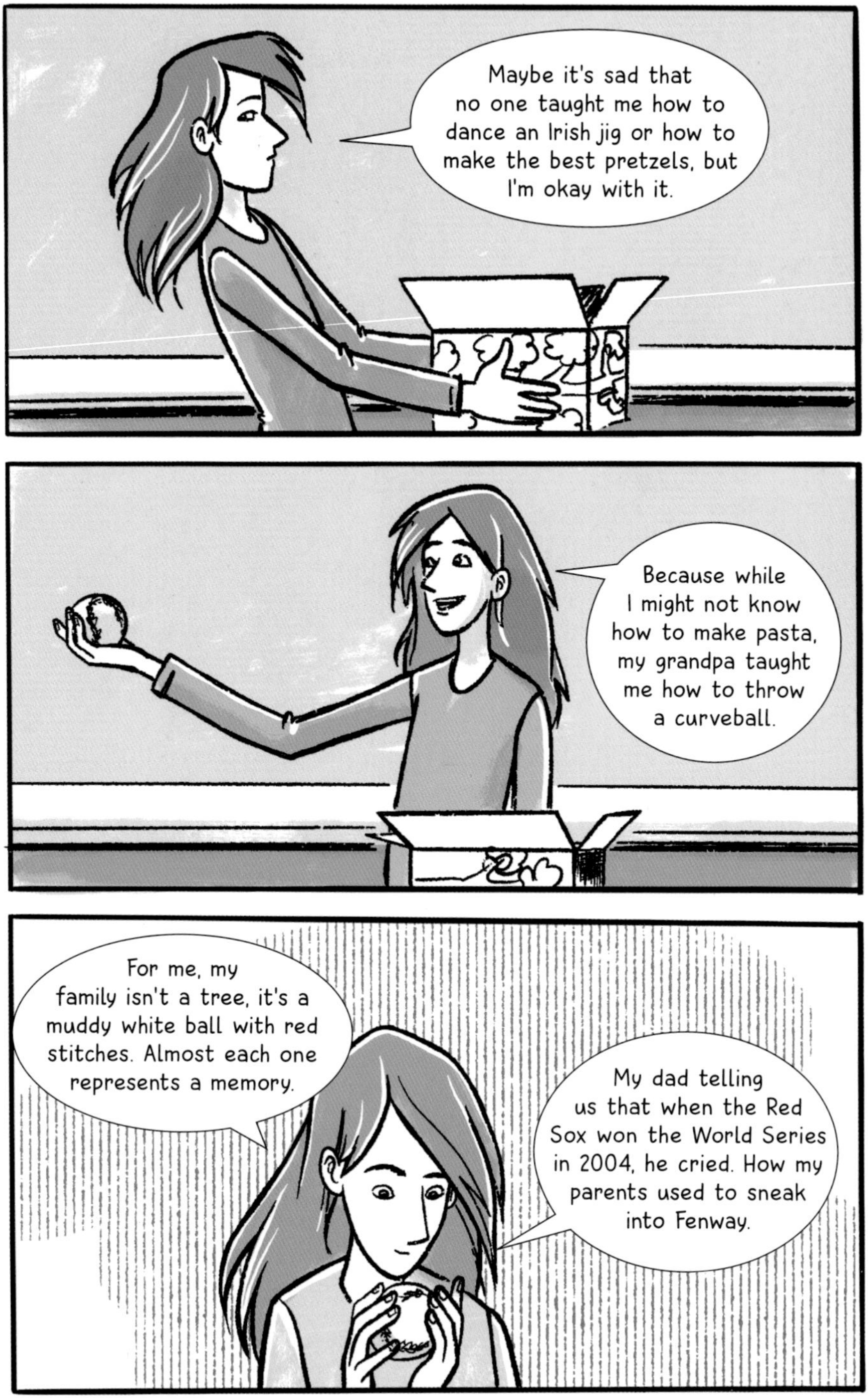
Maybe it's sad that no one taught me how to dance an Irish jig or how to make the best pretzels, but I'm okay with it.
Because while I might not know how to make pasta, my grandpa taught me how to throw a curveball.
For me, my family isn't a tree, it's a muddy white ball with red stitches. Almost each one represents a memory.
My dad telling us that when the Red Sox won the World Series in 2004, he cried. How my parents used to sneak into Fenway.

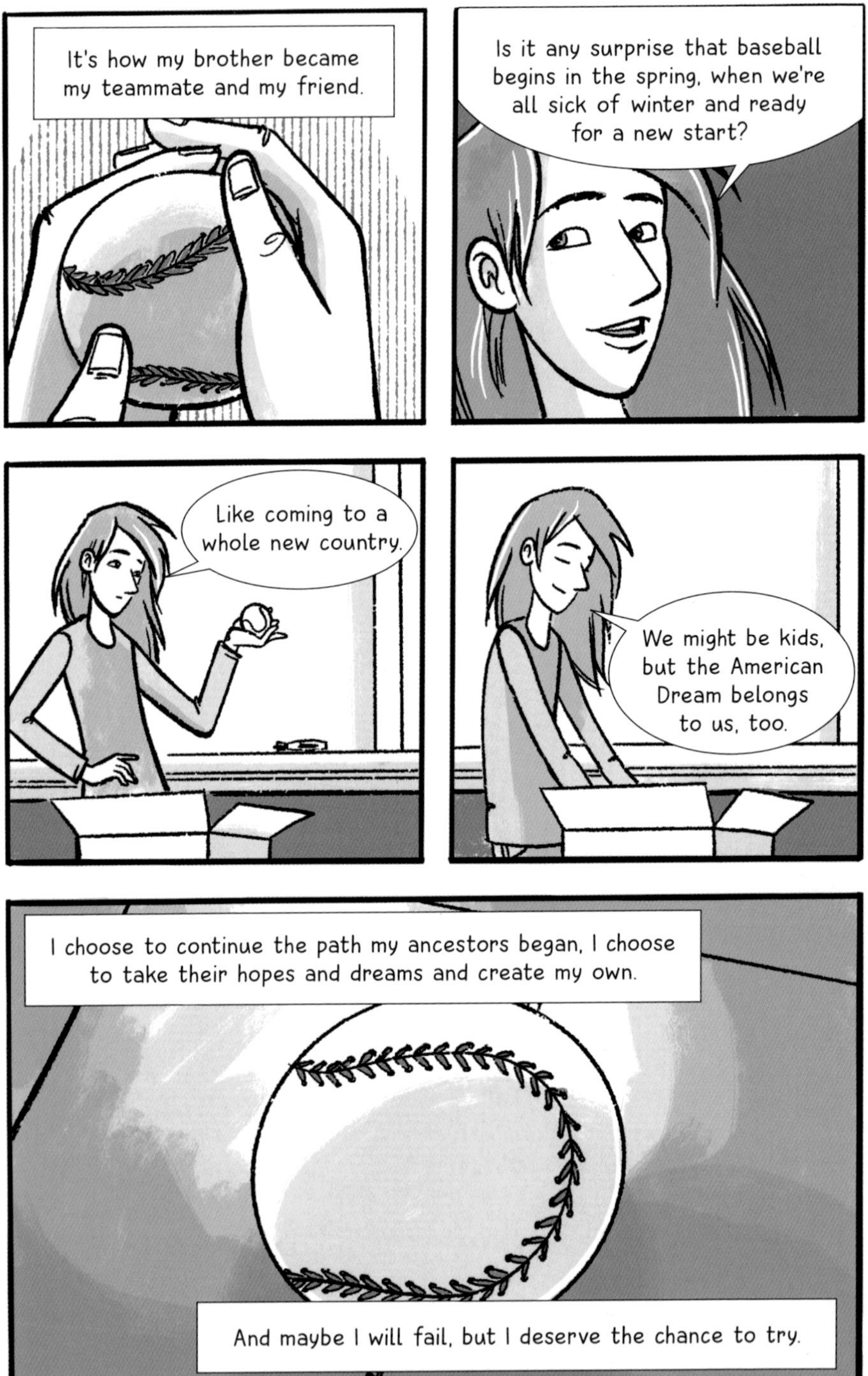
It's how my brother became my teammate and my friend.
Is it any surprise that baseball begins in the spring, when we're all sick of winter and ready for a new start?
Like coming to a whole new country.
We might be kids, but the American Dream belongs to us, too.
I choose to continue the path my ancestors began, I choose to take their hopes and dreams and create my own.
And maybe I will fail, but I deserve the chance to try.

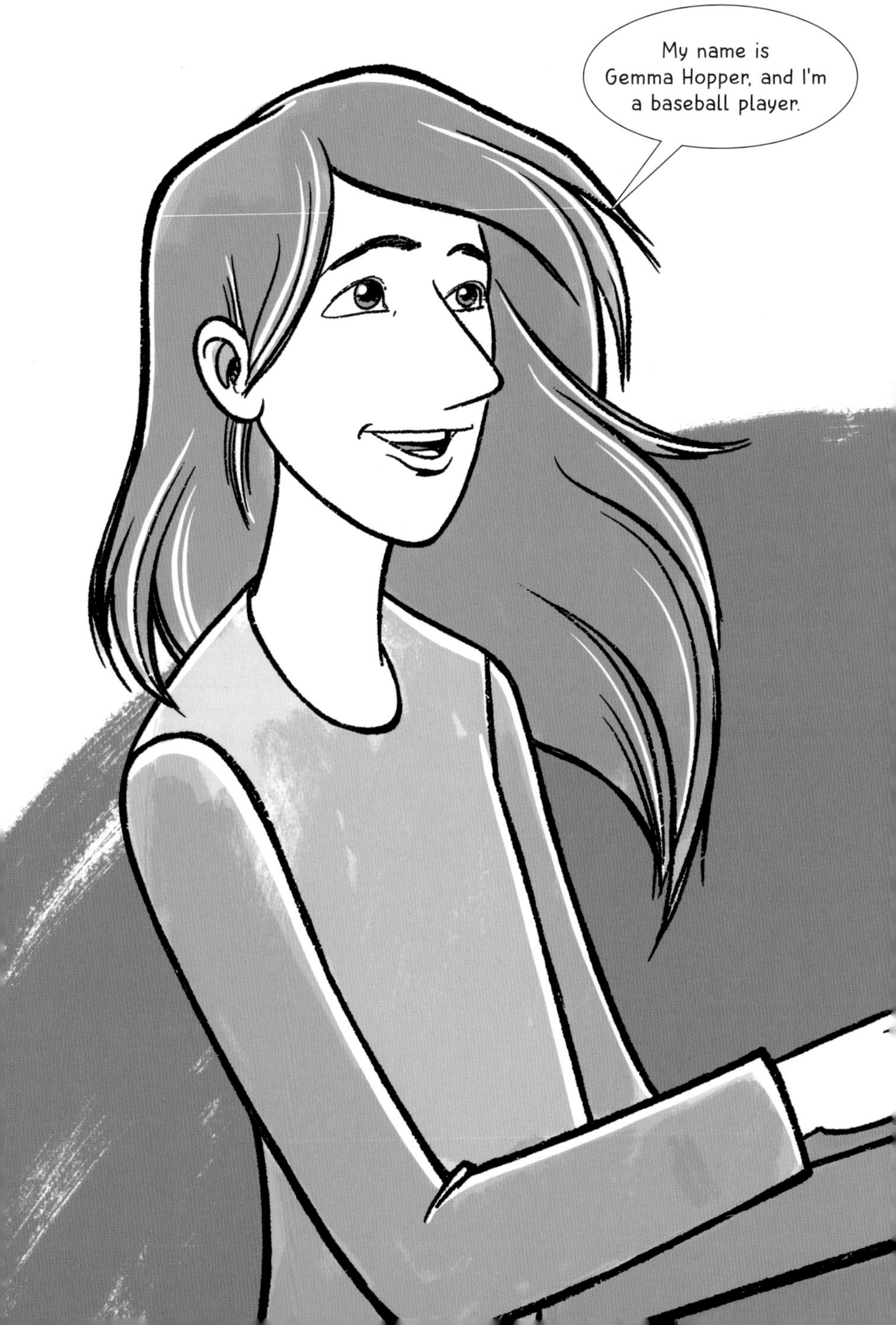
My name is Gemma Hopper, and I'm a baseball player.

Hello. Brie here!
Thanks so much for reading. There's a lot of love in this book...

Most especially, my Love for baseball.

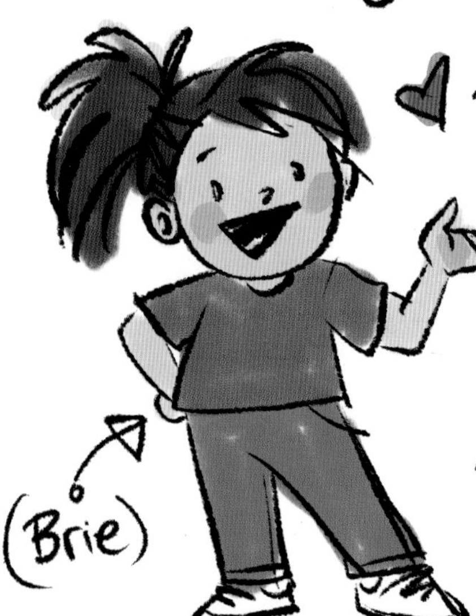
(Brie)

Why baseball?

because

BASEBALL IS MAGIC!

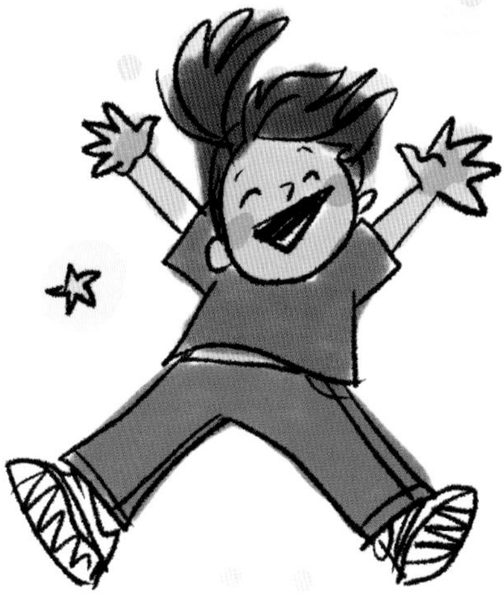

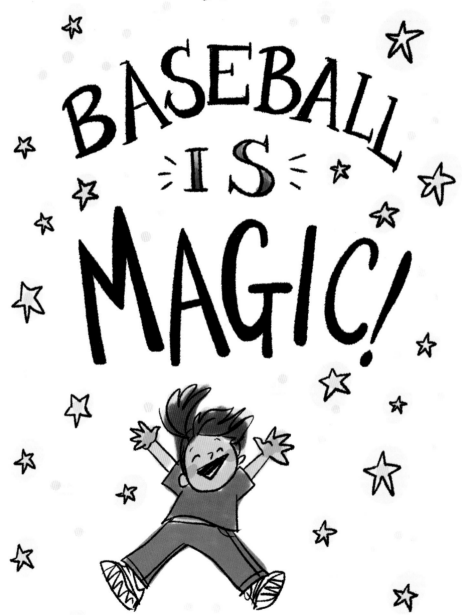

I could watch baseball forever. I don't even have to like the teams playing. BUT...

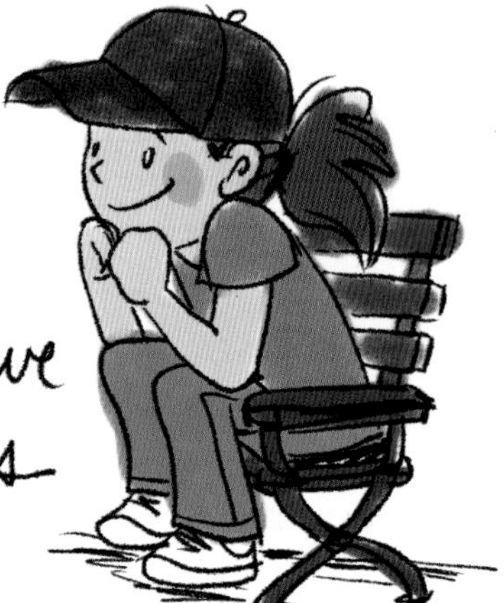

when it's <u>your team</u> taking the field, those are the moments that live forever.

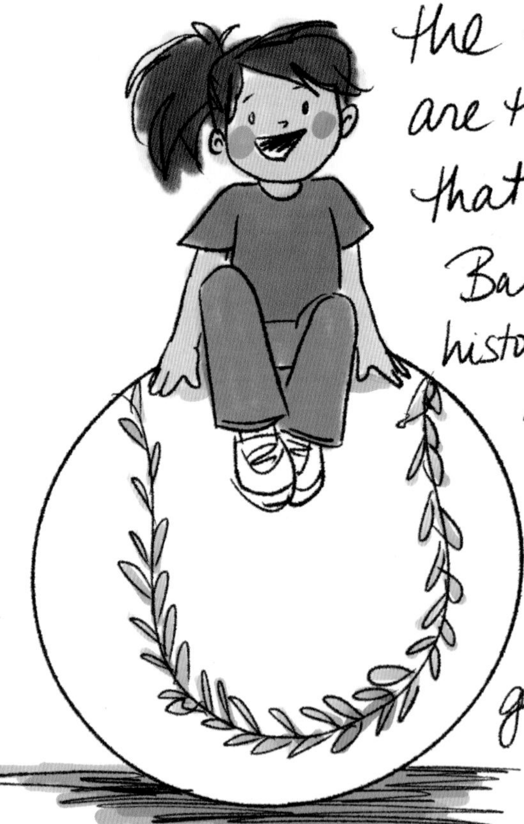

Baseball has a history. It's a generational soap opera. You can share it with your great-grandpa and your baby cousin.

I could keep rounding these bases, but I'm out of room.

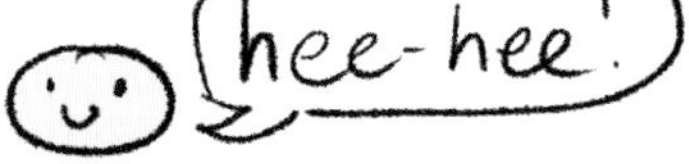
hee-hee!

So as I say thank you to baseball, I must give

HUGE THANKS TO:

· ERIN CLARKE ·
· MACKENZIE BRADY WATSON ·
· JEN VALERO ·
· GIANNA LAKENAUTH ·
· APRIL WARD ·
· LISA LEVENTER ·
· ARTIE BENNETT ·

FIND YOUR VOICE
WITH ONE OF THESE RELATABLE GRAPHIC NOVELS

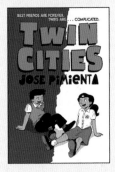

PRESENTED BY **RH** 📖 **GRAPHIC**

🐦 📷 @RHKIDSGRAPHIC

A GRAPHIC NOVEL ON EVERY BOOKSHELF